Love & Coffee

By Bryce Main

Dedication.

Every book, published either in electronic or printed form, is a journey. The chances are the author will have benefitted from the help and advice of any number of people, either directly or indirectly, somewhere along the line. Love & Coffee would not have seen the light of day were it not for the support and encouragement of the writer Denise M. Main, the sculptor Shaun Main, the personal trainer and nutritionist Chris Main, and a hundred and one other very talented people who liked what they read before they even saw this published paperback.

A large slice of thanks must also go to the highly creative **designer Darren Scott, founder of Truth Design in Manchester.** His contribution to the cover concept and artwork for both the ebook and the paperback was large, and more than just the icing on the cake.

A note about spelling: Although I may eventually have readers all over the world, I live in the UK, write in the UK and, therefore, spell in the UK. Any differences in the spelling of certain words in Love & Coffee may be due to language and cultural differences. They are not necessarily incorrect spellings of the words themselves, and are definitely not meant to cause offence. Have a nice day.

Episodes	Page

The fly on the wall

Love & Coffee didn't start off as a book. It began life as a guy scribbling a few lines here and there to pass the time in his favourite coffee shop. Waiting for a damned Americano to get cool enough to drink. Not gulp. Just sip now and again, nice and slow, while his brain said hello to the morning.

A funny thing happens while you wait for something like that. You get to looking around. Not obviously so other folk see you doing it. Not blatantly so they wonder why the hell you're looking at them. But slyly.

You come to an agreement with the guys in control of your central and peripheral vision that as long as they don't tell you all the details of what they do and see…you can't be held accountable. Plausible deniability. And when that happens something else happens. All the guilt you felt before because you were looking at folk getting ready to meet the day disappears.

And when that happens, folk tend to open up to you. Not intentionally. Not deliberately. But somewhere in between the lines. Somewhere in between the actions. Then the change takes place.

You become the fly on the wall. The piece of furniture. The witness to all the good and bad that happens in their lives. And you learn things pretty fast.

Things like everybody wants to be happy. And everybody wants to be loved. Some folk want to remember. And others just want to forget.

And somehow, here, everybody gets the chance to get back in touch with whatever makes them want to wake up in the morning and get out of bed.

They get the chance to go some place where the heart beats a little steadier. The smile stretches a little wider. The tears fall a little less. And the breathing shifts down a gear or two.

For a while, they hand over control to someone who always seems to know more about them than anyone should. Someone who helps them partake of the finest damned drink on the planet.

Someone called Little Italy.

Welcome to Love & Coffee.

Be cool...

Goodbye Hello

Sometimes a new day needs a new door to walk through. A change of pace...a change of place...a change of face. Just like this morning. Goodbye generic cafe haunt. Hello feelgood coffee shop. Right in the city centre.

Maybe I find it by chance. Maybe it finds me. Who the Hell knows. I hit the city centre too late for dawn. Too early for work. The sun tries to force itself out from behind the northern clouds. It's almost a fair fight. I catch a waft of strong coffee coming from round the corner.

I see the tables and umbrellas first. I see the relaxed patrons second. I see the open doorway third. A sign on the door says: The best damned drink on the planet. I see folk relaxing in the semi-shade. The rich aroma of Italian coffee blended with continental ambiance in the foreground. Classical sounds and low conversation in the background. A taste to die for, accompanied by music to come alive to.

I pass over the threshold and walk up to the bar. It's a fifty-fifty morning. Half the tables are empty. Waiting for the regulars. Waiting for the newbies.

I feel like a kid on the first day of school. A stranger in a strange land. I look across the counter and see dark eyes locked onto me. Long lashes. Dark curly hair framing the kind of face that any guy would cross the street for. Just so he could get a closer look.

Well...you gonna just stand there and look, or you gonna put your mouth in gear, she says. I put my mouth in gear. Double espresso, I say. She nods and the ghost of a smile shows up in her eyes. Everybody's first time should be special, she says. Like a date with destiny, she says. I guess you must be The New Guy. You guessed right, I say. And you? Rosalee, she says. My friends call me Little Italy. What do you do, she says. I write, I say.

She turns away and faces a stainless steel machine. It looks all kinds of ready, willing and able. She turns back and hands me a small white cup full of a dark, steamy liquid. I grab some silver and push it across the glass top. She shakes her head. On the house, she says. Just this once. We can say we're introduced now. This might be the start of a beautiful friendship, I say.

She raises an eyebrow. You like Casablanca, she says. It's a curse, I say. Now she smiles. Full face. Nice to meet you New Guy, she says. You too, Little Italy, I say. I turn and make for a slot against the far wall near the corner. Sit down, back to the wall. Eyes on full alert.

I reach down, lift up, and take a first sip of espresso. It hits my taste buds and disappears down my neck before I even get the chance to say wow!

I look over at Little Italy and she's looking at a space above my head. I turn and see a box on the wall. I get the feeling that somewhere inside the box the number 1 comes to life. I close my eyes.

The curtains open and Bobby Zimmerman is standing at the mike. Guitar strapped on. Harmonica in the harness. Shelter From The Storm in the air.

A new coffee shop. An old Dylan.

Be cool…

I guess that means I'm a regular

Good morning Tuesday. It's 8am on this side of the world. It's been over a month since I was in the city centre, so I feel like a stranger when I walk into the coffee shop.

A second visit won't get me a second glance. Surely I don't warrant a double take. Then I come up against Little Italy. So…the usual, she says with a smile. I raise an eyebrow. Surprise surprise. I guess that means I'm a regular, I say. Oh, you got a long way to go down that road, she says. I just got a good memory. But let's say you're on the right track, she says.

There's a young Italian-looking man standing beside her. He's got hair on his head. I have hair on my face. We nearly have something in common. This is Chico, says Little Italy. He's Brazilian. Just like my coffee, I say. Naaah…your coffee is Arabica, she says. Could be from Africa. Could be from the Caribbean. Maybe even China.

Chico smiles. She knows her coffee, he says. It's a symbiotic relationship, says Little Italy. I stroke my chin. Symbiotic, I say slowly. I think I'll make that my word of the day. All the right letters fall in all the right places, she says. And make all the right sounds, I say.

Little Italy brings the verbal dancing to a halt. You look like you could do with a large Americano with an extra shot, she says. You look like you know your customers, I say.

Chico does the necessary with the stainless steel machine behind them. I slip Little Italy some silver and take the tall mug to a spot in the corner. Life as a human being pretending to be a fly on the wall is complicated. An image of Jeff Goldblum swoops into my mind. I quickly swat it away and look around the room.

In a far corner Sweethearts are indulging in a quiet spot of mutually agreeable face-eating. Never speak with your mouth full, my mother used to say. I silently reply…yes, but what if your mouth is full with someone else's tongue. My mother doesn't reply. The intervening years in her coffin have diminished her ability to hold a decent conversation.

As I raise my Americano for a sip & sigh, the door opens and The Bookworm walks in. Large leather satchel strapped over shoulder and chest. Fast gait. Worn sneakers. Elephant cord pants. Heavy wool duffle coat. Toggle fastenings. Circular frame glasses. Hair unkempt but stylishly acceptable.

He whispers something to Little Italy and gestures with the index finger of his right hand. It points to the chalk board behind her. She answers. He nods. She smiles. He blushes.

A minute later he takes his hot chocolate to a table near the door to the gents toilet. Something in the way he moves makes me think it's a good idea. He sits, puts the chocolate at the far side of the table. Reaches into his satchel. Takes out an old, leather bound volume. Opens it and begins to read.

Little Italy watches him from behind the bar. Turns to look at the Sweethearts who are now looking at each other, then nods at the box on the wall. The box has a love of all things old. From deep inside it pulls up number 79 and slides it carefully onto the turntable.

The curtains open. The Flamingos are on stage. I only have eyes for you, dear. Little Italy nods in satisfaction. The Bookworm lovingly turns another page.

Be cool…

The Rucksack Guy and The Curly Haired Blonde

Good morning Thursday. The green tea is in the cup...and the law is in the coffee shop. The boys in blue are wearing black bulletproofs and the girls behind the bar are wearing new black tees. On the front: The best coffee on the whole damned planet. On the back: Served by the best baristas.

The uniformed threesome sit with their lattes locked down safe and warm. Next to a curious individual typing furiously on an iPad. Onboard keyboard. No problem. Even has the sound of a manual machine. Just for effect. Just for atmosphere. Even got a bell on the return. The things you can do with an app these days.

The posse of lawmen speaks casual. Acts natural. Feels comfortable. A guy with a rucksack stands in front of Little Italy at the bar. He can't find his coffee money. He fumbles. He blushes. He finds and breathes a sigh of relief. All will soon be right in his double espresso world.

Outside, slow trams slither through the city centre. Inside, slow music oozes through the box on the wall. A little instrumental. Something from James Newton Howard. The Prologue from The Lady In The Water. Perfect for the lady in the coffee shop. Perfect for Little Italy. The piano solo just about sets the tone. Notes flow like lethargic ripples. Allowing the heart to slow. Pulse to settle. Giving life a chance to take a break.

Rucksack Guy takes his double espresso from her. Thanks her. Turns and looks for a space to chill. Take the weight off his boots. Give his bones a rest. Think about where he's been and where he's headed. Maybe somewhere special. Maybe nowhere in particular. Just as long as it's as far away as possible from the one he left behind.

He still has her photograph in the bottom of his rucksack. In a metal case to keep it safe and unblemished. Away from sight. Never away from mind. Never away from memory. Too painful to look at. Too precious to get rid of.

He looks down at his rocket fuel, picks up the cup and takes a sip. As the liquid hits his tongue the door opens. Curly Haired Blonde walks in. Four inch heels. Skin tight leopard print pants. Ramones tee. Black leather biker jacket. Matching leopard shoulder bag. Chewing gum. Hips and lips moving in perfect harmony.

Rucksack Guy feels his pulse speed up. Just a touch. Maybe this is what he needs. A little distraction. A little me space. A little me time.

He sees Little Italy looking at him. Sees her head slowly moving from side to side. Sees her mouth shaping the words…too soon…too soon. Sees her look at the box on the wall and nod. The box gets the message and number 20 steps up and onto the turntable.

The curtains open. Lady in the Water drains away. Fleetwood Mac pours on stage. They go their own way. Little Italy looks at Rucksack Guy. He's smiling.

Be cool…

When The Man comes around

Good morning Tuesday. You ever sat down...leaned back...closed your eyes...and breathed in deeply as a little early morning coffee shop jazz filtered through the skin? It's a whole new patchwork quilt kinda comfort blanket. Wrap it around you. Feel the warmth seep into the bones.

Life may come kicking and screaming into the world. But easing yourself into the day deserves a more sedate approach. More considered. More pick me up slowly and put me down gently.

It might not be sunny on the outside, but it sure as Hell is on the inside. Inside the coffee shop the warmth is dripping off the walls. A serious, sweating, roly-poly of a man is servicing the mini-me coffee machine. It's old and cold. It doesn't produce the goods like it used to. It's espresso deficient. Latte challenged. Minus Mocha and sans steam.

Little Italy is sympathetic. Empathetic. She knows that Big Brother is by her side. Not he of the Georgie-boy and 1984. Not Apple's cinema commercial's hammer-throwing beauties. This Big Brother is a stainless steel behemoth. The patron saint of the finest coffee creations. Large, shining, with whistles and bells and fast-action knobs, buttons and levers.

From the box on the wall the track shifts and music from the movie The Piano oozes like sweat from pores. It's carried on pregnant air molecules to grateful ears. The score is haunting. The composer is Michael Nyman. The soundtrack album is rated in the top 100 of all time.

Who would have guessed? Who could have known? Who else but Little Italy? She knows that every now and then all the possible combinations of musical notes in the known world come together to work a little magic. All the sharps and flats put on a show, take a bow, and disappear into the wings. Until the next time.

She knows this. And so does The Man in Black. The Man sitting by the window. Not facing the world outside. Facing the one inside. Facing everyone who comes in looking for refuge and caffeine. When this man comes to town and heads for the coffee shop, folk move sideways and give up their sidewalk space.

When he reaches the door, he always finds it open. He doesn't even go to the bar to order a drink. Little Italy always has one waiting for him. Large Americano. Four sugars. One short squeeze of toffee syrup.

Sitting on a table that has reserved written all over it. He always drinks coffee. He always stays an hour. Not a skinny second more. He always leaves a mouthful in the bottom of the cup when he goes. And nobody ever sees him vacate the premises.

I can see him now. Sipping slowly. Right leg crossed over left. White skin. Black under black over black outfit. Neat black hair with a Superman curl at the forehead. Ice blue eyes scanning the room. Little Italy sees the scan. She nods at the box on the wall and the box shifts gear. Slides number 54 onto the turntable.

The curtains open. Johnny Cash is standing at the mike. Acoustic strapped on. Fully loaded. Everybody sits up and listens when the man comes around.

The Man in Black's gaze rests on Little Italy. He smiles. She smiles. He winks. She nods. Head down. When it comes back up…he's gone.

Be cool…

Thank you George

Good morning Tuesday...and hello Mr. Blue Sky. Sorry Jeff. Thanks George. Here comes the sun. No more winter overcoats. Not here. Not now. Well...not today anyway.

It's short sleeves not short tempers. Long smiles not long faces. Make love not hate. Make peace not war. Today I can feel the slow, slow...quick, quick slow of a blended start to the day. One pot of the steaming green infusion stuff, followed by a dark triple espresso. Bring me down then take me up. Pause for thought then feet don't fail me now.

I can feel the calm wash over me. I can hear the sound of the aircon pushing the notes into the background. I dial the volume of my own internal music speaker down a notch. Natural noise reduction technology kicks in and the blood coursing through my veins slows from a race to a jog. Then a casual walk.

Little Italy passes by the table. Sees the effect. Sees the smile. I'll leave it fifteen minutes before I bring the espresso, she says. That okay? All I can manage is a nod. I'm too busy chilling from the inside out. I look around.

Standing at the bar is Hawaiian Shirt Bob. He looks like a bit part player from Hawaii Five O. Only he's so big he's more like Hawaii Ten O. He's a single guy heart in a double guy body. Love is a stranger and the last time he was kissed it was by his cousin. He was sixteen and she was a nightmare in a floral frock and a panty girdle.

But that was then. This is now. And now he's getting Goo-Goo Eyes from someone at a table over by the stairs leading to the balcony. Freckles is showing an interest. The look but don't touch kind.

She's six feet three inches tall. Thin as a rake, and pretty as a picture. She's a size junkie and lonely as Hell. Small guys need not apply.

No matter how drop dead handsome they are. No matter how hilarious they are. No matter how goddam clever they are. As long as they're big, they'll be on her radar. As long as they got a smile that makes her go weak at the knees, they'll be on her wish list. She stopped having a to-do list a long, long time ago.

Hawaiian Shirt Bob shuffles forward to the head of the queue. Little Italy's gaze travels up…and up. She smiles. Hello Bob, she says. You got bigger, she says. Yeah, last time you saw me I was a dwarf, he says. A fast laugh escapes Little Italy's mouth. The usual, she says. The usual, he says.

She turns and lifts down an extra large white mug from the shelf above the stainless steel coffee machine. Big enough for two lattes. Fills it up and puts a smiley face in chocolate powder on the top.

Somebody's giving you Goo-Goo Eyes, she whispers. Nods in Freckles' general direction. Hawaiian Shirt Bob turns. Looks. Blushes. Turns back quick. The lady needs a refill, she says. Give her this from me. Hands Bob another double latte. Winks. Hawaiian Shirt Bob grabs both mugs. Turns. Takes a deep breath. Good old Elvis. It's now or never. Takes a step forward.

Behind him, Little Italy looks at the box on the wall. The box has a big idea. Reaches down deep. Brings up number 109. Slips it on the turntable.

The curtains open. The Drifters are on stage. And the top of the stairs is just a few notes away. Freckles looks at Hawaiian Shirt Bob and smiles. The future is walking right towards her.

Be cool…

The Frightened Man walks in

Good morning Wednesday. Halfway through the week. Halfway through my breakfast of green tea and carrot cake. Ain't half hot, mum.

Empty coffee shops carry the ghosts of past drinkers. From my spot over in the corner I can see their shadows. Hear their murmured conversations. I can't tune them out. Can't turn them down. Can't switch them off. They're peripheral sound and vision. Visible and audible when the light bounces off the edge of your eye and the soundwaves get twisted in the right direction.

Little Italy says the world comes through her coffee shop doors. Arriving bent out of shape. Leaving bent back in again. She says they all leave an emotional residue. An echo. That's what you see, she says. That's what you hear.

I look at all the chairs. I wonder what happens when full-bodied folk come in and want to sit down. Do all the ghosts move over? Get up and walk out? Or do they just stand around, waiting for another free seat to inhabit.

I take a bite of carrot cake and wash it down with a mouthful of warm tea. Empty of milk. Full of antioxidants. As the cake slides down, the door opens and The Frightened Man walks in. Eyes darting everywhere. Hands constantly brushing tiny invisible spiders off his clothes. Ready to hit the deck at the slightest loud noise. Scared of everything and everyone.

The only reason he leaves the safety of his home every morning is to come here. Take a journey of Hell from one sanctuary to another. Feel the eyes of other travellers stare at him. Feel their bodies brush up against him on the tram.

The only reason he puts up with the horror of all that, is so he can see Little Italy. Then he can look into her eyes and know she understands. Then he can drink a large espresso with three extra shots. And talk to the ghosts.

Hey you, says Little Italy. Hey you too, says The Frightened Man. She smiles. He begins to relax. His shoulders sag. His hands slow down. His eyes chill out. The spiders go into hiding. For the time being.

Little Italy watches him take his espresso and give her a tentative nod. Watches him turn and choose a table right in the middle of the floor. Watches him sit down, breathe deeply, look around, and smile.

The Frightened Man nods and smiles at the empty tables around him. Greeting their ghostly inhabitants. Responding as they greet him. Then he begins to speak. Softly in a whisper. Recounting his adventures. Asking them about theirs.

A small voice to the left of me speaks. Haven't seen him in here for a while, says the voice. I turn. The table is empty. I turn back, look at The Frightened Man. He's laughing. I see Little Italy looking at me. She nods towards the box on the wall. The box has a history of making the right choice. It chooses number 3. A small vinyl disc slips onto the turntable. A little crackle comes through the speakers.

The curtains open. The Who are on stage. Roger is out front. See me...feel me.

The small voice to the left of me speaks again. I wonder if he knows I'm here, it says. I don't bother turning. Oh he knows, I say. He knows.

Be cool...

The Boys in Blue frog march The Shifty Dude

Good morning Thursday. When I cross the portal, the coffee shop is Continental. Instrumental. Sentimental. There's a little Rodriguez in the air.

Spanish magic on six strings with ten fingers and one genius, oozing from the wall. A touch of flamenco. A taste of the gipsy caves. I breathe slowly and deeply and look to the left. Scanning the seats. Perusing the people.

I stop at the middle-aged professor. Old-school intellectual with a new school iPad. White hair. Same shirt as yesterday. Deep in thought.

I hear a commotion and look back outside. Boys in blue frog-marching a shifty dude somewhere quiet for a good finger wag talking to in the back of a black and white van. No prying eyes. Naughty boy. Menacing tattoos. Sneer on his face.

The box on the wall changes gear and develops a sunny disposition. ELO gives Manuel the elbow and Mister Blue Sky makes the pulse jump. Good old Jeff. Can't beat a modern classic.

Willowy Blonde stands by the counter, waiting for her caffeine hit. Hey you with the pretty face. Frowning at the human race. Willowy Blonde fingertaps her denim-coated left thigh in time with the music.

Tight beat. Tight jeans tucked into cowboy boots. Loose blue jacket over black tee with a slogan on the front. She turns. Jacket opens. Slogan reads: "Love & Coffee. Everything else is bollocks!" She glares at the room. The room glares back.

Willowy Blonde snaps her head around and faces Little Italy. All I need is a black Americano, three sugars and the truth, she says. Little Italy knows about Willowy Blonde. Knows the story behind her. Knows the attitude is all a front. False as a pair of silicone implants.

Everybody's got a defence mechanism. Everybody's got something they're scared of.

Little Italy knows what Willowy Blonde's scared of and she keeps it well and truly locked up. It's not the kind of secret that anyone should have to tell. So she cuts her a break the size of the Grand Canyon. You found a gig yet, she says. Willowy Blonde shakes her head. Bust my ass…bust my bass, she says. Neck's cracked, she says. Band's got a stand-in, she says.

Little Italy looks at her. Two heartbeats. Wait here, she says and disappears into the back office. Comes back a minute later with a black case. Opens it up. Sitting inside is a Rickenbacker 4003. Midnight Blue. Looks brand spanking new.

Willowy Blonde's jaw drops. You play, she says. Little Italy winks and closes the case. Hands it to Willowy Blonde. Her name's Alice, she says. Give her back when you get yours fixed up, she says. No hurry, she says. Now go sit down in the corner, I'll bring you over your Americano, she says. Sugar's on the table. You'll have to figure out the truth for yourself.

Willowy Blonde has a tear in her eye. Wipes it away. Moves to the corner hugging the bass. Sits down and wipes away another tear. Little Italy takes over a steaming Americano. No charge. No words. Walks away and looks at the box on the wall.

The box doesn't need to be told twice. Reaches down. Brings number 149 up and slides it onto the turntable. The curtains open. The Beatles are on stage. Ringo, sticks and vocals, sings with a little help from his friends.

Willowy Blonde smiles at the room. The room smiles back. Nice one Mr. Starkey.

Be cool…

The Moaning Man gets a break

Good morning Friday 13th. It's don't bother about black cats day. Walk under ladders day. Keep your superstitions to yourself and give me a damned break day.

It's the kinda day where you ask yourself a question. Do I want three espressos, or only two?

I walk across the square to the coffee shop and pass by the soft-shoe tap dancer. Moving to his own internal rhythm. Feet shuffling to meet the beat. Listen to the heel and toe clicks. Black tap shoes. Black pants with a high Spanish waist. Black open neck shirt. Black waistcoat. Black felt Derby. White face paint over dark skin. He has a box at his feet and a sign propped against the box. The sign says: "My name is Solomon Grey. Pleased to meet you. Have a nice day!"

I toss some silver in the box and give him the nod. He gives me a sideways shuffle and a Cincinnati backward move. Tips the hat and smiles.

I walk to the coffee shop with an extra spring in my step. I step on every concrete crack along the way and nearly make it to the door. No trips. No falls. No bad luck pianos dropping from a great height.

Just outside the shop I see a bundle of clothes on the floor wrapped around The Moaning Man. Ten feet from the entrance. He looks in pain. Out of luck. Out of cash. I tripped up, he says. They don't mend the slabs anymore, he says.

I help him to a vacant outside table. He smells like he hasn't had a bath for a year. A couple on a nearby table get up and move indoors.

The Moaning Man is wearing a tattered army greatcoat. It's a survivor from World War Something. But not for much longer. It's on its last legs. Just like him.

I go inside. There's no queue at the bar. I walk up to Little Italy. I see you've met Charlie, she says, frowning.

He looks sad, I say. Give me the biggest coffee to go that you've got, I say. Hot and sweet.

She nods, turn, grabs a container, pours in an Americano and four sugars. Pots the top on and hands it to me. This one's on me, I say. He looks like he could do with a bath and a decent bed, I say. She smiles. Already taken care of, she says, putting down the phone.

What's his story, I say. Little Italy shakes her head. Never got over the love of his life, she says. Car accident in the sixties, she says. She was in her twenties. Just lost his way, she says.

I pay and take the coffee outside where The Moaning Man has stopped moaning and is now grimacing and rubbing his right knee. He sees the coffee and perks up.

Just then, a van pulls up and a burly guy with tattoos gets out. He smiles. Charlie, he says, like a long lost friend. Who are you, I say. Nephew, he says. Come on uncle…let's get you sorted out. He helps Charlie out of the chair and into the van. Charlie nods at me from the passenger seat. Holds up his coffee-to-go and smiles.

Big Red comes out and fumigates the chair as I wave goodbye to The Moaning Man and head back inside. Give me what Charlie had, I say to Little Italy. I give her the price times two and look for a vacant space. Little Italy looks at the box on the wall. The box reaches down. Picks up number 29 and puts it on the turntable.

The curtains open. Elvis is on stage singing Love Me Tender. I look at the seat where The Moaning Man sat. Sometimes love never comes.

Sometimes it never goes away.

Be cool…

You must remember this

Good morning Friday. It's the 4th of July and I feel quietly independent. I'm a stand-in for a bald eagle a million miles from home. I used to be a Yankee in King Arthur's Court. But that was a lifetime ago. Here...now...a large, dark colonial Americano calls to me as I enter the coffee shop.

I walk through the door and flip back in time. It's theme day and the theme is Casablanca in the Forties. I'm in Rick's Café Américain. Little Italy has put on her best French frock. Resistance is futile, she says. That's okay by me, I say. I'm The Big Easy.

Sam comes out of the box on the wall. The piano echoes like warm memories in a cold empty church. You must remember this, he sings. I remember, I whisper. Only too damned well. Bergman stands behind me with The Frenchman by her side. He looks like a goddam hero in a cool white suit. She looks like a song unsung and a lifetime full of Southern Comfort.

I take my Americano and feel the lump in my throat move south and take up temporary residence in the pit of my stomach. Of all the coffee joints in all the towns in all the world, they walk in here. They only have eyes for each other. They're on the run. On the lam. But at least they had Paris.

I see the fat man in the corner. White suit. Turkish coffee. Lifting up the cup. Weighing up the pros and cons. I move to a table against the wall. Little Italy serves a shifty looking small guy with eyes like Peter Lorre. He grabs the first available cappuccino and makes for the balcony. I can see the bulge under his jacket. It doesn't look friendly.

The door opens and a tall GI Joe in full combat gear walks in. Looks like Clint. Walks up to Little Italy. Where's the small guy with buggy eyes, he says. Little Italy shoots a look up to the balcony. You want to go up, you pay the price. Clint's eyes narrow even more. He drawls...there's a price? There's always a price, she says.

26

What's your poison, she says. Americano, he says. What else would it be, he says. Make it a large one. Little Italy makes it the largest one she has and hands it to him. A crooked smile wipes itself across his face as he turns and heads for the balcony.

The sound of a chair being pushed back comes from somewhere near the back wall. I look. See a young, dark haired guy stand up. He's with a blonde who looks up at him like he's the best damned thing since sliced bread. He clears his throat and begins to sing.

I hear a voice shove itself into the back of my head. Shoves the singer out. The room goes kinda fuzzy. The voice gets louder. I blink. Look up. Little Italy is standing in front of my table. Smiling. I look around. Casablanca has disappeared. So has the dark haired singer.

Everything that flipped back has now flipped forward again. Little Italy lifts an eyebrow. I think you got lost there for a while, she says. I'll get you another hot Americano, she says. That one's gone cold, she says.

As she walks away she looks at the box on the wall. The box is a sucker for Motown.

The curtains open. Number 143 is already on the turntable. The Temptations are already on stage singing. Or is it just my imagination?

Great moves. Great harmonies.

Be cool…

The Hermit steps back in time

Good morning Wednesday. I never realised how hypnotic a smile was until now. It can reach out, catch and make a single, magic moment in time last…and last.

It can tell the rest of the world to go to Hell while more important things are happening in the space between two sets of eyes.

There are new Lovers in the coffee shop. New hands attracted to each other like magnets. No need for nervous laughter.

These lovers are straight down to business. They are Antony and Cleopatra. Lancelot and Guinevere. Bogart and Bacall. He knows how to whistle. She knows how to have and have not.

That's all they need to know for now. Everything else is unnecessary.

To their right, The Hermit shuffles through the doorway, gold on his fingers. He sees The Lovers and steps back in time. Back to when his trousers were pressed, his wife was alive and his future was bright. Back to when the love in his heart wasn't a faded memory of a feeling he used to know well. Back to when his home was bright and happy and not the solitary confinement it is now.

He doesn't come here to remember what it's like to live amongst people. He doesn't come here to take a break from his loneliness.

He comes here to take a break from his abstinence. He indulges in caffeine. That's all. And only here. Nowhere else.

I asked Little Italy one month ago to the day. Is he homeless? She gave me the full skinny. He's extremely comfortably off, she said. He's not filthy stinking rich, but he's not far off, she said. He just doesn't like people, she said. But he likes coffee. It's the only love affair he has left.

I see The Hermit talking to Little Italy. I see her smile. Take down a special box from above the stainless steel machine.

The box containing her extra EXTRA strong blend. The blend that puts hairs on chests. Makes eyeballs bulge. Gives blood a damned good reason to rush even faster through the veins.

She makes up a cupful and follows him to the most faraway table on the floor. The one with the 'do not disturb' sign on a card sitting on the dark wood.

She waits until he's comfortably sat down, then she places the cup in front of him. Pats his left hand gently. Twice. Leaves.

The Hermit unwraps an old expensive-looking scarf from his neck, runs his fingers through his white hair, takes a deep breath, and begins the ritual. Closes his eyes. Thinks of his wife. Sees her face. Sees her smile. Watches as the smile reaches her eyes. Waits a heartbeat. Then another. Then freeze-frames. Slowly breathes out. Opens his eyes. Reaches for the coffee. Takes a sip. Savours it. Lets loose a slight gasp as his pulse quickens. Prepares for another smile. And another. Until the coffee is finished.

Over behind the bar, Little Italy can see the bliss in his eyes. Understands completely that some desires can never be allowed to disappear. Even with time.

She looks to the box on the wall. The box understands. Reaches way down and brings up number 11.

The curtains open. The Beatles are on stage. McCartney tugs at the heart with The Long and Winding Road.

The Hermit gets up from his chair. Nods at Little Italy. Walks away from the world. Until the next time. Until the next cup.

Be cool…

Tickling the ivories

Good morning Friday. I walk through the square. Through the throng of people. Some rushing to go somewhere. Others rushing to go nowhere. Me strolling to visit my haven. Move over people. Walking stick man coming through.

I have a key. A catalyst. A switch I flick to start the day off on the right note. At the right tempo. Mister Piano Man. Some mornings he sits under the trees, tickling the ivories for anyone who cares to listen. Selling his talent for pennies in a cap. A refugee with a classical repertoire.

I always stop for a minute or two. Open the ears. Slip a few slivers of silver in his cap. He always nods a thank you. Carries on playing. Never misses a note.

I walk around the corner to the coffee shop. Strains of something jazzy floating through the air following me every step of the way. I realise my feet are walking to the bootleg rhythm. They have a musical appreciation that beats the hell out of the rest of my body.

I reach the shop and follow The Tall Guy in ripped jeans and a shapeless knitted jumper through the door. I stay behind him as he heads for the serving part of the bar. Halfway there he slams on the brakes and I rear-end him. I apologise. He apologises. Wrong place, he says. Wrong time, I say. He nods and heads for the door. Fast exit.

Little Italy is four feet away. I shrug. His loss, I say, and smile. He does that every day, she says. Comes in here. Same time. Then turns around and walks out again. Haven't figured out why. It's a mystery, she says. I look at the food shelf. See a vacant space. How come you don't have any slices of carrot cake, I say. That's another mystery, she says.

I grab a pain aux raisins. I know a nice cappuccino that would go well with that, she says. Sounds like a plan, I say. We smile. Great minds think alike.

I load up a tray and head for a vacant table against the wall. Next door to me, Executive Thirty-Something Couple are making an iPhone selfie record of their assignation.

30

Mini stars on a mini screen. iFriends. Or maybe more. Work and pleasure. Impeccably dressed. Exquisitely coiffed. Touching scene. Touching hands.

At the bar, Big Red is serving two Sports Direct Dot Coms in track suits and tees. Two lattes. Two bowls of fruit. Too healthy by half. Too much muscle definition.

At the window chair, The Man In Black sits and lets the world wash over him. Over the years he has learned to live with all the voices in his head. The ones belonging to other folk. All those internal conversations. The soft speakers. The loud screamers. The tearful pleaders. The mad ones and the sad ones. The ones with murderous rage and the ones with suicidal intent.

The Man In Black hears them all and can do nothing about it. That's his gift. That's his curse. Little Italy can see him close his eyes and try to tune them out. Or at least calm them down. So she helps the only way she knows how. She prepares an extra strong espresso. Takes it over to him. He hears her approach. Glances up. Smiles. Nods a thank you. Closes his eyes again.

Little Italy can feel his gratitude. Doesn't need any visible proof. She walks away and shoots a glance at the box on the wall. The box gets the drift. Reaches down. Picks up number 90.

The curtains open. Standing on the stage is Jimmy Cliff. I can see clearly now.

The Man In Black takes a deep breath and lets it out slowly. Opens his eyes and reaches for his espresso.

Be cool...

George rolls his arse

Good morning Tuesday. I love the sound of a smooth alto sax to start off the day…not just to end it. Slow and easy. Soft and gentle. Hitting all the right notes. Touching all the right emotions. Bringing order into chaos. Making the air molecules dance as I walk through the tree-lined square in the centre of the city.

Even from a hundred yards away I can smell the dark, rich aroma of caffeine. Waiting to salve the throats and the minds of those who visit the coffee shop. The saxophonist is called Willie. He salves the souls. He sucks on a rolled-up lit cigarette in between tunes. I figure he only has enough lung power for one tune before the wind bags need a break. I slip him some change and make for the coffee shop.

I walk through the door and the place is light on people but crowded with expectation. Full of possibilities for the coming day. The ghosts of yesterday are sitting at the tables. Filling the chairs. Their conversations mingle in my head with the sound of Sting coming from the box on the wall. They'll soon be on their way as, one by one, the tables fill up with the living of today.

Two sixtysomethings are standing in front of Little Italy. Agnes and George. Agnes is more feminine than masculine. George, the other way round. A pair of dapper, colourful Adam's apples who move to the beat of a different drum.

I liked them the moment I spoke to them months ago. They sat down next door and started up a conversation we never got the chance to finish. Maybe this morning.

Turns out maybe not, as they grab their skinny lattes to go and turn to head for the door after air-kissing Little Italy from three feet away.

Cherio darling, says Agnes. And that'll be enough of that, says George.

He tuts. Rolls his eyes. Rolls his arse. Looks at Little Italy. He's such a tart, he says. He grabs Agnes's arm and steers him towards the door.

Then they spot me and it takes me five minutes to extricate myself. My arse was patted twice and squeezed once in the process.

I turn to Little Italy, a blush on my face. I think you need to cool down, she says. Your arse okay? My arse is fine, I say. In another lifetime it might even be cute, I say. George and Agnes both agree. She raises an eyebrow. But not in this one, she says.

We smile. I order a pot of green tea and slice of lemon cake and load them on a tray. I can feel Little Italy look at the box on the wall. The box never refuses her. It reaches down, brings number 120 up and slides it on the turntable.

The curtains open. The spotlight above the stage shines on The Four Tops. Cue intro. Cue vocals. Can't help myself.

I say my finals to George and Agnes and head for the wingback. Right come on, Sugar Pie, says George. Oh okay Honey Bunch, says Agnes. They disappear into the crowd outside, leaving the shop all the poorer for their absence.

Love is love and it doesn't give a damn who it happens to. Be cool...

Pin Stripe has big plans

Good morning Wednesday. Today it feels like a 'what if' kinda day. Like what if time stood still. Had a time-out. Just for half an hour. No rushing. No panics. Just stillness. Only silence.

Or what if the coffee shop closed its doors to all but those who knew the meaning of real time, non-electronic conversation (oh the irony). Just the noise of vocal cords being exercised. No buttons bring pressed. No screens being viewed. Just old school communication.

What if here, inside the coffee shop, Little Italy wore red instead of black and I sipped espresso instead of green tea, feeling the dark liquid open my eyes just a little more than usual.

I look to the left, where open-necked shirts stand. Out of shape. Waiting to be served. Bags over shoulders. Shorts over hairy, tanned legs with bicycle calves. No doubles at the tables. No meeting eyes deep in love. Only singles, deep in thought. Waiting for the man. Waiting for the woman. Waiting for the right time to get up and leave.

Another what if. What if they stayed? Spoke to the person at the next table. Opened up. Let their guard down. Just for a minute.

I look to the left and I see that The Hermit is sat at one of the outside tables and he's talking to the friends inside his head. Damn, that man is so cool. His dreads animate throughout his selfie conversation as he rolls a fat joint, puts it in his makings tin, puts the tin in his pocket. A little something for later, when he's sat under the trees in the square. A little wacky baccy. A little suck it and see. A little light up, sit down, tune out grass when he's cross-legged on the other kind of grass.

But for the moment, he watches the world go by, exchanges psychological insights with the invisible folk, and drinks from an empty cup left by a previous chair occupant. While three feet away the world goes by oblivious.

Here inside, soft Irish music massages the heart and feeds the soul of a dozen thoughtful listeners. Little Italy's front says 'the best espresso this side of New York'. Her back says 'the best damned coffee this side of the planet'. I wonder about the other side.

The door opens. Pin Stripe walks up to the bar. All business. Black Americano with an extra shot of something to kickstart the day. He looks around. Sees a spot by the window. For thirty minutes he's the MD of a small table and single chair. Corporate empires are built on less.

Pin Stripe has plans. Big plans. The kind of plans that need financial muscle to bring to life. The kind of plans that need talent and expertise and attitude. And time. Time to strike the match. Light the blue touch paper. Get the Hell out of Dodge.

But for now...a steaming hot Americano will do. Four sugars. Ten stirs clockwise. Two taps of the wooden stick to shake off all the drips. Like I said. He's a man with a plan. All he needs is a kickstart. He's in no hurry. He's got all the time in the world. Starting now.

Over behind the bar, Little Italy sees his cogs go round and she looks at the box on the wall. The box has some cogs of its own to put in motion. It reaches way down and plucks up number 152.

The curtains open, The Stones are on the stage. Mick licks his lips. Flicks his locks. Stretches out the first word. Time...is on my side.

Pin Stripe lifts his mug and takes a sip. Nice and slow. Time to be patient. Be smart.

Be cool...

Lola wags her tail

Good morning Friday. We are creatures of habit. We find comfort in regularity. Predictability. We have a preference for the warm and fuzzy. The non-threatening. And when that's taken away, the part of our brain that wants to run for the hills kicks into action and pushes the red panic button.

The professor wasn't in his usual spot today in the coffee shop. He had been usurped. Taken over. Beaten to the punch. He was sitting disconsolate, confused, three tables away. His comfort zone had been invaded. He was a fish. There was no water.

He saw the look of sympathy in my eyes and shrugged. He knew I understood. And as if in tandem understanding, a little Oirish fiddle oozed from the box on the wall. Slow and full of regret. Maybe next time, it said.

The door opened and Maureen O'Hara stood framed against the brightening day. All red hair, padded shoulders and a smile the colour of purity. Untouched by dental decay. Framed by blood red lips. Looking for her Quiet Man. Searching for her John Wayne. Finding only a quiet room. Devoid of her kind of heroism.

The music flipped and the branches of The Joshua Tree swayed in the wind of disappointment. I still haven't found what I'm looking for, they said. U2? Yep...me too. But there's always tomorrow. Until then...Maureen comes in...sits down. Keeps The Professor company. His name's Harry, but he ain't dirty. Make his day.

The door opens and The Girl With Purple Hair comes in. A rare occurrence. A small waif-like creature with a shock of colour. Five minutes ago she was outside on the patio. Drinking latte and attacking a long cigarette. A love-hate relationship. Now she comes inside, following a mixed species duo of Guy and Dog. One smiling, the other sniffing. The urge to lift a leg and leave a calling card is almost too much to resist. Almost.

Little Italy smiles in recognition. The guy is a regular. Lola is something much more profound. She wags her tail gleefully and receives her daily treat. A slice of apple. A mouthful of friendship. By the window, The Man in Black makes a sign in the air with his fingers. Lola sees and understands. They speak each other's language. She runs to him. Sits down. Head up. Waiting.

The Man in Black makes another sign. Lola barks softly. Getting the message. Goes back to the guy she came in with. A little happier. A little wiser.

Little Italy looks at the box on the wall. The box is normally a cat lover. But not when Lola is around. It reaches down and pulls up number 2.

The curtains open. The Kinks are on the stage. Halfway through Lola's namesake song.

Lola walks slowly to The Girl With Purple Hair and head-butts her leg softly. The Girl looks down. Drops a hand. Lola sniffs. Looks round at the guy. Gets the nod. Little Italy laughs.

What's so funny, says The Girl With Purple Hair. You passed the test, says Little Italy. What test, says The Girl. You'll find out, says Little Italy.

Be cool…

Mister Tick Tock slows down

Good morning Tuesday. Time is a villain that sneaks into our lives like a thief in the night. It steals our ability to be the one thing that makes us different from everyone else. Ourselves.

Somewhere in all that time doing other things for other folk, the life we want for ourselves...(and the people we want to be)...gets lost. Mislaid. Time-napped. All those precious minutes, hours and days. All those years working for the man. Or the woman. Gone, never to be regained, returned or seen again.

The coffee shop has an unwelcome visitor this morning. Sitting on a bar stool by the window near the door. The Time Thief. Mister Hurry Up. Mister Get Your Skates On. His gaze passing over everyone in the room. Giving them a nudge. No time to sip. No time to chill out. Get your ass in gear.

Behind the bar, Little Italy clocks him as he gives her customers the eye. She nods at Big Red who takes over the dispensing of caffeine.

With slow deliberation and powerful indignation, she approaches The Time Thief. Stands in front of his stool. Gets in his face. Gets in his space. Who the Hell let you in the door, she says. Folk round here like things slow and easy, she says. You got no place here Mister Tick Tock, she says.

She looks at him. Sat on his four-legged perch. Vacant space in front of him where a coffee or tea should be. I got no place else to be, says The Time Thief. My time is up, he says. My timepiece is all wound-down and broke, he says, tapping the silent ticker strapped to his left wrist. I'm old school, he says. Analogue. Everybody's digital these days, he says. New school, he says.

Little Italy softens. Maybe somebody's trying to tell you something, she says. Maybe the world is too wound up. Maybe it's time you got wound down, she says. Maybe it's time you put time on the back burner, she says. How about a coffee.

The Time Thief looks thoughtful. Raises his right hand. Strokes his grey chin beard slowly. Nods his head. Smiles. Sounds like a plan, he says. Maybe something tall and dark and hot, he says. I got just the thing in mind, she says.

Turns away. Walks behind the bar. Mixes up a steaming Americano with a little squeeze of something cinnamon. Another little squeeze of something special from the top shelf. Adds a heaped sugar. Gives the milk a miss. Walks back and lays it in front of The Time Thief.

He leans forward over the cup and takes in a deep breath. Lets it out slow. Take your time, she says. Walks away. Turns and looks at the box on the wall. Little Italy always has the reins. The box always rides shotgun. It reaches down. Picks up number 140. Slides it on the turntable.

The curtains open. Good old Willie Nelson stands at the mike. Grizzled. Lived-in. Guitar strapped on like a Wild West rig.

The Time Thief takes a sip. Swallows. Closes his eyes. Willie sings. Funny How Time Slips Away.

The Time Thief takes off his broken watch and puts it in his pocket. Rubs his wrist. Feels free. Feels good.

Be cool…

The Mouse has a girl talk

Good morning Wednesday. Have you ever noticed how anti-social social media is? A question laden with irony. Positively dripping with it.

We sit in our own little worlds, talking to the rest of the world yet isolated from it. Our minds focused on buttons rather than faces. Our ears listening to the noise of an incoming email, rather than the sound of an incoming voice. And yet...and yet.

Our heads and hearts reach out to people we will never see and we'll get to know some of them better than their next door neighbours. We smile and laugh with them. Sometimes cry with them.

There is a sadness in the coffee shop this morning. In a faraway corner is The Mouse. A timid creature with short brown hair and pointed features. A beautiful, small, frail creature bursting with want...and need. Pressing buttons furiously. Dabbing away salty tears with a tissue already damp with emotion.

Somewhere at the sharp end of her fingers...maybe at the other end of the world...is another want, another need. Another mind that understands. Sympathises. Reaches out and connects the dots. Holds hands over the net. Speaks words with a silent voice. Gives solace when those around her never do.

Little Italy watches from behind the counter and feels the sadness of The Mouse. She reaches behind and pours a fresh cappuccino. Takes it to The Mouse. You look like you could use a friend, she says.

The Mouse nods and Little Italy pulls up a chair. Time for a little girl talk.

Back at the bar, Big Red steps up to the plate and gets ready to dispense coffee shop TLC to the needy.

For a few minutes at least she is stand-in for the queen of the baristas. But that's okay. You don't get to ride shotgun here without knowing a thing or two about what makes folk tick.

And standing in front of Big Red, looking at the coffee menu chalkboard on the back wall is someone who ticks every damned box on the list when it comes to being a beautiful, weird sonovabitch.

The Button Guy is humming like he always does when he can't make up his mind. The chalkboard is packed full of options. He finally speaks. Can I have a large cafe mocha with double chocolate chip with organic soya milk, an extra shot, and a vanilla squeeze? With a nutmeg dusting on the top? Please?

Big Red looks at him. Blinks. The Button Guy starts fiddling with his buttons. There are hundreds of them. All pinned to the front of his dark woolen jacket. She blinks again. You want that all in the one mug? The Button Guy looks alarmed and starts humming.

Tell you what, says Big Red. Let me make you up one of my very special coffees, she says. It's so strong your toes will curl, she says. You'll love it, she says.

The Button Guy stops fiddling. Somebody cares about what he might like. He drops his shoulders. Relaxes. Smiles. That would be nice, he says.

Two minutes later he's sitting at the table next to The Mouse with a smoking Caramel Macchiato with just a hint of peppermint.

Little Italy gets up from the chair at The Mouse's table, squeezes her hand gently, looks at the box on the wall, walks away, and somewhere inside the number 31 makes a move.

The curtains open. There, on the stage James Taylor puts his silky voice into gear.

Don't worry little Mouse. Don't worry Button Guy. You've got a friend.

Be cool...

The Girl With The Butterfly Tattoo

Good morning Thursday. We fight so hard to bring some kind of order into our lives. Some sort of safety. Some semblance of knowledge. So that, on a good day, one plus one really does equal two.

We forget that chaos is the natural state of affairs. Not the chaos of romantic violence. Not the chaos of fear and despair. But the chaos of beautiful unpredictability. Of wild nonconformity and emotional roller coaster rides.

Today is an order and chaos day. In the coffee shop, The Girl With The Butterfly Tattoo has come to drink and be quietly obsessive. Compulsively neat. Disorderly ordered. Her chair is just so. Her coffee cup even more so. The contents especially so. Nothing is out of place. Nothing that disrupts the harmony. Except her ankle ink. The Papilio Antimachus. The most poisonous butterfly in the world.

I asked her about it once when were next door neighbours on the back wall. He's called Hector, she said. He's my protector, she said. I got him so nobody would mess with me, she said. But every guy you've gone out with you messes with you, I said. I know, she said. Hector's too nice, she said. I think he needs toughening up.

On the other side of the room sits the physical and emotional opposite of The Girl With The Butterfly Tattoo. Smiling in a pile of disarray. Mister Disorderly Conduct. Mister Pierced Everything. He's enjoying his spilled latte and he finds comfort in knowing that his life doesn't conform to the laws of the neat and the tidy.

And yet occasionally he looks at her. And occasionally she looks at him. These are not the looks of repulsion or failure to comprehend. They're something entirely different. A cross-contamination of North and South. Without the interruption of East and West.

No blending of similarities here. This is the rule of precision versus the law of the jungle.

42

Step back folks…this could get messy. There could be pain involved. But there could also be pleasure. No polite conversation. No getting to know you chats. No small talk. This is getting down to business stuff. This is getting your kit off as fast as you can at the earliest possible convenience stuff. This is don't be gentle. Don't be slow. Don't be considerate. This is the fast and the furious. The hot and the sweaty. This is car crash lust.

But only from a distance. Only in the mind. Without the merging of bodily fluids. Because nobody's making a move. Nobody's flicking the on switch. They're too busy being cerebral. Too busy getting laid between their ears.

Behind the bar Little Italy can see this. Plain as day. She knows that unless somebody moves their ass, no sweaty business will get done with these two. So she looks up at the box on the wall and nods. The box has seen this all before. This prelude to a meeting of two different species. It knows the end result. Life finds a way. But time is wasting. So it reaches down and plucks up number 91. Watches as it slides vigorously into place.

The curtains open. Iggy Pop, godfather of punk, is on stage. Bare chest. Raw. Taught as a wire. Stooges at the back. Halfway through a track. Looks a hundred years old. Still has a six pack. Still has a Lust For Life.

Mister Disorderly Conduct looks down at the feet of The Girl With The Butterfly Tattoo. Hector is fast asleep. Time to make a move.

Be cool…

The note in black ink

Good morning Friday. There is a unique pain that some of us feel knowing that, even though we are lapsed Catholics, we still have guilt embedded in our genes. We don't have to do anything to feel it. It's just there.

We forget what the inside of a church looks like, we feel guilty. We see someone in a worse state than ourselves, we feel guilty. We indulge in a secret pleasure, we feel guilty. We smile inside because the weekend is tomorrow and we can stay in bed an extra five minutes and wear pyjamas for the rest of the day...and we feel damned guilty.

Today all that comes to a shuddering, if temporary, halt. Today the jail door opens and I can walk in the sun a free man. The angel in my own personal slammer has paid my bail.

Today, Little Italy hands me an envelope with my green tea. There's a handwritten note on the front. One line. Black ink. It says: 'Sit down...sip your tea...open the envelope...read the card'. I look at it. Look at her. Search her face for some sort of hint. Nothing.

She just smiles and nods towards one of my regular vacant spots. Sometimes you just have to zip the lip and do what you're told.

I walk to the table and nod at The Professor on the way past. He's scratching his head in a way that has nothing to do with itching. His latest equation is obviously not going well. His iPad is misbehaving. His apple is being a pain in the ass. Things do not compute. Even his brown corduroy jacket with leather elbow pads isn't helping.

You can't always rely on the clothes you wear to give you the answers you need, I whisper as I draw level. He looks up. Blinks rapidly and raises a finger in the air. I see a Eureka Moment flash before his eyes. He smiles. Wrong socks, he says. I knew it as soon as I took my first sip of coffee, he says. Should have put the blue ones on. The ones with the exclamation marks, he says.

I try to look sympathetic. Let me guess, I say. You put the red ones with the question marks on? He nods, defeated. Right on the button, he says. Wrong on your feet, I say. He smiles, ruefully. There's always another problem, I say. Another equation. Leave P versus NP for another day. Go get yourself one of these and cogitate, I say, glancing at my green tea. It's my parting shot and the thought walks with me on the journey to my table ten feet away.

Behind me, I hear him scrape the feet of his chair along the black and white tiles and stand up. I sit, arrange my glutes, pour my slightly bitter liquid, take a sip, and open the envelope. A card inside said: Congratulations. Today is your guilt-free day. Enjoy.

I look up at the bar and see The Professor take my advice. Big Red is taking his order. For this morning, at least, green is the new brown. Beside her, Little Italy is looking at the box on the wall. The box is looking chilled out. From deep inside, number 53 ambles up and sets itself down on the turntable.

The curtains open. The Eagles are on the stage. Take it easy.

The Professor comes back to his table with a pot of the green stuff and a chunky muffin bursting with blueberries. Food for thought.

Be cool...

Heels on Wheels doesn't give a damn

Good morning Tuesday. There are those of us who spend our lives wishing we were normal. Wishing we were just like everyone else. And there are those of us who fight tooth and nail to head for the hills whenever normal comes knocking on the door.

Heels on Wheels doesn't give a damn either way. All she wants is someone who wants her. All she wants us someone who can see past the obvious and say hello to the kick inside. And Heels on Wheels is one helluva kick.

Six inch stilettos, four motorised tyres, two useless legs, one lonely heart. Parked in the reserved space by the window of the coffee shop.

I stand at the bar. Order given. Coinage given. How long has she been coming here, I say to Little Italy. Since Noah built his little boat, she says, and fills up my cup. She's waiting for Mister Right, she says. Maybe today's the right day, she says. The world is full of Mister Rights who turn out to be Mister Lefts, I say. She gives me the kinda shrug that says maybe so...maybe no.

Heels on Wheels is sipping something dark and steamy. Looking at the door in between sips like she's waiting for something to happen. But the door is just a dead slab of glass that only comes alive when somebody comes in or goes out. It's looking for a little action. A little push and shove. Just like Heels on Wheels.

Meanwhile, back at the ranch, I grab my skinny latte and head for a vacant spot in the corner. I see everyone. Nobody sees me. Fair exchange no robbery. Just as I sit down I get a little peripheral vision. A little corner of the eye thing.

Three tables away I see OCD Girl. Small, dark and beautiful. Curly hair. Light brown skin. Bright white blouse. All buttoned up. Arranging her stuff on the table. Clockwise three times. Anti-clock once. Don't miss a move. Don't break the groove.

She stops. Turns. Sees my peripheral. Looks away fast.

Another turn anti-clock. Nods at the mug. Now a slow count to thirty to let the cappuccino cool to 155 degrees. No more. No less. That's when the coffee nods back. That's when optimum taste is achieved. That's when she hears the voice in her head say 'damn that's a fine cuppa Joe'. Then it's all systems go. Six gulps. No more. No less. Ten pages of her book. Another six gulps. Another ten pages. A little obsessive. A touch compulsive. But hey…we do what we do to feel good about ourselves, right?

Off to the right, the door swings open and Mister Right, six feet four of muscle and brain squeezes through the space. Heels on Wheels' heart steps up a beat. Then another. Breath catches in her throat. Little Italy looks at the box on the wall. The box acts fast. Reaches down. Pulls up number 80 and slides it onto the turntable.

The curtains open. Etta James stands at the mike. Lush orchestral intro sets the scene. Her sweet voice oozes across the air. Hairs stand on end.

At Last. Mister Right looks at her. She looks at him. The rest of the world excuses itself and disappears out of sight. We're born. We die. And the whole alphabet of life is what happens in between. Be the same. Be different.

Be cool…

The Girl With A Thousand Freckles nods

Good morning Wednesday. Today I walk across the city centre square and the rain wets my face like tears from Heaven. I have an umbrella, but it's a coward and fights to stay in my shoulder bag. Tangled up in the cord from my laptop charger. So I let the wetness touch my skin and feel refreshed.

I grab a national from the newsstand at the corner. The news guy has an umbrella that isn't afraid of the rain. I pay him. Stuff the national inside my jacket. Walk the last twenty yards to the coffee shop.

The usual suspects are huddled around a couple of tables under the awning on the outside. They're friends of Mister Nicotine. I nod. They nod.

I push through the doors and make for the bar and Little Italy. She smiles when she sees me. Why so serious, she says. It's a shit day out there, I say. She shrugs. Shit happens, she says. It's just another day at the office, she says.

She raises an eyebrow. You got a new jacket, she says. I smile. My old one's a coward, I say. It's not brave enough for a day like today. It lets the cold in. It doesn't keep the rain out. And it's blue. Green jackets are warmer, I say. And braver, she says. You need a new drink to celebrate your new jacket, she says.

I look up at the chalkboard on the wall above the stainless steel machine. A cafe mocha jumps out at me. Espresso…liquid chocolate…whipped cream…Belgian chocolate shavings on the top. Damn that sounds good, I say, pointing to it. Little Italy nods. Tastes good too, she says. Go sit down, I'll bring it over, she says.

I turn and make for a vacant spot against the far wall. Two tables away from Romeo and Juliet on the left. Today they're not silent, lost in each other's eyes. Today they're found. Full of sound and movement and conversation. They touch and stroke and laugh and sigh. The rest of the world has gone to Hell.

I sit and take the National out of my jacket. The front is full of celebrity death. The passing away of fame. Not necessarily talent. I flip the pages. Genocide is relegated to a small column on page three. Bigger stories get smaller cover. My mocha appears on the table in front of me. I didn't even hear it arrive.

Off to my left, The Girl With A Thousand Freckles sees me and nods. Red wavy hair moves with the gesture. Her eyes blink slowly. I live on the dark side of the moon. She lives on the bright side of the sun. Maybe in another life. She looks away.

I look down at my mocha. Pick up the cup. Take a sip. Let the taste crawl all over my tongue and slide slowly down my throat. Over in a corner by the window, The Hermit is wearing his best tenth-generation baggy hand-me-downs. He hugs his Americano and disappears into a million memories.

Little Italy knows one or two of those memories and she throws a nod at the box on the wall. The box catches it, reaches down and picks up number 128.

The curtains open. Nat King Cole is standing on stage. Opens his mouth. Out comes a voice to die for. When I fall in love…

The Hermit closes his eyes and remembers.

Be cool…

The ones who want to fit in

Good morning Friday. There are some folk who go through life collecting friends like baseball cards. The more they have, the more popular and valued they feel.

Then there are those who go for quality not quantity. All they need...all they ever want...is someone special...or maybe just a few special someones. They don't go for big numbers. They go for big feelings.

This morning, in the coffee shop, big numbers are by the window. Big feelings are at a table next to the stairs leading up to the gallery. I can hear the sound of laughter and animated conversation as soon as I walk in the door. Big numbers have taken over the six tables on the inside left.

They look like students. They sound like an assault on the ears. Are they happy? Absolutely. This isn't a place for the down at heart. This isn't a section of the room for the romantically challenged. This isn't a collection of emotionally damaged individuals. This is the land of the ones who want to belong. The ones who want to fit in. The ones who want to feel part of the in-crowd. And the more there are of them...the more they fit in...the more valued they feel.

It's popularity by sheer weight of numbers. It's not I am...it's we are. Every one of them has 2,000-plus Facebook friends and they only know 35 of them personally. And nearly all of them are here.

Unlike The Girl With The Butterfly Tattoo. Sitting quietly in a corner by the stairs. Staring at her phone. Waiting for the one call that puts the rest of her life into perspective. Gives it meaning. Soothes the aches and pains. Lifts the spirit. Quickens the pulse. Warms the heart.

Until then she's the odd one out. She's flying solo. She's Sally No Mates. There's no companionship in her life. No laughter. No friends with benefits. At least that's what she thinks.

But friends...real friends...are curious creatures.

Just because you can't see them doesn't mean they're not there. Doesn't mean they don't exist. Just because you can't touch them doesn't mean they can't reach out and touch you.

Technology is a wonderful thing. And sometimes just when you think you're only talking to one person, you find out there's a whole crowd of folk waiting to join in the conversation. Behind the bar, Little Italy warms a teapot then glances at the box on the wall. The box knows the meaning of true friendship. So it reaches down, pulls number 30 up, and slides it on the turntable.

The curtains open. Ben E. King is on stage. First comes that four-note double bass intro. Then the unmistakable voice. Stand by me. The rest is history.

The phone in front of The Girl With The Butterfly Tattoo blinks into life and on the other side of the world a friend hears the song, stops what he's doing, and stands up. Then another friend stands...and another...and another...

Be cool...

The Limping Man's rule

Good morning Wednesday. Good morning slow 12-string guitar and piano in the coffee shop. Unplugged. Nothing shrill...everything soft. A little balm to soothe a lot of pain.

There are those of us who go through life feeling no pain. No aches...no hurts...no sharp, jagged stabbings. Not physically anyway.

And then are those who feel everything. For them the slightest touch is a hammer blow. The merest stroke is an enemy of comfort. For them pain is a constant companion. The only thing that makes the constant bearable is how much. How little. How long. How short. For them a flare up isn't merely a fire. It's a blaze that consumes.

Little Italy's pain is quiet today. They have an arrangement. She leaves it alone. It leaves her alone. Until such times as the silence loses it's grip and has to give way to the sharpness and the noise. Until such times as each movement is a battle.

But today it's merely a struggle. Today the tremor in the hand is almost imperceptible as she serves up my pot of green tea. I apologise for the weight. She apologises for the wait. We both understand and smile.

No apologies are needed for something you can do nothing about.

I look around and hunt for a vacant spot. I don't like being in the middle. I like the edges and the corners. So does The Limping Man. He likes the support of walls at his back. He likes the space to sit down and stretch his left leg out straight without fear of being tripped over. Today it hurts like Hell. He's right behind me in the queue. Standing on one leg. The other pulled up. Pain on his face. Killers in his pocket.

The Limping Man has a rule about pain. It's his damned pain. Nobody else's. He owns it. So if he takes the pills to take away the pain, he doesn't own it any more.

Somebody else does. Somebody who makes pills that take pain away. And if they own his pain, they own him. So the pills stay in his pocket. And the pain stays in his leg. He's a stubborn bastard.

Little Italy looks in his eyes. You got your pills, she says. The Limping Man grimaces and pats his jacket pocket twice. Where's your cane today, she says. No cane…no pain, he says. At least that's the theory, he says. How's that working out, she says. The Limping Man shrugs. Work in progress, he says.

I grab my tray. Spot a table in the corner at the back. Make for it…then stop. Turn. Looks like a good spot, I say to The Limping Man. Plenty of space to stretch out. He looks. Nods. Feel like company, he says. I smile. Sounds like a plan, I say. We both make for the corner.

I turn and look at Little Italy. She looks at the box on the wall. The box knows the score. It reaches down, pulls number 55 up and slides it on the turntable.

The curtains open. A single beam lights the stage. Johnny Cash is standing at the mike. No guitar. No need. Just Hurt.

I turn my head and look at The Limping Man. The pain is gone from his face. For now.

Be cool…

The Thin Lady is emotionally blind

Good morning Thursday. We are a caring species. We care about what the weather's going to do today. We care about how little time we have and how much money we don't have. We care about the place we call home and the stuff we call ours. We care about how we feel and what we do. We even care about whether we care enough.

And then, sitting at the back of the queue, are the ones who should be standing at the front of it. Each other.

The coffee shop is full this morning. Full of life. Full of laughter and conversation. The noise of busy mouths and busy minds. Busy on the surface...not so busy underneath.

It's a caffeine microcosm. And right in the middle is The Thin Lady. Almost devoid of flesh. The clothes she's wearing are almost her only substance. Sitting in front of her, on the table waiting, are a skinny latte and a slice of carrot cake. Untouched. Untasted. The largest slice Little Italy could find.

She sees The Thin Lady look towards the door and search the crowd outside for the slim chance that 'he' might put in an appearance. That 'he' might take a chance and give a damn. She knows that, for as long as she's known The Thin Lady, there have been many men in her life. And they all have one thing in common. Their lack of ability and desire to care for her.

However, as well as being painfully slim, The Thin Lady is also emotionally blind. She cares about every one of them. They care not a fig about her. Not a jot. She's merely a convenience. Except for one of them. The one she's waiting for. The latest one. He's different in every way.

She knew it the instant she saw him for the first time. Yesterday. She knew he had possibilities. Potential. He drank his Americano black. And sweet. That was a good start. He'll come again today. She knows. So she waits.

Little Italy sees her looking at the door again and again.

She knows that, sometimes, the worst thing that can happen is for our deepest desires to come true. She also knows that sometimes it's the best thing that can happen.

So she looks at the box on the wall, and somewhere inside the box, number 151 slips into view, slides onto the turntable and says a soft hello.

The curtains open. Nina Simone, High Priestess of Soul, sits at a grand piano. Her fingers move across the keys. The introduction is unmistakable. So is the voice. So is the song. My Babe Just Cares for Me.

The door opens and Babe walks in. He smiles and sits down at her table. Lifts a fork, spears a small chunk of carrot cake and feeds it to The Thin Lady. She lets the food enter her mouth and slowly makes it hers. Just like he is.

At the counter Little Italy chalks up another small victory. There's no such thing as coincidence. There's only what is.

Be cool...

The King and Queen of Hearts

Good morning Tuesday. The small day. The forgotten day. The day of the week that gets stuffed in between another new beginning and the breathing space halfway through another week.

Misunderstood. Always shoved to the back of the line. Never given the chance to shine. All except inside the coffee shop.

Here, Tuesday is a safe haven. A good news day, when bad news is left outside and the sign on the door says: Don't hurry...don't worry. Come in...have a coffee...take a load off.

It's a day when one table in particular has a reserved sign on it...and Little Italy has a pair of black as night Americanos waiting.

The door opens and she looks up to see the King and Queen of Hearts walk in hand in hand. The Queen looks at Little Italy and the ghost of a smile passes between them as kindred spirits acknowledge each other. They nod and the couple walk to the back of the room where their table awaits. Holding hands. Oozing class.

On the way they pass by The Man In Black, who sees everything but says nothing...and The Professor, who today is wearing his most intelligent bow tie. Even the design probably has an IQ higher than most university graduates.

Little Italy waits until they're seated before she brings their Americanos over. They don't even notice that she's there. They're too busy noticing each other. As she leaves she looks up at the box on the wall and somewhere inside, number 21 slides into its spot.

The curtains open. And there, at the microphone, the gut-wrenching voice of Mister Percy Sledge, singing When a Man Loves a Woman, puts everything into perspective.

Behind the bar Little Italy breathes deep. Sometimes the smallest day of the week is the biggest day.

Be cool...

The Listener searches for a sound

Good morning Wednesday. There are those of us who go through life and the only true voice that they ever hear coming from inside their head is their own. Every other voice is a copycat. A facsimile. A sound belonging to somebody else. Created by somebody else.

Then there are those of us who live their whole lives inside the noise. The noise of a thousand voices all wanting to be heard. All looking for attention. All fighting for the right to exist. What do we do when the voices stop? When the silence comes pounding on the door demanding entry?

Today...in the coffee shop...The Listener is searching for a sound. He sits in a chair at a table smack dab in the centre of the room. He wants as much space around him as possible. He wants every sense he has dialed all the way up and his own personal radar scanning 365 degrees.

He scours the landscape of his imagination looking for company. Hunting for a conversation...a shouting match...the soft whisper of a lover's private confidence. Anything to tell him that he's not alone. That the world inside his head exists because he wishes it to. But all he can hear is the silence.

Behind the bar, Little Italy sees The Listener's eyes rapidly moving back and forth. Sees his fingers twitching with pent up energy. Tapping on the keyboard of the tabletop. So she pays him a visit. Says hello. Reaches out a hand. Holds his tightly in hers. And waits for one of the voices inside her own head to go visiting and work its own special brand of magic.

Then she walks away with a backward glance at the box on the wall. The box puts everything else to one side and reaches out for a small black vinyl disc. Number 107. The disc slips onto the turntable. And gets ready for a little royalty.

The curtains open. Freddie puts in an appearance. And Queen turns everything on its head.

Boom boom clap...boom boom clap...boom boom clap...boom boom clap. We Will Rock You!!

The Listener looks over at Little Italy and smiles for the first time in days. And a voice inside his head laughs and whispers: "buckle up sunshine...it's gonna be a bumpy ride!"

Be cool...

Time is on my side

Good morning Thursday. Every heart is given only so many beats in its life. It can choose whether those beats are fast and furious, slow and easy, or somewhere conveniently in-between.

Few folk know the grand total for each pump. One of them is The Timekeeper. The one who knows every tick and every tock. Every beat and every rhythm. When to keep going…and when to stop.

She's in the coffee shop this morning. Sitting where the tables begin and end. Underneath the box on the wall. Close to the music. Counting every beat except her own. The only one she has no knowledge of. No clue. No foresight. The only person who has that knowledge, who knows the day when her heart will change its constant rhythm, or cease completely, stands behind the bar pouring a triple espresso into a small white cup.

Little Italy walks to where the Timekeeper sits and places the tiny container on the dark tabletop. The Timekeeper looks into her eyes. Of all the time in all the world she regards this as the most important. The most precious.

It's the only opportunity she ever gets to hand time over to someone else. Someone who will one day take over from her and be the new keeper of the seconds and minutes. Hours and days. Weeks and months. Years and decades. Centuries and millennia.

As Little Italy walks slowly back behind the coffee bar, she places her hand over her own heart for a second and feels it move beneath her fingers. Between its beats she feels a second heartbeat. Softer, but just as regular. Just as determined. She reaches the bar, turns and glances at the box on the wall.

The box knows all about time. It knows about what happens on the beats. And what happens in between the beats. And right on cue, it reaches down and picks up number 152.

The curtains open. The stage lights up The Stones.

Mister Jagger eases himself itself into place in front of the mike. Mister Lips & Hips tells another truth. Time Is on My Side.

Little Italy moves on to the next customer. The only thing worse than having too much time is not having enough.

Be cool…

The Matchmaker conjures a sign

Good morning Friday. It's funny how the end of one thing can also be the beginning of something else.

The Matchmaker is in the coffee shop and standing at the bar, taking in the ambience. I'm standing behind her, waiting for my green infusion.

She looks around, her gaze pausing on two small individuals who are sitting alone at either ends of the shop. Lost in their own little worlds, with nothing to think about except the empty chairs on the opposite sides of their tables. Nothing to do but count the thousands of electronic friends they have and wonder why they feel so alone in the crowd. Nobody to touch. Nobody to smile at and see them smile back. Nobody to share more than just a conversation with. Nothing deeper. Nothing more profound.

The Matchmaker sees all this and turns to Little Italy who hands her a medium cappuccino dusted with something dark and aromatic.

There's a small white card perched on the saucer next to the silver spoon. The card has a number, beautifully hand written in red ink, on it. Nothing else. I see it briefly. 155.

The Matchmaker nods at Little Italy and sits at a table equidistant from the two loners. As she walks to her seat I can feel a strange attraction, like the pull of a magnet, following her as she goes. But only for a second. I turn to Little Italy who slowly winks at me and smiles, then nods in the direction of my usual chair.

There, on the table, sits a two-cup teapot waiting for my attention. When I turn back to thank her she had moved away. Someone else's turn. Someone else's time.

I walk to my spot and the two small individuals stand up, fuss with their things, and make for the door. The Matchmaker conjures a sign in the air with her right index finger. I see that, too. Ten feet from the door they collide. Carried items spill onto the floor. She falls. He catches her. They look into each other's eyes. Time freezes.

Little Italy looks at the box on the wall. The box knows immediately what's required. It reaches down. Picks up number 155 and drops it onto the turntable.

The curtains open. A light shines on the stage. Roberta Flack stands at the mike. Sings. The First Time Ever I Saw Your Face.

Time starts up again. The two crash test dummies are still looking into each other's eyes. Frozen. Then magic happens.

For every door that closes…another one opens.

Be cool…

The non-electronic love note

Good morning Monday. It's an umbrella Monday. A hurry and hope the drips don't catch you Monday. Just another manic Monday. No wonder Bob doesn't like it.

Or is it more like a Mama Cass Monday? So good to so many?

It's the beginning of the week rather than the end of the weekend. So maybe it's the turn of a corner rather than more of the same, straight road. Something new to see. Something new to do.

Sitting in the coffee shop...drinking her usual wake up call...The Girl With The Butterfly Tattoo is doing something unusual. She's writing a letter. By hand. A non-electronic love note. In ink.

A slow, thoughtful collection of lines and curves on paper that keep pace with the beat of her heart. A physical link from the embossed surface to her fingers...and her feelings.

A prompt. Maybe this will work. Maybe this will make a difference. Not a typeface flying through the ether. A conversation. Hand made. Hand delivered. From one side of the world to the other.

A butterfly flaps its wings here...a passionate tornado strokes a heart there. Cause and effect. Motion and emotion.

Behind the bar, Little Italy sees the movement of the pen and reaches into a pocket, removing a postage stamp. First class. To anywhere on the planet.

She pours a single espresso, places the stamp on the saucer and hand delivers it to The Girl With The Butterfly Tattoo.

As she walks away she sees Earphones Guy. Oblivious to the sounds of the world. Walk through the door and make for the vacant spot at the head of the non-existent queue.

His rhythm is shaking the drips off his waterproof jacket. His hi-tech phones are dry and his folded mini-umbrella is making a river of rain on the tiled floor.

He reaches the bar, flips the phones off and smiles at Big Red. She can hear the music from the phones sat on his shoulder. It's something new. From somebody big.

63

That who I think it is, she says to Earphones Guy. Depends who you think it is, he says.

Big Red double blinks. Oh, this is your day to be a smartass, she says. Must run in the family, he says, grinning at his sister ear to ear.

Happy Monday, says Little Italy nearby. The usual? Naaah, says Earphones Guy. It's a new week…so make it a new drink, he says. To go with your new boots, says Big Red, nodding down. I saw them when you bounced in the door.

Earphones Guy introduces his new footwear. Say hello to Tom and Jerry, he says. Which one's Tom, says Big Red. The cat, stupid, says Earphones Guy. Big Red double blinks. Shakes her head. You're crazy, she says. Must run in the family, he says. I think it's a cappuccino day, he says.

Big Red turns away to talk to the stainless steel machine. Who's the babe with the Parker pen, says Earphones Guy. She's the Out of Bounds Girl, says Little Italy. She's going left. You go right. Little Italy shoots a glance at the box on the wall. The box responds in usual fashion. Number 68 flies in on a mechanical arm.

The curtains open. Joe Cocker is in front of the mike. Engine running. Arms waving. Unmistakable voice. Unmistakable words. The Letter…

Earphones Guy picks up his cappuccino. Slides over some silver. Puts the change in the tips jar. Winks at his sister. Turns left.

Be cool…

The Timekeeper sits on the balcony

Good afternoon Tuesday. Time is a sneaky thing. It creeps up on you when you least expect it. When you're looking the other way. When the last thing you're thinking about is where the analogue hands or the digital numbers are.

It revels in its sneakiness and does precisely and exactly what it wants. Any time of the day or night.

Earliness or lateness are concepts alien to the coffee shop and everyone in it. It's a come and go when you want kind of place. A stay as long as you like sort of haven. It only has one rule. What Little Italy says goes. No ifs…no buts.

Of course most of the time she doesn't have to say anything. Just a look is enough. A sideways glance. A straight-in-the-eyes stare. I have seen hulking brutes wilt beneath her gaze and depart with what was left of their tail between their legs.

Today, The Timekeeper is sitting on the balcony, looking over a half-empty floor. Ignoring all except one. Someone who comes here to wind down. Chill out. Take a breather. Someone whose time, and breath, are about to run out. Someone I like to call The Fat Man. Large proportions. Large appetite. Large personality. One chair is almost too small. One table is almost too inadequate.

The Timekeeper can feel the irregular beating of his heart. So she waits. But she isn't the only one. Little Italy feels it too. So she acts. Not on my watch, she says under her breath and picks up the phone. Dials up a flashing blue light, then walks to The Fat Man's side. Lays a hand on his shoulder. Keeps time at bay just for a few minutes. Just until the cavalry arrives. Siren blaring. Emergency paramedics burst through the door. Two Heroes in dark green. The Fat Man looks up and a thousand yard stare invades his face. It's five thousand yards to the nearest E&R. He can't see that far.

The coffee lovers look on. The passers by rubberneck. Little Italy looks at the box on the wall and the box can't remember the last time an emergency like this happened here.

65

It reaches down and number 121 leaps into action. Races onto the turntable.

The curtains open. Over to you Mr.Waits. Dark, busted up suit. Dark, busted up voice. The track is Hold on. The goosebumps rise.

The Heroes load The Fat Man into the ambulance. Little Italy receives a rousing applause. A thank you for acting fast. A display of relief that it wasn't any of them.

On goes the siren. Off goes the ambulance. Another life hangs in the balance. The Timekeeper finishes her coffee and leaves the coffee shop. Unfinished business is five thousand yards away.

Be cool...

Dangerous eyes and a heart as big as Kansas

Good morning Wednesday. The halfway house of the week. Where the distance between looking back and looking forward is the same. And a person could be forgiven for feeling like they're in limbo. Just out of sight of the past. Not quite in sight of the future. Perfectly balanced between regret and hope.

The coffee shop is half full this morning. Or half empty. Big Red is behind the bar. Fiery hair and fiery personality. Dangerous eyes and a heart as big as Kansas.

Defender of the hurt. Protector of the weak. Serving up cups of solace to the folk queued up on the other side. A skinny latte for the skinny blonde in cut off jeans and cut off hair. A cappuccino with a smiley face for a frowning three-piece suit with day-glow pink socks. A pot of green tea and two cups for The Secretary and her executive 'friend'.

And there, at the tail end of the line, are Eeny and Meeny. Two individuals fraught with indecision. Here for a time out. A welcome break. Their future together balanced finely on a knife-edge. He favouring one road. She preferring another. Neither wishing to choose. The past and the future. Waiting for double espressos. Nearly their turn...nearly their turn. Down to the green tea for the Secretary and 'friend'.

By the way they touch each other and bend close, it looks like they're friends with benefits. The kind of benefits that take place on the boardroom table when the rest of the staff have gone home for the night. The kind of benefits that might just result in a salary raise for her. And a completely different kind of raise for him. Office romance where everyone wins.

Little Italy walks in from the room at the back. Surveys the scene. Spots the pair and catches the mood in an instant. Without breaking step she looks to the right. Fifteen feet along and eight feet up.

The box on the wall knows the routine. Number 157 takes it's place and lowers itself onto the turntable.

The curtains open. Enter Mr. Sedaka. Not the fast Neil. The slow Breaking Up Is Hard To Do Neil.

Eeny looks at Meeny. Meeny looks at Eeny. Maybe next week. Maybe next year. Maybe never. Don't break up...make up.

Be cool...

The Birthday of The Lost and Forgotten

Good morning Thursday. Today, inside the coffee shop, something is different. Not quite the same as all the other days.

If you lick your finger and stick it in the air, you can feel the soft wind of change. A breeze that gently blows through the door every year. Same time. Same day. Same reason. It's a warm breeze. A happy one. A breeze that, for 24 short hours, makes things seem a bit brighter. A little more hopeful.

It settles on every table before taking itself behind the bar. It moves up the wall, touching the long line of cards standing to attention on the shelves. Moving them slightly. Carefully. Respectfully.

Today the shop is verging on full and, in front of the bar, a long line of caffeine lovers stands smiling. Waiting their turn. Each holding an envelope. Each envelope holding a card. Each card holding a message. Personally written. Personally felt.

They're all here. The Girl with the Butterfly Tattoo behind Romeo and Juliet. The Girl in the Red Beret in front of The Hermit. The Boys and Girls in Blue standing to attention behind The King and Queen of Hearts.

All the lost and the lonely. All the extroverts and introverts. All the folk who sit in silence, all the time trying to quieten down the screaming inside. All the ones who have found the loves of their lives. And the ones who have lost them. And right at the front of the queue stands The Man in Black. Looking into the eyes of Little Italy.

She hands him a double espresso. He hands her an envelope and a single rose in a small vase. She raises the petals to her nose and breathes in the scent, closing her eyes for a second. Then she places the vase on the counter, opens the envelope and reads the writing on the card. She smiles inside and places the card on a special spot on the shelf behind her. Then turns back to face the next in line to receive the next card…and the next…and the next.

Beside her, Big Red rides shotgun and deals out a river of warm, dark liquid. Today, this one day, the tea and the coffee are free. No charge. No change. No worries.

Today is the Birthday of The Lost and the Forgotten. Those who don't have anyone to celebrate their birthday with. Today the coffee shop celebrates it with them. Whoever they are. Wherever they are.

As the last one takes their seat, Little Italy looks at the box on the wall. It has been waiting patiently. Now the waiting is over and Number 13 takes its turn, drops into place on the turntable.

The curtains open. Mr. Bill Withers steps up to the microphone. Lovely Day comes out of his mouth.

To all those who think nobody remembers their birthday...somebody does.

Be cool...

The marvellous thing about coffee

Good morning Tuesday. The marvellous thing about coffee is it never discriminates.

It never questions, assumes or comes to any conclusions. It doesn't care how tall or short you are. How weird or conventional you are. How large your waist is or how small your feet are. It doesn't give a damn what colour or sex you are. And it sure as hell doesn't care what age you are.

The coffee shop's oldest friends are sitting in the window seats, watching the world go by. The Girls have brought cakes. Individual bite-sized buns. Personally baked. Wrapped in silver. And handed to Little Italy to dispense as she sees fit. It's their thing. They do it every year on September 9 to celebrate the coming together, 45 years ago, of two brave individuals. Ladies with heart.

It was a time when coming together wasn't as easy as it is now. When things were difficult and a closet was something you kept your clothes in. Or went to pee. When coming out was something you did before going back in again. Not like now.

And so they celebrate the bad old days. And the good new ones. By baking. And sharing the fruits of their special recipe. That's why the lucky ones who come in first receive their favourite coffee, or tea, and one of The Girls' cakes. And they go to their tables…to drink…and eat…and smile.

Only Little Italy knows the secret ingredient of the tasty morsels. And she's keeping her beautiful lips zipped tight. Everyone deserves a little happiness. Even if it's only five minutes at the start of the day. The perfect beginning to the rest of it.

The Girls look on from their table and see the results of their labour of love on the faces of their drinking companions. They nod to Little Italy and to each other.

Little Italy looks at the box on the wall and the box has a smile as wide as the Grand Canyon.

It sees the scene. It knows the routine. Somewhere inside, number 159 slowly gets to its feet and ambles onto the turntable. Drops into place and adds another smile to the party.

The curtains open. The stage is lit. Herman and his Hermits step right up to the microphone. They start singing. A thought is shared around. Four words. I'm Into Something Good.

The Girls smile and sip their Americanos. And here and there around the room, a lucky few are enjoying a different take on life.

Be cool…

It's a kind of magic

Good morning Wednesday. Every class has its clown. Every pack has its joker. And every comedian has his, or her, little dark corner where tragedy, or depression, or just plain old sadness sits on a rickety little stool. Facing the wall. Until it's time to put on the happy face, turn around, and make the world happy again.

If laughter is the greatest medicine, then these guys must be the best doctors in the world. Shamans extraordinaire. But…and here's the rub. Does great happiness have to come with great sadness? Does there have to be a price to pay for cheering folk up? Do giggles need to come with tears? Do they really have the magic to heal everyone…except themselves?

The Magician is in the coffee shop this morning. Painted happy clown face. Making folk happy with her close-up magic. Her sleight of hand. Going from table to table like a visiting trickster. Offering laughter, jokes, and a small slice of mystery and enjoyment to each customer, free of charge.

A little gasp here and there to go with their lattes. A small gesture in the air and a disappearing Ace of Spades. A little applause, well earned, after her personal show. Then she moves on to the next table…and the next. Until the job is done and the magic is put back in her baggy pockets for another day.

She reaches the bar where Little Italy waits for her. Smiling. Good audience this morning, she says. The Magician nods. They see the tricks, she says. They don't see the real magic, she says. A flick of the wrist and a frown turns into a smile. A gesture in the air, and sadness is transformed into happiness.

You don't need to see something to know it's there, says Little Italy. She gives The Magician her usual payment for keeping the customers satisfied. A steaming black Americano. Three sugars. Hold the milk. One squeeze of toffee syrup. A little touch of barista magic from the top shelf.

The Magician takes the payment, turns and disappears to the farthest table in the shop. A place of shadows. Where nobody can see the look on her real face as she sits down, takes out a mirror and tissue...and wipes off the makeup. Where nobody can see that underneath the happy face is a sad one. Nobody, that is, except Little Italy, who turns and looks at the box on the wall.

The box has seen more than its fair share of sad faces. Of lives without smiles. Right on cue it reaches down and lifts up number 81 and puts it on the turntable without breaking step.

The curtains open. The stage is lit. Smokey Robinson is out front with the Miracles behind. Immaculately dressed. Motown's soul supergroup moving in rhythm and blues.

The Magician wipes away the tears of a clown and goes back to a time when she didn't have to use makeup to be happy. Then she looks into the darkness of the coffee and a smiling face appears. Slowly, the smile is mirrored in her own face. And she remembers. Love isn't just a chemical reaction. It's a kind of magic.

Be cool...

The Mouse is looking concerned

Good morning Thursday. Or will it be? We can plan and guess till we're blue in the face and the cows decide it's time to come home. We can lick our fingers, stick them in the air, and try to figure out which way the wind might blow next. But we never truly know, 100% of the time, what's waiting for us round the next bend. Over the next hill. Or through the next door.

We don't know, with absolute certainty what tomorrow will bring. Or even today. But hey…that's all part of the plan. The grand design. The big kahuna's surprise party. We can be down in the dumps one minute…and up high with our head in the clouds the next.

The most exciting element in life can't be found in any Periodic Table. It's the element of surprise and it's a thing of pure beauty. It's poetry in motion. The zag to our zig. The left uppercut to our right cross. And it kicks like a damned mule.

In the coffee shop, The Mouse is looking concerned. No matter how hard she presses the keys on her mobile lifeline, the answer is…no answer. No reply. Nada. Zilch. She's gone through anger. Gone through tears. Gone through denial.

This morning she's going through worry. Worry that she said something she shouldn't have. Or didn't say something that she should have. Maybe something happened. Maybe he's hurt. Injured. Incommunicado. Or maybe he's had enough. Doesn't care anymore. Found someone new. She can feel the tears return, along with the screaming in her head.

Twenty feet away, Little Italy can see the signs. She knows the symptoms. Time for a little caffeine intervention. A friend in need isn't a pain in the ass. It's a friend indeed. And the deed in question is warm and welcome.

She pours a fresh cappuccino and takes it to The Mouse. Gently puts it on her table and waits.

The Mouse looks up and the tears are just about to fall. Little Italy puts a gentle hand on her shoulder. Reaches into a pocket. Brings out a tissue. Reaches out and dabs away a salty blob threatening to overflow. The Mouse tries to smile but it doesn't work. It looks like pain. Liquid pain.

Little Italy looks at the box on the wall and puts a side order in for a special kind of happiness. The box knows what's on the menu and somewhere inside number 141 takes a hand in the proceedings. Big Kahuna smiles. The element of surprise does its thing. The Mouse's phone dings and the screen leaps to life.

The curtains open. Over to you Lionel Richie.

The door to the coffee shop opens. The Mouse looks up. The stranger looks down. Hello. His eyes smile. Her heart leaps. Distance means nothing when zag meets zig. The journey of a thousand miles has an ending of just a few feet.

Be cool...

The Woman Who Never Forgets

Good morning Friday. I walk double time to the coffee shop. Spits of rain darkening my light duds. A chilly wind whispering in my ear. Little secrets lost in translation.

Remember when the tar used to bubble on a summer road? Remember when you could set your clock on winter knocking on the door? Remember when inner city doorways were neat and tidy and homeless folk had somewhere warm to go to sleep at night? Remember when the world was a safer place to live in?

The Woman Who Never Forgets is standing in front of me in the coffee shop. She fidgets. Draws diagrams in the air. Converses with the demons in her head. And loves a strong, sweet, espresso.

She's eidetic. Magnetic. Alphabetic. She is the A to Z of everything that has ever happened to her. Everything she's ever witnessed. Or heard. Everyone she's ever come into contact with. And they all clamour to be heard and seen in the space between her ears. Never forgotten. Never disappearing into mental oblivion.

The Woman Who Never Forgets shuffles on worn flat-heeled shoes and stands in front of Little Italy. Her turn to receive her regular communion of caffeine and understanding. Liquid fog. Cappuccino style. The one thing that gives the demons reasons to be silent. Reasons to be thoughtful. Reasons to be cheerful.

Little Italy smiles, nods and gives her a blessing like a priest at the altar of morning prayer.

The Woman Who Never Forgets looks around at all the other grateful souls. Sitting at their tables. Thinking deeply. Gesturing wildly. Looking lovingly. Talking at a hundred miles an hour. Or one word a minute.

A quiet table calls to her. Recognises her. It doesn't like noise. It likes silence and inner peace. Something The Woman Who Never Forgets needs. Just for a while. Time to remember The Man Who Went To War And Never Came Back.

As she walks to her space and slowly sits down, welcomed by a grateful chair, Little Italy, ten feet away, looks at the box on the wall. The box never forgets either. Number 56 takes a breath and slips onto the turntable.

The curtains open. One man stands on the stage in front of the mike. This time…this place…this voice…it could only ever be Nat King Cole. Unforgettable.

Some secrets never get lost in translation. Some secrets always know where they are.

Be cool…

Bruce Banner unclenches his fists

Good morning Monday. The rest of the world can be a noisy place. It can scream and yell at us. Get up. Go there. Do this. Say that.

Compared to the sanctuary inside our heads and inside the coffee shop, it's the birthplace of cacophony. The home of discord. A place of caterwauling and raspy raucousness. It jars and scrapes against the peace and quiet.

But here, in my morning haven, the heady aroma of roasted coffee beans combines with the welcome sound of absolutely nothing happening. Nothing bad, anyway. Nothing disturbing. Nothing that upsets the daily ritual of putting things in order. Before the order gets turned on its head when you walk out the door and allow the world to seep back inside again.

Here you can breathe. Here Little Italy oversees the passage of comfort and, with Big Red and Tiny, does her best to keep the worst of life at bay. Just for a while. But sometimes life is a pain in the ass. Like this morning.

Halfway up the room, against the wall, under a painting of a stormy sea, sits Bruce Banner. Red faced outside. Green skin inside. Angry at the world and at himself. Sadness and Power. Nothing ever goes right. Everything always goes wrong.

Little Italy knows the routine. He comes in fuming. He orders double espresso. He sits down and waits for the storm to subside. It doesn't take long. A few sips and the green begins to fade. The bunched-up muscles begin to relax. The Hulk slips into the background once again. Danger over. The world is safe. He takes another few sips and all that remains is the emptiness. The loneliness.

At the door a figure dressed in blue surveys the scene. She's heard of the coffee shop. Heard of Little Italy. Heard it through the grapevine. Maybe here she can find the peace that runs a mile when it sees her. Maybe here the buzzing in her head and the screaming in her heart can run for the hills instead.

She walks in and Big Red nudges Little Italy. Another one, she says, as the Blue Lady digs into her shoulder bag. A little silver for a little dark gold. Double espresso, asks Little Italy. The Blue Lady nods. Big Red works the machine and Little Italy works the box on the wall. Somewhere inside the box number 89 moves onto the turntable.

The curtains open. The stage lights flick on. And all Four Tops sing Reach Out I'll Be There. All four move to the groove.

The Blue Lady looks around the room. Takes a sip of her double espresso. Sees Bruce Banner slowly unclenching his fists and letting his shoulders droop. Looks into his eyes as he raises his head. Sees a flash of green.

Sadness can be the noisiest damned place on earth. Sometimes it can be the quietest.

Be cool…

The Girl In The Long Black Dress

Good morning Tuesday. Like it or not, we're all passionate about something. It might be the job we do or the people love. It might be the way we look or the food we eat. The garden we grow or the hobbies we have.

It's the way we are. It's how we roll. It's how we survive without being bored to death. It makes us feel special. And for that one special thing all we need to do is take a monster truckload of enthusiasm, switch on the internal radio and turn up the volume. All the way round the dial. And drive. Drive like nobody else is on the damned road and the speed limit hasn't been invented.

Little Italy knows passion. She knows how it makes folk feel. How it makes them act. And she knows how they feel when passion takes a hike. When it jumps ship. When it says so long and thanks for all the fish.

The Girl In The Long Black Dress is in the coffee shop this morning. Sitting on the balcony. Overlooking the floor where life comes to take a breather. She looks at all the caffeinerati. Sitting and being sociable. Then she looks through them and out the other side. Like a through and through bullet.

She's a grunt with a thousand yard stare. Battlefield syndrome sufferer in the war that left her feeling nothing. Empty inside. Her passion has gone AWOL. She woke up this morning devoid of that spark of magic.

The spark that used to make the blood rush through her veins. The one that used to say look out world, ready or not, here I come. The one that used to feed the appetite and intoxicate the soul.

Gone with a letter that simply said Goodbye. David. As if it would have been anyone else. No narration. No explanation. No recrimination. Two words said it all.

So she comes here to hide. To escape. To somehow make sense of something that made no sense. How could so much passion mean so little? Disappear so quickly. Leave so much pain.

Below, Little Italy knows that, sometimes, things just aren't what they seemed. She looks to the door as it swings open. David with jeans and t-shirt barges in and frantically looks around. Sees The Girl In The Long Black Dress. Rushes up the stairs. Sees her tears. Feels his own sting his eyes.

I left the letter, he says. The one for my boss, he says. He's a bastard and doesn't deserve any reason, he says. But I thought, she says. I'm leaving the company…starting up my own…he says. She feels the passion return. First from a distance and then roaring back like a tidal wave.

Below, Little Italy nods at the box on the wall. The box has seen the damage that crossed wires can do. So it acts fast and slips number 150 into position.

The curtains open. The stage is lit. The Temptations stand in line singing My Girl.

Never jump quickly to conclusions. Walk slowly. And carry a large apology.

Be cool…

The Girl With Purple Hair gets dumped

Good morning Wednesday. Change is one of those things that happens whether you want it to or not. It has a mind of its own. And it doesn't give a flying frig whether you agree with it or not.

It can be monumental in size. Like the changing of the season or the changing of a partner. Or it can be small and perfectly formed. Like the switching of a coffee mug for a teacup.

This morning, change bumps into me on the way through the coffee shop door. We try to go in at the same time. There's only room for one. My innate politeness gets the better of me and I step up to the bar late. A close second in the race for sublime liquid refreshment.

Before I can open my mouth to order my usual dark passenger, a teapot is sitting in front of me. Warm and filled with green infusion.

Little Italy is also in front of me. Warm and filled with knowledge and mischief. Her lips smile and she brushes an errant curl of hair away from her eyes. Shame, I think. A little imperfection is good for the soul. Her glance shifts to the corner of the room. Just like mine.

There's another change in town and it's sitting next to The Girl With Purple Hair. She got dumped says Little Italy quietly. Thrown on the trash like some piece of garbage.

I look at the face below the purple hair and see the smile. I say my piece. How come the grin? Where are the tears? Where's the heartbreak? The Boy Who's Always There, she says. He's the change, she says. He's the lifelong friend. He's the one who always picks up the pieces. Now he's picking up where the last one left off.

I look at The Girl With Purple Hair and see happiness not sadness. Peace not war. Hope not despair. I see her hands in his. His eyes in hers. I walk past them carrying my first green tea of the day. Not my last.

As I pass, she leans over and whispers something in his ear. Something long and delicious. Don't be a shy boy, she says. Move in my direction.

I sit nearby and see a folded note on my tray. I open it and the handwriting says it all. Number 69. In red ink.

I look at Little Italy. She's looking at the box on the wall. The box always knows the difference between friendship and something so much more. So it reaches down and plucks number 69 from the back of the stack.

The curtains open. The Supremes are on the stage. Miss Diana Ross is leading the line. Working their spangled magic. Taking it slow.

The Boy Who's Always There takes a deep breath. He knows You Can't Hurry Love. He knows you can't hurry The Girl With Purple Hair.

Be cool…

The rebellion of The Predictable Man

Good morning Thursday. This morning, like every morning, I am a creature of routine. One thought politely standing in line behind the next. One action waiting to get the green light after the one before it has done its thing.

Order and movement. The predictable heartbeat of life. A walk to the coffee shop. A pause before ordering. A wave of the left hand to someone who was waiting for me to arrive. A smile. A nod to someone else who knew I was coming even before I did. All the while breathing slowing. Heart rate climbing down. From the low highs to the high lows.

A handover of the usual steaming nectar. From Little Italy to little me. A gentle stroll to the usual chair. The usual table. Another pause before I look at my cup. Before I lift and empty the sugar sachets. One…two. Six stirs clockwise. Always clockwise. No more. No less. Empty sachets to the left of the saucer. Wet spoon to the right.

Then I pick up my cup and take a sip of the one thing that puts everything else into perspective and tells the rest of the world to go to hell. Just for the next half an hour. Just like I did yesterday. Just like I'll do tomorrow.

I look to the right and over by the window. The Predictable Man is performing the one routine that makes everything else he does at any other time of the day or night seem insignificant and unimportant. He rebels. Protests. Mounts the barricades and roars loudly against convention. Gloriously and without thought for consequence.

This day and for one day a year, his routine is to throw predictability out the door. To give it the bum's rush. To put everything the wrong way round. About face. Front to back.

This is the day he remembers the cost of doing everything the same way. Saying the same things. Making the same moves.

This is the day she called him boring…unadventurous…and walked out the door. And thanks to a kid behind the wheel of a ton of speeding metal and full of the joys of booze, this is the day he remembers she never will come back from a hospital bed where she lies in her own little world.

Little Italy knows his sadness. Feels his pain. She looks to the box on the wall and the box knows that, today, only one number fits the bill. So the box reaches way down, brings up number 108 and slides it into place.

The curtains open. The Righteous Brothers stand on stage. Two sharp-dressed, good looking, Southern California guys. Singing Unchained Melody. The only song that means anything to The Predictable Man.

Some people go away too soon. Some memories never go away at all. That's how it should be. Always.

Be cool…

Romeo and Juliet are in the coffee shop

Good morning Friday. No matter which language we speak. No matter which dialect or accent slips off our tongue. No matter whether the words we use confuse or confound. We can always find a way to communicate. To make our feelings known. To open the door to understanding.

We're a resourceful species. Our ingenuity knows no bounds. But despite all the sounds we make. All the words we use. All the vocal inflections we have at our disposal. Nothing beats our ability to look into the eyes of someone we care for and say everything we want to say to them. Without even opening our mouths.

Our eyes are the masters of silent communication. And they have no equals when it comes to the language of love.

Romeo and Juliet are in the coffee shop. No words pass between them. Their lips are reserved for other things. More private things. Deeper things. They sit at their table. Lost in each other's eyes. Found in each other's thoughts. Their cappuccinos sit between them. Not daring to disturb the moment as it lasts...and lasts.

Soft conversations they have. Gentle words that flow between each other and bypass other ears. Their fingertips touch. No more. Hands entwined are for other folk. These two have a deeper love. A love of delicious anticipation.

From behind the bar, Big Red looks at the lovers' table and sees the remains of two small cakes. Her cakes. Lovingly created. Enthusiastically digested. All except for a few crumbs on the plate. Big Red believes that love has an appetite all of its own. And the more you feed it, the more it wants to be fed. She has always believed this.

She looks at Little Italy who nods almost imperceptibly at the box on the wall. No words pass between them but the box knows. It knows that, sometimes, sounds give moments permission to be special. So it gives permission for number 79 to step up to the plate.

The curtains open. The lights on the stage are dimmed. Day outside turns to night inside. The Flamingos appear, singing I Only Have Eyes For You. Romeo and Juliet couldn't agree more.

True love isn't always the words on the lines. Sometimes it's the words between the lines.

Be cool...

Ground Control loses touch with Major Tom

Good morning Tuesday. Some folk are easy to please. All they want for breakfast is to be left alone. To see in the day with as little fuss as possible. To welcome the next fourteen or so hours in the pleasant company of a small black hole.

All they want is a region of space and time where all complicated thinking is put on hold, orbiting the event horizon of their mind. A place where they can be safe. Untouchable. Where they can relax, breathe easy…and listen to the sound of absolutely nothing bad happening. Where they can maybe, just once, see something good. Somewhere like here.

This morning in the coffee shop Ground Control had lost all contact with Major Tom, who is sitting in a quiet corner staring into space. Investigating his interior cosmos. Trying to explore the sights of his own personal universe.

A suited and booted caffeine-loving urban spaceman. Frequent flyer. Gravity defyer. An off-world, inter-planetary thinker with zero stress relations and just one hiccup in his otherwise solitary existence.

The hiccup wears a short red dress and has hips that can make a dying man reach for an oxygen mask for one last gasp of pure air. The hiccup promises one final ride of the merry-go-round on a bicycle made for two. Only today, this bicycle has one passenger.

There he sits. Lights off. Solar engine powered down. All movement reduced to the bare minimum. No warp speed. Waiting…waiting.

She was here yesterday. Two tables and a billion miles away. He sent a signal across the emptiness. Hoping for a glimmer in the dark. Catching nothing but static.

Maybe today…maybe tomorrow.

Little Italy looks on from behind the bar. She's seen it all before. She'll see it all again.

Close encounters of every damned kind. Too close for comfort. Too far away to connect. Everyone too scared to make the first move.

So Little Italy does.

She looks at the box on the wall and somewhere inside the box number 57 floats down and lands on terra firma.

The Curtains open. Step up Simon. Step up Garfunkel. Step up the Sound of Silence.

Life isn't about pulling back. Life is about reaching out. Little Italy knows this to be true. Major Tom looks at his empty coffee cup. Time for a refill.

Be cool…

Dancing The Hairy Mambo with the butterflies

Good morning Wednesday. Here's a thought for the day. If you're full of the joys of romance you've got the same kind of chemical profile in your brain as people with obsessive-compulsive disorder.

But does that mean that before you know it you'll be turning every handle three times before you open every door? Every time? Or looking behind the shower curtain before you go to bed? Every time? Or making sure the contents of your fridge are neat as hell and perfectly lined up?

Some folk get the hots after they get the OCD. Some folk get them the other way around. So…is love a kind of madness? Or a kind of magic?

You can choose your friends. But you can't choose who's going to make you dance The Hairy Mambo with the butterflies inside your guts. You can't choose where or when the wild, beautiful insanity will strike. You can't choose whose eyes you will look into and feel the buzz. The bump in the road. That moment when the ground gives way beneath your feet and life as you know it is about to change forever. Again.

Here's a tip. You can't stop the love bug from munching on your emotions. Any more than you can stop the sun coming up or the moon going down.

Little Italy knows this for a fact. She knows the symptoms. The diagnosis. And the fact that, despite all the latest advances in medical science…there just ain't no cure. All you can do is indulge in a little damage limitation. Or a lot. Either that, or you just sit back and enjoy the ride.

OCD Girl is in this morning. She's got the coffee shop balcony front row to herself. She carries her Latte, with her left hand as always, up the stairs. All 24 of them, personally counted.

She goes to the third table and sits in the chair facing the floor below. As always.

She turns his cup three times clockwise and then takes three sips in quick succession. Then she puts it back on the saucer, takes three long breaths taking in the scene below.

Little Italy looks up to the other side of the balcony, smiles and nods slowly. A voice behind OCD Girl says so you do the three thing too. I used to think I was crazy. I used to think I was the only one.

She looks up. Sees The Three Times Girl. Five Ten. Black Hair. Black tee with a white number 3 on the front. Faded jeans. Red baseball boots. Here it comes. BAAAM!! The Hairy Mambo dance.

Mind if I sit down she asks. OCD Girl's too busy wondering what hit her to answer. So she nods. The rest is sure as Hell going to be history.

Down below, the ghost of a smile says hello to Little Italy. She looks at the box on the wall and feels the buzz. It knows what's coming next. Way down below, number 4 rushes to the surface and appears on the turntable.

The curtains open. Royalty comes onstage and Freddie Mercury lets that voice of his loose. It's A Kind Of Magic.

There are times to be obsessive. Times to be compulsive. And times to just sit back and let the magic happen.

Be cool…

This is Coffee Shop Chess

Good morning Thursday. In the entire history of the coffee shop, only one table has been reserved for something other than drinking caffeine in all its many wonderful forms.

All the other tables are round. This one's square. All the other tables can seat up to four. This one seats only two. Not side by side. Not even at right angles. This is a table of opposites. Of face to face meetings. Of thinking caps and long deliberations. Of slow, purposeful movements and intricate strategies. Of struggle and conquest. Ambush and capture. Where emotional bloodshed and violence are de rigueur. And where no quarter is given or expected.

This is a table served only by Little Italy and frequented by those who love the fray. Who love the battle. Who love the cut and thrust of a damned good punch up. Not because they want it. But because they need it. They need it to get things out of their system. To purge the bad. To feel the good again.

This is Coffee Shop Chess. None of your namby pamby stuff. None of that pushing little wooden men around a board for fun. This is serious stuff. Earnest stuff. Stuff where two people, emotionally damaged, can begin to mend the hurt. Mend the pain.

I see today's players as they face off against each other. I see them as they start the process. The beginning game. Tentative…full of half-accusations. I watch as the minutes go by and they enter into the middle game. Every move a scream inside. Every capture a victory of common sense. I see their end game as the screams grow louder in the silence of the shop. Closer to victory…closer to victory. Then, when mate in one seems like a foregone conclusion, I see Little Italy move to the table and remove both Kings from the board. Nobody loses today she says.

Nobody puts the knife in. Nobody grinds anybody into the dirt.

Coffee Shop Chess isn't about anyone winning she says. It's about letting it all out.

93

It's about opening up the valve on the pressure cooker and letting off steam. And still staying together. Have a coffee she says. On the house she says.

Then she smiles, turns and looks at the box on the wall. The box is a fan of Coffee Shop Chess. Big fan. But it's a bigger fan of Little Italy. Somewhere inside the box number 32 begins its smooth descent onto the turntable.

The curtains open. And there on the stage Van Morrison does what Van the Man always does to bring the war to an end. Have I Told You Lately, he begins. He doesn't need to finish.

The chess players put down their pieces. Surrender to their coffees.

Be cool…

Five feet two of miniature rock and roll

Good morning Friday. No matter how much we love silence, sometimes we just need a little noise in our lives. A little crash, bang, wallop. A little disturbance of the quiet molecules.

It's the old action and reaction thing. Inside every zip the lips there's a shout it from the rooftops fighting to get out. Sometimes it needs a little Rev. King. A little FREE AT LAST!!

Little Italy knows this. That's why every now and then she opens the doors of the coffee shop wide and throws out an invite to those with an inability to keep their voice box in check for more than five minutes at a stretch.

That's why she wears her special occasion slinky red dress and takes the warpaint out for a walk on the wild side. Blood lipstick. Mile-long mysterious lashes. Six inch stilettoes. Backcombed hair. Hello boys smile.

Today's the day and I wouldn't miss it for all the damned Arabica in Brazil. Today, sound is like prayer. And the line at the bar is religiously celebrating life in all its loudness.

I sit in the corner, ears open, eyes drinking in the swathe of colour and conversation. Mouth drinking in a dark brown nectar. Big Tony is at the front of the line. Five feet two inches of miniature goddam rock and roll.

Elvis has entered the building. White peacock jumpsuit. Rhinestones. Gold lame detail. Black hair. Black shades. Your drink sir says Little Italy. Large latte with a smile on top. Thankyouvurymuch says Elvis. Little Italy melts, just a little.

Somewhere down the line there's an argument. A full-blown barney with knobs on. They shout. They scream. They get in each other's face with gusto and venom.

The line looks on and smiles. Life in the raw. Reality coffee. He jabs his finger. She bites his jab. They burst out laughing and hug. The laughter spreads like wildfire. Soon the whole place is burning. Tears running down cheeks. Ribs aching.

Big Red is wearing her extra happy face. Little Italy has a smile a mile wide. She looks at the box on the wall. The Box has a treat in store.

The curtains open. The Crystals are on stage. Number 123 slips onto the turntable. Da Doo Ron Ron comes blazing off the vinyl.

Sometimes you have to appreciate the sound before you can appreciate the silence.

Be cool…

Julio says he is a fashionista

Good morning Monday. The Bow Tie Guy was in the coffee shop this morning. He came in right behind me. Immaculate grey suit. Black brogues. White shirt. Blue spotted bow tie. About 70. He has one of those white moustaches that give him a look of debonair respectability.

Little Italy knows different. She knows the secret. The one that makes his eyes glisten when he remembers she who will not be named. She who lives in the memory but not on the lips. She who has a faded black and white photograph in his wallet.

When he sits and drinks his Americano he takes the photo out and stares at it. Long moments remembering. Then he brushes his moustache with an index finger. Sometimes it catches the tear that has escaped from one of his eyes. Sometimes he misses and it carries on down to his chin.

I look quickly away from his impending embarrassment and up to the bar. Big Red is animated, so is her customer. He had a leopardskin jacket and a pink t-shirt. His jeans are cut offs and he has busted up cowboy boots on.

His name is Julio and he says he is a fashionista. I don't even think he knows what the word means. But he smiles a lot and his teeth are pure white.

Big Red has a throaty laugh. Julio reciprocates. Hey girl, that's what laughter is for he says. He flips a wrist and rests the other hand on his hip. Striking a pose. He takes a long tall latte to a table nearby and gently arranges his arse before moulding it into the chair. He was a busy boy last night.

The Bow Tie Guy's eyes shift from the photo and onto Julio and the ghost of a smile passes over his face. He's a lifelong student of the human condition in all its fascinating forms. He's a watcher now. He used to participate. Not any more...not any more. Aaaah those were the days. Back to the Americano. Back to the photo.

At the door, a giggling couple enter the sanctuary and for a second disturb the memory. Then their infectious display brings another small smile to his lips. His eyes glisten. Another memory of youth. He breathes deeply and has a generous drink.

From behind the bar Little Italy remembers and sighs. She looks to the box on the wall and nods. The box nods back, number 22 takes its turn on the platter.

The curtains open. The unmistakable Miss Streisand takes her place on the stage and turns back the clock. The Way We Were isn't the way we are any more. But right here, right now, that doesn't matter.

Life isn't always about looking forward.

Be cool...

The box knows where The Philosopher goes

Good morning Tuesday. The Philosopher is in the coffee shop this morning. He talks to those who come near. He talks to those who don't come within a damned million miles.

I think it's going to be a rattle and hum kinda day, he says. A shake the tree and see what falls out kind a day, he says. The kinda day that you can poke with a sharp pointy stick till the cows come home and maybe you'll still be none the wiser as to why the Hell you got out of bed and put on the same damned head you had on yesterday.

Hey, I say, sometimes you just have to go with the flow until something happens that makes you believe that life has plans for you.

He nods his head. Absolutely, he says. Big plans. Cosmic maybe. I agree, only not out loud. He coughs. Long and low and hard. Then taps his nose conspiratorially. You know mister…they might just be the kinda plans that make neck hairs stand on end. Yeah, I say, and grown men and women finally figure out there's no such thing as making your own destiny.

He laughs quietly. You might as well sit back and relax mister, he says, 'cos you know that feeling you got in the pit of your stomach? That's life reminding you that you're not in charge. Not in control. Not by a long way. Never have been. Never will be.

I nod. You might be holding the wheel, but you ain't doing any of the steering, he says. All you can do is hold on tight and hope that nobody with a cute smile and a decent pair of gams gets in the way.

Sounds like a plan, I say. Except with the best will in the world, and no matter how many times you turn the damned wheel to avoid the collision, somebody always gets caught in the crossfire, I say. A trainwreck full of emotional damage, he says. Naah, I say. That's just love. Good with the bad. Rough with the smooth. Butterflies with the pain in your guts.

Behind the bar Little Italy sees the conversation and looks curiously at me, tilting her head to one side. Then the smile appears. Slow at first, then wide and warm. She grabs a spare Espresso from the machine and walks over to where I'm sitting. Puts it down in front of me and says who you talking to? Is it him again?

I look to the Philosopher's chair and it's empty. He's taken a hike. Threesomes make him nervous, I say. That's okay she says. I'm only the piano player…don't shoot me. I laugh. She laughs. Maybe he'll come back when I'm gone she says. Yeah…and maybe it's gonna snow Christmas Day this year I say.

She nods at me, nods at the box on the wall and walks away. The box knows where The Philosopher goes. It always knows. On the button. On the dime. It's rerun time. In a heartbeat number 30 slides into place and another conversation begins.

The curtains open. Ben E. King stands on stage behind the mike. Begins to sing. Everybody knows Stand By Me. Everybody knows the song. Everybody knows the words.

From behind the bar Little Italy winks. Just once. But it's enough. All over the world…it's enough.

Be cool…

The Guy With Thunder In His Face cools down

Good morning Wednesday. It's amazing how far you can go just by putting one foot in front of another. Thinking one thought instead of another.

You can be strolling along, smelling the crap instead of the coffee...and before you know it you go from ignorance to knowledge. Bigotry to open-mindedness. Indifference to passion. Friendship to full-blown, gold-star, butterflies in the stomach, "this is THE one" love. L...O...V...E. All capitals.

All from a standing start. All because something...or someone...reached out and switched on your 'decent human being' gene. All because you were zapped with the Vulcan mind meld and transformed into someone worth talking to. Someone worth getting to know. Rather than someone worth crossing the street to avoid.

This morning The Guy With Thunder In His Face is in the coffee shop. I see his eyes and they always look like a storm is brewing in there just waiting to bust out and start a fistfight. Like all the good things in life are fighting to get a word in...even a small one...and failing miserably.

Little Italy sees them too. But she sees way beyond that. She sees the pain and disappointment. The fist against the wall and the snarl against life.

She sees the never against and the why me rage. And below that...way down underneath nearly hidden from sight...she sees The Man With A Smile On His Face. The one who used to be. The one who said hello.

Little Italy sees it all. And once again she promises to set him on the road back. The journey, one emotional foot in front of another...back to the man he used to be. If only for a while.

But for now, he's still the Guy With Thunder In His Face. Sitting in front of an untouched latte. It's cold. Unfeeling. Whatever taste it had has long since disappeared.

The door opens and The One-Eyed Girl comes in. Black leather patch over skin like dark chocolate. Shaved scalp. Body full of chemo. Head full of why me. Heart full of why not me. Beauty and tragedy in the same package. Stands in front of Little Italy and looks with the good right. Mono vision. Stereo sound.

Little Italy smiles. Hot or cold, she says. Cold, says The One-Eyed Girl in a nano-second. Nothing warm in this life, she says. Little Italy raises an eyebrow. Don't be too sure, she says. Life has a habit of giving you a nice warm hug, she says. Just when you least expect it, she says.

Uh-uh, says The One-Eyed girl. Not today, she says. Not the way I feel, she says. Gimme a nice Caramel frap with vanilla and chocolate chips. Cold as ice.

She takes the frap and heads for the vacant spot fifteen feet away from The Guy With Thunder In His Face. She sits. Breathes. Scans the room and touches her patch. This is crazy, she thinks. If I've only got six months left. I need one last damned smile, she thinks.

Over behind the bar, Little Italy sees the thought and looks at the box on the wall. Nods. The box nods back. It knows the symptoms. Knows the signs. So it digs deep and comes up number 92. The vinyl rushes to the top of the stack and hits the turntable running.

The curtains open. Miss Patsy Cline is right at the front of the stage and she's Crazy.

The One-Eyed Girl looks around the room. Spots The Guy With Thunder In His Face. He looks up. Sees her. Keeps looking…keeps looking. And so the journey begins again. One foot in front of the other.

Be cool…

Lola's back in town

Good Morning Thursday. This morning the sun is shining but Autumn is wearing its Winter overcoat. It might be warm in the coffee shop, but there's a cold wind blowing outside.

But a temperature drop meals zilch. Counts for nothing...because Lola is back in town. Petite, sweet and full of the joys of Spring. A multi-seasonal, compact bundle of life. Tongue out. Tail wagging furiously. Followed by her obedient male companion. Just the way it should be. Hello boys...I'm here! Let the petting begin.

Little Italy beams. No male (except maybe one) can bring out that smile. No testosterone-filled, wide shouldered, well-muscled example of masculinity can have the effect that Lola does when she struts her stuff.

Hey girl, you got a new collar, she says. Love the studs, she says. Lola's companion takes the compliment but Hell, Little Italy knows who made the choice. It's the wearer, not the carer. Lola has taste. Class from her nose to her arse.

Lola sees The Man In Black and puts her paws into gear. He laughs, makes a sign in the air and a handful of tiny treats appear. Just like magic. Lola knows his tricks like she knows her men. Obedient. Subservient. Two steps behind.

The door opens and a squeal of feminine delight comes through on a breath of chilly air. Yaaay...it's Lola, one teen says. Who's Lola, says the other.

Hell...she's only the coolest damned dawg on the planet, says the first. You wanna latte or a cappuccino, says the second. Coffee can wait. Lola always comes before drinks, says the first, and walks to The Man In Black's table, bends down and gives Lola a Low Five. Lola responds in kind.

Behind the bar Little Italy reaches down and slips a treat from a counter shelf. Not just any old treat. Not just an M&S treat. This is a Lola treat, made with love and kept for a day like today.

She clicks her fingers. Lola hears, knows the sound and runs to the one person in all creation who knows her better than the man she lives with. She sits at Little Italy's feet, looks up, devotion in her eyes, and waits until Little Italy places the treat gently on her nose. With practiced expertise, she flicks her head, sending the treat into the air, then catches it gently in her mouth.

Little Italy smiles, looks up and nods at the box on the wall. This calls for something special. Number 2. This calls for someone special.

The curtains open. The Kinks are on stage. Ray is on form. And so is Lola.

What's in a name? Sometimes nothing. Sometimes everything. Be cool…

Just a perfect day

Good morning Friday. Just another day in the week? Another brick in the working wall? Not very different to the day before…and the day before that? Same old same old?

Hell no! For some maybe. If that's what floats your boat, fine. Friggin' fandabbydozy. Me? I'm one of the other folk. The alternative individuals. One of the folk who live on the flip side of the coin. The other side of the road. The dark side of the moon.

I like my predictables snuggled up to my surprises. I like my routines cuddled up nicely to my whatthefucks! I like my silences shaking hands with my noises. And I like my dark caffeine mornings taking turns with my healthy green teas. It makes life a damned sight more interesting.

The coffee shop is quiet. Peaceful. Easy on the ears. Easy on the soul. I'm carrying the sound of The Piano Man curling round every molecule of my jacket. I pass him playing a little late night smoky jazz in the square outside where the trees live. Only it's early in the morning and the nicotine fog isn't allowed through the door.

This is a pack-a-day-free zone. No giant Bolivars here, rolled between the thighs of Cuban virgins. But this morning what they do have is music. Music to soothe the soul. Music to caress the heart. Music to put the brakes on the racing pulse.

I pass over the threshold to the sound of a slow Latin guitar. Old School. Little Italy has a dark, thick Espresso waiting for me. Poured to perfection. Timed to the second. Topped with golden coloured 'crema'.

The aroma hits me from ten feet away. She's smiling. You like the music, she asks. I chose it personally, she says. I return the smile, reach into my shoulder bag and pull out a box. Wrapped in black with a blood red bow. I hand it to her slowly. I got a thing for special occasions I say as she sees the box and blushes.

I take my coffee and walk to my usual corner spot.

I look in my peripheral. See her remove the paper. Open the box. Stop all movement. Just stare. At the contents. At me.

She reaches inside and takes out her first birthday gift of the day. She looks up and mouths the words. Thank you. No sound. All meaning. Then she nods at the box on the wall.

The box is well aware what kind of day it is. It doesn't need reminding. It doesn't forget special occasions. So it reaches down and brings number 12 up to the surface. Slow and easy. Slides it onto the turntable. Soft and gentle.

The curtains open. Lou Reed is on the stage. Sat on a barstool. Dark suit. Dark hat. Just a perfect day.

Happiness isn't just about what you get. It's also about what you give.

Be cool…

Wonderful world beautiful people

Good morning Monday. Some days you just have to take the weather out of the equation before you even walk out the front door.

It's dull. It's wet. It's depressing and windy as hell. In fact the only thing in its favour is that it has the good sense to stay outside. Whatever the hell it's like anywhere else in the world, it sure ain't wearing a smile here. Not on the outside anyway.

But that's okay. That's hunky dory. That's damned peachy. Because all the really important stuff in life happens where the forces of nature can't reach. On the inside. Where the weatherman says the wind is a light tropical breeze and there isn't a cloud in the sky.

Inside. Where the only water drops come, not from above, but from the steaming nozzle of a hard working coffee machine.

Inside. Where all the things going on under your skin can have time to breathe and the chance to sort themselves out. Pick themselves up. Dust themselves off. And start all over again.

I can see it all from here on the balcony. Sometimes a different take on life needs a different viewpoint. A different table and chair. Somewhere quiet above the hustle and bustle of the breakfast literati. Way up on the outer edges of the caffeineverse.

I see Heels on Wheels at the counter, shaking off the wetness. Tears from Heaven. Liquid refreshment for the concrete slabs. Big Red gives her a little smile. Little Italy pours her a big Latte and takes it to a table by the wall. Heels on Wheels follows on behind. Rims turning slowly.

She passes by The Priest. Black on black with a slice of white. Sitting at his altar, blessing that which he is about to receive. Double espresso. Hot as Hell.

I spy Tiny (long time no see) sliding a slice of dark chocolate cake onto a plate for The Secretary. A treat before the rest of the week. A last morsel before the start of the diet.

I see all the colour and conversation. All the laughter and thoughtfulness. All the noise and silence.

Then I see Little Italy nod towards the box on the wall. Showtime. Entertainment time. Background sound that somehow wriggles itself into the foreground time. Number 78 time.

The curtains open. Jimmy Cliff is on the stage with a crowd of colourful reggae musicians and singers. I take my glasses off and clean them. Put them back on. I Can See Clearly Now.

It doesn't matter what the weather's like on the outside. What matters is the weather on the inside.

Be cool…

Then I saw her face

Good morning Tuesday. Today isn't a head day. Today is a heart day. A something happened on the way to the office day. A conga drums in the chest day.

A day when all those wild and crazy feelings, poked into life by the dark, rich aroma of love and coffee, grab logic by the throat and lead it politely to the door before kicking its ass onto the wet concrete outside.

A day for feeling a switch move fast to the "Holy Shit' on position somewhere inside. The kind of switch that won't move to the off position again without some kind of wake-the-street screaming match and bloody fight to the death. This is a day for feeling the full force of the world turn upside down.

Walking Stick Man is sitting in a corner of the coffee shop. Emptiness around him. Emptiness inside him. Pain, rejection and a lifetime of 'who gives a shit about you' all joining forces to make him into the man he is today.

And yet…and yet. Despite all their best efforts, he still has a morsel of hope. Still has a small scuffed, kicked-about grain of 'maybe one day' lying on the floor in a dusty corner of his heart. Still has a dream that hasn't been squashed. Hasn't been dumped on from a great height. Hasn't been torn to pieces by life's pack of rabid dogs.

Little Italy sees Walking Stick Man every day. Every morning same time. Same coffee. Every table same chair. Same look in his eyes. Searching. Same wish. Hoping. Same end product. Disappointment.

He never stops looking says Big Red. Little Italy knows. She sees him every day. Knows his story. Big Red sighs. You think he's ever gonna give in? Little Italy knows the answer. Not a cat in hell's chance she says softly. She knows that sometimes things happen right out of the blue. Not because sheer damned coincidence makes them happen. But because somebody somewhere is looking out for you.

The door opens and a gust of wind blows through the room. Kissing the face of Walking Stick Man. He looks up from his Americano and sees her. Breath catches in the throat. Heart slams on the brakes.

Deep down somewhere dark and dusty, a small grain of 'maybe one day' puts on a growth spurt. She catches his eye and two lonely souls recognise each other and begin the dance. Little Italy sees the look and nods to the box on the wall. Time for a little push in the right direction. The box winks back at her, flicks a switch and number 23 drops nicely into place.

The curtains open. The Monkees take the stage. Mickey and the boys give life a little push in the right direction. I can see the thought in Walking Stick Man's mind. I'm A Believer.

Nice one guys. Sometimes love is a light tap. Sometimes it's a sledgehammer blow.

Be cool…

I walk past The Dark Man

Good morning Thursday. Sometimes all it takes is a little nod in the right direction. A slight nudge here and there. A confidential word with the big man upstairs. And all of a sudden what might have been a depressing pain-in-the-ass day turns into one with a smidgen more hope. A tad more optimism. A touch more Mister Blue Skies.

It's trying its best to be sunny as I walk to the coffee shop. Today its best just ain't good enough. But although Autumn is wearing a scarf and an overcoat and holding a brolly, there's a big collective smile in the air.

I pass The Piano Man, playing in a sheltered corner, and slip him some silver. He's playing something slow and vaguely familiar. The leaves are swaying in time. Branches in motion. This is natural rhythm. A sweet beat.

My half-asleep brain searches to match the right notes with the right title. As the coins slip from my hand the curtains open and a digitally remastered black and white movie reels sharply into focus. Good old smart, world-weary Bogie. Beautiful love-trapped Ingrid. Vichy-controlled Casablanca. They don't make movies like that any more. They don't make stars like that any more. Sing it Sam. Sing it Dooley Wilson.

You Must Remember This is ringing in my ears as I reach my own modern-day Little Italy-controlled haven. No war going on here. No Resistance. No letters of passage. Here folk are free to live their own lives. Go their own way. Do their own thing. Without fear of reprisals.

Here the colourfully caffeinated can sit down, tune in, turn off and drop out...and the rest of the world can stay the hell away for a while.

I stand at the bar behind a shaved head sat on top of a long flowing black coat. The Dark Man is in the house. Damn he has style. He whispers something to Little Italy then turns and smiles.

111

So you're the guy who likes to look at people he says. I shrug. Old habits die hard I say. He smiles. So do old sinners he says and walks away with a small white cup and a large French Slice.

My turn next and I don't have to say a word. A pot of green tea appears before me along with a slice of ginger heaven. Little Italy always knows my poison.

I walk past The Dark Man and sit down easy in my usual spot. Just close enough to be far enough away. I don't look up but I can feel his eyes scan the room. Introduce himself to all the mixed up, beat up, screwed up, loved up happy little souls in the room.

I feel Little Italy nod at the box on the wall. She understands. She has sympathy. The box has sympathy too. Somewhere inside, the number 77 slides into place and a little dark music comes out to play.

The curtains open. The stage is set. Mick struts in front of the rest of the Stones and brings his best lips and hips to the party.

Sympathy For The Devil? Not today. Today...in here at least...it's The Devil's day off. And even the angels breathe a sigh of relief.

Be cool...

Today we rise, today we shine

Good morning Friday. Those of a more complicated nature might call it an emotionally drab morning. A boringly suffocated morning. A morning that's had all the joy sucked out of it, leaving just the shell of another dreary day at the end of another dreary week.

Happily we have those of a more positive disposition on hand to show them the error of their ways. To tell their sad faces to bugger off. To kick their tightly shrivelled arses into gear. To give them a glimpse of the bright side of the sun. Not the dark side of the moon. To help them fill their lungs with highly oxygenated optimism. Instead of highly carcinogenic pessimism.

Today we rise. Today we shine. The sun has got his hat on...and he's coming out to play. Clouds can't hide him. Cold can't chill his bones. He's a man with a plan...and he's been the architect of the finest feelgood factor since the Big Bang decided to start the whole damned ball rolling.

Little Italy knows this to be true. Every day in the coffee shop she brings her own special brand of brightness into the lives of those with a heart that beats, blood that flows, and a soul that knows true love when it sees it. Whether it's on the way in. On the way out. Or there for as long as it takes to know what forever feels like.

I sit in my corner spot surrounded by the ghosts of love and coffee. Slowly...ever so slowly....I can hear their voices. See their faces. Little Italy can see them too. Every one who has walked through the door looking for somewhere to escape to. Looking for a break from the ordinary. From the pain and suffering. Searching for the next best one. The next hand to hold. The next life to make a difference to. Or just half an hour's uninterrupted bloody peace and quiet.

A young couple stand in front of her at the bar. Full of smiles in their eyes and butterflies in their guts. Relationship newbies. She wants to squeeze them tight and tell them everything will be alright.

In the end. She wants to prepare them for all the ups and downs life will throw at them.

All the pain and suffering. All the sheer joy and exhilaration they'll feel.

But she doesn't. That's their journey.

Instead, she looks to the box on the wall simply puts in a good word. The box knows the score and somewhere inside number 105 snuggles up to the turntable.

The curtains open. The Cure are on the stage. British through and through. Post-punk. New Wave. Optimistic not tormented. More light less dark.

Friday I'm In Love is her song of the day, and love doesn't care who it happens to. Where it happens. Or when. It just cares. Full point. End of story. Or maybe just the beginning.

Be cool...

The Girl With A Million Freckles blushes

Good morning Monday. There's something deliciously spooky about walking in the half-light. The night is still hanging onto the coat tails of the coming day. Feeling it's tight grip loosen. Light is the newcomer, bullying its way onto the stage. Shoving the moon roughly out of the way with an elbow here...a well aimed boot there.

The coffee shop is full of colour and conversation. Full of energy and preparation. Fuel for a new journey through a new week. Big Red is behind the bar. Dispensing rosy cheek smiles to the caffeinerati...and a no-nonsense glare to those who would even dream of upsetting the morning's atmosphere.

As per usual there are no misbehaves. By her side, Tiny rides shotgun and cuts a fine young John Wayne figure. He even has the talk. He even has the walk. Who needs Maureen O'Hara when you got Big Red.

As I stand at the bar Little Italy appears at my side. Silent as a ghost. Warm as a summer's day. You got a new jacket, she says. Yeah, same old me inside it, I say and smile. That's what counts she says, and moves behind the bar.

Behind me, the door opens and a slip of a girl extricates herself from the chill outside and introduces herself to the inside. The Girl With A Million Freckles. She's a coffee shop virgin. A nervous first-timer. Never been in here before. Never been in love before. Hasn't even dipped her toe in the water. Hasn't even opened her heart to the possibility. Hasn't even felt time stand still. Or gone slow-mo.

Little Italy nudges Big Red. I'll take this one, she says. You take the next. Little Italy looks at Freckles. You look like you could use a smile, she says. Freckles blushes. Is it that obvious, she says. Obvious is good, says Little Italy.

She reaches over to the chrome machine and pours a steaming Americano into a bright white cup.

First one's on the house, she says. Freckles protests. Little Italy insists. You don't argue with that kind of insist.

For the first time that morning, the first time for half a lifetime of mornings, Freckles smiles. And so it begins, thinks Little Italy, and looks at the box on the wall. The box hates endings. Loves beginnings. Somewhere inside, number 14 slides nice and easy into place.

The curtains open. Ella's voice says hello to the day. Fabulous tone. Impeccable diction. Ain't Misbehavin'. What the Hell else would you expect from the Queen of Jazz.

Little Italy looks over at The Girl With A Million Freckles. Sometimes the best love isn't what you know today, but what you'll get to know tomorrow.

Be cool...

The Professor is saving the atmosphere

Good morning Tuesday. Or is it? Sometimes the only good thing that comes out of Tuesday is the fastest road to Wednesday. Today is a missing day.

There are moments in life when you miss someone so much that the pain is like emotional amputation. Like the air gets ripped from your lungs at the mere mention of their name. Like your heart threatens to shatter into a million razor-like glass shards at the slightest memory of the last time you saw them.

You want to get through the day...through the pain...and out the other side, before the memories threaten to cave the walls in around you. And yet...and yet...there are the other Tuesdays.

The ones where missing means the kind of loving you want to run as fast as you can towards. Not away from. Hard, passionate, till-the-end-of-time love. With every breath in your lungs. Every drop of your blood. Every bone in your body. Every beat of your heart.

I sit in the coffee shop, shaking off the shivers of an early morning chill. Warming my hands around a steaming pot of green tea. Looking at Romeo and Juliet. Ten feet away and already I can feel the heat. The passion. No dark and destructive love here. Only fiery. Explosive. Can't sleep a wink for thinking of you love. With the merest touch they light a fuse. With the slightest look they threaten to overflow.

Two seats away The Professor is oblivious. Too busy saving the atmosphere with the formula for a pollutant-free fuel. A hundred miles a gallon. Nearly there. Only one more equation.

Behind the bar, Little Italy knows every equation under the sun. Every formula under the moon. They're all written on a blackboard in The Room of Solutions in the centre of her heart. Only one door. Only one lock. Only one key.

She looks to The Man In Black, sitting by the window. Looking back at her. Maybe she'll get another key cut. One day.

The ghost of a smile passes across her eyes as she turns her head away and looks at the box on the wall. The box takes a deep breath and number 139 unlocks another memory.

The curtains open. Brian Wilson and the other Beach Boys take emotion and harmony to a new level. God Only knows how they do it.

Some folk love with all their heart. Others with all their soul. Some folk say there's no difference between the two. Shows how much they know.

Be cool...

Business Suit has a blind date

Good morning Thursday. Some Thursdays threaten to fill you with that warm, fuzzy glow of anticipation. But all they end up doing is sounding like the day before the day you've been waiting for. All they end up feeling like is the pregnant pause before the birth of another much more interesting weekend.

They're the "are we there yet?" brigade. Friday wannabees. Sitting revving their engines. Big car body. Small car horsepower. Waiting at the lights just around the corner from the final stretch…where things get a damned sight more interesting.

Some Thursdays are like that. But not this one. Not here in the coffee shop. Here anticipation lives and breathes and has a mind of its own. Here it doesn't walk blindly into a wall full of disappointment. Here it waits with baited breath for what's coming next and it makes the hairs on the back of your neck stand up and do the Hairy Mambo dance.

I sit in my usual spot nursing a large cappuccino, staring at the kind of pastry that makes taste buds glad they're alive. Anticipation.

Over by the counter, a tall, slender redhead in a dark suit – all business – looks like she's the first of a twosome to arrive. She scans the room for a spare slice of privacy. Maybe it's all pleasure. She bites her lip nervously. Anticipation.

Blind date, asks Little Italy, knowing the answer. Business Suit blushes and nods slightly. Little Italy nods towards a place in the corner. A place far away from the madding crowd. Privacy Central. A place with two chairs. Side by side. She orders a Skinny Latte and makes for the table. Anticipation. The door opens behind her and The Cultivated Beard walks in wearing matching everything.

He saw Business Suit here yesterday and wanted to pluck up the courage. She saw him and wanted to say yes. He looks around hoping for a smile of recognition. Anticipation.

Little Italy sees him and nods towards Privacy Central.

As he passes the bar, she hands him a double espresso. How did you know, he says. Anticipation, she says.

As he walks towards Business Suit, Little Italy nods towards the box on the wall. The box is an expert at thinking ahead. Already has a track picked out. Number 52. Old Blue Eyes is back in town.

The curtains open. Step up Francis Albert Sinatra. The Chairman of the Board himself. Cue big band intro. Cue perfect pitch voice. Cue Strangers in the Night.

Love isn't always about who you want to know. Sometimes it's about who you want to know you.

Be cool...

Needles and pins

Good morning Friday. When life gives you lemons you either use them to make lukewarm lemonade with a fistful of twist. Or you cut the damned things up, pop a slice & ice in a tall, heavy glass, and pour yourself a large cool Hendrick's.

Fridays are like that. You either reach the end of the week with a sour taste in your mouth. Or you grab the start of the weekend by the throat and calmly christen the hell out of it with whichever hand you have left over. Your choice. Life's too short and death's too long. It's that simple.

This morning I'm welcoming in the day with a large, stiff Americano with an extra shot. Little Italy style. She hands me the nectar and nods to my usual spot. I look and see the corner crowded with the boys and girls in blue. I've been usurped. It's a damned crime. So I head upstairs to the balcony. Always have a Plan B.

I pass by The Girl With The Butterfly Tattoo. Sitting on her ownsome lonesome. I nod. She smiles. It's a different smile to the one she usually wears. Equal measures of mysterious and excited. Shaken but not stirred. Okay I think, I'll bite.

I stop by her spot. You're different today, I say. What's changed. She looks like she's fit to burst. I'm getting a new one, she says. My eyebrows need a little exercise. They head for the ceiling. A new ink? I ask. She nods slowly and smiles. Looks like the cat that's got the cream. It's a Red Admiral, she whispers.

I feel like a conspirator. A tattoo confidante. She looks down and taps her thigh gently. X marks the spot. When? I ask. Outline Saturday, she says. Colour in a week. I don't think I've ever seen her look so happy. I nod and smile. That's gonna cost, I say. Her smile disappears. I get the drift. Small price to pay for happiness.

I take my leave. Walk up to the balcony. Ease myself into Plan B. Survey the scene. Big Red is talking to Pierced Guy. Piercing stare. Pierced nose. He has a twinkle in his eye. But not for her.

121

Beside her, Little Italy takes a deep breath and lets it out slowly. Looks at the box on the wall and nods once. The box loves tattoos and piercings. Hates unrequited love. So it brings number 154 to the rescue.

The curtains open. The vinyl drops onto the turntable. Time turns back to sixty four. The Searchers are on stage. I feel Needles and Pins all over.

Pierced Guy spots The Girl With The Butterfly Tattoo. Stops in his tracks. He with his metal. She with her ink. Match made in Heaven. Maybe.

Be cool…

The Man With Sadness In His Eyes

Good morning Monday. I have a friend who silently thanks the powers above every Monday he wakes up with anything approaching a regular pulse.

Anything resembling a fully-functioning set of lungs. Reasonable heartbeat. Working legs. And a brain that can still put one thought in front of the other without tripping over itself. He figures that if he has at least three out of the five he's got a good chance of making it through to Tuesday. He's an optimist.

The coffee shop is a place where optimism thrives and pessimism gets the hell out of Dodge. If it knows what's good for it. Occasionally it doesn't. Every now and then it needs a little help. A little reminder. Like this morning.

The Man With Sadness In His Eyes is sitting by himself. Surrounded by an aura of despair and a distinct lack of hope. Little Italy knows when he's due. Knows his inside as well as his outside. Knows that the only thing he'll ask for is an Americano. Black. Like his mood. Bitter. No sugar.

But she also knows that, like osmosis, a warm, welcoming glow of hope and optimism will overtake the sadness. Will help him remember that darkness isn't the only colour in his life. Will give him reason to smile when he looks around and sees the other folk nearby. Stripping off their own layers of pessimism. Hanging them over the backs of their chairs. And feeling the tingle of a happy disposition spread through their veins.

Little Italy nods to Big Red, who pours the Americano and adds a touch of her own particular brand of TLC. A little something from the top shelf. A little spark of magic.

The transformation is slow but almost miraculous. For a blissful hour, Eeyore becomes Winnie Pooh. Darkness becomes light. Despair becomes hope.

Even The Professor, sitting three tables away, notices the change.

Normally buried deep in his equations, he surfaces to nod and smile. Enlightenment Equals Much Comfort Squared. Who the hell needs chalk when the blackboard writes its own story.

Behind the bar, Little Italy smiles. Another job well done. She looks at the box on the wall and the box has a little spark of magic of its own. From deep inside, number 59 rises like cream to the top and slides onto the turntable.

The curtains open. Mick and the boys tell another one of life's big truths. You Can't Always Get What You Want.

The Man With Sadness In His Eyes lifts his cup, takes a sip, smiles, and becomes The Man With Hope In His Heart.

Be cool…

The Lord of Second Chances wakes up

Good morning Wednesday. Sometimes you reach the middle of the week and you realise that, since Monday left without even saying goodbye, you haven't really achieved anything worth a damn.

Haven't floated anyone's boat. Haven't rocked anyone's world. Haven't taken Diana's advice and reached out and touched somebody's hand.

Some folk reach the middle of their lives, look back and think the same thing. They stayed quiet when they should have spoken up. They stayed sat down when they should have stood up. They did nothing when they should have done something. Anything.

Taken a risk. Taken a chance. Danced the hairy mambo by the light of the full moon goddammit! Then before they know it, they're halfway through their week...halfway through their life...and all they can see staring them in the face is the same old same old. Nothing changes.

And then it does. Right out of the blue they stumble across the coffee shop. They say hello to Little Italy. And somewhere inside them, the Lord of Second Chances wakes up, opens his eyes and gets his ass into gear. Hello boys...it's boat-floating time.

I see him across the room of the coffee shop. I sit here with my healthy green tea infusion. The What If Man sits there with his dark, sweet Americano and his life of missed opportunities.

What if he'd zigged instead of zagged. What if he'd walked through door A instead of door B. What if he'd said hello to her 10 years ago instead of watching her walk away into somebody else's future. Ten bloody years and he still remembers what she wore. How she looked. What her perfume smelled like. The colour of her eyes. Some things never change.

But thanks to Little Italy and the Lord of Second Chances, some things do.

The door opens and Middle-Aged Beautiful puts a foot gently over the threshold.

Takes a step forward. Then another. Then another. Then she smiles at Little Italy. Big wide and warm.

Little Italy never forgets a face. Always remembers a name. Just like the Lord of Second Chances. And The What If Man. Especially this face. He feels the shock of recognition. The Tingle. No missed opportunity this time. Not a damned chance.

Little Italy sees him rise and she throws a fast look at the box on the wall. The box reaches down to the bottom of a pile, grabs number 104 and slides one of the biggest classics of all time onto the turntable.

The curtains open. The Beatles are on the stage. Fab Three plus Paul. Time to rock the world. Nice and slow. Hey boys. Hey Jude.

Listen to the man. Don't be reticent. Don't be hesitant. When love comes calling…open the damn door!

Be cool…

The Bag Lady is alone in the crowd

Good morning Friday. One day, some bright spark will figure out how to make reaching Monday, Tuesday, Wednesday and Thursday feel as damned good as reaching Friday.

They'll do the math. Discover the formula. Use up a ton of chalk in the process. And come up with a mathematical system that shows how damned different and welcome a Friday is. Physically. Emotionally. Cosmologically. Every damned ally.

Until then, we'll all have to live with the fact that 60 seconds at the beginning of the week is exactly the same as one whole minute at the end of it. That, without a shadow of a doubt, 24 hours is exactly the same length on the day after Sunday as it is the day before Saturday.

Unless, of course, you happen to be in the coffee shop on a Friday morning, in which case all bets are off.

As well as being a Healer of Souls, Little Italy is also a Companion of Time. She is a friend to very tick and every tock. She also knows that, no matter how precious every second is, people should rule time, not the other way around.

The Bag Lady is in the coffee shop. Every Friday she appears. Regular as clockwork. 8am on the dot. Always with the same bag. Louis Vuitton Papillon. Class carrying style. Always with the same sadness. Alone in a crowd could have been a term created especially for her.

The Bag Lady knows this to be true. She looks around at the smiles and grateful relief on the faces of the Thank Fuck It's Friday crew scattered around the shop. Sipping their caffeinated drinks. Thinking of the weekend. Feeling the buzz begin.

They know what makes Fridays different. But The Bag Lady…all she knows is what makes them the same. Same as any other Friday. Except for that one hour slot. 8am to 9am.

I see Little Italy carry a personalised cappuccino to her table.

I see her sit down beside her, whisper something in her ear, then get up and leave. I see her look at the box on the wall. Nod almost imperceptibly then go back to her spot behind the bar. I feel the box get the message and hear the sound of a black disc, number 5, slip onto the turntable.

The curtains open. Bobby McFerrin is on stage. Smile on his face. Smile in his voice. Don't Worry Be Happy.

The Bag Lady takes a sip of her cappuccino and closes her eyes. Then, for an hour or so, she remembers what it's like to feel the buzz.

Nothing ever truly disappears. It just hides in the background until it's needed again.

Be cool...

The tears of The Girl In The Red Beret

Good morning Monday. Everybody's got a favourite day. Number one day. A pick of the week day. A day where the weather can do whatever the hell it wants and it won't make a blind bit of difference.

Some folk like Friday because, well hell, it's Friday, stupid! Some love sitting on the fence on Wednesday and trying to figure out how the second half of the week will go. I got a friend who even likes Tuesday because he thinks it's the worst damned day of the week and he always bets on the underdog. Go figure.

Me? I like Monday. Not just any old Monday. Coffee shop Monday. Where folk rev their engines ready for the coming week. Or put on the brakes after another weekend heavy on the sauce. Light on the sleep.

Sometimes there's a fizz about the place. A sparkle in the air. Other times it's like the whole damned room is one giant comfort blanket. It just kinda wraps itself around you and hugs you till you breathe easy.

This morning Little Italy has the blanket out and before I reach my spot against the far wall I can feel life slam on the brakes. One Americano with an extra shot. Strong and sweet and hard to beat. I sit down. Look around. Put a sip to the lip. And feel the dark, warm liquid say the words I love to hear. "Slow the Hell down, goddammit. Where's the friggin' fire?"

This morning another kind of fire is three tables down. Flame top with auburn hair spilling out from underneath. Smouldering green eyes and a pink cashmere top. The Girl In The Red Beret is sitting in front of an empty cup and an open letter.

I blink and a memory surfaces. What the Hell happened between her and The Penitent Man? I asked one time but Little Italy wouldn't say. What happens in here stays in here, was all she said. Fair enough. It wouldn't be a sanctuary if it didn't keep its secrets.

At the counter, two Newbies are flapping their lips at Big Red. Whatcha want? One says to the other. I dunno, maybe… like…a coffee or something? The other says and giggles loud. Maybe you girls should come back when you made up your mind, says Big Red, and gives them the look.

They blush fast and order two large cappuccinos. All of a sudden they found politeness. Two Big C's coming up says Big Red with a smile.

Behind The Newbies, the queue is packed full of anticipation. At her side, Little Italy looks at the box on the wall, then shifts her gaze to The Girl In The Red Beret, who picks up the letter and reads as the tears well up in her eyes.

And somewhere deep down inside the box number 108 lines up for a repeat performance.

The curtains open. Onstage The Righteous Brothers turn up the dial. Give it to me one more time. This isn't chained heartbreak. This is Unchained Melody.

You can email till the cows come home. Nothing shows emotion like tears on paper.

Be cool…

The Magnet is off his meds

Good morning Tuesday. Astronomers who know their onions say there's no such thing as the centre of the universe. Doesn't exist. Physical impossibility. End of story.

The Magnet, however, knows different. At least as far as his own particular universe is concerned. The centre, of course, is wherever he is. Wherever he parks his celestial butt. Wherever he holds court. It's a damned cosmological fact. No escaping it. As long as he's in spitting distance of you, you're hooked. Like a gravitational force. Locked in orbit around him. Unable to break free. Unable to take your eyes off him. Unable to head off into the dark blue yonder on your own.

I can see him from where I sit on my somewhat less celestial butt. He's not in a corner. Not against a wall. Not right by the window. But right in the centre of the room. Surrounded by his own little tribe of minor astral bodies. Invisible to everyone else. Visible to only him. He talks to them. Tells them of the wonders of a billion star systems. Paints verbal picture of the vast nebula that are guardians of the galaxy. All while sipping gently on his impressive interstellar latte.

A million light years away, behind the bar, Little Italy looks on, sadly, and silently curses the unreliability of self-medication. The Magnet, she knows, is off his meds and off his head. She lifts a phone and dials a number committed to memory.

Ten minutes later two large Guardians of The Magnet's Galaxy enter the coffee shop, nod to Little Italy and walk to the centre of the universe. One bends down and whispers in The Magnet's ear. He frowns at the interruption, pauses, then smiles. He stands up, full of importance, looks over to the bar and says; "My presence is needed elsewhere," then he leaves the shop with the Guardians in tow.

Little Italy prepares a small Americano and takes it to a tiny, waif-like figure sitting in a far corner, dabbing tears from her eyes. Eyes that follow The Magnet until he disappears from view.

131

Don't ask, whispers Little Italy as she passes me by. I zip the lip but silently wonder. She slips a fast glance to the box on the wall and I can feel the soft thud as number 130 hits the spinning surface.

The curtains open. The spotlight hits Ray Charles. Sitting at a piano. Smiling that smile. Blind as a bat. Seeing everything. Singing I Can't Stop Loving You.

Sometimes you can't see the love for the pain. Othertimes you can't see the pain for the love.

Be cool…

All the corporate zombies

Good morning Thursday. You know the feeling. Get up in the morning. Wash. Shave (or not). Throw a cheap, clean outfit on your bones. Throw a cheap, dirty coffee down your neck. Switch on auto-pilot, press GO and an instant later you're at work.

No memory of the journey. Just A to Z at the speed of light and everywhere in between is somewhere down a black hole with a large dose of chronic amnesia and a fistful of painkillers for comfort.

Sometimes Thursdays are a bit like that. Tom Tom mornings. Just programme in the journey. Sit back. Switch brain off. Wait for caffeine.

From my perch on the balcony of the coffee shop I can see them. All the corporate zombies. All the thousand yard stare business soldiers. Not for them the tears of love's labours lost…or the joy of feeling butterflies for the first time. Or the next time. Or the terror of feeling them for the last time.

Not for them the silent subterfuge. The secret glances. Delicious thoughts. These are Little Italy's Lost Children. These are the career automatons. Careering blindly to God knows where (and he ain't telling). Climbing up the endless ladders. Pushing boulders up the mountains.

The Banker is in the coffee shop this morning. Sharp suit. Fast pulse. Slick back hair. Standing at the counter in front of Little Italy. Frontline grunt in the war of the money boys. Desperate to slow down. Just for an hour. A minute. A damned second. Just so he can feel something. Any damned thing except the thrill of making more money. Then more. Then more.

So he finds himself here. Not knowing how the Hell he got here. It's a damned mystery to everyone except Little Italy. Here she welcomes him back home like a prodigal son. Here she dispenses love and coffee. Here she lets him sit and rest and shove all that stone face, rat race, fast pace life somewhere the sun doesn't shine.

Here, The Banker gets the chance to remember what it was like before he put on the suit. The tie. The fat braces. Before he thought greed was good. He sits down at a vacant spot. Sugars his cappuccino. Begins to breathe like oxygen isn't in short supply.

Then he feels a gentle tap on his shoulder. He looks. The Stranger With Red Lips smiles. This seat taken, she asks. He smiles.

Over behind the bar, Little Italy looks at the box on the wall. The box looks on the stack marked 'Liverpool'. Time for number 67.

The curtains open. Cue screams. Cue The Beatles. Cue a look in The Banker's eyes. Money's not the answer he thinks. Can't Buy Me Love.

The Stranger With Red Lips sits down next to The Banker. So...what's your story, she says. No story, he says. Not yet, he says. And so it begins. Ain't life fab.

Be cool...

Coffee with Elvira Mistress of the Dark

Good afternoon Friday. Most coffee shops are nothing if not predictable. You go in. Smell the coffee. Order your poison. Sit down and chill out. Here…in this particular coffee shop…with Little Italy in the driving seat…predictability doesn't even get through the damned door.

You want to start the day in the morning? Fine. You figure out that coming at it sideways in the PM floats your boat more? That's peachy, too. Today isn't just the end of another working week. It's the beginning of Fright Night. One helluva sight night. Put your fangs in and bite night. Scream till you turn white night.

Tonight is Halloween…and armies of scary little monsters will soon be getting ready to come out to play in the dark. Knock on doors all over the world and demand sacrificial sweeties. The more chocolate the better. All dressed up and bloodied. Trick or treat. Ghoul or vamp. Walking dead or Zombie hunter.

And here, in the coffee shop, one or two scary big monsters are joining in the fun. Behind the bar, Little Italy has disappeared and in her place is Elvira Mistress of the Dark. Jet-black beehive. Blood-red lips. Figure hugging, low cut, black dress. Watch the girls glare. Watch the boys drool.

Big Red has transformed into a flaming haired Huntress of the Night. Heroine incarnate. Serving up only the finest Pumpkin Spice Lattes with supernatural flair. Riff Raff and Frank N. Furter stand in front of Elvira, waiting to gulp down a Time Warp Cappuccino.

I look for Brad and Janet. All I can see are a few Christopher Lees, a couple of Walking Deads and a hot as hell Buffy. It's one helluva queue. I smile, look down at my Ghostly Green Tea and think about an afternoon spent in the company of some damned fine human beings.

I look up again and Elvira throws a wink my way.

Somewhere underneath that horror hostess, Little Italy throws a bewitching look at the box on the wall. The box bows down before its mistress and number 93 slithers into place. It's a classic. It's a monster hit.

The curtains open. Bobby "Boris" Picket is on stage with his Monster Mash and his best Karloff voice. He manages 30 seconds. That's as far as he gets before Elvira comes out from behind the bar and does something with her glutes that makes the boys go wild.

Don't be predictable. Don't be foreseeable.

Be cool…

The Man in the Black Flat Cap

Good morning Tuesday. Some days hit you like an adrenalin rush. Fast and furious. Full throttle. Other days ease in nice and slow. Soft and easy like watching the waves lap the shore on a calm day.

You're either the White Rabbit…or you're the Caterpillar. You're either late for a very important date…or you couldn't give a damn and everyone else can go to Hell in a handbasket, while you have a nice smoke. For a while at least.

The coffee shop has no time for the former. All the time in the world for the latter. This morning is like The Mississippi. The Big Easy. You can even see folk slow their walking pace as soon as they step through the doorway.

Behind the counter Little Italy is in charge of the clock. In control of every tick and every tock. The Man in the Black Flat Cap gently takes a regular Americano, no milk, from her hands and ambles double slow time to a spot against the wall. He moves his jaws like he's chewing gum. But he's chewing ideas. Thoughts. Concepts. A thinker and a drinker. A conceptualiser and a fantasiser.

He sits, offloads the leather shoulder bag. Rummages and brings out a pad and pen. Old school. Old tools. Not for him any of this new fangled crap. Not for him the marvels of an electronic age. The only tools he needs are inside his head. Inside his brain.

Fifteen feet away, standing in front of the coffee bar is his polar opposite. Gadget Guy. Electronics seeping out of every pore in his body. He's fully connected. Wi-fi selected. Old school rejected. He's a keyboard kid of the information age. Dancing across the ether at a trillion microbytes a second.

And yet…and yet…he comes in here every morning. Looking for a way to slow down the stream of electronic consciousness just for a bit. Just so he can breathe without breaking out into a Facebook sweat. Just so he can rest his full set of fingers. Just so he can slam on the social networking brakes. Remember when his solo act was a double act.

So he presents himself to Little Italy and smiles. And Little Italy, being the mistress of all things speed-restricted, knows the antidote to a fast-moving life. Two parts caffeine…dark and mysterious…one part sugar and spice and all things nice.

She serves it up and Gadget Guy pays up, unplugs and heads for a corner. Two tables away from The Man in the Black Flat Cap. He likes the look of the old guy's pen and paper. The cut of his jib. The style of his nib.

Little Italy looks at the box on the wall. It's old school, too. Old school and old sounds. Somewhere inside the box, number 88 slips onto the turntable.

The curtains open and Neil Young steps up to the microphone. Guitar and harmonica strapped on. Old man with an old song.

Nice one Neil. When the rest of the world is hi-tech…go low. Be cool…

The Girl Who Doesn't Step On Pavement Cracks

Good morning Wednesday. Some folk need the company of likeminded friends to get them through the day. Others, like Blind Willie, merely need to sit back, relax, and let the sounds of the world wash over them.

His eyes are useless but he sees more than most. He's a visually impaired master of all his senses. Except one. A perfect example of what you've never had you don't miss. His ears are his eyes. So is his nose...and his fingertips.

And his guardian angels are Little Italy, Big Red...and Tiny. Tiny, whose mother has been blind since a drunken driver stole her sight away when she was nine. Tiny, who knew how to sign before he knew how to speak out loud. Tiny, the only one allowed to bring Blind Willie his Honey Americano.

Sometimes the biggest jobs go to the smallest people. Sometimes they go to the tallest. Little Italy makes it. Big Tiny takes it. He walks to Blind Willie's table, careful not spill a drop, and sets it down six inches from the old man's hands. He doesn't have to say a word. Blind Willie heard every step. Tiny has rubber soles but Willie has hearing like a cat. He smiles and nods.

The big guy gets the message, smiles back then goes back to stand guard behind the bar. Mission accomplished.

The hinges squeak on a door closed to deny entry to the chill of the morning. Little Italy doesn't need to look. She knows the sound. Two quick steps over the threshold...a pause for a double-tap heartbeat...then a careful walk 20 feet or so to the bar. The Girl Who Doesn't Step On Pavement Cracks is back.

It's been a month. Seems like yesterday. Hello stranger, where you been, says Big Red. The Girl smiles. Down South, she says. I got a relative who got a disease. Tiny chips in. Not catching is it? For a second The Girl looks worried, then she beams a large one. Naaaah, she says. He's not the generous type.

139

This one's on the house, says Little Italy. Special rate for homecoming regulars. The Girl doesn't say a word. You don't argue with the lady of the house. The hostess with the mostest. She just takes her double-shot espresso and heads for the balcony. Always on the tread. Never on the edge.

As she leaves, Little Italy looks at the box on the wall. The box has its own little peculiarities. Always looks twice to the left before dropping the right track into place. Just like now with number 33.

The curtains open and a spotlight hits a microphone. Standing behind it is Johnny Nash. Sharp dresser. Soul and Reggae singer from Houston, Texas. Ironic as Hell.

Blind Willie blinks. Thinks. I can see clearly now. Smiles, reaches out and gently lifts his cup to his lips. Right on target. Radar like a bat.

Be cool...

The Walking Stick Lady has a birthday

Good morning Friday. The Walking Stick Lady is in the coffee shop this morning. I see her as she walks, three legged, through the door.

There's a slight spring in her step, taking her from A to Aaaaah. From a pained hobble to a celebratory walking limp. Bravery personified with the help of the level of medication that would poleaxe an average bull elephant.

She smiles as she approaches the bar. Behind it, Little Italy is waiting patiently, as she always does for this one customer. The Lady doesn't need to speak. Doesn't need to order. But Little Italy does. Happy Birthday, she says.

The Lady blushes. Her preference is well known. She's a regular. Americano straight up. In a slow minute it sits on the counter top. Steaming hot. She moves a hand to lift the saucer and is stopped by Little Italy. Oh no you don't, she says. I'll bring it over, she says. Just like she always says on this occasion.

Little Italy lifts the saucer, comes out from behind the bar and walks slowly to a table in the corner. A table specially prepared. Pressed white linen over dark oak. Pristine. With a single red rose in a long, slim vase.

She slides a chair out like the perfect gentleman. The Lady eases herself down with a thankful sigh. Parks the walking stick. Looks at the Americano. Anticipation licks her lips. Little Italy produces a small box from behind her back. Wrapped in golden paper. Puts it on the table. Happy Birthday, she whispers. Kisses The Walking Stick Lady softly on the top of her head, then walks away.

As she goes, she glances once at the box on the wall. The box has been waiting, too. Waiting to pull number 110 from deep inside. Where the good stuff lives. The Walking Stick Lady reads the tag on the box. The tag says; 'Everyone should have a special day. This one's yours'.

She gently removes the wrapping paper from the box.

Opens it. Blushes. Looks at Little Italy standing behind the bar. Mouths the words 'thank you'. Closes the box. I don't get to see what's inside. Damn. She puts the box to one side, lifts her Americano and has a sip. Number 29 slides onto the turntable.

The curtains open...The Doors take centre stage...and Jim Morrison begins to sing Light My Fire.

I look over at Little Italy and raise an eyebrow. She smiles and draws a zipper across her lips. I decide to mind my own damned business.

Be cool...

You're so vain

Good morning Monday. Italian is a language that curls the toes and stiffens more than the sinews. Especially when spoken by a beautiful Latin female with full lips and dark lids. The kind of female who would give any boy with even a trace amount of testosterone reason to delay standing up. The kind like Little Italy.

This morning, the boy in question is bad in a good way. Good in a bad way. And full of trouble. The kind of trouble that makes young girls' mothers nervous as hell. The kind that makes young girls giggle and older ones sigh. The kind that Big Red would eat for breakfast. The kind that's standing in front of Little Italy committing emotional suicide.

The Gigolo has tried many times before. He's full of charm. Full of rugged good looks and smooth conversation. Little Italy knows he's also full of shit. Full of broken promises. Bent morals. Twisted romance.

But he makes her smile and think of another time. A time long ago when someone else stood in front of her. Passionate boy that one, she thought. Not a bit of shit in sight. Not a false word tumbling out of his mouth.

So hard to say no. So easy to say yes. So she did. For a while. Until he wanted more. And more. And more. Until she said no. And goodbye. Reluctantly. So long ago.

Now her mind comes back to this one. Standing in front of her. When do you get off, he asks. Never do, she says. But this is where you get off, she says. Nice try but no cigar. Be a nice bad boy and go drink your coffee.

She watches the smile diminish as he takes his espresso and his disappointment and does the long Heartbreak Hotel walk alone across the dance floor of his mind and into a faraway corner.

She turns her head to Big Red. The look says it all. Too young, too predictable and too damned cock sure. The Mistress of Taking Down a Peg or Two strikes again.

143

A look at the box on the wall provides the icing on the cake. The box provides the cherry on the top. Courtesy of number 144. Needle on vinyl. None of your damned digital crap.

The curtains open. Miss Cary Simon is on stage. Maybe it was Mick. Maybe it was James. Maybe it was you. Who the Hell cares. You're so vain.

Little Italy thinks about bad good boys. And good bad boys. And she knows which of the two rocks her boat.

Be cool...

Give peace a damned chance

Good morning Tuesday. Good morning twinkling Christmas lights in colourful store windows. Blazing out into the dim, early morning. Whispering in the ears of passing sleepwalkers. "It's nearly here…it's nearly here".

Good morning approaching daylight. Creeping across the city centre. Bouncing off the buildings. Crawling up the streets.

Good morning warmth and green tea and smiles and an Oirish fiddle playing a slow, sad lament. Carrying with it the memories of old black and white movies with real movie stars. From a time when you didn't count talent by the numbers in the box office. When a celebrity wasn't famous just for being a celebrity. And you didn't measure the passage of time by looking at your wrist.

Here, in the coffee shop, the ghosts of the past mingle with anyone and everyone who has a hankering for leaving at least some of the cares of the world on the other side of the door.

There they are. The cares that everyone has and nobody wants. Looking through the window like starving orphans hoping to attract the attention of the well-fed folk inside. One stern look from Little Italy and they scatter like leaves in the wind. Gathering in doorways. All except one. Cold and lonely. Sad and forgotten. Ripped from its home.

The Woman Who Never Forgets sits on this side of the window. Thinking of a home that sits on the other side. Trying to push away the memories. Trying to breathe easy. Trying to stop the shakes from overwhelming her.

She cups a warm cappuccino in both hands and shakes her head slowly from side to side. As if doing so will disrupt the pictures in her head. But it doesn't. All it does is bring them more into focus. All it does is bring that place right up front of mind. Don't forget me, it says. That place outside the window. The one she can't look at but knows is there. Waiting for her. No escape. Only surrender. Only capitulation.

But for now…for a blissful, glorious hour…The Woman Who Never Forgets puts her trust in the one person who truly understands. The one person who's been there, done that, and got a drawer full of t-shirts for her sins. The one who keeps her safe when her emotions threaten to overwhelm and pound her into the ground. The one who brings her peace.

She takes a long, deep breath…looks up…and Little Italy is returning her gaze. She starts a smile. Little Italy finishes it, then looks at the box on the wall.

The box never forgets either. It nods a reply and somewhere deep inside number 49 is patiently waiting for its turn.

The curtains open. Step up Mr. John Lennon. We know what he's saying. We know what he means.

Sometimes it's not just war that needs peace. Sometimes it's noise. Violence. Pain. Screams. Sometimes it's a situation a million miles away from happiness.

Be cool…

The Cutter taps his box

Good morning Wednesday. Some folk are conspicuous by their presence. Others by their absence. `

This morning, The Cutter is one of the former. Sad, quiet and secretive in his bloody routine. In the right hand pocket of his non-descript jacket there's a small wooden box. In the box there's a razor sharp blade, some antiseptic liquid and a pack of plasters.

He takes care of himself. His cuts heal quickly. Only his scars last. A roadmap to his journey. When the pressure cooker inside threatens to do a Vesuvius, he goes somewhere private and let's off some of the fiery red steam.

But sometimes just one slice isn't enough. Sometimes the pain hangs around, snarling, and the song remains the same. Those are the times when he comes to Little Italy. To the only other being on God's twisted scorched earth who can do what the blade can't.

So here he is. Two tables away. With a large, dark Americano and Little Italy sitting by his side. Holding his hand. Stroking his fingers gently. Not saying a word. Here he is. Head bowed. Eyes closed. Breathing deeply. Waiting for the emotional larva to settle. And it does. For a while.

He opens his eyes and looks at her. Healer. Protector. Friend. You ok now, she asks. He nods and tries for a smile. It's a piss poor attempt, but what the Hell. She smiles, pats the back of his hand and stands up slowly. You go save the rest of the world, he says. I'm okay now.

Fifteen feet away, The Professor is writing formulas on the blackboard of his mind. He makes a mental note. Running out of chalk and where the Hell's the duster? Nothing is ever where it should be, he observes. Just when he was about to help Little Italy save the world again with a cure for emotional distress. He thinks he'll call it Vesuvius Goes To Sleep.

He looks towards The Cutter and wonders if he left the formula with him.

Behind the bar, Big Red is pouring a Double Espresso with an extra shot for The Mouse. Small, timid, nervous...and jumpy as hell.

She's here to get away from all the tomcats of the world. All the hunters who know her name. Know her game. Know her shame.

Little Italy looks at The Cutter then above him to the box on the wall. The box has its own method of keeping things at bay. Just like it has its own method of bringing things close. Right now it chooses the latter. It reaches down and brings number 31 from the bottom of the special occasion stack.

The curtains open. One light illuminates the darkness of the stage. Cue the sound of an acoustic guitar. Cue the unmistakable voice of James Taylor, standing at the mike. Starts to sing.

The Cutter hears the words. Feels the words. Sees Little Italy smile at him. Hears her voice. You Got A Friend. Reaches down. Taps his box. Closes his eyes. You stay there for now, he whispers.

Be cool...

Getting to know you

Good morning Friday. Every time I see strangers meet and strike up a friendship, right out of the blue, I always think of my friend the statistician.

He told me once that a good looking single white male has more chance of being stung on the tongue by a dead bee, than having a great time out on a blind date. On a Friday. In November. In a coffee shop. At breakfast time. Shows how much he knows. Bless his little cotton socks.

It's blind date time three tables away for a pair of likely suspects. Only they don't know it yet. They haven't made the arrangements. Can't even see it coming. Have no idea of the consequences of sitting down together. Within touching distance. Breathing distance. He with his coloured cane. She with her four-legged friend. Both with their dark eyes on. Courtesy of Mr. Ray Charles.

They usually sit apart. Opposite ends of the room in their own little world of heightened senses. But not today. Not this morning. Little Italy has other ideas. Other plans. Setting wheels in motion is her speciality.

Wheel number one. White Stick Man. Mid thirties. Born blind. Drop dead gorgeous. Large Skinny Latte. Wheel number two. Golden Lab Girl. Early thirtysomething.

Turned blind when she turned ten. The day her father died. Medium Americano with a little cold water and two sugars. Bitter sweet.

So here they sit. Together apart. Letting nature take its course. Letting their individual senses detect each other as Little Italy makes the introductions. Carter, she says, meet Eloise. A pause. Eloise, she says, meet Carter. Now you two be good.

She leaves them to their awkward silences, soon to be replaced by comfortable conversation.

The lab licks the cane. The cane doesn't object. Carter and Eloise get to know each other. Get to like what they see with everything except their eyes, and those don't matter much now.

Behind the bar, Big Red smiles inside. Little Italy looks at the box on the wall...and the box already has number 87 picked out and on the way.

The curtains open. James Taylor is on stage. Getting To Know You. Acoustic guitar. Words and music by Rodgers & Hammerstein. Voice all his own.

You don't need eyes to see that, sometimes, the people you don't know are much more interesting than the ones you do.

Be cool...

The Man With The Five Minute Memory

Good morning Tuesday. Or should I say good afternoon? I'm sitting in the coffee shop and I've seen AM change into PM. Watched the day grow from dull and cold to warm and bright. Sipping one sweet Americano after another. And thinking about the past.

Sometimes it's not the things you've got that make you happy. Make you grateful. Make you laugh out loud or shed a tear. Make you feel all warm and fuzzy and glad you're alive.

Sometimes it's the things you used to have. Used to touch. Used to hold tight. Used to feel like you could never live without. Sometimes it's the things you see that remind you of people you used to know and the time you spent with them. A random thought here. A fleeting face there. Out of reach. Unwilling or unable to be caught.

Today, walking towards my table, The Man With The Five Minute Memory is having no such thoughts. He sits down and introduces himself. He's very talkative. Likes meeting new people. Then five minutes later he introduces himself again. Then again five minutes after that.

I know the routine. So we talk in byte-sized chunks of conversation. And when we finish, we start over again. Repetitive strain injury of the ears for me. The whole world in 300 seconds for him. Or what he can remember of it.

He has a guardian angel. His wife. Three tables away. Watching. Giving him a precious slice of independence. Remembering the man he used to be. Before the headaches came and took away the past. When he never forgot anything.

She takes him everywhere and hers is one of the only two faces he never forgets. The other belongs to Little Italy. The woman who brings him the only drink he knows he likes.

Five minutes pass in a blink. He smiles and sticks out his hand. Says hello and tells me his name.

We talk about coffee.

His guardian angel leaves her table, comes over to ours and sits down. The recognition and love in his eyes are obvious. He turns to me and introduces himself. The Man With The Five Minute Memory has his own version of Groundhog Day.

Behind the bar, Little Italy smiles, looks at the box on the wall and somewhere inside, number 160 takes its turn on the stage.

The curtains open and Dooley Wilson sits at a piano in the middle of a crowded Rick's Café. And, As Time Goes By, we remember all the things that a simple kiss can mean.

Some things you never find. Other things you never lose.

Be cool…

The First Lady of Second Chances

Good morning Friday. Darkness has put in another busy shift. Time for it to catch some serious zees. Make way for the cosmic lightbulb lifting its head slowly above the horizon. Trying to warm the concrete. Trying to put a smile on the face of the city centre.

But the wind has a bite like a pissed off terrier. Waking up the homeless sleepy heads and shifting them from automatic to manual.

Here, in the coffee shop, the sign says business as usual. Superglue for the broken hearted. Peace and quiet for the screaming heads. The best damned coffees on God's green earth for everyone who walks through the door.

And second chances for those who screwed up first time round. Those who zigged when they should have zagged. Those who walked away from a good thing when they should have made a beeline for it with open arms. Those who said no when they should have hit the yes button with a sledgehammer till it gave in and begged for mercy.

Sometimes you don't know what you've got till it's gone. Love doesn't walk out any door voluntarily. It has to be pushed. It has to be kicked, punched, hurt, torn apart and left bleeding on the damned dance floor.

That's where Little Italy comes in. The First Lady of Second Chances. The one who picks you up and dusts you off. So you can start all over again and maybe get it right this time.

I see them sitting upstairs. Hard against the balcony railings. The Girl with a Million Freckles and The Boy with Elvis Hair. She tearful and hurt. He guilty and penitent. There's a white card on the table. It was there when they sat down. It has 12 words beautifully written in red ink on it. They say: "Everyone deserves a second chance. This is yours. Don't fuck it up".

Little Italy doesn't mince words. I see her on the way up the stairs to the balcony carrying a tray with two large white coffee cups.

Cappuccinos with a dusting of cocoa powder in the shape of a heart sitting on the foam.

She says something to the pair. I see her lips move but I can't hear the words. They're not for me anyway. Not for my ears. None of my damned business.

She turns and walks away, slowly taking the stairs back down to where the rest of the world is taking another crack at life. As she reaches the bottom step she glances up at the box on the wall and nods ever so slightly.

The box knows the routine. Somewhere deep inside, number 15 rises to the surface and drops gently onto the turntable.

The curtains open. The vinyl starts to spin. Diana Ross and the Supremes, arms outstretched, palms facing the world, killer queens, have only one thing to say. Ignore it at your peril. Stop! In the Name of Love...

I look up. The gap between the pair suddenly left town in a hurry. Like the card says. Everyone deserves a second chance.

Be cool...

The Joker's tears

Good morning Wednesday. Laughter is the best medicine. At least that's what they say. Whoever they are. Personally, I come down on the side of penicillin.

But hey...who the hell can argue with a giggle? Tickles the happy bones. Livens up the tummy muscles. Makes the world seem a bit damned brighter than it is. So here's to the humour merchants, God bless them one and all. Yeah...right.

The Joker's in the coffee shop this morning. Sitting against the wall. Sad...lonely....face like a smacked arse. Little Italy told me once he does stand-up. Top comedian.

Folk come from miles around. By the bus load. Packed tight as sardines. All to hear his one-liners. His witty monologues. His hilarious slices of life. He cracks them up. Makes them forget their unfunny lives. Just for an hour. Sends them home happy. What a routine. What a guy. What a night. Entertainment at its best. They only paid a tenner. The Joker paid a damned sight more.

He sits this morning cradling his cappuccino tenderly. His eyes welling up. His heart crumbling. Anger festering in the pit of his gut. Remembering the only person who made him smile. Who made him laugh till the tears ran down his cheeks. Who got the Big C and didn't want to waste away. Who asked him...pleaded with him...to help her say goodbye and promise never NEVER to stop making folk laugh.

So he kept the promises. Both of them.

Behind the bar, Little Italy looks over at his down-turned face and knows that she can't even begin to share the pain he feels. Knows that nothing she says or does will lessen it or take it away. All she can do is give him the space to put the laughter to one side. No audience. No applause. No encore. Just a small slice of peace and self-forgiveness.

Little Italy sees his empty cup and takes him a fresh one. Unannounced.

As she walks away she looks up at the box on the wall and somewhere inside the box number 81 knows it's time to step onto the stage.

The curtains open and the spotlight falls on Smokey Robinson & The Miracles. He might be smiling, but he's singing Tears Of A Clown.

Laughter and tears. Flip sides of the same coin. Life isn't supposed to be easy. Or hard. It doesn't have an opinion. It doesn't even have a say in the matter. And it sure as Hell doesn't care who it happens to. Or who it leaves behind.

A bit like love.

Be cool...

It's beginning to look a lot like Christmas

Good morning Monday. Good morning December. Okay. Who the hell stole the past year and where did you stash it?

You know that feeling when your body is sitting comfortably about August…and your brain is double-parked next to God knows where, with a Santa hat on the dash and wobbly reindeer hanging from the rearview?

It's beginning to look a lot like Christmas (already) for some folk. For others, it's just another brick in the wall.

Here, in the coffee shop, soon-to-be-celebrants sit next to those with a thousand yard stare. Festive shell shock on their faces. Zero dosh on their bank statements.

To the left, The Girl with Betty Davis Eyes is wearing a red cardigan with Santa's Little Helpers all decked out in green. It's a pre-emptive strike at Christmas style…two weeks early and she doesn't give a damn. She's sitting with The Man With The Clark Gable moustache and she's weak at the knees.

She's not a classic beauty. Not a movie goddess. But she has a tongue like a stingray's barb so she can take care of herself in a barroom brawl. Maybe that's what drew Gable to her. Surely not her BIG baby blues. Toffee with a liquid centre. Tough on the outside, molten love on the inside. Don't get many of them to the pound.

Over behind the bar, Little Italy has a thing for misfits. A thing for opposites that were never meant to attract each other in a million years. But somehow fit just fine.

She's chewing the fat with Little and Large. He's short. She's tall. Like escapees from Dr. Mysterio's Carnival of Unusual Couples. I reckon she's just shy of six feet eight inches tall. Jet hair. Black, full length, figure-hugging coat, open over a black basque, gaucho skirt and cowboy boots. Draws stares like a magnet draws iron filings.

Beside her, the man in her life is around five feet of pristine masculinity in a dark collar-less suit and a gentleman's walking cane.

Wide shoulders, shoes shining like mirrors. Head like a billiard ball. Short on size. Tall on everything else.

Good to see you again, says Little Italy. Been a while. We've been out saving the world from itself says Large. Little nods in agreement. They don't have to order. Big Red has the two triple espressos waiting for them before the coins appear.

As they take them and make for a vacant spot, Little Italy looks at the box on the wall and deep inside Number 148 rises up like cream to the top of the cup.

The curtains open. Billy Joel is already halfway through Just The Way You Are.

Big rule of life. Don't change yourself just to please anyone else.

Be cool…

The boys are back in town

Good morning Wednesday. Today, as the sun rises, I am an inner city renegade. An outer limits desperado. A caffeinated outlaw with a bittersweet tooth.

Drawn like a magnet to the dark side. Surrendering willingly. My love for the lord of the green tannin temporarily usurped. Upended. Twisted, tangled and turned on its head.

I sit in the coffee shop hugging the dregs of a once luxuriant, black Americano and daydreaming for a minute or two of eyes the colour of night. Skin the texture of velvet. Sitting a dozen feet and a million miles away. Dream on, cowboy, whispers a voice to my left.

I look up and Little Italy is holding a fresh cup of mahogany joe, ready, willing and able to bring yours truly out of an early morning reverie. She smiles. I blush. And the moment disappears like smoke in the wind.

By the time I return the smile she's returning to the bar with a clean pair of heels and a slight sway of the hips that would make the blood pump faster in the veins of any creature within a hair's breadth of testosterone. That's Little Italy all over.

I take a furtive sip of the fresh Americano, let it play around my taste buds for a few seconds before feeling it slip down my throat with all the warmth of an old friend.

A raised voice catches my attention and I snap my head up in the direction of the bar. You used to make the best damned Mocha in the whole goddamned town, says The Voice. It used to be so good you'd get folk queuing up sometimes just to stand outside and smell the damned stuff, ain't that right Eugene? Uh huh says Eugene, with a white smile a mile wide interrupted by two solid gold front teeth. Eugene is dancin' like he badly needs to pee.

You go pee baby, says The Voice, I'll get these. Little Italy points to the balcony and Eugene disappears up the stairs like his arse is on fire.

Over by the window, The Man in Black looks on and smiles.

Shakes his head slow. Just like he always does. He looks back down at his book. Soft black leather cover. Gold cross on the front. He licks a forefinger and turns a page.

Two feet away the door opens and the next slice of life waltzes in followed by a blast of Arctic air. Little Italy looks at the box on the wall and points to the new arrivals. The box gets the message. Somewhere inside Number 58 slides into place.

The curtains open. Lizzy takes to the stage. Thin body. Lynott vocals. Half Irish. Half Brazilian. Lock up your daughters. The Boys Are Back In Town.

Be cool…

The carrot-topped mad boys

Good morning Friday. Welcome to the land of thick padded jackets and multi-coloured bobble hats. Of cosy woolly scarves and ripe, rosy cheeks. Of darkness to light. Dullness to bright.

Of forming your own personal misty breath as you scuttle along streets full of glaring shop lights and fast walkers. A hurry here and a scurry there…city centre's the place where they say hey guys…take a walk on the really damp side. Where Heaven's Tears wet the pavements and raise the temperature a notch or two.

The door to the coffee shop is closed to the intermittent breeze. It's a no-go area but the breeze doesn't give a tinker's cuss. It introduces itself to the wood and glass, trying to get in. Stubborn as Hell. It doesn't know when to give up. Doesn't know when to back down.

Every now and then it manages to gently squeeze through the gap and sail in on the coattails of a caffeine worshipper. Every once in a while it sneaks its way into the Church of the Dark Roasted Bean, only to find Little Italy standing there. Waiting. Guardian of the peace and quiet. Upholder of the law of order in a chaotic world.

The breeze doesn't stand a chance. Mumbling. Grumbling. Nature's breath retreats and ruffles the hair of the nearest passer by.

At the bar, waiting for their daily kickstarter of hot, dark juice, are two mirror image individuals. Derek and Clive. The Identical Twins. Carrot-topped mad boys with wild colonial eyes and all the cheek of the Devil on a Sunday with a twinkle in his eye and soft words that drip off his lips like warm, molten honey.

Same size, same weight, same sense of humour, same sense of style. Every sentence one starts the other finishes. We'll have two large, says Derek. Skinny lattes with gingerbread syrup, says Clive. Please, says Derek. I see you've cut out the cussing, says Little Italy. The twins look at each other and smile. Only while we're in, says Clive. Here, says Derek, quickly.

Behind them, waiting her turn, turning her mind over the events of last night, is a shock of white hair with a dark coat. Collar up. Jeans tucked in knee-length boots. Another damned argument. Another slammed door. Another bucket of tears.

Little Italy sees the look. A touch of the morning afters is required. In here the make ups outweigh the break ups. Little Italy knows this to be true.

She smiles, pours a sweet Americano, hands it over and looks at the box on the wall. The box, ever obedient, brings something special up from the basement. Number 29.

The curtains open. The spotlight blasts away the darkness centre stage. Elvis is in the house. Long before the white jumpsuit.

Love is the finest four letter word on the planet. Don't Be Cruel.

Be cool...

The Swans walk in the door

Good morning Monday. Sometimes all you need is half an hour. Thirty minutes out of all the 1440 minutes in every day. Just to press the button so you can stop the world, look around...and separate the carpe from the diem.

Some folk smell the roses. I smell the coffee. Fewer pricks. Coffee is like warmth. A basic human need. An emotional damned requirement. It's got nothing to do with temperature. Nothing to do with heat. Nothing to do with taste. Everything to do with at least 1,800 seconds of peace and quiet. Or fun and laughter.

It's friendship. Safety. Understanding. The celebration of an old love affair or the beginnings of a new one. It's being alone in a crowd because that's the way you like it. Or being in the company of an empty room because that's the way you want it.

This morning, like every morning, Little Italy is exuding warmth and dispensing it to all who walk through the door of the coffee shop. Like The Swans. Standing in front of her. Waiting their turn. Graceful. Elegant. Old in years, young at heart. Mated for life.

He grey haired and neatly dressed. A gentleman in tweeds. She white haired with muted colours from head to toe. Two individuals who, a lifetime ago, became indistinguishable from each other. Two hearts beating as one.

Little Italy has known them all her life. Loved them all her life. Once a month they come to visit. Here. She takes a tray full of coffee and carrot cake to a table against the wall. Their table. Reserved in advance. There are three chairs at the table. Three coffees on the tray. And a month full of conversation to catch up on.

All three sit and no words are spoken until after the first sips are taken. Then a torrent of smiles and words take place.

At the bar, Big Red takes over and watches the three as the warmth of their relationship spreads throughout the room. Touching all who witness.

And for this day, this once-a-month time, she is the one who looks up at the box on the wall and nods gently. The box responds in a way that does justice to Big Red's direction.

It pauses. Brings number 129 off the stack and waits a heartbeat before it slides it onto the turntable. A small preparation for a special moment.

The curtains open. The band strikes up. A young Francis Albert Sinatra is sitting on a barstool, mike in hand.

The Swans look at each other, then at their daughter. All The Way can last half an hour…or a lifetime.

Be cool…

Loneliness is like battery acid

Good morning Wednesday. It's dawn outside the coffee shop and the wind is sheltering like the homeless in shop doorways, trying to escape the wet, bone-chilling start to the day.

Here inside, where warmth and friendship are dispensed like Holy Communion, the room is almost empty. Tables are clean, shiny and full of anticipation. Waiting patiently for life to come visiting. Waiting for the heady aroma of conversation. Laughter, followed by he said she said. Or the welcome sound of silence. The first caffeine-fuelled thoughts of the morning. Private thoughts. Secret thoughts. Never shared aloud. The sound of silence can be deafening.

I can see her. The Quiet Girl. Sat in the corner. Facing the wall. Never raising her head. Never raising her hopes. Never putting one optimistic thought in front of another. Shying away from the company of others. Shielding her eyes like some creature of the night, cowering from the approaching first light.

Don't come close. Don't want to see. Don't want to know.

Loneliness is like battery acid. It corrodes. It tears at the skin and leaves an emotional wound that never quite heals. The ache never goes away. The pain never subsides.

The Quiet Girl has a special place in Little Italy's heart. The kind of place reserved for those who need a little extra space. A little extra love and understanding. A little more time than the others to put herself back together.

Little Italy sees her empty cup. Feels her empty heart. A refill is a million miles away from the medicine she needs. But it's a start. Some kind of a beginning. So she takes The Quiet Girl a second espresso. And then a third. All paid for in advance. All gulped down after the first burning flush has subsided.

Little Italy knows the routine. Knows how long the recovery will take. How deep the hurt has gone. Recuperation of the heart. Of the soul.

How long has it been so far? Nine months? A year maybe? The time doesn't matter. What matters is allowing what's broken to fix itself. To smile once again. Maybe laugh. Hold a conversation without remembering the sound of his voice. Look at another human being without seeing his face.

Until then, Little Italy will wait. She has all the time in the world. She looks at the box on the wall and the box looks at The Quiet Girl. Somewhere inside it, number 158 rises to the surface and eases itself onto an already spinning deck. The volume goes from zero to hero.

The curtains open. The Fab Four are already on stage. The unmistakable voice of McCartney travels softly through the air. This isn't today. This isn't tomorrow.

This is Yesterday.

Be cool…

Take a look at me now

Good morning Thursday. Everybody has somebody they take for granted. A part-of-the-furniture-person. Almost invisible. Almost irrelevant. Almost a ghost in the machine.

Seen but not taken into account. Heard but not taken notice of. A number in the ledger. A noise in the background. A presence absent from conscious thought. Always there. Never given the chance to be missed. Until they're not there any longer. Until you see the empty chair. Notice the silence. Wonder why you feel an ache where there wasn't one before.

The Lady With The Lopsided Fringe is in the coffee shop. Used to be young and in love. Used to be a slip of a girl. Used to be huggy and touchy and feely.

Then the years rolled on and The Boy With The Mile Wide Grin became The Man With The Constant Frown. And without knowing it, he turned into someone who was always there. But just not always thought about. Then bit-by-bit, he faded from conscious attention until the body that she used to hug so tightly became the part-of-the-furniture-person she never touched except by accident.

His mind is no longer a part of hers. Their fingers no longer interlace. Their hearts no longer melt and become one. So here she sits. Four tables away. While the morning comes awake outside and the aroma of roasted coffee beans tries to awaken something on the inside that has been buried for so long.

She looks to the bar where Romeo and Juliet both have the joy of finding love in their hearts and the terror of losing it in their minds. Their romance is a two-headed coin and every day life conspires to toss the coin in the air and see which head comes down on top. His or hers. Heads or tails. Gain or loss. Smiles or tears.

Enjoy it while you can, thinks The Lady With The Lopsided Fringe. Make every day matter. Make every second count. Never lose sight of each other. Never take a moment for granted.

She looks at her cappuccino. Half finished. Half warm. Half enjoyed. Looks at Little Italy looking at her from behind the bar. Both understand the pain of loss. Both know the feeling of regret.

Little Italy finishes serving Romeo and Juliet and looks up at the box on the wall. The box feels the sorrow from 30 feet away. Emotion can travel at the speed of light. Distance is no barrier. Number 75 is already on the turntable.

The curtains open. Against All Odds, Phil Collins is already on the stage and in full flow. Two lessons to learn.

One. Don't lose sight of the person you were. Two. Don't lose touch with the person you fell in love with.

Be cool...

The Cowboy and Calamity Jane

Good morning Monday. Tick tock…tick tock. The sound of the countdown clock. The movements round the face of time gearing up for the big day. Getting ready for a visit from the fat man in the red suit.

You can see it in the eyes of the folk you pass in the street. Anticipation. Even the folk sleeping in doorways wake up early to sort out their Santa hats and squeeze a little more sentiment and coinage from the passers by.

Anticipation. It's nearly Christmas for Christ's sake. Don't give ten pence…give fifty. Don't give fifty pence…give a pound. Anticipation. Pulling in the sympathy vote. Reasons to be bloody thankful. There but for the grace of God go I.

The Cowboy walks right by them and enters the coffee shop like he was walking through the swinging doors of a Wild West saloon. Gambler's hat, handlebar moustache, sheepskin jacket, roughrider denims, tooled-leather boots with pointed toes and jangling spurs.

You expect the piano player to freeze his fingers. You expect the drunken patrons to turn their heads. Duck down behind tables. Make for the back door. Anticipation.

The Cowboy means business. He strolls up to the bar, spurs saying hello to the room. John Wayne style. Faces off in front of Little Italy. Fingers itching. Eyes twitching.

Little Italy throws him back her best sharpshooter stare. No giveaway blink. Just a calmness in her face and a twinkle in her eyes. Hello Cowboy, she says. The usual? The Cowboy breathes nice and slow. Not this morning, he says. I got company. Better make it two double usuals. Dark and fast. She nods.

He turns and looks to the far corner where Calamity Jane sits with a pile of troubles and a heart full of pain.

Little Italy hands over the tray and The Cowboy moseys over to see if he can fix what's broke before the pain gets too much and the breaks get too bad to put back together again.

Calamity looks up as she hears him come close. Over behind the bar, Little Italy turns away and looks at the next one in line. The next one who needs fixing. The next one who needs a damned fine cup of coffee and a few kind words. Just for a while.

She looks at the box on the wall. The box has a hair trigger and an aim like Annie Oakley. It never misses. Somewhere inside number 153 pops its head up and puts on a brave face.

The curtains open. Tammy Wynette is standing behind the mike, looking as beautiful and as ever.

The Cowboy and Calamity look at each other. True love is about standing by your woman and standing by your man. Always. Christmas…New Year…any damned time of the year.

Be cool…

Star-crossed lovers of a different kind

Good morning Tuesday. As I walk into the coffee shop, the box on the wall is halfway through entertaining what few customers there are, with brass band Christmas carols.

Big Red is wearing a sparkly Santa hat with a light on the front that blinks on and off. Tiny has an impressive set of reindeer antlers clipped to his head. I feel I should call him Rudolph. I let the moment pass.

I look for Little Italy. She is nowhere in sight. Where's the boss, I ask. In the office putting on her Christmas outfit, says Big Red. Yeah, says Tiny, it's her once-a-year thing, he says. She makes a special effort, he says. You know what she's like, he says.

I reach inside and pick up a memory of this time last year. Yeah...I know what she's like. A small grin invades my face. Some things you can't stop. Some things you don't want to.

I hear the door open behind me and The Boys come in. Star-crossed lovers of a different kind. A deliriously happy kind. A mate for life and bugger the consequences kind. I liked them the first moment I saw them. So many mornings ago. So much coffee has flowed under the bridge since then.

Harold is tall. Impeccably dressed. Black suit. Silver hair. Pink shirt and tie. Good looking. George, the more handsome of the two, is in herringbone. Sedate. Classy. Careful not to outshine his better half. His funnier half. Sometimes outrageous. Always caring. Always loving.

They take their skinny lattes and park themselves with style around a table ten or so feet away. They see me. Nod and smile. Harold gives a small wave and blows a kiss. I'm tempted to blow one back. Just for the hell of it. Just because it's Christmas...nearly. Instead, I merely nod and smile.

Something Japanese-sounding is coming from the box on the wall. Something beautiful and soft and painfully sad.

I look up to the bar and Big Red is looking at me and pointing to the office. The door is open and through it walks Little Italy. Dressed not in her usual black...but in red. Red on red in red over red under red. Red shoes. Red hair. Red lipstick. A faint hint of red blusher.

There are some things that simply take the breath away. There are other things that take it away, give it a tango around the dance floor, and bring it back home with a rose between its teeth.

The rest of the world is the former. Little Italy is the latter. The Boys applaud. Little Italy doesn't need to glance at the box on the wall. The box is way ahead of her. Number 50 is already sitting comfortably and spinning.

The curtains open. UB40 are in the spotlight. The audience is drinking up red, red wine. Sometimes it's not the taste of the grape but the colour of the juice.

Be cool...

Singing in the rain

Good morning Thursday. Mizzle is a two-sided blade that dampens the clothes and sharpens the senses. It's the bastard child of full-blown rain.

It starts as I leave the tram and stops as I arrive at the coffee shop. With drops so fine and close together there's no space to walk in between them. No room to duck or dive. No opportunity to bob or weave. Everyone gets a share. Nobody escapes.

All except the Umbrella People. The ones who come prepared. Think ahead. Plan and scheme. Miss out on the mizzle. Miss out on the feeling of something on their face other than fresh air. Love is a bit like that.

You can let the mizzle get you and feel just that little more alive. Or you can hide under the umbrella...feel comfy...but miss all the good stuff.

One of the Umbrella People is standing at the bar in front of Little Italy. I can feel his comfort from my usual spot, back against the wall. Not a damp patch on him. Nothing to show he's ever been close to a relationship. Alone in the crowd. Happy in his skin...or so he likes to believe.

Not even the slightest bit interested in coming into contact with the skin of another...or so he thinks.

Little Italy doesn't say a word as she serves him. She knows what he wants. Americano dark. A safe choice. A no-risk choice. Even has the precise price ready and waiting.

As he walks to a free spot the door opens and in walks a tall 30-something umbrella-free zone covered in mizzle from head to foot. Eyes sparkling. Full of deep, peaceful breathing and deep, meaningful intent. She has life written all over her and a who-the-hell-cares attitude written across her face.

She smiles instantly when she sees Little Italy. As she walks to the bar the espresso machine comes alive and pours out a thick, strong stream of double-strength liquid.

Mizzle Girl exchanges a few words with Little Italy, grabs her coffee and makes her way to the balcony.

On the way, she sees Umbrella Guy look at her. Feels his comfort drain away...just a little. Feels a touch of her dampness travel across the space between them and touch his dry forehead. The effect sends a shiver down his spine.

She nods at him and carries on up the stairs. He, alone in his dryness invaded by the merest touch of mizzle, simply watches her ascend and feels his breath quicken.

Behind the bar, little Italy smiles inside and looks over to the box on the wall. The box sends back one of its special occasion nods. Number 147 rises to the surface and slips onto the turntable. Starts spinning.

The curtains open. A single light shines on an old streetlight. Gene Kelly is on stage. Soaking wet. Umbrella nowhere in sight. Singing in the rain. Happy as a clam in mud at high tide.

Sometimes liking someone keeps you inside your comfort zone. Sometimes loving them takes you way out of it. You choose.

Be cool...

The deteriorating mind of Maude

Good morning Friday. It's nearly raining. Nearly cold. And nearly Christmas. I'm walking in a winter wonderland...but only in the music from the box on the wall.

Not a speck of the White stuff is falling yet. Maybe it's keeping itself for the big day. I suspect the only snowballs being thrown until then will be those being thrown down a few elderly necks in the run up to the festival of old Saint Nick.

There you are gran. A nice snowball for you in a pint glass. There you are grandad. A touch of the hard stuff. A tot of rum. A snifter of scotch. Take it easy now. Don't want you both falling over drunk.

Here in the coffee shop my only drinking companions this morning are the voices in my head. They're no strangers. They're old friends. Over by the bar, two more old friends are ordering up the first of the day. Harold and Maude. Americano and Cappuccino. Founding members of the Active OAPs Club.

Up at dawn and down to the tram stop. In to the city centre to look at the busy people. To watch while the rest of the world goes by. To chill out and talk about old times. To drag up the same memories every day.

Do you remember...says Maud. Yes dammit...you told me that five minutes ago, said Harold though his tortoiseshell frames. Don't swear, said Maud. You always swear.

She sips her cappuccino gently and walks slowly back in time inside her rapidly deteriorating mind.

Behind the bar, Little Italy looks on and feels a tear threaten her happiness. She wills it away and looks at the next in line. A fat jolly male with a white beard and a red suit trimmed in white. Hello gorgeous he says. Hello Santa she replies. You're early. Department store Santas are never late, he says. Not good form, he says. Folk need a bit of cheering up, he says.

What about you, says Little Italy...what do YOU need?

175

Santa thinks for a minute then looks over at me. Turns to Little Italy and says, I'll have what he's having. Little Italy smiles, reaches for the green tea and turns to the box on the wall. The box looks at Harold and Maude, puts its best happy face on, and number 34 rises up out of the dark. Not for the first time. Not for the last.

The curtains open. Billy Joel is sitting at a piano. Harold and Maude look at each other. Harold reaches out and pats Maude's hand. Billy sings Just the Way You Are.

Sometimes love and arthritis go together just fine.

Be cool...

Tiny, the tallest Christmas elf

Good morning Tuesday. Well…nearly here…nearly here. How come the faster you want to reach some place the longer it takes to get there? Or maybe somebody's trying to tell you that, once you get there, it won't be all it's cracked up to be.

Maybe they're trying to say that Christmas is better as an ideal rather than a reality. I knew somebody who thought like that. Cold-hearted sour-faced pain in the arse. He just didn't get it. Didn't get that it doesn't matter what the rest of the year is like…THIS nearly-here day does its damndest to make up for all the pain, crap and disappointment that life throws our way for all the other 364 days.

It's the day when you can wake up as early or as late as you damned well like and kick the hell out of pessimism and doubt. When folk who would normally pass each other without as much as a nod of recognition, suddenly find time to smile. Maybe even say a few words.

Here, today, in the coffee shop, there's a Wellwisher at the door. A Greeter dispensing festive bonhomie. Tiny, the tallest, thinnest Christmas Elf ever to wear the colours of nature and the title Santa's Little Helper, is standing on the inside. And to everyone who passes over the portal he smiles and says Merry Christmas.

Of course the reality is that he's not the helper of the fat man in the red suit at all. He's the left hand man of Little Italy. Caffeine Queen and guardian of the lost and lonely. The found and happy. The rich and poverty-stricken. The loveless and the homeless. The new romantics and the old ones. The chatterboxes and the silent, thoughtful ones. The fashionistas and the ragamuffins.

And that simple greeting means that no matter how sad or worried, frowny-faced or bleary-eyed folk are by the time they reach the coffee shop…they're just that little bit happier by the time they reach Little Italy and Big Red standing behind the bar.

Waiting for the orders. Waiting to dispense their own tidings of comfort and joy.

Or sometimes just a little peace and quiet. A little space for the memories to squeeze themselves in.

I see Little Italy look at the box on the wall and give it the kind of nod that can only mean one thing. One song. At this time of year. The box doesn't need to think twice. Number 111 slides up and onto the turntable.

Cue orchestra. Cue a younger version of Old Blue Eyes. Cue the only place in town to partake of the best drink on the planet.

The curtains open. Francis Albert Sinatra is on stage surrounded by a sea of smiling kids. Wouldn't that be a fine thing. No worries. No troubles. Even just for a day. Nice one Frankie.

Have Yourself a Merry Little Christmas.

Be cool…

He has a badge that says Angel

Good morning Monday. The first Monday of the new year. The first drink of 2015 in the coffee shop. The first look around to see who's here…who's late…who's moved on. Who's got a fistful of resolutions to keep or conveniently forget about…and who doesn't give a damn whether the New Year just means the same old same old.

I walk in from a brisk sunny morning and see a stranger with muscles behind the bar. He has a badge that says Angel. He has that busy look of someone who doesn't know quite what to do, so he does a bit of everything in the hope that he does something right.

He smiles. I frown. Where's the boss, I say. He looks flustered. A small slice of panic creeps into his eyes. She's busy, he says. Can I help, he says. Broken English. Italian maybe. I smile. Best to start the New Year off on the right foot I say. Name, rank and serial number, I say. Pardon, he blurts. Eyes dart to the office, a door opens and the cavalry arrives. Black hair, black eyes, black dress….red rose pinned to left breast. Black tights. Red shoes. Ghost of a smile on red lips. A Million Dollars walks the walk, then talks the talk. Don't worry Angel says Little Italy. I got this one.

Angel looks relieved. He stands to one side, turns, and smiles at the next in line. A pair of muscle worshippers, gob-smacked at the sight of Angel's bulging biceps. He speaks. They melt.

Meanwhile, Little Italy bends her head slightly to the left. Usual, she asks. Nope I say. New Year, new drink. Green tea is so last year. She stifles a laugh and gives me the look that says, okay smart boy, let me guess. I pause and keep the words safely locked up behind closed lips.

She gives me the up and down. Waits a heartbeat. Americano she says. I open my lips and the words come tumbling out. On the button, I say. So…black is the new green she says. Coffee is the new tea. Fifteen is the new fourteen I say.

Behind me, the muscle worshippers giggle and take their tall lattes to a table in the corner.

There, they discuss Angel's various physical attributes. They gaze. They sigh.

Where's Tiny I ask. Little Italy's eyes roll up. Singapore, she says. The rest of the world called, she says. He answered, she says. She gives Angel a fast look. He's got the brawn…let's see if he's got the brains, she says. As I turn, pick out a new spot and give my first Americano of the new year a test run, see if it's as good as I remember it from last year.

I see Little Italy look up to the box on the wall. By the time I sit down, the box has number 160 up and running.

The curtains open. It's Casablanca and Rick's Café is full to bursting. Dooley Wilson is at the piano. Conversations take a break. Some memories don't fade. Dooley sings As Time Goes By.

Angel looks at the muscle worshippers. First new fans of the year. First New Year in a new city. He smiles. They sigh. Play it again Sam. You don't have to be at home to feel at home.

Be cool…

Damaged Goods has a secret admirer

Good morning Wednesday. If only every New Year could be a new beginning. A fresh start. A change for the better. An opportunity to wipe the slate clean and start from scratch. A chance to dig a hole somewhere nice and remote and fill it with all the crap that life has thrown at us over the previous year.

Instead, for some of us, it's a day for being reminded that life doesn't come with a manufacturer's guarantee of satisfaction or your money back. What you see is what you get. What doesn't kill you only makes you stronger. Not happier.

Damaged Goods is in the coffee shop. She stands behind me as I queue for my Americano. Emanating vibes that speak of a broken life. Covering up bruises that scream of broken bones. Broken heart. Broken soul. Cracked all the way through and held together with spit and willpower.

And yet…and yet…she wears her name with pride. Two words. Her two words. Damaged Goods. On an oversized button badge pinned over her heart. Red letters on a black background. A heads up for all interested parties. I come with pain and baggage. Approach at your own risk. All except for one.

Little Italy liked her the first moment she saw her. She liked the way she didn't feel sorry for herself or apologise for the wall she put up. Double thickness, double height.

But most of all, she liked her badge of courage. Damaged Goods is a stone cold survivor with a warm liquid centre. Buried deep. And she has an admirer who watches her from a distance. The Fan knows nothing about her but wants to know everything. From the taste of her lips first thing in the morning…to the look in her eyes last thing at night. From the words in her heart…to the pain on her face. From the dreams she used to have…to the nightmares she carries with her. Everything.

If only he had the courage to walk up to her and say hello. Introduce himself. Tell her his name.

Smash down her wall. Give them both a chance. But not yet. Too soon. Too soon. Until then he'll watch as her 'if onlys' fade away and his 'what ifs' mount up.

From behind the bar, Little Italy sees it all. She looks at the box on the wall and the box knows the score. Time for a little 31.

The curtains open. The stage is set. Time for a little James Taylor. It's Mud Slide Slim…and You've Got A Friend.

Damaged Goods looks up. Feels a pair of interested eyes on her. Can't figure out who the Hell they belong to. Doesn't matter. Sometimes the best friends you can have are the ones you haven't met yet.

Be cool…

The Counting Girl is free

Good morning Tuesday. One…two…three…four…locks are on her bedroom door. Five…six…seven…eight…out the window, through the gate.

The Counting Girl is in the coffee shop this morning. They don't know she's gone. They don't know she's free. They don't know she's up, dressed, off down the road, on the tram, and ready for caffeine. Not just any old caffeine. Little Italy's caffeine. Latte with an extra shot. An extra boost. An extra touch of something special only Little Italy knows the recipe for.

I see her walk through the door. Count the tables. Count the chairs. Count the tiles on the floor. Count the people at the bar waiting for their morning liquid peace of mind. Eyes flickering. Fingers a blur. Numbers alive and kicking.

Big Red smiles that special smile of hers. The one reserved for folk who look at the world sideways. The one that says welcome in big capital letters.

The Counting Girl takes a deep breath, her 28th since she walked in, and places her special order. The one that does the trick. Little Italy turns away and makes a few gestures over a large white mug. That's the something special. That's the bit of magic.

Coffee goes in. Mug fills up. The Counting Girl reaches into a leather coat pocket, pulls out some silver, counts it out and hands it over. Her eyes are flickering less. Her fingers are slowing down. She sees a spot in the corner. A little chunk of darkness with a free table. Deep breath. Fifteen steps. Slow sit down.

Then the mist comes. The one that slowly creeps in and covers the numbers. Obscuring them. Hiding them. She takes a sip of her special Latte. The mist gets thicker. Her heartbeat slows. Her breathing too. She looks around. The coffee shop is half full. Maybe three quarters. Hard to tell. Hard to count. Hard to care as the warm liquid takes effect.

Now she sees them for who they are.

Watches the faces. Sees the smiles. The door opens. Running Man comes to the door at a trot. Feet don't fail me now. He's fit. He's fast. He's full of vim and vigour. I'm late…I'm late…for a very important date.

But once over the threshold he slams on the brakes. Looks around and steps down the gears. Changes into Walking Man and puts time on the back burner. Strolls up to the bar and says morning. Morning says Little Italy. The usual? Walking Man smiles. Yeah, he says. Pour it nice and slow. Give it time to settle. You know the routine.

Little Italy nods. She invented the routine. She nods at Big Red and throws a glance at the box on the wall. The box puts the wheels in motion and from deep inside, number 138 eases up to the surface and slides into place.

The curtains open. The Eagles are on stage. Take It Easy. It's time to kick back. Relax. Chill out. The Counting Girl smiles deep inside.

Five…four…three…two…one…silence.

Be cool…

Little Italy has an on-going affair

Good morning Friday. Good morning dampness and chills. Grey skies and empty trees. Warm overcoats and extra tissues. Uninvited gusts of wind batter violently against the coffee shop door.

But here inside the coffee shop, we're safe and sound. Hatches battened and drawbridge up until refugees from the great outdoors arrive and remind us how uncomfortable nature can sometimes be.

But at least nature doesn't lie. Doesn't deceive. Doesn't backbite or falsify, cheat or misinform. It is what it is. It might not be what you want, but at least it's damned honest. Doesn't pull any punches. Tells it like it is.

That's probably why Little Italy has an ongoing affair with nature, whatever the weather. It's true to itself, she says. Just like coffee. What you see is what you get. That's what's so tricky about love, she says. Sometimes you never know what you're going to get.

Sometimes you just have to stick your head out the door and see which way the wind's blowing. Sometimes it just brushes against your check.

Other times it blows you right off your feet. Sometimes the clouds block out the warmth. Other times the sun blasts its way through and God help anything that stands in its way.

Little Italy also has an ongoing affair with love. Anything she can do to give it a shove in the right direction she does with both hands and occasionally a well-aimed pointed toecap. Anything she can say that can make folk feel a little better towards each other she does with a well-placed word, smile or nod of the head.

Like with the pair standing in front of her at the bar. Wrapped up in layers of colourful clothing and hanging on to each other as if their lives depended on it. As if by losing physical contact they'll lose emotional closeness. Little Italy smiles. Get a room, she says. The Colourful Lovers smile. She nudges him. He orders two chocolate raspberry cappuccinos with skimmed milk.

Big Red standing nearby says wow, nobody ever ordered that before. This is a first. There's a first time for everything says Little Italy. Birth, death, love, even chocolate raspberry cappuccinos. You go sit down and I'll bring them over, she says. He hands over the silver and The Colourful Lovers walk hand in hand to a nearby slice of privacy.

Little Italy delivers the goods in heavy white cups and as she turns and walks away, she looks up at the box on the wall. The box has always had an ongoing affair with a special kind of sound. Special kind of music. The kind that brings folk together, not tears them apart. The kind that calls for a soft piano counting keys in a dark, smoky room.

As The Colourful Lovers take their first sips, number 151 slips gently onto the turntable.

The curtains open. The turntable starts to spin. Needle lowers. Nina Simone sits at the piano. Adjusts the microphone. Fingers on keys. Keys count down. Enjoyment goes up. My Babe Just Cares for Me.

The Colourful Lovers have eyes for nobody else. What they see is what they get. And what they feel is what they want.

Be cool…

The bipolar quick-change artist

Good morning Tuesday. For some folk this could be the best day of their lives. The kind of day they can't imagine getting any better. The kind that makes them feel loud and proud and glad to be alive.

For other folk, this might be the kind of day that needs to be binned. Burned. Sacked. Crossed out. Rubbed out and seriously cancelled. The kind of day when they just need to turn on the tap and flush all that pain down the drain. Switch off the cell and tell the world to shove it sideways where the sun doesn't shine. The kind of day when they would give anything to move straight through from twenty four to forty eight without looking back, stopping or passing GO.

But they don't. Instead, they kick all that shit into touch, hold on tight and push the Hell on through. Not because they want to. Not because they have to. But because today, they're too damned pissed off. Yesterday they were in Happyville. Today they're in the toilet. Today, they're standing in front of a river a mile deep, with a bridge a foot wide…and a whole stack of comfort and joy staring at them from the other side.

So they suck it up and shove their emotional baggage in a plastic bag. And they bring it to the only place, and the only person, who gives enough of a shit to put on a welcome smile and leave them alone in a warm corner with the best goddam drink on the planet.

It's bitter cold outside the coffee shop. And inside, standing in front of Little Italy, is The Up and Down Man. Bipolar quick-change artist. Twenty five going on forty. Black cap…black jacket…black jeans…black boots…black outside and inside. Standing behind him is his polar opposite. Little old me. Full of the joys of spring. Hollywood smile. Real pain in the arse.

The Up and Down Man doesn't need to speak. Little Italy knows the drill. One cup. Large. Americano double strength.

He pays his dues and she nods to a vacant spot in a faraway corner. Secret escape. Perfect.

He moves away. I shuffle up and decide on a change of heart. Change of liquid. Change of mood. You decide, I say to Little Italy. Surprise me, I say.

I thought you changed already, she said. I'm a changeable guy, what can I say, I say. She raises one eyebrow. Left. Smiles crookedly and says you go sit down then. I'll bring it to you. What's the damage, I say. Too painful to even contemplate, a voice behind me says.

I turn and see The Girl in the Red Beret. Only this time it's not red. It's green. I nod my approval. New Year…new beret, I say. Old beret…new man, she says. This is Joe, she says. Joe is standing beside her. He has ear buds in. She pulls them out. Two words, she says. Which coffee, she says. He looks confused. Get me the same as you, he says, and puts his ear buds back in.

I walk away and find my usual parking space. Two minutes later Little Italy brings me something hot, dark and spicy. I ask what she calls it. She says it doesn't have a name yet, but it feels like a Magdalena. I think you'll both get on fine, she says…and winks.

As she turns away, she looks The Girl In The Green Beret, then at the box on the wall. Gives it the nod. The box puts in a recall for number 6. It's a popular choice so pretty soon it slides up from the top of the stack and slips onto the turntable.

The curtains open. A spotlight rests on Miss Dusty Springfield. Peroxide blonde. Bouffant hairstyle. Blue-eyed soul icon. You Don't Have To Say You Love Me, she sings.

Sometimes if you can't be with the one you love, love the one you're with. The Girl In The Green Beret knows this to be true.

Be cool…

The Hi-Fi Blonde adjusts her headset

Good morning Monday. It's early and the night hasn't completely shrugged off its overcoat. The morning light is struggling to make itself known and the coffee shop is full of vacant spaces. Waiting to come alive.

Invitations have gone out. Chairs are preparing themselves. Tables have that air of anticipation. The door swings back and forth…back and forth. As one by one…two by two…the caffeinerati arrive. The Latte lovers. The Espresso experts. The Cappuccino cravers.

There's a little jazz in the background. A little Dizzy. Welcoming them in. Palmslaps from the box on the wall. A mental high five here…fistbump there. A transformation takes place. From the drabness and frowns of the outside to the colours and smiles of the inside.

The sheeesh of the coffee machines blends with the hum of the aircon. Expectation on faces. Those who are about to enjoy salute you. A treat for the senses awaits.

Like a maestro, Little Italy stands behind the bar conducting the movement of liquid music. From machine to cup to steady hands and grateful lips. Big Red, her second in command, works the stainless steel machine like an orchestral instrument. Hands and fingers a blur. Dancing to the rhythm of the finest damned drink on the face of God's green earth.

Out on the floor, Angel flexes his muscles and gives the vacant tables an extra wipe. In the queue The Hi-fi Blonde adjusts her headset, calms her hammering heart and wishes for five minutes with Angel somewhere dark and private. A soundproof room where nobody can hear her scream would be nice. Angel is oblivious. Under the control of Little Italy, his bulging arms say look, but don't touch.

The Hi-fi Blonde orders up a large Americano, slides over the silver and slows her breathing as she walk to the table nearest Angel.

189

She's not backwards at being forward this girl. She knows what she likes and likes what she sees. But Angel passes her by. Eyes averted. Muscles twitching. He has his orders. So The Hi-Fi Blonde takes off her headset, breathes in deep, and lets her Americano have a taste of her ruby red lips.

From behind the bar, Little Italy nods at The Angel and throws him the ghost of a smile. That's it, big boy, keep your personality in your pants and your mind on the job, she thinks. Her eyes drift up to the box on the wall. It sits there waiting, knowing what's coming next.

A wink from the boss. A soft instruction. And from somewhere deep inside the box, a track gets the message. Number 142 slips its housing and moves on up to the surface.

The curtains open and The Beatles are standing there. Mop top geniuses. This isn't hello, how are you. This is Hello Goodbye.

Angel turns as he leaves and winks at The Hi-Fi Blonde. Maybe tomorrow. Maybe next week. Maybe never.

Be cool…

The Boy With The Mythical Arms

Good morning Wednesday. Some days life really isn't worth the paper it's not written on. Other days there's a hefty touch of magic in the air. An odour of joy. The whiff of a smile, carried on the backs of molecules.

A feel of the big man upstairs, giving us his A game. An air of the unexpected, blown in from the outside and infecting anyone inside with a frown on their face.

Here, in the coffee shop, you can see it in the eyes. Hear it in the voices. Feel it bouncing off the tables and chairs. Nipping in and out of the nooks and crannies. It's infectious. Contagious. Breathe in and you'll catch it. A light touch and you'll fall under its spell.

Little Italy has a dreamcatcher tattoo that acts like a feelgood barometer. She mentioned it when I told her about mine. Where is it, she asked. Over my heart, I said. Mine too, she said. It's the only place to have it, she said.

The memory fades into the background and I idly touch the space where my heart lives. Just for a second. Through jacket. Through shirt. Through t-shirt. Through ink. Through skin.

The door opens. The Girl with the Butterfly Tattoo walks in arm in arm with an old squeeze. The Boy With The Mythical Arms. Donkey jacket off. Sleeves rolled up. Ink up to his elbows. Red Chinese dragon on the left. Green Chinese Dragon on the right. Twisting and turning. Dangerous protectors of their human host. Beware all who come within biting distance. Except for The Girl with the Butterfly Tattoo. She's got a free backstage pass. She's got access all areas. She's got the thumbs up.

Recognition in Little Italy's eyes. Hello stranger, she says. Haven't seen you in here for a while, she says. He's been travelling the world, says The Girl with the Butterfly Tattoo.

He's just got back, she says.

That calls for a celebration, says Little Italy. How about a nice triple espresso times two.

191

The Boy With The Mythical Arms nods and smiles. Sounds like a plan, he says. The Dragons give the espressos the once over and nod their approval.

As the pair leave for a quiet corner, Little Italy looks at the box on the wall and nods. Just once. The box nods back and number 32 glides up from the depths and onto the turntable.

The curtains part. A light shines on Van the Man. Have I Told You Lately, he sings. And everyone knows the answer.

Sorry Rod. No contest. Can't hold a candle to Mr. Morrison. Nothing personal. It either touches the ears...or it touches the heart.

Be cool...

Let it snow, let it snow, let it snow

Good morning Thursday. White night has given way to Grey day. Freezing all the way Day. Not Picture Box Day where mathematically perfect flakes float down from the sky. Not the remains of Nights in White Satin Day.

This is All Hail Supercooled Crystals Day. Where pissed off angels throw miniature pellets of rock hard precipitation at you from a safe distance. Just for fun. Just for sport. Just for the Hell of it. Accompanied by uproarious laughter heard only by ears turned on and tuned in to the right frequency. Radio Ga Ga. Ninety one FM. Friggin' Mary!

This is Run for Cover Day. Duck into Doorways Day. Coming at you sideways courtesy of a wind on steroids Day.

I can see it from my perch inside the coffee shop. Looking out the window. Watching the hard, white bullets cut down the outsiders like nature's good little machine gun. And right in the middle of it all…right in the eye of the massacre…is The Man in Black. Untouched. Unbloodied. Unbowed. No hurry. No scurry. The hail avoids him like the plague.

He's a no-go area with leather on his back. Leather on his head. Leather on his feet. Denim on his legs. And a rosary under his shirt.

Softly…slowly…he walks to the coffee shop door, opens it, and walks in from the dark to the light. In where Little Italy…and Big Red…and Angel wait. Eyes turned. Smiles switched on and dialled up. Angel flexes his muscles and grabs a white mug. Big Red fires up the coffee machine. Triple espresso. Strong, long and black as Hell. Welcome as Heaven.

Little Italy stands at the end of the line. Where everything starts and everything finishes. The Man in Black tips the brim of his gambler's hat. Silver buckles for a band. A small thank you. A big deal.

He smiles and takes his espresso over to a table by the window. A table that nobody else sits at. He moves the reserved sign to one side, puts the chunky white cup dead centre of the table, sits down and closes his eyes. Sixty seconds exactly. No need to count. Time waits for no man…but it waits for him. He's perfectly synchronised. Life moves at his pace. Little Italy takes a deep breath. Same time, same length as The Man in Black. Just here…just now…all is right with the world for a while.

Outside, the hailstones soften into snowflakes as big as pillowcases. Little Italy looks at the box on the wall and from somewhere inside number 76 slides up and settles on the turntable.

The curtains open and Mister Dean Martin stands at a bar, drink in hand, flames blazing in an open fire. Everyone's warm as toast. Let It Snow!

Nobody croons like Dino. Except maybe Bing.

Be cool…

The Girl With The Elvis Hairstyle

Good morning Friday. Aaaah….the hum of the stainless steel machine in the coffee shop. The feel of cool Latin American rhythms pouring out from the box on the wall. All I need is a fat Cuban cigar, a red guitar, three chords and the truth.

But today I'm unplugged. Unwrapped. Unseen. Today the coat is off and the mojo is on. I am a leaf on the wind. A fly on the wall. I am the Scribbler Continuous. Imperfectly formed but perfectly positioned to watch the streams of the Caffeinerati. Queueing up to receive their liquid communion.

The colourful and the drab. The powerful and the weak. The ones who have nowhere else to go and the other ones who have everywhere else to go. They all come to receive peace, or approval, or silence, or pure joy, from the lady in black called Little Italy.

At the bar, The Girl With The Elvis Hairstyle is wearing an Eskimo jacket…fake fur, pretend Polar…and looking longingly at the pastry selection. She loves them…she loves them not…she loves them…she loves them not.

Today her desire outweighs her diet. Her friend, Japan, scolds her lack of willpower but I can see in her eyes that she longs for a bite. Just a nibble. Just a morsel. They order their Skinny Lattes and scurry into a corner. Elvis with her mouth full, Japan with her stomach empty.

Their place at the bar is taken by Headset Boy with hair the colour of night and wild as a storm at sea. He stands perfectly still hiding the torment in his heart. It wants to rage. It wants to fight. It wants to scream to the heavens. But the headset clamped tight over his ears keeps his emotions in check. White noise goes in the ears. It keeps him calm. Tones him steady. Dials down the volume before it threatens to breach the barrier and break down the dam.

Little Italy's face shows the ghost of concern. She blinks and raises an eyebrow. She knows the score. Knows the signs. She speaks.

Headset Boy doesn't hear. He pulls off his cans. Ears naked, head tilted, he listens. Sorry, he says. I said are you okay, says Little Italy. It's the first human voice Headset Boy has heard since he left behind the impression on a dark pillow. He tries a smile. Doesn't come off. Yeah…fine, he says. Lying through his teeth.

Want the usual, asks Little Italy. He nods. She remembers all her regulars. Remembers their poison. Remembers their preferences. Up comes a pot of green tea. White crockery. Black tray.

Headset Boy climbs up to the balcony to breathe in the green fumes, feel the liquid warm his senses, and think for the hundredth time today about The Girl Who Walked Away.

Little Italy watches his feet on the stairs then turns to the box on the wall. Nods. The box always has something to contribute to the conversation. Number 131 is already on the turntable.

The curtains open. The Everly Brothers are on stage. Don and Phil. Masters of close, unforgettable harmonies. Don't walk away. Turn around. Walk Right Back.

Headset Boy takes a sip of green tea. Sometimes the only thing worse than falling in love is falling out of it.

Be cool…

Happiness is a large Americano

Good morning Monday. As I ride the train into the city centre, a fat ribbon of light blue interrupts the dark horizon. Another night in black satin. Bullied away by the coming dawn.

Ten minutes later I'm walking under naked trees where the only shelter from the icy breath of a February wind is the bland concrete wall behind a half empty coffee shop. Not my coffee shop. Not her coffee shop. Nothing to see here. Move on.

Mine is a hundred yards into the future. Round the corner. First star to the right and straight on past morning. The lights are on. The welcome mat is out. Happiness is a large Americano with steam rising off the surface and a million thoughts and schemes, hopes and dreams, rising up from that dark liquid.

Happiness is a silent nod from Little Italy and an unspoken promise to leave the cares of the world at the door. I hear them knocking…but they can't come in. Not today. Not here. Not ever.

The mere act of taking off a jacket and sitting down is tantamount to a declaration of peace. Lay down your rifles, boys. Hang up your damned gunbelts. The only ammunition here is dark and roasted.

The door opens and The Backpack Pair walk in. Look around. Smile. Pull back the hoods. Take deep breaths. Take a break. He in blue. She in green. Take your time guys. Rest and be thankful.

Little Italy nods to Big Red who steps up to the plate. You two look like you could use a little somethin' somethin', she says. A little comfort and joy, she says. The Backpack Pair smile in unison. Speak in unison. Yeah, they say. Look at each other. Look at Big Red. Double espressos, they say. Big Red nods. Takes their silver. You go sit down, she says. Take the weight of the world off your shoulders, she says. I'll bring your drinks over.

The door opens and a cool draft announces the entrance of The Lonely Man. I've seen him before. Sitting by the window. Looking out on the world. Emptiness written all over his face. Always the same two words repeated over and over. Goodbye…goodbye. A lifetime of regret.

He looks at Little Italy. She smiles. Hello, she says. One word. Changes nothing. Changes everything. It takes a crushing weight to push down a heart. And a single gesture to lift it up.

Little Italy glances at the box on the wall. A small movement. Almost unseen. But the box sees it and acts accordingly. From deep inside Number 60 rises up to the turntable.

The curtain opens and The Beatles are on stage. The Fab Four and a host of fab friends are dressed up in costume…and Sgt. Pepper's Lonely Hearts Club Band begins to play.

The Lonely Man goes back in time. Some things you don't want to remember. Some things you don't want to forget.

Be cool…

The Girl with Express Thumbs

Good morning Monday. I like to welcome in the day slowly. I'm the tortoise, not the hare. The very thought of hitting the ground running as the sun comes up gives me the heebie jeebies.

I like to go somewhere full of conversation or silence. Somewhere with people who know the value of walking in and chilling out. Somewhere with emotional as well as physical space.

Somewhere like here. In the far corner of the coffee shop. Watching all the comings and goings. The too'ings and fro'ings. Where the blushing innocent rub shoulders with the deliciously guilty. Where colourful characters sit side by side with soulful individuals. And where two people can exist across the table from each other and the only sound you'll hear is the clicking of tiny keys as they talk to the world without moving their lips.

The Texterati are bright young things with a future full of speechlessness and repetitive strain injury. They exist in a bubble of typed conversation and obliviousness to the world around them. The distance between them and the folk they're texting to is getting shorter...and shorter. Pretty soon they'll sit across the table and text each other because they've forgotten the art of speech.

One of them is sitting next to me. The Girl with Express Thumbs. Large latte in front of her. Forgotten. Growing colder by the minute. A face full of concentration. Tongue darting in and out between pursed lips. Digits moving at the speed of light. Then pausing for an answer before another stream of consciousness hits the small screen.

I remember when a phone was just a phone. Now it can control your home lighting and heating. Now it can build relationships...or end them. Now it can network with a thousand 'friends' while looking for the nearest pizza joint.

The door opens and The Luddite strolls in and stands in front of Little Italy.

He's young, he's handsome (in a rugged kind of way) and he's completely devoid of anything mobile. Anything electrical. Anything technical. Anything that connects him with the outside world. All he's interested in is the inside world. The one that doesn't rely on batteries or chargers. Smart phones or ringtones.

Little Italy smiles. Usual? Yep, he says and looks around. He spots The Girl with Express Thumbs in a soft armchair against the far wall. He feels a little spark of natural electricity travel down his spine…hears the sound of a white, chunky cup containing a hot double espresso gently landing on the counter…digs out some silver from a trouser pocket.

He takes the cup and strolls over to the table next door to hers and sits down, making as much noise as he possibly can. Textus Interruptus time. The Girl with Express Thumbs looks up. Her digits slow down. Her mouth opens slightly. He smiles. She blushes. Over behind the counter Little Italy takes in a deep breath and nods at the box on the wall. Somewhere deep inside the box number 15 comes to life and slides onto the waiting deck.

Curtains open. Spotlight hits the stage. Diana, Mary and Flo hit the notes. They're not just wonderful. They're Supreme, and they only have one command. Stop! In the Name of Love.

The Luddite winks. She gulps. Thumbs come to a full stop. He says hello. She says hello. Another Texterati bites the dust. For now.

Be cool…

The Girl with Beautiful Blue Eyes

Good morning Tuesday. For some, today is the day of the hidden. The unseen. Secrets hidden away from the world. Words unsaid, trapped between tightly shut lips. For others, today is the day of revealing. Taking a chance. Throwing open doors. Pulling back curtains. Chasing away the darkness. Letting the bright light of day flood in.

The Girl with the Beautiful Blue Eyes is in the coffee shop this morning. The kind of eyes that can make a person stop whatever they're doing. Whoever they're doing it with. And lose themselves in all that blue. The kind of eyes that can throw back all their covers. Knock down all their walls. Breach all their defences. And see the truth inside. No matter how deep it's buried. No matter how much they try to hide it. The Girl with the Beautiful Blue Eyes sees. She sits alone on the balcony, overlooking the throng. Watching. And waiting.

Little Italy sees her search every face. Spread her net wide. Looking for the one with the barricaded heart. The shuttered emotions. The shattered dreams.

Below, out of view, in a faraway corner, with a faraway look, sits The Boy Who Let It Slip Away. If only he'd said something. If only he'd taken a chance. If only he'd opened up. If only he'd been brave. Instead of being terrified. If only he'd smiled. Instead of turning away before the look on his face brought his feelings to the surface. Held them up for ridicule. Up for rejection.

Above him, The Girl with the Beautiful Blue Eyes feels a tingle. Small at first. Faint. Like an echo blown in on the breeze through an open door. Then growing stronger. Louder. Deafening. She feels like covering her ears. But she doesn't. She knows that he's here. Somewhere down below. She stretches her net wider.

Little Italy catches her attention. From behind the bar she nods in the direction of the space hidden beneath the balcony. Out of sight.

But not out of mind.

The Girl with the Beautiful Blue Eyes gets up from her seat, walks down the stairs and turns to face The Boy Who Let It Slip Away. Her eyes meet his and even from where she is, she hears an audible intake of breath, as her gaze penetrates his defences. Shatters his carefully built-up excuses. Plunges deep inside and grabs his outstretched hand, pulling him out of the water. Out of the murky depths. She smiles. His heart gasps. His face blushes.

From behind her, Little Italy brings two dark espressos and gently puts them on the table. As she turns and walks away, she looks up at the box on the wall. From deep inside the box number 80 rises to the surface.

The curtains open. The stage is set. The spotlight comes to life and little Etta James, with a voice so big it breaks the heart and mends the soul, begins to sing. At last.

Little Italy looks at a small photo on a shelf behind the bar. The photo is old. Faded. It is of a man. Smiling. Beneath it is a slip of paper and on the paper is a sentence in blue ink.

The sentence reads: "Just because you can't see something, doesn't mean it's not there."

Be cool…

Romeo gets down on one knee

Good morning Saturday. Not just any old Saturday. This is Valentine's SaturDay. A day when passion bubbles to the surface and overflows in a billion words of love.

A day when a single red rose carries more weight than any damned bouquet. A day when secret admirers can throw off the shackles of hidden affection. Put their hearts before their heads. Throw caution to the wind. And go for it. Go for it and bugger the consequences. Go for it and say it's now or never. Come hold me tight. Kiss me my darling. Be mine tonight.

A day when words that haven't been used often enough can now be used to rekindle an old fire. Or fan the flames of a new one.

Here, in the coffee shop, there's a buzz of romance about the place. There's a touch of magic in the air. You can feel it the moment you walk in the door.

You can see it in the faces of the couples sat side by side, instead of opposite each other. You can smell the odour of emotion flitting from table to table.

You can practically taste it. It's heart thumping and blood pumping.

Today is the day when everyone gets a blank Valentine's SaturDay card with every coffee. Handed out in person by Little Italy…Big Red…and Angel. To take to their tables and write the words they can't say but can put down in ink. Words of hope…or reaffirmation…or just plain damned let's get it on passion.

Some come in pairs.

Like Romeo and Juliet. He in faded jeans and long leather coat. Black, of course. Biker boots and Rolling Stones tongue & lips tee. She in tigerskin tights, six-inch orange spikes, biker jacket with zips and buckles, belts and scuffs. Worn out. Worn in and pre-loved. They take their lattes and their cards and make for a spot against the far wall. Somewhere in the do not disturb zone.

Some come in singles.

Like The Girl With The Butterfly Tattoo. Sending out Valentine wishes through the post or through the ether. A Yin lover waiting or looking for her Yang. Flip sides of the same coin.

She looks over at me and smiles. Points to her left thigh. High up. Taps it twice. Then gives me the thumbs up. I twig. She's had her new ink done. The new butterfly, I ask. I mouth the words silently. She shakes her head and mouths an answer. No…a dragon. We share a secret smile.

Little Italy hands her a double espresso along with a Valentine's SaturDay card and she walks past me to a seat near the window. Just public enough. Just private enough.

She texts her latest Valentine with loving thumbs. I look around and see pens out. Scribbling words of liquid love on white card.

There's a space at the end of the bar with a bowl of Valentine candies. Next to it is an envelope, unopened. Little Italy notices it and raises an eyebrow. She opens it and takes out a card. Reads it. She looks at me. I shrug. Don't ask me I mouth. Looks like you got another admirer.

She looks around, her eyes resting on a table by the window. She smiles and looks at the box on the wall. The box doesn't have to think twice. Number 79 glides softly to the surface.

The curtains open. Sorry Art. You're good…but this is The Flamingos. This is classic doo-wop time. This is I Only Have Eyes for You.

Romeo gets up from his seat. Kneels down in front of Juliet. Opens a small padded box and holds it up to her. And the rest, as they say, is history. Or at least it will be, one day.

Be cool…

The Hawaiian jumping flea

Good morning Wednesday. Today feels like a stand-up-and-be-counted kinda day. The kinda day when anyone who tells you romance is dead and buried should be punched right in the kisser. The kinda day when doing something as off-the-wall as serenading the one you love in public, just for the sheer Hell of it, is not only good for the heart…it's great for the soul. And sometimes…it's great for business, too.

The Ukulele Boy is in the coffee shop this morning with his Hawaiian 'jumping flea'. Four strings and a hundred love song repertoire. He's no George Formby, but that could be seen as a big plus.

Twenty five going on forty, he's a music man with magic fingers. They move at he speed of sound. Up and down the fret. The boy is a wizard with a plectrum. Little Italy knows this to be true. She knows what sits inside the battered case sitting at his feet. She knows its power. Small in size but a giant in stature.

She knows the effect it has on a certain dancer by the name of Ruby Diamond. Sitting this morning at the side of The Ukulele Boy, sipping a double espresso, not fifteen feet away from yours truly.

Behind the bar, Little Italy works the controls of the stainless steel machine like only she knows how. Both hands moving in harmony. Poetry in motion. Some machines have mechanical hearts. This one has soul.

Beside her, looking on and taking everything in, is The Hairless Barista. Nineteen years young and an hour into day-one on the job. Whether he reaches day two is up to Little Italy. But she has faith in him. You can do it, she says. You got the touch, she says. You make a mean espresso, she says.

The Hairless Barista smiles nervously and strokes his gleaming head. A small bead of perspiration makes its way down the left side of his face.

Little Italy reaches out and wipes it away. Her hand brushes his cheek. He blushes and a thank you lodges in his throat. Now, go wipe the tables, she says. But only the empty ones, she says.

She looks up to the box on the wall and slowly shakes her head from side to side. Puts a finger to her ruby reds. The box zips the lip. The Hairless Barista takes a deep breath, grabs a damp cloth, and makes for the vacants.

Twenty feet away, The Ukulele Boy bends down to the case by his feet and unlocks two worn clasps. He takes out the dark wood instrument, sits it high on his chest and strums a sweet rhythm. Ruby Diamond looks on with love in her heart.

She begins to smile. He begins to sing. Heads begin to turn. Hearts begin to melt. Infection spreads. The song is Stand By Me.

He doesn't get to sing the next few lines on his own. One by one, everyone in the coffee shop joins in. And when they finish, the applause can be heard all the way across the square outside.

Ben E. King he isn't. But we don't give a damn. And, more importantly, neither does Ruby Diamond.

Be cool…

Louie The Pug and his human companion

Good morning Monday. Today is a day when wants and needs are as different as chalk and cheese. As far apart as Venus and Mars. One follows the beat of the heart. The other follows the beat of a different kind of drum.

As I walk across the city centre square to the coffee shop, the sun chases away mean clouds and mister blue skies puts in appearance. It's a welcome sight. A hopeful sight. A sight that puts a spring in the step and a smile on the face. A person couldn't want for better weather so early on in the morning. So early on in the year. Wants and needs. Wants and needs.

I cross the road, careful not to step on the tramlines and reach the pavement, careful not to step on the cracks. Turn the corner. Walk a hundred yards. Turn sharp left. And enter the house of the rising sun. Only this one isn't the ruin of many a poor boy, or girl. This one is the making of us all.

I can smell the aroma from a block away. Wafting out the door towards me. Welcome back, it says. Come in and put your feet up, it says. Just what I want. I walk in and step up to the counter. Get the nod and a ghost of a smile from Little Italy.

It's Monday, she says. It must be a double espresso, she says. I don't mind if somebody does all the talking as long as they use all the right words. In all the right order. I stay shtum and pass over the silver. Put the change in the tips jar. Take my dark brown nectar and mosey on over to a spot in the corner. Sit down, chill out, and survey the scenery. Some folk would say the shop is half empty. I say it's half full. Like the glass.

Two tables to my left sits Louie The Pug and his human companion. The Man With The Black French Beret. Silver hair poking from under the rim. Silver moustache poking from under the nose. Black jumper, black jacket, black jeans…white sneakers.

Looking for someone to cheer up. Looking for someone to reach out and touch.

He looks at Little Italy. She cocks her head and nods to a small crumpled shape sitting by the window. The Mouse sits apart from the rest of the world. Crumpled outside. Crumpled inside. Feelings squashed up like a ball of paper looking for a vacant trashcan.

Louie The Pug looks up at The Man With The Black French Beret, who gives him the nod. Louie slips his lead and surreptitiously makes his way to The Mouse. Sits at her feet. Nudges her leg with a paw. Looks up with his huge eyes. Does it again, and again, until The Mouse surfaces from wherever she was.

Louie The Pug rolls over on his back and invites a belly rub. The Mouse stretches down a hand and rubs. A smile invades her face. And the dark thoughts that crumpled her insides unfold slowly and straighten out. And just for a while, the pain of unrequited love slips into the background.

At the bar, Little Italy looks at the box on the wall and nods. Just once. From somewhere deep inside, number 59 rises once more with the truth.

The curtains open. The Stones are on stage. Happiness, albeit temporary, comes courtesy of Mick and the boys. His voice tells the truth. You Can't Always Get What You Want.

Wants and needs. Wants and needs. The Man With The Black French Beret sips his Americano and smiles inside.

Be cool…

The Nervous Man takes a deep breath

Good afternoon Wednesday. There are a million ways to say goodbye for the last time. A million ways to say so long and thanks for all the fish. A million ways to wave farewell, grab your coat, and head for the door before the screaming begins. Or the throwing. Or the tears. Or the celebrations.

But there's only one surefire way to say hello for the first time. Only one unmistakable, unambiguous, undeniable, way to take the first step from being a stranger to being someone more. Sometimes a whole lot more.

You have to step up to the plate. Exercise your vocal chords. And hope for the best. Five letters. One word. Same meaning the whole world over. Doesn't matter why you're saying it. Doesn't matter what language you use or who you're talking to. Doesn't matter where you are or what time it is. Hello doesn't give a tinker's damn. It only has one game in mind. Getting to know you. Getting to know all about you. Getting to like you. Getting to hope you like me.

It's a grey day outside the coffee shop. Inside, it's a different story. I'm sitting against the wall under the box on the wall, looking at a long line of caffeine junkies lined up at the counter. Waiting for their fix.

Head of the queue is The Strawberry Blonde. A tall willowy creature. Long hair. Long coat. Legs that go all the way up my imagination. Orders up a vanilla spice latte with a subtle hint of Indian cardamom and a whipped cream topping. Big Red does the honours while Little Italy prepares a soothing green tea infusion for the next one up.

Halfway along the line I can see The Nervous Man. The stutterer. Practicing his order over and over in his head. Shuffling closer to the point of order. No mistakes between his ears. He hears the words. Perfectly pronounced. Beautifully articulated. If only they sounded on the outside as they did on the inside.

Little Italy turns. Sees him. Smiles. The usual, she says. He nods. Grateful for her understanding. Her perfect timing. He slips her the silver as she hands him a hot double espresso. Today is the day. Today has to be the day, he thinks. Little Italy sees the look in his eyes. Life's too short, she says. Carpe Diem, she says.

The Nervous Man nods, takes a deep breath, and walks over to The Strawberry Blonde. Make it come out alright, he thinks. Please make it come out alright. She looks up. Curiosity in her eyes. He fights off the terror. Opens his mouth. Hello, he says. Hello, she says. And so it begins.

Behind the counter Little Italy nods to the box on the wall. Directly above my head. I can feel the box making a move, just like The Nervous Man. Number 141 is already on the turntable.

The curtains part. Lionel Richie is onstage under a spotlight. Mike in hand. Hello, he says. One word and the Strawberry Blonde smiles.

Sometimes it's not who you know, but who you want to know.

Be cool…

Love the one you're with

Good afternoon Friday. In a perfect world we'd all be with the ones we love. We wouldn't have to figure out who they are. Or where they are. Or how long the gig is going to last. Or whether it's ever going to bloody well take place at all. It would just happen. Like magic. Like it was predestined. Preordained. Prearranged.

Every Yin would spot their own personal Yang across a crowded dance floor and feel their heart do the two-step hairy mambo. Each zig would discover the only zag in all the world that could open the door to a lifelong attraction of opposites. And everyone would live happily ever after. In a perfect world.

Yeah…right.

Until then, we've got hello at one end. Goodbye at the other. And a whole mountain of glorious mixed-up shit in between that goes by the name of life. Here, this afternoon, in the coffee shop, life has an open invitation. An invitation to come in, sit down, partake of the finest goddam drink on the planet and benefit from open heart surgery of the emotional kind with. An invitation to feel the butterflies. Smell the roses. And be completely oblivious to the rest of the world. Courtesy of Little Italy, Big Red, and Angel.

It's mid afternoon and standing on one leg at the head of the queue is Walking Stick Man. Left leg on terra firma. Right leg six inches above the black and white tiled floor. Easing the ache of a twisted ankle. Concern shows large on Little Italy's face. What happened, she says. Life and a concrete step, he says. Smiles ruefully.

I'll bring your cappuccino over, you go sit down, she says. He smiles and hobbles to a table in the corner. Little Italy follows with the nectar. Two tables away iPad Girl is switched on and looking at an iPhoto of a teen with messy hair and a poor attempt at a hairy chin. But he has a nice smile. A warm smile. A smile that isn't in her life anymore. She sighs and switches her tablet to email mode. Reads a few from the inbox. Fires off a few to the outbox. Powers down, sips a skinny Latte and waits. And waits.

The door opens and The Boy With Streaks In His Hair strolls in and gives her the eye. She nods to the bar. Grab a coffee, she mouths. No sound. Just lip movement. He nods and obeys. Do as she asks, he thinks. Don't rock the boat, he thinks.

Little Italy looks at his chin. Take a hint, she says. Grow some fluff, she says. And maybe mess up your hair a bit, she says. The Boy Streaks In His Hair looks confused. Americano, he says. Never mind kid, says Big Red. You'll figure it out, she says.

He spills some silver on the counter, grabs his cup and makes for iPad Girl. They cheek kiss. He wishes it was more. She used to wish it was less.

Little Italy looks at the box on the wall and nods. The box duly obliges and number 106 is already onstage.

The curtains part and Crosby, Stills, Nash and Young are in full flow. Turn up the volume. Turn up the harmonies. Love The One You're With.

iPad Girl makes a decision and smiles. Screw it. Time to take a chance.

Be cool…

The Man In The Brown Derby Hat

Good morning Monday. The winter wind has a bit of a last gasp quality about it as I walk through the square to the coffee shop.

It's as if it knows that it's on the way out and Spring is on the starting blocks. Getting ready to flex its muscles. Getting ready to remember what it used to feel like to be young and alive and full of piss and vinegar. But not yet. Not before the wind and the rain and the snow have said their final hooray.

Before I even reach the door I can smell the odour of sanctity. The breath of the roasted coffee bean. Wafting through the air. I walk in and make for the counter. Only two in the queue. I pass a table, tucked away in the corner by the window. Fenced off. Reserved sign on. The only one in the place with a tablecloth. Pristine white. Almost glowing in the shade.

I reach the number one spot and Little Italy is waiting. The usual, she says. I nod. Comfort in predictability, I say. Don't be Mister Predictable for too long, she says. Ring the changes, she says. Zig instead of Zag, she says. Who's the lucky customer, I say, nodding towards the table in white. There's nobody waiting behind me, so she takes five and tells me the story.

That's reserved for The Man In The Brown Derby Hat, she says. This is his day. First Monday in March every year he comes in, orders two Americanos and sits down at that table, she says. What's the occasion, I say. He used to come in here with his wife, she says. That was their spot. She passed on five years ago today. He can't stop saying goodbye, she says. He's due in any minute.

I take my usual, pay the lady, and look for one of my regular spots. Halfway there I hear the door open. Gently. Like a sigh. I sit down and see Little Italy meet The Man In The Brown Derby Hat and show him to the table in white. She bends slightly and kisses his cheek. He looks embarrassed. Good to see you, she says. Two coffees coming up, she says. You sit down and I'll bring them over.

The Man In The Brown Derby Hat smiles, nods and sits down slowly. Eases the old bones. By the time Little Italy has slipped behind the bar, Big Red has already prepared the two Americanos. She hands them over and Little Italy takes them to the table in white. Hand delivered. No tray. No sugar. No need.

The Man In The Brown Derby Hat nods and removes his headgear. Places it on the table next to his cup. Looks at the other cup. The other chair. The other space. Picks up his cup, takes a sip…and the years fall away.

On her way back to the bar, Little Italy looks at the box on the wall. The box remembers The Lady in the Floral Dress. From deep inside number 24 glides softly to the surface and settles gently on the turntable.

The curtains open and there, under the spotlight, sitting on a barstool, mike in hand, is Francis Albert Sinatra.

Another day it might be Etta. Or Ella. But today, Come Rain or Come Shine, it's Old Blue Eyes. And it doesn't get any better than this.

Be cool…

Spanish Johnny's moustache

Good morning Wednesday. I spill out of the tram at the edge of the city centre square and shove my feet in gear for a fast walk through the rain to the coffee shop. Past the half-empty café with a drain-blocked ocean at the front door.

Past the sign that always says pastries baked fresh here every morning. Past an empty Ferris Wheel full of swaying carriages. Standing like a giant unicycle swaying in the wind. Past the shivering trees throwing drips at anyone in sight. Past bright green grass and brightly lit shops. Through the bully-boy wind, flapping skirts and trouser legs and turning umbrellas inside out. Round the corner and a fast entry through the doors into the best damned sanctuary in town.

Made it. Take a deep breath. Relax the shoulders. Eight steps to the end of the queue. Four people in front of me. Two minutes to wait. One cup full of hot, strong, dark peace of mind. Zero stress. Turn on. Tune in. Sit down. Drop out.

Little Italy sees me and smiles. Serves up a tall skinny latte to a tall skinny blonde and moves on to The Professor. Wild grey hair and staring eyes like Einstein on steroids. Finger in the power socket. Maybe a little early morning illicit substance. Wink wink. Nudge nudge. Say no more!

Big Red catches the next in line. The one in front of me. Hey amigo, she says. Que pasa? That's Spanish Johnny, whispers a soft female voice behind me. He's got the best moustache ever, she says. You wait and see, she says.

Spanish Johnny must have ears like a bat. He turns and looks at me. His moustache is like the eighth wonder of the world. It twirls and curls in all the right places. It's thick, bushy and the perfect catcher's mitt for a frothy cappuccino. He smiles, turns back to Little Italy, slips her some silver and disappears up the stairs to the balcony carrying a cup and a fistful of serviettes. For the mitt.

Before I can turn around to catch a glimpse of The Whisperer, Little Italy has a double espresso lined up in front of me.

I don't need to think. Don't need to ask. All I need to do is pay the piper and enjoy the tune. I do the necessary and make for my spot. I hear soft laughter behind me.

I hang my padded jacket over the back of the chair and sit down. Take a breath. Grab a sugar. And look for The Whisperer. No one in sight.

I look around and over by the corner, next to the window, I see The Girl In The Multicoloured Knitted Hat looking at me. Only for a second. Then she looks down at her cup. Her face carries the remains of a secret smile. She puts it in the bank for another day.

Behind the counter, Little Italy looks at the box on the wall. The box has a mind for something from The Boss. Something like number 94.

The curtains open. Springsteen lines up in front of the E Street Band. Brings the Incident On 57th Street to life with lyrics that are more than one step up from poetry.

Up in the balcony, Spanish Johnny smiles and wipes a line of froth from the end of his moustache. Closes his eyes. Thinks about a girl called Margarita.

Be cool…

The Girl With The Shaven Head sees the truth

Good morning Thursday. Sometimes the loneliest place to be is right in the middle of a crowd. Slap bang in the centre of a gaggle of folk. You look around. Hoping for a friendly face. Searching for another pair of eyes locked onto yours. All you can see is nobody with the slightest interest in you.

Some folk think that's heaven. Just peachy. Absolutely perfect. Their own kind of voluntary solitary confinement. Peace, quiet and bugger off world. For others, it's just another example of Hell on earth. A brick wall of disinterest. Might as well be a leper. Might as well be invisible. Might as well lose the ability to speak or make contact with another human being.

Except…except…for one of the few folk who understand. One of the few who give a damn. Little Italy. Standing behind the bar with the other baristas. Always knowing more than she lets on. Always giving out more than she takes in. Never giving up on anyone who walks through her door.

Like The Girl With The Shaven Head. Black lips. Spider's web earrings. Hairy jumper. Skintight black jeans. Zips everywhere. Black biker boots. Skinny Caramel Latte. Sitting alone in the middle of the room. Surrounded by life. Desperate to be touched by it.

Desperate to know that there's somebody, somewhere, who feels just like she does.

I asked Little Italy a while back for the story behind the story behind the story. Aaaaah…she doesn't know who she is, she said. She thinks she's a solo act, she said. One day she'll discover the truth, she said. That was then. This is now. This is today and she's still looking for a friendly face. A kindred spirit.

I pour myself a cup of steaming green tea. Take a sip. Feel the liquid slide easy down the throat. Hear the door open and look up. So does The Girl With The Shaven Head.

I can hear her gasp from three tables away. She sees a mirror image. Same shaven head. Same face. Same lips. Same outfit. Same facial expression. The Doppelganger walks in. Sees The Girl With The Shaven Head. Sees the outfit. Stops in her tracks. Eyes widen. Mouth opens. Heart skips a beat.

Little Italy walks from behind the bar. Touches The Doppelganger on the shoulder. Why don't you go sit down, she says. I'll bring your Skinny Caramel Latte over, she says.

The Doppelganger doesn't say a word. Doesn't make a sound. Just looks at The Girl With The Shaven Head and blinks slowly. Heart pounding in chest cavity. Blood rushing through veins.

She takes a step forward. Then another. Then another. Until she is standing in front of the table. Stretches out a hand. Hello, she says. My name is Eve, she says. I think you might be my twin sister, she says. The Girl With The Shaven Head takes a deep breath. Holds back a rush of tears. Stands up. Hello, she says. My name is Alice, she says.

A tall mug appears on the table and Little Italy retreats behind the bar. As she goes, she turns to the box on the wall and nods. From deep inside number 16 rises up and slides onto the turntable.

The curtains open. Standing side by side on the stage, Aretha Franklin and Annie Lennox are powering out the words. Sisters, are doin' it for themselves.

The Girls With The Shaven Heads know all the words. Damned straight.

Be cool...

Déjà vu all over again

Good morning Friday. There are some folk who think that déjà vu is just a trick of the brain. An anomaly of the memory. A sensory input cart before the horse. There are others who think that seeing something for the second time...even though we definitely, positively have only just seen it for the first time...is pretty damned cool.

There's more than a whiff of approaching spring in the air this morning. The sun has got his hat on...even though he's still wearing his scarf. The city square is bustling with early morning folk. Straight backs. Not hunched shoulders. Nearly the weekend...nearly the weekend. The wind still bounces off the concrete walls and paving stones. But not with the same venom as a week or so ago. Not with the same sharp vindictiveness. This morning, there's an odour of expectancy. The long wait's nearly over.

As I walk past The Piano Man, playing showtunes under the trees, my first déjà vu taps me on the shoulder. A pre-teen rushes over to the smiling musician. Intent on dropping some coins in a cap at the base of the piano. Parents stand nearby. Teaching offspring how to be appreciative.

The pre-teen stumbles and two silver coins drop from his hand and roll along the slabs. Bounce off the cap. Flash of memory. The exact same scenario repeats in my mind. Same boy. Same parents. Same spilled coins. First time seen...but a repeat performance. A flash of a memory that never existed...or did it?

I walk on without breaking a step. Across the tram tracks. Round the corner. Over the threshold and up to the bar. The warmth welcomes me. Hugs me. Wraps its arms around me. Little Italy says hello again.

Second déjà vu gives me a friendly nudge in the gut as Big Red walks out of the office, smiling. Hair deep red with a silver wave at the front. Very nice, I say. I liked it the first time you did it, I say. This is the first time, she says and raises an eyebrow.

I feel a small itch somewhere inside. Somewhere I can't scratch. You look like you got the déjàs, she says, and hands me a double espresso. How many so far, she says. Two, I say. She frowns. Does a quick internal check. One more, she says. Any minute now, she says. This one feels like a biggie, she says. Better go sit down.

I slip her some silver and grab my morning nectar. Make for one of my spots and sit down real fast. Preparation is everything. Always expect the unexpected.

I take a deep breath and scan the room. Not a déjà in sight. I relax. Drop the shoulders. Loosen the limbs. Take a breath and take a sip. Lean back in the chair….and BOOM… déjà number three hits me like a slap in the face. I know what happens next. I know every bit of it.

The door will open. The Girl with the Mohican will walk in. Face like a fallen angel. Wearing a worn biker's jacket, skinny black jeans, and carrying a small, shivering, short haired Chihuahua called Boris.

The Girl will look at me. The Chihuahua will bark twice.

From behind the bar, Little Italy looks at the box on the wall. The box feels a repeat performance coming on as number 51 slides onto the turntable.

The curtain opens and Etta James is on stage. Holding the mike. The band starts up. Etta sings I Just Want To Make Love To You.

All the men in the audience hold their breaths. A few don't stop there. I hear a noise. Look up. The door opens…and it's déjà vu all over again.

Be cool…

220

The Good Brother

Good morning Monday. It's a well-known fact. An inescapable truth. Many of us are children at the opening and at the closing of our lives. And a few of us are lucky enough to stay children all the way through. Born with the grown up switch permanently off. Born without anyone who knows how to flick it on.

Born without the adult gene.

Standing in front of me in the coffee shop queue this morning is The Good Brother. The Sister is sitting obediently at a table fifteen feet away from me. Smiling and constantly nodding her head. Middle aged and eternally young. Looking at the world through the eyes of a ten year old. Wrinkled and hunched. Pale and small. Bright red wooly coat and white hair under a green bobble hat. Here for her daily treat.

The Good Brother is a giant in comparison. Twice her size, four times her age, and five years younger. Her lifelong companion. Her knight in shining armour. Her friend.

Little Italy wears the look of someone who knows their story. Someone who admires their partnership. The Good Brother doesn't have to order. Never has to order. Always has the same. Two exotic ice cold Frappe Cremes. Espresso base with caramel sauce topped with fresh whipped cream. No matter whether it's the height of summer…or the depths of winter.

It's what she loves. It's what floats her ten year old boat. Makes her smile a mile wide and brings her hands together in a loud, resounding clap. Makes his heart warm to see her glee. He doesn't mind the role he's had to play. Doesn't mind the life he's missed. Doesn't mind the one-sided conversations where all his verbalized thoughts and wishes fall on deaf ears. They bounce off her mind like footballs kicked against a brick wall. Never penetrating. Always coming back for more.

He takes his tray with the two treats to her table. Her eyes watch him every step of the way. Growing wider with anticipation.

He sits down and places her Frappe in front of her. Reaches out and takes her gloves off. Drink slowly, he says. Don't get cream on your nose, he says. She nods, bends forward, and gets a small, white blob on the end of her nose. He huffs…puffs….smiles, and wipes it away with a tissue.

Behind the bar, Little Italy thinks about all the different kinds of love there are. And knows that few come close to the kind shown by The Good Brother. She looks up at the box on the wall. Nods. Time for something different. Something for the child in the adult. Number 112 slides up from way down below and slips onto the turntable.

The curtains open. The lights come on. Expect the unexpected. Johnny Cash is standing at the mike, guitar strapped on. Dressed in black. Singing You Are My Sunshine.

The Good Brother looks at his sister and they both smile. On the outside…and on the inside.

Be cool…

Big Tony and The One

Good morning Wednesday. The Beat Generation is in the house. The Boys in Blue are in the coffee shop this morning. They have a Girl in Blue with them. It's a Unisex police force. One size guards all. One size arrests all. You're safe...you're busted. Three relax around a table while the one with a regulation beard gets lattes for the law.

Two tables away, The Girl with the Butterfly Tattoo sits. Thumbs a blur. Oblivious to the plods nearby. Texting words of love to her latest paramour. Her new beau. Somewhere out in the big wide world. Somewhere in another coffee shop. In another country. It's all she says he says. Like I miss you, she says. I wish you were here, she says. I know, he says. But you know how it is, he says. I go where the gigs are, he says. I'll buy you a new guitar when you come home, she says. Musical blackmail in action. Call the cops.

She looks at The Boys in Blue. Looks away quickly. Sends the bum on the end of her thumb kisses. Bum sends her a question. Can you wire me more cash, he says. Her heart sinks. Sure, she says. Anything you want. Just come home soon, she says. I'm lonely. Love you, he says. Her heart soars. A temporary reprieve.

Over behind the bar, Little Italy senses the desperate car crash of a heart being slowly ripped apart. All she can do is pick up the pieces. All she can do is be there for the nuclear fallout. In the meantime...triple espresso in the short term. Bloody emotional miracle in the long.

Excuse me, says a disembodied voice. Little Italy raises an eyebrow and looks at the vacant space where the next customer should be. She twigs and looks down a few feet. There, in all his glory, stands four feet nothing of Big Tony. She smiles. He winks. Morning handsome, she says. Morning beautiful, he says.

Big Tony has The One with him today. She's the love of his life. The beat in his heart. The blood in his veins. He makes her feel happy. She makes him feel tall. They're a perfect fit.

She's the Yin to his Yang. He's the sun to her moon. She's sat down at a table in the corner. He's reaching up to pay for two cappuccinos. Each dusted with chocolate powder in the shape of a smiley face. I'll bring them over, says Big Red. That's okay, says Big Tony. A man's gotta do what a man's gotta do, he says.

She hands him the tray and he strides over to The One feeling ten feet tall. On the tray, with the two cappuccinos, is one slice of carrot cake. Cut in two. Right down the middle. And two forks. He turns and looks at The One. She looks up and smiles her extra happy smile. The one that makes him go all funny inside.

Over behind the bar, Little Italy smiles inside. She knows that the heart wants what the heart wants. She knows that two halves sometimes make more than just a whole. She knows that Big Tony and The One have the biggest damned hearts she's ever come across. She looks up at the box on the wall. For once, the box is way ahead of her. From deep inside number 35 has already risen up and has slid easy onto the turntable.

The curtain opens. The spotlight interrupts the darkness and picks out The Girl from Tiger Bay. Dame Shirley Bassey. Big name. Big voice. Big Spender.

On his way to the table, Big Tony does a soft shoe shuffle to the music. The One squeals with laughter. Love comes in all shapes and sizes.

Be cool…

Shelter from the storm

Good morning Thursday. Some folk think that anything worth having is worth waiting for. It's a nice, friendly, civilized point of view, make no mistake. But others…well, they see things from a different perspective.

They feel that a minute waited is a minute wasted. They don't hang around for Mister Opportunity to come knocking on their door. They reach out, grab him by the balls and pull the damned door off its hinges with whichever hand they have left over. No point trying to climb on board after the train has gone. Life's too short, death's too long, and true love's too damned hard to find.

But here, in the coffee shop, salvation comes in the shape of Little Italy, Big Red, Angel…and the best damned drink on the face of God's green earth.

Here you can throw caution to the wind and take a chance on somebody else taking a chance on you. Here you can take a deep breath, go for gold, and to hell with the consequences. Here, actions and words are just as loud as each other…or just as quiet. And the noise of an empty heart can be interrupted by the sound of something absolutely unexpected taking place.

Four tables to the left is The Secretary. Impeccably dressed. Impossibly lonely. Half a lifetime spent bringing order to chaos for other folk. All she wants is half an hour somewhere to shut out the chaos of her own life. She keeps her head down. Doesn't look up. No eye contact. Too risky.

Far away on the other side of the room, next to the window on the world, sits The Battered Babe. The only breaks she's had have been bad ones. Broken heart. Broken fingers. Broken arms. And especially for last Christmas, broken collar bone. Slipped on the stairs, doc. Yeah, right.

But here…here…she's safe. Maybe not sound. But safe. For now.

Little Italy sees all the heartache and pain. All the torment and shame. Here, this morning, the sad-eyed boys and girls outnumber the happy smiley people.

They know the directions to the door. Like a hurt animal knows where to go to lay low until the hurt heals. And they know that some hurts don't go away without a fight. Unless they come up against Little Italy. Then they do the right thing, and run like Hell. This is her place. These are her people. God help anyone who thinks different.

She looks up at the box on the wall and nods. Just once. The box in a battle-scarred foot soldier in the war against sadness. It nods back and from deep inside, number 1 rises up.

The curtains part. The light shines on little Bobby Zimmerman. Mike at the ready. Guitar strapped on. Harmonica strapped on. Blood on the Tracks. Shelter From the Storm. Take it away...

There's only one Bob Dylan. Just like there's only one Little Italy.

Be cool...

Little Italy speaks Lolaese

Good morning Friday the 13th. It's cold. Wet. Miserable. Unlucky for sun worshippers and short-sleeved shirts. Not a nice day for happy coincidences and positive thinking.

But a great day for black cats and falling pianos…for feeling nervous and developing an uncanny ability to trip over fresh air. A perfect pessimistic morning for staying in bed and not venturing out into a world that has you in its cross hairs. Just what any successful, well-adjusted Friday the 13th should be. At least that's what it's like outside. Where bad luck and trouble stay looking in through the window. Misting up the glass.

Here, inside the coffee shop, Friday the 13th is a whole different story. Here, monsters run for cover and the best things in life come out to play. Here, it's a day for sunshine and optimists. For light hearts and dark roast Arabica coffee. For putting on your best damned smile and wearing it until the moon comes up.

Lola is here. Standing by the bar. Tail wagging at the speed of happiness. Brushing the floor as she sits looking up at her human companion. Waiting for the nod to go say hello. He looks down. Smiles and nods. Lola scampers round to the end of the bar where Little Italy is waiting with open arms. Kisses and licks. Kisses and licks.

Little Italy smiles. Hey girl, she says. Where you been, she says. Out and about, says Lola. Nothing's lost in translation. Little Italy knows how to speak Lolaese. She's a multi-lingual, multi-species queen of the baristas. It comes with the territory.

Five minutes later, Lola and her human disappear upstairs to the balcony and in their place at the front of the queue is the most accident-prone man on the planet. Mister Black & Blue. Even from twenty feet away, I can see the signs of his catalogue of misfortune. A limp here. A bandage there.

Little Italy frowns and shakes her head.

What happened this time, she says. Mister Black & Blue shrugs. Tripped over the cat, he says. On the stairs, he says. With a tray full of dishes, he says. Little Italy nods over to the far wall. You got a companion in pain, she says.

He turns and looks. Directly under the box on the wall sits The Girl with the Autographed Leg. She tripped over the cat, too, she says. Maybe you have something in common, she says. You should go say hello, she says. I'll bring your coffee over, she says.

Mister Black & Blue blinks...thinks...smiles....then turns and limps over to The Girl with the Autographed Leg. Little Italy smiles and nods at the box on the wall. The box nods back and from deep inside, number 95 rises very carefully to the surface and sits gently on the turntable.

The curtains open. Time for a little irony. Time for a little Elvis. Mister Black & Blue and The Girl with the Autographed Leg begin to laugh. Who knew that Falling In Love With You would be the perfect ice breaker?

Be cool...

Two perfect green roses

Good morning Tuesday. Have you ever smelled the colour green? Or tasted it? Or heard the sound it makes? It smells like dew on freshly mown grass. Tastes like the first pint of cool Guinness halfway through a long, hot day. Sounds like the pipes and fiddle playing a slow lament that brings tears to the eyes.

The colour green is a joyous thing to behind. And today, here in the coffee shop, on the 17th of March, the Feast of Saint Patrick, it outshines every other colour in the spectrum.

Behind the bar sits a green, lean, coffee machine. Helping it dispense its liquid magic are Little Italy and Big Red. Black dresses. Black tights. Black shoes. Green tops. A touch of the Oirish here in the centre of the city. On every table there's a green coffee menu. Emerald options for the finest drink on the planet.

And just because it's today, and not yesterday, and not tomorrow…there's a special offer on Green Tea. Regulars and newbies are lined up at the bar. Some here for the crack of the caffeine hit…others here for the pure joy of drinking the dark brown liquid of their choice whilst wearing something green…modest or outrageous.

The blessed saint would dance in his grave if he had the room. There's a Leprechaun Crew with green top hats, green outfits and orange beards, sitting in the corner trying to sip chocolate-topped cappuccinos without getting brown froth on their beards. They're not succeeding. The hats are cocked at a rakish angle. Held on with elastic and pins.

Over on the left The Secretary sits. A beautifully tailored herringbone suit outlining her slightly fuller figure. A crushing desire not be left out. Not be the one left holding the parcel with no chair to sit on. Just like she used to be at every damned birthday party. Sally no mates.

Over by the bar, Little Italy is serving The Man With The Silver Hair.

He's in his fifties. He has damned good looks and style oozing from every pore. A cup of dark Americano in one hand. Two green roses in the other. He looks around for the one he sees here every morning but has never had the courage to approach. Today is Courage Day. Today is Throw Caution to the Wind Day.

Little Italy sees his search. Knows his intention. She coughs politely, catches his eye and nods in the direction of The Secretary. He thanks her. Winks conspiratorially. Walks to the table where The Secretary sits in all her herringbone loneliness.

Excuse me, he says, standing behind an empty chair. Is this seat taken, he says. The Secretary whispers a reply. No, she says. She feels the hot flush of embarrassment creep into her cheeks.

The Man With The Silver Hair holds out one of the perfect green roses. In that case this must be for you, he says. She takes the rose. Holds it gently. He sits. So...where do we start, he says. I've always believed that beginnings were a good place for that sort of thing, she says, and smiles.

Over behind the bar, Little Italy nods at the box on the wall. The box, bedecked in green, knows what to do next. From deep inside it pulls up number 61.

The curtains open. Spotlight shines on The Dubliners. Lined up and ready to go. Bearded. Grzzled. Singing a sweet love song about somebody called Molly Malone.

The Secretary pins the perfect green rose on the lapel over her left breast. And so begins the introduction to the Dance of the Strangers. Nicely done Saint Padraig. Nicely done.

Be cool...

The Indecisive Twentysomething

Good morning Wednesday. Some days are just better at making you feel crap than others. It's a fact. They don't even have to work hard at it. They're patient. Determined. Sneaky.

They wait until you open your eyes in the morning, then they put the 'let me just get through today' machine in gear and watch as you hang on tight and do the white knuckle ride. All day long. Other days they can put life between two slices of bread, add some good old English mustard, and serve up the best damned feelgood sandwich you've ever tasted. Bar none.

This morning, outside the coffee shop, a constant stream of folk pass by in their white rabbit suits. Trying desperately not to be late for their very important date. Trying not to trip over the sign that says: Don't drop. Don't stop. Alice doesn't live here anymore.

Inside, Little Italy is paying particular attention to a small, thin, indecisive Twentysomething with long curls and a short black dress. Even from fifteen feet away I can see that she's having trouble making up her mind. First it's a Cappuccino. Then it's a long tall Latte.

Next she sees the word Americano on the board on the wall, and it reminds her of the time she was in New York. She says so. I was in New York last year drinking Americanos, she says. Little Italy nods and smiles. Twentysomething bites her bottom lip. Decisions…decisions.

Why not have something different, says Little Italy. Why not have something calming. Something soothing. How about a green tea, she says. Very good for the free radicals, she says. It has antioxidant properties, she says. It even has polyphenols, she says.

Twentysomething likes the idea of antioxidant properties and polyphenols. So she nods and smiles. Decisively.

The Tall Man behind her sighs softly. This could be his opportunity.

Big Red's hands are a blur and in seconds a pot full of steaming green tea is sitting on a tray, along with a white cup and saucer. It all looks very civilised, thinks Twentysomething, and she takes the tray, turns and looks at a sea of empty tables. Which one, she thinks. Over by the window? Over by the loos? Upstairs on the balcony? Decisions…decisions.

A voice behind her whispers, why don't you join me. I promise I won't bite, he says. It's better than standing here trying to make up your mind, he says. Let me make it up for you.

She turns and The Tall Man is standing with a short espresso in his right hand. His left is pointing to a table over against the wall. It has two chairs. It looks ideal. The thought of not having to decide makes her feel free. A weight disappears from her back. Her shoulders relax. She takes a deep breath and nods.

Okay, she says. Sounds like a plan, she says. They both make for the table. He goes left. She goes right. Introductions are made. Names are exchanged. Embarrassment is put on the back burner.

Over behind the bar, Little Italy looks at the box on the wall. The box looks deep inside and comes up with number 12. Of course.

The curtains open and Lou Reed, black suit, black hat, mike in hand, begins to sing. Perfect setting. Perfect song. Perfect Day.

Twentysomething smiles. The best decisions make up their own minds.

Be cool…

Cappuccino with a dark brown smile

Good morning Thursday. A good friend today reminded me about choices. He reminded me about the things that are open for discussion. And the things you don't have a skinny cat in Hell's chance of influencing.

Like…you can choose the career you have…but not the natural talent you were born with. You can choose the friends who make life fabulous, or just more bearable…but not the family who can make it a living Hell. And you can choose who you decide to jump the broom with…but not the one you fall head over heels in love with.

Tomorrow is the first day of Spring and I can taste it in the air as I walk across the square to the coffee shop. It tastes like making a new beginning. Like turning a corner and taking a fresh look at a street you haven't walked down for years. Like looking at the dark clouds being blown away and seeing the sun force its way through like the cavalry racing to the rescue.

My choice this morning…every morning…is simple. I come to the coffee shop and I choose the coffee, or the tea, that will kickstart the day. The one that will slow me down. Chill me out. Cheer me up.

I walk through the door and every damned molecule in my body has a smile on its face. I wait my turn in the queue and use the time to let the aroma of the room put a tick against the first words that will slide past my lips in about 30 seconds time.

I shuffle along and stand opposite Little Italy. Face to face. Cappuccino with a dark brown smile, I say. Good choice, she says. Like you had any say in the matter, she says, and smiles. I retire to a spot in the corner where a good view of the floor and a slice of privacy are both up for grabs.

My eyes come to rest on The Girl with the Butterfly Tattoo.

A single ink grown now into double figures. Cocooned in thoughts of her latest Squeeze.

On the road with his band. Probably on the pull with his bass player. She of the large and pendulous personalities. They came in here for a coffee and a hug on their way to a gig. I saw The Girl with the Butterfly Tattoo looking at The Squeeze looking at the Pendulous Player. I saw her wishing her personalities were as overabundant.

I also saw The Unrequited Love. The one who, even from across the room, hardly ever took his eyes off The Girl with the Butterfly Tattoo. Followed her every movement. But she didn't know he even existed. She didn't know it then. She doesn't know it today.

Over behind the bar, Little Italy knows the way it goes. It goes nowhere. Not without the kind of intervention that moves mountains. The Unrequited Love finishes his latte, stands up and looks over at The Girl with the Butterfly Tattoo.

Little Italy curses silently and looks at the box on the wall. The box knows that look, so it digs deep inside and number 41 rises to the surface and slides onto the turntable.

The curtains open. The spotlights hit the stage. It's October 1962. The Fab Four are in their mop-top youth. Beatlemania is being born, screaming and shouting, with Love Me Do and an unforgettable harmonica riff.

The Girl with the Butterfly Tattoo looks up. You can't choose the one you fall in love with.

Be cool…

The Platinum Blonde and The Beard

Good morning Friday. It's the First Day of Spring. March Equinox. Solar Eclipse Day. A day when new things barge in the door and old things dive out the window. I can feel it in my bones. I might not be able to see the change. But as my old, blind, great granny used to say. No point looking for something when you know for sure it's there.

As I walk across the square to the coffee shop, I don't have to look up to see the sun hiding behind the mood. I can't feel it. Can't see it. But I know it's there. Somewhere above the clouds. Just like it is every day.

Just like when I walk through the coffee shop doors, I know Little Italy will be there. I might not see her first off. But I know that by the time it gets to be my turn, she'll be there. Just like she always is. This isn't predictability. This isn't par for the course. This is reliability. This is peace of mind, with a large slice of sit back, relax and breathe easy.

I go in and I can feel the presence of The Man in Black. I don't have to look. I know he's sitting by the window. Watching the souls who come in. Counting the ones who go out. Marking it all down and reckoning it all up.

He's the black cat in a dark room who isn't there if you look, and obvious as daylight if you don't. Love is a bit like that. You know it's there. Somewhere. But there's no point trying to figure out where it is. It's easier trying to figure out where it isn't.

Might as well just accept that when it's ready it will come find you. Of course every now and then it needs a nudge in the right direction. And that's where Little Italy comes in.

She was born to nudge. Born to say the right things to the right folk at the right time for the right reason. Just like this morning, with The Platinum Blonde and The Beard. Standing in the queue next to each other. She with the floor-length black leather coat and he with the cream jacket, multi-coloured scarf and skinny leg jeans.

They look at each other using peripheral vision dialed up to the max. See but not be seen. But Little Italy sees. Sees their interest. Sees their attraction. So she nudges. Just enough to let them get from A to C without having to figure out how to go through B.

So…two double espressos, she says. Looks like you've both got good taste, she says. The Beard looks at The Platinum Blonde. Great minds think alike, he says. I sometimes have a triple, says The Platinum Blonde.

In that case, let's make them both triples, he says. Two triples coming right up, says Little Italy. I'll bring them over, she says. You two go sit down, she says.

They look at each other. Decision made. They look for a table for two and another two strangers bite the dust.

Little Italy looks at the box on the wall and nods. The box puts the feelers out and up from the depths comes number 52.

The curtains open. Spotlight illuminates Francis Albert Sinatra. Perfect timing. Perfect voice. Perfect strangers in the night.

Little Italy smiles. Over to you guys.

Be cool…

We all hear voices

Good morning Monday. We all hear voices. Most of them come from outside our heads. Out there in the great wide world. They belong to other folk. Real folk. Not us.

And then there are the other voices. The ones that come from inside our heads. The ones that suddenly pop up out of nowhere and act as though they run the show and you're just a witness. An onlooker.

Sometimes they're the backseat driver and you're the one with your foot on the gas. Sometimes they're sitting in the front with the wheel gripped tightly in their hands and a look on their face that wants to make you jump out at the next lights. And run like Hell.

It's dull this morning as I walk to the coffee shop. Dull and cool and cloudy. Overcast and uninteresting.

But that's okay. Warm and interesting is just around the corner. Folk drift past like so much smoke. Heads down. Moving across their own internal landscape. Wishing they were somewhere else. Anywhere else except here.

Two minutes later I'm in the coffee shop, sitting down, with a hot Americano in front of me and a cream coloured wall behind. I take my first sip of darkness and look around. Scan the scene. Eyes on full alert. Peripheral vision controls turned up to the max. In the zone.

I see Little Italy over behind the bar. Service with a smile. Handing a small cup to The Blimp, a large customer who seems to be the same size side to side as he is top to bottom. He casts a giant shadow on the tables nearby.

As The Blimp turns to look for a seat which will never be big enough in a million years, I see his mouth…talking. Having a conversation with someone that nobodybody outside his skin can see.

237

Smiling at first. Then arguing. Nodding his head in agreement one second…then shaking it in anger the next. He speaks out loud. Yes I know, he whispers…we'll go sit over by the window. Well I don't know, he whispers…just don't make a scene. Don't create a fuss. I'll tell you in a minute when we sit down.

The Blimp's mouth is always on the move. The crowd he carries inside scuffle for attention. Scramble to get noticed. Fight to be heard.

I look to Little Italy. I can see concern grow on her face. The Blimp sits down. The chair groans under the weight. He adjusts his massive frame then picks up his double espresso. So daintily. So carefully. Thumb and index finger grip. Pinky finger straight out. Takes a sip and relaxes. Takes a breath and smiles.

I see him mouth the word hello to nobody in the chair opposite. He nods his head slowly. I like it here to, he says. Over behind the bar, Little Italy kicks concern out the door and the ghost of a smile crosses her face.

She looks at the box on the wall and the box has a word with its own internal voices. One in particular looks for number 149 and places it on the turntable.

The curtains open. The lights dim. The spotlight picks out The Beatles. Ringo, behind the drumkit. His voice. His song. With a little help from his friends.

The Blimp knows the words. So do his friends. He looks to Little Italy and nods. Mouths a silent thank you. Little Italy mouths a silent no problem.

Be cool…

Today is Bump Day

Good morning Tuesday. Today is Bump Day. Ever since I can remember I've had a habit of bumping into things. Some would call that just plain clumsy.

Other folk of a more understanding nature, would call it a desire to make contact. Either with other living beings or with a wide selection of the physical objects that populate our lives. A stranger or family member here. A chair or table there.

Sometimes those bumps are intentional. Other times they're the result of dark and mysterious forces at work. Forces that result in a painful clatter...physical or emotional...and leave the Bumpers amongst us bruised, inside or out, (or both) after the experience.

Today, the sun is out as I walk through the square to the coffee shop. The height of summer is still a warm jacket away. But the weather is in training. Like any good athlete, it's doing its warming-up routine. Getting the muscles in gear. Preparing the body and the mind for the exercise ahead.

I dodge and weave between the trees. Between the travellers. Trying not to step on the paving stone cracks. Avoiding spat-out chewing gum. Stepping over sprawling liquid. So far so good. So far so good.

Round the corner. Through the door. Blast of warm air. Blast of warm welcome. Little Italy looks up. Smiles. You look like you could use something different, she says. Just for a change says Big Red, standing beside her. This looks like an ambush, I say. Okay, I'll bite, I say. How about a nice pot of green tea, says Little Italy. You used to like that, she says. I nod and smile. Sounds like a plan, I say.

Bloody Hell, says a voice behind me. How long has it been, says another voice. Oooh, must be ten years, says the first voice. How the Hell are you, says the second voice. Losing touch is a pain in the heart. But finding it again is a morphine drip.

I turn and see The Bump hugging The Girl With The Violin Case.

Long lost pals. Friends reunited. Picking up the threads of a relationship that never died, just went to sleep.

The Bump looks like she's about to book herself into the maternity ward. Pop out a little toddler. The Girl With The Violin Case looks like she's about to book herself into a spot on the corner outside. Pop out a little Mozart.

I pick up my tray and decamp to the corner. Safe and sound. Pour my liquid peace of mind and scan the floor. Friends reunited order a pair of skinny lattes and find themselves a comfy spot to hunker down and catch up.

Behind the bar, Little Italy smiles inside and looks at the box on the wall. The box knows the score and digs deep. Up comes number 140 and eases it onto the turntable.

The curtains open. Spotlight settles on Willie Nelson. At the mike. Guitar strapped on. Bandana tied on. Lived-in face with a lived-in song.

Big Red nudges Little Italy. Funny how time slips away, she says. Maybe that's why so many folk bump into each other, says Little Italy.

Be cool…

The Man With The Lopsided Grin

Good morning Wednesday. There are those who spend their whole lives trying to bring order into a universe that thrives on chaos. They love quiet, sunny days. No wind. No storm. No disruption. No loud voices. No upset emotions.

They exist in a permanent state of trying to put things right when things just want to be put left. They like even...not odd. Straight...not bent. Balanced...not wobbly. Then there are those who love to be different. Who can't be anything else. Who get a kick out of giving convention a bloody nose. Who love injecting a rare touch of screw you into an otherwise boring bloody world. Who wage a constant war against the obsessive compulsives with their straight edges and their tidy minds.

The Man With The Lopsided Grin is in the coffee shop this morning. And his Lop is even more Sided than usual. Even more asymmetrical. Even more askew. It goes from an unbalanced high on the right to a sloping low on the left. He has a lopsided quiff. A lopsided edge on his pulled-out shirt . Lopsided zips on his scuffed leather jacket. Lopsided design on his biker boots.

He sticks his middle finger up at the sound of silence and brings a wild uneasiness wherever he goes.

Behind the bar, Little Italy takes a deep breath and exhales slowly. Somewhere at the back of her neck a warm little tingle interrupts her feeling of cool, calm control. It's always the same when he comes to visit. When someone she sees the least of inhabits the same body as someone she thinks the most of. Especially this one. This wild man. This off-centred individual from the more interesting side of the tracks.

Somewhere underneath her ribcage a small flock of butterflies exercises their wings. But she knows that, for the moment at least, they won't find a way to be free. He's too much of a temptation. Too much of a distraction. Too much of a drug. So she deflects and nudges Big Red.

Do the honors, she says. Americano with an extra shot, she says. I got business in the office, she says. And she turns and walks away. Leaves Big Red to salivate. Leaves her to look into the eyes of The Man With The Lopsided Grin …and tell her own flock of butterflies to settle the Hell down. Shut the Hell up.

Little Italy turns at the door of the office and nods to the box on the wall. Time for a delicious little tease. The box raises an eyebrow and inwardly tuts. But a request is a request. Especially this one. So it digs deep and comes up with number 51. Brings it to the surface. Slides it on the turntable.

The curtains open. Etta James stands at the mike. Band behind her. Voice all the way in front. I just want to make love to you, she sings. Only it's not so much a song. It's more like a taste of things to come.

Little Italy takes a last look at The Man With The Lopsided Grin, before disappearing behind the door. Just because you can't eat…doesn't mean you can't taste.

Be cool…

Four-legged Man coming through

Good morning Thursday. We grow up believing that, on balance, two legs are more than enough for any of us. Man or woman. Sometimes age gives us the added benefit of three legs. Very occasionally, infirmity or accident gives us the extra support of more. Or the deficit of less.

As I walk through the square to the coffee shop this morning, I overtake The Four-legged Man. A slow-moving individual of twisted spine and extra tubular metal appendages. A pre-middle-aged example of blended mobility. Four steps of flesh and bone, aluminium and rubber, in perfect sync. Poetry in motion.

His bag is slung over his shoulder. His hair is tucked under his cap. His left eye is apologetic. His right one has the fierce glare of determination. Look out folks. Four-legged Man coming through. Bugger off out of the way.

He has the power of Moses. He parts the red, white, blue, green, yellow, brown and black sea of people coming towards him and forges ahead. I leave him in my wake and hurry two-legged across the tram tracks.

Around the corner there's a table with my name on it. Delay isn't an option. I have a caffeine deficit that needs seeing to. Topping up. Sorting out. Filling in. What I don't realise is…so does The Four-legged Man. And so do his two and three-legged companions.

By the time I sit down and allow the dark, rich odour of my Americano to caress my nasal cavities, the door is opening and The Four-legged Man is entering, followed by his caffeine crew. They are a motley lot. As colourful and smiley a gaggle of individuals that ever deserved to call themselves lifelong friends.

One in particular looks more than merely a friend. She snuggles up close as he stands in front of Little Italy in all his five feet ten inches of romantic boyfriend.

He's not disabled. He's multi-abled.

He's not on crutches. He's on a tailor-made, hi-tech, 18-degree balance support rig. State-of-the-art. Machine made. Hand painted black with red and yellow flames at the base.

I sip my Americano and look closer at her. She slips her left arm around his waist and looks closer at him. Nuzzles his ear with her nose. Little Italy is a sucker for an odd couple. So she lets the charge slide for their two cappuccinos. The rest of the crew know a good deed when they see it.

So they zip the lip, dig deep, pay up and sit down. The Four-legged Man follows on behind. Last man walking across the floor.

Big Red looks at Little Italy and shakes her head. Smiles. Gives her the thumbs up nice and low so nobody sees. Little Italy shrugs, winks, and looks at the box on the wall. The box will take the odd over the even any day of the week. Except when it comes to music. And then anything's up for grabs. Today's slice of anything on the turntable is number 84.

The curtains open, The Stones are on stage, Keith does the intro that the whole world knows…and Mick does his thing with the lips and the hips. Get yer ya-yas out. It's Jumpin' Jack Flash.

The Four-legged Man struts his stuff. All the way to the table. Be cool…

Heroes are funny buggers

Good morning Friday. Heroes are funny buggers. They have a curious habit of appearing out of nowhere and saving the day.

They have a wonderful knack of coming to the rescue, just when you need them. Galloping over the hill with the cavalry, just in the nick of time. They step up to the plate without a second's hesitation and do what a man's gotta do…or a woman.

They're not developed over time. It's in them right from the start. They're born that way. Born with the hero gene switched on. The one that gives them permission to do something that nobody else is prepared to do and step forward when everyone else is stepping back.

They stick their necks above the parapet when everyone else is sensibly cowering. Foetal position. Scared shitless. Unable to move. Wishing they were anywhere else but right where they are. Just like yours truly.

The painful truth is…I'm no Captain America. No member of the Justice League. No Caped Crusader. No Gamora, Guardian of the Galaxy. But I know a hero when I see one. And I can see one right now. He's small, weedy, not great looking…but if you piss him off he'll turn green and scare the living shit out of you.

He's sitting on a stool by the window in the coffee shop. Minding his own business. Head down. No eye contact. But half an hour ago he was seven feet tall, built like a brick shithouse, and completely invulnerable. At least that's what it seemed like when The Thug With The Crazy Eyes burst through the door and laughed like a maniac at the top of his voice.

Was he dangerous? Who the Hell knew? It took Little Italy about two seconds to move the fifteen feet from where she was to where he was. This is her territory and she takes no prisoners. But The Hero was faster. Although he was smaller on the outside than The Thug With The Crazy Eyes…he was bigger on the inside.

245

He slid protectively between The Thug and Little Italy, looked up at the unwashed intruder and spoke real slow. Go sit outside and I'll bring you a coffee, he said. He didn't move a muscle.

The Thug With The Crazy Eyes lifted a large hand and was about to slap The Hero sideways to Christmas, when The Boys In Blue who were chasing him caught up. Grabbed him by the collar. Hauled him back out of the coffee shop. And marched him out of sight.

It's not often you hear a half-full coffee shop burst out into spontaneous applause. But that's what happened. True as I'm sat right here.

Afterwards, The Hero went back to his table. Back to minding his own business. Only instead of being the little guy in the corner who nobody looks twice at, he's now the guy who every other guy in the place wants to be like. And every other gal in the place wants to be sat next to. One in particular. Pulse quickening. Hope rearing its head. Maybe tomorrow.

That was then. This is now. Little Italy has just finished serving him his third free coffee and as she walks back behind the counter, she nods to the box on the wall. The box loves heroes. Especially unexpected ones. So it picks number 17 from the vinyl collection in the basement and places it personally on the turntable.

The curtains open and David Bowie…cream suit…filmed backdrop of ordinary people performing extraordinary acts…begins to sing Heroes.

The Hero bows his head and the ghost of a smile covers his face.

Be cool…

The Freebie Guy and The Waif

Good morning Tuesday. Time is one of the four things in life we never seem to have enough of. Two of the others, of course, are health and love.

There are never enough hours in any given day. Even if we doubled our quota of 24 to 48, we'd still somehow manage to come up short. Even if we were fit and healthy, we'd still want to lose a bit more weight.

Work a little more out. Gain a bit more muscle. Buy a bigger medicine cabinet. And even if we were madly in love with the perfect partner, there would still be that nagging little doubt in the back of our mind about whether they were as much in love with us.

Life doesn't come with a manufacturer's guarantee of complete satisfaction. And we can't return the goods and claim a full refund if we end up broke and dysfunctional. All we can do is the best we can do. All we can wish for is to be happier and healthier in our skin today than we were yesterday. Earlier in life rather than later. And all we can hope for is that somehow, in spite of it all, we'll fall madly in love with someone who'll fall just as madly in love with us.

It doesn't always work out that way. In fact there are some folk who think that if it ever does work out that way, it should be considered a bloody miracle and shouted from the heavens.

And then…and then…there's the last of the holy 'can't have enough' quartet. The fourth piece of the puzzle. The magic ingredient that helps us get ready for the rest of our day.

Maybe even helps us get through the rest of our lives. The thing that helps us put everything else into perspective. The thing that, when properly blended and prepared, makes up the glue that holds us together…stops us from falling apart. Helps us to add things up. Tie things down. Sort things out.

Those of us who can always put two and two together and come up with any damned number you want, know it as the finest drink on the face of God's green earth.

Those who wouldn't know a good thing if it smacked them round the face, know it by its other description. Coffee.

This morning the weather resembles an introduction to a hurricane. Somewhere, it's threatening to blow the roofs off houses. Somewhere, trees are about to lay down and give up the ghost. Yet here, in the coffee shop, shelter from the storm can be had for the price of a cappuccino and a slice of carrot cake.

Here, a small waif of a girl in a black bobble hat, black wooly jacket, torn jeans and distressed trainers, can ask Little Italy for a warm drink and be treated like a long lost daughter. Free of charge. Paid for by the guy who just left the counter and sat down in the corner. The guy who knows what it's like to have nothing and need a friend.

Little Italy nods in his direction and The Waif turns and puts on her best Sunday smile. It looks like a Monday one. Feels like a Wednesday one. But to The Freebie Guy it looks just fine.

He raises a hand. His fingers call her over. This could be the start of a beautiful friendship.

Behind the bar, Little Italy stops preparing a tall skinny latte for a tall skinny teen, and turns to nod at the box on the wall. The box returns the nod with change and somewhere inside number 1 puts in an appearance.

The curtains open. Bob Dylan stands at the mike. Puts the voice into gear. Shelter From The Storm isn't just a favourite play here. It's a prerequisite for a place that looks after folk it knows…and folk it hasn't even met yet.

The Waif sits down. Little Italy smiles.

Be cool…

The Nasty Boys get their comeuppance

Good morning Wednesday. The first day of April. The day when unfunny jokes are played on unsuspecting folk by uncharitable fools.

The day when a suspect sense of humour has until noon to raise a titter and leave the recipient bewitched, bothered and bewildered. And secretly more than a little pissed off. Oh what a jape. Oh what a jest. Oh how tickled I am.

Except when the tickle crushes your heart. Except when it leaves you with tears stinging your eyes and the shock of being taken for a fool. Once again. Not everyone who comes into the coffee shop has pure intentions. Not everyone plays fair.

Two tables away from me are a couple of jokers. Not the laugh a minute kind. Not the smile a mile wide kind. These are The Nasty Boys. Nasty minds with shriveled up hearts. Squeezing sniggers out of the misadventures of others. I overhear them boast about their latest nasty deed.

See her over there, says Bobby Nasty. A small weasel in a bust-up leather jacket. Who? says Frankie Nasty, a misshapen runt with buck teeth and greasy hair. The one by the window who keeps looking around like she's expecting someone, says Bobby Nasty. I know her sister, he says. I got her phone number, he says. I called her up and asked her out here for a coffee, he says. Like on a blind date, he says. Never been on a date before, he says. This is April Fools Day. She's gonna wait and wait for someone who's never gonna come, he says. Best April Fools joke ever, he says, and they both laugh.

I want to stand up. Walk over to their table. Smile politely. And show them what real nasty violence is. What it feels like. Up front. Repeatedly. But I get sidetracked. From behind the bar, Little Italy catches my eye, shakes her head slowly from side to side. Puts a finger to her lips. And nods in the direction of the window.

I follow the nod and see the victim of The Nasty Boys. The Girl With The Lonely Eyes. Sitting stiff and upright. Beginning to wonder. Beginning to worry. He should have been here by now. Beginning to put two and two together and realising the name of the day and the name of the game. The anger in her eyes. Why was she such a fool as to think that anyone could be interested. Why does she do this to herself. Stupid. So stupid.

She looks around and sees The Nasty Boys staring at her. Hears the words loud and clear, over and over in her head. April Fool. April Fool. April Fool. Then she senses a presence. Hears a voice. Looks up. Sees a stranger. Standing in front of her table, looking down and smiling. Tall Dark And Handsome Guy. Plenty of girlfriends. Never been in love. Ever.

Jet black hair. Deep blue eyes. Close cut beard. Dark jacket. Faded Jeans. Cowboy Boots. Excuse me, he says. Is this seat taken, he says. She blushes. Feels the heat rise. Stammers an answer. No, she says. Feel free, she says.

Next to me, The Cruel Twins' jaws hit the tabletop. Over behind the bar, Little Italy winks at the box on the wall. The box is a sucker for a large slice of justice. So it pulls number 23 from the basement and slides it onto the turntable.

The curtain opens. The Monkees are on stage. Micky Dolenz on drums and lead vocals. Nobody else has a voice like that. I'm A Believer.

Tall Dark And Handsome Guy slings his jacket over the back of his chair. Smiles at The Girl With The Lonely Eyes. Points at the bar. She nods a yes. Little Italy stands in front of The Nasty Boys. Points at the door. They get the message.

It might be April First, but she ain't joking.

Be cool...

Father, Son and Holy Ghost

Good afternoon Friday. Sometimes things happen purely by chance. Other times you get the distinct impression there's a man, or a woman, with a plan guiding the proceedings. The Big Kahuna. The Head Honcho.

Today the day is good but the weather's bad. It's Easter and it drizzles religiously and blesses the concrete. Tears from Heaven. I move fast forward to the coffee shop. Head down. Umbrella up. Muddle through the puddles. Turn the corner. Walk through the door.

I see The Priest with the Black Leather Book sitting at the first table on the right. He's late forties with a touch of early fifties. Young enough to remember the birds. Old enough to steer clear of the bees.

He's wearing the uniform. Black on black. Under black. Over black. With a white slash on the throat. Dog collar? Or God collar? Heaven knows and it's not giving up the skinny without a fight.

Little Italy nods as I pass her. She's laying a cappuccino on The Priest's table. It has a white cover. Looks like an altar. He has a slice of carrot cake next to the coffee.

My mind concocts a metaphor. I dismiss it in a flash. Too risky. Shove up a don't go there sign and walk on to the counter.

Big Red winks. Long time no see, she says. Yeah, like yesterday, I say. We laugh. Let me guess…it's Friday…that would be a green tea, she says. Fat chance, I say. It's Good Friday, I say. That would be a triple espresso. Father, Son and Holy Ghost, I say.

She looks at the priest. You sound like you used to be one of The Boys in Black, she says. Thought about it briefly, I say. For about a second and a half, I say. What changed your mind, she says. Give you one guess, I say. I wink.

She laughs. Turns. Reaches for the handle on the stainless steel machine behind her.

Works her magic and comes back with a small white chunky cup. Full to the brim of dark liquid. I slip her some silver and retreat to a favourite spot. Against the wall. Full 180 degree vision of the room. Eyes front and centre and peripheral left and right.

Little Italy walks slowly back behind the counter. Queen of the Baristas. Blessed with a movement in the hips that would turn any saint into a sinner, and make the confessional the busiest place in the church.

The door opens and a soft breath of a wind heralds the arrival of The Waif. Almost insubstantial. Light coloured full length coat…neck to boots. Eyes taking in everything at a glance. Stopping at The Priest. Moving swiftly on.

Stopping at Little Italy. Moving swiftly on. Stopping at a vague shape in the corner next to the stairs leading up to the balcony. A table for two. Lattes for two. Set up ready and waiting. The Waif looks and lingers. Smiles a couple of heartbeats. Looks back at Little Italy who nods. Just once. Ever so slowly.

The Waif moves over to the corner. The shape moves off his chair. Stands up. No more waiting. No more searching. All she wants is someone to love. Someone to stand by her through thick and thin. Maybe this is the one.

The Priest looks at his book. Little Italy looks at the box on the wall. Doesn't need to put in a request. It's already on the way up and onto the turntable. An old favourite. Number 30.

The curtains part. Ben E. King stands on stage behind the mike. Begins to sing Stand By Me. All the talking stops. All the noise dies down.

Little Italy smiles inside. Sometimes things happen purely by chance. Other times, chance takes a back seat and The Big Kahuna steps up to the plate.

Be cool…

The Scribbler is waiting for his Muse

Good morning Tuesday. We all like to think we're in control. We feel safer when we know that we've got one hand on the wheel, and the other on the stick. Foot on the gas. Eyes on the road. We're in the driving seat and we go where we want. When we want. It feels good. Feels natural. Feels right. And guess what…it's a hundred percent wrong.

Destiny doesn't like to be told what to do. She doesn't like it when her well-laid plans are nudged sideways. She gets pissed off when she's told to go left when she wants to go right. So she rolls her own dice. And they always come up facing the way she wants. Every damned time.

The Scribbler is in the coffee shop today. Waiting for The Muse. Waiting for the one who inspires him. Shows him where to put the ink on the page. The type on the screen. Tells him which words to use. Where they go. How they sound when they're spoken out loud.

The Scribbler sits at a table against the wall. Sipping dark coffee. Looking at a blank screen. Willing The Muse to put in an appearance. Knowing that nothing he does will hurry up the process. She'll arrive when she feels like it. When the time is right.

Then the words will form in The Scribbler's brain. Travel down his arms. Along his fingers, to the keys of his laptop. That's when magic happens. But until then he waits. Stares at the blank screen. Tick tock. Tick tock.

The Scribbler loves words. Adores sentences. Hates waiting. Little Italy loves sounds. The sound of intimate conversation. The sound of early morning laughter. The sound of the hiss and gurgle of the stainless steel giant behind her. The sound of life.

She knows that she's not in control of it all. She knows that it has a heartbeat all of its own. But every now and then, Destiny and Little Italy follow the same path.

Listen to the same music. Have the same goal. And every now and then, Destiny lets her take hold of the steering wheel. Just like now.

Standing in front of her is The Girl With The Butterfly Tattoos. The girl with the ache so far inside you'd get lost just trying to find it. Where's the squeeze, says Little Italy. All squeezed out, says The Girl. All tired out and used up and pissed off and over, she says.

You forgot the cardinal rule, says Little Italy. The one undeniable, irrefutable, uncontestable law of the jungle, she says. Destiny is a river, she says. It goes where it wants, she says. You can step in and go with the flow. Or sit on the bank and watch it flow by.

The Girl With The Butterfly Tattoos bows her head. I know, she says. I screwed up, she says. Another one bites the dust, she says. She looks up.

Little Italy is smiling. Sometimes goodbyes take a hike just to make way for the next hello, she says. Take your cappuccino…go sit down, she says. And she looks at the box on the wall.

From deep inside, the box pulls up a well-used number 103. Slips it on the turntable.

The door opens. Dark hair. Dark glasses. Handsome in a rugged kinda way. Hard in a soft kinda way. A new squeeze looking for his next hello. Or maybe his last one.

The curtains part. Spotlight burst into action. A man stands at the mike. Guitar strapped on. Dark hair. Dark glasses. Dark suit. Voice to die for. Roy Orbison begins to sing. Only the lonely.

The Girl With The Butterfly Tattoos looks up. Sees Dark Hair. Sighs. Breathes deep. Destiny calls.

Be cool…

Bent out of shape, bent out of time

Good morning Wednesday. I can remember when Spring used to mean something special. Something fresh, and green, and full of the joys of new life.

It's a beautiful morning as I walk through the square to the coffee shop. There are folk all around who aren't wearing fewer clothes and more smiles. No more collar-up Winter coats and scarves and padded jackets and hats with earflaps. The warmth is starting to seep back into the world. Or at least my tiny part of it.

But I can remember when I used to remember so much more. The smell of the seasons. The sound of friendship. The faces of those friends whose names tripped off the tip of my tongue. All those things that happened. Those bits and pieces of good times and bad times that stick like flies on gluepaper inside my head.

But not so much anymore. Not like The Woman Who Never Forgets. She hasn't been here for a while. At least not at the same time as yours truly. But she's here now. Standing in line. Conversing with the universe. Drawing symbols in the space in front of her face. Writing in the air with a right index finger that never stopped moving. She's the witness to all that happens.

The whole spectrum of events in her life is there, like her own, personal book of life. Opened up. There for her to read. The full pages of her past. The blank pages of her future.

She shuffles forward. Looks up. Orders a strong, sweet espresso from Little Italy and puts silver on the counter. Exact amount. No change there then. Little Italy asks. You alright Alice? The Woman Who Never Forgets smiles vaguely then disappears into the world running on a loop inside her head.

She turns, looking for the table she had yesterday. Over by the window. Remembering the position of the chair. The way the sunlight hit the table. The spilled sugar from a previous caffeineratti. The mess they left.

Little Italy nudges Angel. Standing beside her.

255

Waiting for his orders. Muscles at the ready.

Little Italy looks at him. Nods at the table mess. Turns to The Woman Who Never Forgets. Don't worry Alice, she says. Angel here will wipe your table, she says. Make it nice and clean and fresh, she says.

The Woman Who Never Forgets loves nice and clean and fresh. So she smiles and nods. Then follows on behind Angel carrying her liquid peace and quiet. Waits while he does his thing with the cloth and the clear-away tray. Then puts her small, white cup on the clean surface. Sits down. Adjusts the chair legs to the position they were on the floor yesterday. And the day before. And the day before that.

She takes a crumpled paper tissue from her pale brown jacket. Dabs a little round her nostrils. Breathes in the aroma from the dark liquid. Sees The Man Who Can Never Remember sitting four tables away. Bent out of shape. Bent out of time. Bent out of every damned emotion from A to Z. Memory Card hung round his neck. Full of numbers. Number 25 says ask the nice lady for a cappuccino. Number 28 says smile at Alice.

Behind the bar, Little Italy sees the scene playing out. Something inside aches. She looks at the box on the wall. The box is never slow to react. From deep inside number 80 rises to the surface. Slides onto the turntable. An old favourite...from an old favourite.

The curtains open. The stage is dark. A light flares. Standing alone at the microphone is little Etta James. Blonde hair. Black eyebrows. Skin the colour of light coffee. Lips the colour of blood. Voice that moves mountains.

At last. For a few precious minutes, The Man Who Can Never Remember...does.

Be cool...

The Girl Who Doesn't Exist

Good morning Thursday. Today is a day of two stories. A game of two halves. On the left side, we have one of The Invisibles. Anonymous. Inconspicuous. Imperceptible. Fading into the background. Becoming part of the furniture.

And on the right side, we have one of The Perceptibles. Apparent. Obvious. Crystal Clear. Standing out like a single cloud in an expanse of blue sky. Somehow you just can't take your eyes off it. So you watch it drift. Fascinated by its shape. Its speed. It's ability to capture your attention. Little realizing that elsewhere in that high ceiling there are other clouds. Tucked away in corners. Visible only if you look closely. Only if you take notice. Only if you give them the time of day.

There's an Invisible in the coffee shop this morning. Tucked away in the farthest corner. Hugging the shadows. Merging with the walls. The Girl Who Doesn't Exist sips her skinny latte slowly and deliberately. Trying desperately not to draw attention.

Little Italy knows her. Knows her craving to avoid prying eyes. Knows the reasons for her head-down posture. Knows the violence that it used to incur at home if she raised her eyes and dared to look. So she has a special place for her. A safe place. Far from the madding crowd. Far from interruption or threat of conversation. And there she sits. Alone. Unbruised.

And then her polar opposite breezes in through the open door fifteen feet away. A Perceptible. Full of noise and colour. Impossible to miss. Impossible to ignore. The Guy Who Moves To The Grove puts in an appearance. Limbs and hips in sync. Fingers clicking. Dark skin. Light feet. Dreads on the head. Eyes on the move. Smiling. Everything moving in rhythm. Ear buds in. Music on. Dancing as he walks. Mouthing the words to the song bouncing around in his head. Full of the joys of life.

Little Italy sees him and smiles. He's infectious. Bodacious. Flirtatious.

He's a fan of the strong stuff. Quadruple espresso. Rocket fuel. Baamalam!! Everyone sees him. He sees them. Then he sees The Girl Who Doesn't Exist.

He looks at Little Italy. Looks at The Girl Who Doesn't Exist. Turns back. What's her deal, he says. What's the cloak of invisibility for, he says. Leave it alone, says Little Italy. Let her be, she says. This is her sanctuary time. Her safe zone. Her escape pod. That's the deal, she says.

The Guy Who Moves To The Grove stops mid-dance. Takes off his ear buds. Unclips his iPod. Walks to where The Girl Who Doesn't Exist is sitting. Puts the iPod and buds on the table in front of her. Walks away. No talk. No explanation. Just in and out of the zone and back to Little Italy.

He picks up his quadruple espresso. Slips over some silver. Moves to a table against the far wall. Switches to the music already in his head. The Girl Who Doesn't Exist looks at the buds. Picks them up. Puts them in.

Little Italy looks at the box on the wall. The box makes a move of its own. Down to the basement. Up with number 47.

The curtains open. The needle falls. And Bobby McFerrin is on the stage. Infectious smile. Grey-streaked dreadlocks. Perfect pitch. Don't Worry, Be Happy.

The Girl Who Doesn't Exist switches on the iPod. Listens. Sits back. Breathes in slowly. Out slowly. And smiles.

Be cool...

Macho Man makes The Mask smile

Good afternoon Friday. The Mask is in the coffee shop today. Like the rest of us, she has about forty three facial muscles, give or take.

Unlike the rest of us, they don't give a damn whether she's happy or sad. Curious or mad. Elated or depressed. They don't twitch. Don't stretch. Don't bend, flex, relax or contract.

It's as if years ago she looked in the mirror, saw a facial expression she really liked, one that captured her essence, and decided to keep it. And so it stayed. Frozen in space and time. Devoid of all movement. And underneath her skin, the muscles hardened. The nerves went to sleep. The outward sign of any personality became unnecessary. She evolved into The Mask.

And here she sits. Over by the window. Wearing the same generic expression she always wears. Blanking out the rest of the world. Except the rest of the world doesn't know what's going on under the surface. Behind the scenes. Between the ears. Under the ribcage. It doesn't know who The Mask used to be.

But Little Italy does. She remembers the vibrant, bubbly, 240-volt electric personality. Remembers the laughter and the non-stop chatter. The colourful outfits and the slinky walk. Some things you never forget.

So she makes a mental note. Enough is enough. Today's the day. Then turns to the next customer at the head of the queue. Macho Man. Tall, dark eyed, great hair, and with the kind of drop-dead gorgeous looks a girl would slit throats to wake up next to. Until he speaks. Then all bets are off.

Little Italy sees The Mask look over. Watch. Skinny Latte to go, sweetie, says Macho Man, softly. Sure honey, says Little Italy. I'll even throw in a fresh-baked pastry for free, if you do me a favour, she says. Consider it a done deal, says Macho Man.

So Little Italy leans over and whispers in his ear. A conversation of a highly personal and confidential nature. Short, sweet and to the point. A ticking timebomb wrapped up in a single sentence. Ending in a playful tap to the cheek. A wink and a nod.

Macho Man smiles. Little Italy looks at the box on the wall and the box flicks a switch. Number 133 moves up fast and slides onto the turntable.

The curtains open. On the stage…Frankie Valli and The Four Seasons. Macho Man grabs his skinny latte and begins his best John Wayne walk to the door. Hips swaying. The Mask looks on. Frankie begins to sing Walk Like A Man.

Macho Man reaches the door, turns to the left, looks at The Mask. Pouts. Kisses the air. Wiggles his buns. Well good luck, pilgrim, he says. Falsetto voice. Then exits stage left. The Mask blinks fast. Mouth opens. Jaw drops.

Then BOOM…from nowhere, a smile the width of Niagara Falls erupts across her face. Muscles and nerves remember. Vocal cords explode. And laughter erupts using all forty three facial muscles. Give or take.

Little Italy smiles. Job done.

Be cool…

The Poet needs a Plan B

Good morning Tuesday. Everyone needs a Plan B. A back-up you keep up your sleeve. Ready and waiting for when Plan A doesn't work out. Or runs out of steam. Or simply reaches the end of the line.

The Poet is in the coffee shop this morning. Seventysomething. Bright white hair a la Spencer Tracy. Circular specs a la John Lennon. White moustache and pointed chin beard. Large, piercing blue eyes. Old on the outside. Young on the inside.

He sits where he can notice everyone without everyone noticing him. In a faraway corner close to a large portrait of a small dog sitting by a young 18th century man leaning on a round table.

The Poet wears a dark open neck shirt under dark lightweight jacket. His white, wiry chest hairs creep up to meet a prominent Adam's Apple. Orange glass rosary beads wind twice around his neck. Tall Americano on steroids sits on the table in front of him. Not too bitter. Not too sweet. Ready to gulp.

He holds an old fountain pen in his right hand. Writing words in the air before he writes them on the open page of a well-thumbed notebook. Even from three tables away I can see the book is nearly full.

He used to have a Plan A. He used to have a wife. And children. He used to have happiness. And satisfaction. That was his life before. Now this is his life after. After Plan A crashed and burned. Now he has Plan B. Now he writes poems about them. About their life together. Beautiful, lyrical, tortured poems. Poems with laughter and tears. Poems that rip the heart and pummel the emotions. Poems that fill volumes. Fill shelves. In a home that's empty of touch and packed full of memories.

Occasionally he writes poems about the coffee shop. Gives them to Little Italy. A poem for a coffee. Fair exchange. No robbery.

I see him write on the page this morning, then tear it out.

The last words on the final leaf of paper. He looks at the words. Reads them slowly. Nods in satisfaction. Stands up. Takes them to Little Italy and hands them over. She has another Americano waiting in payment. He takes it, nods and smiles. She reads. The poem is about a wish to spend one more minute, just sixty seconds, in the company of his wife again. Its title is The Longing.

The Poet walks slowly back to his table. Back to his memories. Little Italy looks at the box on the wall. The box has an old favourite up its sleeve. Number 59.

The curtains open. The Stones are centre stage. Up front is Mick with his lips and hips. Beside and behind are the boys. Thousand year old Keef...ultra cool Charlie...and artist Ronnie.

Little Italy opens a drawer behind the coffee bar and removes a fresh, new notebook. Takes it to The Poet. Lays it gently on the table and walks away without saying a word, as Mick sings You Can't Always Get What You Want.

The Poet smiles. Opens the book and begins to compose another memory. Blank page. Black ink. Ready when you are.

Be cool...

When a man loves a woman...in 3 acts

Good morning Thursday. I used to believe in coincidences. The accidental marriage of random events. The coming together of unrelated happenings. No grand design. Just blind damned luck. That was then. This is now.

I sit in the coffee shop. Listening to a little piano magic. The box on the wall is taking a coffee break and Wolfgang Amadeus is filling in. Guest spot. Unplugged. Something A to G. Something major or minor. Something concerto not sonata. A bit of hard rock star stuff from the seventeen hundreds. Volume low. Peace and quiet high.

Americano grande with a slice of carrot cake sit on the table. I wait for the green light. Wait for the ready steady go. Wait until the pulse slows down a notch. Meanwhile, all around, life makes its sneaky little connections. Sight unseen. There's no such thing as unscripted chaos in this corner of the universe. There's just order of a different kind. All part of the master plan where nothing is off the cuff and everything happens for a reason.

Act One: the door opens and The Kid From Nowhere steps in. Been nowhere. Going nowhere. Scruffy cowboy boots. Torn jeans. Grateful Dead Tee. Hair the colour of old straw. One eye brown. The other one blue. Strolls up to Little Italy and flashes a bent smile and a full set of pearly whites. The lady is not impressed.

You know the answer, she says. Every time, she says. I never asked the question yet, he says. She raises an eyebrow. No need, she says. She's not been here in a year. Grab a coffee, grab a chair and reflect on the universe, she says. Expect the unexpected, she says. The Kid From Nowhere nods, wraps his fingers round a double espresso and retires to a spot against the far wall.

Act Two: an hour and three doubles later the door opens and The Girl With The Two-Tone Hair wafts in. Just like it was yesterday and she needed a cup of the best drink on the whole damned planet.

Only that was last year. Now it's this year. But Little Italy never forgets a face. Or a coffee. Usual, she says. The Girl With The Two-Tone Hair throws her a nod and smiles. Been a while, she says. You don't forget anything, she says.

Act Three: over against the far wall The Kid From Nowhere hears the blast from the past. Now everything clicks into place. He had a feeling when he woke up. The kind of feeling you get when all the pieces are coming together. The kind of feeling you get when the penny drops and the voice repeats over and over…there's no such thing as coincidence…there's no such thing as coincidence.

The Girl With The Two-Tone Hair looks at him. Remembers. Smiles. Walks over and sits down at the table right next door. The Kid From Nowhere listens to the voice. There's no such thing as coincidence. But there is such a thing as second chance. He turns. Smiles. And so it begins.

Behind the bar Little Italy looks at the box on the wall. Break over. The box knows the power of music. Nothing happens by accident. There's no such thing as coincidence. Without even asking, number 38 is already on the turntable.

The curtains open. Percy Sledge is on the stage singing When A Man Loves A Woman. When the man in the attic made this voice, he broke the mould so nobody else could sound so damned good.

Be cool…

Green is the new red

Good morning Monday. A long time ago I knew a kid with epilepsy. He used to wear knee and elbow pads and a crash helmet all the time. He used to have ten or twenty seizures a day.

He'd fall down, stiffen up, and do the full-body shake thing. Black out. Then come to. Get up. Dust himself off. Smile. Carry on playing. Act like nothing happened. Get the Hell on with life. Did he care? I doubt it. Not if the light I saw in his eyes was anything to go by. Some things you can fix. Other things just stay broke. Life goes on.

The Girl In The Green Beret is in the coffee shop this morning. Green is the new red. Just like red was the new black before that. She wears the beret slanting left on her head. She wears her heart on her right sleeve. It's exposed to the elements. Weather-worn. Bruised. Bust up and sore. She's always falling in love. Then falling out of it. She crashes and burns every few months. A new squeeze. A new tease.

Every time she sees a good-looking guy with a tight ass. Every time she sees tall dark and handsome. Or even two out of the three. Sometimes even one. She falls for them every time. Stiffens up. Does the full heart shake thing. Blacks out. Comes to. Gets up. Dusts herself off. Smiles. Carries on living. Carries on loving. Acts like nothing has happened. Gets the hell on with life.

Does she care? Sure. Every damned second. The only thing that helps with the pain is the medicine provided by Little Italy. A large cup of dark roasted TLC. Tender Loving Coffee. Bitter sweet. Sniff first. Sip second. Gulp third. Refill fourth.

Right now she's sitting by the window. Looking out for the next big thing. Maximum vantage point for those coming in. Those going out. Those passing by on the way to God knows where.

Over behind the bar, Little Italy has learned to recognize the signs when Cupid's poison arrow hits home and The Girl In The Green Beret is on the receiving end.

The slight jaw drop. The unblinking stare. The small blush in the cheeks. The mid-air freeze of the coffee cup's journey from the table to the mouth. The tip of the tongue's lick of the lips. The way the head slowly turns like a guided missile to track the potential love interest. Whether he's interested in her or not.

But for now The Girl In The Green Beret is safe. No new squeeze. No arrow notched on the bow. So…time to move on to the next in line. The queue shuffles up. A pair of tanned faces smile and place an order. The Skinny Blondes order two skinny lattes to go. They're doing the walk, talk and sip routine. Buff boys and well-defined muscles are the topics of loud conversation. Wishful thinking is thirsty work.

The Girl In The Green Beret sits alone. Looking…looking. Start it first. Finish it first. Have some fun. Avoid the pain. Get out fast. Unless…unless.

Behind the bar, Little Italy looks up at the box on the wall. Lesson One. You can't put a weight on hurt. Lesson Two. You can't put a time on regret. Lesson Three. You can't feel love at the flick of a switch. The box knows all this and acts accordingly. From deep inside number 55 drifts up and settles on the turntable.

The curtains open. There's a lone microphone on the stage. Standing behind it is Johnny Cash. Unmistakable. Irreplaceable. Legendary voice. Legendary Hurt.

The Girl In The Green Beret breathes deep. Falling down is easy. Getting up gets harder every damned time.

Be cool…

Have I told you lately that I love you

Good morning Tuesday. I remember a time, not so long ago, when you could go into a cafe…ask for a coffee…and that's exactly what you got. A coffee. Black or white.

No extras. No complications. No multiple choices. Just early morning rocket fuel. Liquid ignition. Fresh roast Arabica, boiling water and the best damned taste on the planet. Plain and simple. Like a bust-up red guitar, three well-used chords and the truth. No damned lies.

Now, you got a whole damned orchestra of tastes. You got options up the wazoo. Served up by your own smiling barista. But no matter what they do to it. No matter how much they dress it up with fancy names. Fancy prices. Fancy tastes. Underneath it all, it's still good old coffee. Good old Joe. Still the original sipping breakfast.

It can run…but it can't hide. Just like The Biker Chick. Leathers and zips. Top to toe. Suzi Quatro hairdo. Five feet nothing of bite-yer-head-off-toughness. Emblem on the jacket back. Snarling tiger. Do not approach. Do not chat up. Do not even look twice.

Satchel strap sits across her ample personalities. Inside the satchel sits her life in a laptop. Everyone she knows. Everywhere she's been. Every poem she's ever written. Secret words. Not for public consumption. No cats let out of any bags. No glimpses at a secret life. Carried everywhere she goes. Away from prying eyes.

Except the eyes of the one person who has seen her without her onion layers on. The person who knows that the outside doesn't match the inside.

The person who knows the red guitar, three chords and the truth. Little Italy. Standing in front of her. Behind the counter. Waiting for the word. Waiting for the sign.

The Biker Chick unzips her front and takes out a black leather wallet. Opens it up. Billfold on the right. Faded photo on the left.

A quick glance at the photo. A girl in faded jeans and a white tee. A girl with long blonde hair and a short button nose. Looking into the lens. Eyes full of innocence. Future full of promise.

The Biker Chick can feel her. Deep inside. Somewhere. She flips her eyes to the right. Takes out the billfold. Peels off a ten. Hands it to Little Italy. Doesn't say a word. Just smiles. Little Italy doesn't say a word. Just smiles. Turns and faces the stainless steel machine. Pulls a handle. Introduces a large Americano to the world. Black. Strong. The kind of coffee a girl with faded jeans and a white tee might like.

The Biker Chick takes the tall mug, takes her change, turns and walks to a spare chair by the window. Toughness can stay outside. For the next half an hour she can be who she used to be.

Little Italy watches her walk. The leather pants turn into faded jeans. The leather jacket turns into a white tee. The brown hair turns into blonde. The Biker Chick sits, relaxes and looks out at the world. The tiger goes to sleep. Little Italy stands, relaxes and looks up at the box on the wall. The box gets the nod and pulls up number 32 from way below.

The disc slips onto the turntable.

The curtains open. A single spotlight brightens up the stage. Cue Mr. Morrison. Van the Man. Cue the voice. Have I told you lately.

Today's Biker Chick looks at yesterday's Blonde in Faded Jeans. Sometimes you have to learn to love yourself before you can love anyone else.

Be cool…

The Man In Black writes something in the air

Good morning Wednesday. If I didn't know any better I'd swear I was in a warm country. Maybe somewhere Mediterranean. Possibly with a few palm trees here and there. Accompanied by a strong desire to wear only one layer of clothes.

Sadly, here in a not-so-warm country, we take what we can get. And we're very grateful for any sunshine that happens to come our way. Whether it's the indirect result of planetary warming or not.

I sit against the wall in the coffee shop, looking out a fresh but sunny morning. Bright skies. Bright faces. Sunglass sales go up. Umbrella sales go down. Here inside, the aircon goes on and the jacket comes off.

There's a sea of empty tables in front of me. Except one. The Man In Black. Not Mr. Cash. This is a different Mister. A mysterious Mister. A Mister with gipsy blood in his veins and a spooky knack of knowing stuff he shouldn't know. He's Lola's friend. The Lola with four legs and a talkative personality. Not the Lola who walks like a woman and talks like a man.

The Man In Black always sits by the window. Always speaks with his hands. Makes signs in the air although he can make sounds with his vocal cords. Little Italy knows him from way back. Back in the day. The good old day when every now and then, somebody would come along who had that look in their eyes. Like the look in the eyes of The Man In Black now. The look that's following The Secretary as she walks in the door.

The Man In Black points at her and writes something in the air with the index finger of his left hand. I try to figure out the word he writes but he's too fast. Too sneaky. Too clever. He stops writing and takes a sip of his green tea. The bitter freshness cuts through the clag clinging to the back of his throat.

The Secretary stops in her tracks as if she's just thought of something. As if a new thought had just barged its way into her head.

She smiles inside, then carries on walking to the bar. There's no queue. Just her and Big Red. The Secretary nods. Where's the boss, she says. Big Red nods towards the office. Family business, she says. On the phone, she says. Big Red winks.

A confidence shared. A small secret revealed. A large secret kept safely tucked up and out of sight.

What's it to be, she says. The secretary looks up at the list on the board. She was going to order a skinny latte, like always. Extra ounces…extra pounds. But not this morning. Not today. Today a voice in her head says something else. Words she hasn't used in a long time. Maybe months. Maybe a year.

A pot of green tea, she says. And two slices of carrot cake. Big Red raises an eyebrow. Two slices, she asks. Two, says The Secretary. Separate plates, she says.

Big Red nods. Turns to the stainless steel machine behind her and fills the teapot sitting under a waiting spout. Pops in a bag of the green stuff. Puts it on a tray with the double carrot cake order. You hungry, she says. The Secretary smiles. I always listen to the voices in my head, she says. One of them just put in a request, she says. Who knows, she says, and smiles.

She turns, walks over to The Man In Black by the window. Stops. You hungry, she says. You asking, he says. I'm asking, she says. I'm hungry, he says. She slips him a slice and sits down at the next table. Personal space is a thing of beauty, she thinks.

Just then, Little Italy comes out of the office and looks at the box on the wall as she walks to the bar. The box gets the message and brings up number 115 to sit on the turntable.

The curtains open. The Doors are on stage. Frontman…Jim Morrison. Mister Beautiful. Open necked frilly shirt. Black tight pants. Nothing left to the imagination. Those eyes…that mouth. Both hands grab the mike.

The Man In Black smiles. Thinks. Come on baby, light my fire.

Be cool…

The Dreamer and The Mouse

Good morning Thursday. I once knew a bricklayer who downed tools, picked up a pen, and became a damned fine advertising copywriter. I even heard about an engineer who retired his socket sets and created one helluva new career out of sculpting clay.

That's the thing about dreams. It doesn't matter how long it takes you to get to where you want to be. It doesn't matter how many hats you have to wear before you find the one that fits you best. It doesn't matter who or what you were before you took the plunge. And it doesn't matter how many times you get to tell the rest of the world to go to Hell because this dream's yours mister, or sister, and you're gonna go right ahead and live the damned thing whether they like it or not.

You don't need their permission. You don't need their opinion. And you sure as hell don't need their approval. You just need yours. Plain and simple. To paraphrase Jake and Ellwood; they're not gonna catch you…you're on a mission from God.

The Dreamer is in the coffee shop this morning. He's sitting with a cappuccino that hasn't seen warmth for five or six minutes. He's got that thousand yard stare. The one that all the nineteen year old grunts coming back from patrol in the leech-infested paddy fields in the Tan An Delta in Vietnam had. Live today. Die tomorrow. Except he's nineteen going on thirty.

He's got a bead of sweat running down the right side of his face. And a thick beard that can't make up its mind whether it's full of cool or just plain full of hair. He writes coursework in a local college. He wants to write books in an old vicarage. He used to be shellshocked. Part of him still is.

Little Italy has a soft spot for the shellshocked folk of the world. She treats them extra gentle. Especially the ones who never stop dreaming.

The Dreamer comes here not just for cappuccino and TLC. He comes here so he can see The Mouse. Small and nervous. Always looking. Always twitching. Sharp face. Sharp eyes. Sharp mind.

The Mouse dreams too. She dreams that one day, somehow, she'll wake up with someone who loves her for the person she wishes she was. Beautiful. Relaxed and confident. Someone with style and poise. Not small but not tall. Just right. Just perfect. So there they sit. Ten feet apart. The Dreamer and The Mouse. Each holding the key to the other's dream. The Mouse works in a literary agency.

The Dreamer doesn't give a damn about conventional beauty. He just wants someone to love. Someone who will, in turn, love him. Someone whose beauty lies in the inside more than on the outside. So he watches The Mouse. And he tries to pick up the courage to climb the wall that lies between them. But all he picks up is another cappuccino.

Over behind the bar, Little Italy picks up all the signs that tell of another morning devoid of one small step for The Dreamer...one giant leap for romance. She looks at the box on the wall. The box picks up the nod and digs deep into the vault for number 137. Perfect choice.

The curtains open. The spotlight shines on a four-piece on the stage. The Mamas & the Papas. Harmonies to die for. Mama Cass to listen to. Dream a little dream of me.

The Mouse looks up and sees The Dreamer looking at her. Stops shivering. Calms down. Manages the beginnings of a smile. Small heart becomes big heart.

Little Italy looks on from fifteen feet away. Every dream needs a nudge in the right direction.

Be cool...

The Gimp and The Girl With The Scar On Her Cheek

Good morning Friday. Some things stick with you for life. Like glue. Welded to the soul. Other things get lost and forgotten in the mist five minutes after they fall off your radar. That's just the way it is.

Perfection held no interest for The Gimp. He saw it as boring as hell. Empty of interest. Devoid of fascination. He didn't feel at home in that world. He felt alien. Unsubscribed to their view of life. He travelled through his own world with a left-sided limp.

His view was coloured by the balance he saw in the unbalanced folk around him. He had no time for the physically unblemished. The emotionally stable. The ones who were fit as a butcher's dog and didn't have to cough up the lining of their gut first thing every morning.

His was a world of cracks and imperfections. Mistakes of nature and things that didn't quite add up. His was a rawness and a soreness and an existence that was the result of a simple twist of fate. Or two. One leg normal. The other one short. Spine that wouldn't know straight if it bit him on the arse.

And he loved every second of it. All the pain. All the abnormality. All the struggle to stand up after lying down all night immobile. He hated them. He loved them. They belonged to him. He owned them. They never owned him. Bring it on.

The Gimp is in the coffee shop this morning. He's standing in front of Little Italy about ten degrees off the perpendicular. Leaning on his dragon's head cane. Fire coursing down the shaft. She looks over the bar and down. Love the cane, she says. He nods. Does it bite, she says. He smiles. Big and wide. Naaah, he says. I got her trained well, he says. She only bites folk who piss her off, he says. Little Italy raises an eyebrow. Without waiting for the order, she turns and reaches for a chipped mug on the shelf. Beautifully flawed. Set aside specially for times like this. Times when The Gimp comes to visit.

Little Italy fills the mug with strong, bitter coffee. Accepts his silver. Nods to a space behind him. She's here already, she says. The Gimp turns and there in the corner is The Girl With The Scar On Her Cheek. A long, livid red line stretching from under her left eye, down her cheek and nicking the left side of her mouth. She used to hide it so the world didn't see. Couldn't judge.

Then she met The Gimp. And now she doesn't give a damn what the world thinks. Now her imperfection is a beautiful thing to behold.

The Gimp goes over and sits down. Not opposite her. Beside her. Behind the bar, Little Italy feels a smile change the landscape of her face. She looks at the box on the wall and notices it's tilted. Ever so slightly off the perpendicular. There's a scratch on the wall that used to be hidden. Now it's revealed. The box doesn't mind. For the moment it feels right. From deep inside, number 62 rises up and slides imperfectly onto the turntable.

The curtains open. The stage is dark. The floodlights come on. So do Fleetwood Mac. Buckingham, Fleetwood, the McVies and Nicks. Magic follows on behind. The only way is forward. Never Going Back Again.

Little Italy smiles. The Gimp looks into the eyes of The Girl With The Scar On Her Cheek. The rumour is true. Some things you just can't hide.

Be cool…

The Priest and The Hooker

Good afternoon Monday. The sun has got his hat on. Hip hip hip hooray. He's sat in the middle of Mister Blue Skies. Ain't no disruption here. Ain't no interruption to a sweaty AM or PM. Except maybe for the lack of heat.

This is no shirt-sleeved tropic of Torremolinos. No bare-chested attempt to turn milky white skin a nicer shade of brown. Today is Brisk Day. Cool Day. Gimme another layer of clothing Day. See...the trouble with eyes is they only tell half the story. Sometimes not even that. You might have twenty-twenty vision, but those damned peepers don't give you the full picture.

The Priest is in the coffee shop. At least he looks like a priest. And he sounds like a priest. And he acts like a priest. So he must be a priest. Right? Wrong. Depends on your definition. Just because somebody carries a bible doesn't mean he knows how to pray. Just because he wears a dog collar doesn't mean he wears a God collar. Just because he talks the talk...doesn't mean he walks the walk. What you see isn't what you always get. Sometimes it's a whole lot more. Sometimes it surprises the hell out of you.

The Priest is in his pulpit. On the balcony. Overlooking his flock. Sitting at a table with a triple espresso in front of him. The cup halfway to empty. Waiting for the first confession of the day. Below, the door opens and Little Italy turns her head. She knows the sound of that walk. The noise the stilettoes make on the tiled floor. The Lady moves like a catwalk model. All eyes are on her as she shortens the space from the entrance to the bar.

Walking doesn't even begin to describe the action. The air parts in front of her. The stilettoes click in rhythm. She stops in front of Little Italy and takes a breath. Looks unblinking into Little Italy's eyes. The two smile. Mutual respect. I see you brought Mister Blue Skies with you, said Little Italy. The Lady blinks. Slowly. Dark brown eyes disappear for a second. Reappear between impossibly long lashes.

Little Italy nods in the direction of the balcony. Your first customer of the day is here, she says. At least that's what other folk might think, she says. She slides a double espresso towards The Lady and raises an eyebrow as The Lady slips her some silver. Now you know the rule, says Little Italy.

The Lady smiles and withdraws the silver. She lifts the double espresso and moves to the stairs leading up to the balcony. Takes them slowly. Carefully. Finally reaches the top one, turns left and walks over to The Priest. He stands and holds his hand out. The Lady gives him the double espresso.

They both sit. Look at each other for a heartbeat or two. So, says The Lady…time for confession. The Priest nods…and begins to talk. Below, Little Italy looks over at the box on the wall. The box knows the routine. Pulls number 96 from way down below and places it gently on the turntable.

The curtains open. The man called Dylan is on the stage. Band of followers behind. Acoustic intro. This isn't just playing for the audience. This is Knockin' On Heaven's Door.

Little Italy sighs and pours another double espresso. The trouble with eyes is they only tell half the story. Even if the eyes belong to a penitent priest…or an understanding hooker.

Be cool…

The Two Cowering Twentysomethings

Good morning Tuesday. Today is False Sense of Security Day! Don't Speak Too Soon Day. It's wet, cold, blustery, overcast, and doing its best to rain, snow and hail, all at the same time.

Yesterday's blue skies seem to have given up the ghost and this morning, we are reminded, once again, never to take any damned thing for granted. Just when you thought it was safe to hunt out the Hawaiian shirt…the padded hoodie throws itself at you from the back rack of the wardrobe. Sometimes you just have to take the hint, bend over, and take the punishment.

The walk from the tram to the coffee shop becomes a small struggle for survival against the elements. Umbrellas everywhere are under threat. And then suddenly, the clouds begin to break. A small patch of blue appears. Then another. And another. The wind drops. The rain stops. It's as if The Man Upstairs has decided to cut us a break.

By the time I reach safe haven the sun is poking its head out from behind a medium-sized clump of cotton wool. I shake the drips off at the door like a damp red setter, and walk in to warmth, and smiles, and calmness. It's a safe bet. Or so I think.

Immediately to my right a screaming match is taking place. I freeze on the spot. It's hard to tell who's winning. Two Cowering Sitting Twentysomethings. One He. One She. One Ranting Standing Twentysomething. A She with a glass of water in her hand and murderous revenge in her eyes. I hear something about two-timing double- crossing bastard. The rest is lost in a tirade of hurt and tears…then shock and screams as the water propels itself from the glass, voluntarily it seems, to drench the faces of the two accused. Standing Twentysomething turns and exits stage left.

Sitting Twentysomethings frantically wipe each other and look at Little Italy who has emerged from behind the bar and is carrying two lattes.

Please accept these on the house, she says. Are you okay, she says. He Twentysomething nods dumbly, wishing the ground would swallow them both up. We've never seen her before, says She Twentysomething. She's a complete stranger, she says. We only wanted a coffee, she says.

I know, says Little Italy. She's done this once before, she says. It's a case of mistaken identity, she says. I apologise, she says. She turns and walks through the door to the tables outside. Standing Twentysomething is now sitting at one with her head in her hands. Weeping uncontrollably. Little Italy sits down beside her and says a few words.

Sitting Twentysomething slowly stops weeping and nods four or five times. I see her look up at Little Italy and mouth a 'thank you' and a 'sorry'. Little Italy turns, comes back indoors and walks to the bar. Pours a strong Americano and takes it out to Sitting Twentysomething. No charge.

As she comes back in, she looks at the box on the wall. The box is sympathetic. It pulls out number 7 and slides it on the turntable. The needle hits the vinyl. The crackles hit the speakers.

The curtain opens and Etta James is alone at the mike, singing Stormy Weather. Hair like silver. Voice like gold and sadness all mixed up.

I unfreeze from my spot and finish my walk to the bar. Little Italy looks at me. Shrugs. I look outside. The sunshine is here. Sitting Twentysomething isn't.

I look at the slightly damp pair by the window. Think about tears and anger. Life isn't always fair and love isn't always happy and sometimes innocents get caught in the crossfire.

I turn to Little Italy. Order a large Americano. Double strength.

Be cool…

The Tweedle Boys blow hot and cold

Good morning Wednesday. Today the weather is delusional. Schizophrenic. Contradictory. I'm having a hard time distinguishing between what's real (overcast, wet and windy)…and what's a hallucination (warm, sunny and calm). Or maybe it's the other way around.

My perception of whether to wear cold weather clothes or warm weather duds is being altered on a cellular level. The lines are blurred between my khaki shorts and my double-thick combat trousers.

I walk to the coffee shop with rain clouds above and wet puddled concrete below. The only medicine is caffeine. Lots of it. The only place is the coffee shop.

I cross the square, weaving in between the trees. Turn the corner and head for sanctuary. Two glass doors with a push here brass plate and a glimpse of peace and quiet waiting inside. Standing patiently by the bar, a line of thirsty folk think they're a queue. It's a line of four. Tweedle Dum and Tweedle Dee on the low side. Long Tall Sally on the high side. And yours truly.

Big Red is serving. Dum is having a frappe latte on the way. Milk, ice and chocolate powder. His perception is that it's a day for cooling down. He's overweight and under-dressed. Short-sleeved shirt. Underarm stains. Lightweight slacks. Dee is having a steaming hot Americano. Dark. Four sugars. His belief is that it's a day for warming up. He's cold-sensitive, double-layered and thermalised.

Big Red knows the score. She knows what's what and who's who. She's even got the why figured out. The Tweedle Boys waddle over to the long wall. Near enough to be far away. Far enough to be close at hand. Then Long Tall Sally steps up to the plate. Big Red smiles and looks up. Way up. Long Tall Sally looks straight ahead. She has a perception that she's just the same height as the rest of the world. Eye contact is difficult when you're tall and shy.

Big Red smiles. Hey Sally…down here, she says. Long Tall Sally looks down and returns the smile. Big style. Even blushes. Touches her immaculately cut hair. Flicks it off her face. Somewhere in between her right eyebrow and cheek. It's straight. Somewhere in between black and purple. Or so she perceives. Long Tall Sally orders up a cappuccino with a happy face sprinkled on the top. She slips Big Red some silver. Puts the change in the tips jar. Makes for a seat by the window. Maybe the sun will shine soon. At least that's the impression she gets.

I watch her walk away then turn back. Little Italy is back in the driving seat. Crooked grin on her face. It's a funny kinda day, she says. Just when you think you want an Americano, you figure out you need a green tea, she says.

I got fussy tastebuds, I say. Go figure, I say. Looks like you brought Mister Blue Skies with you, she says, and nods to the door. I look to the right and see a couple of umbrellas go down. Rays strike the concrete. Bounce off the shop windows. As I look back I see her nod at the box on the wall. The box nods back. Inside, number 125 slips off the loader and onto the turntable.

The curtains open. George Harrison stands at the mike. Acoustic strapped on. The remaining Fab Three at his side, but today he's the main man. I take my green tea and head for a spot near Long Tall Sally. I look outside. Yep. Here Comes The Sun.

Be cool…

Moses Fleetwood Walker gets a card

Good morning Friday. Good morning May Day. A day that kicks the old month into touch and says hello to the new one. But it's more than that. I remember a time when maypoles were dusted off and brought out to play. Up and down the country.

I remember watching troupes of colourful Morris Dancers. Strange folk. Hopping around in their weird choreographed rhythmic steps. Bell pads on shins. Waving sticks and coloured handkerchiefs.

I remember when May Day was something special. Maybe a bit pagan. Definitely a bit fun. Now, it's just a bit normal. A bit same old same old. A bit business as usual. And then…and then…

I walk through the city centre square. Turn the corner. And May Day leaps back to life. Right out of nowhere. Just when I thought it was safe to mark the day quietly with an extra shot in my espresso, I walk into a wall of hues.

Outside the coffee shop large table umbrellas are no longer their drab blue. They're multi-coloured. One end of the spectrum to the other. The tables are no longer dark old wood. They're multi-hued covers. Half-full of smiley people. Drinking up coffee. Drinking up atmosphere. It's contagious. Infectious. I feel a grin coming on.

I walk through the doors and see Little Italy, Big Red and Angel. Busy as a good day in Hell. Serving up comfort and joy and all things caffeine. Wearing tops that match the umbrellas outside.

I see a queue of customers. Empty of cappuccinos and lattes. Full of anticipation. Looking at the May Day Specials on the chalk board. Looking at the freshly-baked pastries on the trays. Looking for a spare table to sit and drink and watch the world go by. The young and the restless. The loud and the silent. The ones in love and the ones in lust. The ones who take away and the ones who come to stay.

I shuffle up and eventually take my turn in front of the one who orchestrates it all. Little Italy. Working at half the speed of everyone else. Yet somehow managing to do twice as much.

She sees me looking. Admiring. It's all in the wrist movement, she says. And the anticipation, she says. In that case I guess I better have something special, I say.

I look at the board. Let me choose for you, she says. I never say no to a lady who wants to make me coffee, I say. A minute later I'm holding a syrup and cinnamon latte and Little Italy is holding some coins of the realm. Fair exchange. No robbery.

She nods to the corner where a vacant table waits. Lonely but not for long. I park the cup. Park the arse. And see a folded card on the table. I look around and see folded cards on every table. I pick mine up. It says: "On this day in 1884, Moses Fleetwood Walker became the first black person to play in a professional baseball game in the United States of America. Enjoy your coffee."

I wonder what's on the other cards on the other tables. I look over to Little Italy. Give her the thumbs up. She's looking at a couple sitting by the window. The girl is grinning. She leaps out of her chair. He leaps out of his. They meet and hug. She nods rapidly. Yes, she says. Starts to cry. Little Italy looks at the box on the wall and nods. The box picks out its own May Day selection from deep down in the basement. Number 46.

The curtains open. The Beatles are on stage. There's an orchestra behind. The French horn plays the introduction to La Marseillaise. Anyone who knows the Fab Four knows that sound. Lead vocals, John.

I look at The Two Huggers. Look back at Little Italy. Look all around me. Take a sip of my special edition coffee. Yep. All You Need Is Love.

Be cool…

The Flash dashes into the coffee shop

Good morning Tuesday. I feel the need...the need for speed. I rush towards the week at 100 mph. Sitting in my usual corner in the coffee shop, revving my synapses. Ready to leave slow thinking stalled at the lights.

My fingers twitch in anticipation of a day spent dashing around the keyboard. Scribbly scribbly. Zoom zoom. There goes another slice of creativity. Disappearing under a hail of fingertips. No escape. No retreat. No surrender.

I take the first sip of my steaming green tea. Life takes a sudden u-turn. I feel the brakes slam on. Feel the wheels lock. Smell the rubber burn. Everything inside my skin slows down. Calm descends on body and mind. It ripples through my muscles. Courses through my veins. Breathing slows. Lungs relax. Heart rate drops. Shoulders droop. Senses chill out. I've got that peaceful easy feeling. This isn't Hotel California. It's the little shop of bliss...and I can leave any time I please.

I hear the door open. Look up. The Flash enters the shop so fast it's difficult to see anything but a blur. There may even be atoms that move slower. But there's no red muscle suit. Instead, there's grey business suit. There's no winged helmet. There's dishevelled hair.

There's no heat-resistant armoured spandex. There's stain resistant polyester. He's no superhero. He's more like a junior exec on a mission. Impossible. Get in. Get coffees. Get out. Thirty seconds flat. Forty five tops.

Little Italy looks at him and can see trouble ahead. There may even be tears. He goes from hero to zero in front of her. Smoke comes off his brogues. He takes a deep breath. Fires off an order. Machine pistol-like. Words fall like spent cartridges on the floor. Hot brass.

Twolargeskinnylattestwocappuccinosonewithanextrashotanda hotchocolatewithextravanilla, he says.

Phonedmyorderinhalfanhourago, he says. Little Italy blinks twice. You're the guy on the phone, she says. Yes, he says. Looks at his watch. Running out of time. It's not ready, says Little Italy. Be a couple of minutes. Go sit down, she says.

She sees the panic invade his eyes. Big panic....VERY BIG PANIC!! She comes round the front of the bar holding an espresso. Just made. Extra ingredients. Little Italy style. Grabs The Flash softly by the arm. Guides him to the one free sofa in the place. His brain, still operating at supersonic speed, goes into hiccup mode.

But...but...but...he says. Sit, says Little Italy. He sits. Drink, says Little Italy. He lifts the cup. Empties half the contents down his throat.

Suddenly, The Flash becomes plain young Terry White. Not meta-human Barry Allen. Not the fastest man alive.

This human has discovered Little Italy's special blend of coffee. Slo-Mo Espresso. Doesn't have a kick. Doesn't have a rush. Has two spoons of anti-speed. Slows you down. Holds you up.

Terry White feels his body take a break from major movement. Deceleration takes place. Even taking a breath becomes lung-friendly. He smiles. Little Italy walks back to the bar where Big Red is making up his order. She looks up at the box on the wall. The box reaches down and pulls up number 161.

The curtains open. Simon and Garfunkel are on the stage. Slowing down. The small guitar-playing one and the tall thin one with weird, intellectual hair are singing The 59th Street Bridge Song. And everyone's feeling groovy.

Terry White has forgotten the need for speed. And discovered the need for slo-mo.

Be cool...

Fast Annie throws in her order

Good afternoon Friday. Today is a day of sunshine and showers. Of wild celebrations and bitter disappointments. Of folk proved reassuringly right and others proved desperately wrong. Of election winners and losers.

It's a day when fighters in red corners lose on points to boxers in blue corners. And where those in the North lift their kilts and show their naked arses to those in the South. More importantly, it's a day when The Girl In Red sits across the table from The Guy In Blue. Both enjoying the best damned drink on the planet and looking into each others' big brown eyes.

There's a time and a place for politics. And the time isn't now, when love is in the air. And the place isn't here, where folk care a damned sight more about each other than they do about themselves.

Here in the coffee shop, the haves can sit side by side with the have nots. The socially broken can drink with the financially secure. The emotionally ravaged can hold hands with the physically unbalanced. And Little Italy and friends can make sure that everyone who walks in is given the time, space, and freedom they need, to recharge their batteries and refill their cups.

I sit in the far corner. Looking at all who come and go and all who come and stay. Fast Annie is one of the former. Fortysomething aiming for twenty five. Aim way off. Missing by a mile. Feet never still. Always on the move. Ripped jeans. Ripped body. Ripped heart. All covered by an oversized Parka full of sewn-on badges. Can't stay still with the same squeeze. Can't wait longer than a month before moving on to the next. She almost stands with the brakes on in front of Little Italy. A slight shift of balance from one foot to the other keeping body and soul in motion. Stillness is stagnation. Stillness is failure. Stillness is death.

Fast Annie throws in her order. Little Italy catches it. Fast Annie smiles. Medium cappuccino with toffee syrup and two extra shots, she says. No…make that FOUR extra shots, she says.

Little Italy raises an eyebrow. Doesn't say a word. Fast Annie does. What…you think four's not enough?

Little Italy shakes her head. Too much, she says. Make it three, she says. Fast Annie performs a fast foot shift and nods. A deal's a deal, she says. You know best, she says. Make it three.

Little Italy smiles. Grabs a travelling cappuccino container. Fills it. Says sayonara as Fast Annie grabs it, leaves the correct coinage and disappears into the crowd outside. Feet won't fail her now.

Little Italy looks at the box on the wall and puts in a special request. The box complies. No argument. Number 132 slides into place.

The curtains open. Mr. Morrison steps up to the microphone. This isn't sleepy Jim. This is Van the Man. This is Brown Eyed Girl.

The Guy In Blue looks at his own brown-eyed girl and smiles. Love is a fast intake of breath. It's a slow exhale. It's colour blind and it doesn't give a damn who the Hell it happens to.

Be cool…

Got a pay-it-forward coffee?

Good morning Thursday. It's empty coffee shop quiet. Waiting. Like the calm before the storm. Or the pause after pregnant. Only a handful sit and stare. Or fumble. Or, like me, exercise their digits.

It's a mobile and tablet world, people. Laptop at a stretch. Desktops are like cars up on bricks. Wheels removed. Ain't goin' nowhere, pal. No gas...no class...no cash.

Just like the scrawny teen in the Dead tee just walked in the door. Grateful for a rest. Looking for a latte. Puts down his sack. He's got future. He's got dreams. Only thing he hasn't got is cash.

He looks at Little Italiy behind the bar. Got a Pay it Forward coffee? She gives him the up and down. I butt in. No problemo, I say. I'll pick up the tab. Scrawny Teen smiles and puts out his hand. I shake. Turn and give Little Italy silver for two.

I pick up my green tea with a chocolate twist. Pastry with a touch of honey. He orders a cappuccino. We go our separates. Everybody needs a break. It feels like a deep and meaningful kinda day. Two-thumbs up and both ears open. Chilled out yet plugged in.

Four Boys in Blue are three tables away. They're on the coffee shop protection patrol. Lattes drawn and ready for action. I see the ghost of acknowledgement from one. A hint of a nod. I feel safe and warm and fuzzy.

In twenty or thirty I'll greet the rest of the day. But for now I'll greet a couple of cups of the green stuff and a few chews of freshly-baked heaven.

A Girl in Blue comes in and joins the boys. Big Red brings over a skinny latte.

The uniformed newcomer offers to pay but Big Red waves it away. We're even, she says. We don't shoot the sheriff in here. We don't even shoot the deputies.

The Girl in Blue laughs and puts the headgear on the table next to the latte.

She has buzzcut blonde hair and a pretty face. The Boys act like she's one of the lads. One of the posse. One of the crew. But she knows she isn't. Never will be. She'll always be on the outside looking in. Even though she acts like she's on the inside looking out.

We don't have no internal sexual discrimination. Yeah...like Hell we don't.

So she laughs. Joins in the sarky pisstakes. The crude innuendos. Gives back as good as she gets. To all of them. Except the one with the green eyes and the dimple in his chin. Except him. To him she gives back more. Harder. Faster. Funnier. No holds barred.

It's how she's always operated. Find the guy you're interested in. Then insult him. Give him lip. Give him a hard time. See how he reacts. See if he's interested. See if he walks away. See if he stays and looks at you funny. Kinda sideways. Holds the stare a bit longer. Maybe smiles when nobody else is looking.

So here she is giving him a hard time. Thinking that nobody else can see her interest. Thinking that nobody else can see her watching. But Little Italy can.

She could see it blindfolded a mile away on a moonless night. So she looks at the box on the wall and gives it the green light.

The box steps on the gas and brings number 25 up to the turntable.

The curtains open. The Police are on stage. The singer is Gordon Matthew Thomas Sumner. The stagename is Sting. The song is Every Breath You Take.

Green Eyes looks at The Girl in Blue and sees her looking back at him. And so it begins.

Be cool...

The Boy With The Moon And Stars On His Head

Good morning Friday. It feels like a round peg in a round hole kinda day. A touch of OCD kinda day. Don't step on the pavement cracks kinda day. Obsessive ABC. Compulsive one two three.

Some things just have to go together. No questions asked. Like fresh fruit and green tea. Fiddles and squeeze boxes. Pipes and drums. Everything in its place.

The boys in blue are here again. Only this time they're not sitting. Not drinking. This time they're standing. Mob handed. Near the door. Ready to pounce. On the lookout. On a stakeout. Looking conspicuous by their presence. In amongst the outside tables. Where the chairs are full of electric smokers. And the coughs are full of phlegm.

Suddenly a radio squawks into life. A pair of leggy teens dash past the entrance. Hundred miles an hour.

The boys in blue leap into action. A bit slower. They went that-a-way! Electric smokers act impressed. Exciting start to the day...bloody hell yeah! Unaware that inside, the box on the wall has switched from soft rock to Narcocorrido. Cowboy hats, cowboy boots, guitars, trumpets and badass polka beats.

Every now and then, Little Italy throws in some very good Mexican music about some very bad Mexican boys. Nothing against The Boys in Blue. She just gets an itch that needs scratching. It's only a little itch. But it needs a big scratch.

As the track dies down and she takes a long, deep breath, the door opens and the wind blows in The Boy With The Moon And Stars On His Head. The first time I saw him was a month ago. Black boots. Skinny black jeans. Black tee. Black leather jacket. Freshly shaved head except for three icons. One crescent moon on the right side. Two stars on the left side. Carved from jet black hair.

Now he was back and nothing was new. Nothing, that is, except the scar on his left cheek.

All the way from the edge of his eye to the end of his mouth. Angry as hell. Parting gift from a switchblade last month. Shoulda seen the other fella. Somebody called an ambulance. Shoulda called a priest.

The Boy stands at the bar and strokes the moon three times with his right index finger. Now he can speak. Marocchino, he says. Loud and clear. No ifs, buts, or misunderstandings. Like it's the only word in his vocabulary and he knows it inside out. Back to front.

Little Italy raises an eyebrow. Been months since anyone asked for one of those, she says. You're the second today, she said. You want a cocoa powder shake on the top, she says. The Boy thinks for a coupla heartbeats. Sure, he says. What you got?

Little Italy holds up a card. It has half a dozen icons on it. One of them is a crescent moon. He smiles and points. Perfect, he says, touching his head then turning and scanning the room. Over in the corner, says Little Italy over her shoulder as she makes the Marocchino.

The Boy scopes the corner and sees The Girl With Dreads And Sparkles. Head shaved both sides. Dreads like one helluva mane right up the centre. Over the top and down the back. Sparkles in the dreads that glitter when the light hits them at the right angle. Hits him like a sledgehammer.

Looks like she could do with some company, she says. She hands him the Marocchino and looks at the box on the wall. The box has a trick up its sleeve. Number 145.

The curtains open. A backing crowd is on the stage. All ages, all colours. Right at the front, Bob Marley stands at the mike. Multi-coloured Rasta tam on. Smile on. A million voices. One Love.

The Boy With The Moon And Stars On His Head walks over to The Girl With Dreads and Sparkles. Hands her his Maroccino. She takes a sip. Smiles. Ice broken.

Be cool…

The Girl In The Dark Shades

Good morning Monday. God's tears are falling on Manchester and there's not a dry pavement in sight. Don't know why, there's no sun up in the sky. Stormy weather on the way? Who knows? Sure as Hell feels sad and muggy. Sorry Billie, Ella, Lena and Etta. Ethel Waters beat you to it. Cotton Club. Harlem. 1933.

Fast forward in time. Coffee Shop. City Centre. 2015. The world might be all kinds of wrong but this song is still all kinds of right. Personal choice of Little Italy. Personal favourite of Big Red. Painful memory for The Girl In The Dark Shades. The shades that hide the tears. The shades that turn puffy eyes into mysterious style.

She's an undersized, underloved, beautiful, nervous blonde hiding behind thick hair and sadness the size of a mountain. She has full lips and thin ankles. Long fingers and short nails. She's standing at the counter, mouthing the words of the song. Words impaled in her brain. A pain that doesn't go away. A girlfriend that won't come back. Ever. This is not the time for Rock and Roll. This is not the time for don't worry…be happy. This is the time for lonesome, stab-you-in-the-heart ballads.

The Girl In The Dark Shades shuffles up to the head of the queue. Looks at Big Red. Waits a dozen heartbeats like she was making her mind up. Doesn't fool anyone. She has the same drink every time she comes in. But Big Red is patient. Respectful. She knows that The Girl In The Dark Shades loves to drag out this dance. She knows that eventually she'll turn to the stainless steel machine and make up the same variation on a theme that she always does.

Café Mocha with a touch of orange flavor. Whipped cream and cinnamon. And a spoon for the cream. Every single time. Every single week since way back last Christmas. The first time The Girl came in. Big Red wonders what colour eyes sit behind the shades. Brown or blue? Hazel or green?

The Girl In The Dark Shades comes to a decision. Double espresso with whipped cream, she says.

Big Red does a double take. Eyebrows up. What about the Mocha, she says. The Girl In The Dark Shades reaches up to her eyes. Slowly removes the shades. Hello Heterochromia iridum. Left iris blue. Right iris brown. Both red from crying. I think it's time for a change, she says. Time to move on, she says. Big Red smiles. Nods.

Little Italy appears stage left. Good girl, she says. One double coming up. She turns. Works her magic at the stainless steel machine, and comes back with the best damned double espresso with whipped cream that The Girl In The Dark Shades will ever taste. Until the next one.

She looks at The Girl. Then at the box on the wall. The box looks at the primo selection in the basement. Grabs number 62. Slips it onto the turntable.

The curtains open. Fleetwood Mac are on stage. Lindsey Buckingham sings Never Going Back Again. A song penned for a woman he met on the road. On the bounce. Or so the rumour goes.

The Girl puts the shades in her bag. Takes the espresso. Turns and looks for a new space. A new place. Now she's The Girl With The Beautiful Eyes.

Be cool…

Baby please don't go

Good morning Tuesday. Dampness soaking into jacket day. Rain boulders bouncing off pavement day. Sunshine cowering behind dirty clouds day.

Feeling in the groove. In the flow. In the coffee shop, sneaky peeking at the world.

The atmosphere is noisy. The air is busy. The music is something Cuban. Something Latino. Who the Hell knows. All I know is it's from the heart not the head.

Picture flared red dresses with black frills. Picture skin-tight, arse-hugging material. Picture heels to die for and passion to live for. I look over to the coffee bar and see Little Italy with a fire in her eyes. Sting said it right. Every little thing she does is magic. Even if it's only three minutes of tocaores strumming harsh-sounding flamenco guitars, while I sip a dark, roasted café cubano with a heap of demerara sugar.

I look around. Over by the window, huddled in the corner…watching all…is The Cat. Preening herself. Waiting to be waited on. Waiting to be served. She has a plan for the man who thinks he's the one making all the moves. He thinks he's the one in control. He thinks he's the one pulling all the strings. He thinks he's the one who can end things any time he wants. Poor deluded fool.

Slink she slyly doth The Cat…knowing fully where it's at. See the prowling pussy's Prey…think he'll simply walk away. He doesn't realise the odds are stacked against him. He hasn't twigged that the trap has been sprung. The eyelashes. The breathless words. The blush. The soft stroke of her hand on his. He won't see it coming. Until it's too late. But Little Italy will. She knows the routine. Seen it all before. Knows what's coming next.

The Cat pounces. So…what were you going to say, she says. The Prey is helpless. Frozen in time and space. He takes a breath. I love you, he says. She waits a heartbeat. I know, she says.

293

Over behind the bar, Little Italy can feel his crushing disappointment. Say the damned words, she whispers. Say I love you too. But The Cat stays silent. Looks down at the cappuccino in front of her. The one with the chocolate heart drawn on the foam.

And then The Prey does the unexpected. He plays the surprise card. The last thing in the world The Cat is prepared for. He gets up from the table and walks out the door. No goodbye. No explanation. No so long and thanks for all the fish. Just gets up and heads for the crowd without looking back. Just looking forward.

Little Italy can see the surprise on The Cat's face. She can hear the gasp escape out of her open lips. She knows this wasn't part of the plan. The Prey isn't supposed to walk away. He's supposed to be the hunted, not the hunter. She's supposed to spring the trap, not be caught in it.

Panic sets in. Pulse races. Heart hammers. She stands. Grabs her bag. Makes a move for the door. Only to see him return with a smile on his face. So…this is what it feels like to be The Prey, she thinks.

Over by the bar, Little Italy smiles and nods at the box on the wall. The box slides number 45 onto the turntable.

The curtains open. The Stones are on the stage with Muddy Waters. Mick is in top gear. Muddy is in top form. Low, slow and easy. Four words say it all. Baby Please Don't Go.

The Cat and The Prey look at each other. Let's start again, he says. She nods. They walk back in.

No matter who you are. No matter who you love. No matter how much you think you're in the driving seat. You're probably wrong.

Be cool…

Old Hollywood glam

Good morning Thursday. It's nearly Spring Bank Holiday weekend. When the fat weather controller has a break. When the houses of finance lock up their monies. Lock up their daughters. Put up their rates. Hitch up their skirts. Roll up their sleeves and count up their pennies.

Not yet, though. Here in the world of green tea and brown coffee...of soft, soul-mending sounds and slow, muscle relaxing movements...a small slice of lucre gets you a little piece of heaven. Tucked away in the corner. All yours for half an hour. Or as long as you want.

Where your pulse can slow, your smile can grow and your face can glow with the light of another day doing what floats your boat. Doing what makes your own little peaceful segment of the world go round. And round. Before you have to rejoin the rest of the human race and climb back on the treadmill.

I stand in the queue inside the coffee shop. Cash at the ready. Taste buds standing to attention. Little Italy is dispensing TLC and I breathe a sigh of relief. I mentally prepare. Get ready to be a fly on the wall. A leaf on the wind. I have my cloak of invisibility in my bag. Folded up next to my laptop. I shuffle along until I'm face to face with the Queen of Caffeine.

There's something different about her today. I do a quick scan. A fast up and down. A rapid gander. She says nothing. Waiting for me to make the first move. Say the first word. I take stock. Dark luscious hair...check. Eyes a red-blooded guy could dive into and get lost forever...check. Small Roman nose with a cute tilt...check. Lips you could get slapped in the face just for thinking about...check. No...wait. I slam on the brakes. She smiles. I smile. Lips. Bingo. New colour, I say. New tube, she says. Old colour, she says.

My mind does a back flip. Old Hollywood glam. Taylor. Kelly. Marilyn, of course.

Classic look. Make up of the stars. MGM gloss. 1950's romance in a bullet. Danger Will Robinson…lost in the space between top lip and bottom!

Nice, I say. New lips deserve a new drink, I say. What would you recommend, I say. Be careful what you ask for, she says. But she closes her eyes. Long lashes come together like a pair of Venus Flytraps. Snapping closed.

Go sit down, she says. Let me make it a surprise, she says.

So I nod, and I turn, and I head for a few square feet of privacy against the far wall. Right under a copy of a reproduction of an oil painting of a man in a purple waistcoat. The painting is called The Morning Coffee. I can't think of a better place to say hello to the day.

A full turn of the second hand later, Little Italy comes over with a large, white chunky cup and saucer. The cup is three quarters full of something dark and mysterious, with the initials L.I. floating on the top in cream. She places it down, turns and walks away with a nod to the box on the wall. The box goes back in time and returns with number 56. Slips it onto the turntable.

The curtains open. I raise the cup to my lips. A caffeine bomb explodes in my mouth. On the stage Nat King Cole stands at the mike with a voice that makes the hairs on my neck stand on end.

Unforgettable. Thirteen letters. That's all I need. I don't need to hear any more. The song and the memories and the coffee take over.

Be cool…

The Girl With Betty Davis Eyes feels an itch

Good morning Tuesday. I'm not one for going to the Opera. But this morning I'm one for listening to it. Green tea and Don Giovanni. Thank you Wolfgang Amadeus.

Today there's a Continental cafe atmosphere outside the coffee shop. Smokers and writers sit in the sun. Entertainment for the ears. Fascination for the eyes. Joy for the soul. Time to think and space to be alone in the crowd.

There's something about greeting the day slow and easy that puts all the right shaped pegs in the proper shaped holes. Something about sinking into a comfy leather sofa and letting the aroma of rich, dark coffee massage the senses while the rest of the world goes by at 100 miles an hour. If only they stopped. Listened to the grass grow under the concrete.

I look to the box on the wall and breathe in slowly as Wolfgang switches to Rodriguez and a little Spanish guitar floats through the air. I can almost feel the sun on my face and the warm blood in my veins. Almost.

I look to the bar where Big Red is busy cleaning the stainless steel machine. She wipes it down lovingly with a damp cloth till it gleams. In front of her, Little Italy is serving up a cappuccino to The Girl With Betty Davis Eyes. Large dark orbs in a face that looks like a child. She has brown curls like Shirley Temple and brown skin like Shirley Bassey. The minute she walks in the joint (boom boom) I can see she's a little on the compact side. A little on the nervous side, too.

Little Italy can see it. So she says a few words. Smiles a few smiles. Pours a nice frothy cappuccino and throws in a slice of carrot cake. I can see The Girl With Betty Davis Eyes visibly relax.

Shoulders drop. Tension fades away. She slides her tray off the glass bar top, turns, and looks around for a safe haven. I smile.

She smiles, makes a decision and walks towards me. Nice and slow. Sits next door. Safety in numbers. So far we got two.

I don't plan on growing into a crowd, so I make a mental note to self. Don't smile at anyone else. Especially anyone with peepers the size of Alaska.

I get the feeling she's looking for someone to get friendly with. All I want to do is drink my green tea, empty my pot, feel vaguely healthy for it…and head for the hills.

I hear the door open and catch the newcomer in my peripheral. I hear Little Italy's voice. Hey you, she says. I look up. Hey you too, says The Cowboy. I've seen him before. They greet each other like long lost pals. She does small talk. He's big. He does tall talk. He looks the part.

Tooled leather brown cowboy boots. Lived in jeans. Sheepskin jacket. Three day beard. Thick moustache turned up either end. Six foot four. Hollywood smile. Tom Selleck look-alike.

Beside me, The Girl With Betty Davis Eyes catches her breath. She won't catch The Cowboy though. He's on his way out the swinging door. Disappearing into the sunrise with a double espresso. Little Italy looks up at the box on the wall. Winks. The box fast draws number 116 from the basement. Sets it easy on the turntable.

The curtains open. Willie Nelson is on stage. Grizzled face. Grey beard. Long hair. Legend. Great voice. Great advice. Mamas Don't Let Your Babies Grow Up To Be Cowboys.

Little Italy looks at The Girl With Betty Davis Eyes. The Girl looks down at her cappuccino. Takes a bite of her carrot cake. Thinks about Tom Selleck. Feels an itch she can't scratch.

Be cool…

The Man In Black has a birthday

Good morning Monday. A day of births and celebrations. A day of counting the cards and counting the years. Of well feelings and well wishes. Of friends and families.

It's early in the coffee shop and The Man In Black is on the warm side of the window. A low, solitary horn echoes from the box on the wall. The Man loves jazz and jazz loves the Man. A little soft piano joins the melody. On the table in front of him is a triple espresso and a single card. The cup has a tag on the handle. The tag says drink me. The card says Today is your Happy Day. Put it in a box and keep it somewhere safe.

He looks at the counter where Little Italy's smile says everything anyone needs to hear on a day like this. Standing in front of her is The Secretary. Dialling up another song on a mobile distraction. White buds in. Black eyeliner on. Sharp Specsavers and rounded derrière. She looks at Little Italy and wonders if the smile is for her.

Not today baby girl. Not today. This one has a reserved sign on it. Cut to The Man In Black. He looks at the cup handle. Looks at the card. Looks at Little Italy and smiles. This is a man who doesn't smile. Doesn't frown. His face doesn't say much of anything. Neither does his voice. But today his face says everything.

His eyes twinkle. His lips stretch. His vocal cords step back in time and remember what his own laughter sounds like. His skin remembers an expression that doesn't normally put in an appearance. He wonders, not for the first time, how Little Italy knows the things she knows. How she can tell at a glance who needs helping and who needs leaving alone. He wonders why hers is the only internal voice he can't hear. She's a blank. A silence. A vacant space where there should be form and substance.

But he doesn't wonder for long. He knows that, with her, there are some questions that shouldn't be asked. Some answers that shouldn't be sought.

So he gives her a smile and a nod and takes a sip of the dark, strong liquid in the cup. Enough said. Enough done.

Meanwhile, back at the bar, Mother and Son take their turn. She's small, white haired, heavyset, wearing a bright red coat. She has fat legs and old comfy trainers and she's leaning on a battered walking frame on wheels. He's tall, unshaven, with greasy brown hair and an old duffel coat. Creased jeans and old boots. He watches her every move. Ready to catch her if she stumbles. She scolds him for fussing so much.

They have green tea and a cream scone cut in two to share. They amble slowly to a table at the bottom of the stairs. Arguing all the way. Little Italy looks on. Shaking her head slowly. Then she looks at the box on the wall. Somewhere inside, the box dials up number 12. The only number that means any damned thing today.

The curtains open. Lou Reed walks onstage. Light shines on a piano. He sits down and begins to play. Perfect atmosphere. Perfect song. Perfect Day.

The Man In Black looks at Little Italy, lifts his cup and mouths thank you. She mouths Happy Birthday. He doesn't know how she knows. He doesn't need to.

Be cool...

George has a secret

Good morning Wednesday. Silence is a funny thing. It's sneaky. Premeditated. It can creep up on you in the middle of a wall of noise, and banish all sound. Right when you least expect it. Right when you most need it.

Today is a banishing day. At least for a while. The coffee shop has it's own brand of sound. It's polite. Soft. It doesn't interrupt thought or speech. And if you want to be alone in your own little bubble, it understands. Doesn't complain. It just turns down the volume and gives your silence room to breathe. Time to be heard. Space to be comfortable.

The Cowboy knows this. He sits in the corner. Headgear on and working to full capacity. Arms folded. Eyes closed. Legs outstretched and crossed at the ankles. Not sleeping. Just keeping the silence in. The world out. His own little white noise and coffee status quo.

Little Italy slips quietly by and puts a do not disturb sign on his table. She's a dedicated follower of silence. A fan of the old internal landscape. The grassy bank. The slow moving stream. The sun on her face and the wind in her hair.

That's on the inside. On the outside it's a whole different story. She's the wind in the sail. She's the power that turns the wheel. The gas in the engine. The reason folk come here in the first place. Folk like Gorgeous George. Thirty five years old and too bloody handsome for his own good.

Gorgeous George has a secret. A damned big one. The kind of big that makes him think he'll burst just trying to keep it all inside. So he tells someone. He lets the cat out of the bag. Just once. Just with one person. Someone so special and so trustworthy that he knows wild horses couldn't drag it from her. Ever.

Gorgeous George is talking to her right now. Right here. Fifteen feet away from where I'm sat with my triple espresso. Raw caffeine with muscles.

Rocket fuel on steroids. Sometimes you need an extra shot or two to kickstart the day.

Little Italy looks surprised. What…no new squeeze, she says. Gorgeous George shrugs. You know how it is, he says. Sometimes you just have to be squeeze-free, he says. Sometimes life makes too much noise and you just need a slice of silence to get by, he says.

So I pack up my troubles and come here, he says. I can see a table with your name on it, says Little Italy. Nods in the direction of a mahogany round table sat under the painting called The Lonely Dog. I'll pour you a cup of the usual and bring it over, she says. Sounds like a plan, he says, turns and walk away.

She follows a minute later with a large cappuccino with a powdered chocolate smiley face on the top. Puts it down. Turns and heads back to the bar. Looks over her shoulder halfway there. Sees The Cowboy. Brim pulled down. Edges of his mouth pulled up. She nods at the box on the wall. The box reaches down, pulls up number 72 and slips it on the turntable.

The curtains open. The Steve Miller band is on stage. The Joker is on form.

Little Italy looks at The Cowboy and right on cue he whistles. The whistle cuts through Gorgeous George's silence like a bullet from an 1860 .44 Army Colt Revolver. He doesn't bat an eyelid.

Be cool…

The Man Who Smiles At Everyone

Good morning Thursday. I see The Man Who Smiles At
Everyone walking through the door of the coffee shop. I saw him for
the first time months ago. I thought he had a physical affliction. Or a
mental aberration. Then I thought he might have an infectious
disease. Like an airborne happy virus.

I saw him smile at folk then I saw them smile back. Like he
breathed his happy virus all over them.

Then he smiled at me and I smiled back. I had become
infected. It felt good. No sweating or coughing. No feeling like shit or
looking like death warmed up. More like life warmed up.

Now, I have become infected again. He does have a certain
style. The Man Who Smiles At Everyone is a bit of a dandy.
Impeccably suited and booted. Lightweight three-piece. Grey with a
faint stripe. White shirt. Maroon patterned tie with Windsor knot.
Shiny black brogues with a mirror polish. Moustache with upturned
ends and a small goatee beard. Closely trimmed. Not a hair out of
place. Hollywood teeth.

He walks past The Professor who looks up from trying to
solve another one of the world's greatest mathematical problems,
smiles and waves. Little Italy has a ring on her finger that wasn't there
yesterday. An escapee sunray dives into the shop and glints off the
Rock of Gibraltar sitting snugly on her left hand.

Fourth proximal digit.

She says nothing. It says everything. The Man Who Smiles At
Everyone spots it and smiles even wider. You got hitched, he says.
Nope, she says. Looking after it for a friend, she says. Some rock, he
says. Some friend, she says. I think I'll take my poison black today, he
says.

He slips her some silver, lifts a freshly poured Americano and
heads for the only vacant leather wingback chair in the place.
Chesterfield. Dark antique chestnut. An original. Not a copy. Just like
The Man Who Smiles At Everyone.

Just like Little Italy. She turns, faces the next in line, and her heart sinks. The Girl in the Red Beret is standing with mascara streaks down her cheeks.

Little Italy sighs. She knows that, despite all that love inside, another twosome has bit the dust and become a onesome. A lonesome. Another eggshell-walking relationship has gone south.

Not again, she says. The Girl in the Red Beret nods slowly. Doesn't say a word. Little Italy whispers. Go sit in the corner, she says. I'll bring you over a nice cup of tea, she says.

The Girl in the Red Beret turns, scans the room, spots the corner table and walks slowly towards it. Almost in a daze.

Little Italy fills a four-cup pot with boiling water and throws in a pair of green tea sachets. Puts it on a tray with two cups. Turns to her left and asks Big Red to take over the reins.

Then she takes the tray to the table in the corner. Sits down next to The Girl in the Red Beret. Pours two cups of green tea. No milk. Glances up at the box on the wall. Waits for the floodgates to open. The box reaches down deep. Picks up number 56 and slips it onto the turntable.

The curtains open. Nat King Cole is on stage, standing at the mike. Unseen orchestra does a slow, melancholy intro. Nat begins to sing. Irreplaceable voice. Unforgettable Smile.

Little Italy nudges The Girl in the Red Beret. Nods in the direction of The Man Who Smiles At Everyone. He smiles at her. She smiles at him. Just a small one. But it's a start.

Be cool…

The Talking Man and his listening chair

Good morning Monday. For some of us conversation is like a drug. Communicating, even if it's with ourselves, is the only way we move from one minute of the day, or night, to the next.

The Talking Man is in the coffee shop and his mouth is on overdrive. Today's subject: the price of honey and the industrious nature of bees. I hear his words, passed conspiratorially from his lips to the chair by his side. The chair isn't a good talker, but it is a good listener, as all chairs are. They come from a long line of good listeners. Trees.

Trees are, without doubt, the most attentive listeners in the world. Since the first tree pushed up from underneath the ground they have listened to everything the world has had to say. Sometimes agreeing. Sometimes not. And now, here in the shop, The Talking Man and his listening chair are continuing that tradition.

Nearby, however, no listening is taking place. No talking. Just silence of mind and silence of mouth. On one chair, at one table, there is a communication veto. A silence so profound that even the synapses of the brain are having a time out.

This is a moment of anti-sound and The Girl In The Bubble is it's owner. Inside her bubble she is safe. Nobody can reach her. Nobody can hurt her, break her heart or terrify her spirit.

The Talking Man sees this and strikes up a conversation, but his words bounce like paper rocks against the impenetrable shield of her bubble. They fall on the floor and roll under nearby tables. Useless. Barren.

The box on the wall sees this and sends out warning signals to Little Italy, busy creating magic at the stainless steel machine. She hears and shakes her head sadly. Sometimes there are just questions. No answers. Not in this part of the coffee shop, anyway.

But upstairs in the gallery, looking down on The Girl In The Bubble, trying not to be seen, is The St-St-St-Stuttering Boy.

He carries a card with him. The card says; A large macchiato with a small squeeze of vanilla syrup, please.

He shows the card to Little Italy or Big Red, so he doesn't have to speak when he orders. So he doesn't have to delay the process. So he doesn't have to go red in the face and want to scream inside. He just digs inside his jacket pocket. Pulls out the silent order. Smiles and keeps his trap mercifully shut.

He knows that the beautiful baristas behind the bar understand. They don't even look at his card anymore. The usual, they ask. He smiles and nods. They fiddle with the stainless steel machine and produce the liquid that makes his taste buds sing. He pays and goes upstairs. All without saying a word. And now here he is. On the balcony. Looking at a kindred spirit who doesn't know he exists.

Little Italy sees him stare and she looks at the box on the wall. The box feels his sadness and it reaches down, pulls number 108 from the basement and places it on the turntable.

The curtains open. The Righteous Brothers are on stage. Unchained Melody is the first song that eases past their lips.

A tiny tear escapes from the left eye of The Girl In The Bubble and a memory forces its way through a tiny crack in the bubble wall. The crack grows and a few tables away The Talking Man falls silent.

Be cool…

The Penitent Man and Layla

Good morning Tuesday. Anyone can feel guilt, but nobody apologises quite like a Catholic. We of the Church of Rome are experts when it comes to believing that we're to blame for, well, everything.

Our ability to say sorry for anything that isn't even remotely our fault is breathtaking. We are the apologists extraordinaire. We don't feel puddles of guilt, we feel oceans of the damned stuff. And we do it automatically.

Nobody persuades or strong-arms us into it. Nobody prods, pushes, shoves or drags us kicking and screaming into it. We go willingly...some of us even happily.

The Penitent Man is in the coffee shop this morning, sitting alone surrounded by acres of guilty space. I can see him as I stand in the queue. Waiting for my liquid peace of mind. He wears his guilt like a hair shirt. He wasn't always like that. There was a time when he was at peace with himself and everyone else. There was a time when he was happy in his skin and his guilt took a place on the back burner.

But that was before The Incident. Now his guilt is like a mountain. An ocean. A dark sky pregnant with rain clouds. He sighs and looks at the bar.

Standing before Little Italy is Layla. Black haired. Olive skinned. A sultry beauty. Even the deep scar that runs the length of her left cheek is exquisite. Layla has a bigger scar. An uglier scar. But that one's on the inside. The man who gave her the outside scar with the edge of a broken bottle has his guilt. And various long-term injuries. But the inside scar. That's from someone much younger. Someone innocent. No guilt there. Only a wound that will never heal. And a love that will never die.

Little Italy has a special place in her heart for Layla. So...is it the small espresso, or the tall latte, she says. Something in the middle, says Layla, brushing the curls from the front of her eyes.

Cappuccino it is then, says Little Italy. Raises an eyebrow. Raises a smile. Layla nods.

The door opens and in comes someone for whom guilt is an alien concept. A strange fruit. Except for one secret. One desire. The Professor walks slowly to the bar. He cogitates as he perambulates. A learned man with learned feet, learned brain cells and a lifetime of politeness. His cerebral cortex is infused with highly focused intelligence. It's in his blood. His DNA. As is Layla. But not this one.

Little Italy hands over the Cappuccino. Takes the silver. Glances at the box on the wall. Somewhere deep inside the box the number 83 steps up to the plate and onto the turntable.

The curtains open. Derek and the Dominos take to the stage. Eric Clapton takes to the mike. Only one song on his mind. Only one name. Layla.

Little Italy watches The Professor as he walks to his chair. Sometimes guilt is an infrequent visitor. Other times it's a lifelong passenger.

Be cool...

In memory of The Beekeeper and Lazarus

Good morning Monday. Friendships come in all shapes and sizes. There are a million and one reasons why two creatures, however similar or different, should decide to stick around and keep each other company.

Today is June 15. The day when I remember The Beekeeper and his Dead Bee Routine. It's also the day for marvelling at the determination of friendship to survive despite all the odds.

I witnessed the routine the first time I came to the shop. A raw young virgin in the world of social tea and coffee drinking. I can see it even now. Fresh in my mind after all this time.

A raggedy smiling man was standing in the queue at the bar, hands cupped closed as if holding something precious.

He spoke softly. Slowly. Conspiratorially. His eyes pointed to a secret wrapped in grimy flesh. Wanna see a miracle, he said. It was that kinda day. Sure I said. Buy me a coffee and I'll show you, he said. Americano on the rocks, he said. I smiled and nodded.

I turned to a woman behind the bar, who said nothing. Just served up the price of the miracle and left me to watch as The Beekeeper slowly opened his palms to reveal a bee. No movement. No life. He bent close to the tiny body and blew. Gently.

Suddenly the bee twitched, juddered, and began to crawl around his hand. Say hello to Lazarus, he said. He's my friend and professional business associate, he said. Lazarus seemed to look up at me and nod his head.

The Beekeeper took his coffee and left...Lazarus hiding in a fold of his old army coat.

That was then. This is now. Every June 15 I remember the friends and I buy myself two Americanos, on the rocks. One for me, the other for the old man and his small associate.

Little Italy serves me. Just like the first time. I take them to my table. Sit down. And wait. That was three years ago. I only saw them that first time. Never since.

But here's the strangest damned thing. I'm sitting this morning, waiting, when a voice comes in from the left. Female. Kinda gruff. But kinda kind.

You're waiting for him, she says. I turn and see dark hair. Tight curls. Streak of white like a skunk. Olive skin. Dark eyes. Twinkle. Plain black t-shirt. Silver crucifix on silver chain. Faded jeans. Slim figure. Not an ounce of fat. Early fifties.

Elaborate, I say. The guy with the bee, she says. He said you'd be here today, she said. He told me to give you a message. So give, I said. He said to tell you he was here yesterday, she said. He got the date wrong, she said. He told me to say don't worry about him. He'll get by with a little help from his little friend.

When she says all that she gets up and walks out. No goodbye. I can see Little Italy watch her as she goes. Then she looks at the box on the wall and nods. The box watches the door close, then it reaches down and pulls number 149 to the surface. Slides it onto the turntable.

The curtains open. The Beatles are on stage. Ringo is the Starr man today singing With A Little Help From My Friends. I reflect for a minute on the sad fact that there are only two of the four Fabs left.

I lift up my Americano. Take a sip. Think of The Beekeeper and Lazarus. And smile.

Be cool...

The love of The Mirror Image Blondes

Good morning Thursday. As I walk through the square to the coffee shop, the sound of a lonely piano drifts through the air. It floats gently and bounces off the shops on one side and the buses on the other. Says hello and bounces back again. Back to the black and whites. Back to the player. Back to the music in his head.

I reach The Piano Man's pitch on the concrete stage. Drop some silver in a plastic box down by the side of the music machine. His fingers murmur thanks as they travel slowly up the scales. I don't know the music. I only know the effect. The hairs on the back of my neck think seriously about standing up.

Then I'm past and round the corner before the thought translates into action. A hundred feet later I walk through the door of the place I know as sanctuary and twenty feet later I'm standing in front of the woman I know as Little Italy.

I don't even have to state my case. The stainless steel maker of the dark liquid has already been given its instructions and in the space of a bunch of heartbeats I'm on my way to one of a few regular spots I have.

This morning's vacant space winner goes to the small rectangle in the corner on the right. Up against the wall. Three tables away from The Mirror Image Blondes. Facially different. Alike in all other respects. Short cropped hair. Alabaster skin.

Leopardskin jackets. Black leggings. Heads bent forward melting into each other's space. Fingers touching. Stroking. Unaware of the rest of the world. Uncaring of their judgemental thoughts. Lost in their own love. Too damned right.

They drink the same booze. Eat the same food. Watch the same movies. Read the same books. The only difference is their taste in coffee. One has a double espresso with crème. The other has a cappuccino with a squirt of something special. Little Italy is the only outsider who knows which coffee goes to which twin.

Love isn't a chemical reaction. It doesn't live and die in the limbic system. Sweet nothings have no sexual preference. They are what they are and to Hell with anyone who says different. Behind the bar, Little Italy looks on and smiles. Looks on and likes. Looks on and considers this another job well done.

She flicks her eyes at the box on the wall. A casual movement but one full of intent and instruction. The box considers itself well and truly instructed. From the depths number 79 rises to the surface and hits the spinning deck.

Curtains part. On the stage, spotlights illuminates The Flamingos rolling back the years, singing I Only Have Eyes for You. The year is 1954. The Mirror Image Blondes look into each other's eyes. Life doesn't happen to you. You happen to it.

Be cool…

Closed for refurbishment

Good morning Thursday. Some folk think that change for change's sake is never a good thing. They believe that there has to be a damned good logical reason tucked in there somewhere to explain all the disruption. To give an excuse for all that out with the old and in with the new.

Of course that's utter bollocks. Sometimes the best change happens for no good reason other than we simply wake up one morning and feel like swapping the chairs around. Changing the colours. Just for the Hell of it. Just to see what it looks like. Right is the new left. Upholstered is the new plain wood. Strange is the new familiar.

I haven't been to the coffee shop in over a month. My walk across the city centre square is full of expectation, but interrupted by a hairy, raggedy bundle of dirty clothes wrapped around a guy who could be anywhere between thirty and eighty. The grime of half a lifetime spent sleeping outdoors cakes his face. His eyes zero in on mine like an Exocet missile. He has his target.

I move to my left to avoid. He moves to his right to capture. I feint to my right. He dodges to his left. We're joined by an unseen cord in a curious danse macabre that has only one outcome. Face to face. Noses a foot apart.

His right hand held out. Nails bitten to the quick. My right hand held in. Nails digging into my wallet.

I sigh and dig deep. Good old Catholic guilt wins again. I pull out a few high value coins. Hand them over and turn to go. Stop. Turn back. Will you get yourself something to eat with that, I say. Mind your own fuckin' business, he says and walks off. I smile. Serves me right for asking.

I cross the road, turner the corner, and see a crowd gathered at the coffee shop entrance. They look like they lost something priceless.

There's a sign on the door. I step to the front and read it. I recognise the handwriting. It belongs to Little Italy. Sorry folks, it says. Closed for refurbishment. Open again in a couple of weeks, it says. All is not lost. Watch this space, it says.

I turn to go. Hope is a sick bitch when she walks away and that's a fact. I hear the sound of an approaching engine. Loud. I look up. A cappuccino-coloured, fast-moving van screeches to a halt at the kerb. There's a sign on the side. Love & Coffee, it says. Little Italy beeps the horn. Smiles. A flap on the side opens and Big Red is standing ready to serve up the best goddam drink on the planet.

The crowd smiles. Some of them even break out into spontaneous cheers. Little Italy looks out at a sea of heads. Moves to the back. Reaches up to a shelf where a mobile version of the box on the wall is sitting. Waiting for instructions.

She turns the dial. The box hits the station. Tunes into Blood, Sweat & Tears. Turns the volume up on You've Made Me So Very Happy.

The mobile stainless steel machine behind her comes to life and, in a few minutes, a long string of happy coffee drinkers make their way to sit on the benches around the square.

As far as Little Italy's concerned, when you can't come to the mountain, the mountain damned well comes to you. See you on the flip side.

Be cool…

The End (for now…)

Coming soon

There's only one thing better than one cup of coffee…and that's two.

By the same token, there's only one thing more enjoyable than one Love & Coffee…and that's another one.

Love & Coffee, The Refill, is presently bubbling away nicely and should be coming your way shortly. There may even be chocolate biscuits on the side.

In the meantime…here's a little sip to soothe the tickle in your thirst.

First impressions

Good morning Monday. It's true what they say. You don't get a second chance to make a first impression.

Today, my journey through the city centre square to the coffee shop is happening in fifth gear. My feet are doing double time. Today is the grand opening. The unwrapping of the refurbishment. The day when the old place throws back the covers and says "Hey guys…whaddya think?"

The first thing I see as I turn the corner is the entrance. New patio…new umbrellas…new tables and chairs. More colour…more comfort…more kickass atmosphere. And jam packed full.

The second thing I see is the new door. Rich mahogany with toughened glass. I look through and see the third thing. A new layout. Bar on the left instead of on the right. Freestanding tables and chairs. Booths for quiet conversations of a more intimate nature. Dark leather sofas to sink in and chill out.

Old was chalk. This is cheese. This is the big kahuna of new. This is the last word in first impressions.

I look in front of the bar. I see all the old familiar faces. All the young familiar regulars.

I look behind the bar and I see Little Italy and Big Red, working the Hell out of the stainless steel machine.

I love the look of the place. The sound. The smell. But what I think about interior décor doesn't amount to a hill of beans in this crazy world. There are only two things that really matter. The people…and the coffee.

I look to my right. Over against the wall in a leather wingback chair sits The Stranger. Forty five. Fifty maybe. Tanned, wrinkled skin. The world looks like it lives on his face and looks through his eyes. Fifteen feet away and I can still see they're Paul Newman blue. He's looking around. Taking in the scenery. First impressions.

He sees me see him and nods. Just the once. Then he lifts a glass espresso cup up to his lips. Takes a hit. Settles the cup back down. Pushes his shoulders back against the chair. Closes his eyes….and smiles. First impressions.

I look behind the bar and see Little Italy looking at me. In that instant I know everything is good. All is as it should be. And the new place is just as good as the old place. Only better.

Behind me, the door opens. The Waif steps into view. A long, tall, elegant creature. White hair, white outfit, porcelain skin. Eyes as black as coal. She looks at Little Italy. Little Italy nods towards The Stranger. The Waif breathes deep. First impressions.

Chalk another one up to being in the right place at the right time for the right reason. There's no such thing as coincidence.

I see Little Italy look up to the box on the wall. The box looks down and I can see it pause for thought. Make up its mind. Today is opening day. Time for something a bit special.

The curtains open. The spotlight hits Martha Reeves and the Vandellas on the stage. Three mikes. Three voices. A million hairs suddenly stand on end. Time for a little classic Motown. Number 202. Time for a little Dancing in the Street.

Little Italy looks around the new joint. You don't need to be at home to feel at home. Sometimes all you need is a friendly face…a friendly space…a little music…and the best damned drink on the planet.

Be cool…

About the author

My name is Bryce Main. I'm somewhere above primary school age and below pensionable age (just). I'm Scottish by birth, live in the UK, and am happily married to the author Denise M. Main. She's English by birth.

Together we have managed, somehow, to bring up two sons who are better looking, better natured, and more intelligent than I ever was at their age, or any other age.

Love & Coffee isn't the first book I've written, but it's the first one I've published. It's available in eBook form and printed paperback.

That doesn't mean I like it more than the others…it just means I like coffee more than is probably good for me.

For most of my life I've had the opinion that it's the best damned drink on the planet and, judging by the number of coffee shops scattered around the globe, I'm not alone in that opinion.

If you enjoy Love & Coffee, please feel free to spread the word…even if (sometimes) you'd rather have a nice cup of tea.

Email: brycemain@virginmedia.com
Web: brycemainauthor.com

Printed in Great Britain
by Amazon

THE STRANGE SIDE OF MIDNIGHT

Ben Hammott

The Strange Side of Midnight
Ben Hammott

Author can be contacted at **benhammott@gmail.com**
Author website **www.benhammottbooks.com**

Chapter 1

Sinister Mansion

KALLISTO CROWE, A ONCE successful supernatural thriller and horror novelist who had now fallen out of favor with his once loyal readers, his agent, and publisher, drove along the driveway that weaved through the forest and halted at the wrought iron gates barring the track. The faded lettering of the wooden plaque fixed to one of the brick posts revealed the name of the building glimpsed through the bars, Hagsdell Manor.

Plucking the bunch of large iron keys from the passenger seat, Crowe climbed out and approached the gates. Peering through the rusty, paint-neglected railings, his eyes took in the distant building that was to be his new home. He found it just as impressive as the first time he had viewed it a few weeks before. West and east wings of the building led off from the slightly off-center domed tower dominating the facade.

Still finding it difficult to believe he would be living in such a grand house—and being paid to do so—he unlocked the gates. Hinges screamed out for lubrication when they swung open. Adding the task to his to-do list, Crowe climbed back into his car, drove through and pulled to a stop outside the main entrance set in the east wing. Eager to begin exploring the house he had so far only seen a small part of, he immediately started unloading the car and stacked everything in the spacious hallway before deciding where it would all go.

When the car had been emptied, Crowe picked up a box of his unsold books and grunted from the weight; he should have packed them in smaller boxes. Though aware that all they would do was gather dust, as they have been doing for years, and really should be thrown away, it wasn't something he could bring himself to do. It was his first book, and they held a special affection to him; though why he had to keep four boxes of the same title was a mystery even to him.

As he hefted them up the creaking staircase, he glanced at the title scrawled in black marker pen in his handwriting. *My first masterpiece – Ghosts of Crowley Manor,* and cringed slightly. It hadn't been the bestseller he had envisioned. Out of the five hundred copies he had paid to have printed, he had sold exactly fifty-three. Luckily, his following book, *Haunted,* showed enough potential to persuade an agent to take him on. After some revision and, at times, hard edits, Haunted was picked up by a mid-range publishing house and sold a respectable number of copies, putting him firmly on the publishing map. His next two books did even better, selling so well he was able to give up his day job as a document archivist for the British Library and become a full-time writer. Although assembling, cataloging, preserving, and managing valuable collections of historical information had its enjoyable moments, he found creating works of fiction a more pleasurable and rewarding profession.

After three more book successes, things began spiraling sharply downward. His imaginative author-juices had evaporated to become as dry and barren as any sand-swept desert. When his next two books flopped, his agent, diplomatically, had advised him to take some time off to try and regain his writing mojo. With hefty mortgage payments and no new titles to top up his waning royalties, Crowe had no option other than to sell the house he had purchased on the back of his relatively short-lived success and search for a cheaper place to live.

As it happened, a builder friend of his, Peter Jones, had purchased a large plot of land in the countryside with some crumbling ruins set on some open ground and a grade II listed mansion positioned at the south end of an ancient sprawling forest. Hagsdell was a modest, mansion-sized dwelling that needed some *remedial* building work, including sorting out the subsidence caused by tree roots undermining the foundations that had sent cracks creeping up one end of the house. Though none of the repairs were severe enough to threaten the building's structure, they would need doing before it could be resold if Peter decided to do so. It was also badly in need of modernization.

As Peter didn't want the hassle of navigating through the red tape minefield that would arise from English Heritage overseeing the repairs, his interest in purchasing the property firmly laid in the attached land, where he intended to build ten large, luxury houses. Another problem that would deter possible future buyers was a proviso in the deeds stipulating that all the furniture, paintings, ornaments, etc., were to remain in the house. If that weren't off-putting enough, another nail in the coffin of its salability now the prime land would no longer be part of the package, were further peculiar stipulations. Firstly, it decreed children were forbidden to live in the house. Secondly, it must not remain unoccupied for an extended length of time, and to ensure the occupation of Hagsdell at all times, a caretaker had to be hired to take care of the building and contents. The only silver lining was that funds had been set aside by the deceased Sinister family to pay the caretaker's wages.

With little interest in the house, Peter's proposal to Crowe was that he would install a new kitchen, upgrade the plumbing and wiring, and he could move in as its new caretaker, rent-free. Crowe had jumped at the generous offer and said he would move in as soon as the renovations were completed. With the caretaker wages and no rent or mortgage to pay, he was able to put the bulk of his belongings into storage and just bring his essential knick-knacks, which included his first baby, *Ghosts of Crowley Manor.*

Placing the box of unsold books on the floor, Crowe opened the attic door. Assaulted by a whoosh of ancient, musty air that caused him to gasp, he stepped back until it had settled. His eyes followed the dusty treads up the narrow wooden staircase and gazed at the pitched roof timbered with wide boards. Though originally painted white, they were now the shade of old parchment. The stifling air that drifted down seemed to be starved of oxygen and slightly asphyxiating. Leaving the door open to let fresh air seep inside, he returned downstairs and carried the remaining three boxes of his failed masterpiece upstairs. The last one he kept hold of and poked his head into the small stairwell. The air was now a lot fresher. He climbed to the attic and gazing around, marveled at the sheer number of objects cluttering the large space, none of which he was permitted to throw away. Peter had warned him it was jam-packed with some of the previous occupants' belongings, but he hadn't expected there to be so much.

Light seeped into the gloom from a round window at the far end, highlighting the floating dust motes the incoming fresh air had disturbed. He placed the book box to one side and moved through the attic. Everything was old and covered in years of accumulated dust. An Aladdin's cave of antiques. There was a row of framed paintings leaning against each other, a child's rocking horse, a pram stacked with china dolls, tea chests full of toys, linen, and clothes, stacks of old books, wooden steamer trunks, two tall cupboards, and a plethora of other objects.

Walking further into the room, Crowe stroked his hand along the toy horse's mane, setting it into a creaking, rocking motion. He halted at one of the tea chests filled to the brim with antique toys; metal with no plastic in sight. Lifting out the one on top, he found it to be heavier than expected, made of cast iron. He blew off the accrued dust, setting it adrift to glint in the sun's rays. It was a circus toy, a red carriage with seven blue-clad figures sat on top. Six played musical instruments, and the seventh held the reins that drove the two white horses. The front legs of the twin steeds had small wheels attached to their hooves, their back legs raised slightly, allowing it to be pushed along on the carriage's four yellow wheels. Though it showed signs of being played with— scuffs and scrapes—it was in decent condition. A glance in the chest revealed it to be crammed with circus-themed toys, including circus animals—lions, elephants, and the like, clowns, acrobats, and a ringmaster, all with small metal wheels on their feet.

Returning the toy to the box, Crowe moved on. After sidling through a gap between the stacks of discarded possessions, he halted at a large cabinet adorned with strange mythical beasts, demons, and devils. Fascinated by the creepy, lifelike carvings, Crowe felt his writer's imagination tingle. He could write a truly spine-chilling tale around this piece of macabre furniture alone. Stroking his hand over the dusty details, he pondered how he could move it downstairs. *Maybe he could borrow a couple of Pete's workers to help him?*

Excited by the prospect, he gripped the twin demon-head door handles and twisted. The doors refused to open. After blowing the dust away from the lock plate, he stared at the keyhole fashioned inside the mouth of a snarling beast. Though Pete had given him a bunch of house keys, he couldn't remember any that might fit this strange lock. Though temporarily thwarted to discover what was inside, he was determined to find out. He put a hand to the top of the cabinet and pushed, rocking it slightly. Whatever lay within, it had no weight. Probably some old clothes he thought. He'd get it downstairs and then worry about opening it.

Turning his back on the cabinet, he sighed at the amount of stuff he would have to reposition to create a gap large enough for it to be taken out. With possible storylines already swirling around his imagination, he knew it would be worth the effort and set about the task.

Chapter 2

Strange Painting

"YOU NEED TO LIFT your end a tad," instructed Crowe.

Struggling from the weight of the solid piece of furniture they were trying to maneuver down the narrow attic staircase, Fred frowned at Crowe. "I thought you said this bloody thing wasn't heavy?"

Crowe shrugged. "Sorry, it seemed lighter when I rocked it."

"Trust me, it isn't."

"I can vouch for that," moaned Charlie who supported the top end of the cupboard.

Bent over awkwardly at the top of the attic staircase, Charlie adjusted his grip and stumbled when he stepped onto a lower tread hidden from his vision by the large piece of furniture. Carried by gravity, the cabinet's top edge bounced down the steps. When the base slammed into Fred's chest, he shot through the attic door and crashed into the banister overlooking the hallway. With the weight of the cupboard pressed against his ribs, Fred glanced worriedly at the creaking balustrade he hoped wouldn't break and then below at the floor he would plummet to if it did.

Crowe rushed forward, took the cabinet's weight, and shifted it away from Fred.

Rubbing his chest when the pressure was released, Fred tapped the rail. "It's a good job it's quality workmanship, anything modern would have broken and seen me sent below."

Struggling with the weight, Crowe asked, "You okay, Fred?"

Fred nodded and gripped the base again, taking some of the weight off of Crowe.

"I'm also fine," quipped Charlie sarcastically.

Fred rolled his eyes. "Can you pick up your end without dropping it this time?"

"I'll try, but no promises."

When Charlie had raised the top, they slowly inched it through the doorway and turned. When it was free of the stairs, they lowered it to the floor.

"I hope it's not damaged." Crowe moved to the top and examined the cabinet where it had bounced down the stairs. Charlie and Fred tilted it to the side so he could check underneath. "A dent or two, but nothing serious."

"They knew how to build things in those days," said Fred. "Quality workmanship and materials, not like the chipboard and MDF crap they use today."

"And it has," said Crowe, running a hand over the cabinet. "I wonder how old it is?"

"Got to be a hundred years at least," offered Charlie.

"Older, I think," said Fred, grimacing at the eerie carvings. "You sure you want this downstairs where you can see it?"

"Don't say that, he might get us to take it back up," groaned Charlie." It was a struggle to shift when gravity was on our side. It'll be a damn sight harder when it's working against us."

Crowe smiled. "Don't fret, Charlie. I want it downstairs where I can see it. I'm hoping it'll provide me with inspiration for a new book."

"Oh, right," exclaimed Charlie. "Pete said you write ghost stories."

"Yeah, kind of. Supernatural thrillers and a bit of horror."

Fred studied the cabinet's ghoulish adornments. "I guess you have plenty of food-for-thought in this strange antique."

Crowe glanced at the carvings Fred focused on. "That's what I'm hoping."

"If you do write a book about this cabinet, will we be in it as we're moving it?"

"Maybe," answered Crowe. "I've still not fully worked out the plot yet."

"Come on then, let's get this bloody thing downstairs," urged Fred. Pete only gave us an hour for lunch, and half that's gone already."

With the three of them sharing the weight, they carried the cabinet downstairs and into the living room where Crowe had set up his writing desk and computer.

"Put it over there, to the right of the hearth," instructed Crowe, pointing to the space he had cleared earlier. In full view of his desk, he'd be able to glance at it for inspiration while he wrote.

The two men placed the bottom edge on the floor, and when they hoisted it upright, something shifted inside.

"Sounds like something's come loose," said Fred. "Must've 'appened when Charlie dropped it."

"Don't blame me," defended Charlie. "Might just be something inside sliding about."

"Either way, it's not a problem," reassured Crowe. "It's the outside I'm more interested in, though I would like to take a peek inside to satisfy my curiosity as to what it might contain."

Fred crouched to examine the lock. "A shame there's no key because this ain't no ordinary cupboard, and a sure bet there's something weird inside it."

"Looking at those spooky carvings, I'm sure it's nothing I'd like to see," commented Charlie. "Wouldn't surprise me if it was full of skeletons."

Crowe grinned. "I hope so."

Fred's grumbling stomach reminded him he was hungry. "Right, that's us done. If we 'urry we can grab a sandwich and a cuppa before dinner break's over with."

"Thanks again, guys." Crowe gave them each twenty pounds. "I never would have got it down without your help."

"As long as you don't want it taken back up again, you're welcome." Fred slipped the money in his pocket.

Crowe walked them to the front door.

"That key must be 'ere somewhere, ya want to 'ave a rummage around for it," advised Fred, stepping outside into the sunlight.

Crowe squinted from the brightness after the gloom of the house. "It's on my to-do list."

"Cheers, then, and good luck."

Crowe glanced at the approaching gray clouds; rain was on its way. He shut the door and returned to the living room.

Standing in front of the cabinet, he ran his eyes over the demonic carvings and wondered who had created such a thing and for what purpose. What he did know was that before he could concentrate on writing his new novel, he needed to find out what was inside or face the constant distraction. God knows it didn't take much nowadays, and probably the reason for the poor reception for his last two books. Playing games on his PC and PlayStation, and watching TV and movies had been his downfall, but no more. No, he would find the key and open the cabinet to find out what it contained. Hopefully, whatever was inside, would be something unusual enough to kickstart his writing mojo.

Feeling more excited about writing than he had for a long time, Crowe glanced around the room for a likely hiding place for the key. He had already gone through the desk before he and Pete had shifted it in here from the study. This room had a fireplace, and with the winter months almost here, he had a feeling he would need its warmth when the cold weather hit, especially if it turned out to be as chilly as the previous winter.

Carrying out a room-by-room search, he eventually found a strange-looking key tucked inside a teapot in the kitchen dresser. Almost running back to the living room clutching the key, Crowe crossed to the cabinet, inserted it into the lock and turned it. The satisfying clicks of the locking mechanism releasing brought a smile to his lips. He stepped back when the twin doors creaked open an inch with a sound like a moan coming from the bottom of a deep well. Attributing it to the wood reacting to the fresh air, he was about to step forward and open the doors when the right-hand one creaked open further with a shrill squeak of protesting hinges. Committing the eerie sounds and his anxious feelings to memory to be typed out later, he peered into the dark interior.

Something barely perceptible was inside at the back and Crowe immediately felt he was being watched. Shaking off the apprehension that had ridiculously claimed his common sense, he approached the cabinet, pulled the other door open wide and gazed upon the object inside; a painting, almost the width and height of the interior space. Crowe got the impression the work of art was the sole reason for the cabinet's creation; to conceal it.

Breathing in the mustiness that seeped from the cabinet's interior, he leaned inside to examine it. The mood of the image was dark, spooky. The eye he had imagined watching him was, in fact, a full moon floating in the gray, cloudy sky. The moonlit garden was surrounded by trees with a fountain at its center. Recognizing the details, Crowe crossed to the large bay window and gazed out at the fountain and the forest beyond the back of the house. Though his current view was slightly off center to the artist's viewpoint, it was unmistakably a painting of this very garden. Grabbing his phone, he went outside and stood by the back door. He clicked off a few photos and returned inside. Holding the phone out, he compared the images to the picture. Though the fountain and garden in the painting were neater, maintained, and the trees a little smaller than those in the photograph, it was undoubtedly the same view.

Disappointed by the unremarkable painting, he searched the interior for something more inspiring for his starved, creative mind, but it was the only object it contained.

Refocusing on the painting, he ran his eyes over the frame. It too was adorned with some of the entities that decorated the cabinet's exterior, which alluded to them having a connection, but what?

Gripping the sides of the painting, he found it to be firmly attached. After checking every inch of the frame for a fixing, nails or screw heads, brackets or clips, and seeing none, he gripped the edges again and yanked it up. The painting came free and banged against the top of the cupboard. Crowe lifted it out and flipped it over to examine the back. Except for the four, flat prongs in each corner that slipped into the fixing brackets on the rear of the cupboard, it was bare of any detail. He carried it over to the hearth, placed it on the mantelpiece, stood back, and pondered the artwork.

Why was such an unimpressive painting locked inside a cupboard that appears to have been specially constructed to house it, and what was the link between the carvings on both frame and cabinet? They had to hold some significance or why would they be there, so out of odds with the depicted scene? If it had been a painting of some Dante-inspired hell, or something equally macabre, he could understand the addition of the ghoulish adornments, but a scene of an English garden made no sense.

Thinking that maybe researching the house and its previous occupants would shed some light on the mystery, he decided to go and have a chat with Pete the next day to find out what he knew about the former owners. All Pete had told him was the last person living in the house, the only remaining member of the mysterious Sinister family, had died some months ago. With no surviving relatives to take over ownership of the house, it had been put on the market.

With a myriad of thoughts swirling through his mind, he headed to the kitchen to fix himself something to eat.

Chapter 3

Strange Chest

AS CROWE WAS WASHING up his dinner things and pondering the day's strange discoveries, he stared through the window out at the garden scene depicted in the painting. He froze with a plate half rinsed when he remembered something. An object in the cupboard had moved when they had stood it upright, yet the picture was firmly fixed, and there was nothing else inside to account for the shifting item. He dropped the plate in the soapy water, dried his hands, and headed back to the living room.

Halting in front of the open cabinet, Crowe contemplated its empty interior. There had to be a hidden space, a secret compartment containing the object that had shifted. Excited by the prospect, he leaned inside and started tapping. The sides and top produced the expected retorts to his knuckle drumming, the bottom, however, returned hollow thuds.

Crowe knelt and started exploring the piece of wood forming the cabinet floor with his fingers. He prodded, pushed and tried getting a fingernail in the paper-thin joint running around the edges and lifting, all to no avail. Placing his hands on his knees, he stared at the dark-varnished piece of wood, convinced it hid something exciting. Briefly thinking about fetching his toolbox to try jamming a screwdriver into the joint and prizing it free, or smashing it with a hammer, but decided against it. The secret compartment he pictured below the wood cover had to have been designed to be accessed without resulting to vandalism. It would also make a far better piece for his book if he discovered the hidden mechanism that opened it.

Certain the deviously concealed catch, button or lever had to be low down, Crowe roamed his fingers over the lower carvings, pushing, probing, turning, and pulling every detail. When his finger slipped inside the open jaws of a hideous demon, he felt something give. He grabbed a flashlight, laid on the floor, and aimed the light into the demon's mouth. There was a small domed protrusion at the back. He had found it. He slid a finger inside and pressed. When nothing happened, he applied more pressure.

Click!

He climbed to his knees and smiled at the raised front edge of the cabinet floor. Wondering what he would find inside, he raised it up and stared at the small wooden box, about a foot long, half that wide, and about eight inches high, set at an angle to one side. Four catches, two on each of the long edges, held the lid in place. Crowe lifted it out. Though not heavy, it did have some weight. He carried it to the coffee table, sat on the sofa, and released the catches. He removed the lid and laid it aside. Purple velvet was wrapped around an oblong object almost the size of the box's interior. An iron chain, thin and delicate, held the material in place. Leaning closer to examine the wax seal trapping the chain ends, he peered at the strange writing. Though too small to read, it seemed to be old Latin or possibly an even more archaic language, around the circular imprint in the wax. In the middle was the Star of Solomon with arcane symbols in each triangular arm.

Excited to see what the object was, Crowe lifted it out, pushed the empty box back and placed it on the coffee table. He grabbed his phone and snapped off images of the wrapped object and close-ups of the wax seal.

15

Unwilling to break the seal he'd like to keep intact, he collected his toolbox and used wire cutters to cut the chain around the seal. Carefully laying the wax seal to one side, he folded back the flaps of the purple covering. A waft of nauseous stench, like that of a rotting cadaver, assaulted him. He shot back as dizziness and a feeling of great lethargy overwhelmed him. Without the strength or wherewithal to prevent it, he slumped sideways onto the sofa.

Ten minutes passed before the ill effects that had suddenly stricken him began to fade. It took a further five minutes before he was able to sit upright. Experiencing bewilderment by what had happened, he focused his puzzled gaze upon the small casket he had uncovered. As the remnants of the ailment which had seized him dissipated, and his brain-fogginess cleared, he stared apprehensively at the object and the cause of his temporary incapacitation. Certain that something noxious laid within, he tentatively leaned forward. The chest was silver, both in color and substance. It had seven small drawers, three either side and one above a central panel featuring a prominent skull furnished with slanted eye sockets, giving it an evil appearance. The smooth, fluted edged top was absent any decoration. Eight, inch-long legs supported the strange casket.

Keeping his distance, Crowe lowered his vision and focused on something crammed in the gap beneath the base; plants squashed when the casket was placed upon them. Spying nothing else that might account for the substance that had afflicted him, he assumed the vegetation had to be responsible. It needed to be disposed of before he'd be able to investigate the mysterious casket safely.

After collecting some gardening gloves, a plastic bag, a damp tea-towel wrapped around his mouth and nose, and the coal tongs, Crowe was ready.

Cautiously lifting the casket off the plants, he placed it aside to examine the toxic vegetation. Though withered and squashed, he recognized the species from its bell-shaped purple-veined flowers, hairy and wool-like, with a pale, dingy yellow base from his research into poisonous plants for a previous novel. It was Black Henbane. This particular variety was especially nasty and could cause death. With its purportedly magical properties, it has long been associated with witchcraft and a plant most likely to have been used by witches to concoct ointments and potions. In folklore, it was a favorite of those practicing the black arts, rituals of necromancy and the summoning of spirits. In bygone times, it had also been used for medicinal purposes to allegedly cure a series of various ailments and used as an ingredient in anesthetic to put patients to sleep during operations. Also, if Crowe's memory served him well, it was surprisingly good protection against some mythical creatures, including demons, which wouldn't come near it.

Placing the open bag on the floor, Crowe held the coal tongs at arm's length, folded the flaps of velvet material softly over the plants and plucked up the bundle. He put it carefully in the bag and twisted the top closed. After sealing it with tape, he took it outside.

Satisfied the danger was removed, he set about examining the small silver casket. The three drawers along the top were thinner than the ones either side of the skull panel and intrigued Crowe the most as to what they might contain. Wary of more poisonous substances, he leaned back and pulled open the middle, widest drawer. When no toxic gasses or odors wafted out, he moved closer and stared at the miniature set of weapons laying on a bed of padded felt. Surprised by the small but lethal looking objects, Crowe fetched a magnifying glass from his desk drawer and lifted out one of the two short swords. The same star of Solomon symbol present in the wax seal was at the crossed section of the handle and blade. Symbols etched into the blade ran along both sides of its length.

Returning the sword to its imprint in the drawer, he ran his admiring gaze over the two tiny daggers positioned above and below the sword and focused on the equally small blunderbuss type pistol, its proper name was a *dragoon* he recalled from his research into antique weapons. He carefully picked it up and marveled at the intricate workmanship. It seemed to be an exact replica of its full-sized counterpart as if it had been shrunk, miniaturized. He cocked it and used the nib of a pen to pull the trigger. It fired with a dull click. *It actually works!*

Returning the weapon to the drawer, he lifted out the small leather sack. He carefully loosened the drawstring holding it closed and tipped the contents into the palm of his hand. Amazed by the tiny lead balls, the two powder horns, and stumpy sausage wads of pre-made cartridges for speedy loading, he glanced at the pistol with no doubt that when it was charged with the gunpowder, if it were still viable, and loaded correctly, it would fire the balls. But why? What use was such a tiny weapon?

Crowe put the objects back in the sack and returned it in the drawer. Opening one of the larger drawers, he gasped in surprise at what lay inside; a small doll of a child, a little girl. Dressed in a white nightgown, she rested on a soft velvet mattress with her head laid on an embroidered pillow. Fascinated by the doll's lifelike appearance, Crowe used the magnifying glass to peer closer at her small face framed by long dark hair fanned out on the pillow. He couldn't shake the feeling that he was looking at an impossibly tiny girl sleeping and wouldn't have been surprised if she opened her eyes and sat up. He carefully scooped her from her bed and laid her limp form in the palm of his hand. Her features, hands, and tiny bare feet had been rendered in such exquisite detail he wouldn't have believed possible before. He gently brushed her arm with a fingertip. It was soft, slightly warm, and felt like skin but had to be a type of rubber. Crowe gently returned her to the bed drawer and softly—so as not to wake her, he realized—pushed it shut.

Turning his attention to the lid, Crowe tried to open it without success. Another concealed catch, he thought. His fingers went straight to the skull and twisted it. Click! It turned, as he thought it would. He raised the front edge of the lid and looked at the weapons laid out in the top middle drawer, blocking what was beneath. He pulled open the wide, thin drawer and got his greatest shock of all since finding the casket.

Shackled by its wrists and ankles was the creepy figure of a tall, thin...Crowe stared at the face for a clue...ghoul or golem for lack of a more fitting description. With the space too short for its long slender legs to stretch out, they were bunched up, almost to its chest. Aiming the magnifying glass at its nose-less face, he took in its closed eyes and thin mouth. Whatever it was, it was completely hairless, and its skin had a leathery appearance. The tiny iron shackles that tethered its arms and feet to the four corners of its small prison had locks on the bands around its limbs. Pondering the restraints that could only be there to prevent it from being stolen or from escaping; the author in him preferred the latter, he peered closer at one of the locks. Again, it was adorned with the Star of Solomon and in its center, a star-shaped keyhole.

Overloaded with the exciting discoveries, Crowe sat back on the sofa and contemplated the casket's contents which were, to say the least, strange. Is it a child's toy fashioned by some talented miniaturist, or did they have another purpose? He glanced at the cupboard's demonic carvings and its secret compartment. Something sinister perhaps?

He refocused his gaze on the mysterious casket and the five drawers he hadn't yet opened. For the life of him, even with his, at times, overactive imagination, he couldn't guess at what mystifying wonders he'd find in them. Though tempted to open them to find out, he was keen to start writing about what he had discovered so far.

Tomorrow, he would do some research on the house and its previous owners to hopefully shed some light on these strange discoveries. Feeling excited about the cabinet, the small casket and its unfathomable contents that had provided him with the inspiration he desperately needed, Crowe crossed to his desk and resumed writing.

Two hours later, Crowe paused his fingers on the keyboard and reread the last paragraph, made a couple of edits and corrected a spelling mistake. Though he had only written a little over five thousand words so far, he had a good feeling about the book and hadn't been so excited about writing for a long time. Confident this would be the novel to rekindle his popularity as an author, he continued.

Barely ten minutes had passed when he stopped typing and cocked his head at the soft scratching sounds that had distracted him. An almost imperceptible jangle of chains turned his head to the casket. After a few moments had passed without hearing any further sounds, he climbed from his desk chair and crossed to the chest. Staring at the strange, sinister-looking figure chained inside, he focused on its head that was now tilted to the side; it had been upright and facing forward before. He leaned in closer and peered at its slightly open lips that he could have sworn were closed previously. With a certain amount of apprehension, he prodded its chest gently and jumped back in fright when it moved. He laughed inwardly at his ediginess; it must have just shifted from his touch. He closed the weapon drawer and shut the lid which clicked when the hidden catch engaged, returning the skull to its original position.

Crowe moved to the fireplace and wondering how it fitted in with the mysterious casket, examined the painting. Though the slightly spooky trees and lighting created by the artist bathed the scene in a somewhat foreboding atmosphere, to all intents and purposes, it was a rather dull landscape depicting the view from the back of the house.

The frame though was much more stimulating. In each corner was what seemed to be demon faeries in various poses tormenting the skeletons and corpses adorning the straight edges of the frame. Just as the human figures, they were in high bas-relief and encroached over the sides of the frame and painting. Though all were adorned with evil expressions, all were different. There was a red, green, brown, and a particularly evil-looking black one perched on the top right corner, that was stabbing at something with a spear. Leaning closer, Crowe could see it was a similar ghoul figure to the one in the casket.

Fascinated by the amount of detail, Crowe turned his attention to the skeletons and corpses, which varied in height from about two to six inches, and included men, women, and children. Two strange black dogs, wolfish and vicious, were depicted snarling and baring sharp teeth at the red demon faerie. The expressions of the skeletons and rotting cadavers were of terror and pain. Mingled together, they seemed to be clawing at each other, perhaps climbing, as if they were trying to escape some hellish terror. Set in the center at the top of the frame was a clock face with its hands frozen at midnight.

Suspecting there was more to the painting that met the eye, Crowe used the magnifying glass to take a closer look. Starting from the top left corner, he searched along the top and gradually moved down the painting. Halting on the left side of the forest when he noticed a faint detail, he zoomed the magnifying glass back and forth to try and bring it into sharper focus, but without success. He took a photograph of the area with his phone and then crossed to his PC and opened his Dropbox. He navigated to the photo he had just taken and loaded it into Photoshop. After trying a few different enhancing techniques, he met with success. Though faint and a little grainy, it was obviously a headstone. Blurry details of more gravestones indicated the area was filled with them. If Pete was aware there was a graveyard on the land, he hadn't mentioned it. Its inclusion could be another reason why he deemed the house unsaleable. He then noticed something else in the forest to the right of the graveyard. Though little more than a faint smudge, it seemed to be a figure. Wondering if it was just something unintentionally formed by paint stokes, Crowe enlarged the detail and stared at its chilling features. Two tiny dark smudges on its blurry head were unmistakably intended as eyes.

Saving the enhanced image, Crowe closed Photoshop and glanced at the rain pattering the window. Though he was eager to check out the forest to see if the graveyard existed, as it might reveal some information about the previous occupants of the house, he would have to wait for the rain to pass. He switched to his writing program, and after reading the last few paragraphs he had written, resumed typing.

The following morning it was still raining and, typical for the English climate showed no signs of abating. While Crowe sipped his tea, he glanced at the painting. Noticing something, he moved over to it and stared at the possible figure standing in the forest. It was a little clearer than before and slightly larger as if it had moved into the foreground. Wondering if it was his imagination, he crossed to his computer, brought up the photograph of the picture he had taken the day before and printed it out. Collecting it from the printer tray, he crossed to the painting and held it up. Flicking his eyes between the two images, it was clear the painted figure was different.

Scrutinizing the figure, he noticed that a twig protruding from a tree branch in the photo taken the day before, was in front of it, but in the painting, it was obscured by the figure; and was now behind it. A shiver ran down his spine. Puzzled by how it could even be possible, his thoughts flicked to horror novels and movies that featured such an oddity. Some ghost or phantom would gradually move toward the front of the cursed picture before appearing to kill or scare the pants off the unfortunate owner. Is this what he had, a painting featuring some evil entity coming to get him now he had removed it from the cabinet that perhaps had kept it at bay?

Aware he was letting his writer's imagination get the better of him, Crowe pushed the ridiculous thought away. His eyes darted to the hearth when a log being consumed by flames crackled.

Maybe the heat was affecting the oil paint somehow? Heating it up and making certain details clearer. That though, wouldn't explain the twig moving behind the figure. Crowe stared at the mysterious anomaly while he fathomed a possible explanation. Maybe what he was seeing was the ghost of something the artist had painted but then, for some reason, had covered up. The heat from the fire had caused it to materialize through the overpainted layer. Satisfied with his reasoning, which was far more believable than the creepy alternative, he gently touched the figure to see if the paint was soft. It wasn't. Though a little warm, it was as dry and brittle as the rest of the oil paint. He shifted the painting from the mantelpiece and propped it against the cabinet it had been stored in. No doubt when it cooled it would return to normal.

After donning his coat, Crowe nipped outside to collect some logs from the woodshed. With a bundle clutched in his arms, he shouldered the shed door shut and flicked the catch in place with his elbow. While heading back to the house, he glanced into the forest and stared at the spot where the painting figure would be standing. He halted when he thought he saw something slightly paler than the gloomy surroundings. Ignoring the rain drumming on his waterproof coat, he kept his gaze focused on the spot while he edged closer to the fountain for a better viewpoint. A chill ran down his spine. Though indistinct, there seemed to be something there; a tall blurry figure staring at him. Believing it to be nothing more than a trick of the light, he turned away and headed for the back door. Unable to fully dismiss his apprehensiveness, while wiping his wet shoes on the doormat, he glanced back at the forest. If something had been there, it wasn't there any longer. He entered and closed the door behind him.

After stacking the logs by the hearth and removing his wet coat, Crowe crossed to the painting and stared at it again. The figure was still there exactly as before; neither bigger nor smaller. Realizing the picture was beginning to unnerve him, he decided to investigate the anomaly further and went to collect what was required.

Placing the painting on the armchair, he positioned the camera on a stack of books he'd piled up on the coffee table and lined it up until the picture filled the frame. After setting the camera to take a single photograph every minute, he stepped back. If anything happened, it would be recorded.

He waited until the camera had taken its first shot and then retired to bed.

When Crowe awoke, he was pleased to see a sliver of sunshine seeping through the gap in the curtains drawn across the window. He climbed out of bed, his feet gliding into his slippers automatically, and donned his dressing gown. He crossed to the window and drew back the curtains. Bright sunshine flooded the room. After the prolonged bout of rain, he would finally be able to check out the graveyard.

Remembering the painting, he hurried downstairs and entered the living room. Crossing straight to the artwork, he examined it to see if it had changed. To his shock, it had. The figure had moved even closer into the foreground and was now distinct enough to identify it as the ghoul from the casket. For a few moments, he was so stunned he just stared at it. The click of the camera snapped him out of it. He switched it off and stoked the fire, adding a couple of logs to the dying embers.

Feeling perplexed, he went to the kitchen, made himself a cup of tea, and returned to the living room. A worried glance at the painting revealed he hadn't imagined it. The ghoul had moved. He drained his mug, picked up the camera, and removed the SD card. After switching on his PC, he slid the memory card into the reader and transferred the photographs into his pictures folder.

Crowe clicked on the first image, selected sideshow mode and held a finger on the right arrow key to speed through the hundreds of pictures with his gaze glued on the faint figure and gasped when it popped forward. He sat back and stared at the ghoul until he had recovered from the shock. Crowe navigated back until the figure was as it was when he went to bed, and then, one image at a time, scrolled forward. Over five pictures, five minutes in real time, he watched the figure take two steps forward. A cold shiver crept down his spine. He replayed it a few times, watching the feet lift from the ground, the knees bending, and the leg moving forward with each jerky step. It was like he was an unwilling participant in a horror movie. Now certain the ghoul would eventually, however improbable that seemed, emerge from the painting with murderous intent aimed at him, he had to do something to stop that from happening. His eyes flicked to the flames licking at the logs in the hearth. He could burn it. No. That rarely worked in books and movies; it was too simple a solution. He turned his gaze to the cupboard that seemed to have kept it trapped before. He would lock it up again. Confident that would solve the problem, he fetched the painting, hung it back in the cabinet and locked the door.

He returned to his computer and looked for the timestamp on the image currently showing the ghoul, 12:05. It moved at midnight; of course, it would. He'd check tomorrow, and if it hadn't moved, he'd know that locking it in the cabinet had worked.

He took a deep breath to calm his nerves. Breakfast and then he'd head into the forest to find out if the graveyard in the painting existed in the real world; something he now thought was a distinct possibility.

Chapter 4

Strange Graveyard

STEPPING OFF THE GARDEN path formed of large flagstones that led from the house to garden boundary, Crowe passed through the iron gate and entered the forest. He pushed through the wild undergrowth and nettles and headed between the elm, oak, ash, and birch trees. The thickness of some of the heavy-limbed trees hinted they might be a hundred years old or more.

After a short walk, Crowe pushed through a patch of tall bracken and some exceptionally thorny brambles that snagged at his coat, as if trying to prevent him from getting through, and stepped into a clearing filled with gravestones, many positioned at odd angles. Though a section of the graveyard was set on level ground, many of the graves were placed on the sloping sides of the small valley formed by the meeting of two hills. To Crowe, it gave the impression that when the level ground had been filled, the dead had moved out onto less suitable land.

Though many of the headstones were of a similar shape, other designs were scattered amongst them, including a few impressive stone mausoleums.

A small stream, barely a yard wide, meandered through the V created by the irregular sides of the opposing hills. The thick leafy canopy formed by the trees, in as much abundance as the tombstones, shuttered out the light and cast a depressing gloom over the cemetery.

After taking a photograph with his phone, Crowe moved to the nearest headstone and crouched to read the inscription. The stone was old, covered in moss, and green from years of enduring England's cold, damp weather. Brushing and peeling away the moss proved fruitless in revealing the inscription. Though the green top layer was easy to remove, its roots seemed to have penetrated the porous stone and remained to obliterate any words that might be present.

Believing he might have better luck with one of the larger monuments, he moved to an above-ground tomb. Again, he found no evidence of an inscription. After photographing it, Crowe wandered through the graveyard examining other headstones and monuments. Spying a large memorial surrounded by trees on the top of the hill on his left, he climbed up to it. Its circular domed roof was supported by five marble columns resting on the top of a large stone sarcophagus. After he had circumnavigated the tomb without finding any hint of an inscription to allude who was interred within, Crowe gazed around the graveyard. It was more than a little strange that not one of the gravestones was inscribed with the name of the entombed, no dates, nothing. He pulled his coat tighter around his neck when a chilly gust swept around his collar, causing him to shiver.

Catching the sound of heavy machinery carried on the wind, Crowe moved to the far side of the hill and stared down into the valley at Pete's construction site. In preparation for the building work to begin, the remaining walls of the old buildings were being demolished. Other men and machines were involved with clearing the land of trees and bushes and leveling the ground.

Spying Pete supervising the loading of branch-stripped tree trunks onto a long flatbed truck, Crowe decided to go down and chat with him about Hagsdell Manor, its past owners, and the cemetery filled with unmarked tombstones.

Crowe reached the worksite as the trunk-loaded lorry pulled away. Spying Pete heading for his portacabin office, where he would soon be on the phone, something Pete seemed to spend half his life doing, he hurried to intercept him.

"Pete!" called out Crowe when the builder opened his office door.

Pete turned toward the voice and registered surprise at seeing Crowe. "Kallisto. Everything alright up at the house?"

Crowe nodded. "Yeah, everything's great, thanks. I just wanted to ask if you knew anything of its history."

Pete glanced up at the gray clouds when a faint rumble of thunder rolled across the heavens and frowned that the lousy weather would halt work when it arrived. "Come inside."

Crowe followed him into the cabin.

Pete crossed to a small kitchen area set up at one end of the cabin. "You want a cuppa?"

"I'm fine thanks."

As he put a kettle of water on a gas ring to boil and added a teabag to a mug, Pete revealed what he knew. "To tell you the truth, when I purchased the house, I wasn't that interested in it. As you know, it was the land that came with it I wanted. As I mentioned to you before, I did toy with the idea of doing it up and selling it on, but I don't have the patience to deal with those English Heritage busybodies poking their condescending noses into every nook and cranny to ensure I'm doing every expensive thing they insist on. It'd be a damn money pit and a waste of my time. Also, the provisos in the deeds predestined the resale value would be low and a suitable buyer difficult to find without the land I bought it for. That's why you're its caretaker."

"And very grateful I am too, Pete, really. It's a great house, and that strange old cupboard I found in the attic has set my creative juices flowing."

"Glad to hear it." Pete poured hot water into his mug, added milk, and crossed to his desk.

"I've just been having a poke around the old graveyard in the forest..."

"Graveyard?" questioned Pete, surprised by the revelation. "I had no idea there was a graveyard up there." He reached for a rolled-up plan from a shelf and spread it out on his desk."

"It's not overly large, but it is full of graves, which strangely, are unmarked with any inscriptions."

Pete scanned the plan. "As I thought, no graveyard on the plans." He raised his head to Crowe. "You sure it's a graveyard?"

Crowe nodded. "What else could an area crammed full of headstones be?"

Pete shook his head. "Nothing else I suppose." He re-rolled the plan and returned it to the shelf. "Well, that's another nail in the coffin of the salability of that damn house."

"I actually like it. If I had the money, I'd buy it from you."

Pete smiled. "And I'd let you. So, how about you nip back to it and whack out a bestseller so I can be rid of it?"

"I'm trying and have already started. It's actually about the house, which is why I asked you about it."

"What you need to do is nip into town and speak to...oh, what's his name? Sebastian Burche, I think. He works in the local museum part-time, so if he's not there, I'm sure someone can point you in the right direction."

"Cheers. I'll do that tomorrow."

"Well, if that's it, I have some calls to make. Time is money." Pete reached for his mobile.

"I'll leave you to it then, and thanks again." Crowe headed for the door. As he stepped through, Pete called out.

"And good luck with your new book."

"Thanks." Crowe shut the door and hadn't gone ten steps when the heavens opened, drenching him. Clutching the collar of his coat tight around his neck in a vain attempt to prevent the rain from seeping beneath, he hurried across the fields and up the hill, the shortest route back to the manor.

Shutting the door behind him, Crowe slipped off his drenched coat and hung it on a hook to drip dry. He took off his shoes, wet socks, and trousers soaked from the knees down, left them in a heap to deal with later, and entered the living room. He crossed to the red embers in the fireplace, added a couple of logs and warmed himself in the heat from the roaring flames.

When he had banished the chill from his bones, he headed upstairs for a shower and returned half an hour later in what he called his comfy clothes. Tracksuit joggers, a T-shirt, and warm hoody. The unfashionable ensemble was finished off with thick socks and slippers. He shut the living room door to trap the heat inside and gazed around the room while he pondered what to do next. His eyes halted on the silver casket. He'd open another drawer before he returned to his writing.

Chapter 5

The Strange Key

GRASPING THE TINY silver knob of the top left drawer with his fingertips, Crowe slid it open. Only one object was inside; a miniature key. Immediately knowing what the key fitted, his eyes flicked to the lid and pictured the strange figure shackled inside. Though still mystified by it all, he lifted the tiny key from its velvet rest. Turning it over in his fingers, he examined it through the magnifying glass. It seemed to be made of iron. The unadorned stem ended in a circle decorated with the ever-prevalent Star of Solomon associated with the casket. The tip was star-shaped and would fit the identically shaped hole in the locks of the ghoul's shackles.

Though uncertain he should, Crowe opened the casket, slid out the top drawer to reveal the imprisoned ghoul, and slid the key in the lock of the restraint around its right leg. The shackle sprung open with a soft click. He unlocked the remaining three, returned the key to its drawer, and lifted the ghoul out. Placing it in the palm of his hand, the slender, naked figure stretched from the tip of his middle finger to two inches down his wrist. Its long, slim fingers were without fingernails. The absence of any sexual organs was a strong indication whatever this figure represented it wasn't anything human.

"What are you?" asked Crowe aloud.

He lifted one of its arms and let it flop into his palm. There was something inside that acted like bone and jointed like a human limb. An indication it had a skeleton, some type of puppet armature used for models in stop motion photography, perhaps? A limb would be moved, photographed, limb moved again, photographed and so on until the desired movement had been completed. It suddenly clicked. This was what the things in the casket were for. One of the Sinisters must have had an interest in such films and was making one. It explained the figures, the tiny weapon props, everything, almost... He glanced at the cabinet and pictured the painting inside, wondering where that fitted in. *Maybe it was a backdrop for the puppet characters to perform against?* It seemed a reasonable explanation and would explain its blandness if not the ghoul's ghostly image moving within it. He remembered the other paintings stored in the loft. *Maybe there were others depicting a variety of backdrop scenes? But why was this painting alone stored in the strange cabinet?*

If the filming was done in the cabinet in some director's arty manner, and the forest scene was the last to be filmed, it could have been left there? Though not totally convinced of his somewhat plausible explanations, without more information it would have to do. After returning the ghoul figure to the casket, he went to his desk and typed for a few hours before retiring to bed.

Chapter 6

A Strange Night

BATHED BY THE RUDDY glow of the dying embers in the hearth, the casket's weapon drawer slid open. The lid raised a sliver. Bright white eyes appeared in the dark gap and peered out. A slender arm lifted the lid higher. The ghoul poked its head out. After peering around the room cast in the moonlight's gray hue filtering through the window, it climbed out. The ghoul turned to the weapon drawer and chose the sword and the pistol before walking to the edge of the table and jumping to the floor. It padded softly across to the door and slithered underneath.

Deep in slumber, Crowe dreams of the success of his new book and soaks up the lavish praise from his peers, his fans, and those in the publishing world. His dream flicks to the exterior of a London movie theatre as a limousine pulls up. With a beautiful actress on his arm, he climbs out and walks up the red carpet. Waving copies of his book, hundreds of his fans cheer, screaming excitedly, calling out his name, and requesting autographs.

As Crowe and his date enter the theatre about to screen the premiere of the movie based on his book, the VIP guests give him a standing ovation. He sits at the front as the lights dim and slips on his 3D glasses. The screen flickers like the static garbage of an old television set. In the center, a shape slowly appears, gradually becoming more distinct.

Crowe is confused, this wasn't in the film he had viewed at the movie director's private screening. He recognizes the slender figure of the ghoul when it grows in size as if running toward the screen. It gets larger and larger and then dives out with its long, taloned fingers stretched out, clawing for Crowe's throat.

Sweating, Crowe gasps, and whips off his glasses. The screen is dark now. A sliver of light appears in the distance when a door creaks slowly open. The rectangle of light grows, a spotlight probing the darkness. The shadowy figure of the ghoul emerges, framed in the doorway. It stands there, its eyes staring. Suddenly, it vanishes. Crowe's eyes follow the light that now protrudes from the screen and creeps along the floor. Slightly puzzled by the effect because his 3D viewing glasses are off, he continues to follow its menacing advance to the seat next to him. He turns to his date and screams at seeing the slender ghoul sitting beside him. Its head lunges at him. Its mouth stretches open impossibly wide and slips over his face.

Screaming, Crowe awoke fighting the blankets. He rolled off the bed and came to his senses when he slammed against the floor. He laid there while his breathing calmed. Crowe had never experienced such a realistic nightmare. Aware that it had been fueled by the casket's contents, he was willing to forgive it if its inspiration produced a book even as half as successful as the one in his dreams.

He cocked an ear to the sounds of the grandfather clock downstairs chiming midnight. As the last chime faded, a scuttling turned Crowe's head to the floorboards by the bedroom door. He saw nothing except a dust fairy disturbed by a draft, dancing lazily across the boards through a shaft of moonlight. Faint scampering tip-taps on the floor directed his gaze beneath the bed. Something too quick to identify, nothing more than a fleeting shadow darker than the gloom, moved from the floor to the bed. Crowe's eyes flicked over the network of wire and springs of the antique bed when they creaked as if something had landed on them. His anxiousness increased when the depressions in the mattress and the compression of spring creaks crept toward him.

Crowe slowly raised his head above the bed to see what was coming. He froze at the sight of the tall, slender ghoul striding purposely closer, a sword in one hand, a pistol in the other. Screeching when it saw him, it sprinted and leaped. Crowe reacted to the vicious menace when it landed on his face, gripped his nose with its knees like it was riding a bronco, and stabbed the sword furiously at his face, slicing and carving off chunks of flesh. He grabbed the murderous ghoul and flung it across the room. He heard it crash into the large wardrobe and drop to the floor. The tip-tap of its feet on the floorboards rushing at him revealed it wasn't injured.

Keen to get off the dark-cloaked floor, Crowe scrambled onto the bed. His hand reached for the bedside light and flicked the switch. Darkness remained. Absent any suitable weapons to ward off the approaching peril, he snatched up the lamp that had failed him, yanked the electric cord from its socket, and threw it at the running footsteps. The bulb smashed with a resounding pop that sounded too loud for its small size. Fear had heightened his senses. The lamp slid across the floor until the wall brought it to a halt.

Silence.

Had he killed it?

A flash of lightning bathed the room briefly in stark light and glinted off the tiny glass shards littering the floor. It revealed no glimpse of the ghoul, alive or dead. Loud rumbling thunder vibrated the windows. Crowe forced his rapid breathing to a more normal rate. His frightened gaze swept the gloom. Bedsprings creaked when he crawled to the bottom of the bed and peered down at the floor. The ghoul wasn't there. His head jerked to a new sound, footsteps crunching glass.

It wasn't dead.

It was coming for him.

He backed away from the edge when it drew near. His frantic search for something to fight off the demon revealed nothing ideal for the task. He dashed to the head of the bed, grabbed a pillow to use as a shield, and to perhaps smother the fiend, and faced the side its attack would come from. With pillow raised to fend it off, he waited. The footsteps ceased, leaving behind a deathly silence far worse than the sounds of its movements. At least its footsteps had identified where it was, now soundless, it could be anywhere.

Crowe cautiously leaned forward and peered down at the floor. Nothing. A stabbing pain to his cheek moved his fingers to investigate and came away bloody. Fear turned his head to the direction he thought the attack had come from. The ghoul stood on the headboard, a bloodied sword in one hand, a pistol in the other. It raised the tiny gun, aimed it at Crowe's face and pulled the trigger. A bright flash. A loud explosion. The minute, deadly ball entered his forehead. Blood trickled from the small wound.

Lightning greeted Crowe when he screamed and sat bolt upright in bed. Breathing heavily and glistening with fear-produced sweat, he clutched a hand to his rapidly pumping heart.

"What the hell?"

As he calmed, he gazed around the room, his eyes ending on the rain pattering against the window highlighted by the moon's pale glow. He had never before experienced such a lifelike nightmare. Aware the cause was because his head was swimming with thoughts of the mysterious casket, the strange figures, and their storylines in his new book, he reached for the bedside lamp, which he was glad was where it should be, on the bedside table and not smashed on the floor, and switched it on. Its light revealed the normality of the room. Knowing he would find it difficult to get back to sleep if he didn't check the casket, he swung his feet over the side of the bed and eased them into his slippers. He put on his dressing gown and went downstairs.

The casket was just as he had left it. The creepy ghoul in the position he had placed it in. He closed the lid and pushed the weapon drawer shut. He moved to the fireplace and added a couple more logs to keep it burning through the night so he wouldn't have to relight it in the morning, which wasn't far away. He switched off the light and closed the door behind him.

Oblivious of the tall, slender figure standing in the corner of the room observing him, Crowe hung his dressing gown on the hook on the back of the bedroom door and moved to the window. For a few moments, he stared at the creepy forest that surrounded the house. When lightning flashed and lit up the bedroom, there was no sign of the tall figure. As thunder rattled the window, Crowe crossed to the bed, kicked off his slippers, and slid under the thick duvet. After banishing all thoughts of the casket and its contents from his thoughts, he drifted back off to sleep.

Chapter 7

Strange Revelations

THE STORM HAD PASSED through the night leaving a bright sunny morning, so Crowe decided to walk the two miles to town—God knows he needed the exercise; sitting at a desk typing wasn't exactly a strenuous occupation for keeping a body fit and healthy. He entered the main road and strolled past the usual makeup of shops prevalent in all British towns. People busy with their own lives and errands crisscrossed the street and entered stores with a purpose and exited with their purchases.

Crowe smiled warmly at a couple of older women sitting at one of the three tables outside a café and entered a side street that the information sign heralding the location of the town's museum pointed down. He climbed the few steps leading up to the entrance, pulled open the door and entered.

His gaze around the surprisingly exhibit-sparse interior picked out a man hunched over an open display case at the far side of the room. Crowe headed over and peered into the display case. "Bronze age weapons if I'm not mistaken."

Startled by the voice, the man almost smacked his head on the display's glass lid. Recovered from his shock, he looked at his unexpected visitor. "You are correct, sir. And fine specimens they are too." He held out a bronze axe. "Obviously the handle is a reproduction, but the bronze head is genuine. I have a talented carpenter who makes any bits I need. Though not all my peers agree, I feel it shows off their usage and original appearance to a heightened degree. Kids nowadays aren't always interested in *boring* history now they have their computers, game consoles and, in my opinion, something invented by the devil, mobile phones that are permanently stuck in their hands texting, facebooking and tweeting nonsense to their social media *friends*." He paused his ramble to draw breath. "Go on, you can hold it. I'm all for giving visitors hands-on experiences so they can, I hope, in some way feel the history of the object and get a sense of who might have used it all those thousands of years ago."

Crowe took the axe and turned it over in his hands. The nicks along the blade edge showed signs of wear, causing him to wonder who had used it last and for what. He held the handle and posed a chopping motion. "It's heavier than I would have thought."

"They had to be strong and tough in those days to survive," commented the curator. "Everything they used or ate had to be gathered or hunted. No superstores or online shopping in the Bronze age."

"Simpler, but vastly more dangerous times," commented Crowe, handing the axe back. "I'm looking for Sebastian Burche."

"Then you need look no further. How can I be of service?" Sebastian reached into the display case and laid the weapon in its place above the information card furnishing details about the object.

"I've just moved in as caretaker of Hagsdell Manor and..."

Sebastian smacked his head into the tilted display lid. With a slightly shocked expression, he looked at Crowe as he rubbed the back of his head. "You have?"

Somewhat perplexed by the man's reaction, Crowe nodded. "I've been there a few days now."

Sebastian shifted out from under the lid and closed it. "I thought a developer purchased Hagsdell?"

"He did," Crowe confirmed. "But he's only interested in the land in the valley below that came with the house. He did some basic modernization but other than that, he's leaving the house alone. Too much hassle, red tape, and hoops to jump through with English Heritage to make it worth his while. And, to complicate matters further, there's a clause in the deeds that prohibits the furniture and other stuff from being removed from the premises."

"Interesting," uttered Sebastian, contemplating the news. "It must be full of antiques."

Crowe nodded. "Apart from a few of my modern knick-knacks, nothing but."

Sebastian leaned back against the display. "So, how are you finding living in the old manor?"

"It's a bit creepy at times, but I like it. I'm a writer of the supernatural and horror, so being surrounded by history is an ideal setting to gain inspiration."

"Oh, I'm sure it is."

"Have you ever visited the manor, Sebastian?"

Sebastian shook his head. "I've walked through the forest and seen the outside, but never set foot across the threshold."

"Then you'll have to visit so I can give you a grand tour."

Sebastian perked up at the invitation. "I'd love too, thank you..."

Crowe held out his hand. "Kallisto Crowe."

Sebastian shook the offered hand. "Kallisto, an unusual old name you don't often hear nowadays."

Crowe smiled. "Blame my parents."

"Great author name though."

"That's what my agent said."

"So, do I call you *Kall* for short?" asked Sebastian.

"I'd rather you didn't. I prefer Crowe."

"Splendid. Now we have dispensed with the introductions, tell me how I can be of help."

"I was wondering if you know anything about the history of the manor or its past occupants, the Sinisters?"

Sebastian rubbed his chin. "Not a lot, given that it's been there for nigh on four hundred years and they are the only family, until you moved in, who have lived there."

"It's that old?" exclaimed Crowe.

"Not in the form you see now, but yes, there's been a dwelling on that site for almost four hundred years and always owned by the Sinister family, as was the forest and the surrounding land."

"Astonishing."

"By all accounts, the Sinisters were a private family, keeping very much to themselves. They only ventured into town on rare occasions, having servants to do their bidding—shopping for supplies, cleaning, and upkeeping the grounds and house. They lived in the valley on the far side of the forest in homes the family built to house them. Ruins now and where the builder who purchased Hagsdell Manor is currently working. Going to build some large luxury houses according to the planning application he submitted."

"That's a shame as I was hoping to find out more about the Sinisters."

"Not all is lost as there are a few scant records pertaining to them. Here's what I'll do. I'll check the archives and gather any relevant information and then come and see you up at the manor to show you what I've found."

"Sounds ideal, if you don't mind?"

"Not at all, it'll be a pleasure. Shall we say around seven o'clock?"

"Tonight, you mean?" asked Crowe, surprised Sebastian would have the information ready by then.

"Of course. I may be an avid fan of the past, but I live firmly in the present. To tell you the truth, I'm chomping at the bit to see inside the old manor."

"Tonight it is then. I'll see you about seven. I'll cook us something."

"Splendid." As Sebastian escorted him to the exit, Crowe commented on the emptiness of the museum. "It's normally full of exhibits," explained Sebastian, "but we're clearing it out for our annual witch exhibition, something we do every year as Halloween approaches. In fact, it's our busiest time of year. Apart from school trips, when the kids have no choice about visiting, witches, ghosts, and goblins seem to be the only thing to entice them to voluntarily set foot through the door. We also sell Halloween related items to help finance the museum, so there's that."

"A strange thing for a museum specializing in local history to set up, though," commented Crowe.

"Not at all. We have a history of pagan worship and witches in the area. Visit the town square and you'll see a stake, not the original of course, where quite a few witches, alleged or real, who knows, were burned."

"Interesting for such a small town," said Crowe. "I'll bear that in mind as maybe some of their stories will provide me with an idea for a future book."

"Just let me know if you want to learn more as, unlike the Sinister family, we have quite a bit of information on our past resident witches. There's even a legend hereabouts that one still lives in the heart of the forest attached to the manor. An old crone named Griselda Poison, though, except for fleeting glimpses of a shadowy figure moving through the forest, no one I know of has set eyes upon her."

Crowe smiled. "Spooky, but certainly food for thought book-wise." He shook Sebastian's hand. "Thanks again for your help."

"Glad to be of service old boy. I'll see you tonight at about seven, and I'll bring the wine."

They said their goodbyes and Crowe went to do some food shopping before returning to the manor.

Entering the manor, Crowe nudged the door closed with his rump and headed for the kitchen. He placed the four plastic shopping bags he had lugged all the way from town and shook his fingers the bag handles had dug into. With hindsight, he would have taken the car. After putting away the shopping, he made a cup of tea and went to the living room.

Even though it was sunny day, whatever the temperature outside, the interior of the old house always remained a few degrees lower. After feeding the fire with some fresh logs to ward off the chill, he sipped his tea and turned his gaze upon the casket. It was time to open another of its drawers before getting back to his writing. He sat on the sofa, pulled the small chest a little closer, and ran his eyes over the drawers. Selecting the one bottom right, he lifted the small hanging handle and slid it open.

Again, Crowe was astounded by what was inside. Two strange dogs, black as midnight and just as creepy, with matching orange stripes running along their backs, lay on a velvet pad. Their powerful back legs were longer than their front ones, and all four were tipped with talons. Their sleek bodies bore a slight similarity to a greyhound, but their heads looked more reptilian. Crowe carefully picked one up. Its coat was amazingly lifelike, so much so that he thought it had to be some type of real hair. Its padded paws and claws were expertly rendered. Focusing the magnifying glass on the dog's head, its pointed back ears, and eyes that he pulled open, Crowe marveled at the attention to detail. Gently folding back the skin around its jaws, he examined the gums and teeth, which appeared as lifelike as any real animal's. He spread the jaws open with his fingers and, as he'd expected, the talented modelmaker had included a tongue. As with the little girl doll, Crowe received the impression of a strange-looking real dog miniaturized.

He carefully returned it to its drawer and pushed it closed. It was time he did some more writing. He crossed to his desk, powered up his PC, and continued with his new novel.

After writing for three hours, and pleased with the way the storyline was evolving, Crowe took a break for a snack and a cup of tea. As he ate, his thoughts pondered the manor's previous occupants, the Sinister family. Even their unusual name was spot on for a creepy horror story. Gazing around the living room, he realized there were no photographs of the Sinisters, which he found a tad odd. By all accounts and the number of gravestones in their private cemetery, their lineage stretched back many generations so one would expect to see a few portraits dotted around the house. Wondering if there were any stored in the attic, Crowe headed upstairs to see if he could find any. While he was doing that he'd also search for any film-making equipment to explain the intricate models stored in the casket.

After rummaging through the plethora of knick-knacks, and thrice foiled by locked steamer trunks that prevented him from discovering their contents, he found a flat, one foot square by four inches deep wooden box. Resting it on one of the locked trunks, Crowe released the two catches and lifted the lid. Bingo! It contained photographs. Deciding to go through them downstairs, he closed the box and placed it by the top of the stairs.

When a further hour's exploration failed to produce any movie-making equipment, and the paintings of landscapes and still life he doubted could be used as backdrops, he called an end to his search, collected the box and headed downstairs.

Crowe glanced at the photographs and two painted portrait miniatures he'd spread out on the dining table. The Sinisters certainly lived up to their name. All seemed to be prime candidates plucked straight out of central casting for scary characters to star in a spooky horror movie. Identified by their names written on the back, he picked up the one featuring a past patriarch of the family, Solomon Sinister, posing with his wife, Eldora, and daughter, Clara. Solomon, who was way beyond spooky, stared into the camera lens with, what seemed to Crowe, an expression of murderous intent aimed at the photographer. His wife's expression, only slightly less homicidal, matched that of their child. Placing it on the table face down, he picked up a family photograph picturing two children wearing what seemed to be handmade Halloween masks. Their stiff arms straight down by their sides, their unsettling, expressionless mask faces and holes for eyes staring at the camera. The image was only slightly less disconcerting than the photo featuring Solomon and co.

Aware time was getting on, and he still had dinner to prepare, he flicked through the remainder of the family portraits and group photographs, thankfully more normal than the previous two. They showed groups of children, family groups, and individual members of the Sinister clan through the generations since photography had become common. There was even a couple of the house showing views of how it looked in days gone by.

Crowe headed for the kitchen and began preparing dinner for himself and Sebastian.

Chapter 8

Strange Family

AFTER THEY HAD EATEN in the dining room and cleared away the dinner things, Crowe and Sebastian retired to the living room. Having been given a tour of the house shortly after his arrival, Sebastian again glanced at the spooky-looking cabinet when he entered.

Deciding to hold back on showing Sebastian the casket or the strange painting, Crowe did tell him about the macabre cabinet he had brought down from the attic to use as inspiration for his novel.

"Here are the photographs I mentioned at dinner," said Crowe, handing them to Sebastian.

"Ah, the Sinister family portraits," said Sebastian, taking the photos and plonking himself in an armchair. "My, that Solomon Sinister sure lives up to his name. I've never seen such a creepy individual."

"My thoughts exactly," commented Crowe, watching his guest flick through the photographs.

Sebastian laid the images aside and reached for his briefcase. "As I said when we first met, there's not a lot of info about the Sinisters on record, but what there is you might find interesting." He pulled a folder of papers from his case and opened it. "Though it's not known where the original

47

Sinisters came from when they arrived here almost four hundred years ago, there are records of some of the family joining them from America. Salem, Massachusetts in January 1692, in fact."

"Just as the Salem witch trials were starting, interesting," commented Crowe.

Sebastian smiled. "I was sure you'd make the link and find it intriguing. What's even more interesting is that strange things started happening shortly after their arrival. Strange lights and figures in the forest at night. Sheep and cattle missing or found with their throats ripped. People suddenly becoming ill or going missing, stillbirths, et cetera, et cetera.

"As in many small communities in the era, the villagers were a suspicious bunch by all accounts. They suspected the Sinisters were up to no good and rumors started spreading of them practicing witchcraft and other arcane chicanery. Joining in the witchcraft craze that was rippling through Europe, the villagers seized the chance to be rid of those they thought responsible for the strange goings-on. Accusations of witchcraft and devil sorcery were flung at seven members of the family, five women, including two girls aged thirteen and fifteen, and two men.

"The resulting trials, such as they were, saw all seven burned at the stake in the village square. However, responsible or not, the ridding of the seven Sinisters failed to alleviate the villagers' misfortunes, in fact, they worsened. Nearly every soul was wiped out by a plague-like ailment that swept through the village precisely seven days after the Sinisters had been burned at the stake. Those few who escaped the blight fled never to return. For many years it remained a ghost town, but gradually as memories faded, people started repopulating Hagstown. Over the following years, it steadily grew into the thriving community we see today. All the while watched over by the Sinisters, who kept their distance from the townsfolk.

"Unfortunately, there's a break in the records until 1852, when Conrad and Eliza Sinister arrive in England aboard the steamship *London Merchant*, also outbound from America, location unknown. They joined the Sinisters at the manor and bore a son, Solomon," Sebastian nodded at the photographs. "The creepy man in the photo. He later married Eldora, who was suspected of being his cousin, and they started their own family to keep the Sinister name going. The family began to decline when the females became barren, cursed some say. Unable to keep the family line going, it slowly petered out until the last of the Sinisters died a few months ago."

"You said the information was sparse, but I could base a book about what you've just told me."

"They certainly are...were, an eccentric family with, it seems, a lot of dark history."

"Just mulling over ideas for my book, you mentioned the legend of a witch living in the forest when we first met, was she rumored to be a Sinister?"

"Details are sketchy. It's possible, but who knows. For many years she was accredited with being accountable for almost every piece of bad luck or crime that happened in the area over the last hundred years or so. There are even two recorded witch hunts that saw townsmen enter the forest to seek her out, capture and administer their own brand of justice upon her, burning at the stake. However, not all returned, and the witch's lair was never discovered by any that lived to tell the tale. Rumors of the evil witch and other death-dealing devils stalking the forest kept everyone away. Even today, the locals, including myself, are wary of venturing too deep inside."

"Again, as possible storylines for my book, are there any legends of faeries, ghouls or other strange or mythical creatures inhabiting the forest?"

Sebastian nodded enthusiastically. "Most undoubtedly faeries and not good ones either. Devilish imps and such have been glimpsed throughout the ages in and around the edges of the forest. Though that was long ago and can probably be attributed to people's imagination running wild, mistaking birds and small forest creatures for something menacing because, as we know, there's no such thing as faeries and like creatures outside fiction."

"Of course," agreed Crowe with less conviction.

Sebastian pulled folded papers from the file folder and spread them out on the coffee table. "Are you aware of how Hag's Hollow Forest got its name?"

Crowe shook his head. "No idea."

"It originates from an ancient hollow oak tree shaped like a crippled old hag that stands alone in a dip in the forest."

With raised eyebrows, Crowe looked at Sebastian. "Is that true?"

Sebastian shrugged and smoothed the creases from the old blueprint he had unfolded. "Though I've never seen it for myself, I believe it exists. Something else for you to check out, although that would mean going deeper into the forest."

"It's not something that worries me," said Crowe.

"Rather you than me. I wouldn't call myself overly superstitious, but there's something about that ancient forest that doesn't sit well with me. I went in there once but soon turned back. The deeper you venture, the more ominous it becomes. I truly believe there's something ancient and unworldly living in the forest that doesn't bode well for those that intrude too far into its territory."

"It's only superstition passed down through the years. Some large forests, especially one as ancient as Hag's Hollow, can be naturally ominous and our imaginations do the rest. You're in it now, and you're fine."

"Barely. This house is on the fringes, the forest goes on for miles. I imagine there are many places within where few humans have trod, and of them probably none are still alive today. Some areas I suspect have never been explored."

Crowe smiled. "All the more reason for me to take a ramble then."

"Good luck with that. If you do find Hag's Hollow Oak, please take a photo so I can finally see it and include it in my witch exhibition."

"Don't worry, if I find it and it's as impressive as I'm visualizing, I'll be taking lots." Crowe scanned the large piece of paper on the coffee table. "Now, what have you got here, the manor building plans?"

"Yes, the only surviving blueprint I could find. It's the architect's 1885 perspective design for adding the west wing to the left of the tower. The central section was the original modern house before the east wing was added. As you can see, it shows, more or less, how it looks now. Eleven bedrooms, ten on the first floor and one on the ground floor for a sickly aunt I believe lived to be over a hundred, an even more amazing feat for those days when the average lifespan was fifty-six. The drawing room marked on the plan is now the living room we are in currently, and the pavilion is no more, destroyed in a storm that felled a tree onto it."

"Is it possible I can get a copy of this?"

"Certainly. I would have done one for you, but the plan printer at the planning office was on the blink. As soon as it's repaired, I'll get a copy to you."

"Thanks, Sebastian, appreciated. It'll help me to keep track of the rooms while I'm writing."

"You're welcome, old boy."

The hall grandfather clock struck the hour of ten.

"Oh, well, time for me to get going," said Sebastian.

Crowe walked him to the front door. "Thanks for coming and for the info on the Sinisters."

"My pleasure and I hope it will be of use. If there's anything else I can help you with, let me know."

"Thanks, I'll be sure to."

When Sebastian walked to his car, Crowe glanced over at the forest edge with the uneasy feeling he was being watched. The sound of Sebastian's car starting drew him from the thought. He waved as Sebastian steered around the fountain and drove away. With one last look at the forest, he went inside and closed the door.

Chapter 9

Potions and Parchment

ELECTING TO OPEN ANOTHER casket drawer before deciding on his itinerary for the day, Crowe selected the one bottom left and pulled it open. It had been sectioned off into small cubbyholes and in each sat a tiny glass bottle filled with a variety of colored liquids and powders. He ran his eyes over their many different shapes and designs. There were square, round, hexogen, triangle, bulbous, tall, fat, and pyramid-shaped bottles.

Selecting one at random, he lifted out a square bottle, held it up and admired the blue intensity of the liquid contents, that glowed when it caught the light. Amazed that it was even possible to make such miniature glass containers, he focused the magnifying glass on the intricate, raised geometric patterns that covered each side. Absent any label to identify its contents, which Crowe sensed wasn't just color-tinted water, he refrained from unstopping its tiny cork and giving it a sniff.

He returned the bottle to its snug partition and turned his attention to the long thin compartment situated at the front of the drawer. He carefully plucked out the scroll resting inside. It felt like parchment. Intrigued to find out if anything was written on it, he slid off the red ribbon and unrolled it. Strange letters interspersed with pictograms filled the page. He roamed the magnifying glass over the parchment and zoomed in on one of the small drawings decorating the margins, which he had first thought were insects. Now enlarged, he could see he had been mistaken; they were faeries, sprites, or imps. Most had wings. None were the cute, human-like figures one imagined when thinking of the fairy type of creatures from folklore or the Disneyfied versions. These depictions were much darker, grotesque even.

After he had taken closeup photographs of the parchment, Crowe re-rolled it and replaced it in the drawer. He took a photo of the drawer full of jars, closed it, and sat there for a few moments contemplating the casket and its contents. He was beginning to doubt that, from what little he knew about the Sinisters, any would be involved in anything like making a stop motion movie.

But what else could the strange objects be used for?

With his thoughts recalling his conversation with Sebastian the night before, he decided that checking out the Hag Tree should be a priority, book-plot-wise, before he wrote much more as he would probably want to include it. When rain pitter-pattered the window, he crossed to it and tilted his face skyward. The gray clouds overhead spewing the deluge earthward seemed in no hurry to move on. Reluctant to go exploring in such weather, Crowe decided to wait for it to improve before setting out. He headed to his desk and continued his writing.

Chapter 10

Strange Creatures

WHEN AFTERNOON ARRIVED, CROWE halted his writing and made something to eat. With his appetite sated, he glanced out at the wet weather keeping him indoors. Deciding to open the final casket drawer, he sat by the coffee table and pulled it open, smiling at the regular sized bunch of keys inside. Confident he knew which locks they fitted, he headed to the attic.

Choosing a tall steamer trunk to open first, he tried the keys in the lock until it clicked open. The bottom of the door scraped along the floorboards and released a musty, slightly decayed smell when Crowe pulled it open. Revealed were five mahogany drawers and a top compartment concealed by the lid. Starting at the top, he raised the cover previously held closed by the top lip of the door and gasped. Stepping back abruptly from the sight he beheld, he barged into a stack of tea chests, almost toppling the top one to the floor.

Hardly believing his eyes, he stared in disbelief at the strange creature behind the sheet of glass spanning the width and breadth of the inner compartment. He moved closer and ran his stunned gaze over the small, human-like body and its stretched-out wings. It was a damn faerie. Crowe almost pressed his nose against the glass as his fascinated observation took in the strange creature's details. Its tiny arms, hands, fingers, feet, and toes, though slightly more elongated than a human's, were similar in appearance and number to his own.

Its longer-by-proportion middle finger was tipped with a dark-brown talon. Its face, however, bore little parallel to human form. The ball-shaped head was wider in proportion to its body, its small eyes set further apart, and its ears barely oval cavities in the side of its skull. Its mouth filling the bottom half of its face, had thin lips, a shade darker than the rest of its olive-green skin, and was pulled back, like a snarl, exposing two rows of wide, blunt teeth. Turning his attention to the wings spread out from the back, he noticed they were leathery, bat-like.

In the compartment below were two more similar sized creatures encased in glass-fronted wooden boxes. One had wings, the other none. Crowe lifted out the box containing the winged beast and read the faded label stuck to the glass.

Red Devil Faerie (Dangerous) Captured 1893 north of Satan's Hollow.

Believing them to be models, he admired the creator's attention to detail. The Red Devil Faerie did indeed look dangerous. Two horns, sharp and straight, protruded from the front of its skull, giving it its devilish appearance and hence its name. Its red skin, a tail, long and tipped with thorny protrusions, and its four-clawed hands and feet aided the demonic illusion. The long thin head sported two slanted eyes set closer together than the green creature's, and its mouth was smaller. The nose was narrow, pointed, and slightly hooked. The jutting chin looked like a pointed beard. Stretched tight over its skeletal frame, the skin revealed shapes of ribs and joints. The Devil Faerie's wings were black, a little larger than the green-skinned creature's, and more pointed.

Crowe placed it back in the trunk and examined the wingless faerie for a few moments; another small horror he was glad wasn't real, before reading the yellowed label partly coming unstuck from the glass.

Lesser Faerie. (Workhorse, slave of others more powerful. Threat level, medium) Captured 1891 in the kitchen.

The next drawer down contained pliers, a small hammer and a selection of other tools, bottles of liquid, jars of powders, a scalpel with spare blades, and a tin of small tacks.

Pulling open the third drawer released a stronger waft of musty decay and focused Crowe's eyes upon the creature splayed out angel-like on the board it was pinned to. Its brown, humanoid body was about fifteen inches in length and its wingspan about seven inches, causing Crowe to doubt they were large enough to get it airborne. Like the other faerie creatures, this one also had a mummified appearance but was more goblin-like—shorter, fatter, stocky, with muscular arms and legs. Its tiny shriveled genitalia identified it as a male. He leaned closer and sniffed the tiny corpse. Old, musty with a faint hint of chemicals, possibly embalming fluid. The information label stuck in the bottom right corner read:

Faerie Goblin. (Brutal, savage, and strong. Usually hunts in groups. Avoid.) Captured winter 1893 by Hag's Hollow Oak.

Either side of the faerie goblin were things not included with the other two, clothes and weapons. Brown trousers and a short sleeveless tunic fashioned from animal skin—possibly rat. The weapons consisted of a bow, complete with a quiver of arrows, and a sheathed knife. Crowe pulled the knife from its leathery pouch with his fingertips. The serrated blade appeared to be bone, and thin strips of hide were wrapped around the top to form a grip.

After replacing the knife, Crowe leaned back to take stock of his latest weird discoveries since setting foot in Hagsdell Manor. Though it was all too possible to imagine these were the corpses of real faeries, he knew how inconceivable that was. Such things didn't exist outside the imagination of stories, movies, and myths. The talented creator of the casket models had to be responsible for their exquisite workmanship. The reason why was still a mystery.

Crowe closed and relocked the faerie trunk and moved to another steamer trunk. This one was flatter and smaller than the others with a handle on one of its longest edges. Placing it on the floor, Crowe knelt and tried each key until he found the one that released the lock. He flicked open the catches at either end and opened it. Glad to see it didn't contain more strange creatures, he ran his eyes over the no-less strange contents. Fixed to the underneath of the lid were two rows of eight small glass vials containing blue, green, red, and amber liquids. In the middle between the two bottle groups was a dagger in the shape of a cross. Runes and the Star of Solomon were etched into the blade. Two larger bottles with thin necks contained white powder with gray flecks, which their labels identified as iron and salt.

In the deeper base of the trunk were a selection of snares and traps, including a small version of a bear trap, with wicked shark-like metal teeth. This was also covered in symbols and the Solomon Star. In the middle was a stack of wire mesh. Crowe gripped the mesh's handle and lifted it out. It appeared to be a flattened cage. A sharp jerk unfolded it into a cage of small gapped wire mesh. A door at one end would allow the creature to be trapped to enter, and a metal pressure plate around the opening of a second inner wall dividing the bait chamber would spring-shut the door. If a creature crawled, flew, or walked, the small pressure plate opening meant it couldn't avoid setting the trap when it passed through.

Crowe again ran his perplexed gaze over the objects that seemed to have been created and collected together for one purpose only, to capture the creatures he had viewed in the previous trunk, and then at the cage that he held. It was a faerie trap.

Pondering the purpose of the strange objects, Crowe slid open the trunk's bottom drawer. It contained a single item; a cardboard tube two inches wide and eighteen inches long. Crowe lifted it out and gazed into its open end. There was something rolled up inside. It expanded a few inches when he slid it out and placed it on the top of the trunk. He carefully unrolled the yellowed paper and stared at the design labeled Hag's Hollow Forest. It was a map of the whole forest. His gaze wandered from the drawing of Hagsdell Manor deeper into the woods and came to a halt on a single tree set in a small clearing. Neat handwriting revealed it to be the Hag's Hollow Oak. To the right and a half mile deeper into the trees, was a detail marked *Faerie Realm*.

Other details included the locations of Satan's Hollow, Devil's Cauldron, the Demon Hole, and one that especially piqued Crowe's interest, Witch's Bog.

Assuming the Sinisters, who had owned the forest, had given everything within a satanic themed name, it was a glimpse into their macabre psyche. No wonder the villagers thought they were up to no good.

After returning the map to its protective tube, he placed it aside to take downstairs to photograph. A glance at his watch revealed he had spent too much time in the attic. He collapsed the cage, put it back in its compartment, and closed the trunk. With his thoughts swirling with these latest discoveries and how they would fit into his book, he went downstairs to start preparing dinner.

Chapter 11

Hag's Hollow Oak

EAGER TO CHECK OUT Hag's Hollow, the following morning Crowe decided he would do it today. He would also investigate the location labeled as Faerie Realm on the map. Though he wasn't sure what he would find there, faeries, though that would be great for his book and probably his career, wasn't what he expected to discover.

Crowe closed the back door behind him and glanced at the fountain when he strolled past. No doubt it was once a pleasing feature, but now it was little more than a foul breeding ground for mosquitoes, algae, and the green slime that choked the stagnant pool and covered its graceful posed figures, leaving the stone nymphs and oversized fish mere ghostly images of their former proud selves.

He pulled a compass from his pocket as he neared the edge of the forest and flicked open its brass cover. According to the map he needed to head north for a mile and then turn northwest for about half a mile to reach Hag's Hollow. Leaving the early morning sun behind, Crowe stepped into the shade-cloaked forest stabbed by streaks of both shadow and bright rays. Shivering when a gust of chilled autumn air slipped beneath his coat, he zipped it up tight to his neck. Regularly checking his compass to ensure he remained on track, he walked deeper into the ancient forest where few had tread.

Layers of leaves, brown, brittle, and rotting, crunched with his every step, as if he walked over cereal, pressing them deeper into the soft leaf mold they were destined to become. Trees and branches of yesteryear toppled by past storms littered the forest floor in various states of decay, more so for those that had lain there the longest, home for a myriad of insects and providing nutrition for the mushrooms and fungus taking root on their dying limbs.

Though leaves put into motion by an invisible force occasionally scudded over the ground, causing some to take brief flights into the air before again settling with their many brethren, the only movement of the living came from an occasional bird startling in a tree or a squirrel foraging for lost nuts it had previously hidden.

Crowe breathed in the air rich with the fragrance of leaves, loam, dampness, and decay. The wet soil beneath the thick carpet of leaves occasionally released wispy strands of heady, rot-tainted mist.

As he traveled farther into the forest, the trees became larger, their branches thicker, longer. He tilted his head and gazed up dark ancient trunks boldly rising heavenward. His eyes scanned the gnarled, twisting limbs interlocking with their neighbors like mythical giants linking arms together in a defensive pose to protect their home.

With more of the daylight gradually becoming blocked by the larger, bough-heavy trees the deeper he ventured, the woodland became bathed in a twilight atmosphere and an ominous hush interspersed with sounds of creaking limbs. Leaves shifted by the wind rustled from afar and headed toward Crowe like an invisible creature slithering along the ground.

Judging he had journeyed about a mile, Crowe paused to check his GPS position on his phone, but it proved impossible to get a satellite lock with the signal blocked by the leafy canopy. Confident he had reached his turning point, he headed northwest.

Unobserved by Crowe, the shadowy figure paused the collecting of herbs and fungi and watched him move away. After a few moments of contemplating the stranger, they followed him.

Reaching an area where the trees thinned, allowing brambles and bracken to flourish with dominant, wild abandonment, Crowe pushed through and climbed a slight rise. Halting at the top of the ridge, his gaze wandered down the sharp sloping sides of the deep dell and focused on the wide, stubby tree shrouded in shadow at the bottom. He had arrived at Hag's Hollow Oak.

Switching on his flashlight, he searched for the easiest route down. His brow creased with concern when he recognized the pale blooms of the tall plants thriving on its bowl-shaped sides as white hemlock, one of England's five most poisonous plants which could prove fatal if ingested. Though sparser near the top, they grew in thick, close-knit clumps nearer the boggy ground at the base of the dip.

Noticing a slightly less steep section, he walked around the deep depression and carefully climbed down, almost slipping twice. He passed through the hemlock slowly, disturbing it as little as possible. His feet squished into the boggy ground at the bottom when he made his way to the tree at its center.

Set on a small hump of firmer ground, the ancient oak tree's roots spread out from around its base like limbs that gave the impression they could come to life at any moment and grab him. The light he aimed at the heavily gnarled trunk picked out the pale, bulbous, cancerous growths adorning it. Expecting to discover one that vaguely looked like a hag's face, he examined each one without avail. Wondering why it had received its Hag nametag, Crowe moved around the trunk and almost staggered back in surprise when he came face to face with the tree's namesake.

Crowe stared at the grotesque, evil-looking face formed in the pale knot of the twisted branch curving out from the trunk. Its eyes—two holes slightly lopsided—peered back at him with such a menacing stare, a chill slithered down his backbone. The nose formed from a ridge of bark, pointed and long, reached over the tree-formed open mouth set in a permanent scream or, thought Crowe, more likely frozen in the act of issuing a dreadful curse when she was turned into a tree by a more powerful and skilled necromancer. He smiled at his writer's imagination imbuing the hag tree with a former life.

Moving to the side, Crowe ran his gaze over the stooped body, crooked and hunchbacked. The impression of an arm was formed by the thin branch growing out from the shoulder formation. It ended in crooked twig fingers formed in a grasping claw. When he brushed a hand over its hunched back, the bark, rough and gnarled with age, like the skin of an old man but harder and coarser, he sensed the tree's ancientness through his touch.

Sensing eyes upon him, he surveyed the ridge. Turning full circle, the flashlight's beam roamed through the blackness and across the dark figure the light failed to highlight. Having failed to pick out the cause of his unease, he put it down to the dell's oppressive atmosphere.

Returning his attention back upon the hag tree, Crowe looked at the impression of a long dress given by the splayed branch and noticed a gap, a rip in the bark dress. He crouched and shone the light inside. The hag was indeed hollow, explaining the second part of this feature's designation. Poking his head in the space filled with the cloying stench of damp earth and wood decay, he glanced at the white filigree fungus of heart rot highlighted starkly in the torch beam. Crowe recognized the Death Cap mushrooms growing in the dank earth at the back of the hollow trunk. He had used them as a device to kill off a character in one of his more successful books. If eaten, symptoms would begin to appear several hours after eating. Starting with severe vomiting, diarrhea, and stomach pains, it then passed, furnishing the unsuspecting victim with a false sense of a full recovery. A few days later they'll die of kidney or liver failure. His research also revealed the Death Cap had caused the most recorded fatalities for a poisonous species in the UK, as there is no known antidote.

Climbing to his feet, Crowe took photographs of the hag tree from all angles with his phone. When he had finished, he clambered out of the dip and headed for his next forest destination, the Faerie Realm.

Chapter 12

Faerie Realm

AS CROWE APPROACHED THE location of the feature highlighted as Faerie Realm on the map, he arrived at a wall formed of tall thorny shrubs. A shorter variety at the forefront was adorned with bright red berries and wicked inch-long thorns set in groups of three, which ran the length of every stem of the vicious looking plant. Behind it, rising taller than him, Crowe took in the equally thorny barrier of shrubs sporting clumps of purple berries. Doubting even a rat would get through the impenetrable barrier unscathed, he knew he would be ripped to shreds in the attempt. He stepped back and gazed both ways along the curving thorny wall he assumed surrounded the area marked as the Faerie Realm. It seemed out of place in the forest, unnatural, as if it had been planted with a purpose. It reminded Crowe of the thorny barrier the wicked witch had placed around Sleeping Beauty in the popularized Disney spin of the original darker version of the fairy tale.

Determined to find a way through, Crowe walked its circumference and halted at a tree fallen across the barrier; a natural bridge for him to make use of. Though the vicious barb-lined tendrils encroached partway over the broad trunk, if he was careful, there seemed to be enough room for him to sidle past unscathed. He climbed up the root end of the tree and cautiously walked along its length. Covered in lichen, moss and damp decay, it wasn't the firmest surface he would wish for while navigating through bushes armed with razor-sharp defenses. A fall might not kill him, but it would be painful and probably leave him with a few scars. He wasn't the most handsome of men, so face scars would only add to his anti-attractiveness.

Taking one slow, careful step at a time, Crowe ducked, twisted and stepped over the barbed branches. On reaching the bough end of the tree, he slithered between two close-knit branches and was free of the thorns. He jumped down, his feet sinking into the thick leaf layers. Before him stood a ring of ancient oaks, each bent slightly, leaning toward each other, their thick, heavy limbs twisted around others of its kind; a natural roof of oak branches casting darkness over what dwelled beneath.

Crowe approached the oak circle and passed between their massive trunks. The close-knit clump of trees caused the sunlight to fade to a twilit glow, bathing Crowe and the surroundings in oppressive gloom. Along with the drop of temperature within the tree circle, the woodland seemed ominously quiet. He tilted his gaze to the creaking branches overhead, giving the impression they were drawing closer, cutting off the tiny slivers of daylight that still managed to penetrate their tightly entwined limbs.

The atmosphere, now heavy with foreboding, wrapped Crowe in heightened anxiety. Wind wailing between distorted trunks carried the sickly stench of decay and cast his nervous glance at every creak of tree and rustle of leaves. Spooky, mysterious sounds coming from all directions did nothing to alleviate his rising trepidation that he had entered another realm where few humans had dared to tread.

Fighting back what he knew was an unfounded sense of unease—he was still in the forest and could leave any time he wished—Crowe reached into his pocket and pulled out his flashlight. He felt the stub of the small button and heard the reassuring click under his thumb when he pressed it. The beam of portable, comforting faux sunlight cut through the darkness, banishing the fright-inducing shadows within its reach.

Startled when something big and dark screeched close-by and flapped across his path, Crowe yelped in surprise and ducked as he followed it with the light.

The large rook swooped in a circle and landed on the fence a short distance away. Focusing its dark, beady eyes upon the intruder, the rook observed the human, as if curious about why it had come and what it was about to do.

Human and bird stared at each other for a few moments, then, as if losing interest, the rook jumped into the air with a loud caw. Perhaps a warning to other forest dwellers of the human's unwelcome presence in this wilderness it shouldn't have entered, before disappearing into the darkness.

Whispers faint and menacing began... *"Something's coming."*

"It's a man human."

"What's it doing here?"

"Will it set us free?"

"Quiet the lot of you!" snapped an authoritative voice.

Recovering from his fright and glad the evil looking bird had departed; Crowe moved the light beam over the fence he approached.

"It's coming."

"I warned you."

Thwack! A painful moan. Silence.

Made of iron and covered in rust, the chest-high fence ringed a clear area of grass dotted with bright woodland flowers that grew up to the barrier but not one shoot of grass or tendril of shrub passed beyond it. Though Crowe thought flowering plants at this time of year a little unusual, especially in such a sunlight-starved area, he paid it little heed as, according to the map, this was the realm of the faeries, and if so, he should expect to see things a little strange for it to be labeled as such.

A little disappointed by the unimpressive piece of ground devoid of any faerie life or small houses made from brightly colored toadstools, Crowe walked around the edge looking for a gate that would allow him to enter. After traversing the entire circumference, he had failed to find one.

Placing a hand on the cold, rusty metal, he shook the fence. Though it wobbled slightly, releasing flakes of rust, it seemed firm. He placed a foot on the bottom cross rail and hoisted himself up.

"Conceal yourselves," ordered the voice of authority.

With a tearing screech of metal, the fence section he balanced on broke free from its posts and toppled forward, sending Crowe spilling to the ground with his feet poking outside the fenced circle.

"The circle is broken."

"The realm of humans is ours again."

"If I have to tell you lot again...!"

Unhurt by the fall, Crowe got to his knees and glanced at the broken end of the fence. It was hollow with a white granular substance trickling out. He reached out and rubbed the coarse powder between two fingers; it felt like salt. A cautious taste confirmed it. Perplexed at why someone would go to the bother of filling an iron fence with salt, he climbed to his feet, Stepping fully into the circle, he glanced around.

"Oh, crap!" He was no longer in Hag's Hollow forest!

A bridge of stone, ancient, almost a ruin, and covered in moss and lichen, led from the small hillock he now stood upon, across a noxious and festering river, to a forest displaying no similarity to the one he had just inexplicitly vacated. Trees, ancient, evil, gnarled, and twisted into menacing shapes, sported arm-like branches with splayed claws formed of sharp, finger-slender twigs, posed ready to grasp anyone who dared come within their reach. An unnatural mist hugging the forest floor swirled and sent out vaporous fingers lacking the substance to grasp anything, added to the unnerving strange sort of wrongness that permeated this land he had somehow stumbled into and, to all intents and purposes, should not exist.

Darkly foreboding cracks, like that of tree trunks snapping, echoed through the forest and jerked Crowe's head toward the sounds. Leaves rustled like the whisperings of foul, unimaginable creatures communicating.

Turning his worried gaze behind, Crowe noticed the dismal bog stretched the reach of the dim light before it faded into darkness. His eyes flicked to the only visible tie to the real world, the section of rusty iron fence, however, this too had changed, it was now huge. Each of the metal bars was almost as wide as he was tall. Ducking under the end that rested on a rock, he crossed to its base and climbed over the bottom rail. A few more steps carried him outside the circle.

He stared in amazement when the dark landscape around him morphed back into the real world. He turned around. Everything was back to normal, well as normal as it could be given that he was standing in a strange ring of oaks at the entrance to the realm of the faeries which, if his imagination wasn't tricking him, he now suspected was real. To test his disbelieving common sense, he stepped over the fence again and observed the dark realm materialize into existence once more. Even though he knew it was impossible, he had discovered some sort of doorway—a portal to a different world—the Faerie Realm.

Gazing around at the bleak, dark landscape, he was certain the fairies usually depicted as cute, beautiful and benevolent winged, human-like creatures, weren't the type that lived here. No. Things evil and monstrous dwelt in this realm. Faeries of the kind he had found in the Sinisters' attic.

Though common sense bade him to return to the real world, Crowe's stronger inquisitiveness led him around the giant piece of fencing and across the bridge. Things barely glimpsed when they rose toward the river's viscous, pestilent surface, sent ripples skulking across the stagnant water and shivers down Crowe's spine.

He halted at the far side and flicked his anxious gaze behind him. Reassured that if danger threatened, a fast sprint would carry him to safety, he took a deep breath to pluck up his waning courage and continued into the creepy forest. Though the occasional unnerving distant booming crack and the wind creaking the dead branches continued, the forest was surprisingly quiet, as if it held its breath. There was no sign of life; no birds, and no evidence of any forest dwellers scampering across the forest floor or through the trees.

A short anxiety-filled distance later, the trees changed to thin, spindly growths tightly packed together. On rounding a bend, the path he followed ended at a set of stone steps rising gently into the distance. Above the distant fog that shrouded his view of the landscape, Crowe glimpsed the faint outline of something tall and imposing; a tower.

"The human has trespassed far enough, capture him," whispered the authoritative voice.

As he pondered going to investigate the structure, a rustling in the trees to his left turned his head. A group of five creatures bounded along thin branches toward him. When they arrived at the break in the trees that formed the path, they jumped into the air and fluttered to the ground on wings inadequate to keep them airborne for long and stared at him. After a brief unintelligible conversation, they headed for him. In jumping, flying motions, they raced across the ground brandishing vicious snarls and sharp blades.

Momentarily taken aback, Crowe stared at the weird creatures. There were four brown ones armed with knives and a blue one who carried a bow and a quiver of arrows on its back and had a patch over one eye. If they were faeries, they weren't the tiny ones he had visualized from fairytale lore. These were almost as big as him and infinitely more intimidating. Recovering from his shock at the sight of real, living faerie creatures, he staggered back, turned, and fled.

The faeries followed.

Crowe raced back through the forest and glanced behind when he reached the stone bridge. Their movement might seem ungainly, but the faeries were damn fast and only a short distance away from catching him. Adrenalin spurred him across the stone bridge. With the sounds of pursuit alarmingly close, Crowe sped for the giant piece of fallen fence, dodged around it and jumped through the invisible portal.

He tripped on landing and rolled across the leaves until an abrupt meeting with an oak halted him. Panting heavily, his eyes flicked to the flower-strewn ground inside the fenced circle when areas of grass bent back, forming five small depressions.

The faeries felt a tingling sensation when they stepped onto the magic mound and turned their bewildered expressions on the large piece of fallen iron fence.

"It's true! The barrier is broken. We can cross to the human world again."

One of them fluttered its wings and rose above the grass. *"Is it safe though?"*

"Where be the human?" said another, joining its comrade in the air and turning full circle.

Outside the barrier, Crowe cocked an ear to the faeries' barely audible whispers which he failed to understand. Faerie talk, he assumed, because they were faeries and they were talking. He was still trying to come to terms with all this sudden strangeness.

One of those still on the ground pointed at the break in the barrier that had trapped them for so long. "It must be outside the circle." It narrowed its eyes and scowled at a patch of blurred, undulating air. "It watches us."

"Let's get it. I longs to taste human flesh again," said another, running a drooling tongue over its teeth in anticipation. "The small ones are especially tasty."

"Be cautious," advised the one-eyed faerie on the ground. "Those humans be a devious race. This could be another sneaky trap of theirs."

"Aye, we all knows what happened last time they came to our realm, they murdered our king and trapped us here."

"Now the barrier is down, they'll suffer greatly for their crimes," said another.

When the faeries started moving slowly toward the fence, their progress identified by the trails they formed in the grass, Crowe's first instinct was to flee, but his eyes flicked to the barrier he had broken. He had written enough about occult practices, demons, and the like to realize that both the iron fence and the salt that filled it must have a purpose. Perhaps to trap the faeries within; iron and salt. Aware he'd be responsible for setting them free if he didn't do something, he lunged back into the circle and grabbed the fallen fence section.

Both human and faerie wore the same astonished expression as each race materialized before the other. Surprised the faeries were now normal fairy size, Crowe took in their tiny clothing and small weapons, which reminded him of the ones in the strange casket. Recovering quickly from the shock when one of them fluttered into the air and flew at him jerkily with a sword ready to slice and stab, he raised the now normal size fence from the ground and dragged it into place as best he could, making sure the broken ends touched the fence posts to bridge the gap. He dodged back when the five faeries neared the barrier, all of whom vanished as soon as his hand parted from the fence.

The faeries halted a short distance away from the feared barrier when the human disappeared.

"One of us needs to test it," stated the sword-wielding faerie, landing on the ground with a thump.

"That someone won't be me," stated the fattest faerie, taking a step back to reinforce his cowardice in case the others hadn't picked up on it.

The authoritative sword faerie rested the tip of his sword on the ground, placed his hands atop the pommel and turned to the faerie armed with a bow and a quiver of arrows and a patch over his left eye.

"Now, I knows ya to be afraid of nothing in this realm or the next, Deadeye, so hows about ya steps up to the barrier and gives it a poke?"

Deadeye shrugged, took three paces forward and jabbed a finger at the fence. He screamed when sparks sizzled from the area of his touch. He screamed again when he shot backward and became airborne faster than any arrow he had ever fired.

The other four followed his trajectory over the river, into the branches of a tree and finally his plummet to the ground. Deadeye's groans announced he had survived the rapid flight. His hurried rush back to his comrades revealed his blackened finger and smoking hair.

Sword faerie contemplated the problem. Though the iron barrier was all but invisible, the air it occupied on the edges of human and faerie world was slightly blurred, revealing the barriers weakness and its presence. When he noticed another disturbance in the air, he peered at the fuzzy image of the human approaching the barrier.

He again turned to Deadeye. "If the human appears again, loose an arrow at it."

Deadeye notched an arrow in his bow, drew it back, and waited.

When after a few moments the faeries failed to appear, Crowe wondered if having been unable to follow him, they had given up the chase and left. In order to find out, he moved forward and stretched a hand toward the fence.

As soon as the human materialized, Deadeye let loose an arrow. When the miniature barbed missile was a few inches away from Crowe's eye, it fizzled with sparks into a puff of ash that was carried away on the wind.

Sword wielder cursed. Nothing of theirs could cross the barrier while it was intact. They needed to somehow tear it down.

Though his senses begged him to turn and flee, Crowe couldn't resist the opportunity of observing the small creatures, who, like the arrow that had just been fired at him, he now assumed were unable to pass through the barrier. Realizing the opportunity before him, he kept one hand on the fence and fished his phone from his pocket with the other. A video of the faeries would surely go viral on YouTube. Also, if released at the appropriate time, it would be great publicity for the book he was currently writing, which would now include this magic portal and the faeries trapped within. Switching his phone to video mode, he filmed them.

The faerie armed with a sword spoke, what sounded like gibberish to Crowe, to one of its brown-skinned comrades, who then promptly disappeared back through the portal into the faerie realm.

Crowe zoomed in for some close-up shots, capturing their faces, clothing, and weapons. When the faerie returned with a length of rope attached to a grappling hook, he sensed they were up to something and focused the camera on it. It swung the grappling rope around a few times and let fly at the fence. It clanged against the top and bounced off. Crowe realized they were attempting to pull it down to break the protective circle. Keen to keep them trapped within, he stopped recording and returned the phone to his pocket. When the grappling hook was thrown again, he grabbed and yanked it. Expecting the rope to be pulled from the faerie's grasp, he was surprised when the faerie kept a firm hold and was pulled off his feet. With a spectacular but brief display of sparks, it disintegrated into a shower of ash when it breached the invisible barrier.

Feeling guilty for being responsible for killing a faerie, however vicious it was, Crowe looked at the others waving their weapons at him angrily. He glanced at the thread-thick rope and the tiny grappling hook swaying on its end. Surprised it hadn't disintegrated like the faerie, Crowe wondered if the reason was that he was human and able to cross the barrier, so anything that passed through with him would survive. He wrapped the thin rope around one end of the fence and the post and tied it in place so it couldn't fall or be pulled away.

Two more faeries appeared through the portal, a larger red one, and a small green type. Both flew near to the barrier entrapping them and stared at Crowe. Hoping he had done enough to keep them imprisoned, Crowe removed his hand from the fence and backed away.

When the faeries made no further attempts to breach the barrier, Crowe walked away and climbed onto the fallen tree bridge. Glancing back at the faerie rope securing the fence in place, he focused his concerned gaze upon the wisps of smoke coming from it. When a spark fizzled into the air, he realized it wouldn't hold them at bay for long. He rushed across the bridge and headed home. He needed to take another look at Solomon Sinister's books and the faerie items he had found in the attic to find out if there were any way to repair the damage he'd unwittingly done. If the faeries crossed over to the human world, it could prove disastrous for those living nearby and perhaps even further afield if they spread out. It was something he couldn't let happen. Whatever it took, he would re-trap the faeries in their own realm.

Sparks slowly spluttered along the length of faerie rope and burst into a spray of colored light. Released from its tether, the fence section tilted and fell.

The red faerie, whose name was Redweedle, materialized into the human world, the first faerie to do so for nigh on a hundred human years. After gazing around, a smirk formed on its cruel lips. It spun with a purpose and returned to its realm. There were preparations to make.

When night began creeping through the forest, seven bursts of light briefly lit up the gloom within the circle of oaks. The fluttering and scampering of faeries across the ground moved toward the fallen tree. Its dying branches trembled when they climbed its boughs and rushed along its trunk. The movements of the seven faeries faded into the distance when they followed the trail left by the human that had set them free.

Chapter 13

Strange Skirmish

SITTING AT HIS COMPUTER typing up the day's events into coherent story form to fit in with what he had written so far, Crowe glanced at the window when movement from the corner of his eye distracted him. Jittery from his encounter with the faeries earlier, who he was sure he hadn't seen the last of, he climbed from his chair and crossed to the window. Bathed in moonlight and shadow, the trees at the edge of the forest were put into motion by gusts of wind, swaying their branches a little ominously he thought in his present nervous condition. He had locked all exterior doors and pulled the shutters across all the windows except the one he presently gazed through and the hall window whose shutter was broken. Noticing the rain highlighted in the moonlight, he wondered if faeries were like butterflies and couldn't fly in such weather. Doubting that was so, he gazed around the garden for any sign of them.

Spying nothing amiss, he was about to return to his writing when a tinkle of glass on the floorboards in the room above tilted his face to the ceiling. His apprehensive gaze followed the soft pattering footsteps moving across the upstairs floorboards.

The faeries were here!

Though he had been expecting them, their presence and their unknown reason for coming, which he thought wouldn't be anything good for his health, scared him.

Controlling his fear, Crowe hurried into the hall, grabbed the gas lighter from the small table against the wall and moved to the star of Solomon sign within a circle formed in salt on the floor. A preparation he had made earlier after consulting Solomon's notes and research. He carefully stepped into the middle, lit the candles set at each star point before focusing his gaze up the staircase and on the eyes peering through the balcony rails at him. When they moved to the top of the stairs and started climbing down, he pulled the flat wooden box nearer and raised the lid. He lifted out the iron dagger shaped into a cross and hoping his defensive preparations would work, he waited for them to come.

When a beam of bright light traveled across the hall, Crowe turned to the window behind him and glimpsed a car pulling into the drive. Wondering who it was and what they wanted, he listened to the engine fade. A car door slammed shut. Hurried footsteps crunched across the gravel and climbed the steps to the front door. The booms of the iron knocker being struck three times echoed through the house.

Realizing the danger to the person who had come calling, Crowe shouted, "Go away! Run!"

Ignoring his warning, a woman's voice asked, "Is that you, Mr. Crowe? I'm Sebastian's daughter, Arabella. I have the house plans you wanted."

Crowe's eyes flicked to movement on the stairs. Three faeries split off from the group and rushed back upstairs. *They're going after her.* Cursing her inopportune arrival, Crowe snatched up a jar, tipped a handful of its contents into his palm and flung the mixture of salt and iron filings at the four faeries approaching the bottom of the stairs. As soon as the powders left his hand, he sprinted for the door, slid back the bolts and pulled it open.

Arabella smiled. "Good evening, Mr. Crowe, I..." her words were brought to an abrupt halt when he grabbed her wrist, yanked her inside and slammed the door closed.

Ignoring her surprised gasp, he slid the bolts home and dragged her toward the magic protective symbol.

"Do exactly as I say," Crowe ordered.

Flummoxed and a little scared by the unexpected turn of events, Arabella let herself be dragged across the hall.

Flicking his gaze at the faeries suffering from the effects of the salt and iron thrown at them, he pointed at the symbol on the floor. "Tread carefully, so you don't disturb the salt."

Wondering what the hell was happening, she carefully followed Crowe into the center of the symbol.

"We'll be safe within the circle."

Arabella looked at the man she thought quite mad. "Safe from what?"

Crowe turned her around to face the stairs. "Them!"

Arabella gasped in shock and stumbled back into Crowe, her foot almost sliding through a salt line as she stared in horror at the small, shrieking creatures flittering about erratically and brushing hands over their bodies as if beating at invisible flames. With a shaking hand, she pointed the long cardboard tube at the creatures on the bottom of the stairs. "Are those...*faeries*?"

"Unfortunately they are, and not the good kind. There are also three more that went outside after you, which explains my dragging you inside more forcefully than I would have liked on our first meeting."

Crowe bent down and picked up a jar from the floor. "Take this. It's a mixture of salt and iron filings. I don't know why, but the faeries seem to hate both. Tip some into your hand and throw it at them if they come too close."

Trying to make sense of what was happening, Arabella took the jar and glanced around at the four faeries that had now surrounded them. In her opinion, they were already too close.

"And be careful not to break the salt lines. I know it's a bit cramped in here, but I wasn't expecting company."

"And I wasn't expecting to be standing in a magic circle surrounded by things that shouldn't exist."

"Even so, you seem to be taking the shock rather well."

"Believe me, it's all an act. Inside I'm screaming like a frightened schoolgirl watching a scary movie with the lights out on Halloween."

"Which is only a few days away," Crowe realized, glancing around at the faeries and wondering what their next move would be. "If we remain calm, we should be okay."

"I'm trying, but it's not easy."

Crowe knew exactly what she meant.

"But the faeries," Arabella's eyes flicked to the stairs. "Are they real? They seem to be, but faeries aren't real, are they?"

"As real as you and me." Crowe noticed the faeries that had gathered to plan their next move were splitting up again. "I'll fill you in later, but now we need to be prepared for their attack. I think the protection symbol will keep us safe, but it's not something I've had experience of before, so it could all be mumbo-jumbo and completely useless. However, they didn't like the salt and iron I threw at them a moment ago, so that gives me some confidence we'll be safe as long as we stay within the circle."

Having trouble taking it all in, Arabella looked down at her feet and shuffled away from the salt lines a few inches, and then at the dagger, Crowe held. "And what's that for?"

Crowe held up the dagger cross. "In case the salt symbol fails."

"Oh," uttered Arabella worriedly. "Can't we make a dash out the front door? My car's outside. We can run for it and drive away."

Crowe shrugged his head at the window. "A sound plan in theory, but there's a problem."

Arabella looked at the window Crowe pointed at. One faerie hovered outside, and two others stood on the sill with their faces pressed against the glass. "Oh."

"Here they come," he warned.

Arabella focused on the faerie scampering across the floorboards toward them. Though she found it hard to believe she was looking at a real living breathing faerie, the evidence was impossible to refute. She took in its clothing, the patch over its eye and the arrow notched in the bow it held aimed straight at her. "That can't be good."

Crowe glanced at the faerie archer. "It's okay. I don't think the arrow can pass over the symbol."

"Your uncertainty isn't inspiring me with confidence."

Deadeye drew back the bow and let the arrow fly. It sizzled into dust when it entered the invisible barrier produced by the magic protection symbol.

"See, I was right," bragged Crowe.

"I have a feeling you're as surprised as me that your words rung true. What do we do now?"

"Try throwing some salt at it to see what it does," suggested Crowe, keeping his eye on the other three who seemed content, for the moment, to keep their distance and observe.

Tucking the cardboard tube under her arm, Arabella sprinkled some of the salt and iron filings mixture into her palm and threw it at the archer.

Deadeye dodged back and ran, but he wasn't fast enough to avoid it all. He screeched when the substance rained down on him, stumbled to the floor and rolled.

"It didn't like that," said Arabella, a little less worried now she had a defense against them. "What are the others doing?"

"Nothing. Just watching. I think they're waiting for something."

"That also doesn't sound good," answered Arabella.

A rapid fluttering of wings directed their gazes up the stairs and upon the red faerie flying down them. Their eyes followed its approach, turning to keep it in view when it flew around them. It dived for the floor and hovering a short distance away from the protection symbol, examined it for a few moments. It looked at Crowe and Arabella in turn and then spoke.

"What did it say?" asked Arabella.

"I've no idea, I don't speak Faerie."

It was obviously an order as immediately two of the smaller faeries moved to the front door. While one slid back the bolt at the bottom, the other flutter-climbed to the top bolt and drew it back. Both then grabbed the handle and pushed it down. A fluttering of their wings creaked it open. The three faeries outside helped push the door wide open.

Redweedle glanced at the two humans briefly before flying to the entrance.

"Did it just smile at us?" asked Arabella.

"I think it was more of a sneer. Get ready, they're up to something."

"And how am I supposed to prepare for something when I have no idea what it will be?"

Crowe shrugged. "Just prepare for the worst, I suppose."

"Great," uttered Arabella, pouring some salt and iron into her palm.

Redweedle spoke loudly, a call to something outside.

A faerie necromancer, ugly, evil and black, flew through the doorway, his black cloak decorated with strange mystical symbols fluttered behind him. Halting just inside, he glanced condescendingly at Crowe and Arabella before turning to face outside. He raised the gnarled, twisted wooden staff in a hand tipped with long sharp fingernails and pointed it up at the sky. A sequence of strange chanting phrases spewed from his mouth.

A flash of lightning lit up the house interior and the worried faces of its two human occupants. The loud clap of thunder that rattled the windows violently in their frames increased their anxiety.

"It's performing magic," uttered Crowe, enthralled.

"I'd calm your obvious excitement because if it is magic, I doubt it's the good kind and its result won't be anything favorable to us."

Captivated by the actual spells he witnessed being cast, Crowe made a mental note of every detail to be recalled later for his book, if he lived to finish it.

The wind grew in strength and whipped around the house. Dragging leaves and twigs in its wake, the conjured storm clattered them against the windows in passing.

Keeping his staff aimed outside, the necromancer faerie backed up until he was halfway into the hall. After shooting an evil sneer at the two humans, he jerked his staff at the symbol on the floor. The wind dived through the entrance and screamed around the room.

Crowe and Arabella covered their faces with their hands to protect them against the wind, leaves, dust, and twigs bombarding them.

"Uh-oh!"

Keeping her face covered, Arabella turned to Crowe. "What?"

"Look at the floor."

Arabella looked at the wind slowly shifting the salt, wiping away the symbol. "What do we do?"

Crowe shrugged. "I'm open to suggestions."

Arabella gazed around fearfully, looking for a way out of their predicament before the symbol was destroyed. "I hope your characters in your books fair better than we are."

Crowe shook his head. "Not usually. Most die." He looked at the window as a possible escape route and noticed things were about to get a lot worse. A tall, pale figure rushed toward the house. "We need to move now!"

"At last, he speaks sense," uttered Arabella. "Which way and where to?"

Having seen the fear appear on the human's face when he looked at the window, one of the brown faeries, keeping clear of the storm whirling around the center of the room, moved to the window to find out the cause. He looked out, saw what was coming and jerked his head to the red faerie. His shrill, piercing screech cut through the noise of the wind and alerted Redweedle to the danger, who fluttered to the side and peered through the window. Fear spread across his face. He shot to the door to inform the necromancer of the imminent threat.

Peering through the maelstrom of windborne debris, Crowe searched for the faeries and a safe direction to flee. Without warning the wind battering them ceased. Both stared at the wizard faerie who had aimed its staff back outside and was uttering a chant that funneled the raging storm into a tightly wound maelstrom of wind, thunder, and lightning.

Crowe shot a glance at the window and saw what was coming. Though he recognized the pale, slender creature as the ghoul from the casket, this version was taller than a doorway and much more frightening. The ghoul skewed to the side and slid backward when the twisting, swirling tornado blasted it. Pushing through, it jumped free, ran for the house, and dived through the window. The brown faerie, too terrified to flee, was plucked from the windowsill as the ghoul entered and rolled across the floor. It jumped to its feet and flung the faerie across the room, sending it crashing into a wall. As the dead faerie fell to the floor as limp as a rag doll, the ghoul turned its wrath upon the two nearest faeries. Snatching them from the air, it squeezed, crunching their bones under the pressure. Discarding the broken forms, it rushed at Redweedle. A flash of light shot from the necromancer's staff and exploded in front of its face. Temporally blinded, the ghoul dropped to a crouch. Arrows fired at an extraordinary rate by Deadeye, peppered its head.

Recognizing that the battle was lost and more worryingly there was a high chance of him losing his life, Redweedle ordered the retreat. When the others followed Redweedle outside, the ghoul gave chase. It grabbed two more faeries before they were through the door. One it crushed in its fist, the other it bit off its head and spat it out. The ghoul glanced at Crowe and Arabella as it scooped up the faerie corpses before rushing outside.

Stunned by what had just taken place, for a few moments, Crowe and Arabella were unable to move, they just stared at the doorway.

Arabella broke the silence. "What the hell just happened, and what was that thing that just saved us?"

"I think it was a ghoul."

"A ghoul?"

Crowe nodded. "I don't think they'll be back tonight, but let's get this place shuttered up and restore the protection symbol, and then I'll explain everything. I also need a drink."

Arabella screwed the lid back on the salt jar and handed it to Crowe. "After what I've just been through, just hand me a bottle."

Crowe held out his hand. "Kallisto Crowe."

Still baffled, Arabella gently shook his hand. "Arabella Burche. Sebastian said I might find you a little strange, but this..." she swept the cardboard tube around at the chaos, "...gives strange a whole new meaning."

Crowe smiled. "I assure you this is not what I do on a normal night."

"Glad to hear it," replied Arabella, gazing around the hallway; twigs and leaves were everywhere. "Go find something to board up the window, but first fetch me a broom, and I'll start clearing a space for your magical salt drawing, and this time, make it a little bigger."

Crowe formed a surprise expression. "After all that's just happened, you're not fleeing?"

"Though common sense dictates that's exactly what I should do, I want to hear your explanation for all this first. Faeries and *things* I've just witnessed shouldn't exist, and yet they obviously do. They also don't seem to look kindly upon us human folk, or maybe it's just you that they don't like, either way, I believe it's in my best interest to find out as much as I can about them and the threat they pose, and then I'll probably flee."

"That's very reasonable of you. To tell the truth, I could do with sharing the strange happenings I've been encountering lately."

"Well, let's get this place sorted first and then we can sit down with a drink, and you can reveal all."

An hour later, Crowe had explained to Arabella what had happened to him since moving into Hagsdell manner. He also showed her the casket and the strange objects inside.

Cradling the ghoul model from the casket in her hands, Arabella looked at Crowe." So, to get this straight, you're telling me this thing is somehow linked to that creature that killed the faeries?

"I'm not sure how, but yes, I believe it is. I think it's a ghoul."

"But why did it help us? Where did it come from, and where did it go?"

Crowe shrugged "I assume it came out from the painting I told you about as it's not there now. After witnessing it saving us, I think it might be a guardian for the house or its residents, maybe both. Alternatively, it could just really hate faeries."

Arabella placed the ghoul back in the casket. "One thing I'm sure of is that you've opened Pandora's box and need to find a way of closing it before more of those faeries get free and someone gets hurt or killed."

"I know, it's something I've been working on. After going through Solomon's archives, I think I've found a solution." Crowe topped up his and Arabella's drink. "You've heard the legend about the witch living in the forest?"

Arabella nodded. "Griselda Poison."

"Yes, well I now believe it might not just be a myth, and she actually exists. I'm going to seek her out and ask for her help."

A little stunned, Arabella sipped her drink. "Well, good luck with that because if the stories about her are true, and she is real, you might be better off facing the faeries on your own."

"Thanks for the encouragement."

Arabella glanced at the clock. "Goodness, it's late." She stood. "I have to get going."

Crowe walked her to the door and checked the area outside was clear. "Thanks for the house plans and everything. I promise our next meeting will be less strange and frantic."

Arabella smiled. "Let's hope so, and I think you owe me dinner for what you put me through tonight."

"It's the least I can do," replied Crowe. "As soon as things have calmed down here, I'll ring you."

Arabella climbed into her car and started the engine. She rolled down the window. "Be careful."

Crowe nodded. "My middle name."

Arabella rolled her eyes and drove away.

When she had gone, Crowe peered into the forest. Certain the ghoul wasn't far away, he called out. "Thank you for your help."

An owl hooted in reply.

Crowe entered the house and closed the door.

Chapter 14

Griselda Poison

KEEN TO SORT OUT the faerie problem before it got worse, the following morning Crowe headed into the forest. Utilizing the image of the forest map on his phone for reference, he made his way to Witch's Bog.

Halting at the edge of the boggy ground, Crowe stared at the stinking, festering expanse of stagnant black soup. Areas of fine mist tinged with the smell of the decay that formed it floated across the pond ringed with thick, dark mud. An occasional air bubble plopped to the surface and sent out delicate ripples. If the witch's house was nearby, he saw no sign of it. Keeping clear of the uninviting mud, he carried on around its circumference.

The caw of a raven turned his head. The black bird sat on a post leaning at an angle watching him, but it wasn't the bird responsible for the surprised expression upon his face, but the wooden bridge that hadn't been there a moment before. The raven took flight when he approached and settled in the twisted bough of a dead tree rising from the foul swamp.

Retracing his steps, Crowe halted at the end of the rickety old bridge and gazed along its length to where it disappeared into a bank of thick mist. Though concerned the bridge had appeared out of nowhere, its magical appearance decreed it was sure to lead to the witch's house he sought. He carefully placed a foot on the first warped board and applied some weight. It creaked and sagged alarmingly but otherwise held firm. Wishing there were rails he could grip to prevent his plummet into the foul bog if a board broke, he cautiously walked across.

After passing through the mist, a dwelling perched on the side of a small, rocky island, emerged into view. Little more than a ramshackle hut; a mishmash of angled wooden props protruding from the water supported the end of the house and its attached veranda overhanging the bog. A sagging pitched roof of wooden tiles rested on walls formed of warped and twisted weatherboards. Two windows glowed with reddish lights, giving the impression of evil eyes watching him. A fleeting movement of a shadow crossing one of them indicated someone, or something, was at home and awake.

Crowe pushed aside the thought of returning home; he needed to do this, and nervously walked to the end of the bridge. A rowboat, half in the bog and half on the bank, rested beside the bridge. The rotten, slime-covered planking and its submerged stern identified it as no longer being sea— or bog—worthy. He stepped onto dry land and followed the sloping path around the large tree dangling its moss-draped branches over the bog.

The path led to the precariously leaning porch jutting from the front of the shack, which was set into a creaking, trembling motion when Crowe climbed the three steps. As he pondered whether knocking on the flimsy, distorted door would send it tumbling from its rusty hinges, it menacingly creaked open. He peered into the darkness within. The only light came from a sliver of red filtering beneath the door on the far side.

Apprehensive about entering, Crow remained where he was.

"If ya ain't coming in, I'll shut the door," said a croaky voice. "Ya be letting out all me heat, and logs don't collect themselves."

"Er, I've come to see…"

"It be flippin' obvious who ya come to see, Kallisto Crowe, cause as ya may 'ave noticed, this festering bog ain't exactly prime real estate, and I be the only one who lives hereabouts. So put ya legs in gear, step across me threshold and shut the door, or go away and leave me in peace."

Reluctantly, Crowe stepped across Griselda Poison's threshold and shut the door.

Wondering whether he should reach for his flashlight and switch it on, Crowe gazed around the room lit by weak rays of light probing the darkness through the many thin gaps between the wall boards. Gusts creaked the roof and walls. A scampering jerked Crowe's nervous gaze to something unseen moving across the floorboards.

Crowe focused on an indistinct shape in the corner he believed to be Griselda. "A light would be welcome," he uttered in a shaky voice.

"Too damn right, it would," said Griselda from an entirely different direction. "But this ain't no fancy dwelling wiv that electricity ya 'ave in ya grand mansion."

Crowe spun to face the voice but saw only shadow. "A candle then."

"Did ya brings any wiv ya?"

Crowe turned to the voice that now came from the far side of the room. "Er…no!"

"Something else, then? A gift for me as be the custom when ya seeks the services of a witch?"

"Sorry…again no."

Griselda snorted. "Ya not very good at this, are ya, Crowe?"

"Seems I am not. It's my first time meeting a witch."

"Unladen with gifts, it might be ya last."

Worried by the threat, Crowe asked, "As you know my name, do you also know why I'm here?"

"I've been watching ya wanderings through my forest, so I knows all I need to know."

Crowe frowned. "Was that a yes?"

"It well may be, let's find out. You've come for one of me famous love potions that'll make ya irresistible to women that won't give ya a second glance looking as ugly as ya surely are."

"Er...no, not at all."

"Are ya sure? cause me love potions are the best around."

"Yes, I'm certain, and I'm sure they are. I have..."

"No, don't tell me. Ya want to know next week's lottery numbers, that's it. Ya want to cheat the system and be rich from the deceit."

"Um...another no I'm afraid."

"And afraid ya should be. Ya keeps changing what ya come fer, don't ya, so I looks foolish. I should turn ya into something small and hideous like a toad or a cockroach."

"You can do that?" asked Crowe, astonished.

"You bet ya lack of gift giving I can. Wiv the right potions and spells I can do almost anything."

"What about faeries?"

Candles dotted around the room sprung into flame, highlighting Griselda shooting across the room. She stopped abruptly with her nose almost touching Crowe's.

"Faeries! What do ya know of faeries?"

Crowe, unable to move, as if he had been paralyzed, stared along the length of the long, crooked, hairy and wart-adorned nose into Griselda's red piercing eyes. "Not a lot really, except that they live in the Faerie Realm in the forest and er...they are now free."

"Free? Impossible! They're guarded by a protection ring of me own design."

"Ye...about that. I might have...er...broken the ring."

"What!?" snarled Griselda.

"I didn't mean to. It was an accident. It broke when I was climbing over. And, in my defense, the fence is rather old and rusty. I bet it hasn't had a coat of paint for years. If you'd maintained it properly, stuff like this would never have happened."

Griselda spun away. "Why in Satan's name were ya climbing over it?"

"I got this map, and it said it was the realm of the faeries, but it looked like a normal patch of flowery grass, so I climbed over. That's when it broke, and I entered the Faerie Realm..."

Griselda shot back nose-to-nose to Crowe.

"I wish you wouldn't do that. It's quite disconcerting."

"Ya visited the Faerie Realm?"

Crowe went to nod but couldn't move his head. "Only briefly."

"Tell me ya weren't seen and ya didn't lay ya eyes upon any faeries or theirs upon you!"

"Um...well, I saw a few. Five, perhaps six. Seven, I think. They chased me through the portal—or whatever it is—and to stop them getting into our world, I put the fence back. Unfortunately, it didn't work, and some came through."

Griselda stepped back, slipped a long fingernail up Crowe's nostril forcing him to his tiptoes. "I should kill ya for what you've done."

"I'd rather you didn't."

"It took the Sinisters and me thirteen years to learn their ways and trap 'em, and then ya comes along and poof, in a few minutes undoes it all. Death is the only fittin' punishment."

"I'd be keen to argue that point. I can help. I have all of Solomon's research. Together we can trap them again. That's why I'm here to seek your help."

Griselda released her hold. "I was young then, look at me now. Old, ugly, and weak."

Crowe scrunched his nose that seemed to have been stretched out of shape. "I'd argue about the weak bit."

Griselda glared at him. "But not the old and ugly reference, aye?"

"Er...sorry, but not having known your former younger self, I have nothing to compare your now to then."

"That's easily remedied."

Griselda spun amidst a puff of smoke that suddenly appeared.

Unable to believe the transformation that had happened before his eyes, Crowe gawped at the beautiful woman. Dark, raven black hair framed a roundish, beautiful face. Large breasts thrust out from a flowing low-necked gown of silk and lace.

"Is this more to your liking?"

Crowe's attempt to nod enthusiastically failed. "Yes...much."

Griselda moved closer and brushed her lips against his. "Do you want to kiss me?" Her voice soft and sultry.

Without waiting for an answer, she planted her lips on his.

Smitten and unable to resist, Crowe responded in kind.

When he felt a change; fewer teeth filling her mouth, the sweet taste of her lips pressed against his now rancid, his eyes shot open. The hag had returned. Unable to move or push her away, he fought his gag reflexes and waited for Griselda to finish.

Breathing heavily, Griselda staggered back. "Wow! That was rather pleasant. I haven't been kissed fer many a year." She looked at Crowe's shocked, disgusted expression and smiled a gap-toothed grin. "I see ya also enjoyed it." She nodded coyly behind her. "We could retire to me bedchamber."

Crowe glanced at the bedroom door. The death the witch had threatened him with earlier sounded preferable to the torment she now had in mind for him.

A click of her fingers released Crowe from his temporary paralysis, allowing him to frantically wipe her foul spittle from his mouth. When he had removed as much as was possible without the aid of a bottle of mouthwash and a stiff-bristled scrubbing brush, he looked at the ugly hag.

"How could someone so sexy and beautiful have turned into..." he looked her up and down, "...you."

Griselda shrugged, sending a ripple down her lopsided hunchback. "Spells and magic takes their toll."

"You must have been performing them constantly."

"That's enough about me. We need to find a way to fix ya stupidity and re-trap the faeries. They've had about five hundred faerie years of festering hatred against humans, and I don't expect it'll be long afore they start dishing out their revenge."

"If their attack against me at Hagsdell Manor is anything to go by, they've already started."

Griselda's astonished eyebrows flipped up her warty-wrinkled forehead. "And ya survived?"

Crowe nodded. "Barely, but yes. I used some of the Sinisters' weapons and a magic salt circle."

"And now ya here, *gift-less* I might add, to seek my help."

"Tell me what you want, and I'll be happy to get it for you next time we meet."

"Hmm, I'll have to think about that." Griselda struck her crooked staff on the floor, sending a sharp echo through the creaking shack. "We need to formulate a plan. Let's go through to the other room where we'll be more comfortable." She moved across the room.

Crowe glanced anxiously at the door she headed for. "Er...is that your bedroom?"

"Calm ya passion, Crowe. There'll be plenty of time for that later after we've dealt with the faeries ya let loose."

Crowe shuddered at the thought as he followed her through to the back room and was pleasantly surprised by the coziness that greeted him. A fire roared in a stone hearth, spreading warmth and a red glow across the room which was filled with many strange objects; bottles of colored liquids, weird things in jars he didn't dwell on, and an assortment of herbs and plants, some of the poisonous variety Crowe noticed, hung from ceiling beams. A tree growing at one side of the room, its wide trunk disappearing through the roof constructed around it, had been hollowed out and shelves stacked with books filled the space. A long, low cupboard was positioned along the wall fitted with two windows, and a tall cupboard was at the far end beside a deeply padded armchair.

Griselda shuffled over to the tree bookshelf and pulled out an ancient dusty tome, which she dropped onto the table in the middle of the room, sending up a cloud of dust probably as ancient as the book it had settled on.

"Right Crowe, to business," announced Griselda, lighting a hand-carved pipe stuffed with tobacco and blowing out a noxious cloud of pungent fog. "We need to correct ya cock-up before it gets any worse." Turning her attention to the book, she thumbed through its pages.

Coughing when he drew near to the table, Crowe waved away the foul-smelling smoke and looked at the book Griselda flicked through. It was covered in strange writing, symbols, and drawings of all manner of things. "Not so much a cock-up, more an innocent accident," he defended.

Griselda's loud, and in Crowe's opinion, much exaggerated, snorting guffaw, sent a ripple down her humpback. "*Innocent accident!* Ya trespass on land clearly marked on the map ya had as the Faerie Realm, vandalize the protection barrier and go wandering around their kingdom wiv ne'er a thought to the consequences. *Then*, if that wasn't bad enough, ya lead the evil little devils back to the world of humans. In my book, and anyone else's who has any common sense, that's a catastrophic disaster of humongous proportions."

"Well...putting it like that it's obviously going to sound bad. All I did was break a fence and do a bit of exploring. As I said before, that fence was in bad condition, all rusty and rotten. And, in my defense, there were no signs saying *keep out* or anything."

"That's as maybe, but whatever the cause the damage is done. We need to fix it before the faeries venture into Hagstown and start killing folk."

"They'll do that, kill people?"

Griselda crossed to the side and poured out two drinks. "Too right they will, and they'll enjoy it. They be evil creatures, and they have a grudge to settle after old Solomon killed their king and, with my help, trapped them in their realm. That's why they probably attacked ya last night. You're living in the Sinister house, so they probably believe ya to be a Sinister, which ain't good for ya health, any which way ya look at it." She handed Crowe a glass.

Crowe looked at the purple liquid warily. "Can't we just repair the fence, or put up a new one?"

Griselda gazed at him scornfully. "Ya really think we'd be able to get anywhere near it now they've discovered their route to the human world is open again? No, they'll be after all the resources on offer here, which includes human flesh—they especially like the young ones. If ya think they won't guard it, ya stupider than I already believe ya to be. We set foot anywhere near it now, and we'll be dead before ya can say, *sorry it's all my fault*, which it undoubtedly is." Placing a boney finger on the base of Crowe's glass, she pushed it toward his mouth. "Drink up. It's only blackcurrant homemade by me own fair hands. You'll be needin' the energy." She gulped hers down in one go and smacked her lips. "Delicious."

Crowe sighed. "I think it's best we don't dwell on who's to blame; the person responsible for the upkeep of the barrier or me, and concentrate on how to fix it." He gulped down his drink as he glanced at the page Griselda had stopped on. "And how do we do that exactly?"

Griselda tapped the page as she looked at Crowe with a sly smirk on her thin lips. "Quite simple, really. Ya needs to enter the Faerie Realm, seek out the faerie king, cut off his head, and bring it back to the human world without being slaughtered horribly in the process."

Crowe's mouth dropped open. "You can't be serious?"

Griselda nodded and smiled. "There are consequences to ya actions. *You* set them free, so *you* must fix it."

Shocked, Crowe looked at the book. "You said it was simple. There was nothing simple in what you just told me."

"Yeah, well, I may have honey-coated it a bit. You'll be fine, and ya won't be alone as I'll be coming wiv ya. I could do wiv a vacation from this dreary bog hole."

"But we'll die."

Griselda nodded. "Possibly, but Solomon did it, and he survived. Well, when I say survived, he completed the quest."

"And then what happened to him?" asked Crowe, not sure he wanted to know.

"He died three minutes later. Well, if truth be told, nearer two actually, but I thought I'd round it up."

"And he died how?"

"In agony," replied Griselda nonchalantly. "I've never witnessed anyone scream and writhe in acute pain as much as Solomon did when he dragged his broken, ripped body back into our world and emptied the faerie king's severed head from the bloody sack his crushed and maimed hands could barely grip."

"Oh, great. That's really going to encourage me to repeat the process. No way am I going back to faerie land." He shook his head. "Nah-uh."

"Oh believe me, you're going, willingly or not."

"You can't make me go," argued Crowe, with less conviction then he intended.

"Oh I can, and I will if need be, but it'll be less unpleasant for ya if ya go voluntarily. Besides, that drink ya just supped down contained a particularly nasty venom of me own concoction," she stated proudly, "that should start reacting in extremely agonizing and unpleasant ways in about thirty-six hours, give or take. Mixing potions ain't an exact science, well not fer me anyways. Also, depending on the time of year, or day for that matter, the ingredients were picked, and the ratios mixed, governs how long before it takes effect. I don't measure ya see, just chuck it all in. *Near enough is good enough* is what me old ma used to say, God bless her evil black heart."

"You poisoned me!?"

Griselda nodded. "Sorry, wasn't I clear enough?"

Crowe slumped into a chair. "But why would you do such a thing?"

"Well, apart from me being an evil witch, me name should have given ya a clue as to me nature."

Crowe groaned. "That still doesn't explain *why* you did it."

"Because I knew you'd chicken out of venturing into the Faerie Realm with me to fix what you've done, that's why. Now, ya 'ave no choice 'cause if ya don't go ya won't get the antidote, and you'll die a horribly painful death."

Crowe glanced around at the many bottles of unfathomable potions, none of which were labeled. One of them contained the antidote, but which one? Resigned to his fate now firmly in the witch's hands, he turned to Griselda. "Then I guess I have no choice but to try."

Griselda smiled. "I had not a doubt ya would." She slapped Crowe on the shoulder. "Ya wait and see, it'll be a fun adventure. We'll have to be in disguise though, so the faeries don't recognize us as human."

Crowe doubted that would be a problem in Griselda's case. "What, like wigs, beards, and different clothes sort of disguises?"

Griselda shook her head. "I was thinking of something a bit more elaborate."

Crowe sighed. "I'm not going to like this, am I?"

Griselda chuckled merrily. "I'd be shocked if ya did." She rubbed her hands together gleefully as she crossed to a tall cupboard and pulled it open. "Now, what shall I wear?"

"If I've only got thirty-six hours before your poison kills me, when do we leave?"

"Tonight."

"Tonight!?"

Griselda looked at Crowe. "We enter the Faerie Realm on the stroke of midnight. Not a second before or after."

Crowe rolled his eyes. "Of course we do. But if the portal, or whatever it's called, is guarded by faeries, how do we get past them?"

"There's more than one way in, three that I know of, but only two ways out. There's probably more but I ain't ever found them."

"And this one we're going to use is nearby?" Crowe's stomach was already churning, whether from fear from what he was about to do, or the witch's poison, he wasn't sure.

"It is, but first we need to go to Hagsdell Manor as we need to collect the things we'll need."

"Some of Solomon's weapons?" asked Crowe.

"No, they're only good in this world, too big for where we're going. We'll need something else. You'll see when we get there."

"I can't wait."

"That's the spirit." Griselda stuffed some clothes into a bag that seemed too small to fit them all in, grabbed her wonky staff, and turned to Crowe. "Ya ready? Because we've lots to do and little time to do it in."

"Not really." Crowe stood and headed for the door.

"I tell ya, it might sound daunting, but it'll be fun, just wait and see if I'm not right."

"Is that the pep talk you gave Solomon before he went in?"

Griselda thought for a moment. "Ya know, I think it was something along those lines."

Crowe sighed.

Crowe unlocked the door of Hagsdell Manor and waved Griselda inside.

Her gaze around the entrance hall ended on the salt-drawn symbol on the floor. "Apart from the amateur attempt at creating a protection circle, little has changed since me last visit."

Crowe closed the door. "It might not be up to your standard, but it worked."

Griselda's eyebrows rose in surprise. "Then ya were lucky. Now, we need to find an old cabinet adorned with…"

"…demons and other macabre decorations" finished Crowe.

Griselda's recently lowered eyebrows rose again when she looked at Crowe. "Ya found it?"

"Found it, unlocked it, and examined its contents."

"Ah, but I bet you didn't find the secret compartment."

"Wrong, found it and the casket inside," said Crowe smugly.

"Then what are we waiting for, lead me to it."

Crowe pointed at the living room. "It's in there."

Griselda barged through the door into the living room. Spying the casket on the coffee table, she crossed to the sofa, sat down and dragged the casket nearer. She glanced at Crowe when he entered. "Everything's still inside?"

Crowe nodded. Maybe now he would discover the purpose of the casket's strange objects.

Griselda pulled the weapon drawer out and checked the contents. "Good, we'll be needing some of these."

Wearing a puzzled expression, Crowe said, "But they're tiny."

"Here they are, but not in the Faerie Realm. You've been there so ya must know you're not the same size there as ya be here. You'd be a giant if ya didn't shrink. The same with the faeries when they come here, they get proportionately bigger, or we'd never see them; they'd be the size of fleas."

Crowe recalled the huge iron fence. So it wasn't *it* that had changed size, but *him*. "But how can that be, my clothes still fitted me."

Griselda shrugged. "It's magic, it don't need no understanding. It's like time travel, you'd go mad trying to figure it all out. Ya just 'ave ta know it's there and fathom what it does. Human weapons don't change size, so they're no good, but faerie weapons do, which is why they can bring them through."

Still mystified, Crowe watched Griselda open the drawer with the little girl doll inside, pulling it out of the casket completely. Smiling warmly at the girl, she placed the bed on the coffee table. She then pulled out a drawer Crowe hadn't noticed before in the side of the bed. Fishing out the clothes and weapons inside, she laid them out on the bottom of the bed. Taking a syringe half-full of purple liquid from the small bag at her waist, she placed the tip above the girl's mouth and pressed the plunger to force a single drop out.

Intrigued, Crowe sat next to Griselda and watched the purple droplet that rested on the doll's tiny lips, slither inside her mouth. He gasped a few moments later when the *doll* sat up and drew in long deep breaths. Realizing his mouth was open, Crowe shut it.

"Hello, Ellie. Long time no see."

The tiny girl turned her head to the voice. "Griselda. What's wrong?"

Griselda jabbed at thumb at Crowe. "He broke the protection barrier and showed the faeries the exit portal."

Too stunned to voice his defense, Crowe stared at the impossibly small girl scowling at him.

"And he still lives?" uttered Ellie, apparently surprised by this fact.

"For now," said Griselda. "To be fair, it was an accident, the fence was old, rusty, and he's an idiot. However, for all his many faults, he's also volunteered to put things right and kill the faerie king."

Crowe snapped out of his shock. "Not so much volunteered as poisoned into submission." He stabbed an accusing finger at Griselda. "By her."

Ellie smiled at the witch. "Griselda, you didn't?"

"I did," she said a little proudly. "He needed the extra encouragement."

"Still no luck with my cure, then?"

Griselda shook her head. "Soon, hopefully."

Ellie took a deep breath. "I'm sure you're doing your best. I assume as I know more about the Faerie Realm than anyone else this side of it, you want me to help you and the idiot."

"Griselda nodded. "He'll need it if he's going to stand any chance of success."

Ellie climbed out of her bed and glanced at the clothes and weapons Griselda had laid out for her. "Revive Satan and Lucifer while I get dressed."

As Ellie shunned her nightie and started dressing, Griselda opened the dog drawer and revived them with the purple potion.

Crowe watched with fascination the strange dogs leaping out of the drawer and bounding over to the girl, whom they licked and nuzzled; a reunion of friends.

Griselda turned to Crowe. "What did ya do with the painting that was inside the cabinet?"

"I took it out but put it back when something strange appeared and started getting bigger."

"Yes, yes, that was the ghoul, it's normal. Where is it?"

"I'll get it." Crowe moved to the cabinet, unlocked it and cautiously opened the door. When nothing jumped out at him, he unhooked the painting, in which he was glad to see there was still no sign of the ghostly ghoulish figure, and carried it over to Griselda.

"Hold it up so I can look at it."

Crowe did as he was ordered.

"Good, it's here," said Griselda after scanning the painting.

Crowe glanced worryingly around the room. "What do you mean, it's here?"

"Not, *here*, here, stupid, but not in the painting." She nodded her head at the window. "Out there. Ya summoned it when ya took the painting out of the cabinet."

Crowe sighed and placed the painting aside. "Again, no warning signs, so not my fault."

"No, due to ya freeing the faeries, it's a good thing. It takes the ghoul a few days to get where it's going and as you've already set it in motion, and there's no sign of it in the painting, it should be somewhere close by."

Crowe peered nervously out the window and scanned the trees. "That may sound more comforting to you than it does to me. The last time it was here, it smashed through my window and killed some of the faeries attacking me."

"Ah, so that's how ya survived," commented Griselda. "I knew it couldn't be your crude salt circle responsible."

"Best we move on," suggested Crowe.

When Griselda lifted the top of the casket and reached inside, Crowe remembered his horrific nightmare the tiny ghoul featured heavily in and grabbed her arm. "You're not going to bring that thing to life?"

"Don't be stupid, it's a doll. I told ya, the ghoul's outside somewhere waiting until it's needed."

Deciding to go with the flow, Crowe released his grip on her arm and observed.

Griselda lifted out the ghoul doll and ripped open its chest with a fingernail. Her fingers probed inside and pulled out an object that looked like a miniature trumpet, two inches in length. She held it out to Crowe. "Go out the back and blow it three times."

Crowe held the tiny trumpet in his fingers. "Why?"

Griselda fished a large antique pocket watch from her bag and glanced at it. "If you're going to question every little task I ask of ya, we'll never make it to the portal in time. If we don't get there by twelve, when the portal will open for a short time, we'll have to wait until tomorrow night, and I'm sure I don't need to remind ya that the sands of time are filtering away your thirty-six, no my mistake, it's now a little under thirty-four hours."

Sighing, Crowe stood. "I'm going. I blow it three times, yes?"

Griselda nodded. "Three short bursts."

Crowe glanced at Ellie, who was now dressed in a short brown tunic and was busy strapping a sword over her back. Thinking she looked very warrior-like, Crowe headed outside.

He took a few steps away from the back door, put the small trumpet to his lips, and blew. Nothing happened. Crowe tried again. Nothing. He drew in a deep breath to fill his lungs and blew. Except for his spittle bubbling out the end, it didn't make a sound. He crossed to the living room window and tapped on the glass to attract Griselda's attention. When she looked at him, he pointed to the trumpet. "It's not working."

Griselda rolled her eyes. "It's fine. Turn around."

Crowe turned and came face to face with the ghoul who was bent over looking at him. Crowe staggered back, banging his head against the window. The grin that appeared on the ghoul's face lacked the expression of mirth commonly associated with curled up lips, which it severely lacked, its mouth just a gap in the front of its head.

The ghoul stood up straight and looked at the door when Griselda appeared. "If you and Ghoul are finished playing, it's time we got a move on."

Rubbing the back of his head, Crowe moved over to Griselda and glanced at Ellie sitting on her shoulder and Satan and Lucifer chasing each other playfully across her hump. "You could have told me it made a sound I couldn't hear and, more importantly, warned me about what I was summoning."

Griselda smiled. "Wouldn't have been as entertaining for me if I had." She plucked the trumpet from Crowe's fingers, dropped it into the small bag slung around her waist, and headed for the forest.

Crowe hurried to catch up with Griselda. The ghoul followed.

"Is Ghoul its name?"

Griselda glanced at Crowe. "It's what I call it, but ya can call it whats ya like as I doubt it cares."

Crowe glanced behind at the ghoul. It still wore that creepy serial killer smile. "Ghoul is fine and very fitting."

"Yes, I thought so," said Griselda.

Chapter 15

Devil's Cauldron

"SO, WHAT'S WITH ALL this faerie king beheading business?" asked Crowe, shining his flashlight around the gloomy, creepy forest. "How will his death help us to trap the faeries?"

Griselda stepped over a fallen tree before answering. "When a faerie king dies, every subject under his rule must return to the kingdom. They have no choice because if they don't return quickly, they'll die. Their heads explode, I think."

"So, to get this straight in my mind, when the king is dead, and his head is brought to the human world, all the faeries that are here in our world will return to their own land before their heads explode, and then you will trap them again?"

"That's the theory behind the plan. It worked before, however, that time I had trained Solomon for months before he entered; time wasn't as in short supply then as the village had been abandoned. You, I haven't trained at all, which means ya chances of success are really, really, slim."

"Your pep talks definitely need some honing. You don't have to honey coat it, but a few sugar sprinkles would be acceptable."

"Best ya expects the worse then it might not seem as bad when ya encounters it."

A thwack rang out, turning Griselda and Crowe to discover the cause. Ghoul rubbed his head and behind it, a branch swayed.

"Is Ghoul coming through with us?"

"No, he remains here to protect the villagers from the faeries ya set free," called out Ellie.

He looked at the girl who had spoken, and to save him from more embarrassment and ridicule from Griselda, Crowe thought it was opportune to change the subject. "As you have wings, I assume you're a faerie?"

"I am now, but I was once human just like you and hope to be again someday."

"Then how come you're so small? The faeries that came to my house were bigger. You're only about four inches tall, they were about three or four times your size."

Because they are true Faerie, I'm not," replied Ellie. "Unlike them, I don't grow when I pass through the portal."

"And how did this come about? Did you enter the portal?"

"Not voluntarily. During one of the faeries' raiding parties, they killed my parents and kidnapped me and some other children. I was one of the lucky ones. Instead of being killed and eaten—we're quite a delicacy for the faerie palate—I became a slave and was studied so they could learn more about human ways to discover our weaknesses. If you remain in their land for longer than five faerie years, which equals one human year, which I did, you remain like them size-wise."

"But you obviously escaped. And where does the ghoul fit into this?" asked Crowe, keen to find out as much as possible about the situation he had become involved in.

Ellie glanced at the slender creature following. "When Solomon entered the Faerie Realm to claim the king's head, Griselda summoned the ghoul to protect the rest of the

Sinister family. I met Solomon while he was carrying out his task. I helped him and came back through with him. Unfortunately, Griselda was unable to reverse the faerie magic, and I remain like this. When the faeries were defeated, and the portal closed, she magicked me to a dormant state to be recalled when she found a cure."

"But if you were with Solomon way back then, you'd be an old woman, or dead by now," queried Crowe.

"A side effect of faerie magic is longevity," explained Ellie. "Once you're one of them, and don't stray from their land for a prolonged amount of time, you don't age very much."

"Which is why I had to put her to sleep, to prevent her from aging while she was here," added Griselda.

"That doesn't seem fair," commented Crowe. "Stay in the Faerie Realm and live an extended life or stay here in a magic Sleeping Beauty type sleep forever."

"I might have found a solution," explained Griselda. "I've recently learned of a powerful wizard dwelling in the distant lands adjoining the goblin kingdom, over the mountains bordering the Faerie Realm, who might be able to reverse the effects. However, finding him in the perilous lands fraught with danger and filled with all manner of dangerous creatures will be a daunting task."

"Good job we won't be heading in that direction then," uttered Crowe, worried by the sly look Griselda now aimed at him.

Distracted by movement on her hump, he watched the dogs move onto Griselda's shoulder and lie down beside Ellie. "Are the *dogs* from the Faerie Realm?"

"No, from here originally. Taken by the faeries when they were puppies. Like me, they were kept too long in their realm and were transformed into their present form on one of the faerie king's whims," explained Ellie. "When he became bored with them, I befriended them, and we bonded, so I brought them back with me when Solomon rescued me. They hate faeries as much as I do."

"We're here," stated Griselda, pushing through a tall patch of ferns.

Crowe and Ghoul followed her through and halted at the base of a vast gray rock. Griselda moved around the edge and pointed her staff at a dark opening. "We go in there."

Crowe crossed to the chest high cave entrance and shone his flashlight inside. "That doesn't look so bad."

Griselda smirked. "As you have the only light, Crowe, lead us in."

He held out the flashlight to Griselda. "Be my guest."

"Stop mucking about and get inside." She glanced up at the moonlit sky. "We only have a few minutes left."

Aware of the poison coursing through his veins, Crowe crouched and entered the downward sloping tunnel. As soon as he was inside, he heard a faint rushing. "Is that a waterfall or something?"

Griselda prodded his backside with her staff. "Get a move on, and you'll find out."

Ghoul dropped to its hands and knees to fit through the entrance and crawled after Griselda.

With the sounds of the rushing water getting louder with his every stooped-over step, Crowe entered a cavern tall enough for even Ghoul to stand upright in. He crossed to the source of the rushing water. Three meters below the rim of the two-meter-wide pit, a maelstrom of water converging from three directions formed an angry, white-frothed whirlpool. "I pity anyone who falls in there."

"Falling's not gonna be a problem," stated Griselda. "We'll be jumping in." An uttered spell caused the tip of her staff to glow. She grabbed Crow's flashlight, switched it off, and added it to her bag. "It'll be the size of a car if *you* carry it through."

His face a mask of shock and terror, Crowe looked at the witch. "That's the entrance?"

"Yep, the Devil's Cauldron."

"You can't be serious. We'll be killed."

"Well in your case, you're damned if ya does and damned if ya doesn't," said Griselda, adding a grin.

"I'd rather die from your poison than risk entering that hell hole."

"I assure ya, if that were hellfire instead of water, it'd be a less painful way to die than experiencing the agony you'll endure from my skillfully concocted poison." She pulled out the pocket watch from her bag and flicked it open. "It's almost time." She turned her face to Ellie on her shoulder. "You and the dogs go first."

"Okay, we'll see you on the other side," said Ellie, showing none of Crowe's reluctance to enter the whirlpool, they climbed onto Griselda's hand.

"Crowe, you go second. Jump when I say."

Crowe backed away. "Nah-uh. No way."

Griselda ignored him. "I'll go next." She turned to Ghoul. "Ya know what to do. When we're in, head for Hagstown and protect it from the faeries."

Ghoul nodded.

Griselda looked at her watch when it started chiming midnight and stretched her hand out over the pit. Ellie dived, and the dogs leaped off.

Crowe cautiously took a step forward to watch them disappear into the raging torrent of water.

"Your turn, Crowe."

Crowe turned to the voice, but Griselda wasn't there. Something slammed into his back. He screamed when he fell. As he twisted, he glimpsed Griselda lowering her foot responsible for kicking him into the Devil's Cauldron and the smirk on her lips. Though extremely annoyed and terrified, he had the sense to grab a lungful of air before he hit the water. Sure he was about to drown if he wasn't smashed to a pulp by the rocky sides of the terrible chute, the whirlpool dragged him under. The last sight he saw was the glow from

Griselda's staff and her billowing skirt when she jumped into the pool. It wasn't an image he wouldn't have wished on anyone to take to their grave. The current grabbed him and swept him underground.

Chapter 16

A Strange Bunch

LIT BY INTERMITTENT FLASHES of Griselda's staff light, Crowe tumbled through the rushing water and caught glimpses of the rocky chute he sped through. Praying he wouldn't be scraped against the rough surfaces, he concentrated on keeping his mouth—that desperately wanted to scream—tightly shut. His lungs began to burn. His brain detected the rising level of carbon dioxide, and inadvisably issued a command to breathe, something Crowe tried desperately to resist. He did though release small amounts of carbon dioxide infused air to release the pressure and burning sensation. Aware he wouldn't last much longer before his brain worked out that the body it controlled was dying by not breathing while in the water, so it might as well enforce the command to breathe in the hope it survived, Crowe urged the end of the tunnel to arrive quickly.

Just as his mouth opened to gulp air that wasn't there and fill it with water, the darkness around him became lighter. He felt a falling sensation and a breeze on his face. Spluttering out water, he glimpsed dark, angry clouds above him. He drew in a much-needed deep breath of oxygen and promptly closed his mouth when he again splashed into water. His feet touched something solid. His swiveling gaze around the gloom picked out weeds waving in the current and rocky gravel beneath his feet. He wasn't in the tunnel anymore. Moonlight sparkled on the surface. He looked up as something splashed into the water nearby. It was the witch. She sank with her dress wrapped around her upper body. Suppressing a gag, Crowe turned away from her hairy legs and sprung off the gravel bottom. As soon as his head was above water, he gulped down air and looked around to get his bearings. He spied Ellie and her two dogs disappearing into bushes lining the grassy bank. As Griselda appeared beside him, he swam for the shore and climbed out. Once on dry land, a wave of nausea swept over him.

"It's just the effects of passing through the portal, it lessens each time," Griselda explained as she climbed from the water.

The queasiness symptoms passed as speedily as they had appeared only to be replaced by ailments more painful. Cramp from every part of his body seized him, doubling him over.

"That though is something entirely different," informed Griselda as the cramps seized her also.

The symptoms dissipated a few moments later.

"That wasn't so bad was it," stated Griselda, glancing around. "The bit through the tunnel was quite fun, actually."

Thinking her mad, Crowe turned his head toward her. His mouth dropped open. His eyes flicked from the pool from the hole high in the cliff they had been ejected from to the pool it cascaded into. There was no sign of the witch.

"You okay, Crowe?" asked the beautiful, shapely woman in Griselda's voice.

"You're Griselda? The ugly old, warty witch who poisoned..."

"Yes, I know who she is and what she did, and yes, I am her." Griselda's harsh tones morphed into a voice far more elegant and refined to match her appealing form. "It's the disguise I told you about."

"Bu...you're beautiful."

"Those are words I've not heard in an extremely long time."

"What about my disguise?"

"You're already wearing it," answered the now beautiful Griselda. "Well, not so much wearing, more *being* it."

Crowe looked at his hands that were no longer hands. "Paws! Why have I got paws?"

"They're an essential part of your disguise," Griselda informed him, grinning. "Look in the pool."

Crowe moved to the water, looked at his reflection, and gasped in shock. "I'm a rat!"

"And in a rat-ish sort of way, very appealing to a female of the species I should think."

If Crowe had heard, he ignored the compliment. "But why a rat? Why couldn't I be...I don't know, something better looking and more heroic?"

"Because then you would stand out. We don't want to bring attention to ourselves while we're here. There are many rats like you here, so you'll fit right in."

Crowe glanced at Griselda 2.0 and scanned the luscious curves of her young womanly body. "And you won't attract attention looking like that?"

"Oh, I certainly hope so, but the right kind of attention. A distraction away from our mission."

Crowe sagged. "But a rat. I'm not happy."

"Tell me about it," uttered Griselda. "These breasts were supposed to be two sizes bigger and look at my buttocks..." she turned to show Crowe, "...a little plumper than what I envisioned."

Crowe then noticed he had something else, a tail. He picked up the tip and looked at its long pink form. "And what am I supposed to do with this?"

Griselda shrugged distractedly; she was too busy admiring her new form. "Rat type things I expect." She fluttered her wings and lifted off the ground a few feet. "At least they work."

"Oh, have I got wings?" asked Crowe excitedly. "I can feel something on my back. I suppose if I can fly it won't be so bad." He twisted his head in an attempt to see.

"Er...not exactly. It's a saddle," Griselda informed him.

"A saddle? Why do I have a saddle?"

"You can't expect me to walk dressed like this?"

"But you have wings, why not fly?"

"They're more for show than for flying. Yes, they'll keep me in the air for short periods, but no good for prolonged flight."

Their heads turned to the sounds of something approaching. Satan and Lucifer bounded through the bushes with Ellie flying close behind. Now the correct faerie size in proportion to Griselda and Crowe, she landed gently on the ground beside Griselda and eyed her up and down. "Nice." She then turned to Crowe and chuckled. "You are naughty, Griselda."

Griselda beamed. "I know."

Ellie turned serious. "I've scouted ahead, and all seems clear."

"Good, then time we got moving." Griselda turned to Crowe. "Get on all fours."

Crowed sighed. "Do I have to?"

"Afraid so. We need to blend in and riding you will help. Rats are used as beasts of burden here. They also do all the more unpleasant and strenuous stuff the other faeries don't want to do."

"I don't want to do them either."

Griselda chuckled. "Just get down. You're wasting what little time you have left."

"Quit complaining, Crowe. You're the reason we're here," reminded Ellie.

Reluctantly, Crowe dropped onto his front paws, and Griselda climbed onto the saddle.

"Tally ho," called out Griselda, nudging Crowe into motion with her knees.

"You don't have to enjoy it quite so much," moaned Crowe, moving forward.

"I'm on vacation, so I'm going to enjoy it as much as I can before I have to return to that depressing bog again."

"Why don't you move if you hate living there so much?" suggested Crowe.

"Because there aren't many places an ugly, warty witch will fit in or be welcomed. Besides, I still need to sort out Ellie's problem. Maybe when that's done, I'll think about relocating."

"Somewhere a long way from me would be preferable."

Griselda leaned forward and tweaked Crowe's rat ear. "You don't mean that. Before meeting me, when was the last time you had such an exciting adventure?"

"Exciting! You poisoned me a few minutes after we met and turned me into a rat that's now carrying you around a strange land full of evil, murderous faeries."

Griselda smiled. "You're welcome."

Trying to flip his uncontrollable tail at Griselda, he missed and struck his own rump. Wincing from the slap, he headed through the trees. "Do we have far to go?"

"It's not the distance you should be worried about, but what lies in between," replied Griselda.

"Should I probe for further details?" asked Crowe.

"Probably best we leave it as a surprise."

Halting at the top of a rise, the unlikely trio gazed down at the landscape stretching toward an ominous black tower in the far distance.

Griselda pointed a slender manicured finger at the tower. "That's our goal. It's where the faerie king lives."

Crowe gazed worriedly at the lofty pillar of stone. "It's taller than I imagined, and I don't suppose he's the only one living there."

"You suppose right," said Ellie. "It's well guarded, inside and out."

"Let's not worry about breaching the tower just yet," advised Griselda. "We have to reach it first, and the journey is fraught with danger."

"Such as?" inquired Crowe, gazing below. Though uncertain he wanted to know, he thought it best to have an inkling of what he was about to face.

Griselda directed her finger at the forest at the bottom of the hill they stood upon. "Our first task is to pass through Nightmare Forest, and on its far side, Death Valley, and then the Swamp of the Dead. If we're still alive, we have perhaps the most dangerous part of our travels, The Underwurld, or as some call it, the Cavern of Lost Souls."

Crowe examined Griselda's face—something he would have thought twice about doing in her original guise—for signs she was making it all up. "Who names these places?"

"That, I'm afraid," answered Griselda, "is information lost to time."

"Even so, I get the feeling whoever was responsible wasn't much fun at parties."

"If you're finished with your questions, I'll continue?"

Crowe nodded.

"Once we've passed through The Underwurld, we're only a hop, skip and a jump from the King's Tower."

"I don't like to be a moaner," moaned Crowe, "but is there a less hazardous route we could take?"

"Perhaps, but it would take too long," said Griselda. "I fear the faeries are already making plans to invade the human world and it's up to us to stop them before that happens. And knowing their sick sense of humor, I also believe they will do it on All Hallow' Eve, which is only two nights away. We have no choice, we go straight through, or we'll never reach the tower in time to prevent their murderous rampage. Hagstown will be first to be conquered, and then they'll spread out. Their plan, before Solomon and I stopped them, was to conquer the human world and make it their own. I don't expect they've had a change of their black hearts since then."

"I don't like it, but I'm assuming you know best," relented Crowe.

"I usually do," said Griselda, nudging Crowe forward with her long, shapely legs.

To save her strength for what lay ahead, Ellie flitted over to Crowe and straddled his neck. They started down the hill with Lucifer and Satan on either flank as protection.

After Ghoul had observed Griselda being sucked under by the maelstrom of water, and thinking what a strange race the humans were, it turned away from the pit and crawled back along the tunnel.

Emerging into the forest, it climbed to its feet and stretched out its aching back. Not that Ghoul actually had any muscles to ache, but it had seen humans do it, so was just trying to fit in. With a mission to attend to, it pushed through the surrounding bushes and headed through the forest to Hagstown.

Chapter 17

Nightmare Forest

"SO," SAID CROWE, PAUSING to scratch at his hindquarters with a rear leg, "why is it called Nightmare Forest?"

Ellie rolled her eyes. "Because it's full of nightmarish things, dummy."

"You've been in it before then, to see these nightmarish things?"

"Not exactly, but I've heard stories when I was imprisoned here. Not one of them described what hides within as being anything good."

"And these stories were first-hand accounts, were they?" pressed Crowe.

"I don't think so, as most who go in are never seen again."

"If that is the case, couldn't they just be made up stories? It's simply a creepy dark forest people tell scary tales about."

Ellie shrugged. "Anything's possible, I suppose."

Griselda sucked on the pipe she had lit and let out a stream of foul smoke before adding her own two penn'orth to the conversation. "What you must realize Crowe, and rather quickly I might add, is that we are no longer in our world. Here, anything is possible. Anyone who roams these lands and ignores its legends, stories and overheard conversations about evil things living in forests or wherever isn't going to survive for very long."

Crowe twitched his whiskers. "Just saying the only thing that might be remotely scary about this forest is its name. That doesn't mean I won't be on my guard."

"Make sure you are," warned Griselda. "because if you're stupid enough to get yourself killed, I'll have to walk with these legs that are more suited to being admired than anything too strenuous."

A distant shriek; long, piercing, and unnatural, made them all peer into the gloom-soaked forest for signs of whatever had made it.

"And I suppose that's just wind howling through the trees?" quipped Ellie.

"I'm really hoping it was," replied Crowe anxiously.

"Standing here gawping and contemplating what might be isn't achieving anything. Take us in, Crowe."

As Crowe entered the forest, Ellie whistled a command to her dogs. With ears raised, they moved forward and swiveled their heads to every sound.

They wandered cautiously through ancient thick-trunked trees—tall, black and gnarled. Twisted branches reached down from their malformed trunks like menacing limbs waiting to snatch them from the forest floor. Deep-throated cracks, the cause none of the nervous trio could explain, reverberated through the forest. The wind howled through the trees, shaking their intimidating twig-adorned branches, and rustled leaves into motion across the forest floor as if something moved beneath them. The smell of dampness and decaying vegetation filled the moist, cloying air.

With no path to follow, they kept heading as straight at the trees would allow, stepping over roots, both small and large, and under some that formed arches. Arriving at a clearing, they gazed at the most massive tree they had ever laid their eyes upon; gigantic did not do it justice.

Crowe was about to voice his astonishment when Ellie leaned down to his ear and whispered, "Don't speak or make a sound." She pointed over Crowe's head and stabbed a finger at the dark openings in the tree's massive trunk. "Things live within."

Mindful these *things* wouldn't be anything he would want to meet, Crowe stared worriedly at the leaves, twigs, and branches littering the ground ahead of him. Dead and brittle, they didn't bode well for a stealthy crossing. His gaze searching for a path less prone to alert any horrors within earshot of his every paw fall, flicked across yellowed bones strewn around the clearing. The many grooves in each were grisly evidence all had been ferociously gnawed. A good indication the creatures who had made the giant tree their home had sharp teeth and were not herbivores.

He turned his head to whisper to Ellie who was still leaning over him. "It might be advisable to retreat and seek a safer route around the tree?"

Ellie's sharp eyes scanned the surrounding forest and glimpsed dark shapes skulking through the gloom. "What makes you think there's anything less dangerous out there? No, press on, but slow and steady."

Crowe nodded his long, whiskered snout and raising a front paw, moved it forward and gently lowered it to the ground. When it had sunk through the leaf layers and touched solid earth, he moved a back leg in the same slow manner. His other front paw was next.

"When Ellie said slow and steady, she didn't mean torturously so," admonished Griselda. "You'll have to move a bit quicker, or we'll be here all day."

A little peeved; he had only been trying not to get them all killed, Crowe increased his speed and the robotic jerking movements moving one leg at a time produced.

Jolted from side to side by her ride's clunky progress, Griselda rolled her eyes but let him get on with it. If she moaned again, he'd only sulk.

When they drew level with the titanic tree, Crowe turned his face to one of the many holes and peered inside. Though he saw nothing within, his sensitive rat nose picked out the rank stench of rotten meat, feces, and urine emanating from the opening.

He froze a few cautious erratic steps later and, along with Griselda and Ellie, observed the tail attached to the rear end of the animal backing out from one of the holes lowest to the ground. Unaware of their presence, its rump appeared as the beast continued reversing out from the opening. Its thin, greyhound-like body and six legs, jointed on its trunk, followed. When its head appeared, they saw it was dragging a bone covered in lacerations, blood, and bits of gristle.

Frozen to the spot by fear of detection, Crowe watched the badger-sized creature draw closer, grunting and groaning with the awkward, large-jointed limb it hauled. When it bumped into Crowe's front leg, it stopped and raised its head in a confused manner. Unable to turn its head with the bone clenched in its jaws, it shuffled its rear end around. Upon seeing the rat, the bone dropped to the ground when its jaws parted in surprise. Apparently unafraid of the larger creature it faced, it snarled at Crowe, who flinched away from the vicious beast, his eyes fixated on the snake-like head and small eyes staring back at him. Spreading its jaws wide to display its flesh-ripping teeth, the creature screeched and dived at Crowe's neck.

Uncertain how a rat was supposed to guard against such an attack, he dodged away, Ellie headed in the opposite direction. She leaped from Crowe's head and slipped the sword from the scabbard strapped across her back. Twisting in the air, she landed straddling the creature's back. Gripping its fur with her free hand, she stabbed the sword repeatedly into its flesh. Each withdrawal of the blade eliciting a spray of blood from the wound it left behind. She rode the creature to the ground when it toppled onto its side. After a few labored breaths and jerks, it was dead.

Smiling proudly at Ellie, Griselda silently clapped.

Crowe stared in astonishment at the beast Ellie had killed, seemingly, in the blink of an eye. He shifted his eyes to Ellie when she cleaned the blade on the beast's fur and slipped it back into its scabbard. Crowe was just about to thank her when shrieks and growls coming from the tree holes distracted him. He cocked his ears to the scampering of many sets of clawed feet approaching far too quickly.

Griselda nudged Crowe with her legs. "The time for stealth is over, run!"

As soon as Ellie had flittered back onto his neck and gripped an ear to hold on to, Crowe spurted forward.

A creature shot from a hole higher in the tree and headed straight for Griselda.

When Ellie let out a series of shrill whistles aimed at the dogs, Lucifer bounded for the creature. Snatching it from the air, he bit down on its neck and cast its limp corpse aside. Satan joined Lucifer, and both headed for the creatures emerging from the tree.

Griselda and Ellie glanced back at the creatures emerging swiftly from the tree's many openings. Their snarling heads darted around the clearing before focusing on the fleeing intruders they all looked upon as prey. While a couple chose the effortless meal their fallen comrade offered, the majority chased after them.

Lucifer and Satan bowled into the creatures, tumbling the leaders off their long legs. Their attack was swift and vicious, biting and flinging the dead and dying predators into the trees.

Fearing the vicious threat among them, those that were able, gave the dogs' snapping jaws a wide berth and continued the pursuit of their fleeing prey.

Crowe rushed through the forest. Dodging left and right around the trees and leaping over roots and fallen branches in his way. If it weren't for the danger closing in behind him, he would have thought the pace exhilarating. He had no idea rats could run so fast.

The six spindly legs of the creatures carried them faster. They snapped at the tail that Crowe desperately tried to keep from their reach. Finding the fifth limb challenging to control, he swished it all directions and swiped one of the beasts. The creature fell and rolled. Unhurt by its tumble, it jumped back to its feet and continued the chase.

Ellie watched the creatures moving alongside; they were planning to outflank them before they attacked. She turned to Griselda, who had her staff raised to poke any that came within reach and thrust out a hand. "Pistol!"

Griselda fished a hand into her waist bag, pulled out the pistol, and handed it to Ellie.

Ellie aimed at the nearest creature and fired. The slug entered its eye and ricocheted around its skull cavity, turning parts of its brain to mush. Its legs collapsed beneath it and sent it tumbling. It crashed into a comrade, sending it sprawling with a crack of breaking limbs. It attempted to continue the chase, but with two broken legs, it wasn't going anywhere fast. When the two creatures behind it noticed their wounded comrade, they snarled at it and attacked. There was no room for the weak in their pack.

Ellie aimed at another and pulled the trigger. The slug entered its mouth and crashing through teeth exited from the back of its head in a spray of blood. The creature was dead before it hit the ground and feasted on by its comrades shortly after.

One of the creatures on the other side lunged at Crowe's shoulder with jaws spread ready to bite. It received a sharp jab to its head from Griselda's staff. Dazed, it shot beneath Crowe's belly and promptly got trampled by the rat's rear legs.

Crowe cursed when his back paws stumbled on something and sent his rear end precariously close to tripping. Recovering quickly, he risked a glance behind. A shot rang out, taking down another creature. Wondering how Ellie could hit anything with his erratic movements, he turned his gaze away from the two dogs drawing level to protect them, allowing him to concentrate on what lay ahead.

Crowe peered through the trees that seemed to end a short distance ahead. They were almost through the forest. When he bounded free of the trees onto a patch of barren soil, all hope of escape from the vicious creatures faded. He dug all four sets of claws into the earth. His rear end slewed to the side when his front legs snatched at a root and gripped on tight. For a few seconds, his back paws grabbed nothing but air.

Griselda shot forward when her ride abruptly halted. Turning her head to the side, she peered into the deep ravine and spied its rocky bottom far below. Gripping Crowe tighter with her legs to stop herself from sliding off, her free hand grasped a handful of fur. She held on as Crowe hauled himself back onto land.

Ellie simply rose into the air and continued aiming at the creatures that had stopped at the edge of the forest, but she didn't waste ammo firing at them. Hearing the barks and howls of her dogs from among the trees, she whistled them to her. They bounded from the forest and halting in front of Crowe, turned and snarled warnings at the creatures to remain where they were or face the consequences.

Griselda righted herself and rubbed Crowe's head. "You did well for a rat."

"I'm not your pet, so lay off the petting." Panting heavily, he looked at the crack in the earth too wide to leap across even if he could pluck up the courage to do so. The forest he had hoped to see the last of continued on its far side. "We need to find a way across before they attack again."

Griselda studied the creatures at the forest edge. "Though I don't know why, they don't seem eager to leave the trees, but you're right, Crowe, we need to get across."

"I'll go high to see if I can spot anything," offered Ellie, who promptly soared straight up on her small but efficient wings.

Crowe turned his head and nodded at Griselda's hand clutching a tuft of his fur tightly. "You can stop ripping out my hair now we're in no danger of falling into the ravine."

Griselda released her hold. "I'd say sorry, but I wouldn't mean it."

Crowe rolled his beady rat eyes.

"There's a bridge not too far away," called out Ellie, pointing to the right, when she landed on Crowe's neck.

Crowe shot a fearful look at the screeching fiends in the forest before moving at a fast gait with the two dogs keeping pace. Though the forest creatures followed their progress, none of them ventured from the tree line.

As they approached the bridge, they came across a dense bush formed of leafless intertwined branches; thick, crooked and black, that all but blocked the width of the clear area between forest and ravine. Crowe headed for the ravine side; he'd rather risk the drop than coming within grabbing distance of the foul beasts obviously waiting for such an opportunity.

Ellie noticed the creatures had fallen silent when they neared the bush. Wondering the cause, she ran her eyes over the strange thicket. Though it emitted an ominous aura, she could see through the gaps between its spindly, thorny branches. Satisfied nothing was concealed within to ambush them, she returned her vigil upon the forest creatures now watching them in silent anticipation.

Hugging the side of the bush, Crowe cautiously padded along the narrow strip of ground along the top of the deep gorge. He yelped when something poked him sharply in the side. Jerking involuntarily, he almost lost his footing on the ravine edge.

"Careful, Crowe," warned Griselda who had a perfect view down the precipitous side of the gorge. "It's only a twig."

"Damn sharp twig," moaned Crowe.

Griselda studied the bush adorned with pointed twig tips when it rustled. It seemed out of place compared to the surrounding leafy vegetation. As did the bones that littered its base; something had fed here. However, she surmised, they were in a different realm and should expect everything to be weird compared to their world.

Relieved to have passed by safely, Crowe headed for the bridge a short distance away and noticed another similar dark-branched bush ahead. The few ancient, weather-worn gravestones dotted around the ground either side of the bridge entrance, didn't instill confidence in any of them that this was a safe place to linger.

Crowe halted where the arched stone bridge met land and gazed along its sagged, lichen-covered cobbled surface spanning the ravine. Worried by its visibly weakened condition, he sought reassurance from his companions. "Do you think it's safe? It looks like it could collapse at any minute."

"It is fine," assured Griselda. "It's probably been standing for thousands of years."

"That's what worries me," uttered Crowe, taking in the crumbling stonework of its side walls that seemed too weak to prevent anyone from falling over the edge if they stumbled into them.

Creaks and clacks turned their heads first to one of the strange bushes a short distance away and then to the other they had passed by a few moments ago. Both were in motion. Their thin, twisted branches disentangled from each other. A group of twigs fell free from the central mass and rose up into a form equipped with ten, multi-jointed twig legs, a thin body and a head that looked like pieces of gnarled bark. Its eye holes looked at them. Its wooden jaws clacked together.

The forest creatures screeched excitedly.

Edging toward them, the dogs barked and snarled at the anthropomorphic shrubs. Ellie whistled for them to remain close.

As more of the twig monsters began to take shape, Crowe's fear of them far outweighed any doubts he'd had about the structural integrity of the bridge; he scampered across.

Ellie glanced behind to make sure Lucifer and Satan were following. Her eyes flicked to the bush creatures in pursuit. "They're coming!"

Crowe almost stumbled when a deep booming voice came from below.

"Who be crossing my bridge without paying my toll?"

"It's a Bridge Troll," exclaimed Ellie, her face a mask of concern.

"You have got to be kidding me," uttered Crowe. "A Bridge Troll?"

Crowe spurted forward and focused fearfully on the giant hand that appeared and gripped one of the side walls, dislodging more rocks and explaining its state of disrepair. A second hand followed.

Slowly, a huge head rose out of the ravine and turned to look at them. Its tongue hungrily licked its lips at the sight of the juicy, succulent rat, which it imagined squirming in its cavernous mouth as it chewed, and the stringier female appetizer on its back. Keen to taste both, it reached out a hand to snatch them up.

Crowe's paws skidded on the cobbles when he tried to prevent slamming into the hand moving toward him.

"Don't stop!" urged Ellie. "Those twig monsters are almost upon us."

Changing tactics, Crowe scooted forward and leaped onto a side wall. Trying to avoid looking down into the ravine the rocks he dislodged tumbled into, he sprung off and landed on the back of the troll's hand. He ran up its arm to the elbow then jumped off. As soon as his paws landed on the bridge, he sprinted away. When the two dogs rushed underneath the hand, one of them snapped at a troll finger, drawing blood, before racing away.

The troll roared in frustration as he clambered onto the bridge, crushing four of the twig monsters in the process and sending the remaining fleeing back the way they had come. Ignoring the unappetizing creatures, the troll lunged at the more succulent trespassers trying to escape paying his toll.

"Faster, Crowe," screamed Griselda, her staff slapping his side, urging him to move faster like a jockey nearing the finish line.

The dogs avoided the troll's latest attempt to grab them by jumping onto the sidewalls and rushing along them. Crowe yelled and stumbled to the ground when the fist slammed into the bridge and trapped his tail. The mighty thump sent vibrations rippling through the cobbles.

Feeling the bridge sag even more, Crowe looked back. His vision was filled with the troll's large ugly face as it scrambled along the bridge on his knees toward him.

Accompanied by Griselda's panicked screams to get moving, Crowe climbed onto his paws and ran.

Unable to stand the troll's punishment anymore, the ancient bridge began to crumble. The walls toppled into the abyss when the supporting arch caved in. Scrabbling for a grip it didn't find, the troll slipped into the rapidly forming gap. The bridge collapsed in a rippling motion that sped both ways along its length and quickly caught up with fleeing trio.

As the dogs sped past him, Crowe's paws scrambled for a purchase on the slippery cobbles. As they slid backward, Griselda and Ellie fluttered into the air.

"Let's try and pull him up," shouted Ellie, grabbing one of Crowe's ears.

Though she thought the effort useless, Griselda nevertheless, grabbed his other ear. Flapping their wings frantically, they tugged.

Crowe desperately fought for leverage on the stones collapsing beneath him. When he saw the dogs waiting at the end of the bridge, he whipped his tail at them. Both jumped for it and gripped it in their mouths. With all four limbs cycling furiously, and with the others' painful, combined efforts, he slowly moved forward.

Unable to halt his plummet, the troll stared up at the rat's delicious plump rump it would never feast upon. It roared in frustration.

Crowe finally managed to drag himself onto solid ground. Hearing the troll roar they turned to watch it fall.

Breathless, Crowe said, "That's the last we'll see of him."

Griselda peered into the deep void. "I wouldn't be so sure of that; trolls are tough as granite. It'll survive the fall and climb back up."

Ellie glanced at the ruined bridge and the twig creatures trapped on the far side. "If it wants to remain a Bridge Troll, the repair work will keep it busy for a while."

Crowe looked at the dogs licking his throbbing tail. "Thanks, boys." He then turned to Griselda and Ellie. "And thanks to you two also. Not sure I would have made it without your help."

Griselda huffed and nodded at Ellie. "It's her you want to thank; I would've let you fall."

Crowe smiled at Griselda. "And yet you didn't, so my appreciation stands."

Griselda shrugged. "Yours to waste as you want." She turned her attention to the forest in front. "I don't suppose there's anything less savage in there than what we've left behind, but time's a-wastin', and we need to keep moving." She climbed onto Crowe's back. "Mush!"

Crowe sighed, and with Ellie straddling his neck and her loyal dogs guarding his flanks, he followed the track leading into the forest.

Standing at the edge of the forest overlooking the Hagstown, Ghoul searched for a suitable vantage point to keep a lookout. It had to be near to the town as possible, high up yet offer concealment. His gaze over the humans going about their business unaware they were about to face an attack from things unknown to them, halted on the tall water tower. Set on the outskirts, it seemed ideal.

Moving stealthily from tree to tree and bush to bush, Ghoul made its way down to the tower unseen. Though the bottom of the access ladder was too high for humans to reach without aid, it presented no problem to the tall ghoul. It reached up, grabbed it, and hauled its lanky form up the side of the tower. Lying down on its domed top, Ghoul kept watch over the town and the surrounding landscape for signs of the faeries.

Chapter 18

The Faerie King

THE FAERIE KING, Mortgrimmest Slithe, exited from his private chambers and headed for his throne. He sat, smoothed out his royal attire, and nodded to his advisor.

Hemlock Mildew promptly turned to face the guards by the door at the far end of the expansive throne room. "Show them in."

Just as swiftly, the guards pulled the doors open to allow the three waiting faeries to enter.

The king and his advisor watched Redweedle, Blackroot, and Deadeye walk the length of the hall, the slapping of their feet on the stone floor echoed around the cavernous space.

Hemlock raised a hand when they drew near the king. "Halt and speak at the king's request."

The three faeries looked nervously at their king. All were aware of his quick temper and swiftness to dish out harsh punishment to those that displeased him, which, apparently, was all too easy to do. The dungeons were full of those that had upset him.

Gripping the human skulls attached to the arms of his throne, the king leaned forward and scowled at each of his visitors in turn. He raised a hand and extended a finger at Redweedle. "Make your report."

"Yes, my king," replied Redweedle bowing. "It's true, the portal to the human world is open again."

The king glanced at his advisor with excitement in his eyes.

"As instructed by your learned advisor," continued Redweedle, never one to shy away from a bit of boot-licking to ingratiate himself into a superior's favor. "I and six others passed through into the human world and made our way to the home of our sworn enemies, the Sinisters. We entered the house, something we easily achieved considering the previous difficulties we encountered when Solomon was alive and likely an indication the passage of time has dulled their powers. Except for a token defense in the form of a crudely fashioned protection circle, easily disposed of by our accompanying mage with a storm spell, the humans in the house offered no viable methods of defense to cause us any concern."

The king shuffled forward excitedly. "So, you were able to kill the last of the Sinister linage."

Redweedle directed his eyes at his feet. "Not exactly..."

"What do you mean, *not exactly*, either you did, or you didn't. Which is it?"

Fearing the king's reaction from the information they had to impart, Redweedle turned to his comrade beside him and whispered, "You tell him."

Blackroot shook his head vigorously. "Not bloody likely. He elected you as spokesman."

Redweedle glanced at the faerie on his other side and then at the king. "If it pleases your highness, Deadeye here is better suited to explain what happened as he was charged with the killing."

Deadeye's face registered surprise at the news. "I was?"

"See, he freely admits it," said Redweedle.

The king sighed. "I don't care who tells me as long as someone does, and quickly before my temper is lost."

Redweedle and Blackroot took a step back, leaving Deadeye to face any wrath the king might be about to dish out.

After glancing behind at his companions, Deadeye looked at the king. "Well, sire, it went like this. The mage destroyed the magic circle the two humans cowered within…"

"…there were only two?" questioned the king.

Deadeye nodded. "It was only a small circle, barely enough for one, really."

"And you came across no other Sinisters in the house?" queried Hemlock.

Redweedle stepped forward. "No, sir, just the two, a man and a woman."

"Who you promptly killed, yes?" asked the king.

Redweedle waved a hand at Deadeye to continue and stepped back.

Feeling the king's abrasive stare upon him, Deadeye continued. "Like I just said, the mage destroyed the circle. We were about to viciously murder them—we had arrows, knives, swords, and spears ready to do the job—when lo and behold," he gestured surprise with a raising of his arms, "out of nowhere, this ghoul crashes through the window that my two companions behind me were supposed to be guarding and starts attacking us." He shakes his head in dismay.

Shock and fear registered on both Redweedle and Blackroot's face when the king narrowed his eyes at them.

"Er…my lord, that's not exactly true…"

Mortgrimmest raised a hand to silence Redweedle's outburst and nodded for Deadeye to continue.

"Knowing the information I alone had gathered, and how invaluable it would be in defeating the humans, I made a rapid retreat to make my report to you, my king."

His exaggerated bow that nearly saw his nose scraping the floor, left his two companions, who had shuffled behind him to be out of direct view of the king in the hope they'd be forgotten, fully exposed.

"Though I am, to put it mildly, deeply annoyed some of the Sinister clan still draws breath, I can see that you, Deadeye, acted according to your instructions." The king turned to the other two who had shuffled backward a few more steps nearer the exit. "Which cannot be said about your two incompetent accomplices tasked with guarding the perimeter and thus solely responsible for letting the ghoul in and its resulting murderous rampage."

Redweedle lurched forward and dropped to his knees. "But, my liege, even if it was our fault, which it most certainly wasn't, we were incapable of defeating one as powerful as the ghoul."

Mortgrimmest slouched back in his throne and smiled cruelly. "Now you have admitted you were incapable of carrying out your assigned task, you leave me with only one option."

Deadeye smirked. His two companions whimpered.

"Well, two actually," added the king.

Hemlock leaned toward his king. "Actually sire, as king you can have as many options as you want."

The king beamed. "True, but two are adequate in this instance." He focused on the frightened, whimpering faeries. "Would you like to hear what your punishment will be?"

Though both didn't, Redweedle answered the king's rhetorical question. "If it pleases you, my king."

"Not sure if *pleases* is the right word, but it's certainly entertaining. I am considering one of two options. One, I have you both beheaded. Yes, a quick and relatively painless demise, but it makes such a mess, and it's freezing outside, as usual, so I'd rather not venture out. Option two, you are hanged here in my throne room where I can witness your demise in comfort.

"Knowing how much you'll enjoy the entertainment of a double beheading, sire, there might be a third option. Some form of befitting punishment that is beneficial to the realm, but quite unpleasant for them both, and then you can have them beheaded when the weather warms up."

"Some sort of community service?" questioned Mortgrimmest.

"Exactly, sire."

"But what?" The King stroked his chin as he considered the possibilities. After a few minutes, a smirk formed on his cruel lips when an appropriate punishment came to him.

After informing Redweedle and Blackroot of their punishment, the king grinned as he watched them being escorted from the throne room before turning to Deadeye. "Now that unsavory matter, which I have to admit I thoroughly enjoyed, has been completed satisfactorily, we need to work out our next step pertaining to the death of the surviving Sinisters and our invasion of the human world."

"I believe sending in a small party of skilled assassins to kill any remaining members of the Sinister clan would meet with better success than an all-out raid at this juncture, my king," proffered Deadeye.

The king glanced at Hemlock for his thoughts.

Hemlock nodded. "I agree. Also, because it has been many decades since we were there last, it might be advantageous to our planned invasion that when their primary task is completed, the incursion party reconnoiter the area and visit Hagstown to ascertain the effectiveness of the human defenses."

The king nodded enthusiastically at Hemlock. "I assume you have someone in mind?"

"I do indeed, sire. I believe my six highly skilled and ruthless assassins, the Phantoms, fit the brief perfectly," replied Hemlock proudly. "Predicting they might be needed, I have them standing by ready for your approval."

"Then call them in," ordered the king.

Hemlock grinned. "They are already here, in this room, my liege."

Both the king and Deadeye glanced around the throne room but, except for the three of them and the two guards by the door, it was absent anyone else.

"You jest, Hemlock," stated the king. "We are alone."

Smiling smugly, Hemlock faced the room. "Phantoms, reveal yourselves."

As if by magic, five black-clad figures melted out of the dark areas.

Both the king and Deadeye were impressed.

With a puzzled frown, the king looked at his advisor. "You said there were six, I see only five."

Hemlock beamed proudly. "Please sire, turn to your left."

The king turned and jumped at the sight of the assassin standing beside him.

"As you can see, my masters of stealth and shadow are able to infiltrate the most securely guarded fortress with ease. I call them my Magnificent Six," bragged Hemlock. "Disposing of the Sinisters, or anyone else you desire will pose them no problem."

The king waved away the assassin who was too close to provide him with any comfort and watched it join the others lined up behind Deadeye. He glared worriedly at the Phantoms armed with a variety of deadly weapons before turning to his advisor he trusted less each day. "Though I'm not a fan of your theatrics, Hemlock, they do seem proficient for the required task."

"Thank you, my liege."

"However," he looked straight at Deadeye, "as you have recently been to the human world and inside the home of the Sinisters, I charge you with leading this murderous mission."

Hemlock's smugness turned to dismay.

Though Deadeye was reluctant to do so, he thought it advisable to his health that he accepted and bowed. "Thank you, my king. I won't let you down."

"For your sake, you had better not."

"Er...sire," uttered Hemlock. "It really isn't necessary for Deadeye, who lacks the many years of intensive training my Phantoms have endured, to be involved at all."

The king scowled at Hemlock. "Are you arguing with my decision?"

Hemlock shook his head vigorously. "No, not at all. I just think Deadeye's services, whatever they might entail, would be better served elsewhere. My Phantoms are not used to working with less capable accomplices."

The king narrowed his eyes at his advisor. "So, Hemlock, are you saying that your highly skilled trained assassins you are so proud of, are imperfect?"

Realizing he had been backed into a corner, Hemlock sighed. "Not at all, sire."

Suspecting his advisor coveted his throne, and that his shadowy assassins were perhaps part of his plan to take it in the near future, the king smiled at Hemlock's discomfort as he sat back in his throne. "Then it's settled. Deadeye will be in total charge of the mission." His gaze scanned the six assassins and Deadeye. "I will refer to them as *my* Magnificent *Seven.*"

"Yes, my king," conceded Hemlock dismally.

"Well, my Magnificent Seven, what are you waiting for? Go and do as your king commands. Kill the Sinisters and reconnoiter Hagstown to discover its defenses and weaknesses, and then report back directly to me."

As one, the six Phantoms bowed, with Deadeye copying them after a short delay, and shuffled backward three paces as protocol decreed, before turning and exiting the room.

The king turned his attention back to his advisor. "While they are carrying out their mission, Hemlock, you are to confer with the commander of my army and start planning for a full invasion into the human world."

Hemlock bowed. "As you command, my king." He backed away and left through a side door.

Pleased with the way things were progressing, Mortgrimmest climbed down from his throne, exited through the door opposite the one taken by Hemlock, and entered his private quarters where his harem waited to administer their many charms upon him.

Chapter 19

Nightmare Forest 2.0

CONSTRUCTED AROUND LARGE TREES and the occasional outthrust of rock, the wheel-rutted track led them along its winding path through the forest. While Crowe concentrated on not twisting one of his four ankles in the deep grooves made by rat-drawn wagons long ago, and the uneven ground between them pitted with the indents of burdened rat paws, Griselda and Ellie scanned the darkness that lived amongst the trees for signs of danger. Though they heard things stalking them either side of the track—rushed movements over brittle leaves, the crack of twigs caused by misplaced footfalls, causing the dogs to growl threateningly—they failed to catch sight of the things that had produced them.

A small stream meandered around the trees and followed alongside the road. Further along, it flowed into a square pool formed of square-cut rocks; a watering hole for beasts of burden and their masters to drink from. It overflowed from a dip in its far side to continue on its journey.

Crowe halted when he spotted something in front and to the right of the track. "There's a building up ahead," he informed his passengers.

Dragging their gazes from the forest, Griselda and Ellie checked it out. Even from this distance, they could see it was a ruin.

"Keep to the track, Crowe. No one lives in the Forest any more, but get ready to run if danger threatens," advised Griselda.

"No need to worry on that score," uttered Crowe, "my legs have been coiled like springs ever since we entered this godforsaken place."

Sharing his gaze between the track and the building, Crowe continued on.

When they draw level, they saw it was a windmill perched on the top of a twisted outcrop of dark rock located on the far side of the widening stream. Describing its condition as ramshackle would be doing its derelict appearance an injustice. The crumbling stonework that still managed to cling in place leaned at an angle. Its four wooden-framed sails hung with ragged canvas that flapped in the breeze like bat wings. Beneath the rock outcrop it perched on, walls had been built to form a dwelling. The dark openings of both the house and the windmill caused them all to envisage an unwelcoming presence concealed within.

Griselda glanced at the growling dogs who also sensed the ominous stance of the ruin. She nudged Crowe with her legs and whispered, "Move on."

Crowe, who hadn't realized he had stopped, pressed on.

The creature inside that had been observing the strangers, crawled from the darkness that had concealed it and perched in one of the windmill's openings to watch them move away. Deciding they would make for an easy meal, he turned to its brethren waiting impatiently behind and signaled the call to attack with a high-pitched screech.

Griselda, Ellie, Crowe, and the dogs turned their heads behind when the screech reached them and watched the stream of creatures fly out from the windmill. They shot into the sky and formed a dark, menacing cloud. After swirling around a few times, they dived for the trees.

Griselda was about to urge Crowe to run, when he bolted forward, almost spilling her from his back.

"Are they bats?" called out Crowe, leaping over a mushroom festooned log stretching across the track.

"If you know of a species of bat that has the appearance of a termite, the head of a piranha, claws a tiger would envy, and a voracious appetite for flesh, then yes, they're bats," replied Griselda.

"They're Termitenators," uttered Ellie, peering at the approaching swarm.

Crowe groaned. "Why does it seem that everything living here is trying to kill us?"

"Probably because they are," said Ellie. Noticing Lucifer and Satan dropping back to guard their rear against the threat they couldn't possibly defeat, she signaled for them to keep pace with Crowe and turned to Griselda. "Did you bring the scattergun?"

Griselda thrust a hand into her bag. "I brought everything." She pulled out a weapon too long to fit into the bag and handed it to Ellie.

Ellie aimed the splayed end barrel at the oncoming cloud and fired.

Dead and wounded Termitenators struck by the deadly blast of iron pellets rained to the ground.

Ellie shifted the gun toward Griselda, who quickly shoved a fresh sausage of primed gunpowder and pellets into the barrel and rammed it down with her staff.

"I don't have enough to kill them all," advised Griselda, peering into her bag. "Nine remaining."

Ellie took aim. "Even if we had a never-ending supply, they're too small and fast to be able to hit them all." She fired again. More Termitenators dropped to the ground. "Maybe the forest will slow them down," Ellie suggested to Griselda as the witch reloaded the weapon.

"I was hoping we could avoid that," uttered Griselda, her eyes scanning the edges of the track.

"As was I, but if we stay in the open, we might as well stop and offer ourselves up to the fiends to get our deaths over with as quickly as possible."

"I choose the forest," said Crowe. "At least we'll stand a chance in there."

Griselda wasn't so sure, but a glance back at the oncoming flock of certain death revealed they had no other option. "The forest it is."

Crowe turned and headed amongst the trees.

Separating into smaller clusters, the Termitenators followed.

Crowe's rat body and limbs proved ideal for sprinting around the trees and over obstacles in his path. Trusting those on his back to hold the flying fiends at bay until they could find a way to lose them, he concentrated on running. He glanced at the dogs either side, keeping pace with him. Satan leaped at a Termitenator shooting in from the side and plucked it from the air. He crushed it in its jaws before devouring it while on the move. Crowe was glad of their company.

Ellie glanced around at the flying devils who had begun to encircle them. If they attacked from all directions at once, they wouldn't survive. She fired off a shot, killing most of a small group and turned to Griselda. "We need to find somewhere we can fight them off, and fast."

Griselda rammed a fresh cartridge into the scattergun and peered ahead through the trees as she uttered an incantation to improve her sight through the gloom. About one hundred yards distance, her Hawk Sight picked out a group of rocks with a dark mass at its center, a cave. She leaned forward and yanked Crowe's left ear to the side. "Turn until I stop pulling and then head straight. There's a cave up ahead we need to reach."

Wincing from the painful ear tug, Crowe veered left until Griselda released her grip and then rushed forward. He spurted for the cave entrance when he glimpsed it, leaped inside and skidded to a halt.

As soon as they were in, Ellie flew from his back and joined the dogs guarding the entrance. She fired at the first wave of Termitenators heading inside. The pellets ripped through their bodies and shredded their wings, driving any that had avoided the onslaught back.

"I think we're safe for the moment," Ellie informed her companions. "They're staying back."

Griselda slid from the saddle when Crowe slumped to the ground for a much-needed rest. Taking position beside Ellie, she looked out at the Termitenators. Some hovered, others swooped around the trees, and others roosted on branches. All were watching them. "I wonder why they aren't attacking?"

Ellie slapped her weapon proudly. "Probably because they realize how expert a shot I am with this."

Creasing her brow, Griselda shook her head. "If they all attacked at once, we wouldn't stand a chance, no matter what weapons we had. No, something else is keeping them at bay." She turned to gaze around their refuge. Though not large, the cave stretched into the hillside for an unknown distance.

Griselda walked around Crowe and peered into the dark tunnel. Though her Hawk Sight spell was wearing off, she picked out gruesome white objects littering the passage. Something lived in here.

Crowe raised his head and followed Griselda's gaze down the tunnel. "What's the plan? We wait here for those things outside to leave or do we head deeper and search for another exit?"

Griselda turned to face him. "I'd prefer to wait, but I don't think those things outside will be leaving anytime soon."

"The tunnel it is then." Worried about the poison in his blood and the time ticking away, Crowe climbed to his feet. "As much as I'd like to rest, let's keep moving."

"We might not be alone in here," warned Griselda.

"I know. My rat eyes are a definite improvement over my human ones. I saw the bones." He jerked his head at Ellie. "Whatever's in there, I'm sure it's nothing our resident monster killer can't handle."

With a smile and an affirming nod, Griselda called out to Ellie. "We're heading into the tunnel."

Ellie backed away from the entrance, her eyes never leaving the creatures outside. "I'll keep to the rear for a while to make sure they don't follow."

"I don't think an attack from that direction will be the problem," commented Griselda.

Ellie glanced at her questioningly.

"I spotted bones up ahead, lots of them."

"All aboard! This rat is leaving the station."

Griselda climbed onto Crowe's back.

To keep her eye on the Termitenators, Ellie fluttered backward when Crowe moved off with her dogs keeping pace.

Crowe picked a path through the scattered bones and tried not to dwell on the deep grooves on each that could have only been made by large teeth and claws.

When the entrance grew distant, and the Termitenators showed no signs of following, Ellie returned to her position straddling Crowe's neck and swapped the scattergun for her bow and arrow.

To light their route deeper underground, Griselda pulled a lighted lantern from her bag and hooked it over the tip of her staff.

Chapter 20

Phantoms

IMPRESSED BY THE STEALTHY movements of Hemlock's Phantoms skulking through the forest without making a sound on the leafy carpet, Deadeye raised a fist to halt them when the Sinister house came into view. He scanned the grounds and windows for signs of anyone at home. All seemed quiet. After peering into the forest for the ghoul he feared was close by, he turned to give the Phantoms his instructions. He sighed when he saw no sign of them. "Show yourselves," he ordered in a firm but hushed voice.

The six assassins creepily oozed from the surrounding darkness and encircled him. Made nervous by their too-close proximity, he stepped back and bumped into one before pushing past. "Right, here's what we're going to do." He found it quite disconcerting being stared at by eyes concealed behind dark gauze covering the eye slits in their black balaclavas; Phantoms was a well-deserved description. "We enter the house, do a room-by-room search, and kill any Sinisters we find. I also suggest we cut off their heads to show to the king to prove the successful outcome of our mission, thus reaping the rewards of his appreciation."

Receiving no indication, not even a nod, from the Phantoms he knew despised him, he turned back to the house and pointed out the broken upstairs window. "That's how we gained entry before; however, I suggest we seek an alternative entry point in case traps have been laid. A downstairs window should suffice."

Deadeye turned to ensure the Phantoms understood and again found them absent. He sighed. "Show yourselves."

When, after a few moments they had failed to do so, he refocused on the house and spied two entering through the front door, and the others spread out climbing the sheer front walls of the house, jimmying open windows and slipping inside. Eager to partake in the demise of any Sinister that would curry huge favor with the king, he hurried to the house.

Though reluctant to admit it, the Phantoms had carried out their task with speed and thoroughness. When Deadeye entered the house through the front door, they were gathered in the hallway shaking their heads at each other.

"I assume your head shaking indicates the Sinisters aren't at home." Deadeye was surprised when one of the Phantoms answered with a nod. Reluctant to take his eyes off them in case they vanished into the shadows again, he issued his next orders. "We'll head for Hagstown to check out the human defenses. While we're there, as none of you know what they look like, I'll keep a lookout for any Sinisters and kill them if possible. If not, I will follow them and signal for your assistance with a call from a Fanged Dervil." He gazed at each faceless Phantom in turn. "Understood?"

Each faceless Phantom nodded, reluctantly it seemed to Deadeye.

Without making a sound or waiting for him, the Phantoms exited the house. They had vanished into the night by the time Deadeye stepped outside. He headed for Hagstown.

Sitting on top of the water tower with his head continually turning to gaze over the all-but-deserted streets of Hagstown below—most of its unsuspecting residents had retired to their warm beds for the night—Ghoul focused on the only signs of life, an inn spilling yellow light onto the dimly lit street. It briefly watched the human shapes within moving past the windows before turning its head to follow a van driving along the perimeter road. When it pulled to a halt at the top of the railway embankment, three men climbed out. After collecting equipment from the rear of the vehicle, they disappeared down the hill. The glow of electric light appeared a few moments later. Dismissing the activity as unimportant, Ghoul continued its vigil.

When a short while later, it sensed the approach of something menacing that tuned its attention toward the edge of town. At first, it saw nothing out of the ordinary, but as it peered into the shadowy areas, it picked out dark things moving stealthily. The faeries had arrived. Believing correctly that the black-clad faeries were assassins on a murderous mission, Ghoul jumped to the ground and went to intercept them.

Splitting up when they reached Hagstown's outskirts, the six faerie assassins set off through the streets, around the perimeter, and over rooftops to discover what defenses the humans had in place to thwart the soon-to-arrive faerie invasion force.

The faerie assassin known as Phantom 3—Hemlock had decided that stripping them of their birth names and shedding all contact with their past lives, which included their friends and families, would help hone them into better killers without all the emotional baggage to distract them—climbed the side of a building and deftly moved along the rooftops. When he had infiltrated halfway into the village without meeting any obstacles, he was surprised by the humans' lack of defenses. It seemed that with the passage of time, they had forgotten how dangerous the threat living nearby could be. When he jumped across a gap between two houses, he was snatched from the air. With a hand gripping him around the waist, Phantom 3's surprised stare focused on the ghoul's face almost close enough to headbutt. Years of training held at bay any fear he might have felt and darted his hand to one of the two swords strapped to his back. With a blur of motion, the weapon was slid from its scabbard and the point thrust between the ghoul's eyes with enough force to sink into the ghoul's head up to the hilt.

Surprised by the assassin's swiftness, Ghoul went boss-eyed when he looked at the protruding hilt. Being a creature born of magic, which was the only thing that could kill it, the blade penetrating its head was little more than a slight discomfort. He pulled it free and slung it over the rooftops. A second discomfort came from the second sword pushed through its chest. When it reached a hand behind its back and touched the blade sticking out, an idea formed. Aware he couldn't leave any faerie bodies behind for the townsfolk to discover, it would be an ideal place to store the assassin squirming to be free of his grip until he could dispose of it somewhere it would never be found. Flipping the assassin over his head, it impaled him on his own sword. Phantom 3 uttered a painful grunt and fell limp. After shaking his shoulders to check the corpse wouldn't slip free, Ghoul went to look for the assassin's murderous friends.

With no way of telling if Hemlock's invisible killers were nearby or already off checking the town's defenses, Deadeye halted on the hill overlooking the cluster of human dwellings. He roamed his gaze along its empty streets and at the three humans working by the train tracks. Spying no sign of the six Phantoms, which didn't surprise him, he peered into the shadows around him. "If you are there, reveal yourselves?" he whispered. When they didn't materialize, he headed below.

Also surprised by the lack of any human defenses against their kind, Deadeye strolled through the deserted streets and gazed at the windows curtained against the outside world while those within were deep in slumber.

Footsteps drifting from a side street, alerted him to someone's approach. A peek around the corner revealed a human walking his dog. Deadeye flipped open the lid of a black plastic trash bin and climbed inside. Though he could kill the old man and his pet easily, the foul deed would alert the townsfolk to their menacing activity and put them on their guard.

Harry Smythe rounded the corner. When his dog squatted to do its business on the thin strip of grass dotted with trees lining the edge of the path, he lit a cigarette and patiently waited for Samson to finish. After the dog had scratched ineffectively at the grass to cover its lopsided pyramid of steaming spoils, Harry pulled a plastic bag from his pocket and slipping a hand inside, crouched and picked up the sizable pile; its foul stench assaulting his nostrils before he twisted the top shut, temporarily sealing the smell inside. Crossing to the row of trash bins his master headed for, Samson sniffed one of them and jumped up, his tail wagging excitedly. Resting his front paws on the top, he growled.

"Leave the rats alone, Samson," ordered Harry, yanking the dog away as he dropped the disgusting parcel inside. Tugging away the dog that pulled on his lead to head back to whatever he found of interest in the bin, Harry headed home along the street.

Deadeye raised the bin lid slightly and peered out. When he saw the man and his dog disappear into a side street, he climbed out. Glad to be free of the stinking bin made stinkier by the smelly object the human had dropped on him, he continued his walk through the town.

To ensure his mission was a success and to ingratiate himself into favor with his ill-tempered king, he needed to track down the surviving Sinisters. Deadeye's gaze roamed over the humans' cars parked bumper-to-bumper along the streets in the hope he'd recognize the one he had seen parked outside the Sinister house on his first visit, which was absent when he and the Phantoms had visited a short while ago.

As the king would look favorably on whoever killed the Sinisters, his original thoughts had pictured him ending their lives personally, but now he began to rethink the plan. If he could capture the remaining Sinisters alive and present them to the king for him to end their lives by his own hand, he would be sure to bestow generous rewards upon that faerie responsible, *him*. Pleased with his new strategy, Deadeye headed for the building where some of the humans had assembled within.

After Arabella had explained the strange events at Crowe's house the previous night, Sebastian sat back in his seat and glanced around at the other patrons in the Witch's Gibbet Inn while he supped his ale. Wiping the froth from his mouth with the back of his hand, he gazed at his daughter with an excited glint in his eye. "I knew it. Faeries *are* real and *are* living in Hag's Hollow Forest."

"Yes, but Father, in case you didn't grasp the danger they pose from what I just told you, the faeries aren't of the good variety. They would have killed Crowe and me if that ghoul thing hadn't turned up to save us."

"Quite so, quite so, but evil or not, don't you see what this means? Creatures of lore and legend are real and living barely a stone's throw from where we sit." He leaned forward again. "If I could prove their existence, I'd be famous. A photograph is no good though—too easily faked. We'll have to capture one, alive if possible. You said they aren't very big, so they should be easy enough to trap."

"Father, listen to yourself. Didn't you hear me? The faeries are dangerous and seem to hate humans enough to want to kill them. You try and catch one, and you'll likely be the one killed. They may be small, but they are many. You wouldn't stand a chance."

"Mere details to be overcome, my dear. Anyway, if they are as dangerous as you believe, it would be advantageous to capture one to study. We need to learn their weaknesses and thus protect ourselves against them. Do you really think if I stood up now and warned everyone here there's a likelihood we are about to be attacked by faeries; they would believe me? Of course they wouldn't. They would laugh and label me crazy. However, if I could show them a live one, indisputable proof they exist, then they'd have no choice other than to believe they are real and would be more amenable to enact any plan we can come up with to protect ourselves and the town against them."

Arabella sighed and gazed around at the people enjoying their night out, unaware of the nearby threat that would shortly—if Crowe's plan failed—threaten them, their families and their friends' existence. She turned back to her father. "Putting it like that, then I can see the sense of capturing one, but how would we even go about such a thing? I know they live in the forest, but Crowe didn't tell me where and it's too vast to search."

"I agree, that's why we'll set a trap for them. Don't worry my dear, I have it all worked out. It's a cunning plan that can't possibly fail."

Arabella wasn't so confident, but if they were going save lives, what other choice did they have. "Okay, I suppose you'd better tell me."

Jumping up to the windowsill, Deadeye peered inside the Witch's Gibbet Inn and cast his gaze over the humans. He couldn't believe his luck when he spied the woman he had encountered in the Sinister house. He had found her. Spying no sign of the male Sinister, he moved away from the window while he deliberated his next move. Though he would have preferred to capture the woman on his own, his size compared to hers was against him. The Phantoms help would be required to ensure the kidnapping was a success. Another foul-up would likely see him killed at the king's angry request.

Unwilling to stray too far away from the inn lest the Sinister woman slipped away, Deadeye flew up to the roof. Cupping his hands to his mouth, he mimicked the shrill call of a Fanged Dervil; a small rodent creature of the Faerie Realm that sported two elongated teeth. The Phantoms would recognize the signal and, if they adhered to his instruction, come to his assistance.

Just when he thought they weren't coming, they appeared out of the darkness around him. Noticing one was missing, he decided five would be sufficient for the task. He informed them of his plan.

Ghoul looked in the direction the strange call had come from. It climbed the side of the nearby furniture store and crossed to the far side of the flat roof with the dead Phantom flopping wildly on its back like a puppet cut from its strings. Concealed behind a small structure with a single door, it gazed along the street and stared at the faeries assembled on the roof of a building with light shining from its windows. Certain their purpose for gathering there bode ill against the humans within, Ghoul jumped down. Planning to attack them from behind, it made its way around the buildings.

Sebastian held the inn door open for his daughter and followed her out onto the street. Arabella tugged her coat collar tighter to ward off the chill air and slipped a hand through her father's arm, and they headed home. They had preparations to make if they were going to save the town, and that included seeking the assistance of Crowe. They turned down a side street, little more than an alley between two shops, and halted with startled gasps when two small black-clothed figures emerged from the shadows in front of them.

Frightened and fascinated by their sudden appearance, Sebastian stared at the two small figures hovering in the air. "Faeries," he exclaimed excitedly.

"The bad kind, remember." Arabella tugged her father away and turned him around to flee from the threat, but three more faeries hovering in the alley behind them blocked their retreat. Movement on her left directed her gaze upon another faerie she recognized from the house, the one-eyed faerie who had shot an arrow at her. Without the protection circle, this time the missile it aimed at her chest wouldn't fail to find its target.

"What do you want?" she demanded.

The one-eyed faerie said something too soft and intelligible for her to understand. A dull thwack rang out. Her father collapsed unconscious to the ground. Arabella glanced at the cudgel-wielding faerie responsible and swung her handbag at it, which it easily dodged. The others sprung upon her. While some tied her hands behind her back, another wrapped a gag over her mouth. She ceased her struggles when she was lifted into the air by the five ninja-like faeries. Glancing down at the alley rapidly receding, she forced herself to remain still lest she slipped from their grasp and be dashed on the ground, a heap of broken bones and blood.

Ghoul ran up the far slope of the inn roof and dived with an arm outstretched to snatch the woman from the faeries' grasp. Its fingers swiped past a foot too short. Its landing on the roof smashed slates. It grabbed the gutter when it slid over the edge and swung back onto the roof. Its sprint after the faeries cracked more slates and dislodged others, sending them sliding down the roof to smash on the street below.

Glancing back at the ghoul, Deadeye noticed the missing Phantom stuck limply to its back. He aimed his bow at the menace and fired off three arrows in quick succession. Though all three found a target in the ghoul's chest, the creature showed no sign they caused it any pain. Realizing his arrows wouldn't stop it, he flew to the Phantom holding the woman's left leg, tapped the assassin's shoulder to get his attention and pointed back at the ghoul in pursuit. Unfazed by the creature's great size in contrast to his own, Phantom 5 thrust Arabella's foot into Deadeye's hands and flew off to intercept it.

Though certain the Phantom would be killed, Deadeye hoped the skirmish would delay the ghoul long enough for them to make their escape. If they could reach the portal and return to the Faerie Realm, they'd be safe.

As the black-clad faerie broke away from the pack and headed for it, Ghoul followed its approach. When it drew two swords from its back and swished them menacingly, Ghoul snatched up a slate from the roof and threw it Frisbee-style.

With no time to avoid the spinning missile, Phantom 5 lashed at it with the swords, chopping it into small harmless pieces. The smile hidden beneath his hood disappeared when he noticed another slate whizzing through the air too close to defend against. It sliced through his neck and parted his head from his body with his shocked expression frozen on his face.

Ghoul grabbed the falling body and kicked at the head rolling down the slope of the roof. Pulling the three arrows from its chest, it dropped two of them and pressing the limp, headless corpse against its chest, pinned it in place with the other.

The head sailed through the air, clipped the side of Deadeye's head and landed on Arabella, who raised her head to see what had just arrived. The scream that sprung to her lips was stifled by the gag. She gazed between the one-eyed faerie and the ninja-type one holding her ankles and spied the ghoul that had saved them before running along the rooftops in pursuit. Feeling hope from its presence, she watched one-eye knock the head off.

With the five of them needed to carry the weighty human, one on each limb and one supporting her from beneath, Deadeye was unable to order another Phantom away to attack the ghoul. To escape from its clutches, they needed another distraction to slow it down. A distant hoot directed his gaze at the lights on the horizon moving swiftly toward Hagstown. Focusing on the workmen beside the track, who had stopped working and gazed at the oncoming train, an idea formed as to how he might achieve that. He quickly informed the remaining Phantoms of his hastily constructed plan. They slid down the roof and fluttered their wings to land softly on the ground.

Reaching the end of the row of houses, Ghoul jumped down and sped along the street after its quarry. Concern flashed across its face when the faeries veered away from the direct route leading to the forest. Wondering their purpose for doing so, it continued in pursuit.

Stepping back from the track beside the signal they were repairing, the men gazed along the rails at the approaching night train heading across country.

As they glided toward the three unsuspecting workmen, the two phantoms holding Arabella's arms drew their cudgels. Flying a few feet from the ground, the feet of the one beneath swept through the long grass covering the embankment they swooped down, they came up behind the unsuspecting workmen. The two front Phantoms swung their cudgels at the heads of two men, spilling them to the ground across one track. The Phantom beneath Arabella kicked out his legs at the third man who stumbled forward and tripped, banging his head on the far rail when he crashed to the ground. With their job done, they sped up the far embankment and headed for the forest.

Noticing she was close enough to the ground to survive the fall if she could get free of the faeries' grip, Arabella struggled violently.

About to put his cudgel away, Phantom 1 swung it at Arabella's head, ceasing her movements immediately. Satisfied the human was unconscious, he pocketed the weapon.

Arriving at the outskirts of town, Ghoul spied the faeries heading for the forest and veered toward them. Leaping down the embankment, it landed on the track and was about to rush up the far side when it noticed something lying across the rails; three humans. Now aware of what the faeries had done, Ghoul bolted along the track as the train hurtled nearer.

To check on the workmen he had been informed were off the tracks, the train driver peered through the curved windscreen. Highlighted in the glow of the temporary work lights, he saw three men sprawled across the tracks. His hand activated the brake lever. Iron wheels screeched on iron rails as they tried to halt the speeding train. The driver frantically stared at the men and the rapidly decreasing distance between the train and knew it wouldn't stop in time. His eyes shot wide open when he spied a tall, pale figure running along the tracks toward him. He watched on incredulously when the...thing, scooped up the three men and leaped to the side a split second before the train would have hit them.

Releasing his hand from the brake, the driver opened the side window, stuck his head out and gazed back at the creature placing the men gently on the grassy bank. When it looked at him, the driver nodded his thanks. Whatever the strange beast was, it had saved three lives; in his book that labeled him as a friend.

Aware no one would believe what he'd just witnessed and might cause his employers to doubt his sanity, thus putting his job at risk, the driver decided to keep what had just happened to himself. He did though ring the local authorities to inform them he had spotted three men who seemed to be unconscious lying beside the track and gave their location.

As soon as the train had whizzed past, Ghoul crossed the rails and rushed up the embankment. Although there was no sign of the faeries or their kidnap victim, it knew where they were heading. It entered the forest and headed on a direct route for the portal to the Faerie Realm. If it didn't reach it before the human was taken through, her chances of survival would be slim.

Pleased the ghoul had been delayed, and confident they could now get the woman safely in their realm before it caught up with them, Deadeye wondered what his reward would be. When the Phantoms' flight began to slow from the exhaustion of carrying the massive human, he didn't berate them. Partly because he was also feeling the strain, and partly because now they had the Sinister woman in their clutches, the Phantoms could murder him and inform the king he'd been killed in battle; something the king wouldn't bat an eye over when presented with the prize they were bringing to him. He had already noticed them looking at him oddly, or rather he sensed their looks were odd, it was impossible to tell with their features concealed. Also, if it were possible to carry the woman on his own, and murder the Phantoms before they could retaliate, he would have no qualms about killing them and claiming the glory of the catch for himself.

"We're almost there," commented Deadeye cheerily to the Phantoms. "When we present the king with his prize, he is sure to shower us all with generous rewards. Plenty for all is what I'm saying. Gold, jewels or whatever it is you deadly assassins crave."

Though each Phantom glanced at him, even the one beneath that moved his head to the side to do so, Deadeye didn't sense any grateful smiles among them. No, he pictured looks of the murderous kind. He'd have to watch his back for their knives that might soon be planted in it.

Ignoring the undergrowth and branches whipping at it, Ghoul's long legs carried it swiftly through the forest. Created from earth, potions, and spells, Griselda had not furnished it with muscles, lungs or any other internal organs when she had magically brought it into being it, so fatigue wasn't a problem. It swerved around ancient oaks, soared over fallen trees and boughs and lifted leaves from the ground that briefly followed in its wake before settling back to earth.

With muscles screaming to be released of the burden they carried, the tired faeries were finding it hard to remain airborne and gradually lowered until the one underneath was forced to run along the ground.

Deadeye peered ahead at the thorny hedge surrounding the ring of oaks approaching slower than he would have liked. In their exhausted state, they wouldn't be able to fly over it; they'd have to use the fallen tree, slowing their progress further.

The cracks of snapping twigs turned his gaze behind and to the left at something pale speeding toward their destination. The ghoul was back. It was now a race to see who would reach the portal first. With the unburdened ghoul at an advantage, the odds were that it would win.

Realizing their tired wings were slowing them down, Deadeye issued an order. "To the ground. Use your feet."

As if they had practiced the maneuver a hundred times, the Phantoms raised the human above their heads and dropped to forest floor. Though the ten sets of legs increased their speed slightly, Deadeye doubted it would be fast enough to beat the long-legged ghoul. Confident four of them could support the human's weight now they were on the ground, Deadeye decided on a delaying tactic that might slow it down enough for them to reach the portal first. "You beneath, go kill the ghoul."

Surprised by the assassin's swiftness and willingness to accept and act on an order without argument; Hemlock had obviously trained them well, and from what he knew of the advisor—probably brutally—the Phantom dived to the side. Twisting as he rolled across the leafy forest floor, he jumped to his feet and sprinted for the ghoul.

Confident that would be the last time he saw the murderous faerie unless it was its corpse, Deadeye turned his attention to those who would survive a little longer. "Run deadly Phantoms. Run like you've never run before."

The Phantom beside him turned his covered face at Deadeye and shook his head in an unmistakably derisory manner.

When they neared nature's spike-laden barrier, they steered around its circumference for the fallen tree. Their bridge to safety.

Spying the extensive roots of the tree torn from the earth, Deadeye thought that if the assassin he'd sent to battle with the ghoul could delay him even for a short time—thirty seconds, a minute would be better—they might actually make it.

Keeping trees between him and the ghoul to hide its approach, Phantom 2 drew a handful of throwing knives from the well-stocked bandolier across his chest and ran up the trunk of a chestnut tree. He sped along a branch and as soon as the ghoul came within range, let fly the deadly blades in quick succession.

Unaware of the ambush ahead, Ghoul shared its gaze between the fleeing faeries it caught glimpses of through the trees and its prime objective, the thorny ring protecting the faerie portal. Though Ghoul registered the seven knives when they struck, three in its face, three grouped close to where its would-be-killer thought its heart should be, and one in the chest of the faerie assassin corpse pinned skewwhiff to his chest, it didn't break its stride. Homing in on the rustling leaves in the tree coming up fast, he jumped into its leafy boughs. It grabbed the black-clad faerie around his neck, dropped to the ground, and continued running. It gazed at the assassin that sliced twin blades at him savagely, the magic it was infused with, healed the wounds as quickly as they were made. Imagining a look of shocked surprise on its would-be-killer's shrouded face, Ghoul swung him around its head and propelled him through the air. Phantom 2 frantically flapped wings in an effort to slow his flight but failed miserably.

The three Phantoms and Deadeye climbed the roots onto the bridge-trunk and raced across it.

Almost there, thought Deadeye.

They and the woman they carried almost toppled into the needle-like spikes of the bushes when something thudded onto the trunk in front of them with an awful breaking of bones and brought them skidding to a halt.

"Don't stop, kick him over the side," yelled Deadeye, aware his delaying tactic had failed, and the ghoul would soon be upon them.

The three disapproving black-clad faces that jerked at him indicated the lack of remorse they felt for their victims didn't apply to one of their own. Though he didn't have time for it, Deadeye sensed a bit of placating might get them moving again rather than an order. "Or we can step over him and return for his broken body later so he can have a proper burial."

With the sounds of the large, pale and angry ghoul homing in on their position, the Phantoms stepped over their fallen comrade and rushed along the tree bridge.

Before the faeries had vacated the trunk, thorny creepers snaked around Phantom 2's corpse and dragged it into their mass; a faerie growbag that would supply them with welcome nourishment.

Deadeye and the remaining Phantoms jumped down from the end of the tree bridge, their wings fluttering their burden gently to the ground. When they sprinted for the ring of oaks and headed for the portal, a moon-cast shadow swept over them. Deadeye and the Phantoms glanced up at the ghoul who sailed over the barrier and dropped toward them.

Reacting to the threat quickly, Phantom 6 indicated to Phantom 4 beside him, to take the full weight of Arabella's top half. Drawing his swords, he flew off to attack the ghoul.

Struggling with the weight of the human's front half on his own, Phantom 4 faltered and almost tripped when the ghoul thudded to the ground a short distance away. Fearing for his life, Deadeye glanced at the ghoul, the two limp Phantoms hanging from it, one headless, and the Phantom rushing at it with his swords swinging menacingly. Fearing the lone Phantom wouldn't last long and the ghoul would soon be upon him, Deadeye grabbed the woman's right leg and barged the Phantom who held it away. "Go help your comrade."

Phantom 1 turned away and joined the attack.

"You at the front," called out Deadeye. "I don't care how we do it, drag her if we have to, but get this damn human in the portal, now!"

Both straining with her weight, they carried, dragged and bumped Arabella across the clearing and through the broken fence ringing the portal.

Deadeye smiled; they were going to make it. Three more steps and they were in. He glanced behind to see how the battled fared and noticed the ghoul looking at them as it swiped a hand at its attackers. Swept aside and off their feet, the two Phantoms smashed into the surrounding oak trees with a dreadful crunching of bones. As their limp forms dropped to the ground, Ghoul lurched forward a few strides and dived with its hands outstretched for their human captive.

Deadeye screamed and shoved the human forward, forcing Phantom 4 in front to topple into the invisible portal. Propelled by his panicked, adrenalin-fueled feet pawing at the ground, Deadeye pushed harder. Bit by bit, the woman disappeared from the head down to her feet. As he slipped through the portal, Deadeye turned his fear filled-face to the fingers curling around him.

Ghoul thudded to the ground as its fingers closed on air. After sliding across the grass a short distance, it came to a halt. It sat up and looked at the empty space the woman had disappeared into. It was an entrance Griselda had forbidden it to pass through. It had failed. The human was in the Faerie Realm and as good as dead now. With nothing more it could do for her, Ghoul climbed to its feet and headed back to Hagstown to continue its vigil.

Lying on the ground beside the woman and panting heavily from his recent exertions and near-death escape, Deadeye glanced at the Phantom climbing to his feet. If the assassin loathed him before he had inadvertently gotten his comrades killed, he'd hate him with a vengeance now. Taking advantage of the assassin's temporary befuddlement of passing through the portal, something he had acclimatized to, Deadeye drew his knife as he stood, moved behind Phantom 4 and slit his throat. When he pushed the dying assassin aside, he noticed the perplexed expressions plastered on the four Tronks ordered to guard the portal.

When the dead Phantom flopped to the ground, Deadeye nodded at it. "Human imposter sent to infiltrate our realm and kill our king."

The guards glanced dubiously at the small corpse, at the larger unconscious human female, and then back at Deadeye wiping his blade clean on the dead phantom's black attire.

Deadeye shrugged as he put away his cleaned knife. "They're training children now to do their murderous deeds," he explained. "Devious creatures those humans."

The deviousness of the humans was something they all agreed on.

"Now," exclaimed Deadeye, looking at each Tronk before pointing at one. "You, go fetch a wagon so I can transport this human to the king, whose direct orders I am acting under."

Undecided about what he should do, the Tronk turned to his comrades for advice. A non-commital shrug from each was of no help. "We ordered to remain here and guard the portal to stop humans passing through," stated the indecisive Tronk.

Deadeye gesticulated at the dead Phantom. "Which indeed they have."

The Tronk glanced at the corpse doubtfully. "So say you, but I must stay at my post."

Deadeye glared at the reluctant Tronk. "If that's the way you want to play it, it's fine by me, but I'll have no choice other than to inform the king of your insubordination as my orders are his orders. However, if you think the king, as forgiving and merciful as we all know he is, will forgive your transgression and not have you killed in some no doubt horrible and agonizing method of his choosing, then I will go and fetch the wagon myself."

When Deadeye took a step forward, the Tronk spoke, "Now hold there a minute. I suppose if you be speaking for the king, then obey I must. But you stay here, so four still guarding portal?"

"If that's what you want, I will," replied Deadeye.

The Tronk scratched his head. "I not sure it is and not sure it isn't. You got me turned all around."

Deadeye pointed towards the city. "Which is something I suggest you do if you want me to report favorably on your behavior to the king."

Muttering under his breath, the Tronk turned away and strode off.

Deadeye sat on the Phantom's corpse, took a pipe from his pocket and lit it. Releasing a long, satisfying stream of smoke, he glanced at the unconscious woman and smiled. He had done it. When he presented one of the last remaining members of the Sinister clan to the king, he'll be showered in gold. It was a good plan of his to capture the human. The king would enjoy the sport of killing her.

He took another long drag of the pungent smoke into his lungs and savored the sensation before setting it free. *It had been a good day that could only get better.*

Chapter 21

Goblins Lair

CROWE TURNED A BEND in the tunnel and continued down the sloping path into the unknown. The faint sound of dripping water they'd all heard for a while now became louder as they ventured deeper into the shaft. Hoping it wasn't another feature like the Devil's Cauldron, he stepped tentatively into a cavern. All three gazed around the vast space and the underground lake weakly lit by subdued sunlight entering through holes in its high roof. Their eyes shot to a loud splash in the water. Ripples set into motion by whatever creature had dived in expanded across the surface. All imagined something vicious and nasty was responsible.

Crowe followed the wake trail created by something moving beneath the surface. "I guess swimming across isn't an option."

"I'm truly hoping that won't be necessary," muttered Griselda softly, concentrating on the bones piled outside a dark foreboding entrance a short distance away. The skulls among the many disarrayed skeletons were mostly of the goblin variety.

Ellie shushed the dogs to silence when they growled at whatever menace they sensed within.

Water drips splashed into the pool from the hundreds of stalactites hanging from the ceiling. Just as many stalagmites jutted from the shore. Mineral-formed columns rose around and from within the pool like cathedral pillars.

At the far side of the lake, that was impossible to reach without a boat, was an opening shrouded in darkness and what might be a jetty extending out from the rising shore nearby.

More accessible was the large opening directly opposite the tunnel they'd just traveled through, which led into an even larger cavern. A small stream feeding the lake came from that direction. Though weak daylight seeped through gaps in the roof to reveal rocks and patches of ground covered in green moss, the areas that remained shrouded in darkness were interspersed with a green glow of unknown origin. It was an altogether more inviting outlook than the darker cavern with its lake creature and whatever horror dwelt in the bone scattered lair.

Griselda nudged Crowe into movement.

Picking his steps carefully, Crowe padded stealthily past the dark entrance that they all willed to remain empty.

Unbeknown to the three travelers passing through this underground world, the creatures that had made the cave their home—a species uninspiringly termed Cave Dwellers, because, logically enough, they lived in caves and rarely ventured above ground unless hunger forced them to—had been aware of the intruders' presence since they had entered their domain. Cave Dwellers might lack the sensitive sight of those they observed hungrily, but they made up for this deficiency with acute hearing and a nose that a bloodhound would envy. Even in pitch-blackness, they could pinpoint the exact position of all five prey.

Though eager to feast—food had been in short supply since the goblins left—the Cave Dwellers remained hidden and followed the interlopers' tantalizing scents and sounds of their movements past their lair. Now they knew what direction the food was traveling in they could set up an ambush; their preferred method of taking down prey. Taking their alpha's lead, the six Cave Dwellers turned away and headed deeper into their lair before scuttling into a smaller side tunnel.

Relieved to have left the gloomy cavern behind, Crowe entered one much brighter and continued alongside the stream where strange fungi with orange bell-shaped tops and red stems thrived along its banks. Satan sniffed at one and obviously not liking its scent, jumped back with a yelp, and rubbed a paw furiously at its nose.

From her higher vantage point, Griselda cast her eyes over the florescent growths thriving near the cavern walls. Huddled in groups of six, they also seemed to be a species of mushroom or toadstool she had never encountered before. They were growing near stubby, branchless trees as dark as the gloom that tried to conceal them. Filaments with glowing ends the same color as the fluorescent mushrooms sprouted from the trunks. Though Griselda was tempted to collect some specimens, their unknown toxicity and the possibility they might be harmful to touch stayed her hand.

Focusing on the only other exit from the cavern she could see, Ellie pointed it out to Griselda. "It looks like something lived down here at one time."

Griselda stared at the simply carved stonework they headed for. "I'm assuming because of the skeletons back there, it's part of the goblins' domain before the faeries defeated them and drove the survivors away."

"Are you certain they're gone?" asked Crowe, picturing the vicious goblins from books and films; his only reference. All seemed to hate humans and had an unsettling craving to eat them. That he was now in the guise of a rat was something he didn't think would deter them from an easy meal.

Griselda tapped Ellie on the shoulder. "Did you hear of any goblin sightings in the Faerie Realm during your stay here?"

Ellie shook her head. "Plenty of other foul creatures that would make an encounter with a goblin a preferable occurrence, but no mention of any goblins. After their brutal defeat at the hands of the faeries, I don't think they would dare set foot on their lost lands again. At least not without good reason and a huge army."

"That's one thing in our favor then...I think," uttered Crowe, not sure he liked the idea of encountering creatures so terrifying it made a meeting with the monstrous goblins he pictured preferable.

"If that's the entrance to one of their abandoned subterranean lairs, then there's bound to be an exit or two leading above ground," offered Griselda.

Crowe climbed the steps formed over an arched tunnel the stream poured from, headed for the entrance, and passed through its doorway.

Just inside were the rotted remains of the thick, wooden, iron-strapped door that once barricaded the entrance. The stone wall facing out into the cavern was filled with angled slits of the type used by archers to fire arrows out at an attacking enemy. Positioned in the middle of the room was a rusty brazier with a pile of ash and charcoal around its base that would have offered warmth for any creature stationed here. On the far wall, a few stone steps led up to another doorway with its sturdy door hanging askew from its buckled top hinge.

Ellie took in the defensive nature of the entrance. "Goblins or not, whatever lived here were guarding against some threat."

"A threat I hope is now long dead," muttered Crowe, avoiding a second glance at the worrying deep claw marks on the door's surface when he stepped past.

The room was littered with pieces of simple wooden furniture, table, chairs and what may have been a rack for storing weapons, now resting on the floor, and a possible serving counter in the corner with racks of empty shelves behind and a narrow archway leading into an adjoining room. Empty clay jars and flagons, some shattered and others intact, were distributed throughout the room.

Crowe nudged a rusty sword with a paw. "I think this might have been a guards' restroom. Somewhere for them to drink and relax when not on duty next door."

"Very civilized for goblins," said Griselda.

They exited through the doorway on the far side of the room into a corridor that doglegged a few times. The source of the sounds of rushing water that had become louder with every step was revealed when they entered a large cavern rising many stories. At the far end, a waterfall tumbled down a craggy drop into a pool, whose runoff formed a stream that disappeared beneath the floor they stood on. Again, dim light penetrated the darkness through a hole in the roof to bathe the surroundings in diffused light.

"I think this might be the goblins' lair, or one of them," offered Ellie.

They turned their gazes to the goblin architecture that towered both side walls. On the right side, a sloping columned porch reached out toward the stream with steps leading to what seemed to be the main entrance. Balconies adorned the stacked dwellings covering the façade. Dark openings hinted at the many rooms the goblins once occupied.

Though similar in design to its impressive counterpart opposite, the left side had steps rising into the distance at its base. A porch, simpler in design than the one on the right, was the main entrance for the dwellings on that side.

Crowe, amazed by what the goblins had built, thought the few entrances made the buildings easier to defend. He had always pictured goblins as nasty, malevolent creatures living in dark, damp caves emitting a foul stench. But here, the waterfall, the stream with plants and trees lining its banks—though admittedly mostly now dead, rotted and black—and vegetation covering some of the buildings must have provided a pleasant scene at one time. Even in its present neglected state, it was impressive.

"Goblins built *this*?" asked Crowe for confirmation.

"They did," answered Ellie. "Like many of the species who live in the Faerie Realm, and who are thought to be mythical creatures of legend and fairy stories in our world, the goblins have been given a bit of a bad rap by authors and scriptwriters. Yes, the evil, vicious type you're probably imagining do make up the minority, but some of them are quite intelligent and others talented in a wide range of skills."

Crowe again swept his gaze over the vast number of buildings stretching into the distance. "I'm finding it hard to believe how huge this place is. It's like an underground city, which I imagine goes deep into the rock, so we see only a fraction of its true size. Hundreds of goblins must have lived here?"

"More like thousands," replied Griselda. "Goblins breed like rats."

It was something Crowe hadn't considered before. "There are female goblins?"

Griselda rolled her eyes. "Of course there are females. Where do you think they all come from, stork deliveries?"

Crowe shrugged, causing his passengers to grab his fur to steady themselves. "Yeah, I suppose there must be females. Funny that I never thought of it before."

"Hilarious," quipped Ellie. "Let's get a move on." She pointed to the left path. "Those steps might lead above ground."

Crowe headed for the stairway. The two dogs, who had sat patiently waiting for the others to move, followed alongside.

Observing their prey from high up, the alpha Cave Dweller barked hushed instructions to its pack. Its six subordinates split into two groups of three. While three scuttled across the sides of the building and jumped from balcony to balcony to overtake the unsuspecting travelers below, the other three kept to the shadows and prepared for their headfirst climb down to attack from behind.

Satan halted and focused on the small piece of masonry clattering down the side of the building. When it dropped to the ground beside him, he gazed up and scanned the towering buildings. Though his eyes searched the gloom shrouding the highest reaches, they failed to pick out any movement.

Noticing Satan wasn't by Crowe's side, Ellie glanced back and spied him with his head pointed skywards. She glanced at Griselda. "Look at Satan."

Griselda followed Satan's gaze to the lofty heights of the goblin dwellings. "Maybe he heard a bat or something?"

"All the same, let's be on our guard." Ellie whistled Satan to her and notched an arrow in her bow.

As Satan padded alongside him, Crowe noticed he continually glanced upwards and wondered what was capturing his attention. Trusting those riding on his back would warn him of any danger, he continued plodding up the steps.

The three Cave Dwellers that had moved in front of their prey crawled down the side of the building and hiding in the darkness beside the steps, they waited for their alpha's command to attack.

The alpha of the small pack observed the actions of its minions below. Once they had killed the intruders, he would join them and take first pick of the food on offer.

The three Cave Dwellers positioned behind climbed down and dropped silently onto the steps. They glanced up at their leader and receiving a nod of his head to begin the attack, they sprang into motion. With their claws retracted, their padded paws barely made a sound on the steps they rushed up.

To distract their prey from looking behind, the alpha raised its snout and uttered a high-pitched cry. On hearing the signal, the three Cave Dwellers in front moved out from their places of concealment into full view of the group climbing the steps.

Though the humans hadn't heard the alpha's high-pitched battle cry, the dogs had. Both jerked their heads up the side of the building. When Satan noticed another three creatures coming up from behind, he barked a warning. Ellie looked back at the creatures bounding up toward them.

All tipped with claws you wouldn't want to get close to, their powerful rear limbs and long, twice-jointed arms sped them up the steps. Small spikes jutted from the side of their heads below their black, glossy eyes. Their layer of brown skin ended at the jaws that protruded out; pink and raw, it looked like a baboon's ass filled with teeth—a long tongue in place of a tail.

Crowe slowed when the formidable beasts appeared ahead. "We've got a problem."

Griselda slipped the scattergun from her bag.

"Don't stop!" commanded Ellie, "There's three more coming up behind us." She halted the dogs' movements toward the three creatures coming up from the rear with a sharp whistle. "Satan. Lucifer." When the dogs looked at her, she jerked a thumb at the Cave Dwellers in front. When they sprinted past Crowe and ran up the steps to attack them, she turned to Griselda. "Keep Crowe moving. I'll handle the three attacking from the rear."

Trusting Ellie knew what she was doing, Griselda nodded and watched her fly off. She grabbed Crowe's fur with both hands and urged him on. "Stop, and we die."

Crowe stared at the creatures ahead and saw a not too dissimilar fate from that direction also. "I hope you know what you're doing."

Griselda shrugged. "Guess we'll soon find out."

As Ellie flew toward the dangerous, vicious creatures, she fired off arrows as quickly as she could load them. The first two found their target, one in the shoulder of the beast on the left, the second stuck in the front leg of the one in the middle. Without breaking its stride, it promptly seized it in its teeth, ripped it out and snapped it between its jaws before snarling at her. Snapping orders at those beside it, the middle Cave Dweller carried on up the steps while the others split off to each side.

Ellie watched the creatures break formation. One ran up the side of the building as effortlessly as if it was flat ground, while the other dived over the side. Once its claws scraping gouges in the stone halted its slide, it continued its pursuit along the vertical side of the steps.

Ellie decided to first concentrate on the creature bounding toward her. She fired two arrows in quick succession, which it avoided by leaping onto the building and then back onto the path. Changing tactics, she flapped her small wings furiously and flew into the air. Changing direction when it saw her coming, the Cave Dweller on the side of the building swiped a claw at Ellie. Glimpsing movement above her and cursing her stupidity, Ellie dodged under the sharp-clawed limb and thrust the arrow she was loading into the bow into the creature's eye. She ran across its back as it screeched and jumped off, glancing back at the falling beast as she flew behind the one rushing up the steps. *One down, five to go.*

Griselda aimed the scattergun at the two creatures ahead but couldn't risk firing as she might hit the dogs almost upon them. She hooked the gun strap over Crowe's ear, fished in her bag and pulled out a pistol. Squinting her left eye, she aimed it at one of the creatures jumping in and out of the gun sight with Crowe's movements. "Can't you run less jerkily; I'm trying to aim here?"

"You ever tried controlling four legs and a tail, it isn't easy."

"Get me closer then, so the target's bigger."

"Though it's against my screaming common sense, it's exactly what I'm doing."

Crowe watched the two dogs attack the snarling creatures three times their size. Satan grabbed the claw that swiped at him, bit hard, and held on when the creature screeched and tried to shake him free. Satan ripped off a chunk of flesh as it dodged the jaws snapping at him, ran under its belly and bit a rear leg. The creature stumbled and slid down a few steps. Leaping onto its back, Satan clamped his jaws around the creature's neck. Ripping at the flesh furiously, blood sprayed from the wounds he inflicted upon it. In its haste to rid itself of its attacker, the creature rolled off the steps and fell. Satan jumped off before he was dragged over and rushed to help Lucifer.

Spying the twin of the animal attacking him coming to help, the Cave Dweller swiped a paw at Satan. It caught the dog around the side of the head and sent him flying. Dazed by the blow, Satan tumbled down the steps and landed motionless.

Hanging by his teeth from the creature's side, Lucifer tried to climb onto its back. In pain from the damage the animals had inflicted upon it, the Cave Dweller slammed its body against the building. Smacked against the stone, Lucifer released his grip and slumped to the floor. Free of the hindrance, the creature bounded for its main prey.

Worried about the dogs he couldn't see moving and annoyed by the scattergun hanging from his ear constantly slapping against his head, Crowe focused on the Cave Dweller about to attack. "Shoot it!" he yelled.

Griselda was attempting to do just that but couldn't keep the creature in the gunsight. Juggling with judging

Crowe's movements, she pulled the trigger when the creature's head appeared in the crosshairs.

The Cave Dweller flinched from the burning pain when something skimmed along its skull. Snarling at the thing responsible on the rat's back, it jumped onto the wall, bounded twice and pushed off with claws outstretched to receive Griselda's flesh.

"Use your knife!" Crowe yelled. Spurting forward, he dived beneath the airborne creature.

Heeding Crowe's instruction, Griselda shoved the pistol in her bag and snatched out her knife. Almost toppling off when her ride slammed to the steps, she gazed at the creature's claws directly above her. Unable to change its flight path that was now too high, the Cave Dweller slashed out a claw at Griselda. She ducked to the side to avoid its talons and thrust her knife into its flesh. The creature's momentum dragged its belly along the sharp blade. Its innards slurped out when it hit the steps. As it lay dying, it watched its guts slither wetly down the treads.

Crowe relieved gaze behind at the dying creature was dragged away when Griselda grabbed his ear that didn't have a weapon hanging from it and jerked his head to face forward. "There's another one to deal with."

Crowe focused on the creature preparing to attack. "Can't you just shoot it now we're not moving."

"I knew I brought you along for a reason." Gripping the knife in her teeth, Griselda pulled the pistol from her bag, aimed between the creature's eyes and squeezed the trigger.

The Cave Dweller's head jerked when something struck. It felt intense throbbing pain between its eyes but continued its attack.

Crowe noticed the bullet hole between the creature's eyes, so knew Griselda hadn't missed. By rights, it should be dead, but it wasn't playing ball. He lowered his head to the side and flicked it up, sending the scattergun flipping toward Griselda. "Try this."

Griselda snatched the weapon from the air with one hand and a fresh cartridge from her bag with the other, she rammed it home with her fist, flipped it over, aimed and fired. So close was the creature, the tightly grouped pellets shredded the skin from its face, leaving its pale, bloodied skull peppered with small holes. It dropped to the steps a paw's length from Crowe and lay still.

Thankful the threat was over; Crowe turned his thoughts to his friends as he bounded over to check how the dogs had fared in the attack. "How's Ellie doing?"

Griselda twisted in the saddle. She spied a dead creature on the steps with an arrow sticking from its eye and another frantically dodging the volley of arrows Ellie fired at it while flying erratically behind it. "I can only see one creature still alive, so she seems to be doing okay."

Crowe halted beside Lucifer and sniffed him.

"Is he dead?" asked Griselda.

"No, he's still breathing." Crowe examined Lucifer's body and limbs. "I can't see any wounds, but he might have internal injuries."

"Let's check Satan before we work out what can be done for him."

As if hearing his name, Satan raised his head and stood up. Though he seemed a little unsteady on his feet, he seemed unscathed. When he noticed Lucifer's unmoving form, he rushed over and nuzzled his head with his nose while whining sadly. Lucifer opened his eyes and licked his brother's face. After rubbing noses, Lucifer struggled to his feet.

Griselda smiled warmly at the dogs. "Thankfully, they both seem fine."

A scape of claws on stone too close for comfort, jerked Crowe's head to the Cave Dweller climbing over the side of the steps, its neck bloody and ripped. "Hold on tight!" was his shouted instruction to Griselda when he shot forward and rammed the creature before it was fully upright, knocking it onto its side with its back legs dangling over the void. Crowe jumped on it before it could recover, bit down on its neck and ripped out its throat. The creature's dying struggles sent it toppling over the edge.

Crowe spat out the chunk of flesh and peering over the side, watched the creature smash onto the ground below. It slid into the stream and leaving behind a bloody trail, was carried away by the current.

"I do believe you're getting the hang of your rat body," said Griselda, scratching behind his ear. "You okay?"

Enjoying the sensation, Crowe tilted his head slightly to gain the full effect of Griselda's attention. "My undercarriage is a bit bruised, but I'll live. Although I'm not sure for how much longer with so many dangerous creatures inhabiting this godforsaken world."

"Now you understand why we can't let the faeries cross over because if they do, it'll only be a matter of time before the other foul creatures populating this world find their way through."

"Yes, I get it. Now if you could just scratch down and to the right slightly..."

Cursing the creature's adeptness for dodging her arrows that were fast depleting, Ellie paused with one notched ready to fire. She needed to get closer to reduce its flight and thus shorten the creature's reaction time. Keeping her eyes and weapon aimed at the Cave Dweller, she flew closer.

Looking back to check how Ellie was faring, Griselda spotted the sudden appearance of another creature, a little larger than the others, climbing down toward Ellie. Griselda jumped to her feet, ran along Crowe's back, and flapping her wings furiously, sprang into the air.

Noticing movement from the side, the alpha turned its head and growled at Griselda. Dodging the claw reaching for her, Griselda rammed the barrel of the scattergun into the creature's mouth splintering its teeth and pulled the trigger. The creature's head exploded in a spray of bone fragments, brain tissue, and blood. With no anchor against the powerful blast, Griselda shot backward and slammed against the building. Crowe slipped beneath her as she fell. Though dazed, Griselda had enough wits about her to grab a handful of fur to prevent her from falling off when Crowe rushed forward.

Distracted by Griselda and Crowe's appearance, the final Cave Dweller turned away from Ellie to face the more significant threat. It snarled at Crowe as they each rushed at the other. Seizing her chance while the creature was distracted, Ellie slung the bow over her shoulder, grabbed two arrows, and flew onto the creature's head. Leaning forward, she gazed into the creature's surprised eyes and then with all the strength she could muster, stabbed an arrow in each.

Crowe skidded to a halt when the legs of the creature it ran toward buckled, spilling it to the ground, and backed up a step to avoid it crashing into him. As the corpse slid down the steps, Ellie gripped the shafts protruding from its eyes and rode it like a macabre sleigh. When it slipped over the edge, she yanked the arrows out and took flight, shaking off the speared eyeball skewered to one of them before returning them both to the quiver on her back. When Ellie noticed the dogs weren't with them, she cast a concerned glance up the steps at Lucifer lying beside Satan. "Are the dogs okay?"

"Like me, a bit bruised," informed Crowe, "but otherwise unhurt."

Griselda shifted into a sitting position on Crowe's back. "I'm also fine."

Ellie looked at Griselda, noticing her disheveled hair and slightly dazed appearance. "Good to hear."

Crowe gazed around. "Are they all dead?"

"I believe so," said Ellie, gathering up any reusable arrows. "I'll just collect these, and then we'll head out of here before more arrive." She flew off to retrieve more arrows littering the stairs and protruding from Cave Dweller corpses.

Though he'd like nothing more than to lie on the steps and rest, the thought that more of the creatures might be on their way persuaded him that would be inadvisable. He waited for Ellie to return and then climbed up to the dogs. After Ellie had made a fuss of them and checked they were okay, they continued their journey up the steps.

Chapter 22

Swamp of the Dead

CROWE HAULED HIS EXHAUSTED body over the last step and along with those having a less arduous journey on his back, stared at the arched exit at the end of a stone path. Its half-open door revealed a sliver of unwelcoming gloom on its far side.

Ellie stroked Crowe's head. "I know you want to rest, but not here."

Wearily, Crowe headed for the door. He forced it open with a screech of protesting hinges echoing throughout the goblin world they were about to leave behind. The tortured shriek ceased when one of the rusty fasteners broke, halting its swing and leaving its bottom edge resting skew-whiff on the ground. They all turned their heads to gaze down the steep steps when the door's call was answered by a multitude of squeals, screams and unearthly growls. When creatures of varying sizes, species and viciousness poured from the dark openings and crawled down or moved along the buildings and up the steps, Crowe forced his body through the sagging door and ran.

Griselda grabbed her staff and lit the lantern dangling from its tip. Its light revealed a landscape as dark and foreboding as any they had so far traveled through since entering the Faerie Realm. The path Crowe dashed along was bordered on both sides by a foul-smelling swamp that reeked of decay and dampened the air.

"You must feel at home, Griselda," said Crowe, his breathing labored.

"Just concentrate on your footing and leave the witticisms to me."

Trees, more snaking roots than trunks, protruded from the swamp and stretched dark, dead branches over the path. Given life by the wind howling across the murky landscape, shuddering their twisted limbs, it was easy to imagine them wading through the water on root-formed legs to snatch them up and pull them into their mass to be devoured as human fertilizer.

"What do we do?" asked Ellie, twisting her head to Griselda and then at the opening they fled from. "Those things will be through that door at any moment, and there are too many to fight."

"Oh, fighting them won't be the problem," countered Griselda, "it's not getting killed in the process that is."

"From someone...who is supposed to...be a wise woman, that wasn't very wise...or helpful," said Crowe between panting breaths.

"I'd save your breath for running faster and not wasting them on ridiculing me," cautioned Griselda.

"He wasn't wrong though," commented Ellie.

Griselda sighed. "It's been a long day."

"One we've all shared in," added Crowe.

Griselda tapped her bag. "I've got some spurs in here somewhere I've a mind to slip on."

Crowe remained silent and concentrated on keeping his footing on the slippery, winding path.

Griselda uttered an intelligible incantation to bring forth her Hawk Sight and peered into the farthest reaches of the dark and dismal swamp. When she spotted something that might save them, she leaned around Ellie to speak into Crowe's ear. "We'll reach a tree bent over the path shortly. Nip beneath and then head north-east."

Crowe glanced at the foul swamp. "Okay two things: One, I've no idea which way is north-east and two, you want me to enter *that*?!"

"Don't worry, I'll direct you. There's a hidden path beneath the surface. The bog will only be a few inches deep."

"It will still stink. I'll get covered in it."

Screams, shrills, and screeches frightening enough to curdle the blood erupted behind them."

"They're here," stated Ellie needlessly.

"A little smelly and dirty or very much dead—your choice Crowe."

Muttering obscenities from his predicament, Crowe shot under the tree stretching over the path and following the direction of Griselda's pointed staff, jumped into the swamp. Dirty, foul muck splashed his face when he struck the water. Skidding in the mud below the surface, Crowe scrabbled all four of his limbs for a purchase to prevent him from sliding into deeper foulness. Finding a grip, he surged forward. Every splash of paw sprayed him with more filth and rose a fresh wave of rotten stench his heaving breath couldn't avoid sucking into his lungs.

Spying their prey's diversion, some of the creatures chose a more direct route than the path and traveled through the trees, jumping from one dead growth to another. When one grabbed at a branch too flimsy to hold its weight, it snapped with a loud crack and sent it plummeting into the swamp with a splash. It rose to the surface, spluttered out the filthy water and swam for the bank. A creature that looked like a cross between a catfish, an alligator, and a walrus, erupted from the water and clamped its widely spread jaws down on the unfortunate interloper. As blood fountained from the trapped creature's wounds, its screams of agony and terror were abruptly silenced when it was dragged under. After a few bubbles rose to the surface, the only evidence to tell of what had happened were the bloody ripples spreading across the pond.

Excited screeches of alarm emanated from those that had witnessed the death of their comrade. These increased in ferocity when other swamp reptiles shot from the water and started grabbing them in their jaws as they leaped from perch to perch.

Deciding it was too dangerous to continue the hunt, those in the trees quickly reversed direction. Plucked from the air by the amphibious monsters' jaws, most never made it back to the safety of the path.

"I never thought I'd be so relieved to see the sudden appearance of vicious amphibians," commented Ellie, turning her head toward each land creature's agonizing demise.

"We're not out of danger yet," warned Griselda.

The survivors of the feeding frenzy glanced back, shooting nervous glances at the reptiles slaughtering their comrades. They decided to follow their prey's trail and stepped apprehensively onto the submerged swamp path.

"Won't those things in the swamp attack us?" asked Crowe, his rat brow creased with concern as he glanced fearfully into the swamp's murky depths.

"I'm sure they will if they notice us," replied Ellie, who flew over Griselda and landed on Crowe's rump. Notching an arrow still bloodied from its last victim, she aimed it back along the trail and fired at the lead creature. The bolt struck its chest and flopped the dying beast to the side. It splashed into the water and slipped below until two smaller water creatures grabbed the easy meal and began a tug of war with the carcass. Ellie's second and third arrows saw two more dead and slowed the now less-enthusiastic creatures behind to a cautious walk.

Observing the swimming creatures circling for prey, Crowe voiced his concern, "Maybe we should find an alternative, less perilous route."

"Cease your whining," scolded Griselda. "Even if there were another route, which there isn't, it'd be just as perilous as the one we're currently traversing. I've still got my Hawk

Sight active, so I can see them coming, in fact, there's one on its way as I speak. Get ready to follow my orders."

Crowe was about to ask for clarification on what these orders might entail so he could prepare himself, when something shot from the water on his left, spraying him with foul swamp muck.

"Drop to the ground!" yelled Griselda.

Crowe dropped onto his belly and groaned when foulness washed over his face.

Griselda slipped to the side and hung on. Dodging the massive teeth-lined jaws of the reptilian horror snapping at her, it sailed harmlessly over them.

"On your feet and run. There're more coming."

Crowe was on his feet and running before Griselda's shout echoing through the swamp had dissipated.

Noticing its brethren's failed attempt to grab a snack, another of the reptilian swamp creatures decided on a different tactic. It swam ahead of the fleeing feast and turning parallel to the path, swam deeper. Flipping around when it neared the bottom, it powered for the surface.

"Another one's coming from ahead," warned Griselda.

"What shall I do?" shrilled Crowe.

"I'm not sure," replied Griselda.

The creature exploded from the surface in a spray of pungent filth. Its hard landing on the muddy path sent shockwaves rippling through its blubbery mass and sent it sliding toward its prey.

Crowe gulped in terror at the snapping jaws heading straight for him. Hoping his claws would find purchase in the slippery mud, he sprung over the creature's head and bounded along its back. Avoiding the tail that slapped at him, he jumped back to the path and continued his sprint away from the horrors infesting the foul swamp.

Copying the rat's evasive maneuver, the dogs bounded over the creature's head.

Almost toppled from the saddle upon landing, Griselda checked that Ellie and the dogs were still with them before focusing ahead. "There's a fork coming up. Take the left one that will lead us to higher ground."

Keen to be free of this latest living nightmare, Crowe rushed along the left-hand trail and was thankful when the rising ground carried him free of the swamp. Pausing at the top of the small incline, they gazed back to see the land creatures fear of the reptiles had outweighed their desire to gratify their hunger. All had been driven back. Though some remained on the main path screeching and hissing at them and the circling amphibians, most had given up the chase and returned to the abandoned goblins lair.

When Crowe laid down on the grass to catch his breath and rest his aching legs, Griselda slid off the saddle and gazed in the direction they needed to travel. The swamp continued around the mound they were on, and after being funneled through a gorge lined with ruins, it formed an unpleasant, stagnant stream without current or movement. Evident by their ruinous conditions, the dwellings had been abandoned eons ago. The structure on the left leaned precariously over the swamp. The only thing preventing it from toppling further was a pillar of masonry tilted in the opposite direction, propping it up. On the right-hand side of the stream, another stone pillar leaned at a crazy angle, and behind this, a colossal head carved from a block of stone overlooked the surroundings. Ugly, monstrous and deformed, either by the inept hand of those who had chipped away the rock to form the features or an accurate representation of the species that once lived here, their ruler perhaps, or a god they worshipped, either way, it was an unnerving sight. The ground around both sets of buildings was littered with blocks of fallen masonry. Plants, moss, lichen, bushes, creepers, and trees were endeavoring to reclaim the land the buildings' creators had stolen from them.

Crowe ran his worried gaze over the darkness filling the interiors behind the many openings covering the walls of the buildings. "Do you think there might be more of those creatures from the goblins' lair living inside?"

"I doubt it," answered Ellie. "They are creatures of darkness, it's far too light here." Crowe let out a loud sigh of relief and glanced at the dogs lying on the grass beside him. Though both looked at the buildings, their relaxed demeanor was an indication they didn't sense any menace coming from the structures. It was a good sign. His relief was swiftly dashed when Ellie continued, "If anything lives here, it will be a completely different type of monstrosity that has taken up residence."

Griselda pointed her staff at a tall building behind the giant head. "If that's empty, it would make a good place to rest for a few hours."

Ellie scanned the building Griselda focused on. "I agree. It looks easy to defend if anything comes calling."

Crowe turned his worried features to the girls. "And if it's not empty, what then? I don't think my legs or lungs could stand another long sprint."

"We will be fine," assured Griselda, "and you need to rest for what's coming."

Crowe was about to ask for details but thought better of it; he really didn't want to know.

"I'll walk to save your strength," said Griselda, setting off down the far side of the rise.

"I would fly, but my wings are still tired from before, and I hardly weigh anything," said Ellie, settling herself around his neck.

Crowe climbed to his feet and followed Griselda and the dogs to the ruins.

The stream that stunk of rot that cloyed their nostrils was only a few inches deep in places and easily crossed. Stone steps, cracked, uneven, littered with weeds, and encroached by branches of the bushes growing either side, provided them with a moderately easy path up the slope to the entrance of the building Griselda had deemed suitable for their temporary stay.

Griselda led them through the opening and stepped into a room devoid of furniture. To leave her hands free to work the scattergun she pulled from her wonderous bag, she propped her staff in the saddle with the lantern hanging just past Crowe's head to light their way. She passed Ellie the pistol and crossed to the far exit.

They entered a corridor lined with doorways. A buzzing produced by things unseen pricked up the dogs' ears. Worried they might be injured by a sudden attack in the confined space, Ellie bade Satan and Lucifer to guard their rear. Cautiously, and with senses on high alert, they made their way along the corridor.

Apart from a few items of wood and stone furniture, including some extremely uncomfortable looking and strange shaped stone chairs, and foliage encroaching through openings, the first three rooms were empty, the fourth was where the majority of the buzzing sounds came from.

Griselda and Ellie cautiously peered around the edge of the doorway and stared at the source of the buzzing. A pulsating growth situated in a corner filled a third of the room. Crawling over it was a species of winged insects they hadn't seen before, which in this strange world shouldn't have been as much as a surprise as it was. The long, thin bodies of the mouse-sized creatures ended with a tail curled like a scorpion's and tipped with a wicked slender sting half the length of its torso. Two feelers protruding out between its large orange eyes wavered in the air clicking the crab-like claw each was tipped with. The elongated snout was all mouth formed of four toothless jaw sections and a long black tongue. Their eyes flicked to the insects flying out the single window and others returning with scraps of meaty spoils from successful hunts. The severed limbs and other body parts of their small victims were carried into the nest to feed those within.

"What is it?" whispered Crowe, wondering what had caused them to linger at the doorway.

Griselda leaned nearer to Crowe and whispered her reply. "Insects you don't want to mess with. If we keep out of their way, hopefully, they will ignore us."

Crowe glanced into the room as he passed. When Griselda had mentioned insects, he had been relieved, nothing that couldn't be swatted away if need be. Now seeing their red and yellow striped bodies and the long stings they sported, which he thought would be a hundred times more painful than a wasp's, and its venom probably deadly, he changed his mind. There must be thousands living in the massive nest. He hurried past and almost bumped into Griselda who had stopped to gaze up a flight of stone steps.

"We go up," she whispered.

Though Crowe dreaded hauling his tired body up the stairs, he nodded.

Ignoring the corridors that stretched off from each landing where the stairs changed direction, they headed through the hallway on the top floor and entered the room at its end. Window openings in two walls looked over the landscape below. One looked over the swamp they had recently passed and the other on the route they had yet to travel, but a tall tree growing out from the hillside the building was built against, blocked the view.

Griselda pulled her staff from the saddle and propped it against the wall by the doorway. "Crowe, get some rest. Sleep if you can as I doubt our journey tomorrow will be any less strenuous than it was today."

Crowe was glad of the opportunity. He laid down along one wall and was so exhausted he fell asleep almost immediately.

Griselda crossed to Ellie, who had perched in the window. "I'll take first watch while you and the dogs rest. I'll swap with you in three hours, but we'll let Crowe rest; he has a big day tomorrow."

Ellie nodded knowingly. "We set off at dawn then?"

"Yes, we need to get through the Underwurld before the morrow's night falls or we might not be able to complete our mission before the faeries begin their invasion."

Knowing what dwelt there, Ellie wasn't sure they would make it through at all, but also aware they had to risk it, she kept her doubts to herself and snuggled between the two dogs sleeping beside Crowe.

Griselda crossed to the doorway, turned the lantern down to a soft glow and with the scattergun aimed along the corridor, she kept watch.

Chapter 23

The King's Reward

WAITING EXPECTANTLY FOR THE arrival of deadeye and his mysterious gift he had been informed his Magnificent Seven had brought back from the human world, King Mortgrimmest turned to his advisor.

"I wonder what they've got me," he said excitedly. "I do like surprises."

"You do, my liege," nodded Hemlock. "I told you my Phantoms wouldn't let you down."

The faerie king glared at Hemlock. "*Whose* Phantoms?"

Hiding his sigh and his displeasure—he had spent years homing his Phantoms skills, whereas the king hadn't even known of their existence until a short while ago—Hemlock answered, "*Your* Phantoms, my king."

King Mortgrimmest grinned at his advisor's acquiescence, which he knew didn't come easily where his beloved assassins were involved. They were something he'd have to take care of before Hemlock applied their skills on him. "And don't forget Deadeye, to whom I charged with leading them. I'm certain he played no small part in their success."

"It's not something I'm likely to forget, sire."

Scowling at his advisor as he pondered the remark for signs of insubordination, Mortgrimmest's thoughts were interrupted when the doors to his throne room abruptly opened, almost knocking the guards off their feet so vigorously were they thrown back. The rumble of cartwheels on the stone floor heralded the entrance of Deadeye leading the rat hitched to the wagon by the reins.

The king nudged his advisor with an elbow more forcefully than was strictly necessary; he hadn't forgotten Hemlock's previous remark yet. "Deadeye certainly knows how to make an entrance, eh?"

"He does indeed," replied Hemlock, rubbing his arm as his peering eyes narrowed in their search for his Phantoms, who were so stealthy they were probably already in the room. It would soon be time to fulfill the main reason for their existence. He turned his gaze slyly upon the king who had risen to his huge hairy feet in an attempt to peer into the back of the cart.

"Damn, it's covered up," uttered Mortgrimmest, plonking his ample backside back down onto his throne and watching Deadeye draw closer.

Trying unsuccessfully to hide his pleased expression, Deadeye halted the rat at the bottom of the steps leading up to the throne his king was perched excitedly upon and performed an exaggerated sweeping bow that rolled Hemlock's eyes.

"My king, I am happy to report that the mission was a total success where I was concerned."

Sensing trouble, Hemlock narrowed his eyes further.

"Yes, yes, but what have you brought me," said the impatient king, eager to see his gift.

Deadeye moved to the side of the cart and swept a hand over the covered object. "Perhaps, my king, you would like to unwrap your gift personally?"

Hemlock leaned closer to Mortgrimmest. "I'm not sure that would be advisable, sire. It might be a trap."

Mortgrimmest glared at his advisor as he stood. "Not all of my subjects are as conniving and backstabbing as you, Hemlock." Rubbing his hands in anticipation, Mortgrimmest approached the back of the cart and took the corner of the cover Deadeye handed him.

"Give it a good tug, and your present will be revealed, sire," instructed Deadeye.

The king yanked off the cover and, letting it slither to the ground, gasped on seeing the human female.

"I present to you, my king, one of the last surviving members of the Sinister family."

The king dragged his gaze from the human and looked at Deadeye. "You're certain she's a Sinister?"

Though he had absolutely no idea–something he wasn't about to admit—Deadeye nodded vigorously. "She was in the Sinister house when I was there before, and she bears an uncanny resemblance to the family portraits in the house." He smiled inwardly at his quick thinking and the credible lie he had pulled from nowhere.

Mortgrimmest turned his gaze back upon the woman. "Splendid. Is she alive?"

"Most certainly. Unconscious is all. I thought you would like the pleasure of ending her life personally."

The king nodded at the cruel images his brain conjured. "Indeed, I would. In a manner most unpleasant, bloody, and painful. However, I require her to be alert to experience every evil thing I have in mind for her." He pointed at one of his throne guards. "Have her taken to the dungeons and looked after. Also, have the physician visit her and attend to any wounds. I want her in perfect health for her agonizing death."

The guard nodded. "It will be done, my king." His overly loud voice echoed around the throne room as he grabbed the rat's reins and led the cart to the exit.

Mortgrimmest, in an unprecedented act of familiarity for someone outside his harem, put an arm around Deadeye. "You have done exceedingly well, Deadeye. Even passing my lofty and often unachievable expectations."

"Thank you, sire," replied Deadeye graciously, wondering what his reward would be but expecting it to be substantial.

"It is an achievement that will not go unrewarded, I assure you," continued the king.

It was music to Deadeye's ears. Believing a little groveling could only improve the amount he was about to receive, he said, "Your praise is reward enough, my king."

The king released his arm and looked at Deadeye with a wide smirk. "Then that is what you will have. "Well done, Deadeye."

Deadeye's mouth dropped open in shock as he watched the king return to his throne.

Hemlock smiled smugly. The king would not find his Phantoms so cheaply rewarded.

"Er...when I said your praise is enough, it really was a figure of speech. A show of reverence, my king."

"Oh, I'm always open for a bit of bootlicking—something you should probably work on as it really wasn't that impressive—but going back on my decisions, not so much. The matter is closed."

Deadeye sighed.

"Please, sire, don't forget the part my...*your*" Hemlock corrected quickly "expertly trained Phantoms—which took many years—played in capturing the Sinister woman."

The king looked about nervously. "Are they here?"

"Most definitely. Like shadows in the night, they move invisibly through..."

"Enough with the annoying hyperbole, Hemlock. Call them forth."

Pouting, Hemlock glanced around the room. "Phantoms, reveal yourselves."

All eyes except for Deadeye's scanned the room for the assassins they expected to mysteriously appear. The king even looked behind his throne.

"Er...their appearance, except perhaps as phantoms of the ghostly kind, is going to be rather difficult, impossible even," advised Deadeye.

"Explain yourself," ordered Hemlock.

"All are dead," answered Deadeye.

"What?! All dead?" uttered Hemlock disbelievingly.

Deadeye nodded. "Every murderous one."

Hemlock huffed. "You surely jest."

Deadeye shook his head. "Nope. Every single one of your assassins is deceased." He sliced a finger along his throat for emphasis.

Shocked by the news, Hemlock staggered and almost collapsed to his knees.

Mortgrimmest's grin, wider and merrier than his usual sneer, was instigated by two good bits of news; first, Hemlock's murderous Phantoms were dead, so no longer a threat, and second, he didn't like dishing out rewards to living faeries, so he wasn't about to reward corpses. He turned his gaze upon the bearer of this good news. Perhaps Deadeye did deserve something after all. But first to prolong his advisor's obvious distress. "How did they die?"

"Very badly," my king.

Hemlock groaned.

Wonderful The king refrained from rubbing his hands together in glee. "Did they suffer greatly before their lives were extinguished?"

Sensing Mortgrimmest's enjoyment of the Phantoms demise, Deadeye played along. "Oh, yes, sire. Their deaths were long, slow, and brutal. Their girlish, agonized screams are still ringing in my head."

Now scowling from the ridicule of his beloved Phantoms, and suspicious of Deadeye's part in their demise, Hemlock probed further. "And what was the cause of their deaths?"

"Inadequate training, I imagine."

The king guffawed loudly. That remark alone merited Deadeye a reward.

Hemlock wasn't as amused. "And yet you survived. How is that?"

Deadeye shrugged. "Probably because you didn't train me."

The king tipped from his throne and collapsed to his knees in laughter, tears streaming down his face.

Hemlock narrowed his murderous eyes at the giggling fool. Barely suppressing the urge to plunge the knife he kept concealed beneath his cloak into the king's back, he focused his wrath on the one-eyed jester. "You declare your mission a success, when it wasn't, as there are still members of the Sinister family alive and well."

"There is one surviving Sinister I know of, a man, who, like the woman I alone captured, also wasn't at the house when we visited. Doubting the untested abilities of your years-trained Phantoms, Hemlock, I decided to keep them together and tasked them with seeking out the male Sinister while I went after the female. As has been recently proven, my endeavors were entirely successful, your Phantoms, not so much." Deadeye turned away from the fuming advisor and focused on the king's mirth-warped face, who was busy mopping away laughter tears from his cheeks with a corner of Hemlock's cloak. "However, if it pleases my king, I will again enter the human world to seek out and kill or capture the remaining Sinister, but this time, with a group of my choosing who I can trust to do what I ask of them and who have not suffered the inadequate training of your advisor."

Suppressing his giggles, the king nodded. "Do as you see fit, Deadeye, with my undenied approval. If you can bring him back here, then do so, but if that proves impossible, kill him and bring me back his head."

Deadeye bowed. "Your wish is my command, sire."

The king glared at his advisor. "If only all my subjects were as loyal..."

Believing his audience had been concluded, Deadeye shuffled backward.

The king's voice halted him. "Before you go Deadeye, here's a reward for your loyalty and entertainment. Kill the remaining Sinister, and there will be more." He reached for something under his cloak and threw it to Deadeye.

Catching it, Deadeye jangled the bag of gold coins. It wasn't as much as he had hoped for, but it was more than the nothing he thought he was going to receive a few moments ago. Picking his words carefully, he answered, "Thank you, my king. Just the right amount to fit in my trouser pocket, but not weighty enough to pull them down around my ankles."

The king burst out laughing. "Normally I'd have you split open from neck to navel for a remark like that, but I like you, Deadeye. You make me laugh. So, I'll let it slip, this once."

"Much appreciated, my king," said Deadeye, "as red isn't really my color. He shuffled back the required steps before turning and heading for the exit.

The king looked at his fuming, sour-faced advisor. "That was fun."

"For some of us."

"Oh, cheer up, Hemlock. You can soon train some more killers."

"No, sire, I can't. It took me seven years to train the last ones."

"Didn't last long though, did they. Maybe you need to train the next lot for a few years longer, or," he nodded at Deadeye stepping through the doorway at the end of the room. "Ask him to train them. He out-survived your assassins, so he must be doing something right."

Hemlock narrowed his eyes on Deadeye's back as the door swung closed. *The only thing I'll be asking from him is the bloodied heart I cut from his chest.* "Yes, sire. It's something I will contemplate."

"Well, go contemplate it somewhere else as I can't sit here all day having fun," declared the king, standing. "I have important king duties to perform."

Hemlock glanced toward the door of the harem longingly and looked forward to the day it would be his. When the door thudded closed behind Mortgrimmest Hemlock fumed at how things had gone wrong so quickly. That accursed Deadeye—of whom he was sure had something do to with the deaths of his precious Phantoms—might be the death of him if he didn't act quickly. Maybe it's time to reinstate the trainees that failed to achieve the rank of Phantom. Surely his slightly-less-murderous Sprites would be able to kill one ludicrous faerie. For devil's sake, he didn't even have two eyes. Attack from his blind side and he wouldn't see them coming.

Glancing scornfully back at the king's chamber, Hemlock turned away. Once the Deadeye problem had been resolved, he would turn his attention back to ousting Mortgrimmest and taking his place, then the kingdom would be his. Confident he would be victorious and shortly be sitting upon the throne, he headed for his chambers to send coded messages to his Sprites. Soon, all his troubles would be over.

Chapter 24

Creatures of the Night

SLAZAR, ONE OF THE night creatures known as Demoniacs and feared by all who encountered them, stirred from his slumber when moonlight seeped into the room. Hanging upside down from the ceiling, he gazed around at his twilight-bathed roosting brethren beginning to stir. To avoid the crushing mass exodus that would shortly occur, Slazar dropped, spread his membranous wings and swooped smoothly through the window. A flap back and forth in a figure 8 motion with his wingtips, hovered him effortlessly while he waited for the others to emerge from their slumber.

Noticing something out of place, Slazar pondered the orange glow coming from an opening high up in the building opposite. A flick of his wings glided it closer. While swooping past he peered through the front opening. In the dimly lit interior, he spied something unexpected, prey. Landing gently in the tree at the end of the building, he crawled along a thick branch and halting at its end, peered into the room through the side window. Slazar's hungry eyes took in the sleeping forms he was keen to feast on.

The chubby rat across the room seemed especially meaty and succulent. Confident he could murder them all in their sleep before they were aware of his presence, Slazer poked his evil head and shoulders through the window. He was just about to leap on the nearest unsuspecting victim and dispatch each swiftly with a slash of claws when screeches and shrill cries from his waking brethren pouring from their roost halted him. A soft foot scape on the floor turned his gaze to another, larger faerie by the doorway and upon the weapon it grasped. He backed out swiftly before he was spotted. Concealed by the tree's leafy bough, he observed the faerie cross to the window and peer out.

Though with one of them awake and armed, it would make the unexpected feast more challenging to acquire, Slazar still thought the delicious rewards worth the effort. To ensure success though, he would need help. With plenty of food on offer, he could afford to be generous and share the welcomed bounty. Moving to the far side of the tree, he dived off and flying in a wide circle headed for the dark mass swooping through the sky.

When Slazar's keen eyes picked out those it sought amongst the wing to wing pack, he dived into the throng. While communicating his discovery to a few handpicked cohorts who usually hunted with him, he joined his brethren swooping around in a majestic dance. When the group headed off to their usual hunting grounds, thirteen of them joined with Slazar peeling off from the pack.

Griselda peered out at the impressive display the mass of giant vicious bats enacted. Their erratic movements were mimicked by all as if they had linked together to form a single entity. Though she found the show captivating, she was relieved when they headed north. She crossed to Ellie and nudged her awake. "Your turn to take watch."

Ellie nodded as she yawned and stretched away the aftereffects of sleep. Feeling her stir, Satan opened his eyes and raised his head. Ellie scratched behind his ears. "It's okay, boy, go back to sleep."

Obeying her command, Satan rested his head back on one of Crowe's front legs and closed his eyes. As Griselda sat in the corner to rest, Ellie climbed to her feet and crossed to the doorway. After checking the pistol was operational and fully loaded, she stood guard.

The fourteen Demoniacs that had peeled off from the mass dived for the building their prey had sought refuge within. Hugging the walls, they sped alongside the towering construction. While eight led by Slazar headed away from the building, the remaining six led by Jeckel continued on.

When Jeckel's group neared the end of the building, they spread their wings to slow their flight and silently perched on the wall a short distance below the room where their attack would shortly take place. Ordering his excited comrades eager to taste faerie flesh to silence, Jeckel glanced up at the opening they would enter when Slazar gave the signal.

After leading his band of ravenous brethren around in a short, steep curve, Slazar shot through an opening at the far end of the building a level below the one their prey occupied. Landing on the floor with a skidding scrape of claws, he waited for the others to enter. After dispensing orders to his comrades, he reiterated the need for silence, and if any of them alerted the faeries to their presence, death upon those responsible would shortly follow.

Gazing around at the hungry group, Slazar focused on Formiddia—a female he often took as a mate and who would share in his rat feast—and indicated for her to fall in beside him before entering the corridor. With the others following, he silently climbed the steps to the upper level. Poking his head through the doorway at the top, he gazed along the corridor. Except for a dim orange glow at the far end highlighting the small, armed faerie keeping watch, the passage was cloaked in reassuring darkness. Glaring behind menacingly at the others to warn them to stealth, he slunk into the corridor and climbed the wall. When the others were in position, they crept along the ceiling, walls, and floor on their wing elbow and feet claws.

Aware the signal to attack would soon come, Jeckel raised his snout to the window where the faeries and rat resided and breathed in their delicious meaty aroma. Their flesh would provide a banquet none of them had experienced for a long time. The days of feeding on the never-ending supply of succulent goblins had long since passed, and something they all wished would return. If he had to eat another piece of fruit, vegetable or a foul-tasting tree slug again, he might be tempted to rip out his own throat in protest, or preferably something less drastic like feasting on one of his weaker brethren; the younglings were always an easy target if their protective parents weren't nearby.

Slouched against the wall and wishing the dawn would hurry up and arrive so they could get moving, Ellie twitched her nose from the wafting stench that now assaulted her nostrils. Curious as to the cause, she pushed away from the wall and, thinking one of the others might have bottom-burped, she stuck her head further into the room and sniffed the air. Whatever the source of the smell, it wasn't coming from in here, but the corridor. She took a step along the passage and sniffed. It definitely emanated from this direction. The air was also musty, a little like wet fur tainted with urine. Hearing something padding softly on the floor, she stepped back to see Satan and Lucifer approaching. Their sensitive noses had also detected the odor. When they growled along the corridor, Ellie feared the worst and whispered, "Lucifer, wake the others."

Gently biting Crowe's paw to wake him, Crowe opened his eyes and saw Lucifer and then Ellie in the doorway looking at him with a finger on her lips, warning him to remain quiet. He glanced at Griselda, who awoke to Lucifer's wet tongue licking her face.

Immediately recognizing it was still dark and so another reason other than the arrival of dawn had prompted her to be awoken, Griselda grabbed the scattergun from the floor as she climbed to her feet. Noticing the worried expression Ellie gave her, she crossed to the corridor and glanced along its dark length.

"Do you smell it?" asked Ellie softly.

Griselda nodded and swiftly brought her Hawk Sight into play. She gasped at the terrifying Demoniacs creeping along the walls, floor, and ceiling. Dragging Ellie with her, she backed into the room.

The scared look on Griselda's face frightened Ellie. "What is it?"

"Demoniacs!"

When the faerie at the end of the corridor started acting oddly, and the two black beasts appeared and growled in their direction, Slazar knew their plan to catch them by surprise had failed. The appearance of the larger faerie and the fearful look on her face confirmed they had been detected. As they all retreated into the room, Slazar shrilled his signal for those waiting outside to attack and led his small group surging forward.

Griselda rushed to the window. They needed to leave, and the corridor wasn't an option. She looked below for a way to climb down. Her fear increased at seeing more Demoniacs crawling up toward them. She dodged back inside when they snarled at her and glanced at the others looking at her for instruction. "There are more of them out there. We're trapped."

Though Crowe had no idea what Demoniacs were, the terror Ellie and Griselda expressed was evidence enough they were something to be feared. "What do we do?"

Trying to ignore the scraping of fast-moving claws on stone from the corridor and outside, Griselda focused on the tree by the side window; it was their only hope. "Crowe.

Climb down the tree. Ellie. Order your dogs to follow him, then fly out and pick off as many as you can from the walls with your pistol and bow."

No one argued with her.

While Ellie spoke to her dogs, Crowe crossed to the window. Trusting his rat legs wouldn't let him down, he climbed through the window and jumped onto the tree. He scrambled along the creaking branch that swayed when the dogs landed behind him. Trying not to look down at the ground far below, Crowe began his climb. When his glance behind revealed the dogs, who weren't built for climbing, were having trouble negotiating the branches, he called out, "Satan. Lucifer. Get on my back."

The dogs didn't hesitate. They leaped onto his back and grasping a mouthful of fur in their jaws, held on as Crowe climbed from branch to branch during his swift descent.

When Ellie flew out the window to confront the menace, Jeckel swiped a wing at her. Engulfed in the leathery cloak, she was pulled toward the fiend's teeth-filled mouth spread wide to receive her. She snatched the knife from her belt, dragged its sharp blade down the wing, squeezed through the slit and flew away. As soon as she was out of its reach, she spun and aimed her pistol at Jeckel, who was examining his ruined wing while trying to keep himself airborne. The bullet entered the back of his head and sent his corpse spiraling to the ground. A further two shots sent two more Demoniacs plummeting earthwards.

As she brought the fourth into her gun sight, the remaining two, keen to avoid the same deadly fate, leaped from the wall and dropped headfirst with wings tucked tight to their bodies. Ellie's gaze followed their rapid fall. They spread their wings, glided away from the building and headed back toward her. The loud retort of the scattergun from inside the room she had recently vacated indicated Griselda was occupied with fighting her own battle.

Hoping the spray of pellets would hit multiple victims, Griselda aimed at the center of the frightening mass of Demoniacs in the corridor and fired. Squeals from various sources indicated a few had been hit. One that had suffered the worst, its head an ugly mess of blood and ragged flesh, fell from the ceiling onto a comrade, tangling it in its dying agony fueled lashing of wings and claws.

Griselda reloaded as she rushed to the window in the side wall. A glance down the tree revealed the dogs hanging preciously onto Crowe's back while he climbed down the branches. They were making good progress. Aiming the weapon at the doorway, she waited for more of the monsters to show themselves. If she didn't slow them down, they would never make it. A gunshot outside turned her head to the window. The Demoniac that had been Ellie's target dropped from the sky.

Suffering only a few minor flesh wounds, Slazar pondered his next move as he glanced at Spinx crawling out from beneath his dead comrade. Wondering if the armed faerie responsible had fled or was waiting for them in ambush, he ordered two of his companions into the room to find out.

Seemingly ignorant of the danger, or the promise of faerie flesh had overwhelmed their common sense, the two Demoniacs scrambled forward. Vying to be the first through the doorway to grab the choicest meal, they both tried to squeeze through the opening too small to accommodate them both at the same time. A loud blast ended their struggles and sprayed their blood and shredded flesh over the corridor wall.

Realizing to attack from this direction through the constricting entrance would see more of them killed, and perhaps the escape of their prey, Slazar ordered Spinx to remain on guard here in case they retreated and instructed the other two to follow him and Formiddia outside.

Griselda reloaded as the two dead Demoniacs slumped to the floor in a gruesome, bloody embrace. Cocking an ear to the doorway, she detected the sounds of the others moving away. Convinced they wouldn't give up so easily, Griselda ran to the window in the front wall and dived through. Flapping her wings furiously to halt her fall and hold her steady, she was aware they would only keep her airborne for a few minutes at most before her muscles became too tired. She flew toward Ellie and the two demon bats attacking her from front and behind. Slinging the rifle strap over a shoulder, she grabbed her knife.

Surprised when something landed on its back, the Demoniac flapped its wings rapidly to support the extra weight and jerked its head behind to stare into the face of the larger faerie. Gripping the bat with her knees, Griselda plunged the knife deep into its back and twisted. A second stab pieced its heart and silenced its terrible shrieks. She leaped off the falling creature and looked for Ellie.

With no time to reload the pistol, Ellie swapped it for her bow. Thankful for Griselda's help, Ellie concentrated on the remaining Demoniac. She darted under the creature's claws intending to grasp her and deftly circled beneath it. She aimed the arrow at its chest and fired. A swift downward swoop carried it out of the missile's path. The Demonic lunged at Ellie. She flew backward to keep free of its clutches while notching another arrow. Doubting she would get another chance to reload before it was upon her if she missed, she slowed her flight and waited until it was close enough to smell its foul stench before firing. The arrow entered its eye and pierced its brain. With momentum carrying the dead bat onward, Ellie stepped onto its head and ran along its back before diving off. She spun and watched the dead creature slam into the building with enough force to crunch bone before its mangled corpse dropped to the ground far below.

"Nicely done," praised Griselda, moving to hover beside Ellie.

Ellie grinned. "Yes, I thought so."

"We're not out of the woods yet," warned Griselda, pointing at the objects of her concern.

Ellie turned her head to the four Demoniacs flying out from the building.

"Persistent buggers," commented Ellie, using the lull of battle to reload her pistol. She glanced at Griselda's scattergun. "You locked and loaded?"

Griselda nodded as she dropped slightly, her wing muscles weakening. "I'm not sure I can remain airborne for much longer. Maybe one shot and I'm done."

Ellie observed the Demoniacs split up to attack from different directions. "Luckily there's only four then. If you take care of one, I'll handle the other three."

Griselda grinned and slapped her weapon fondly. "That, we can do."

Wary of the faerie weapons that could strike from afar, and wondering where the tasty rat was, Slazar led his group from the building and flew in a wide berth around the waiting faeries watching them. His scanning eyes and roving ears picked out the movement of branches in the tree growing beside the end of the building. His piercing eyes gazed into the foliage and picked out the rat climbing down.

Signaling for two of his comrades to attack the faeries, he called Formiddia to him and informed her they would be going after the rat. They flapped their wings and swooped toward the tree.

Hearing gunshots and the squeals of injured Demoniacs, Crowe hoped Ellie and Griselda would kill them all and not be harmed in the process. Apart from not wanting to lose his new-found friends, if by some miracle he survived Griselda's poison, he would be lost and stuck forever in this strange, terrifying land he had no idea how to escape from. A violent rustle of branches above caused him to halt and gaze up. Through gaps between the leaves, he glimpsed something moving and then a Demoniac's frightening face staring down at him. Fear of the thing climbing down prompted him to get moving again. A second rustling below halted him again and turned his gaze to another Demoniac climbing up. He was trapped.

Sensing the danger, Satan and Lucifer released their jaw grips on Crowe's fur and growled at the imminent threats. With no weapon, Crowe was without any means of fighting them off. He'd have to use his brains, something he didn't find encouraging in this strange, life-threatening situation. Holding his panic at bay and trying to quell the fear threatening to overwhelm him, Crowe glanced around. Maybe he could find a sharp branch to use as a spear to fend them off, or one he could use as a club.

The gnarled, twisted twigs offered nothing pointy or stout enough to be suitable to use as either. Keen to have something in his hand when they reached him, Crowe grabbed a long, curled branch and tugged at it to snap it off, but it was too bendy to break. Its flexibility though, did give him an idea. He lowered his back to a thick bough nearby. "Satan. Lucifer. Get off." The dogs jumped off and warily shared their glances between the two approaching creatures.

Ignoring the beast above him for the moment, as down was the route they needed to travel, Crowe climbed nearer to the creature below. Spying a suitable branch for his crazy plan, he anchored his rear paws against the tree and, gripping the branch with teeth and front legs, hauled it back as far as he could. Worried his teeth would be pulled from their gums with the strain, Crowe peered over the top of the bough at the approaching Demoniac all but hidden by the abundant foliage between them. The strain was such, he struggled to prevent the branch from springing back. The creature climbed steadily closer. His terror begged him to let go, but he had to wait until the Demoniac was in the optimum position for his trap to work. When its head appeared over the top of the branch he strained to hold, that position had almost been reached.

Anticipating the glorious taste of rat flesh, Slazar climbed toward it. There was no escape for it now. The claws on the tips of its wing joints and its clawed back limbs carried it eagerly nearer his prey. When his head rose above a bough, and he stared into the terrified eyes of his meal, he noticed the rat biting down on a branch. Pondering at the rodent's madness, he climbed higher to launch his attack. Although he preferred his meals eaten alive, the circumstance of being stuck high in a tree made that inadvisable. A quick kill and feasting on the warm carcass were acceptable alternatives.

Crowe released the branch. It whiplashed straight for the Demoniac.

When the branch struck him in the chest with enough force to crack ribs and send him flying backward with a piercing shriek, Slazar gazed in shock at the tree growing farther away. He flapped his wings furiously, but with broken bones, it was agony he found too intense to tolerate. Hoping he would survive the rough landing, he stretched his wings as wide as he was able to try and slow his fall and waited for the ground to arrive.

Ecstatic that his plan had worked and if the breaking of bones he had heard were as severe as he imagined it was, the Demoniac was no longer a threat, Crowe focused his gaze above at the dogs' growls and snarling barks they directed at the creature two branches above them. Worried they'd be injured or knocked from the tree if they battled the beast, he called them to him. When they were safely on his back, he continued his descent.

Hearing Slazar's pained yell. Formiddia searched for him below. Spying no sign of him, she shifted to the end of the branch and peered down. Spotting him spiraling too fast toward the ground to avoid serious injury or death, she leaped from the tree. With her body held straight and rigid with wings pressed tight to her sides, she plummeted like a stone.

The wind whistled over Formiddia, vibrating her leathery wings with a constant thrumming as she sped toward Slazar. She gazed at him worriedly as she passed and, spreading her wings wide, swooped beneath him. Flapping madly to slow her descent, she gently supported Slazar's weight on her back. Turning his head to look her, he nodded, his pained grimace informing her of his agony when he folded in his own wings to avoid interfering with her flying. Flapping in long powerful sweeps to keep them both in the air, she glided to the ground and landed in a patch of tall, wild grass. She gently slid him off onto the ground and began examining his wounds to see if she could do anything to alleviate his pain.

When the four Demoniacs split up, Ellie and Griselda picked their targets and attacked the two they headed for them. Ellie fired off a shot and cursed the creature when it dodged her arrow and flew straight at her with claws spread menacingly. With no time to reload, she turned and fled.

Sensing its slower faerie prey was no match for its greater wingspan speeding it ever nearer, Ellie's pursuer shrieked a frightening call of triumph as if it already tasted the meal soon to be his.

Aware she couldn't outfly the creature in the open, Ellie turned for the building and shot through a window opening in the hope the confining rooms and corridors would slow it down. She sped through corridors, down stairways, and through rooms but still the creature gained on her.

Spying Ellie entering the building with a creature in hot pursuit, Griselda was left with her Demoniac to contend with. Her wings were becoming too tired to support her for much longer, so she needed to act fast. She aimed the scattergun at the fast-approving creature and fired. The demon was prepared for the onslaught and dropped like a stone and swooped up behind her. With no time to reload, she flipped the scattergun over, held it like a club and spun to face the threat. With the Demonic almost upon her, Griselda swung the weapon at its head and struck it with enough force to snap its neck with a loud crack of bone that sent it spiraling below.

The excited shrieks coming from inside the building worried Griselda that Ellie was in trouble, so she went to help. Her erratic, wing-tired flight warned her she wouldn't remain airborne for much longer. Focusing her Hawk Sight, she glimpsed Ellie and the creature's movements from within. Griselda headed for the end of the building and holding onto the wall beside an opening, leaned inside and called out, "Ellie, come to me." She tapped the scattergun's stock on the side of the exit to direct Ellie to her.

Hearing Griselda's instruction, Ellie followed the constant taps echoing through the building. A worried glance behind revealed the creature was almost upon her. If she didn't do something quickly, she'd never reach Griselda, who she assumed was waiting to ambush it. Shooting along the corridor that would lead her to the room the source of the tapping came from, she glanced behind and knew she would never make it. She swerved into a room and found it buzzing with the insects they had seen earlier. With them congregated around the window, there would be no safe escape that way. She darted for the nest and thrust off with her feet to boost her speed. The larger Demoniac swiped out a wing claw at its prey when it suddenly changed direction. Unable to turn in time it crashed into the nest, splitting it open.

Angry insects poured from the rip and homed in on the creature responsible. They jabbed it with their stingers, pumping their fatal venom into the Demoniac. Covered in the insects like a second skin, the agonized Demoniac screeched as it fell to the floor. Insects dived into its mouth and injected their poison into its tongue.

Bored at waiting in the building, Spinx, the lone Demoniac Slazar had ordered to remain on guard, turned its head to the sound of shrieking a few floors below and hurried off to investigate.

After witnessing the agonized demise of the Demoniac, Ellie made a swift exit from the room before the insects turned their wrath upon her and crashed straight into another Demoniac. Both fell to the floor. Ellie quickly untangled herself from the creature's flapping wings and fled. The Demoniac righted itself, sprinted along the floor and lifted into the air.

Tired from her struggles, Ellie glanced at the end of the corridor and the fast-approaching opening the tap-tapping came from. She glanced behind at the pursuing Demoniac and twisted away from the claw reaching out to grab her. Missing the doorway to the room where Griselda waited, Ellie flew to the end of the passage, darted up, her feet running up the wall, and flipped over. Flying upside down, she shot over the Demoniac's back.

Turning his head to keep the faerie in view, Spinx failed to notice the end of the corridor until he crashed into it. Keen to continue the chase before its prey gained too much of a lead, he picked up its crumpled form, ran along the corridor and leaped into the air. He smoothly turned into the room the faerie had entered and found her resting on a windowsill with her back to him. With two silent flaps of its wings, Spinx reached the window and was about to grab her in his open jaws when she jumped and dropped from sight. When his head passed through the opening, he looked down and saw her hovering a short distance below.

When the Demoniac's body emerged from the window, Griselda leaped onto its back, wrapped an arm around its neck and showed it the knife she then pressed against its throat. Surprised by the unexpected passenger and the knife that briefly flashed in front of his face, Spinx was about to roll over to dislodge its attacker when the blade was pressed against his throat. When the pain of it slicing him open failed to materialize, he thought it best he waited to find out what his unwelcome passenger wanted.

Wondering what Griselda was up to but trusting she knew what she was doing, Ellie flew alongside her. "What's your plan?"

Keeping the knife edge pressed against the creature's throat, Griselda nodded behind her. "Wings tired so I'm going to ride this thing down to the ground."

Ellie's eyebrows rose in surprise. "And you think it'll cooperate?"

Griselda grinned. "I'm certain it will as we've come to an understanding." She glanced over at the tree. "Go check on the others, and I'll meet you all at the bottom."

"Good luck," said Ellie, flying off.

Even though she knew it wouldn't understand, Griselda spoke to the Demoniac. "If you don't want to die, this is what is going to happen. You will take me to the ground and then fly away and leave us alone. Because if I ever see you again," she pressed the knife tighter against its skin, "You will regret the encounter." Pointing below, she nudged it with her knees. "Down!"

Although having no understanding of the sounds uttered by the faerie on its back, Spinx understood the threat pressed against his throat, and the finger pointed below. Assuming that was where the faerie wanted to go, he altered the angle of its wings and gently spiraled to the ground in wide circles.

On her approach to the tree, Ellie headed for the branches set into movement by Crowe's decent. When she drew level with him, she slowed her flight to match his progress and checked the dogs clinging to his back were okay.

Crowe looked at Ellie. Pleased to see she was okay he was about to inquire after Griselda when he noticed something behind her in the sky that widened his rat eyes in astonishment. "Am I seeing things, or is that Griselda riding on the back of a Demoniac?"

Ellie glanced behind at the two unlikely temporary allies. "It is. She's going to meet us at the bottom."

Glancing down the trunk, Crowe was relieved to see the bottom wasn't too far away now. "What's the plan when we're all back on the ground?"

Ellie shrugged. "The usual, I suppose. We run really, really fast from any of the foul creatures no doubt waiting down there to eat us!"

Crowe sighed.

Chapter 25

Underwurld

AFTER NEGOTIATING THROUGH THE ravine strewn with boulders, dead trees and the occasional bones of creatures consumed by others quicker, stronger or more adept at hunting, Griselda called a halt and stared ahead at the foreboding entrance to the Underwurld.

The gloom-shrouded opening was situated beneath a giant tree straddling rocks that rose steeply on both sides. Its dark brown trunk was dotted with patches of moss, and its branches hung with creepers swaying eerily in the breeze funneled through the gorge. The gnarled crooked trunk leaned its twisted boughs toward them as if waiting to drag them in.

"There it is," stated Griselda. "The last leg of our journey. Once we reach the other side, we only have the tower, its guards and the beheading of the faerie king to contend with. We are practically back home."

Wondering what vicious monsters dwelled within and waited for them to enter, Crowe stared anxiously at the unwelcoming darkness of the tunnel entrance. "If it goes as simply as you've just said it, I'll be very much surprised."

Griselda smiled. "Not as much as I will be."

"I guess we've no choice but to head on through," said Ellie, not relishing the prospect.

"Any idea what lives in there?" asked Crowe.

"Nothing good, I expect," replied Ellie. "The tunnels were originally dug by the Moleeki—a sort of a cross between a dwarf and a mole. Apparently, the mountain was a fruitful source of gold, precious gems and iron. Once the Moleeki had exhausted the mine of anything worth their effort, they abandoned the mountain and moved on. The Demoniacs then moved in but were eventually ousted by the rats during the Great Rat Rebellion that lasted almost four years. The uprising came about when the rats became fed up with being used as the faeries pack mules, and slaves, doing all their dirty jobs."

"I can sympathize with them there," muttered Crowe, rolling his shoulders to shift the straps of the saddle chaffing his skin.

Ellie continued, "Commanded by their self-proclaimed ruler, the Rat King led them to freedom and set up camp in the tunnels. During the hours of darkness, bands of armed rats would enter the city to steal food and supplies and slaughter any faerie or creature that got in their way. Though there were many skirmishes between the rats and the faerie army over the years, it wasn't until an all-out offensive, which included every able-bodied faerie; male and female, drafted into the army, when the Rat King and his band of cutthroats were killed, driven off, or once more enslaved to do the faeries bidding. By all accounts, the final days of the Rat War were long, brutal and saw hundreds killed on both sides."

"Aren't the faeries worried about another uprising?" asked Crowe.

"Most definitely," answered Ellie. "That's why they now control the rat population. Males have a potion added to their food that renders them impotent. They have special breeding pens to uphold the status quo of the number of rats needed, which now fetch a high price for those having the need of a rat servant."

"Sounds barbaric," said Crowe.

"Barbarity is rife in this world and would be in ours too if the faeries ever mount a successful invasion," warned Griselda. "Now, if Ellie has finished her history lesson, let us enter."

Though he would rather do the contrary, Crowe knew what lay behind him, which didn't include a way home as the design of the portal they had come through was a one-way route. Forlornly pessimistic what lay ahead would prove any less life-threatening than the creatures he had thus far encountered, he headed for the entrance.

Sensing unfamiliar scents from within, Satan and Lucifer growled at the dark opening they padded toward.

As they passed beneath the tree, Griselda pushed aside the hanging vines in her way with the blunderbuss. "Slow and steady everyone. Be ready for anything."

After checking her pistol was loaded and close at hand, Ellie notched an arrow in her bow, ready to draw back and fire at anything that threatened them.

When they were in the tunnel, Griselda lit the lantern hanging from the tip of her staff propped in the saddle, and with her eyes peeled for danger and her ears straining for sounds of any creatures moving about, she peered ahead.

After traveling along a twisting, descending tunnel, their route leveled out and continued further into the mountain. Though side passages led off from the main, wider route, except for peering nervously into their dark depths as they passed them by, they ignored them.

Upon entering a cavern, they halted and stared at what must be the bones of hundreds of rats piled either side of the wooden walkways leading to the far side. Glinting in the yellow glow of the lamplight, the white bones and eyeless skulls continually shifted as if even after all these years they hadn't settled into permanent resting positions. The eerie grinding of bone across bone was accompanied by unseen things scuttering through the darkness shrouding most of the vast cavern.

Griselda reached into her magic bag and pulled out Crowe's flashlight. She switched it on and swept its bright light through the darkness, enabling them to see its hidden details. The steeply angled walls met at a point far above them. Thick wooden beams and trusses reinforced unstable areas of the walls and high galleried walkways led to further tunnels. Large nets fashioned from thin wire, leftovers from the traps the rats had set for the faeries attacking their nest, hung from the walls and proved to be an ideal framework for spiders to spin their webs from. The walkways at ground level they needed to cross to the other side, were set on different levels with simple wooden stairs accessing each.

Though Griselda jerked the light to each sound of movement, except for brief, fleeting shadows, she wasn't quick enough to highlight the creatures responsible. "I suggest we keep moving."

In total agreement, Crowe approached the front walkway and cautiously crossed. Though the boards bent slightly from their weight, they seemed firm. The steps he climbed creaked alarmingly but held.

With Ellie's bow scanning the darkness for danger, and Griselda's blunderbuss following the flashlight beam she aimed around the cavern, they reached the far exit without incident, which brought relief to them all.

Quickening his pace slightly to leave the bone cavern behind, Crowe moved through the tunnel that was wider and higher than the previous ones they had traveled through. In places, the rough-hewn walls covered in pick marks wielded by the Moleeki hundreds of years earlier were slick with moisture seeping through the rock.

The sounds of water drips heralded their entry into another cavern. Though not as tall as the bone cavern, it was wider and longer. Calcium icicles formed of minerals leaching through the rock had choked the arched ceiling with dark, pointed stalactites. The floor, though less infested, was adorned with its fair share of stalagmites and stone columns where the two sets of formations had met. Smooth, glossy flowstone formations covered the lower walls and most of the floor. A pool fed by water drips stretched to the far exit. Sodden and now below the surface, was the wooden walkway the Moleeki had used to easily pass through the chamber they had seen fit to leave in its natural state.

"It's stunning," exclaimed Ellie.

Crowe glanced at the plethora of sharp stone teeth they'd have to pass beneath and then at the few evident in the clear pool that had broken free. "Beauty may have a dark side if one drops while we're under it."

Griselda gazed around at the formations captured in the light beam she roamed over them. "Stop being such a worrywart, Crowe. They have been here for thousands of years, so I see no reason why they would decide to fall when we pass beneath."

Crowe shrugged, swaying Griselda. "Just the way our luck has been going is all."

"We're alive," stated Ellie. "Can't get luckier than that."

Crowe couldn't argue with the sentiment. He padded over to where Satan and Lucifer were drinking and stared at the submerged walkway six inches below the water and two yards away from the edge of the pool. He'd have to leap to reach it. "The water looks freezing."

"Then I suggest you don't dilly-dally when you paddle through it," advised Griselda.

"All right for you, your feet are not going to get wet and cold," moaned Crowe.

"You forget you are a rat. Rats don't feel the cold."

Surprised by this revelation, Crowe twisted his head to look at Griselda. "Is that true or another of your lies to coax me into doing something I'd rather not?"

A scuttling from behind, like crabs sidling over concrete, directed Griselda's gaze back along the tunnel they had recently emerged from. "Just jump in before whatever is creeping up on us arrives. It will be your fat rump that will be bitten first."

Crowe glanced worriedly back along the tunnel before turning to face the pool. He sprung and gasped when the freezing water numbed his paws and ankles, his weight pushing the waterlogged walkway in a little deeper. Griselda had lied *again*. Keen to be back on dry land and out from under the stone spikes he imagined breaking free and impaling him, and if they did, hopefully, the lying witch as well, he started moving across the saturated boards that trembled with each step, sending ripples expanding out across the surface. Algae, green, thick and slippery as ice, covered the boards, adding another obstacle to make his journey even more precarious, causing him to slip and stumble more than once, almost submerging more of his body into the frigid water leeching his warmth.

Satan and Lucifer leaped from the shore to the unstable wooden path and followed Crowe across.

Crowe climbed onto dry land and glad to be free of the water, shook each leg, in turn, to dislodge the liquid from his fur.

"See, that wasn't so bad," said Griselda.

Muttering under his breath nothing that could be ascribed as painting Griselda in a flattering or charitable light, Crowe carried on.

The creatures, though small, were plentiful and equipped with the necessary sharp appendages to hunt and devour the unexpected bounty that had entered their domain. Their claws scuttled them along the tunnel floor and around the walls when they reached the flooded chamber.

Conscious they were being pursued by things they didn't want to meet, Crowe increased his pace through the winding tunnel littered with many side passages. He skidded to a halt when a metal barrier the height and width of the shaft appeared from the darkness. Crowe gazed at the handle-less rusty iron door set in the wall, the corner at the bottom was bent back where something had obviously forced entry at one time—the faeries he assumed—during their quashing of the Great Rat Rebellion. Moving nearer, he peered through the metal rungs barring the small lookout window. "The tunnel continues on the other side, but there's no handle to open it."

"It wouldn't be much of a defense if all the enemy had to do was turn a handle to gain entry, would it?" said Griselda, shooting a worried glance behind. By the gradually increasing volume of the sounds, it wouldn't be long before whatever was coming arrived. She turned to Ellie. "Do you think you can squeeze through the gap at the bottom and open it?"

"I'll give it go." Ellie slipped off her weapons and flew to the barrier. She laid on the ground and squeezed through headfirst.

Crowe looked back at the growling dogs and nervously along the tunnel the approaching sounds moved through.

Griselda slid off her ride's back and crossing to the barrier, aimed the flashlight through the barred window. "Can you see what's holding it shut?"

Ellie appeared at the window. "There are two bolts and a locking bar, all rusty. I'm going to try to free them."

"Quick as you can then, we don't have much time."

Ellie moved to the top bolt that was almost as thick as her arm and placing her feet on the edge of the door for leverage, grabbed the bolt knob and heaved. Groaning with the strain, the rust anchoring it in place slowly relented its hold and the bolt squealed out of its recess. Panting from the effort, she called out to Griselda. "Top bolt's free, moving to the bottom one."

With no way to help Ellie, Griselda joined the dogs and Crowe staring back along the tunnel.

Crowe glanced at her. "You got anything in that magic sack of yours we can use to kill what's coming or hold them back until Ellie's unlocked the door?"

"Most creatures are afraid of fire..." Griselda fished in her seemingly bottomless bag of items, pulled out a large flask and threw it at the tunnel wall.

Fragments of flask flew in all directions when it smashed, showering the surrounding area with liquid.

"Lamp oil," Griselda informed Crowe as she produced a box of matches and held one ready to strike.

A clunk of metal behind them was followed by Ellie's voice. "Bottom bolt freed. Only the locking bar to go."

Wrinkling his nose from the acrid fumes given off by the flammable oil, Crowe dragged his gaze away from the sounds of the scuttling creatures about to appear around the tunnel's curve and focused on the match Griselda held against the striker. "Wouldn't now be a good time to set it ablaze?"

"You let me worry about that." Griselda glanced at the dogs who sensed the imminent arrival of the creatures and inched forward, ears back, legs crouched ready to spring. "Call the dogs to heel before they attack, or I won't be able to light the oil."

"Satan. Lucifer. On me," Crowe ordered, backing toward the barrier he hoped Ellie would soon have open.

The two dogs turned their heads to look at Crowe but didn't move.

"Satan. Lucifer. Here!" called out Ellie sternly, her voice muffled by the barrier and strained from her efforts of struggling with the locking bar.

Though reluctant to do so, Satan and Lucifer approached the door. Lucifer stuck his head through the small bottom opening and tried to shuffle through to Ellie, but he was too large.

"Away," ordered Ellie, worried the iron bar would fall on his head when it was free. Placing her feet on one of the door's cross struts, she gripped the round two-inch-wide bar and lifted. She needed to raise it four inches to be free of the half-looped brackets attached to the door and frame. Flapping her wings furiously to help with her burden, the bar ground against its brackets as it slowly lifted.

The creatures rushed around the corner in a creamy mass of viciousness. When those at the front saw the faerie and the rat, they shrilled cries of anticipated pleasure of the feast to come.

Crowe stared fearfully at the oncoming hoard. Though their pale, furry bodies were only the size of hamsters, their four long and spindly multi-articulated legs, held them a foot from the ground. Each swayed their two shorter front arm limbs in the air menacingly, snapping together the pincers each were tipped with. Equipped with four eyes protruding on stalks from the back of their heads that seemed to be all mouth and teeth, Crowe had no doubt they were designed to see in the dark. A clang of metal striking the floor behind the barrier signaled Ellie had released the locking bar. The door would soon be open; an escape route they desperately needed. But to ensure their escape, they needed to hold the creatures back.

"Now, Griselda" Crowe screamed, backing away.

Ignoring the rat's frightened girlish shriek, Griselda concentrated on the approaching creatures whose constant clicking of pincers was beginning to annoy her. She had to time her move exactly to take down as many as possible. Her hand began to tremble, almost prematurely striking the match. She lifted it away from the striker, forced her rising fear to a manageable level, and watched the legs of the frontline creatures enter the flammable puddle. When they were just about to step from the near edge of liquid, and within leaping distance, she struck the match. As it sizzled into life, she flung it at the puddle of oil and stepped back.

The oil whooshed into flame and devoured every creature within reach. The creatures' shrill, painful cries filled the tunnel. They contorted in agony as the flames consumed them, the smell of their burning fur and cooking flesh filled the passage. Those behind lucky enough to escape the flareup backed away from the heat.

Ellie's voice coming from the barred window turned Crowe and Griselda around. "I could do with some help to open this door if you're not too busy."

They rushed over and pushed the stubborn door open. The dogs bounded through first to be made a fuss of by Ellie. After passing through, Griselda closed and re-bolted the door. The bent back section at its base wouldn't stop the small creatures from getting through when the flames died down but funneled into the small gap, it would slow them down.

Tired from her exertions, Ellie flew onto Crowe's neck, retrieved her weapons and again kept vigil for anything that might attack from the front.

"Well done, Ellie," praised Griselda, climbing into the saddle. "Now let's move before the oil burns away, and they are back on our trail."

The thought of the creatures nipping at his rump spurred Crowe into motion. "I assume moving slow and cautious has gone out the window now?"

"It has," concurred Griselda. "We flee as fast as your powerful stumpy rat legs can carry us."

"Amen to that," uttered Ellie, checking her dogs were keeping pace.

With the flashlight held by Griselda lighting their way, they headed for the heart of the mountain.

Chapter 26

Just Run!

IMPATIENT TO CATCH THEIR escaping prey, a few of the long-legged monstrosities found themselves jostled ever nearer the dying flames by those behind them. With no choice other than to risk leaping over the approaching fire that threatened to roast them alive, they jumped through it. Though a couple stumbled on landing and rolled across the floor with a clacking of limbs, the others landed surefootedly and headed for the door. With only room for one of them to fit through the gap at a time, a brief scuffle took place between the first two to reach it. When the smaller of the two had its front leg snipped off, it relented and hobbled after the larger creature once it had passed through.

Seeing their brethren's success and worried they would reach the food before them, the rest of the creatures shrieked excitedly when they jumped through the flames and joined the log jam backing up behind the breach in the door.

Hearing the faint shrieks of the creatures drifting along the sound-carrying passageways, and with no more lamp oil to fend them off, Griselda hoped they didn't come across any more obstacles that would impede their escape. Crowe was doing well in his rat-form now he had become more accustomed to it and carried them swiftly through the tunnels. There was hope for them yet. To save the little lamp oil they might need if the flashlight batteries failed, Griselda extinguished the flame and hung the lamp on the saddle.

The twitching of his whiskers was what first alerted Crowe to the danger they rushed toward. The awful stench wafting from ahead, like rotten cabbage and maggot riddled corpses, confirmed it and slowed his pace. "Trouble ahead," he announced anxiously just as the offensive odor assaulted Ellie and Griselda.

The dogs' sensitive noses set them to whining when it washed over them also.

Ellie drew an arrow back in her bow and prepared to fire it at whatever foul creature creating the slithering squelches made its appearance.

"Ideas anyone?" inquired Crowe who had slowed his pace to a walk.

Alerted by the barking dogs, Griselda glanced behind and picked up the clicks of clawed feet on the tunnel floor. They couldn't go back. She turned forward. "Whatever you do Crowe, don't stop!" She aimed the flashlight ahead and picked out a dark patch in the tunnel wall. "Head for side passage up on the left. It is our only chance as those furry crabby things are behind us and coming up fast."

Against all his survival instincts, Crowe sprinted for the side passage and the unknown emanator of the disgusting stench. When it appeared in the flashlight's beam, all were shocked by what they witnessed. Hurtling toward them was a mass of tentacles. Amongst the writhing form, grotesque, malformed heads of various shapes and sizes appeared to snarl teeth-lined jaws at them before disappearing beneath the rolling bundle of shiny limbs. It was impossible to tell if the abomination filling the tunnel was more than one creature entwined with its brethren or a single grotesque many-headed entity.

Crowe shot a fearful gaze at the opening they both headed for and knew it would be a close-run race for whoever reached it first.

Aware her arrows weren't going to damage the creature enough to halt it, Ellie lowered her bow and drew her sword. Holding it ready for the close quarter battle she feared was about to come, she gripped Crowe's ear with her free hand when he pushed all his adrenalin-fueled strength into his limbs to propel them forward and hopefully to safety.

Having no noses, the putrid stench had no effect on the creatures in pursuit that had once again sighted their prey. The first few through the flames had successfully managed to maintain their head start and stared hungrily at the bobbing rat rump they gained on.

Tentacles reaching out from the rolling ball of monstrosity for the prey it hungered for, slapped on the floor when they were dragged beneath its ever-rolling mass to be quickly replaced with more.

Trying to close his nostrils against the putrid smell was all but useless as the reek was so awfully pungent Crowe could taste it. It was all he could do to suppress his gagging reflex battling to evict the foulness from his throat. Aware a single misstep would doom them all, he concentrated on his footing and the distance between them, the side turning and the Lovecraftian Cthulhu horror waving tentacles at him, ready to grab as soon as they were within reach. Which would happen in 5, 4, 3, 2, 1.

Seconds before he clashed with the creature, Crowe leaped onto the wall opposite the opening and springing off, dived into the side passage. Ellie slashed her sword at the slick limbs aiming to curl around them, slicing clean through. The severed limbs sprayed dark blood as they were yanked out of reach for others to rapidly replace them.

When the dogs bounded beneath Crowe's flight through the air, Satan snapped at a madly writhing limb searching for prey and clamped it in his jaws. He had the sense to release it when it dragged him toward one of the open-mouthed heads slavering for flesh.

Griselda ducked under a tentacle, sliced at another with her knife and shoved the barrel of her blunderbuss into the mouth of the head that shot out on a long neck to bite her. It exploded when she pulled the trigger and caused the rest of the creature's heads to screech in pain, an indication all of them were connected.

Stumbling on the floor when he landed, and almost crushing the two dogs that appeared out from beneath him and raced ahead, Crowe regained his footing and sped away from the tentacled menace.

When the rat disappeared into the side passage, and the leading creatures saw the ravenous monster, they tried to halt their forward dash but skidded and tumbled across the floor. The visible heads screeched at the fresh source of food and sent out tentacles to snatch them up. Two were fed into mouths before the others dodged from their reach. With a wary eye on the threat rolling toward them, the creatures retreated.

When their excited shrieking brethren arrived and saw those in front had halted their chase for the food, they jumped over them and saw the reason why. Tentacles plucked them from the air and stuffed them into hungry mouths. When others saw the threat, they tried to stop, but the momentum of those behind shoved them forward into the arms of the beast to be swiftly devoured.

Hearing the creatures' dreadful screeches, Griselda glanced behind and was pleased to see the monster gorging itself on them, a fate they had all narrowly escaped. She directed her gaze and the flashlight forward and wondered if they would be so lucky with the next horror they met.

Having barely recovered from his latest encounter with a subterranean horror, Crowe noticed the dogs prick up their ears. When he heard a faint buzzing growing louder with every hurried step, he assumed he was about to face another.

On entering a circular cavern hollowed out of the mountain by the Moleekis' inexhaustive thirst for precious minerals, Crowe halted. They all gazed at the pulsating cocoons adorning the walls and the large central pillar the miners had left to support the ceiling. Lit by the roaming flashlight and the green glowing slug-like creatures occupying the walls spaces between the bulging sacks, all noticed the things living within moving about. The constant low droning that came from each indicated each contained a significant number of creatures.

Sensing the danger, Satan and Lucifer remained by Crowe's side.

"Stinger nests," whispered Ellie. "Imagine a hornet with claws, and you'll get the picture. They are practically blind, so if we move through without making a sound, we should be okay." She turned to Griselda. "Best kill the flashlight in case they detect it."

Griselda switched off the light, leaving their surroundings lit by the ghostly green glow of the wall creatures busy chomping on the lichen and lapping at the calcium-rich moisture leaking through the rock.

"What about those things on the wall," asked Crowe quietly, staring at one of the eight-inch maggot-like monstrosities that had turned its flat face to him. Though lacking in the eyes department, it had an impressive selection of teeth. Three large curved ones along the bottom of its round mouth-face, and smaller ones around the mucus-oozing opening in the center.

"Cave Leeches," replied Ellie. "Don't get too near as they can leap on their prey."

"Thanks for the warning," whispered Crowe. "Bloodsuckers, I assume."

"Well, yes, they'll happily drain your arteries dry if they get the chance, but they are easily dislodged with a poke from something sharp. However, them sucking your blood isn't what should concern you, as their mouths are also their birth canal. As soon as they latch onto your skin, they make a hole and inject their young inside to feed and grow, eating you from the inside out."

Crowe shivered from the horrible, agonizing death he pictured.

Ellie flew down to the dogs and straddled Lucifer's back. Placing a finger to her lips, she warned them to remain silent. She mouthed *follow me* to Crowe and set Lucifer into motion.

Griselda leaned forward and spoke quietly into Crowe's ear. "Get ready to run if the Stingers detect us."

"Good advice," whispered Ellie. "Apparently, their sting is excruciating and potent enough to paralyze a full-grown Orc. But what comes next is much worse. They dissect their victims alive and carry the pieces to their nests to feed their young or themselves.

"Be assured, ready to run has been a permanent condition of mine lately, more so now after hearing that disturbing snippet of information."

Ellie hushed Crowe when they approached the first nest, which they passed without incident. Crowe shared his fearful gaze between the cocoons and the leeches that turned their heads and creepily watched them. They bunched up their spawn-filled bodies like a concertina, prepared to spring from the wall if the intruders came within range. With the measurement of their leaping ability unknown, Crowe worried as he was the largest target, he would be the focus of any attack.

Though eyeless, the receptors encircling the leeches' heads detected the carbon dioxide the humans breathed out. Prepared to attack if the opportunity arose, the young inside sensed their parents' anticipation and started squirming excitedly at the prospect of being born and taking their first feed.

Ellie halted the dogs when a few Stingers crawled from the openings in the side of their nests, spread out over the waxy surfaces and flexed their wings.

Though Crowe had seen a few frightening creatures since setting foot in the Faerie Realm, he thought the species he stared at now was the one that scared him the most. Though only the length from his wrist to his fingertip, its compact size was equipped with, what seemed to Crowe, an overabundance of murderous appendages. Its long, curved head, dark brown and glossy like its body, was enclosed in a carapace ridged with raised protrusions. Short, hooked tentacles hung from the sides and below the single, milky orange eye set at the front. Two stag beetle-like pincers were positioned either side of its mouth. It had no legs, just two arm appendages whose end sections were scythes that looked sharp enough to slice through any prey with ease. As if that wasn't enough for its deadly needs, the end section of its body was tipped with a second, larger mouth sporting four curved teeth and a slightly longer stinger to inject a paralyzing venom into any unfortunate victim.

The Stingers fluttered into the air. Thankfully, taking no notice of the trespasses, they flew over their heads to the cave leeches.

Fascinated to see how the Stingers fared against the leeches, Crowe waited for the forthcoming battle and was surprised when it didn't materialize. Hovering by the leeches, the Stingers bowed their head toward them. The leeches stretched out from the wall and with retching motions, deposited the mucus seeping from their mouths onto the top of the Stingers heads, where it collected between the raised ridges. When they had finished secreting the foul mucus, the leeches retracted, and the Stingers buzzed back to their nests and disappeared inside with their revolting payload. A little astounded by what he had witnessed, Crowe supposed the two creatures worked together for mutual benefit. Perhaps the mucus was a food substance the Stingers craved, and in return, they protected the leeches from predators. Which, if that were the case, begged the question, what creature would risk feeding on such deadly prey with equally vicious protectors and expect to survive? Hoping he wouldn't get to find out, Crowe again followed Ellie and the dogs when they started moving.

When more Stingers began emerging from their nests to collect the leech mucus, indicating it might be a daily feeding ritual, the intruders creeping through their domain kept their movements slow and silent in the hope they would reach the far exit without detection.

Slithering sounds coming from the tunnel Ellie headed for, halted her and Crowe while they assessed the threat it posed to them. Unnerving with the hundreds of deadly insects flying over them, which luckily, through disinterest or limited vision, still left them alone, they focused on the tunnel mouth to see what was about to arrive.

Pale faces at the end of long bodies emerged from the darkness into the leeches' glow and turned their heads around the cavern.

Sensing the new arrivals, the Cave Leeches started swaying their heads around in a circle, uttering high pitched warbles and flashed between red and their original green glow.

"What in hell's name are those things?" uttered Crowe in a whisper.

Ellie shrugged. "I don't know every creature that lives in this crazy world, but if you need to label them, Tunnel Vipers seems appropriate."

As if this was their cue to attack, the newly named vipers snaked along the base of the wall. With surprising speed, they slithered up the walls and homed in on the nearest leeches. The Cave Leeches, obviously afraid of what was coming, increased their circular head motions and heightened the pitch of their fearful cries.

When the vipers were a short distance from their chosen victims, a pink, glistening tube extended from the hole located above their mouths and bulging briefly, fired a black, glutinous blob at the leeches' heads. Splattered with the black that seemed to have a life of its own, the leeches struggled frantically and chomped at the gluttonous strands seeping over their faces and covering their heads, muffling their pitiful cries. Tongues unfurled from the vipers' spread wide jaws and darted at their selected prey. Just before each one struck, the tongue tip split into four lashes and like fingers, wrapped around the leech and yanked it from the wall. In a blur of movement, the trapped creature was pulled into the viper's mouth. As soon as its meal was securely clamped in its jaws, the viper dropped to the floor and speedily slithered back through the tunnel.

Not all the hunting vipers were as successful. Some of the leeches seized the opportunity to birth their young. They leaped upon their attackers, injected their offspring, and had a quick drink of blood before returning to the wall. Unable to resist the unexplainable urge to climb, the infected viper crawled up the wall and grabbed a rock protrusion on the ceiling with its jaws. Soon to become another of the many wilted husks adorning the cavern roof, it hung there limply while the young now in its care feasted on its internal organs.

As other infected vipers headed for the ceiling, the leeches' cries for help were finally answered. The attack of their food source was a regular occurrence, and the Stingers were aware that to attack too early would prevent the leeches from birthing their young and thus reduce their number. If this continued, their valuable source of protein would disappear, something they weren't prepared to let happen. The leech eaters also provided them with an alternative source of nourishment, so it was important they culled them wisely.

Judging enough time had passed for what needed to be done, Stingers armed with wickedly long stingers, poured from the nests. The retaliation was swift, brutal, and organized. Their scythe-like arms ripped, stabbed and sliced at the vipers. Others attacked with their pincers and tail mouths, biting, tearing and injecting venom. Dead, dying and paralyzed vipers dropped to the floor. When sufficient numbers had been killed, the Stingers retreated and let the survivors slither away to return during the next feeding cycle.

"It's time we left," whispered Ellie as the wasps began dissecting the vipers on the ground.

Crowe agreed and with the dogs keeping pace copied her dash for the exit, along the tunnel, and past the many holes in the walls the vipers had come slithering from.

Chapter 27

Captured

AFTER TRAVERSING THROUGH MORE twisting tunnels, the fleeing group entered a large cavern. Crowe slowed his rush and glanced around at the smashed, rotten and overturned wooden tables and benches strewn across the room. "It looks like it might have been a mess hall."

"It's certainly messy," uttered Ellie.

Satan and Lucifer moved through the room, sniffing the strange scents on everything. Crowe moved over to the low circular wall set to one side of the room, which he thought might be a well. He could do with a drink. However, when he peered in and smelt the sickening stench of rotten food and decaying flesh emanating from the hole, he forgot about his thirst.

Leaning to the side, Griselda stared into the dark hole and cocked an ear to the sounds of things shuffling about far below. "I think it might be a feeding tube."

Holding a paw across his nose, Crowe asked, "A feeding tube for what?"

"Whatever foul creatures dwell down there, obviously," said Griselda, glancing around the room. "Who or whatever ate here would have thrown their scraps down the hole."

"Probably the rats when they were here," offered Ellie. "Rumors are they enslaved a tribe of Hobkrakkens to do their bidding."

"Hobkrakkens?" inquired Crowe, glancing at the feeding tube anxiously.

Dragging the information from her encyclopedia-like knowledge of the Faerie Realm and its inhabitants, Ellie explained what she knew about the Hobkrakkens. "Ugly creatures about a seven on the vicious scale and strong for their size. Compared to our Faerie Realm appearance, they are about the size of an adult chimpanzee standing upright. They are underground dwellers, blind but well equipped with other heightened senses to move adeptly through the dark as easily as we do in the light."

"Doesn't sound like a creature I'd like to meet, so how about we keep moving?"

"Probably best," agreed Griselda.

When Crowe headed for the exit on the far side of the room, he noticed Satan and Lucifer standing in the archway, ears erect and growling. "That doesn't bode well."

"I'll check it out." Ellie flew over to the exit and stared along the dark passage. At first, she couldn't hear anything, but when she cocked an ear along the tunnel, she detected distant shrieks gradually becoming louder. She glanced back at the others. "Trouble's coming."

Crowe sighed. "Nothing new there then."

"It might be Hobkrakkens," added Ellie.

Griselda stared back at the entrance they had just come through when Hobkrakken shrieks came from that direction also. "Not good."

With their terrified gazes jerking between the only two exits the spine-chilling shrieks and cries emanated from, Crowe, Griselda, and Ellie knew they were trapped. Quickly formulating a plan, Griselda whipped off her bag and knelt. "Ellie, you and the dogs climb in."

Surprised by the request, Ellie argued, "What about you two, you'll never hold them off on your own? I can help."

"We won't hold them off even with an army, and I need you safe to finish our mission in case we don't survive. I don't have time to argue. Get in, or it is likely we will all die."

Reluctantly yielding to Griselda's demands, Ellie ordered the dogs inside and then followed them through.

Amazed by what he was witnessing, Crowe watched the bag opening grow to accommodate the dogs and Ellie's bulk and return to normal once they were inside. Hearing the shrieks getting worriedly nearer, he dived for the bag and forced his head inside before becoming stuck. Shock peeled his eyes wide open when he stared at a room filled with shelves containing hundreds of objects. At one end, Ellie sat on an armchair by an open fire drinking what seemed to be hot chocolate, and Satan and Lucifer lying on a rug beside her licking the marrow from the large bone they each had.

A strange winged creature that, by the addition of horns and red scaly skin, was probably a demon, flew at him and started pushing his nose and yelled, "Out! Out! You're too big."

The vision disappeared when he was yanked out.

"What in hell's name do you think you're doing?" scolded Griselda, dropping his tail.

Crowe was still stunned by what he had just seen. "Getting in the bag."

"My bag might be magic, but it has its limits, and the size of your fat body is one of them." She snatched up her bag and hung it around her waist. "We fend for ourselves."

"If like me, you were aware of my despicably lacking fending capabilities, you'd sound more worried."

Griselda forced a smile. "I don't know, you have done rather well so far."

"Like your magic bag, my run of good luck also has its limits." Remembering what he had seen, he pointed at her bag. "There's a whole room in there, full of stuff, and a demon!"

"Of course, he is my storekeeper. We are linked telepathically. I think of what I require, and the demon picks it out and hands it to me. "What did you think I did, shoved a hand in and scrambled around hoping to find the correct object?"

Crowe shrugged. "Never really gave it much thought. This magic business is beyond me."

"That is because magic is a paradox beyond comprehension for those who have not mastered its inconsistencies." Piercing shrieks and scrambling footsteps alerted Griselda they had run out of time. "Quick, we must conceal ourselves until we can think of a way out of our current predicament."

"And where do you suggest I secret myself," Crowe asked, waving a paw around the room decidedly absent any handy cubbyhole, cupboard or any other suitable place of concealment his rat body would squeeze behind or into."

Griselda grabbed her staff from the saddle and swiftly glanced around the room. "I see two options for you, behind an overturned table…"

"No good. If the Hobkrakkens senses are as good as Ellie indicated, they'll soon sniff me out."

"Option two it is then; get in the feeding tube and hang on until I have led them away."

Crowe looked at the pipe worriedly. "And if I fall?"

Griselda grimaced. "It doesn't bear thinking about, but if your luck holds out, you will die when you hit the bottom. Your only alternative is to wait here and fight what is coming. That is if you are confident you can fight off what sounds like…" she cocked an ear at the rapidly approaching shrieks and terrifying screams, "…about thirty to fifty bloodthirsty and extremely vicious Hobkrakkens."

"Alright, alright. I'll get in the pipe," moaned Crowe, peering into the foul feeding tube with disgust. "Just don't waste time leading them away as I'm not sure how long I'll be able to hang on. My paws are small and, well, the rest of me isn't."

Griselda rolled her eyes. "I wasn't planning on having a tea party with them." She pointed at the doorway they had entered. "When they are here, I will lead them back that way. As soon as they are gone, head through the other door and try to find the exit and wait for me there. As soon as I am able, I will double back and catch up with you."

Crowe nodded." Thanks, Griselda. I'm aware you could fly over them and escape, so I appreciate you're not abandoning me."

"Oh, stop it, you will get me all teary-eyed. Besides, we still have a quest to complete, and it stands a better chance of success with your help."

"No one could ever accuse you of being sentimental," Crowe quipped.

"And live to say it a second time if I am within earshot. Now quick, into the pipe, they are almost upon us."

While Crowe climbed into the pipe, Griselda placed herself in the middle of the room between both doorways. Though he was tempted to watch what was about to happen, Crowe gripped the top of the tube and hung from his front paws. Worried his long head was visible above the top and wishing rats had longer limbs or shorter snouts, he turned it to the side, almost brushing his nose in the foul encrustation covering the inner walls.

Griselda, slightly taken aback by the Hobkrakkens' sightless faces when they appeared, turned to watch them entering from both doorways either end of the room and spread out. They sniffed the air and directed their noses and ears around the room.

To get their attention, Griselda called out, "Hello, foul creatures."

Surprised by the voice, the Hobkrakkens halted and warily turned their faces to the sound. Trying to determine the source by its scent, they sniffed when they moved closer.

"Now, if you will all be good boys..." then noticing a couple with saggy breasts, Griselda added, "...and girls, and follow me, the sooner I can be rid of you, and the awful reek you are collectively giving off, the better."

Crowe wished Griselda would stop toying with the creatures and lead them away. His paws supported a lot of weight and, with hindsight, he would have removed the saddle and put something over his nose; the stench had increased tenfold inside and was making his eyes water. Shuffling sounds from below cast a teary eye down the tube and into its foreboding darkness. Unsure if it was the pipe's acoustics or the noises really were getting nearer, he focused on what was going on in the room so he could climb out and flee at the first opportunity.

Griselda observed the sniffing creatures spread out and gradually surround her. She shook her head in dismay. "Look, you lot. You might be blind, but I am not. I can see what you are doing; the old, and rather unimpressive 'sneak around and rush your prey all at once' maneuver. I tell you now, it is not going to work."

Unable to understand the strange sounds the intruder uttered, the Hobkrakkens continued with their doomed-to-failure plan.

Crowe sighed. *Come on, woman, rush from the room already.* A scrape of claw on the tube below elevated his already heightened fear up another notch, with very few notches left to go. Something was undeniably climbing the pipe.

Aware they were going to make their move at any moment, Griselda focused on one slightly larger and a whole lot uglier than the others. The abundant scars covering his face and body indicated him as a battle-hardened veteran and probably if the rabble had such a thing, their likely commander.

The scarred Hobkrakken known as Slobslurper by his friends, which admittedly were few, shook his head to detach the long-tailed string of globulous snot dangling from his nose and aimed his unseeing eyes at the creature they were about to attack. When the snot missile whipped across the face of the Hobkrakken standing beside him, its tongue snaked out to lap it up and drag the glutinous thread into its mouth. Hobkrakkens weren't a species that wasted food, whatever unsavory form it came in.

When the ravenous circle had been completed, Slobslurper grunted a command. They rushed at the food that all hoped to get of taste of.

Griselda bent her legs, flapped her wings and jumped into the air free of the creatures' clawing grasps. Hovering above them, she observed them collide into a snarling tangled mess of slashing claws and snapping teeth that ripped flesh before they realized they were attacking one another.

When the throng parted, the wounded, of which there were many around the inner circle who had suffered the full brunt of the savagery, whimpered from the sounds of their brethren's hungry tongues slithering over ravenous teeth longing to chew anything edible, even if it was the flesh of one of their own. Acutely aware they were now victims, the wounded crawled away and searched for a gap in the circle of murderous intent they could escape through but found none. As if a silent signal had been given, they were set upon and torn apart as all fought for a share of the feast.

The snarls and excited shrieks caused Crowe to wonder what was happening. Concerned that Griselda had been caught, he risked a peek above the feeding tube. A mass of monstrosities crowded around something that blood and lumps of flesh sprayed from. Glimpsing movement, he spied Griselda hovering in the gloom above them. Relieved she was safe, he watched her fly for the far doorway, then ducked again before he was spotted.

"Come on, you lot," goaded Griselda, heading for the exit she wanted to lead them through. "You are eating gristly old mutton when you could be eating prime juicy steak."

Those scrabbling unsuccessfully for a share of the spoils turned to her voice and sniffed her scent drifting through the room. Licking blood from his fingers, Slobslurper barged his way to the front and aimed his face in Griselda's direction. When she moved nearer the door, his bellowed command set the others on her trail.

Though pleased her plan was working, Griselda noticed a few had moved away from the main pack to devour the morsels they had won. Others fought over their comrades' bones already picked clean, and some were desperate enough to lap at the blood from the floor, which gave her an idea. She drew her knife, pricked her thumb and waved it about. That got their attention.

Griselda smiled. They have probably never smelt such sweet blood. When she noticed one of the stragglers paying undue attention to the feeding chute, its nose raised, nostrils flaring as it sniffed the air while moving closer to Crowe's place of concealment, she flew above it and squeezed a drop of blood from her thumb. Even before it had splattered on the floor, the inquisitive Hobkrakken had aimed its nose at it and followed it down. It leaped on the red splatter and lapped the stone clean. Waving her bloody thumb at it, Griselda coaxed it to over to the others. Delighted to see all their noses and ugly eyeless faces pointed in her direction, Griselda shook her thumb, splattering some of those below with bloody goodness, which was promptly licked up by the first tongues to find them.

She glanced over at Crowe's paws gripping the pipe's lip. "Crowe, I am leaving."

Griselda swooped low over the heads of the creatures that wanted to eat her and flew through the doorway, shaking free a breadcrumb trail of delicious blood splatters for them to follow.

Crowe had never been so glad to hear Griselda's words. His tired paws were already beginning to slip. He cocked an ear to the Hobkrakkens' shrieks and the shuffling of their feet through the exit. A deep, menacing growl that sounded far too close for comfort caused him to glance below. He gasped in fright when the pale form of a Hobkrakken appeared from the darkness, its arms and legs splayed wide to grip the pipe walls. Moving one set of limbs at a time, the Hobkrakken gradually drew nearer. Crowe glimpsed another climbing behind it, and the multiple sounds of shuffling legs lower down the pipe indicated more were coming.

The last Hobkrakken to step through the door after Griselda halted, and spun toward the gasp that had emanated from somewhere in the room. It raised its ugly nose and flared its snotty nostrils to seek out a scent. Snarling when it found it, it followed the trail to its source.

Crowe's fear of what was coming from below overrode his fear of what might still be above. Hoping all the Hobkrakkens had left the room, he heaved his body up and came face to face with one almost upon him. The foul creature slashed out a claw. Crowe instinctively dodged away. One of his front legs slipped from the rim. He dropped into the tube until his remaining latched-on paw halted his fall. Hanging from one limb, he whipped his tail at the Hobkrakken below that was making a wild grab for his rear leg. He screamed when the one above bit his paw gripping the pipe. Jerking it from the creature's mouth, Crowe fell.

He crashed into the topmost creature, sending them both colliding with the next in line. In a concertina-like effect that dislodged all those below, they plummeted down the chute. Their screams and shrieks faded as they slipped into the foul bowels of the Underwurld.

Worried she had taken a wrong turn—she hadn't been concentrating on the route when they'd fled along it a short while before—Griselda was relieved when she spotted the Cave Viper holes in the tunnel walls. She zoomed past the entrances to their nests and entered the Stingers cavern with the ravenous Hobkrakkens close on her heels. Spying none of the deadly insects flittering about, Griselda flew to the nearest nest and whacked it with her staff, eliciting an angry drone from the Stingers inside. She moved through the room, repeating the process.

Believing their nests were under attack, the lethal Stingers poured from each and were surprised to see the Hobkrakkens running around their cavern screeching. Grateful for the unexpected bounty, they attacked.

Also surprised by the appearance of so many incubators for their young, the Cave Leeches sprung from the walls, latched onto their chosen surrogate, and injected their young. If the newly infected Hobkrakkens had sight, they would be wearing glazed looks as they bumped into the walls and climbed to the ceiling.

Dodging and fending off any Stingers that came too close, Griselda headed for the exit and flew over the vipers that had been drawn to the commotion and slithered into the cavern to discover the cause. Grasping the opportunity of the flesh on offer, they attacked the rapidly retreating Hobkrakkens heading for the exit.

Leaving the painful cries of the dying Hobkrakkens behind, Griselda flew along the tunnel. To rest her tired wings in case she needed them in an emergency, she landed on the ground and sprinted back to the mess hall.

Crossing to the feeding chute and seeing no sign of Crowe, Griselda held her bag near the ground, opened the flap and summoned forth Ellie and her dogs.

After emerging from the bag, Ellie glanced around. "What happened and where's Crowe?"

"Crowe hid in the feeding tube while I led the Hobkrakkens back to the Stingers, who seemed pleased to see them. I told Crowe to head for the exit as soon as the room was clear, so I suggest we go catch up with him."

Griselda fastened the bag back around her waist, and with the dogs bounding ahead, they left the chamber.

After navigating through the warren of tunnels using a draft of fresh air as their guide, which they hoped would lead them to an exit, breathless from their sprint and flight, Griselda, Ellie and the two dogs halted by the exterior opening welcoming sunlight flooded through.

Griselda glanced around the Moleeikis grand entrance hall, but there was no sign of Crowe.

"I'll see if he's waiting outside." Ellie flittered through the tall doorway and returned a few moments later wearing a worried frown. "He's not there."

"Damn!" uttered, Griselda. If Crowe had gotten out, he would be waiting here for us. "He couldn't have made it. The Hobkrakkens must have got him."

"You don't know that," argued Ellie, unwilling to believe Crowe was dead. "He could have taken a wrong turn or be hiding somewhere."

Griselda shrugged. "Either way, we don't have the time to search the whole mountain for him. There must be miles of tunnels on multiple levels."

"We can use the dogs to track him," suggested Ellie.

"We would still have to find the start of his trail. That could take us all the way back to the mess hall. It is too far and too dangerous. No, time is running out. We need to focus on our primary objective and hope if Crowe is alive, which I sadly doubt, he finds a way out."

Though reluctant to leave without knowing Crowe's fate, Ellie recognized that Griselda was right. If the faeries invaded Hagstown, many would be killed. The fate of the many outweighed the fate of one. "Just in case he still lives and manages to escape, I'll leave him a message to let him know we're alive and have headed for the city. Maybe then he can catch us up."

"Be quick about it then," relented Griselda.

Ellie picked up a piece of rock and scratched an arrow pointing at the exit on the floor. Underneath she wrote, *G & E gone to the city. Find us.*

"That should do it," stated Ellie, admiring her handiwork.

"To the city then."

Calling the dogs to her, Ellie followed Griselda to the exit.

"It is a shame Crowe is no longer with us," commented Griselda.

"Yes, he's been a great help, which has surprised me. I'll miss him."

"As will I," muttered Griselda. "Without him, one of us will have to chop off the king's head. Worse than that, I've lost my ride."

Ellie rolled her eyes. "The city's not far now, so I expect you'll survive."

They headed through the entrance and left the horrors of the Underwurld behind.

Chapter 28

Roasted Rat

GRADUALLY REGAINING CONSCIOUSNESS, Crowe experienced a bobbing sensation. It slowly dawned on him that he was hanging from something and his limbs that were attached to it hurt. The last thing he recalled was falling down the feeding tube and the abrupt halt when the Hobkrakkens he fell with cushioned his fall. They hadn't been so fortunate when the unforgiving ground halted their plummets with cracks of broken bones and crushed bodies. He had then climbed off the pile of writhing, broken creatures, and turned toward a noise. He had briefly glimpsed a strange piggish-looking creature swinging a wooden club at his head, before feeling excruciating pain and then blackness until he had awoken a few moments ago.

As Crowe's faculties returned, his brain pounded as a result of the hard-swung club, causing him to wince from the pain every bouncing flop of his hung-back head brought. His nose wrinkled at the foul stench currently dwelling in his nostrils. Forcing his heavy eyelids apart, he focused his bleary eyes on the equally foul sight of a Hobkrakken's butt cheeks barely an arm's length from his face. Averting his gaze, Crowe cast his gaze skyward at the wooden stake resting on the creature's shoulder. A fresh wave of pain coursed through his fuddled brain when he raised his battered head and gazed at his limbs tied to the stout pole and another Hobkrakken supporting the far end.

Feeling tugs on his tail, he moved his head to the side. Three Hobkrakken young played with his unruly appendage. Although their creamy glazed-over eyes indicated them to be as blind as the adults, two of them had no trouble avoiding the tip of his tail the third whipped at them in the game they were enjoying.

He turned his attention to his predicament and wondered why he had been tied to a stake, where was he being taken and why haven't the savage Hobkrakkens killed and eaten him already? The last quandary was the only one he was pleased about.

Directing his gaze ahead past the smelly Hobkrakken currently scratching his grubby fingers at its equally grubby posterior, Crowe focused on the orange glow spilling from the opening they seemed to be heading for.

As they passed through the doorway, he noticed the two large guards either side of the entrance staring at him weren't blind, and neither were they Hobkrakkens. They were much worse and the same species as the one that had knocked him unconscious. All muscle, snout and a killing temperament if their cruel snarls and plethora of weapons they were decked out with were any indication. Glowering at the Hobkrakken at the front struggling with Crowe's weight, one guard prodded it savagely with the butt of his spear, almost causing the creature to stumble to the ground before it reclaimed its footing and increased its pace.

Sensing the nearby guards, the children abandoned the rat tail game they had been playing and fled in the opposite direction. The other guard slammed the thick wooden door closed. Its booming crash against the doorframe echoed around the chamber. Crowe narrowly avoided trapping the children's plaything in the door when he yanked his tail tip into the room. Wearing a disappointed expression brought about by his failed attempt to trap it in the door, the scowling guard jabbed Crowe in the side as punishment for spoiling his fun.

Yelping in pain from the blow, Crowe groaned when his smelly short-legged carriers banged his back on the stone steps as they rushed down them. When they sped across level ground at the base, Crowe gazed around the room lit by flaming torches dotted around the large chamber. The flesh-stripped bones scattered across the floor failed to instill any hope his wouldn't soon be joining them. The variety of skulls indicted whatever had stripped them clean of flesh wasn't fussy about what creature they ate. A plump rat like him would probably be a welcome special on the menu.

An enthusiastic clapping heralding his arrival seemed to indicate he had reached his destination, wherever that might be. His rough landing on the ground and the two scared Hobkrakken retreating to the side of the room confirmed it. When the weight of the stave rolled his limbs painfully to the ground, Crowe stared at the thing excited to see him. Though it was the same species as the intolerant hog guards, this individual was much larger and a whole lot uglier. Though unfamiliar with the creature or the name of its species, its excitement from his arrival probably didn't bode well for his continued existence.

What Crowe's terrified gaze beheld was a Trottersnipe, sometimes referred to by the lesser-informed as a HogGoblin, a forerunner of the later evolved Hobgoblin, but the two are vastly different. Trottersnipes were bigger, stronger, and extremely malicious. They hated vegetables of every description with a vengeance, especially green ones, and had an insatiable craving for flesh of any variety. It is rumored they would eat their own limbs if they became hungry enough.

Wearing a huge smile that turned his wide ugly mouth into a sneer, the self-proclaimed Trottersnipe dictator, and cruel ruler of the Hobkrakken, Gruntzswiller Bragsnort dragged his quivering bulk from his throne and over to the prize laid before him. He was of the murderous Bragsnort linage renowned for their laziness as much as their brutality;

their family motto was: *Why do it yourself when you can force someone else to. If they refuse, kill them and feast on their bones.* Making for a somewhat larger crest than decorum decreed. Crowe yelped when stubby fingers, each tipped with a hog's hoof, prodded his stomach and roughly groped the meatiness of his flesh.

Sliding a tongue over its salivating lips, the stinky beast moved to Crowe's head and stared him in the eyes. "I shall enjoy eating you, rat."

Almost gagging from the swine's foul breath whooshing over his face, Crowe was surprised he could understand a couple of words from the otherwise unintelligible, guttural grunts, *eating* and *shall*. Fearing the hog monster was contemplating eating him now, Crow struggled against his bonds and received a swift kick to the spine from the guard that had lunged forward to administer the punishment.

Settling down to avoid another kick, Crowe turned his head to the sound of clacking and watched a tall, skinny hog creature slowly approaching. He sported a long, scraggly white beard, and saggy wrinkles covered his face like gnarled tree bark. His acutely bent back necessitated him to raise his head to look forward. After hobbling slowly over, using a twisted staff for support, which he jabbed in Crowe's stomach when he spoke. "Hmmm, delicious and a fine feast for our dictator and his closest trusted allies to partake of."

Gruntzswiller scowled at his advisor vying for a taste of rat flesh.

Sensing the dictator's contemptuous gaze upon him, Gristlekrak Jerkmolder—no noble lineage to speak of— quickly directed the tyrant's thoughts to other matters less threatening to his wellbeing. Throwing his spindly arms up in an exaggerated display of mock bewilderment, he exclaimed, "But how will such a large piece of meat be cooked?"

"We'll spit roast it," stated Gruntzswiller. "Have it taken to the dungeon while the fire and roasting spit is prepared."

As the dictator returned to his throne, Gristlekrak snapped his fingers at the two Hobkrakken rat bearers. "To the dungeons with it."

While Gristlekrak headed back to his position beside the throne at an excruciatingly slow, hobbling pace, the two Hobkrakken bearers rushed over, heaved the rat-weighted pole onto their shoulders and transported Crowe speedily from the room.

Gruntzswiller's hungry eyes followed the rat's departure. He couldn't wait to tuck into its juicy meat. Rat was his favorite food, with chicken that tasted like rat, coming a close second. If there were such a thing as a rat the size of a Great Spiklephant, he would be in hog heaven. Rat meat would be a welcome change from faerie flesh. Though his Hobkrakken minions headed into the city most nights to forage and hunt for food, they mostly returned with faeries that were so small and scrawny he needed handfuls to alleviate his hunger. Aware his Trottersnipe comrades would expect a share of the rat feast, he'd make sure their helpings were considerably less than his own. Rationed to his closest aides, he could assure the prime meat would last for a couple days, three if he was especially stingy with their portions. Aware of the consequences he would reap upon them, they wouldn't dare complain. He smiled; it was fun being a ruthless dictator. His army of Hobkrakkens, who were also a never-ending supply of food as they bred like rats—shame they didn't taste like them—did his bidding without question. Life was good.

The Trottersnipes had stumbled across this refuge when they had been forced to flee from their homeland when Gruntzswiller's coup to overthrow the current dictator had failed miserably. Some backstabbing Trottersnipe out to line his own pockets had betrayed him. When he had walked into the trap set for him, he had barely escaped with his life and a few of his loyal followers.

They had roamed these strange lands for months before coming across these old mines. The discovery of the blind Hobkrakkens living in its lowest depths, which they had promptly enslaved, was a bonus Gruntzswiller had never expected. Any that complained about their harsh treatment were swiftly silenced and added to the day's menu.

With only sixteen followers, death, usually a result of his murderous temperament, had caused their ranks to slowly dwindle. To increase their numbers, he had ordered one of his subordinates to breed with a female Hobkrakken. The result, neither Trottersnipe nor Hobkrakken, had been far from satisfactory. Because of the constant stream of snot oozing from its skew-whiff snout, Gristlekrak had labeled it a Snotterkrakken. Gruntzswiller had used stronger expletives. An affront to his eyes, he had it banished it to the deepest dungeon where he wouldn't have to be assaulted by the sight of the grotesque abomination again. He shivered with revulsion when the long-repressed image of its form again intruded into his thoughts.

Seeking a distraction, Gruntzswiller turned to Gristlekrak who had just arrived beside him a little out of breath from his short walk. Deciding a little fun was in order, he discreetly tore a button from his food-stained robe and rolled it along the floor. "Oh, dear, I've popped a button. Be a good hog and fetch it, Gris."

Gristlekrak stared at the button spinning in a circle before clattering to the floor. Though only a few yards away, it seemed like leagues to him. "I could, but if you require the button urgently, it would be quicker to ask a guard to fetch it."

Gruntzswiller shook his massive head. "No hurry, Gris. Take your time."

He watched Gristlekrak take his first step on his long journey and grinned. Being a dictator was good. Sighing, he sat back and ran a hand over the skulls and bones design fashioned into the arms of his throne. Carved from a solid block of stone for him by the Hobkrakken, it was surprisingly well made and ornate given their blindness. Relaxing while he watched Gristlekrak struggle across the floor, he thought about the upcoming rat feast.

Chapter 29

Imprisoned

AS CROWE WAS UNCOMFORTABLY conveyed through dark and dingy corridors by his uncaring carriers, they passed Hobkrakkens running in the opposite direction with armloads of firewood. When they were forced to a halt and to hug to the wall to avoid the four Hobkrakkens heading in the opposite direction transporting a wide load, Crowe stared fearfully at the iron spit they carried between them and winced at the sharp pole the roasting meat would be impaled on. His fate was no longer a mystery.

After being carried down umpteen flights of stairs, each level becoming colder, gloomier and damper than the previous, they moved through a corridor lit by flaming torches distributed along its length. On either side were rows of grim, depressing cells.

Hearing something approach, Dungborn Shittinstiff, a Trottersnipe banished to the deep dark realm as jailor for a year; punishment for spilling the king's wine during an extremely robustious night of drinking and debauchery, put down the book he had been reading and went to see who had disturbed him.

Even by his species' lower-than-low standards, Dungborn was a particularly loathsome example of its male population. He glanced at the rat carried by two skinny Hobkrakkens and called them to a halt with a raised hand. After briefly examining the captive, he ushered the rat-bearers into an empty cell where they promptly dumped the prisoner on the slimy floor, slid the stake free and departed.

So long had he been without decent food, the craving to feast on delicious rat flesh overwhelmed Dungborn as he eyed the meaty rodent. Knowing the only part of it he would receive would be the delicious aroma of its sizzling fat wafting down to him, which would likely drive him even crazier, he considered taking a bite. However, fearing the king's malicious wrath if he discovered someone had taken a taste of his feast without permission, if he did risk it, it would have to from somewhere where it would not be noticed. He focused on the rat's head; its tongue perhaps?

With hunger driving his thoughts and suppressing the dangers of his inadvisable action, Dungborn approached the bound creature's head. He slipped the grubby knife from the waistband of the filthy cloth wrapped around his midriff which probably had initially been a more extensive piece of clothing, but so little now remained it was difficult to tell. Staring at the rat staring back at him, Dungborn worked out the steps needed to secure the dainty morsel he coveted. *A swift, powerful kick to the head to stun the rat, crouch, force open its jaws, grab the tongue, stretch it out, a quick slice of his blade and the deed would be completed. Then return to his room to eat it. Simple.*

Snarling at the creature he suspected by the drool dribbling from its cracked lips and the dirty dagger in its hand was up to no good, he watched it approach. When it launched a foot at his head, he jerked his mouth at it and chomped down his jaws.

Screaming in pain and realizing his chance of a snack had failed miserably, Dungborn hopped to the door leaving a trail of blood.

Sniffing up a long stringy drool of snot and smelling the delicious aroma of blood, the creature imprisoned in the cell opposite opened its eyes and glimpsed the rat as Dungborn hopped into the corridor and locked the door. Its tongue caressed its teeth at the sight of the red goodness leaking from the jailor's toeless foot.

Feeling evil eyes upon him, Dungborn glanced fearfully through the rusty bars at the two small orbs in the darkness, reflecting the torchlight that failed to reach the back of the cell and quickly hopped away.

Listening to the Jailor's painfilled moans, hopping footstep, and the jangle of keys moving away along the corridor, Crowe spat out the filthy, foul tasting toes covered in years of accumulated muck so thick it was crusty, and retched the blood and foulness from his mouth. After he had evicted as much as he could without a prolonged rinse with a powerful detergent, he turned his thoughts to escape. Jerking his body back and forth, he managed to turn and view the complete cell and, in the process, scrub a clean streak in the squalor covering the floor. The windowless damp walls were streaked with green slime and brown fouler substances Crowe was reluctant to dwell on. Manacles fastened to the end of chains hanging from the back wall waited patiently for their next guests. The yellowed bones of their previous attendees scattered on the floor below revealed a worrying lack of care by their jailor.

A movement in the corner where walls and ceiling met, focused his attention on a squirming creamy mass of wriggling creatures that had the appearance of giant maggots. He followed a trail of them down the wall and noticed a bunch of them chewing on waste deposited by a previous guest of Dungborn.

What Crowe observed was a marvelous addition of the dungeon's designers. The maggot species' scientific name was Excremental but was often referred to by any prisoners unlucky enough to be forced to eat them or starve to death, as Crapmaggots. They happily fed on waste, human or otherwise, whether it be solid, liquid or any consistency in-between, they lapped it up. Not only were they waste disposals, but also food for the unfortunate prisoners.

Though no creature who had tasted them would call them flavorsome, they offered essential protein, albeit with an adverse bad breath side effect. Their inclusion saved the jailor from the messy and unpleasant job of slopping out the cells and feeding the prisoners. If the incarcerated were thirsty, they lapped up the moisture seeping from the walls. The cells were ingeniously self-sufficient.

Turning away from the maggots he suspected he soon might be providing with fresh sustenance if his churning stomach was any indication, Crowe considered his options. If Griselda had survived and returned to the Mess Hall to find him gone, she would have assumed he'd fled and would have gone to catch up with him. When, and if, she realized her mistake, she would believe he had been killed and eaten, something about to ring true, meaning he couldn't expect rescue from that quarter. He was on his own. Which worried him immensely.

Thinking that getting his limbs free was a first good step, Crowe moved his front paws and mouth closer together until he could scratch at them with his incisors. Jerking his head up and down repeatedly, he proceeded to slice through the rope.

As soon as the rope parted, Crowe unwrapped it from his limbs. He then curled into a ball to untie the binding around his back legs. Lacking an opposable thumb, Crowe struggled to unknot the rope pulled tight by his weight hanging on it. When he finally succeeded and was free, he stretched out his aching back and shook his limbs to get the blood circulating again.

Turning his thoughts to escape, he moved to the back wall where he had noticed the crumbling cement between the stone blocks. The crack led up to one of the chains attached by a metal plate to the wall. Hoping there was a corridor on the other side, he gripped the chain and tugged. After a few tries, he managed to yank the stone free. It dropped to the floor with a booming thud. Worried the jailor had heard the crash and would come to investigate, Crowe cocked an ear to the door. Detecting no hopping footstep or jangling of keys, he made short work of dislodging more. A large rock, too heavy to lift out, posed a problem. A shove with his shoulder slid the stone in a few inches. A few more painful shoulder jolts pushed it right through, and it dropped from sight. Breathing in the fresher air that wafted through the hole now big enough for him to fit his head through, Crowe pondered the lacking sound of the rock crashing to the floor on the other side. He poked his head through and looking down, discovered the reason why. The wall was built on the edge of a ravine. The darkness filling the void hid its depth. The distant echoing crash of the dislodged rock hitting bottom a few moments later indicated it was too deep to jump down. Turning his head left and right revealed no handy ledge against the wall he could sidle along to safety.

Disappointed his first escape attempt had failed, Crowe gazed around the cell for another solution. Deciding the ancient door might be his best option, he crossed to it and peered through the small, barred window. When his restricted view revealed no sign of his jailor, he shook the bars. The door rattled but remained firm. Doubting shoulder-barging it would do any good, he was about to examine the door and frame for any weaknesses when he noticed eyes staring at him from the gloom shrouding the cell directly across from him. The floor to ceiling bars along the front with a door set in the middle allowed him full view inside.

Wondering what species of creature its occupant was and if it might be able to help him with his escape somehow, Crowe called out to it. "Hi. I know you probably can't understand me, but if by some slim chance you can, how about we both try to escape?"

When no response was forthcoming, Crowe stepped back from the door to examine it and nudged one of Dungborn's toes, sending it into a spiraling roll. Thinking he might be able to make friends with his fellow prisoner by offering it food, he gingerly picked up the toe, moved to the door and stuck his paw through.

"Are you hungry? I've got some food if you want it," he called out, watching the eyes.

A deep sniff—more like a growl in reverse—came from the darkness.

Crowe waved the toe about to spread its foul scent and then hoping the creature wasn't fussy about what it ate or too hygienically minded, lobbed the grubby toe. The disgusting digit clanged against one of the metal bars and dropped to the floor where the light from the flickering torch ended, and the darkness began. Focusing on the eyes, Crowe followed them when the creature shuffled over to the unappetizing treat. Another sniff from the darkness was followed by a clawed hand snatching up the toe. Crowe grimaced at the crunching of bone coming from the gloom.

Believing it to be the first step to making friends with his fellow captive, Crowe retrieved another toe from the floor and threw it into the creature's cell. It sped through the bars and bounced across the floor until it was snatched up and stuffed into its mouth. Though he had three more toes available, Crowe decided to save them as bribes for later. Pondering how he could enlist the creature's help, his eyes rested on the manacles. A few moments of deep thought produced an idea. He separated the chain from the stone block and tied the wall fixing end around the bars. Dangling the other end in his paw poked through the viewing window, he swung it at the opposite cell.

"Grab it and pull, and I'll give you more food," he instructed.

The owner of the puzzled eyes looking at him from the shadows remained still.

Wondering how to make the creature understand what he wanted it to do, Crowe conceived a plan he was particularly pleased with and, if he said so himself, quite clever and a little bit cunning.

He forced one of Dungborn's toes in a chain link near the barred window and pointed at it. "Food."

The growling sniff from the darkness indicated food was something the creature understood, or it at least smelt the disgusting aroma emanating from the never washed digit and found it appetizing.

Crowe swung the chain back and forth and lobbed the end at the creature's cell. It clanged against the bars and dropped. The beast lunged from the darkness and grabbed it before it struck the floor.

Seeing the creature for the first time, and probably every time after if he was unlucky enough to set eyes on it again, Crowe experienced shock, revulsion and the urge to scratch out his eyes to remove the offensive vision. The thing was so grotesque it slandered ugliness. Though the creature's face bore some resemblance to a mishmash of Hobkrakken and Trottersnipe, it had the appearance of being pulled inside out and twisted upside down before being bashed repeatedly against a hard surface for a prolonged time. One of its arms was a withered stump and the other overlong and bulging with muscles. Its short stumpy legs were way out of proportion to its massive, rotund and wrinkled body bristling with patches of random spiky hair adorning its flabby frame. With the absence of a neck, the enormous squashed head rested between its shoulders.

Brought back to his senses by metal clangs, Crowe watched Snotterkrakken tug the chain taut; its biceps bulging with the strain.

The creature grunted.

The door creaked.

Dungborn yelled.

After retiring to his room, a cell he had decorated with a few items to make his yearlong penitence a little more comfortable; a bed formed from a wooden pallet decked with lice-ridden straw, a small table beside the bed to rest a candle holder and his only book, *The Adventures of Licky and Alfie.* Reading it again and again always made him smile. The humorous story and colorful pictures he never tired of looking at were the only pleasure he garnered from his miserable existence down here. Dungborn grabbed a piece of material that was more filth than cloth and bandaged his bleeding foot.

Wincing when he knotted the makeshift bandage already sending germs flowing into his bloodstream, Dungborn admired his handiwork and wondered if his toes would grow back. Confident they would, he pulled the cork from the bottle of faerie wine he had pilfered on one of his night forays into the city for food that wasn't crapmaggot and took a long swig. He removed it from his lips and cocked a grimy, wax-caked ear to the door at the sound of jangling chains. Believing another prisoner was being brought down for him to care for, and marveling how busy it was today, he hobbled out into the corridor.

"What in hell's name ya think ya be doing?" Dungborn yelled when he saw what two of his three prisoners were up to.

Unable to see the perplexed jailor, Crowe thought it would be obvious to anyone what they were up to, they were trying to escape. He then realized he'd understood what had been said. *Was the hog creature speaking English? Doubtful.* Assuming faerie magic must be responsible, he stepped back from the creaking door when it began to bulge from the strain his partner in crime applied to it. The lock shrieked as it tried to keep the door secured. The bars groaned when they bent. Wood cracked and splintered. The door rattled into its frame when the window bars exploded from the door and clanged against Snotterkrakken's cell bars. Expecting the door to have been pulled from its hinges, Crowe gawked in dismay at the splintered opening. Although now without its bars, it was still too small for him to fit through. He sighed when the jailor's face appeared in the opening and stared in shock at the destruction to the door under his charge.

"Wanton vandalism, that is," accused Dungborn angrily, fingering the splintered window frame. He yelped when a sliver of wood stabbed his finger and glared at Crowe. "You're gonna 'ave to pay fer that."

Still shocked that he understood what the smelly jailor said, Crowe hid the destruction he had caused to the back wall with his body and replied in what he assumed was English, but with the unfathomable way magic worked in this Realm, might be Hobkrakken. "That, my grubby little friend, will be rather difficult as I suspect I am shortly to be joining the flesh-stripped bones littering your leader's floor."

Dungborn rubbed his chin as he pondered the dilemma. If the news of the escape attempt and the resulting damage to the door reached the dictator's ears, he would be the one that paid; in pain and suffering.

"However," Crowe continued when it seemed his jailor had understood. "I have a solution you might find acceptable."

Dungborn looked at his prisoner hopefully. "Ya do?"

Crowe nodded. "With my help, we could swap another door deeper in this disgusting, dank place you call home, for this one, and then no one will be the wiser, as I expect it's not a place any of the foul creatures living above would be keen to explore."

Dungborn nodded knowingly. "Ya right there. No one comes ta visit me. Months at a time I'm on me lonesome down 'ere."

"So, my stinky friend, unlock the door and we'll get started."

Reaching for his keys hung at his waist, Dungborn halted and looked at Crowe, his eyes narrowed with mistrust. "I knows what ya be doing. Ya be tricking me. I comes in there, ya overpowers me and kills me before ya runs off."

Crowe sighed. His jailor wasn't as stupid as he looked, which was a surprise. "Not necessarily, I might just walk away fast."

As the puzzled expression formed on Dungborn's features, Crowe rushed at the door and shot a grasping paw through at the jailor's neck. If he could strangle him and force him to hand over the keys, he'd be free.

Dungborn though had other ideas and dodged out of reach.

"Ya has ta gets up earlier than that ta catch Dungborn Shittinstiff out," bragged Dungborn, whose moment of smugness waned when he noticed the rat grinning.

The low, rumbling growl behind him slowly turned his head. He whimpered at the sight of Snotterkrakken's snot-dripping face pressed against the bars close enough for them both to smell each other's rancid breaths. Noticing one of his missing toes between Snotterkrakken's teeth, his bladder opened when it was crunched into swallowable chunks. He gasped for air when a hairy hand grabbed his neck in a vicelike grip.

Peering through the opening of his cell, Crowe watched Dungborn's life drain from his bulging eyes. When the jailor fell limp, his murderer tried to pull the corpse through the bars, but, like a square peg fitting in a round hole, it wasn't happening.

Crowe jabbed a paw at the jailor's keys. "The keys! Give them to me, and I'll set you free. Then you can eat him."

Snotterkrakken's look at Crowe was filled with incomprehension. When the jailor's arm was dragged through the bars, its mouth was filled with Dungborn's flesh. With the limb—including the bones—devoured, the ravenous Snotterkrakken again tugged at the corpse to get the main feast into its cell. Unable to resist the pressure, the cracking of Dungborn's skull echoed along the corridor. His ribs were next to crack. The pelvis proved the most stubborn and only after a good, hard yank, did Dungborn finally enter Snotterkrakken's lair.

Crowe turned his disgusted gaze to the bunch of keys dislodged from the jailor's waist clanging to the floor. Giving up on any help from his murderous friend, he pondered on how he could reach them.

Chapter 30

Appetizer

IT WAS WITH HIS usual impatience that Gruntzswiller observed the spit being prepared. The Hobkrakkens tasked with its construction, jumped at every instruction their Dictator barked at them, causing them to make even more mistakes. By the time it was finished, and the logs at its base were set to flame, every one of them wanted to roast their cruel leader on it.

Rising from his chair, Gruntzswiller crossed to the table placed beside the spit and began dipping a trotter finger in the oils and basting sauces prepared to spread over the rats roasting hide. Tasting each and finding three he liked, he indicated his choice to his Trottersnipe underling responsible for cooking the feast.

"A fine choice my evil dictator," beamed Bogsniffer. "Those flavors will enhance the delicious taste of succulent rat flesh and yet, not overpower it. Under your guidance, it will prove to be a magnificent feast."

Gruntzswiller scowled at his subordinate Trottersnipe. "Well, Bogsniffer, if your cooking is as finely honed as your groveling, we are indeed in for a tasty banquet."

Bogsniffer bowed. "Of that, sir, you can be assured."

Returning to his throne, Gruntzswiller kicked the staff his sleeping advisor rested on while he slept; he dozed off at least ten times a day.

Springing awake as quickly as his frail body and mind would allow, Gristlekrak was brought back to the real world and hid his disappointment that the cruel, and at times, creative torturing he had been administering to Gruntzswiller, had only been a pleasant dream.

"Good sleep, Gristle?" asked Gruntzswiller, grinning.

"It was, and I'm hoping my dream comes true."

"Raunchy was it?" inquired Gruntzswiller.

Gristlekrak smiled. "It certainly was for me." He glanced at the fire crackling away beneath the spit. When it settled to red embers, it would be ready for a rat roasting. "Shall I fetch dinner?"

Gruntzswiller's expression turned to shock. "I'd starve to death if you went. It'd probably take you a year. Send someone quicker."

"I didn't plan on going myself." Gristlekrak laughed at the thought. "I'd likely flop to the ground dead from exhaustion before I got anywhere near the dungeons."

Though tempted to change his mind by that pleasurable outcome and send him, Gruntzswiller resisted. He desired roasted rat meat far more than Gristlekrak's demise. However, after the rat was eaten...

Pointing his staff at one of the dictator's Trottersnipe followers positioned around the throne, Gristlekrak stated his order. "Take two Hobkrakkens and go fetch the rat. And be quick about it. Your dictator is hungry."

Muttering something that included, *he's always bloody hungry...* and, *wring Gristlekrak's scrawny neck and suck his brain out through a straw*, the guard headed for the door with Gristlekrak staring daggers at his back.

Gristlekrak added the Trottersnipe's name, Offalslick, to his mental list of those to be tortured in his dreams and turned to Gruntzswiller. "Your bidding has been done, oh great one. Soon we will be breathing in the delicious aroma of roasting rat."

"Bring me my appetizer. I'll snack while I'm waiting."

Bowing his head slightly, Gristlekrak turned to a door set in the side of the room. When a clap of his bony hands failed to produce the desired effect, he stamped the staff on the floor and shouted, "Bring forth the dictator's table."

The door opened immediately. With one at each corner, the Hobkrakkens that had been waiting for the command jogged in carrying a large table set for one.

Gruntzswiller rubbed his hands together and slurped in the drool oozing over his lips. As soon as the table was placed before him, he lifted the lid from the large serving platter and hungrily ran his eyes over his appetizer; six faeries presented in six coffin-shaped serving dishes. He speared one with a fork and examined it; de-winged and lightly charred, just how he liked them. It was just a shame they weren't bigger. Sighing with pleasure from the satisfying crunch when he bit off its head, he held it between its teeth and sucked out the brain. After it had slithered down his throat like a succulent slimy oyster, he crunched the head, shoved in the rest of the body and chewed.

Salivating from the aroma of the grilled delicacies, Gruntzswiller's not-so-loyal followers watched him eat. All thought how good it must be to be the dictator, and all wanted their turn. Each wondering if they could harvest the support of the others if they moved against him, they looked at each other with knowing winks and nods.

Noticing the Trottersnipes exchanging glances, Gristlekrak rolled his eyes. They had been doing the same thing for years and yet not one of them had made a move to kill Gruntzswiller and usurp his position. He eyed the feasting hog and wondered if he still had it in him for such a risky maneuver. A recurring painful spasm that clawed along his spine and distorted his face into an agonized grimace indicated he probably hadn't.

With faerie legs dangling from his lips, Gruntzswiller glanced at Gristlekrak. "If you insist on making those faces while I'm eating, then turn away. You're putting me off me appetizer."

"Sorry, sir." Contorted in agony, Gristlekrak turned away. He couldn't wait to get back to his dreams, which in his present mood, were going to be particularly brutal for some.

Chapter 31

Jailbreak

WHEN THE INKLING OF an idea formed, Crowe dragged his gaze away from the out-of-reach keys, grabbed the end of his tail and fed it under the door. Though an awkward maneuver with his back pressed to the door, he twisted his face to the opening and ordered the tip of his tail to move to the keys. The unruly appendage thrummed across the bars of the monstrous creature's cell opposite. Distracted from its feast, Snotterkrakken jerked its ugly face to the sound, the morsel of Dungborn hanging from its bloody lips quivered with the movement. After glancing at Crowe's face pressed to the splintered opening opposite, it returned to its meal.

Urging the tail to do as it was instructed, Crowe swished it along the floor and called it to a halt when it brushed against the keys. With his intention to thread the tail through the key ring, he lifted it up and bent the tip into a hook. Attempting to manipulate it through the ring was like holding a high-pressure water hose on full blast held six feet from the end. Swaying erratically under his control, he dived the tip at the keys as it passed. To his utter amazement, the tail slipped through the key ring and lifted it from the ground.

Crowe's delight faded when his fellow prisoner crashed against the bars of its cell and darted a hand at his tail. Scarcely jerking it from the Snotterkrakken's grasping reach in time, the keys clanged against the wall on his side. Keeping his obviously appetizing appendage out of the slobbering creature's reach, he scraped it, and the keys, along the wall toward the door. As soon as they were at the opening, he twisted his shoulder, fed a paw through the window and grabbed them. He pulled his tail into the cell and fed each key into the keyhole until one sprung the lock. He pulled the door open and stepped out. He was free. His head shot to the approaching footsteps; someone was coming.

Snotterkrakken snarled at those about to make their appearance around the corner. Crowe needed a distraction while he made his escape, and his ugly vicious friend would be the one to provide it.

Conscious of the imminent arrival of the footsteps' owners, Crowe collected the keys from his cell door. Keeping as far away as possible from the creature pressed against its bars watching him, he unlocked its cell door and pulled it open until it butted against his open cell door to form a barrier across the corridor between him, Snotterkrakken, and those about to arrive. Though the Snotterkrakken stared at the open doorway, it made no move to exit the gloomy, dank cell that had been its home for as long as it could remember.

Crowe directed his gaze upon the hog creature that appeared at the end of the corridor and then at the two accompanying Hobkrakkens carrying the long pole they would use to transport him to his painful demise. Surprise registered on their faces at seeing him out of his cell.

Offalslick's horror at seeing the rat he had been sent to fetch free, morphed into acute fear bordering on panic with the realization of the disastrous consequences that would befall him if it escaped. Gruntzswiller's reaction when he was informed rat was off the menu, didn't bear thinking about, but at the very least, if he were lucky, he'd be spit roasted alive and eaten in its place as punishment.

"He's escaping! Get him," screamed Offalslick, sprinting forward.

Acutely aware they'd also be blamed if the dictator's meal failed to arrive, the two Hobkrakkens dropped the pole and rushed to help procure its capture.

In an attempt to entice the Snotterkrakken from its home, Crowe nipped into his cell and snatched up the last of Dungborn's toes, the now only recognizable parts of him. He returned to the corridor and with the three creatures almost upon him, lobbed the filthy digits onto the floor the far side of the makeshift barrier.

Spying the tasty snacks, Snotterkrakken lunged from its cell and crashed into Offalslick, sending him slamming against the wall. Turning to the frightened shrieks, it shot out its good arm, grabbed the nearest Hobkrakken, and squeezed. The snapping of its neck echoed like a gunshot. Noticing the second Hobkrakken fleeing back along the corridor, Snotterkrakken threw its dead comrade at it. The corpse missile slammed into the fleeing creature's back and sent it sprawling. Its face connecting with the floor knocked it unconscious; merciful oblivion for the desecration about to be reaped upon it and its dead comrade.

Dazed by his abrupt meeting with the wall, Offalslick staggered about the corridor. When he unwittingly kicked the toe from the Snotterkrakken's grasp, the creature snarled at him. Noticing Snotterkrakken for the first time, Offalslick stared into the ugliest and by far the most grotesque thing he'd ever had the misfortune to lay his eyes upon. He turned and fled.

In an awkward, lunging gait, Snotterkrakken's stubby legs carried it after the fleeing Trottersnipe. Its deformed elongated arm swiped at Offalslick, who screamed from the claws raking deep gashes down his back. In a stumbling, falling motion, Snotterkrakken jumped onto Offalslick and

271

knocked him to the floor. Offalslick's bones cracked, and his lungs almost burst from his throat when the obese creature flattened him. Unable to breathe, the last thing he was conscious of was the creature looking hungrily at his finger trotters and bending his arm back until it snapped so he could bite them off one at a time. After enjoying the finger snacks, Snotterkrakken turned its ravenous hunger to Offalslick's more meaty parts. It had never eaten so well. Licking the dribbling blood-tainted snot from his lips, it tucked in.

Crowe had witnessed little of Offalslick's ghastly demises or the two Hobkrakkens, as he had fled in the opposite direction almost as soon as they had appeared. When he rushed past the gloomy stinking cells, he noticed a face, drawn by the commotion, pressed against the bars of one of them. He skidded to a halt on the slimy floor and returned to the occupied cell.

Frightened and shocked by the reappearance of the large rodent she had watched run past a few moments ago, the prisoner stepped back from the bars and received a second shock when it spoke.

"Arabella?"

Wondering how the rat knew her name, Arabella stared at it worryingly.

Crow put his front paws on the bars and peered through. "Don't be scared. It's me, Crowe."

Not so long ago she would have thought it impossible, but after what she had witnessed in Hagsdell manor and since her kidnapping and incarceration, she knew anything was possible, however unbelievable. "But you're a rat, and you're talking."

"You're in the faeries world now, expect the unexpected and go with it or you'll likely not last long." He shot a look along the corridor at the gruesome feeding sounds Snotterkrakken produced. "I'll explain later, but first I need to get you out of there. Hold on."

To avoid alerting the feeding leviathan to his approach, Crowe moved stealthily back along the passage. Trying to ignore the grisly sounds of chomping flesh, cracking bones, and slurping tongue, he reached for the keys he had left in the keyhole and grasping the bunch to prevent them from chinking against each other, he slowly eased the key out. He grimaced when it scraped on the lock and froze when the creature slowly turned his head.

With blood mingled with snot dribbling down its face, Snotterkrakken glanced at Crowe for a few moments. After a failed attempt at a smile for the one that had introduced it to the delicious taste of pork and set it free, it turned away and continued eating.

Sighing with relief, Crowe retrieved the keys and rushed back to Arabella.

As he tried each key in the lock, Arabella pressed her head against the bars and peered at the strange figure along the corridor. "What is that thing?"

Crowe shrugged as he tried another key. "I'd be surprised if anyone knew. It seems like a combination of more than one species." He glanced at its distant form. "Just another poor creature suffering through no fault of its own I should imagine." The lock clicked. Crowe pulled the door open. "Now let's get out of here before more of those creature's intent on having me for dinner arrive, a fate you might also have been destined for."

Arabella stepped from her prison and looked at the feasting creature. "How will we get out with that thing blocking our way?"

"I'm hoping there's another exit in the other direction. "Crowe crouched on all fours. "Climb on, and we'll get going."

Arabella looked at the saddle. "You sure?"

"I am. We can travel faster if you're riding me and if anything attacks it'll attack me first."

Arabella smiled as she climbed onto his back. "That's very chivalrous of you."

"Yes, I thought so too. Now hold on and be ready for anything." Crowe sprinted forward.

After licking the last remnants of flesh and blood from a thigh bone, Snotterkrakken dropped it onto the pile of similar stripped bones and burped. Still hungry, it shuffled over to the two Hobkrakkens. When it prodded them with a finger to find the meatiest parts, one stirred. A hammer blow from its fist exploded its skull and sprayed the corridor with blood and brain. Satisfied the creature was dead, Snotterkrakken tore off an arm and chomped off a large piece of flesh, which was promptly spat out. It tasted worse than the Crapmaggots it had been forced to survive on for years, and taste-wise bore no comparison to the flavorsome Trottersnipe flesh. Craving more pork, it moved along the corridor its bulk almost filled in search of some.

Chapter 32

Raiding Party

After fleeing through maze-like corridors, Crowe halted at a junction. When a glance both ways revealed nothing to distinguish the merits of either, he turned his head to look at Arabella. "I guess it's pot luck, so I'm thinking of heading right."

Arabella shrugged. "I'm way out of my depth here, so I'll go along with whatever mad scheme you come up with if it gets me back home to my normal, uneventful life."

"Amen to that. You wouldn't believe half the things I've seen since entering this world," uttered Crowe, heading along the passage.

"I'm riding on a talking rat who's actually a human, through dungeons located in the realm of the faeries. Believe me, my disposition of disbelief has been radically altered, and now I'll believe anything."

Crowe headed along the right-hand passage.

A short distance later, he halted at the bottom of a staircase that spiraled up. He cocked an ear and sniffed the foul air drifting down. Believing it to be clear of any menace, Crowe ascended. The staircase opened onto another corridor with a choice of three directions, left, right, and straight across. As he considered his options, he focused his senses on the approaching voices and footsteps drifting from the passage directly opposite. Backing down the stairs until the curve hid them, they waited.

"A good raid it was," stated Spewspawn, glancing at the faerie corpses, crates, and lingering on the barrels of faerie wine they'd pilfered from the city. "And we only lost three Hobkrakken to the Slitherings this time."

"Yessum, hardly any at all," agreed Jockelstrap, also casting his coveting eyes on the barrels. "I 'as an inkling two of them there casks of wine will go missing afore Gruntzswiller gets his greedy paws on 'em."

"Too damn right," moaned Spewspawn. "It's not fair that we takes all the risks entering the city, murdering faeries for his table and stealing stuff, and he damn well goes and hogs most of it, leaving us, his loyal followers he swore he'd look after, with a few measly scraps to fight over."

"Ain't fair is right," agreed Jockelstrap. "About time one of us slit the greedy hog's throat and took his place." He turned to his comrade. "You'd make a much better leader than that gluttonous pig. You should kill 'im, it's ya hell given right."

Smiling at the thought of becoming the dictator, Spewspawn smiled. "Yeah, ya be right, Jocky. I'd be a great, and a fair to my friends type of leader. Ya knows what, I might just do that when I see 'im next. Slit his flabby throat, and then we'll roast his fat meaty rump at a celebration feast."

"Yous can count on me, Spew. I'm behind ya all the way."

"I knows ya will be mate. But first, we'd better 'urry up and get this stuff back for greedy paws to pick over. We're already late getting back, and we all knows how his highness hates to be kept waiting." He savagely prodded the Hobkrakken weighed down with a large chest in front of him. "Faster ya lazy lot of good-fer-nuffinks."

Increasing their pace, the raiding party emerged from the passage and turned right.

Contemplating what he had overheard, Crowe waited until their footsteps had faded before stepping out from the stairwell. "That was a raiding party returning from the city with their spoils." He looked in the direction they had come from. "That means there must be a way out in that direction."

"You actually understand what they said?" inquired Arabella in surprise. "It was all gibberish to me."

"I did, although I didn't when I first arrived here. I assume the longer us humans are in this world, the more we understand it and the creatures dwelling here. Probably some sort of built-in magic so everyone can understand everyone else. You wait and see; you'll soon be conversing fluently with the foulest of creatures." Crowe headed along the passage the raiding party had emerged from.

"Great, I can't wait," muttered Arabella, gripping the saddle when her ride jerked forward.

Snotterkrakken's snotty nose wasn't the best at sniffing out scents, but its addition of four ears, two Hobkrakken and two Trottersnipe, though lopsided and positioned oddly, including one protruding from its heavily wrinkled forehead, compensated for its slime-choked nasal passages. Twitching with every sound that drifted through the levels, it slowly homed in on them and was led to stone steps rising toward the sounds. Undaunted by the narrowness of the stairway, it hauled its ample bulk up the steps, rubbing away the slime oozing from the walls in the process. On reaching the top, it plopped from the stairwell with a slithering squelch of slime-greased flesh and turned its hungry attention upon the figures it glimpsed disappearing around a curve in the corridor. It grinned serial-killer-like at the sight of the delicious hog at the back. Keen to tuck in, it goaded its short legs into a sprint and darted after its food in a gangly, loping motion that threatened to topple it onto his gut with every step.

Still picturing himself sat on the throne with his loyal subjects attending to his every whim, Spewspawn was brought from his imagined dictatorship by thumping footsteps coming up behind him.

"What ya think that be?" asked Jockelstrap, peering apprehensively back along the corridor.

Spewspawn was contemplating the same conundrum. "If I didn't knows better, I'd say it was one of those giant doubled-trunked Spiklephants that live over the mountains, but I ain't never seen one round 'ere and no way it'd fit in these passages."

"Maybe a baby one would?" offered Jockelstrap.

Fretting about the floor that jumped with every footstep, Spewspawn turned to his friend. "Whatever it is, I'm picturing something big and heavy with whopping great feet, so I suggest most forcefully we moves before it tramples us."

"Good idea," agreed Jockelstrap. "That's why you'll make a good leader. Ya got them there brains I've heard rumors about."

"And yet ya stands there motionless," stated Spewspawn, giving his friend a forceful shove. "Run!"

Barging aside the Hobkrakkens impeding his rush from danger when he passed, Jockelstrap had the foresight to grab a cask of wine before whatever was coming arrived. The loudness of its footsteps and the increased floor trembles indicted it was almost upon them.

Admiring his comrade's intuitive action in the face of danger, Spewspawn also snatched a barrel from a surprised Hobkrakken's grasp and fled with the precious liquid gripped firmly in his arms.

The perplexed blind Hobkrakkens, though at a loss as to what was happening, assumed the shaking floor and the fast-approaching pounding footfalls weren't anything good, decided they had better flee. Dropping their cargo, which, except for the one in front, proved fatal to those who tripped and stumbled over the unseen obstacles.

Rounding the bend, Snotterkrakken saw the stumbling bad tasting Hobkrakkens climbing to their feet and ahead of them the fleeing pork treats. Without pausing its ungainly running stride, it trampled over the Hobkrakkens and objects strewn in its path. Focusing past the lone Hobkrakken still on its feet and on the tasty Trottersnipes, it rushed after them.

Having witnessed the terrible screams and the sounds of the breaking limbs of his crushed and trampled comrades, the surviving Hobkrakken panicked in fear of the unseen horror behind. He careened into walls, stumbled to the floor and rolled. In his frenzied haste to escape, he had gotten himself turned around and unsure what direction the echoing thudding footsteps came from, ran straight toward them. Realizing his mistake too late, a mass of sweaty flesh engulfed him.

Snotterkrakken barely gave the Hobkrakken a glance when it rushed past. Squashed against the wall, the unfortunate creature became entangled in mounds of quivering flesh and dragged along with it.

Spewspawn glanced behind at the dreadful screams and immediately regretted doing so when he set his terrified gaze upon the mountain of flesh barreling toward him. An even worse sight was the drooling lips of the ugly, distorted face staring hungrily back at him. He turned away and screamed out to his mate. "Jocky, we needs to find a door that huge creature chasing us won't fit through. And whatever ya do, don't look back."

Looking back was the last thing on Jockelstrap's mind. "There's a room just around the corner with a door," he shouted back.

"Take it," ordered Spewspawn.

Skidding around a sharp right-hand corner and then hard left, Jockelstrap headed for the door in the left wall, shoved it open and with his friend hard on his heels, rushed inside.

Spewspawn kicked the door closed with his foot and glanced around the room. "Quick, grab the table!" he ordered. "We'll barricade the door with it." Putting the wine cask down by the side wall, he crossed to the table. "I'm sure what's coming is too big to fit through the door but better safe than sorry."

Shaking his head in admiration of his friend's quick thinking, Jockelstrap placed his wine down. "Again, he proves what a good leader he'll be."

"Just grab the other end," urged Spewspawn frantically, aware of the approaching thundering footsteps rattling the door in its frame and vibrating the floor beneath their quivering legs.

They hurried the table over to the door and jammed it against it. Standing back to admire their handiwork, Jockelstrap nodded. "That'll do it. It's never getting through that door now."

Though Snotterkrakken tried to slow down to navigate around the corner, momentum and inertia conspired against it and sent it crashing into the wall. Unable to stand the great force thrust against it, the ancient wall shattered. Rocks and debris exploded out like missiles.

Shocked by the abrupt and unfathomable implosion of the wall, the two Trottersnipes mimicked statues as rocks, both large, small, and bits too tiny to mention whizzed past them. Miraculously, when all had settled, they remained unscathed. A condition that wasn't destined to last for long.

Snotterkrakken stumbled over the rocks littering the floor and emerged from the dust cloud created by its destruction. When it noticed the two agape pork snacks standing there, it whooped with glee and punched the closest one in the face, breaking every bone and cartilage in the vicinity of the blow that sent him slamming into the far wall.

Crossing to the remaining snack that screamed in terror and had sprung a leak from its groin, Snotterkrakken gripped Jockelstrap around the waist and snatched him to his face. Licking snotty lips, it gazed hungrily at the wriggling, leaking, pork feast. Deciding to save the brain until last, it clamped its jaws around the snack's neck and bit off a large chunk. Savoring the porky taste, Snotterkrakken vowed to never eat another Crapmaggot for as long as it lived. From now on, every meal would be pork. Pleased the snack had stopped screaming the high-pitched shriek that tingled its plethora of oddly placed hearing attachments, it lowered its head for another delightful mouthful.

Slowing when he detected faint voices coming from an opening seeping an orange glow into the corridor, Crowe instructed Arabella to remain quiet while he crept ahead to investigate. Peering around the door frame, Crowe observed two Hobkrakken guards sat at a small table playing some sort of game involving teeth, a dice and a wooden board divided into grooved sections. A brazier glowing with embers beside them threw warmth into the cold, damp room. Directing his eyes to the iron door barred with wooden locking beams behind them, the only other exit in the room and most likely the exit from this subterranean hell Crowe sought, he backed into the corridor before whispering to Arabella.

"There's another door, but it's guarded by two Hobkrakkens, which we need to find a way past. They are blind, so I'm thinking I might, with your help, be able to creep up on them and overpower them. Knocking them out might be the best solution."

"I can't say I'm overjoyed by the prospect, but if it gets us out of here, what do you need me to do?"

"Distract them while I creep up behind them. I noticed a pile of logs, so I'll use one as a club."

"But you won't kill them, will you? I know they're foul creatures who'd probably eat us both if they got the chance, but it's still murder anyway you look at it."

"Just a tap hard enough to knock them senseless while we make our escape is all," assured Crowe, though he had no idea how hard a tap was required to achieve that without crushing their skulls. "You creep in, position yourself on the left side of the room, and distract them while I creep behind them, grab a log, tap tap, job done."

"Any ideas on how I should distract them? They're blind, so flashing some of my womanly charms won't work."

Crowe grinned. "It might for me."

Arabella swung her leg free of the saddle and slid to the floor, "Just for future reference, a rat grin looks more like a creepy sneer than a joyous smile."

"I doubt that will stop me though. But seriously, stamp your foot, whistle, sing, anything that will draw their attention away from me."

"And if they attack me, what then?"

"I'm hoping they'll be too surprised for that to happen. I only need a few seconds to knock them out, but if they do, run, and I'll protect you. I might not look it, but I've become quite a dab hand at fighting all manner of vicious creatures lately. A couple of blind Hobkrakkens will be easy."

"Okay," uttered Arabella doubtfully. "But don't hang about in there."

"I won't. You go in first, and I'll follow. Just don't make any noise until…"

"I'm not an idiot, I know what to do," interrupted Arabella, striding for the guard room.

Unaware of the intruders who had stepped through the door, the Hobkrakkens carried on with their game. Skyle threw the dice and then ran a finger across the single raised dot on its uppermost surface. When disappointment formed on his face, he narrowed his eyeless sockets at his opponent and called out, "Six!"

Frowning at Skyle suspiciously, Liceridden reached out a hand to check there really were six dots showing on the dice. Flinching worriedly when he heard fingers shuffling across the tabletop toward the dice, Skyle swiped at the incriminating cube, sending it rattling across the floor.

Arabella froze when the dice hit the wall beside her and clattered to the floor by her feet. Wondering if a fight was about to break out, she watched the two creatures arguing. If it did, it would provide the perfect cover for their task. Her eyes flicked to Crowe heading across the room, his attention focused on the squabbling Hobkrakkens.

Listening to their bickering and cheating accusations, Crowe made his way past the Hobkrakkens. He hugged the shelf unit along the wall stacked with weapons; swords, knives, bows, and arrows, two garottes but no handy club to save him collecting one from the woodpile. His tail, as unruly as ever, brushed against the shelf, caught the tip of a sword handle, and dragged it a few inches.

The Hobkrakkens' arguing ceased. Their heads spun to the screeching sound. Their noses sniffed the air. Arabella rolled her eyes. Crowe gulped.

Chairs scraped on the floor when the two Hobkrakkens, sensing an intruder in their midst, abruptly stood.

"Who be there?" asked Liceridden, grabbing the nearby sword leaning against the wall.

"Reveal ya self," demanded Skyle, picking up the wicked short sword he had propped against a table leg within easy reach.

Crowe remained still and silent.

The two Hobkrakkens approached him, their heads turning this way and that, noses sniffing the air, ears alert. When they were only three steps away from Crowe, they sliced their blades through the air before them, seeking him out. They spun when something struck the wall at the end of the room and clattered to the floor.

Noticing the dice rolling to a stop, Crowe nodded his thanks to Arabella. When the creatures moved to investigate the new sound, Crowe grabbed his tail with one paw to keep it out of mischief and crept nearer the log pile. He reached it without further detection and selected a suitable club. The Hobkrakkens were now too far away to risk sneaking the distance, especially as they were now aware someone was in the room.

Detecting Crowe's problem, Arabella came to his assistance. "Oi, you two, I'm over here."

The Hobkrakkens spun, almost slicing each other with their swords, and looked where the voice had come from.

"Well?" said Arabella, "what are you waiting for? You want a piece of me or not?"

Now they had homed in on the intruder's position, they rushed forward before she moved.

Crowe had the makeshift club raised ready and struck the nearest creature as soon as it was within range. Shrieking in pain, Skyle's sword clanged to the ground when he shot his hands to his throbbing head.

Arabella again rolled her eyes. How the man-rat had survived for so long in this vicious, creature-infested world was beyond her.

Realizing a harder tap was needed to produce unconsciousness, Crowe put more effort behind the blow aimed at the other Hobkrakken, who worriedly darted his head about for sounds of whoever had attacked his comrade. Liceridden groaned when something struck his head.

Crowe sighed when he too failed to go down.

Dazed by the blow, Liceridden staggered back and forth waving his sword wildly to defend against his attacker. His cheating partner shrieked when the blade sliced his arm. Believing the intruder was responsible, Skyle drew his knife and flailing it about madly, he attacked, opening a deep cut across Liceridden's stomach. Liceridden retaliated with whirling, erratic sword swipes of his own until both received fatal wounds and dropped to the floor, dead.

Crowe placed the log back on the pile. "That didn't go quite as planned."

"That's the understatement of the year," uttered Arabella, crossing to the armament rack. "I'll grab a weapon while you open the door."

Stepping all four limbs over the bloody corpses, Crowe unbarred the door and pulled it open. Chilled air whooshed in and flickered the torch flames. It was a good sign. Flowing air indicated an exit of some kind. He peered along the dark passage that led off to God knows where.

"It's a tunnel," he called out to Arabella, who was strapping on a sword.

She added a dagger, grabbed a bow and a quiver of arrows, crossed to the door and peered inside. "It's pitch-black. We'll need a light."

"No need, I'm a rat. I can see in the dark."

"Well I can't. If you think I'm entering somewhere that might be crawling with horrors, especially the eight-legged variety, without a light, think again." Before Crowe could stop her, she had grabbed a flaming torch from its wall sconce. She deftly swung onto Crowe's back and declared, "Now, I'm ready. Take us into the unknown."

"Just don't singe my fur is all I ask."

"Why? It's not like you'll need it when you get back, is it?"

"It's not the loss of my fur I'm concerned about, it's the burning pain that comes with it."

Arabella leaned forward and scratched him behind the ear. "I promise to be careful, Mr. Grumpy Rat."

"I wasn't moaning, just asking is all, and your sword is digging in my back." Crowe stepped through the doorway and headed along the tunnel.

Arabella adjusted her sword scabbard and turning serious, gazed into the darkness and wondered what danger they might encounter ahead. Realizing in this dangerous world, it was probably impossible to imagine, she rested a hand on her sword and prepared for the worst.

Chapter 33

Spookravens

STILL ANGRY WITH THE king, Hemlock Mildew slammed the door of his chamber occupying one of the small towers perched on the sides of the tall central tower. Crossing to the window, he stared down at the gathered faerie army undergoing last minute training. Having learned from their previous disastrous forays into the human world, there would be no mistakes this time. The humans wouldn't know what had hit them before it was too late. They would attack in force while they slept.

Glancing at the sun shortly to dip behind the mountains, Hemlock spun away from the window and sat at his desk. He picked up a quill, dipped it in the ink pot, and wrote a coded message on a small parchment pad only he and his Sprites could decipher.

URGENT! Imperative we meet in secret to discuss a mission suitable for your particularly well-trained skills. 10 o'clock tonight. Stone circle. Tell no one.

Satisfied with the message, he copied it out five times. He rolled up the small notes tightly and sealed them with his secret wax seal. He exited his room, climbed the narrow, winding stairs to the roof space, and crossed to a pole fixed across thc middle of the circular room. He tilted his head to the dark interior of the sharply pitched roof and called out, "Come to me one through six."

Scarcely discernable in the darkness that cloaked the roof space, six of the twelve Spookravens leaped from their perch, glided down and landed on the pole. Admiring his message carriers that were more dark smoke than grabbable substance, he delivered his instructions. "Each of you will deliver a message to one of my Sprites." Their beady red eyes turned to the handful of small scrolls their master held up. "As I place one upon you, I will proclaim the identifying number of the Sprite you are to visit."

Starting at one end of the line, he placed the first scroll onto the Spookraven's back. It sunk into its fog-formed mass. "Deliver to Sprite number 1."

He moved to the next Spookraven and issued its payload. "Deliver to Sprite number 2."

When he had dished out all six, Hemlock pointed at the opening in the wall. "To your task my spirit birds."

The Spookravens sprung from the pole in sequence, and flapping mist-formed wings, flew through the window. When the last one had taken flight, Hemlock watched them for a few moments before returning to his room to prepare for tonight's meeting.

Striding along the line of soldiers he was trying to kick into shape for the forthcoming battle against the humans, Drill Sergeant, Sternly Gobshout, strode over to one of his raw recruits and snatched the crossbow he was about to fire at the human-shaped target from his hands.

Surprised by the action, and rubbing his thumb scratched by the sudden theft of his weapon, Scratchy Bottom turned to his superior. "What was I doing wrong, Sarge? I was holding it like you taught us; elbow tight against the chest, arm locked, and eye peering along the shaft."

"It's not how ya was holding the damn weapon, stupid, it was what ya had it loaded with." He nodded at the silver bolt primed ready to fire. "Ya see the markings on the shaft there?"

Bottom nodded. "Very pretty. Much nicer than those plain old wooden ones the others are firing."

"Which is exactly my point. You shouldn't have it. Where'd ya get it?" demanded the Drill Sergeant, narrowing his eyes at the nervous soldier.

"Well, Sarge, I was at the end of the ammo queue with the others when you started yelling if we didn't 'urry up and get on the target range, they'd be bloody hell to pay. And we all know how severe your punishments can be. Poor Growley Thumper is still running laps around the city, and that was two days ago."

Gobshout's eyebrows rose in surprise. "He is? I thought I told him he could stop?"

Bottom shook his head. "You must have forgotten with all the punishments you've been slinging about lately."

Calling a soldier to him, Sergeant Gobshout ordered him to go and inform Thumper his punishment was over, to stop running, and if required, visit the sickbay. As the soldier ran off to carry out his order, Gobshout refocused back on Bottom. "Continue."

"Like I was saying, with me being at the back end of the queue and you yelling your head off threatening all manner of horrible penalties, I was worried if I were last it wouldn't bode well for me. It was then I noticed this rack of arrows with no queue, so I went over, grabbed a handful, and rushed to the target range. I was just about to fire one at the human's eye on the target, when you snatched it from me, almost ripping my thumb off in the process." He held up said wounded digit to prove his point.

Gobshout peered at the almost invisible tiny red mark and rolled his eyes. "Well, Bottom, what you have here..." he slapped the crossbow for effect and almost lost an ear when it fired—both of their surprised expressions followed the arrow's trajectory high into the air. The strange black bird it struck exploded in an impressive display of showering sparks and soot. "...is a magic arrow."

"Wow! Very pretty, Sarge" exclaimed Bottom. "Like fireworks." He pointed his finger at another of the strange birds. "Please, Sarge, can you shoot that one too, so I can see the fireworks again?"

Gobshout's anxious gaze flicked to the small tower where the owner of the strange birds resided. Relieved to see its windows absent Hemlock's gaze witnessing his blunder, he thrust the weapon back into Bottom's hands. "Return the magic arrows and get the proper ones before I have ya hung up by ya supposedly injured thumb from the city gibbet."

Staring after the Drill Sergeant, Bottom shook his head as he sucked his sore thumb. *The Sarge is extra grumpy today.* Sensing he had better do as instructed, he picked up the pretty arrows he had stuck in the grass and headed for the ammo stores to swap them for the plain boring type.

———◆——◆—O—◆——◆———

Silhouetted by the rising moon, Hemlock's six Sprites raced across rooftops, leaped over the gaps between buildings, tightrope-walked across washing lines stretched from one side of the street to the other, jumped down to balconies and landed on the paved ground with barely a sound.

Disappointed they hadn't been chosen to join their trainer's elite Phantoms, the six Sprites continually honed their skills in the hope that if one of the Phantoms were injured or killed, then one of them would be chosen to replace them. Nearly every evening, they met and practiced their stealthy routines. As Sprite 1 led them through the dark streets busy with faeries returning home from their places of work, he dipped into their pockets and took whatever he found, threw it behind for the others to catch and replace in its owner's pocket. So light-fingered, swift and invisible in their shadowy attire, their victims were oblivious to their reversed pickpocketing.

Reaching the edge of the city, the six Sprites climbed the city wall, weaved past guards patrolling the top, who only detected a slight breeze from their passing, and dived off. Gliding on their wings, they swooped for a row of trees and landed on branches so softly, not a leaf rustled. A little out of breath from their exercise, they slipped off their hoods while they rested.

"That was our best time yet," said Sprite 1 proudly, real name Zagan Black.

Spike Trumple, designated as Sprite 4, mopped the sweat from his face with his mask. "Yes. Let's see those Phantoms match that."

Sprite 6 was the only female faerie to be initiated into the group. Lezabel Dewsweet shook her long raven hair to put some life back into the flatly confined tresses and gazed back at the city. Narrowing her eyes when she noticed something. She pointed them out to the boys. "Are they Hemlock's Spookravens?"

The other Sprites pulled back leafy branches to look.

"They're coming this way," stated Pikey Lodestone, designated Sprite 2.

Zagan smiled. "Finally, he sends for us."

"I only see five," stated Sprite 3, Moxie Draven had the sharpest eyes of them all, so if he said there were five, five there were.

"Strange," uttered Pikey.

Sprite 5, Pax Plunket, stared worriedly at the five approaching birds. "One of us is about to be left on the shelf."

Zagan glanced at Lezabel, certain it would be her, before refocusing on Hemlock's spooky carrier birds. Once assigned a target, the Spookravens would seek it out and only return to its roost once the message it had been entrusted with was in the recipient's hand.

The five Spookravens glided down to the trees, and each landed beside their designated beneficiary. Nobody was more surprised than Zagan when none of the birds landed beside him.

Following the others' lead, Lezabel thrust her hand into the Spookraven's body, gripped the scroll hidden within and pulled it out. As each bird was released of its burden, it took flight and headed back to the city.

Fuming he had been left out, Zagan watched the others break the seals and read their messages. Moments later, chemicals woven into the seals—activated once broken—caused the parchments to smolder, creating wisps of smoke before bursting into flames and devouring the secret orders which were promptly discarded to avoid burnt fingers.

"Well, what is it?" asked Zagan.

"You know we can't tell you, Zag," said Spike.

Zagan nodded.

"I can't believe you aren't included," uttered Pax, bewildered by the turn of events. "You're the best of us of all."

"I wouldn't fret about it, Zag," reassured Pikey. "Hemlock's probably saving you for something special."

Feeling a little uncomfortable by the silence that followed, Moxie said, "We had better get going, or we'll be late."

As the others jumped to the ground, Lezabel looked at Zagan, who was obviously upset and brooding. "You okay, Zag?"

"I'm fine," he spat. "You had better go, or you'll be late for whatever secret mission Hemlock's got planned for you."

"I'm sure there's a good reason why he chose to exclude you, maybe..."

"I'm not interested in your attempt at consolation. Just leave."

Knowing in his present mood Zagan couldn't be reasoned with, Lezabel dropped from the tree and caught up with the others. Maybe he'd be in a better mood tomorrow.

After Zagan had watched them leave, he searched the skies for the approach of a waylaid black bird but glimpsed none. He swung to the ground and headed home.

On his way back from the successful meeting with his Sprites at the stone circle, Hemlock contemplated the non-appearance of one of his Spookravens to deliver its note to Zagan. It was something that had never occurred before, and he was concerned that someone might have somehow intercepted the message, but who? Though confident if that were the case, the party responsible would never be able to break his complicated secret code, he would have to be on his guard. Making a mental note to seek out Zagan the following day, he headed back to the city.

Hemlock paused on hearing faint female voices. Wondering what they were doing outside the city gates at this time of night during curfew, he snuck closer to investigate.

Hidden behind bushes, Griselda and Ellie peered down the hill at the city below and focused on the main gate with its abundance of soldiers guarding the entrance and more patrolling the top of the wall.

"Is it usual for there to be so many guards?" asked Griselda.

"No, only if they're on alert," replied Ellie. "Must have something to do with the reopening of the portal and the fear of a human attack."

"We'll have to risk it as we haven't got the time to wait around." She looked at Ellie with Lucifer and Satan waiting patiently beside her. "What about you and your dogs, will you be recognized?"

Ellie shrugged, scratching Lucifer behind an ear when he nuzzled against her waist. "It's possible, I suppose. I was there for nigh on eight faerie years, and the dogs are quite distinctive."

293

Griselda slipped the bag from her waist. "That's what I thought."

Ellie glanced at the bag.

"I'll stand a better chance of getting inside the city if you're not with me. It won't be for long. You should be able to blend in once we're through, but I think we should leave the dogs hidden."

Ellie knew Griselda was right. "I don't mind. Your storekeeper's a great host. I'd barely entered last time when he had me sat by a fire drinking hot chocolate." Ellie ushered the dogs inside and looked at Griselda. "As soon as you think it's safe, let me know, and we'll go kill the king together."

Griselda nodded. As soon as Ellie had entered, she reattached the bag around her waist and headed for the city gate.

Wide-eyed in surprise at what he had just witnessed, Hemlock watched the beautiful faux-faerie head for the city and set his mind to thinking how he could turn this unexpected event to his advantage.

Approaching the gate at a leisurely stroll while swinging her hips seductively, Griselda smiled coyly when the guards turned their gazes upon her. Mouths dropped open. Hearts fluttered. Knees trembled. Lips whistled.

"Hello, boys," she said when she reached the guard-choked gate. "Nice evening for a stroll in the refreshing night air."

"Who are you?" asked guard chief, Stubby Stouthobble, pushing to the front and brandishing a spear in her direction.

Smiling seductively, Griselda gently pushed the pointed tip away and looked at the faerie guard, his squat, tubby appearance made it look as if someone had dropped a heavy weight on his head from a great height. "I am a beautiful breath of fresh air come to brighten up your dreary lives."

"What she say?" asked Mufflewort, a guard at the back, standing on tiptoes to see over the shoulders of those in front.

"Dutiful death of flesh rum frighten scup your bleary knives, I think," said his friend Strangleweed, picking a lump of wax from his ear and wiping it off on the guard's tunic in front. "Whatever that means."

"She may talk gibberish, but she sure is a looker," commented Flipgibbert Marrowbone.

"What's ya name?" demanded Stubby, not one to be swayed from his duty by a pretty face and an oh-so-shapely body.

"Flancy Gigabeth," replied Griselda.

"What she say?" asked Mufflewort.

"Fancy Big Beth," replied Strangleweed.

"Isn't Big Beth the chief's wife's name," asked Spoiledrotten, a row in front.

"That it is," confirmed Flipgibbert. "As you all know, I'm not fussy when it comes to female company. I've kissed a lot of horrible, ugly things, some who I wasn't even sure were faeries, but I draw a line, wide and thick, which I'll never dare to cross when it comes to the chief's wife. I assure you, she's nothing to be fancied from any angle."

"Shush ya gibberings and listen, the lot of yous," scolded Grumpy Nutthumper, his gaze never leaving the beautiful stranger the chief interrogated.

Stubby narrowed his suspicious eyes. "Well, Flancy Gigabeth, what's ya business being out at this time of night when there's a curfew on."

"There's a curfew? Silly me. Sorry, I hadn't heard. But now you have kindly informed me there is, I'd better rush home and lock my beautiful, vulnerable body behind closed doors." Griselda went to step around the inquisitive guard chief but was stopped by the spear he placed across her ample chest.

"Not so fast, missy," threatened Stubby. "Something about ya ain't right. There's no doubting you're pretty with everything in the right place and in desirable proportions, certain to turn the heads of any red-blooded man faerie ya pass and probably incite the crashing of a few wagons in the process, but I ain't never laid eyes on ya before. A sight I'd be sure to remember and revisit in me head from time to time. In my thinking, this all adds up to ya not being from around here, and something that's making me suspicion hackles stand to attention ramrod stiff. The gist of it is that you're coming with me to the guardhouse until I'm satisfied you are who ya say you are, and I've established exactly what you're up to. Grab her boys! But gently."

A mad rush to have the honor of escorting such a gorgeous faerie to their guardroom, resulted in the over-enthusiastic guards tumbling to the floor in an entwined heap. Disgusted by their unprofessionalism, Stubby shook his head.

Griselda was just about to make a run for it when someone grabbed her arm. "What seems to be the matter, my dear?" inquired Hemlock.

Surprised by the faerie's sudden appearance, Griselda was unsure how to react.

Hemlock turned his scolding gaze upon Stubby. "Well, chief?"

"You're saying ya know this beautiful faerie, Mr. Mildew, sir?" inquired Stubby, also taken aback by the King's advisor's unexpected presence.

"I should think so, she's my niece visiting me for a few days from Raventown."

"Ah..." exclaimed Stubby. That explains the mystery of why I ain't never seen her prettiness cavorting around the city before."

Hemlock turned his attention to the guards untangling themselves and climbing to their feet. "Now, if you'll have your soldiers create a path, we'll get out of your way so you can continue your excellent job of guarding the city against undesirable interlopers and assassins." He squeezed Griselda's arm when he spoke the last word.

Stubby saluted sharply. "Yes, sir, Mr. Hemlock." He turned to his subordinates. "Make way, make way."

The guards parted. Still holding Griselda's arm, Hemlock led her through the gap.

Zagan was fueling his disappointment and drowning his sorrows in faerie ale when his glance around at the loud rabble in the inn focused on the two fairies walking past the window. After a few moments contemplation, he headed for the exit.

When they were well out of earshot of the guards and anyone else, Hemlock pulled Griselda into a side alley.

"I know why you're here and don't bother denying it. I want you to succeed in your mission and will help you achieve it."

Surprised and mistrustful of the man's informed knowledge and proposal, Griselda asked, "And what is it you want to help me with?"

"Killing the King," he whispered.

Griselda raised her well-trimmed eyebrows. "And if that were true, hypothetically, you are okay with that?"

Hemlock nodded vigorously. "Let's not play games. Killing the King is something I've often contemplated doing but never followed through, which is why I want to help you succeed. I have the King's ear—not physically of course—It's not like I chopped it off and have it in my pocket or hanging around my neck on a silver chain, or anything so grisly. I'm Hemlock Mildew, his advisor, which means I can gain you an audience with him. And if this isn't a suicide mission, which I doubt it is, once you've completed your murderous deed, I can help you escape."

Though not totally convinced she could trust the advisor, if he could help them get to the king, it would make their mission less problematic. "Okay, I'm interested."

"Super," said Hemlock, releasing his hold on her arm. "Then let's go to my private chambers where we can discuss things without fear of being overheard, and where you can let Ellie and her dogs out. She'll vouch for my position as we've met before."

Wondering how Hemlock knew so much, Griselda followed him through the streets toward the king's tower.

After noticing Hemlock skulk pass the window accompanied by a beautiful faerie, Zagan had slipped from the Inn and followed them. If the opportunity arose, he'd ask Hemlock why he'd been excluded from the secret meeting.

Having seen and heard everything, Zagan observed Hemlock, and the pretty faerie enter the tower. Discovering that he was a traitor didn't overly surprise him. Training a band of skilled assassins, you would expect the man to have a dark side. Torn between his loyalty to his master, his fellow Sprites who he assumed were somehow mixed up in Hemlock's nefarious activities, and his king, Zagan contemplated the merits of staying faithful to each. Making his decision, he headed into the night.

Chapter 34

Snotterkrakken

THE SATISFIED BURP TRUMPETING from Snotterkrakken's bloodstained mouth echoed around the partly destroyed chamber. Rubbing its bulbous tummy, it noticed a grubby foot protruding from its fleshy folds. Yanking it free with a sweaty squelch, it held aloft the gasping-for-air Hobkrakken who had stared into Death's face sight wasn't required to gaze upon.

Welcoming the scythe Death swung at him to bring an end to his torment and carry him hopefully to a better place, Scripesprickle was confused when the blade that was about to add his soul to the countless it had culled, swished harmlessly by. Sighing at the sight of Death—its skeletal eye sockets and lipless jaws depicting astonishment and disappointment matching his own—the Hobkrakken was once again dragged back into the miserable dark world of never-ending despair.

Sensing he was being held upside down and observed by something that made being sightless preferable, the helpless Hobkrakken waited to find out what new brand of misery he was about to endure.

Recognizing the creature that tasted so foul it made the taste of Crapmaggots desirable, Snotterkrakken shivered in revulsion at the memory and flung Scripesprickle away. His head connected with the wall, abruptly ending his flight and sent him flopping unconscious to the rubble-littered floor.

Gazing around for something else to munch on, Snotterkrakken noticed red liquid that looked suspiciously like blood leaking from a barrel knocked on its side. It lumbered over, picked it up, and licked the dribble. Its eyes widened in delight. It wasn't blood, but it was almost as tasty. It tugged the cork free, held the opening above its tilted back head, and poured the faerie wine down its gullet.

After gulping it all down, Snotterkrakken dropped the empty barrel and hiccupped. Swaying from the effects of the delicious red fluid, its blurry eyes focused on a second barrel, which took three tries before it successfully grabbed it. A groan directed its attention on the unpalatable creature sitting up and rubbing the lump on his head. Swaying unsteadily and through alcohol-glazed eyes, Snotterkrakken watched Scripesprickle climb to his feet. Stumbling over the rubble and table fragments scattered throughout the room, the Hobkrakken felt his way along the wall. On reaching the wooden door, Scripesprickle's fumbling fingers found the handle, pulled the door open and disappeared through it.

As it had observed the Hobkrakken, the inkling of an idea had begun to develop at the fringes of Snotterkrakken's brain and slowly form cohesion. Except for the jailor, Dungborn, every time it had seen the tasty pork treats, they had been accompanied by one or more of these inedible creatures, so if it followed this one, it should lead it to more Trottersnipe feasts.

Pleased with the first plan its brain had ever conceived, it tucked the full wine barrel under an arm and headed for the door designed for creatures much smaller. The frame splintered, and the surrounding stonework crumbled when it forced its large bulk through the opening. Shaking free the dust and rubble, Snotterkrakken followed the Hobkrakken in a staggering drunken gait.

Hearing the destruction of the doorway behind it, Scripesprickle increased his pace to escape the thing in pursuit. He rushed along corridors, up stone steps, and through various levels, but couldn't escape the thudding footfalls of his lumbering pursuer. Hoping leading it to other Trottersnipes the creature seemed to enjoy eating would distract it long enough for him to escape, he headed for the meeting hall where they habitually congregated.

Growing impatient from the non-appearance of the rat to roast, Gruntzswiller turned his gaze away from the glowing red embers beneath the roasting spit and barked an order at one of his Trottersnipe minions. "Krakbone! Go find out what's happened to Offalslick and tell him I am, to put it mildly, irked with the delay."

Pleased to be out from the increasing angry temperament of the dictator, Flunkmonkey headed for the exit and was promptly sent flying backward when the door burst open and slammed back against the wall with a resounding crash.

With his senses blinded by fear, Scripesprickle was unaware of the Trottersnipe on the floor he trampled over during his rush into the room.

Surprised by the Hobkrakken's sudden entrance, the two lazy Trottersnipe guards slouched against the wall were slow to react. Lunging forward, they thrust out their spears to block the Hobkrakken's path.

Powered by fear of what was coming, Scripesprickle ducked under the spears and heading for Gruntzswiller shouted, "A monster comes!"

Unaware of the Hobkrakken's intentions and glad of the excitement to break up the boredom, two of the Trottersnipe guards beside the dictator's chair, rushed around the roasting spit to intercept him. Scripesprickle weaved around them and exited the room through a side door, almost bowling over Gristlekrak heading for the meeting hall. Pondering the creature's strange behavior and the look of dread plastered on its face, Gristlekrak entered the meeting hall and joined those within staring at the far door as thundering footsteps approached.

With worried frowns, the two door guards raised their spears and backed away from the entrance.

"Take another step backward, and it'll be you two roasting on this spit for my dinner," yelled Gruntzswiller. Aware the threat was backed up by years of cruelty, the two guards halted their nervous retreat. "In fact, you two can go find out what's coming and stop it before it arrives."

The two anxious guards looked at each other worryingly before stepping around Krakbone getting to his feet and going into the corridor.

Sensing caution might be in order, Gristlekrak remained by the side door for a quick retreat if needed.

All eyes and ears focused on the main entrance when two Trottersnipe screams rang out. Simultaneously, the thundering footsteps and terrified screams ended abruptly. A satisfied grunting squeal that sent a fearful shiver down every spine in the room was followed by the gruesome sounds of something feasting. Recovering from his abrupt meeting with the door, Krakbone joined his nervous comrades staring at the doorway.

Gruntzswiller recalled what the terrified Hobkrakken had uttered during his flee from the room. *'A monster comes!'* Realizing the Hobkrakken had led whatever was outside, here, he vowed to seek out vengeance upon him after he had handled the current situation confronting him. He glanced around at his few remaining guards; all wore fearful looks. "You lot! Guard the door and kill whatever enters." Not one of them made a move. "If I have to tell you again, you'll all regret it!"

Mumbling obscenities under their breaths, the Trottersnipes headed halfway across the room and formed a line facing the door.

Gruntzswiller turned to his cowering advisor. "Gristlekrak. Fetch some Hobkrakkens and arm them."

Gristlekrak nodded. "How many?"

Gruntzswiller glanced toward the disturbing sounds seeping into the room from the far corridor. "As many as you can muster. Order half to come up behind whatever's out there and the remainder to enter through the doorway you're currently cowering in. And Gristlekrak, I don't care how painful it is, hobble as fast as you can. If that thing reaches me before the Hobkrakkens arrive, I'll crush every bone in your body and chuck you on the fire."

Also mumbling evil thoughts aimed at the dictator, Gristlekrak hobbled away to do his bidding as fast as his arthritic s limbs were able.

The silence that followed the ghastly sounds of flesh and bone being ripped from their comrades and devoured, proved to be more unnerving. At least when whatever outside was eating they knew where it was. The defensive line of Trottersnipes gasped, and the two in its direct path stepped aside when the head of one of the guards bounced into the room like a clumsily thrown bowling ball and rolled along the floor until it came to a halt on the red embers of the fire pit. Its flesh sizzled. The aroma of roasting pork drifted through the room. Grunting, sniffing snorts came from the corridor. Heavy footsteps followed.

Sniffing the delicious aroma, Snotterkrakken followed the scent and peeked around the door frame into the room it emanated from.

The seven Trottersnipes faced with confronting the creature that had just appeared gasped in equal amounts of fear and revulsion. Bogsniffer, who was not a fighter, was especially horrified. Cooking was his forte in life. Having long ago given up his dream of opening a restaurant, he now turned his culinary skills on preparing his dictators' meals, not that the glutinous hog appreciated it. Unable to comprehend the abomination it was faced with, Bogsniffer tried to turn and flee. He failed. Terror rooted his feet to the spot. Deciding on a new tactic, he fainted and collapsed to the floor.

Two of Bogsniffer's companions envied his comatose state if not his head smashing to the floor with a loud crack. Three others despised his cowardice for taking the easy way out and leaving them a Trottersnipe short to fend off the creature stepping through the door and hungrily eyeing them.

The seventh, Mucktrimple, who was a tad more optimistic than his brethren, seized the opportunity his unconscious comrade offered and shouted, "Quick, grab Bogsniffer."

Though confused by the order, it was something all were in favor of if it meant delaying the attack none were certain they would survive. The four Trottersnipes did as requested, and each grabbed a limb.

"Throw him," ordered Mucktrimple, pointing at the hideous monster heading for them.

The Trottersnipes swung Bogsniffer's limp form and let go.

Blissfully unaware of what was happening, Bogsniffer sailed through the air.

Though excited by the seven tasty treats lined up before him, Snotterkrakken was more interested in the cause of the delicious aroma currently working its way up its snot-choked nasal passages. It had barely taken three steps into the room to investigate when one of the pork treats was thrown at him. His malformed muscular arm snatched it from the air by the ankles. Swinging the unconscious Trottersnipe around its head, he rushed at the Trottersnipes who had thrown it. Wielded like a club, a bat and a hammer, Bogsniffer's head connected with various body parts of his all too conscious comrades with resounding cracks that rattled his brain in his skull.

When the last Trottersnipe in its way had succumbed to the onslaught, Snotterkrakken focused on the fire the smell of roasting flesh stemmed from. Noticing the lone Trottersnipe climb from a large chair and skulk away, Snotterkrakken swung the makeshift weapon around its head and with a flick of its wrist, let Bogsniffer fly across the room.

Gruntzswiller had observed the brief battle with deep anxiety. As his last comrade fell, he decided cowardice in the face of such a monstrous entity would serve him better than bravery and climbed from his chair. His low sneaking creep to a side exit was brought to a painful halt when Bogsniffer collided with the back of his head.

Bogsniffer's already battered and cracked skull exploded on contact with his dictator's. Dazed by the blow that sent him spilling to the floor, Gruntzswiller tried to regain his footing but slipped on the blood and brains sprayed across the floor.

Snotterkrakken halted by the glowing embers of the roasting pit and plucked the charred head from the fire. Juggling the sizzling feast in its hands, it sunk in its teeth and took a large bite. It almost swooned from the heavenly taste of cooked meat and the hot juices sliding down its throat and dribbling down its chins. It continued eating when Hobkrakkens poured into the room from entrances around the room.

Led by Scripesprickle whom Gristlekrak had nominated as leader—something Scripesprickle suspected was punishment for almost bowling him over earlier—the Hobkrakkens armed with spears, knives, swords, and daggers, rushed into the meeting hall. Surprised at finding the unconscious Trottersnipe guards littered around the room, the Hobkrakkens turned their attention on Snotterkrakken by the spit. Though none could see it, their senses were so acute they each pictured a diverse variety of monstrosities feeding on the cooked flesh of a Trottersnipe.

Aware the creature he had led to this room detested Hobkrakken flesh, Scripesprickle formed an idea; a chance to be out from under the Trottersnipes' cruel reign of terror. After ordering some of his comrades to disarm the unconscious guards and take them to the dungeon, he crossed to Gruntzswiller crawling toward an exit. He raised his spear in two hands and thrust it down with such force it slid though Gruntzswiller's fleshy leg and pinned him to the floor.

Gruntzswiller screamed and glared at the Hobkrakken responsible when he stepped into his view. "You'll die for that, very slowly," he threatened.

Scripesprickle shrugged. "Die I might, but not by your trotters." He reached out a hand for a comrade's sword. "Know this. Your body will be roasted on the spit you had us prepare, and then that fiend, and we will feast on your flesh."

Fear like he had never experienced before swept through Gruntzswiller. So desperate was he to get away, he yanked his pinned leg. Tearing flesh sent a fresh wave of agony coursing through him. Dragging himself forward, he saw the shadow of the Hobkrakken raising the sword and bringing it down. He grunted when the point entered his back and sliding deeper, it pierced his evil heart. Blood gurgled from his mouth as life left him.

Scripesprickle yanked the sword free. Their reign of terror was over. He turned his attention on the feeding monster he doubted they would be able to kill so easily, and then swept his sightless eyes over his nearest comrades. "Strip him and put him on the spit. Roasted dictator is on the menu tonight."

Nervous hurrahs accompanied their setting to the tasks.

Dropping his weapon, Scripesprickle warily crossed to the creature he had sensed approaching to find out what they were doing. He bowed. "Oh, great one. Let us serve you, and a feast in your honor we will prepare."

Snotterkrakken, who had been observing the Hobkrakkens, wondered what the foul-tasting creatures were doing. When one approached and spoke, it understood a few words. Though unable to join the words into a cohesive sentence to fathom out what was said, it sensed the strange unpalatable creatures meant no harm and nodded. Stepping back when they dragged the unclothed Trottersnipe over to the hot coals, it plonked into the chair recently vacated by the corpse being impaled lengthwise on the large metal spike. When the four Hobkrakkens struggled to lift it on the spit rests, it stepped forward and helped. Sitting back down, it watched two Hobkrakkens turn the spit while another basted it. The room was soon filled with the tantalizing scent of roasted pork.

Scripesprickle stopped in front of Snotterkrakken. After bowing, he raised his hands into the air. "Hail to our new leader, the slayer of Trottersnipe and Hobkrakken friend." He lowered his arms and in a continuous waving motion, raised them again.

Weapons throughout the room clattered to the floor when the other Hobkrakkens joined in the rejoicing. "Hail to our new leader."

Sucking an eyeball from the Trottersnipe skull it was reluctant to discard until it had been stripped clean, Snotterkrakken decided it would do good by its new-found friends, the first it had ever had.

Snotterkrakken smiled and for the first time in its miserable life, experienced happiness.

Panting from his rushed painful exertions, Gristlekrak halted by the door of the meeting hall and listened to the Hobkrakkens voices. Detecting something had gone horribly amiss, he peered into the room. Ignoring the waving and chanting Hobkrakkens, he noticed something that brought a smile to his lips; Gruntzswiller being roasted on the spit. He thought the apple stuffed in his mouth was a nice touch. His only regret was the cruel hog wasn't still alive. When he turned his attention to the object of the Hobkrakkens worship, he almost spewed forth his meager lunch. He backed into the corridor and hobbled along it. It was time to leave this miserable place before he too suffered the same fate as his slowly charring leader.

Chapter 35

Exit Tunnel

HEADING CAUTIOUSLY ALONG THE dark, damp tunnel, Arabella held the torch high and peered into the gloom for any danger that might threaten. Crowe also looked ahead, cocking his ears for telltale sounds of creatures moving in the darkness, but except for the hundreds of red-striped cockroach-type insects disturbed by their passing scuttling creepily over the walls, all seemed quiet. Spying a side turning ahead, he slowed and peered down its dark length lit by the torch Arabella aimed into the opening. Pleased to see no eyes reflecting the flames, Crowe studied the tracks on the floor. As the majority carried straight on, and the draft washing over them stronger from that direction, he followed them.

After rounding a few bends in the tunnel, they were halted by a sturdy metal grill blocking their path and beyond freedom from the danger-filled underground world behind them. Both peered through the bars at the moonlight-bathed rocky landscape outside.

Arabella slid from Crowe's back and approached the gate set into the iron framework. It rattled when she shook it to test its strength. "Rusty, but strong." She turned her attention to the two large locks holding it firmly closed. "With hindsight, we would have searched the guardroom back there for keys."

Crowe studied the locks. "With no way to pass through without them, I'll have to nip back and find them. You wait here as I'll be quicker on my own."

"Okay, be careful."

Crowe turned around and sprinted back along the tunnel.

After Arabella had watched him disappear into the darkness, she turned back to the gate and looked at the freedom that eluded her by the thickness of the metal bars.

Bounding along the tunnel, Crowe soon arrived back in the guardroom. After patting down the two Hobkrakken cadavers and finding no keys, he focused on searching the room and discovered a single large key hanging on a nail hammered into the side of a shelf unit. Grabbing it in his mouth, he fled back through the tunnel.

Hearing footsteps in the darkness she was confident were Crowe's, Arabella turned and glimpsed his eyes reflecting the torch flames before he appeared. She took the key from his mouth, unlocked the gate, and pulled it open. They both stepped outside into the cool, night air.

"Where to next?" asked Arabella.

"We need to get into the city to link up with the others I told you about, Griselda and Ellie, if they are still alive. As the Hobkrakkens discovered a way to sneak in and out, I guess we follow their tracks and hope for the best."

After locking the gate and throwing away the key to delay any would-be pursuers, Arabella climbed back into the saddle. With his eyes on the ground, Crowe followed the path worn by years of passing footsteps.

After crossing through a rocky landscape, they entered an area filled with strange trees that seemed to be all roots or creepers entwined to form trunks and branches. Though leafless, long strands of green stalks hung from their tops. Alert for danger, Crowe followed the trail winding around the creepy growths and noticed what he first thought to be red-budded flowers, but when they moved, he realized they were a type of insect. He watched their six-legged bodies scuttle up and down the hanging fronds and freeze with their red buds aimed at him when he drew near. Though eyeless, the way their heads turned to follow his movements indicated they knew precisely where he was. Crowe wasn't fooled by the lack of a visible mouth that he was sure was concealed by the tightly bunched petals that would spring open to reveal a vicious set of jaws if food was in the offing. Keeping a wary distance, he continued along the trail.

The source of the foul cloying stench of sewage becoming stronger with each step was revealed when they crossed through a fast flowing but shallow stream and reached a towering cliff of rock. Lumpy fluid, brown and syrupy, oozed from a large round opening into a pool of fermenting sewage overflowing down the side of a rocky embankment into the stream they had just crossed. The swift current carried the putrid effluents away.

Crowe gazed worriedly at the bubbling pool of filth and the bent back bars of the iron-gated entrance on the far side, which seemed to be the Hobkrakkens' secret way into the city. "No way am I swimming through that filth."

Arabella tapped Crowe on the shoulder and pointed over to one side where she spotted something hidden amongst the bushes. "You may not have to."

Gazing in the indicated direction, Crowe spotted the end of a wide wooden plank. He crossed to it and examined the board. It was undoubtedly what the Hobkrakken raiders used to bridge the sewage pool. "Give me a hand."

Arabella climbed down and together they manhandled the thick plank over to the pool and guided one end onto the lip of the sewer outlet.

"I'll cross first," Arabella volunteered, stepping onto the makeshift bridge. She crossed over and looked back at Crowe. "It seems strong enough."

Crowe crossed, and though the plank bent and creaked alarmingly, it held his weight.

"Do we leave the bridge or pull it over so nothing can follow us?" asked Arabella.

Crowe peered along the dark and smelly sewer passage. "No, leave it. We might need to make a hasty retreat and having to waste time resetting the bridge might get us killed. Climb aboard, and we'll see where this foul tunnel leads."

Once Arabella had climbed into the saddle, Crowe stepped onto one of the raised sides that funneled the sewage along its middle and headed inside. They hadn't traveled far when the rough rock walls turned to stone blocks forming an arched tunnel. Away from the opening, the stench emanating from the flowing filth was overpowering and something they were forced to endure as they followed its gently curving path.

Conscious of the flaming torch lighting her way, Arabella worried it might ignite the methane she imagined filling the putrid air. She drew comfort from it not having done so already, and her fear of journeying through pitch blackness and not being able to see anything attacking persuaded her the risk was worth taking.

When the tunnel led them into a large space with its floor covered in a pool of sewage fed by two large outlets on the far side, one barred with a metal grill and the other open, Crowe had no option other than to enter the flowing sludge. Luckily it wasn't deep, coming halfway up his legs. Trying to hold his tail free of the filth and his nose raised as high as possible, his paws sunk into the thick layer of something he preferred not to name covering the floor as he made his way over to the open tunnel. He spied the missing metal grill partly submerged in the pool, which he assumed the Hobkrakkens had removed.

Passing through, he entered a longer cavern with three similar openings at the far end and two small high outlets trickling waste into the three converging rivers of filth. The battling eddies had caused banks of glistening excrement to form along the sides and a triangular island of brown sludge reaching out from the wall between the two openings behind them. Keen to be free of the brown lumps bumping against his legs, Crowe pressed on to the far end of the space and headed for the left-hand outlet that had its iron grill bent back. He passed through into a tunnel slightly larger than the one they had just trekked through and stepped free of the sewage stream onto the raised walkway along its edge. The sound of splashing water drifted out from the darkness prevalent outside the ring of Arabella's flickering torch.

After shaking his legs to free his fur of the disgusting congealed lumps adhered to them, he turned his head to his passenger. "It might stink in here, but it seems free of danger, so I think we'll be okay."

The next chamber they arrived at revealed the source of the splashing water, or to be precise, splashing waste. A *wastefall* of lumpy filth pouring from a high outlet into a circular pool that emptied into the passage they had had just passed through. The walkway led to stone steps leading up to a platform that wrapped around the room. Crowe climbed to the top and passed through the arched opening positioned to one side of the foul deluge.

Filth cascading down a sloped, stepped ramp, formed the sewage stream feeding the wastefall. A filtering grill across the end of the stream was backed up with debris that included rotten, broken barrels, branches and smashed skeletons of unrecognizable creatures matted into a sludgy mass of foulness.

Crowe continued along the walkway and climbed a set of stone steps doglegging to a higher level. Barrels, crates, sacks, and a plethora of other items were stacked along the raised walkway beside the flowing sewage fed by a row of smaller outlets set along the wall.

Arabella ran her eyes over the stacked items. "The Hobkrakkens' stash of pilfered loot I imagine."

Crowe thought the same. "It could mean we're getting close to the city."

"Breathing fresh air again sounds awfully inviting," commented Arabella as Crowe stepped around and over the stolen goods and climbed the iron spiral staircase in the far corner.

The next subterranean room they entered surprised them both. The side walls were formed of large metal grills that continued below the surface of what seemed to be a deep pool the size of the chamber. The foul glutinous liquid filling it gurgled and churned as fresh waste entered below the surface. Slightly cleaner air was coming in through the higher grills and swirled the foul stench around the room and out the exit. A metal ramp led to a raised platform in the middle with two chains wrapped around manually operated winches linked to the top of a large drawbridge presently in the closed position.

Curious as to the purpose of the barrier, Crowe crossed to the raised platform and peered into the large metal grill set in the floor, which he thought might be an overflow outlet if the room flooded. A nudge of the lever connected to both winches lowered the drawbridge with a loud shrieking of metal and rattling of chains. Its resounding clang against the edge of the platform reverberated through the sewer.

"That was noisier than I would have liked," muttered Crowe, fearing someone or something would have heard it.

"The Hobkrakken thieves must come this way, so if there were any danger of it alerting the faeries to their presence, surely they would leave it open?" offered Arabella.

"It's not the faeries hearing it that particularly worries me, it's the reason why there's a need for a drawbridge that can be opened from this side, negating its use as a defense barrier from an attacking force."

Arabella stared at the dark opening. "You think it was to keep something in?"

Crowe padded softly for the doorway and peered through. "I do now."

Arabella held the torch behind so as not to impede Crowe's rat sight. "You see anything?"

"If you mean anything with teeth, then no, only a long room, but stay alert. My rat senses are picking up something other than sewage."

Gripping her sword tighter, Arabella held the torch higher to spread the light as far as possible when Crowe tentatively crossed the threshold.

Oddly angled arches with solid stone supports positioned throughout the room gave the impression they held some great weight. A small outlet trickled water—clearer than any thus far encountered—into a narrow gully set in the floor that emptied into the square pool set to one side. A few steps running the length of the room led to a flat area hugging the side wall interspaced with angled reinforcing pillars. An indication they were nearing the surface came from the thick roots that snaked down the wall, across the floor and dipped their sucking tendrils into the pool, and what might be faint daylight seeping through the distant arched opening.

Crowe paused at an area littered with splintered bones and recognized what he thought to be Hobkrakken skulls scattered amongst them. He turned his attention to the large chain formed of links larger than his paws, attached to one of the thick stone columns. "What do you think that's connected to?" voiced Crowe softly.

"Something long dead I hope," answered Arabella glancing fearfully at the many dark patches surrounding them; perfect places for something to hide in ambush.

Pattering feet and the clanking of chains halted Crowe's cautious progress through the bone graveyard and turned his anxious gaze to the worrying sounds.

Both listened to the alarming sound of chains being dragged unhurriedly across the ground. Growls, low and fearsome, heralded the arrival of eyes in the darkness reflecting the torchlight. Though he picked out faint traces of the creatures' forms, Crowe had no idea what species it was. Having learned since entering this world it was inadvisable to wait and find out, Arabella was almost toppled from the saddle when he lurched forward. Scattering bones in his path he bounded swiftly across the room. The increased speed of the dragging chains and claws clacking on stone indicated the creatures were in pursuit.

Twisting her head to see what chased them, Arabella shivered in fear when she glimpsed the creatures slithering in and out of the torchlight she was unable to hold still.

The length of a family car, the hide of the meter-thick creatures were covered in a pattern of lines that, now they had been spotted, glowed red. Spikes, longer on their rear section, adorned the back of their bodies. Their raised front section sported arms with hooked claws. Their long, thin heads had three eyes either side, two feelers and two long horns that swept back over their bodies. Two tentacle appendages wavered from their jaws. Legless, they scuttled along on their many, single-clawed feet. It had the appearance of a giant bug one might encounter in an alien world, which Arabella remembered, this was.

Its horse size four-limbed upper body, that was also its head, sprouted spikes, both long and short. When it noticed her looking at it, it spread its foremost spikes back and splayed its spike-adorned jaws as it bellowed a terrifying shriek. The length of chain attached to the metal hoop around its body clanked and skittered along behind it.

Noticing the creatures were gaining on them and were about to cut across to attack, Arabella yelled, "Turn left!"

Trusting his passenger, Crowe dodged left around one of the many arched support columns and heard something crash into the stone close behind him with a grunted squeal.

Picking itself up from the ground, the creature shook its fuzzy head, dislodging the stone scrapings and dust its spikes had gouged from the pillar and rejoined its pack continuing after its prey.

Keeping her eye on the five creatures and wishing she had a weapon powerful enough to stop the terrible beasts, Arabella informed Crowe to turn back toward the exit. Doing as instructed, he bounded for it.

"Watch what you're doing!" warned Redweedle, grabbing hold of the sides of the boat tipping preciously to one side. "You nearly pitched me into that filth."

Blackroot hoisted the dense congealed mass of muck from the pile backed up against the sewer's primary filter trap and slopped it into the metal tray set in the middle of the boat. He scowled at Redweedle at the other end of the excrement tray. "Cease ya moaning, Weedle, and start shoveling the sewage into the boat. The longer we take, the more it piles up."

As if to reinforce his argument, a gurgling from one of the many pipes protruding from the wall at the far end of the sewage lake they floated in, spewed out a fresh outpour of chunky foulness. Lumps rode the rippling waves across the pond and collected against the reeking obstruction they had been tasked to clear.

Gagging from the raised stench, Redweedle pulled the cloth wrapped around his face higher over his nose.

"It could be worse. We could have had our heads chopped off already."

"If I had a knife handy I'd gladly chop off my nose to be free of this disgusting stench. I also believe death would be preferable to this punishment."

Blackroot raised the five-pronged scoop threateningly. "Carry on moaning instead of working and dead you'll be."

Redweedle thrust his scoop into the mound of waste and grunted with the weight as he shoveled some into the boat. Brown sludge oozed into the indent he had created with a disgusting slurp. When Redweedle stabbed his scoop into the pile for a second load, Blackroot continued removing the blockage from his side. The obstruction was so large it would take them days to clear.

Both froze when the clanging of chains and screeching resounded through the chamber.

"What was that?" asked Blackroot, staring across the room.

Thankful for the distraction, Redweedle dropped his pooper-scooper into the boat. "Something's disturbed the Slitherings. Grab an oar and let's go find out what."

They rowed to shore.

Sebastian Burche awoke and surveyed his surroundings. His blurry eyes revealed he was in the hospital emergency ward. The throbbing pain in his head reminded him of the attack and the faeries responsible. Climbing from the bed, he pulled back the curtain and glanced around the busy waiting room. Spying the reception desk, he headed for it.

"Is my daughter Arabella Burche here?"

The receptionist glanced at the cubical Sebastian had heralded from and then at Sebastian. "Has the doctor examined you?"

"I've no idea, I just woke up. I need to find my daughter."

"Please return to your aid station, and I'll ring her for you if you give me her number."

"No, you don't understand. She was with me when I was attacked. When I was found, was she brought here?"

The receptionist shrugged and pulled Sebastian's admittance record from a pile. "According to this, you were found by Ginny Southland who was heading home from the Witch's Gibbet Inn and noticed you unconscious in an alley. He rung for an ambulance and you were brought here. There is no mention of your daughter." Looking up from the file, she stared after Sebastian rushing for the exit. "Mr. Burche, you need to see the doctor before..."

Ignoring the receptionist, Sebastian barged through the double doors and over to the taxi pulling up to drop someone off. Barely had the passenger exited the cab when Sebastian climbed in.

"Take me to Hagsdell Manor and fast!" demanded Sebastian.

"The driver turned to look at his flustered passenger. "Now that's a first. I've never dropped anyone off at the Manor before."

"I don't mean to be rude, but I'm in a hurry, so can we please dispense with the chit-chat and get going."

The driver shrugged. "Just making conversation is all." He pulled away from the hospital building, edged into the traffic and headed for Hagsdell Manor.

Wincing from the throbbing pain, Sebastian gingerly felt the bruising bump on his head. Hoping Arabella was okay, he rung her mobile. As he feared, there was no answer. Glancing out at the forest bordering the edge of town, Sebastian wondered what the faeries wanted with her. Fearing it wasn't anything good, he knew he had to find her.

* * *

With the Slitherings close on his heels, Crowe dodged around a column, jumped over the one that slithered across his path, and headed through the archway. His gaze around the dark room picked out a single exit barred by an iron portcullis with no obvious way to open it. He rushed over to the metal barrier, gripped it with his front paws and heaved. It was either too heavy for him to raise or it was locked in place. He searched around for a mechanism to open it but found none.

"Hurry, Crowe, they're coming," urged Arabella, gazing behind at the foul creatures crawling through the archway.

"I'm trying, but I see no way of opening it." Aware there must be some way of opening it for the Hobkrakkens' raiding party to get through, he desperately searched either side of the portcullis.

"I suggest you look harder because time's running out fast."

Crowe's frantic search spied a rope draped through the bottom of the portcullis. His gaze followed its length and discovered the other end was tied to a lever attached to a drum a chain was wrapped around. He snatched at the rope. As his paw was about to grab it, it was pulled from his grasp.

Swinging the end of the rope around playfully, Redweedle peered through the barrier and glanced at the approaching Slitherings. "It looks like someone is having a spot of trouble."

Though both were surprised to see the faerie, Arabella was even more surprised she had understood what he had said.

Hoping the faerie would help them, Crowe blurted out, "Open the gate!"

"Now why would..."

"Hey, you're the female we saw in the Sinister house," exclaimed Blackroot, stepping into view.

Redweedle stepped to the side and noticed the human female sat atop the rat. His eyes flicked between Arabella and Crowe as his brain went into overdrive to compute the reason for them being here. "Interesting." He scrutinized Crowe. "And I'm predicting you're no normal rat. If I had to guess, you are the man who was with this woman in your house."

With the creatures almost upon them, Crowe didn't have the time to argue. "Yes, yes, correct. But if you don't open this door, we'll be food for those things behind us."

"You're here to kill the king, just as Solomon did before," accused Redweedle.

Crowe remained silent.

Redweedle turned to Blackroot. "Help them."

"What? But they want to kill the king!"

Crowe turned to face the five Slitherings almost upon them.

Arabella raised her sword ready to swipe at them.

Redweedle narrowed his eyes at his companion and nodded. "Exactly."

The penny dropped for Blackroot. "Oh, right. If he's dead, he can't have us beheaded." He crossed to one of the two levers jutting from the floor and yanked it down.

The metallic grinding of some hidden mechanism put into motion was followed by the clanking of chains.

The five Slitherings opened their jaws wide and leaped at the rat.

Crowe flinched tight against the barrier. Arabella screamed.

The Slitherings were yanked to a halt barely a hand width from Crowe.

"Calm your frightened trembling humans, you're safe by the gate."

Crowe and Arabella dragged their terrified gazes away from the snarling, snapping creatures and looked at Redweedle.

Redweedle nodded to Blackroot, who had his hand on the lever connected to the chains. "Unless of course, Blackroot lengthens their tethers."

Blackroot swiftly jerked the lever down and up.

Crowe pressed tighter against the gate when the creatures lunged forward an inch. "What do you want?"

"Answers. Are you here to kill our king?"

Seeing no point in lying in their present predicament, Crowe nodded.

"Excellent." Redweedle rubbed his sewage-stained hands together in glee. "Then I'll help you."

Crowe's whiskers twitched in surprise. "You will?"

Redweedle nodded and turned to Blackroot. "Open the gate."

Redweedle pulled the second lever. The gate began to rise. As soon as the gap was large enough for them both to fit through, Crowe passed under. It clanged closed when Blackroot returned the lever to its original position.

With their prey now out of their reach, the Slitherings screeched frustratingly and crawled away.

"Thank you," said Crowe to the faeries.

"Our pleasure. I assume with you here so soon after the reopening of the portal and the gathering army up above, that time is of the essence?"

Worried by the news the faerie army was already making preparations, Crowe nodded. "It is."

"As I thought," said Redweedle. "Saving your lives was not purely a charitable act. We saved yours in the hope you can save ours. But first, so you can understand our eagerness to see the king dead and thus trust our judgment, I will explain the reason. Our work in the sewers is part of our punishment for upsetting the king. The other part is exceedingly more drastic. We are due to be beheaded at an unspecified date in the near future. That all goes away if the king dies. Even by faeries immoral standards, Mortgrimmest is not a good king. Tyrannical at best, he is a ruthless leader that many would be pleased to see dethroned. It is something I have thought long and hard about doing but lack the bravery to carry it out. The gist of this contemplation is that I have the perfect plan, which is relatively risk-free, and everything you need to achieve this outcome. If you are serious about this endeavor, then join with me, follow my instructions, and together we'll see it done. What do you say?"

Arabella halted Crowe's translation, "It's alright, I understand them now, and I can't see we have any other option than to join with them."

Crowe digested Redweedle's speech for a few moments longer before he replied. "As we know nothing of the Faerie Realm, the way it works or how to achieve my goal, I would be a fool not to take you up on your offer."

"Splendid," exclaimed Redweedle. "Follow me."

As they set off after their two new faerie friends, Arabella whispered in Crowe's ear. "Do you believe we can we trust them?"

"Difficult to say, but they seem to want the same as us, and they did save us from those creatures, so I'm willing to go along with them to see what happens."

"Just be careful."

"My middle name." Crowe padded after Redweedle and Blackroot.

The two faeries led their unlikely companions through the mazelike sewer tunnels. Blackroot glanced behind at the rat and the human female and nudged Redweedle. "Are you certain involving them in this plan of yours is a good idea?"

"If you mean helping them to kill the king so we can end our punishment and not be beheaded when the whim takes him, then yes, I am certain. We are only alive now because Hemlock stepped in and saved us. He wants the king removed from the throne as much as we do so he can take his place, so I expect we will be well rewarded for our part in the king's downfall when Hemlock takes the throne."

"Okay, but just to check, you really do have a plan to achieve this much-anticipated outcome?"

"Of course. And if I say so myself, it's almost foolproof." Redweedle brought them to a halt beside a wooden door and turned to speak to them. "We are about to enter the king's tower, so no talking and move stealthily. We have a lot of floors to climb and will be traveling up the back staircase. It's rarely used since the king had an elevator installed, one of the few human inventions we have imported into our culture, so I don't expect to encounter anyone. However, if we do, let me handle it."

Crowe and Arabella nodded their understanding and followed the faerie through the door. Following behind, Blackroot closed it when they were through.

Out of breath from their ascent up the hundreds of steps, they paused on one of the many landings.

When he'd got his breath back, Redweedle instructed Blackroot to go collect the few items they would need to carry out his plan. After he had gone through the door identical to every other on each landing, Redweedle turned to Crowe and Arabella.

"We are almost there but to get where we're going we need to pass through to the other side of the tower."

"And where exactly is it we are going?" inquired Crowe.

"The place we need to be. Trust me, and we'll all get what we want from this."

Redweedle led them up two more flights of stairs and through a door into the tower proper.

Led by mounted cavalry troops atop rats, the faerie army marched three abreast through the throng-lined city streets. To rousing cheers from the city dwellers, the invasion force passed through the city's main gates and headed for the portal.

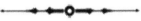

As the taxi drove away from the manor, Sebastian rushed to the front door and rapped the iron knocker. When the booms throughout the house had faded, and no one had answered, he turned the handle. It was unlocked. Sebastian pushed it open and peered inside. Though he didn't expect Crowe to be home—Arabella had told him he planned to seek out the forest witch's help and do whatever was needed to trap the faeries he had unwittingly set free—he called out his name to check, "Crowe, it's Sebastian. Are you home?"

Receiving no answer, he entered and headed for the living room. He saw the forest map taped to the wall as soon as he stepped into the room. He crossed to it and picked out the location of the Faerie Realm. Certain that was where the faerie kidnappers had taken his daughter, he committed the coordinates to memory. Aware he would need some sort of defense against the faeries if he were going to stand any chance of rescuing Arabella, he pondered what his daughter had told him about the night she and Crowe had encountered them; she had used a mixture of salt and iron filings.

Sebastian returned to the hall. Noticing the salt drawn protection symbol on the floor, he crossed to it and crouched beside the items placed in its center. They were exactly what he needed. He slipped the two jars of salt and iron into his pockets and picked up the dagger shaped like a cross and examined the symbols on its blade. Believing the symbols imbued the weapon with some sort of power—magic perhaps—that would help him fight the faeries if a close-quarters battle was unavoidable, he took that also. At a loss at how he could prepare himself further, Sebastian exited the house and headed into the forest.

Astounded by the room they had entered, Crowe and Arabella gazed around at the shelves that stretched from the floor to the ceiling fifty meters above them. Moonlight streamed through the glass dome spanning the center of the circular, arched roof. Reached via wooden staircases dotted around the circumference, tiers of walkways lined the bookshelves.

"When you think of faeries you don't picture them reading books, let alone a library this extensive," commented Arabella.

Seeing the look of wonder on the human's face, Redweedle proudly announced, "We have books dating back many thousands of years, I believe faerie culture dates back further than human civilization."

"Impressive," uttered Crowe, thinking it would take many lifetimes to read them all.

"This way," prompted Redweedle.

The albino rat known as Skirax the White; deformed with a raised shoulder that pushed his head to one side, halted his flicking through the yellowed pages of a large ancient tome when footsteps drifted up to him. His full-length white robe tied with a belt around his waist, swished up dust as he crossed to the balcony and peered down. His paw rested on the dagger at his belt while his sharp red eyes followed the three forms moving across the room. Pondering the strange threesome, he wondered what a faerie, a rat and a human were doing skulking through the tower. Once they had exited through a door on the far side, he returned to the book.

He had spent many years searching through thousands of books, many so ancient and forgotten, no faerie remained alive that had read them. Skirax had discovered many secrets and learned much about the faerie and human worlds. Unknown by but a few, in the distant past, faerie explorers had traveled to the human world to observe and learn their ways. It was these long-dead explorers means of travel he searched for. Ever since the drastic outcome of the Rat Wars, he had been searching for a better life for his pack, and somewhere in this vast library was the means to fulfill that goal. He sought the whereabouts of the Lost Portal, which most believed to be a myth. Skirax thought otherwise, and he would die seeking it rather than give up.

Coming to the end of the book, he replaced it in its empty slot in the bookcase and drew out another just as ancient and large. Dust rose from its cover when he placed it on the table. A swipe of a paw removed what remained. Skirax smiled when he read the title. *The Travels and Explorations of Absinia Livingstone into the World of Humans.*

He had found it. Skirax excitedly turned to the first chapter and began reading.

The rat cavalry was first through the portal, then three at a time, the faerie soldiers appeared in the human world. Fighting the groggy effects of passing through the magic gateway, they were directed by the waiting Tronk guard to head through the oak ring. Another Tronk ushered them across the tree bridge in single file. When they were free of the prickly barrier, they jumped down and moved back into formation with the waiting cavalry at the front; they would be first to reach Hagstown and charge through it, leaving chaos, destruction, and death in its wake. The foot soldiers would then enter to capture and kill any humans that resisted. When all the soldiers were through and lined up, they set off for Hagstown to begin their invasion of the human world.

Moving more swiftly than those relying on their two legs, the rat cavalry pulled ahead.

Keeping vigil over the town upon his ad hoc watchtower, Ghoul watched fascinated at the human children below dressed in strange macabre-themed costumes going from door to door. There were ghosts, monsters, ghouls, goblins, werewolves, vampires, and others he failed to recognize. The quality of the outfits ranged from laughable to impressive. Wondering if the humans had learned of the faerie threat and this was part of their unfathomable defense, he didn't hold out much hope of their survival if that was the case.

Sensing something amiss, Ghoul switched his attention to the forest. Something was happening. He pictured the portal that any danger to the townsfolk would come from. *Was the faerie army here already?* His gaze refocused on the excited children moving in the streets and what would become of them when the faerie army swept through the town. The lucky ones would be slaughtered in the first wave. Those taken prisoner would be roasted and eaten. The adults would suffer similar fates. Deciding it was better to preempt the faerie threat at its source rather than wait for it to reach Hagstown, Ghoul jumped from the tower and headed for the forest to intercept them.

After being led through a series of corridors and rooms, Redweedle ushered Crowe and Arabella through a doorway similar to all the others they had already passed through. Crowe entered the chamber whose walls were lined with pigeonhole shelves and glanced over the many scrolls stored in each.

"We're here," stated Redweedle.

"And where exactly is *here*?" asked Crowe.

Redweedle tilted his head. "Below the throne room." He moved to the far end and pointed at the ceiling. "Directly above sits the king on his throne."

Crowe tilted his head to the ceiling. "That's all well and good, but how do I cut off his head if I'm not in the same room as him?"

Redweedle smirked. "That is where my cunning plan comes into play. While we are waiting for Blackroot to join us with the essential items we'll need, I'll explain all."

Crowe and Arabella gathered around Redweedle.

CHAPTER 36

The King's Head

UNAWARE THEY WERE BEING followed by Hemlock's Sprite Assassins, Deadeye and his motley band of evildoers headed for the palace to present themselves to the king before heading off on their mission to seek out and kill who they thought was the last remaining member of the Sinister family.

Pausing momentarily outside the throne room while the king was informed of their arrival, they were soon ushered inside and began approaching the king sat upon his throne. They were only halfway through the room when the door behind them opened, and a guard sprinted past. Wondering what was happening, Deadeye observed the guard kneel at the bottom of the steps leading up to the throne and speak to the king in hushed tones too quiet for him to hear. The astonished expression that appeared on the king's face indicated that whatever he had been told, it was something unusual.

Once the king had spoken to one of his private guards, the soldier walked briskly up to Deadeye and raised a hand to halt him and his band. "An urgent matter has just presented itself. Move aside while the king deals with it."

Doing as ordered, Deadeye and his men moved to the side of the room. They looked at the door when the sounds of footsteps and clinking of chain grew nearer. The guards pulled the doors open. Hemlock entered with a beautiful faerie manacled to the opposite end of the chain the king's advisor held.

All eyes in the room followed their progress toward the king.

Sitting forward on his throne, King Mortgrimmest watched his advisor and his pretty prisoner approach and halt at the bottom of the steps. "Well, Hemlock, you have finally surprised me." His eyes flicked to Griselda. "Why have you brought me the pretty faerie?"

Hemlock yanked the chain, staggering Griselda closer, and waved a hand at her. "This, my liege, is a false vision of beauty. This is no faerie, but a human assassin come to part you from your head."

Fear flicked across Mortgrimmest's face as he sat upright. "Guards, surround her."

His private guards left their positions around the throne and formed a semi-circle around Griselda with their spears pointed at her.

Satisfied the human assassin was covered, Mortgrimmest relaxed. "Are you certain she's human as she looks very faerie-like to me?"

"I am sire. Her true identity is well known to us as she was partly responsible for your predecessor's demise. This is the Sinisters' witch, Griselda Poison."

Gasps escaped the lips of everyone in the room when Griselda shunned her disguise and morphed into her true form. Lithe limbs twisted, and smooth, taut blemish-free skin sagged into wrinkles and erupted with warts. Silky golden tresses became straggly and black streaked with gray. Her posture hunched when the lump forming on her back forced her to stoop. When the transformation was complete, the beautiful faerie all had admired was no more. She had been claimed by the ugly, withered hunchbacked crone who all found offensive to gaze directly upon.

The guards took a cautious step back.

"Hold your positions, or you'll suffer the consequences," ordered Mortgrimmest, glaring at his nervous guards before turning his reluctant attention back on Griselda. "Can the ugly hag speak our language?"

"Yes, she can," spat Griselda, "Though ya probably won't like what I 'ave to say."

The king shrugged. "Nevertheless, I'll hear it anyway."

"Your reign is about to come to an abrupt and rather messy end as I mean to chop off ya head and once again banish the faeries to their own realm."

The king snorted. "And how do you plan to do that, witch? You're shackled, without a weapon, and surrounded by my best guards who will stab you full of holes before you've taken more than a step toward me."

Griselda shrugged. "If they are ya best, I've nothing to worry about."

Apprehensive about how things were progressing, a guard by the door nipped out to gather reinforcements.

Though nervous from the witch's assured manner, Mortgrimmest was confident she would be dead before she could carry out her threat. "I am surprised you came to carry out this dangerous deed on your own. Were no other humans brave enough to face the task?"

Griselda smiled. "Who said I was alone? Maybe my comrades are at this moment enacting their part in my plan, and my capture was a ruse to distract ya from our true intentions."

Concealed in the shadowy parts of the room and unsure about what they should do, the Sprites observed everything taking place.

Frowning worriedly, Mortgrimmest forced his eyes to scrutinize Griselda's face for evidence she was lying but failed to detect any. He turned to Hemlock. "Did you see any other humans or accomplices?"

Hemlock shook his head. "Only her, sire. She's bluffing."

Griselda released the catch on her waist bag. As soon as it hit the floor, Ellie sprung forth armed with a pistol which she aimed at the king.

Griselda was about to make her move on Mortgrimmest when the rush of footsteps converging on the throne room halted her. The three doors around the room burst open as the city guards poured in.

"Surround the witch," shouted Stubby Stouthobble.

The soldiers surrounded Griselda and the king's guards at the front with a ring of menace four faeries deep.

Five faerie necromancers flew over the soldiers and hovered in front of the armed barrier. Primed to fire, their enchanted staffs sparkled with deadly magic.

Griselda sighed, picked up her bag, and refastened it around her waist. She looked at Hemlock. "You ready?"

Hemlock nodded and avoiding gazing at the king staring suspicious daggers at him, he sheltered behind a stone pillar.

Realizing Hemlock was in league with Griselda, and she was about to make her move, Mortgrimmest yelled, "Kill the witch!"

As the king's command echoed through the room, Griselda's shackles slipped from her thin bony arms and clanged to the floor. Her hand shot into her bag and emerged gripping her staff. When the king's private guards took a step nearer and thrust their spears at her, she uttered an unintelligible spell and slammed the staff on the floor. A bright flash filled the room. The circular blast wave that emanated from the top of her staff knocked the guards and soldiers off their feet and slammed them against the walls. Those that weren't knocked unconscious dropped to the floor groaning from the ordeal. The faerie necromancers convulsed wildly as if from an electric shock when the bolts of magic they had shot at the witch were turned against them when Griselda's spell swept over them. When the magic gripping them dissipated in a shower of bright sparks, they dropped to the floor unconscious.

Thrown into the back of his throne, Mortgrimmest blinked while his eyes recovered from the bright flash. When his sight returned, he saw no sign of the witch until she dropped onto his lap pulling a sword from her bag. Before he could utter more than a surprised grunt, the sword swung at his neck.

Zagan rushed from his nearby place of concealment and blocked Griselda's sword with his own, halting it a hairbreadth from the king's neck. He kicked Griselda in the chest, sending her toppling onto the floor and sliding painfully down the steps. He was upon her before she had time to recover and thrust his sword at her heart.

"Stop!" Yelled Hemlock.

Zagan's sword halted with its tip pricking Griselda's skin. He pulled a loaded mini crossbow from beneath his tunic and aimed it at his traitorous master.

Unable to keep out of the affray any longer now one of their own was involved, the Sprites emerged from their hiding places and moved to stand beside Zagan.

"What are you doing?" asked Lezabel Dewsweet.

Zagan had already detected his fellow Sprites were in the room, so he wasn't surprised when they finally revealed themselves. "My duty. Protecting the king." Zagan scowled at Hemlock. "I am no longer your pupil, Hemlock. You are a traitor. My loyalty rests with my king who you have plotted with the witch to murder. When you failed to request my attendance at your secret meeting with the other Sprites, I was, to put it mildly, disappointed. When I noticed you and this witch in her faerie disguise walking through the city, I followed to ask the reason for my exclusion. However, instead, I learned that you were joining forces with her to assassinate the king. To thwart your plan, I made it my mission to protect my king and acted when Griselda made her move, and here we are. Your traitorous plan has failed, the king is safe, and you will both now face the consequences, which I assume will be severe."

Shocked by the sudden turn of events, Hemlock glanced at his other Sprites. "Are you still with me?"

Indecision masked their faces as they battled with their loyalty to Hemlock and the king. Their intrinsic faerie nature to obey their ruler won out.

"We are with Zagan, we support our king," said Moxie Draven.

The others nodded their agreement and turned their weapons on Hemlock.

"Bravo!" exclaimed the king, clapping. He glared at his mistrustful advisor. "It seems your Sprites are better trained, and I suspect, more loyal to me than your Phantoms were Hemlock."

Ignoring the king, Hemlock focused on Zagan and the cross bolt he had aimed at his heart. "I don't understand. I did send a Spookraven with a message for you to come to the meeting. You are my best Sprite and the son I never had. I would never purposely leave you out of my plans. The reason why the message failed to be delivered is beyond me, but the only way it could have failed in its task is if the Spookraven had been killed."

Zagan shrugged. "That's as maybe, Hemlock, but I've played my hand and will see it through to its conclusion. I've chosen to loyally serve the faerie king and serve him I will."

Hemlock nodded. "That is as it should be." A barely perceptible nod at Griselda caused her to squirm. Distracted, Zagan shifted his gaze from Hemlock to the witch. Hemlock swiftly slipped the sword from beneath his robe, sprung up the steps with surprising agility and swung it at the king's neck.

The king's head still wore its surprised look when it toppled into his lap, rolled off and bounced down the steps.

A shocked gasp rippled throughout the hall.

Zagan shifted the crossbow to aim at Hemlock again.

Hemlock let the bloodied sword clatter to the floor and turned to address the shocked onlookers. "With the untimely death of the tyrant king, and in the absence of anyone else suitable, as the former king's not-so-trusted advisor, I declare myself ruler of the Faerie Realm." His glance around at the those gathered detected a worrying lack of enthusiasm for his new role. To placate them, he added, "I swear to rule with a more lenient hand than my cruel predecessor. My first command as your king will be to set free all the political and wrongly imprisoned faeries arrested and imprisoned by Mortgrimmest, so they can rejoin their families and friends. Support my reign, and I promise I will do right by you all."

A muted acquiescence rippled through the guards recovering from Griselda's magic blast. Most had suffered or knew those who had, from the king's tyrannical rule, and none of them had particularly liked Mortgrimmest.

Hemlock turned to his Sprites. "As I am now king, you Sprites serve me. Release Griselda."

Zagan looked at the king's decapitated head and then back at Hemlock. "Yes, my king." He lowered the crossbow, removed his blade from the witch's throat, and held out a hand to Griselda. Although a little shaken, Griselda grasped Zagan's hand and allowed herself to be helped to her feet.

"My second decree will be that we cease our attacks on the human world. No good can come of this and the resulting deaths to both sides. I have seen the humans' destructive weapons, and if they declare war on us and manage to discover a way to bring them through to our world, we will all be obliterated, and our city destroyed. We have no need to venture into the world of humans when our world is so vast and much of it unexplored. This is where we should focus our attention. Leave the humans to their world, and hopefully, they'll leave our world to us."

Griselda nodded. "Wise words indeed and ones I'm in favor of. As very few humans know of this world, if I'm allowed to return to mine, and ya never invade ours, we can live in peace apart."

Griselda impaled the king's head on her sword and lifted it up.

A little surprised by the unexpected turn of events, and much annoyed that his promised reward from the king would now never materialize, Deadeye ordered his men to attack the witch and Hemlock. They halted when five of the six black-clad Sprites who still had a mission to fulfill, confronted them. Both sides aimed their weapons at each other.

"Sprites! Cease your course of action and consider your mission rescinded," ordered Hemlock.

The Sprites lowered their weapons and stepped back.

Deadeye and his gang turned their weapons on Griselda.

Griselda raised her staff and aimed her words at Deadeye. "I have no quarrel with you unless ya make it so. I'm leaving with the king's head. If ya tries to stop me, you'll regret it with ya dying breaths."

Deadeye glanced at the king's head impaled on Griselda's sword and her raised staff, a power he couldn't defeat. He shrugged, released the pressure on his bowstring, and lowered the weapon. "I guess the damage is done now, so anything we do isn't going to change that."

He stepped back and waved a hand at the exit. The route littered with groaning and befuddled guards still not fully recovered from the witch's magic blast.

Griselda turned to Ellie. "Let's go."

They hadn't taken more than a few steps when a loud explosion lifted the king's corpse and his throne into the air. The blast wave rippled across the floor, toppling everyone present off their feet and spraying debris across the room. Smoke and dust engulfed the king as he dropped through the hole in the floor.

In the scroll chamber beneath the throne room, Crowe, Arabella, Redweedle, and Blackroot covered their ears with their hands and waited for the fuse they had lit to reach the explosives Redweedle had fashioned.

Redweedle glanced around the corner of the scroll rack he had taken refuge behind at the fizzing cord. It climbed up the line, reached the gathering of the six fuses hanging from the six packs of explosive stuck to the ceiling in a circle, and shot up each of them. Hoping he had judged the correct quantity of explosive to carry out the task, he dodged behind his shelter and crossed his fingers.

The sound of the explosion was deafening. The blast wave struck the ground and spread out. Scrolls dragged from their cubby holes flew through the air. Racks toppled and slid along the floor. Dust, rubble, and smoke rolled through the room.

When the rubble flying past their hiding places had ceased, they peered out at the king's throne dropping through the hole blasted in the ceiling and crashing to the floor.

Before the smoke and dust had cleared, Redweedle thrust an axe into Crowe's paws and pushed him forward. "Quick, before the king recovers."

Crowe's ears were ringing so much he barely heard Redweedle. He gripped the axe in his teeth, climbed over a toppled scroll rack and rushed to the throne. Engulfed in dust and acrid smoke, he stood on his hind legs, grabbed the axe from his mouth and was about to swing it at the hazy form of the king's neck when the smoke cleared.

With puzzlement creasing his rat face, Crowe glanced back at his companions peeking from their shelters. "There's a problem. The king's head is missing."

"What do you mean, *missing*?" Redweedle approached the throne and stared the king's headless corpse. "Oh," he sighed. "What a waste of an excellent plan."

Their heads tilted to the sounds of commotion above them.

A little dazed, Griselda and Ellie climbed to their feet, moved to the hole and peered in.

"Crowe!" Griselda's surprised expression matched the rat's looking up at her. "I thought you were dead."

Wondering why she had shunned her disguise, Crowe focused on the head impaled on her sword blade. It was Griselda who had beaten him to it. "I nearly was a few times."

Noticing Crowe gazing at the head and guessing his thoughts, she said, "Hemlock did it, not me. He's king now."

Redweedle and Blackroot high-fived at hearing the welcome news."

Griselda briefly glanced at the two celebrating faeries before focusing back on Crowe. "As it's going to be difficult for you to climb up here, is there a way out from down there?"

Crowe turned to Redweedle. "Is there a quicker way out than backtracking through the sewers?"

Redweedle nodded. "There's a substantially more direct route."

"Then we'll take it," said Griselda.

"You'll need to hurry," added Blackroot. "Our army is heading for the portal and might even be through by now."

"Move aside, we're coming down."

Crowe backed away from the hole and told Arabella to climb on his back.

"Ellie, down ya go." As Ellie jumped into the hole, Griselda turned to Hemlock, who was brushing off the dust covering him. "We're heading for the portal to complete the task, but if you can get someone through first to recall ya army before they reach the town and start their killing spree, I urge ya to do it."

"I'll send someone immediately."

"Good luck with ya reign, King Hemlock. Hopefully, human and faerie will never meet again."

"Be assured, we won't be using the portal to invade your world again."

"Good, and neither will we." Griselda jumped into the hole and nodded at the two faeries she assumed had been helping Crowe. She glanced at Ellie straddling Crowe's neck and then at the stranger on his back.

This is Arabella, a friend of mine the faeries kidnapped, who I rescued from the dungeon," explained Crowe. "What's the plan?"

"We run." Arabella edged back when Griselda climbed into the saddle.

"Now why doesn't that surprise me." Crowe nodded at Redweedle. "Lead the way."

Flying ahead, Redweedle led them around the debris littering the floor and to the exit.

Blackroot, not sure what he should do, called out, "I'll stay and explain things to our new king." He glanced up when footsteps shuffled toward the hole.

In the throne room, the faces gathered around the hole in the floor peered down at the decapitated king still sat upon his throne.

"I've never seen him look so agreeable," commented Deadeye.

Hemlock was slightly miffed he now had no throne to sit on to reinforce his new role.

"Are we not going after them?" asked Zagan when the humans fled.

Hemlock shook his head. "What's done is done. Let them flee back to their lands. If Griselda is true to her word, which I trust she will be, she'll seal the portal again, hopefully forever this time. Faeries and humans were never meant to mix. Let them have their lands, and we'll keep ours." He glanced around at his new subjects. "As your new king, I have roles for you all. My Sprites will be my personal guards with Zagan as their commander. Deadeye, though we started off on the wrong foot, you have proved yourself a worthy and, I might add, a cunning adversary I would be a fool not to make use of. You will form an elite band of commandos from faeries of your choosing, to be sent on special missions I have in mind to improve and perhaps expand the kingdom I now rule over."

"Will the pay be good?" queried Deadeye, narrowing his good eye.

"With the bonus scheme I have in mind if you are successful in your endeavors; exceptional."

Deadeye grinned. "Then I'm in, my king."

Though a little disappointed by Deadeye's lackluster bow, Hemlock let it slide. "To ensure my reign is a long one and I don't lose my head from any human reprisals, your first task is to recall my army and ensure the humans pass safely through the portal to their own world."

Deadeye repeated his lackluster bow. "Yes, my liege." After gathering up his band of nefarious comrades, they dived through the windows and flew over the city toward the portal.

"Now, someone please bring me a chair to use until I have my throne back. Zagan, you and your Sprites head below to the dungeon and release all the prisoners."

His subjects rushed from the throne-less throne room to do his bidding.

Hemlock turned his attention upon Blackroot below. "I assume you and Redweedle are responsible for this mess."

A little sheepishly, Blackroot nodded. "We were trying to repay you for delaying our executions by killing the king for you."

"That's as may be, and though your intentions were good, your resulting actions denied me my throne and left a damn great hole in my floor."

Blackroot gazed around at the destruction before looking back at Hemlock. "Please, my king, allow me to take charge of the repairs. I come from a long line of builders and will soon have everything back to normal. I've also noticed your tower is in desperate need of repairs; something your predecessor ignored, before parts of it start crumbling down around your ears. And don't get me started on that poor excuse for an elevator that I'm surprised hasn't plummeted its passengers to certain doom, there's also..."

"Yes, yes, I get the picture," interrupted Hemlock. "To ensure my tower doesn't collapse around me, I am making you the city's chief architect. Put together a list of the most urgent repairs, and I'll see what funds remain in the coffers to pay for them."

Blackroot's bow was far more impressive than Deadeye's had been. "Thank you, sire. I am honored."

"And tell Redweedle I wish to speak to him upon his return."

"Yes, my king." Bowing again, Blackroot backed up, almost tripping over the rubble, and went to seek out Redweedle to tell him his good news.

Hemlock sighed at the simple wooden chair brought to him. It was not the throne he imagined he would be sitting on. He sat and, turning his thoughts to more positive matters, smiled. *Finally, at long last, life was almost as it should be. I will be a moral and fair king and look after my people. Maybe someday I will take a queen who will bear me children to continue my dynasty.* His eyes flicked to the harem door. *But not just yet. Yes, life was definitely on the up.*

Skirax the White had observed the death of the king and Hemlock's subsequent usurping. Backing into the gloom shrouding the high balcony running the length of the throne room, he contemplated what he had just witnessed. Hemlock declaring himself king had given him an idea. Shifting the satchel filled with stolen books to a more comfortable position over his shoulder, he turned away and headed off to carry out the latest addition to his plan that had been many years in the making.

CHAPTER 37

Invasion

THE SOLDIERS GLANCED WARILY around the forest they marched through. It wasn't the humans that unduly concerned them but the ghoul they had been warned about. That it had managed to kill all six of Hemlock's professionally trained Phantom assassins was a worry they all dwelled on. Their training, such as it was, was amateur in comparison.

Their sergeant's recent words of encouragement, which had fallen a little flat, had told them that although the ghoul might be a skilled fighter, magical and almost impossible to kill, they had numbers on their side. If they encountered the practically invincible ghoul, they would overwhelm it and hack it to pieces, job done. Yes, a few would die in the process, but danger is what they signed up for.

Not one of the soldiers felt invigorated or reassured by their sergeant's pep talk.

Deadeye angled his wings and swooping down landed softly on the ground by the portal and the Tronks guarding it against unlawful use. After telling the guards *by order of the king* the humans soon to arrive are to be allowed to return to their world unhindered, he and his comrades disappeared through the portal.

Redweedle led Crowe and his passengers through the tower and halted at a large door. He slid it open and ushered Crowe inside. The large wooden box creaked and swayed when he stepped in. A glance out the window—a hole cut in the back wall—revealed the city landscape far below.

Redweedle entered and slid the door shut.

"Is this thing safe?" asked Crowe.

Redweedle shrugged. "As safe as the old rope attached to it."

Three levers labeled, UP, DOWN, and STOP were situated on a side wall. Redweedle pulled the DOWN lever down then returned it to its original position.

When the DOWN bell rang in the hut built precariously on the edge of the tower, the faerie tasked with its operation released the break on the drum fixed flatways to the roof via a spindle in its center. To set the rat fixed to the pole attached to the cogged wheel beside the drum into motion, he prodded it with a stick and slowly the rope attached to the elevator was fed out.

After a brief delay, the crudely constructed transportation device—more akin to a dumbwaiter—lurched alarmingly and began its trembling descent.

Noticing the passengers' nervousness, Redweedle reassured them, "We'll soon be at the bottom."

"Not too soon I hope," worried Crowe, spreading his paws to stabilize himself against the erratic swaying of the creaking construction.

All were relieved when the elevator banged to a halt on solid ground a few minutes later, and they were able to get off.

From their high vantage point, Redweedle pointed out the route they needed to take before turning to Crowe. "Good luck and thanks for your help, even if it didn't turn out quite as expected."

"Likewise," replied Crowe.

"Though I'd like a few moments chat-chatting with your new friend, Crowe, we're running out of time and need to get moving as fast as your rat legs will carry us," urged Griselda.

Taking point, Crowe began his dash through the streets.

Redweedle watched them go before reentering the elevator and riding it up.

Blackroot greeted him when he stepped off at the top.

After explaining in excited tones that Hemlock had made him the city's chief architect, Blackroot informed him that the Hemlock wanted to see him. Redweedle went to find out what his new king wanted. Accompanied by two others he had hired to help him, he halted outside the throne room and knocked.

Hemlock glanced at the door when the guards opened it and focused on the large chair the two faeries struggled with.

Redweedle bowed when he reached the king. "Sire, please accept my humble gift as a temporary replacement until your throne is restored.

Climbing from the uncomfortable wooden chair, Hemlock ran his gaze over the red velvet covering the deeply padded armchair, and the scrolled, gold-leafed adornments. He back-kicked the wooden chair, sending it crashing into the hole and pointed at the recently chair-vacated place. "I accept your gift, Redweedle, put it there."

When the chair was positioned correctly, the two laborers left.

Hemlock sighed with pleasure when he sat and sunk into the plush, cushioned seat.

"I most humbly apologize for my part in the destruction of your..."

"Yes, yes, no matter," interrupted Hemlock, waving a dismissive hand. "Your intentions were good." He stared straight at Redweedle. "I like you, Redweedle, always have.

There's not many that can be trusted to do what is right, but I believe you are one of them. If you swear to serve my subjects and me in a fair and just manner, I'd like you to become my chief advisor to help me run this great kingdom."

Taken aback, it took a few moments before Redweedle could speak. "My king, I swear to you my loyalty and my promise that I will serve you and our realm with integrity and fairmindedness so all may live in harmony, something which has long been absent from this kingdom." He finished with a deep and impressive bow.

Hemlock smiled. "Then I appoint you, Redweedle, as my chief advisor. And as your first task for me, could you please rustle me up some grub, all this usurping has given me an appetite, and grab something for yourself while you're at it as I'm sure all that blowing up my throne room business has affected you likewise."

Redweedle grinned as his bowed. "You are correct there, sire. I'm famished."

Astounded faerie onlookers watched with mouths agape when the speeding rodent with its strange passengers passed them by. Those in Crowe's path dodged aside to avoid being bowled over or trampled. Those on his back gripped on even tighter when their ride rounded a corner and leaped over a cart blocking the street.

Glad to be free of the city, Crowe sprinted through the gates and headed for the portal.

Panting from his sprint through the forest, Sebastian rushed past ancient trees he would generally have halted to admire. Hearing the approaching thuds of many footsteps pounding the forest floor, Sebastian believed caution was in order and hid amongst a group of bushes gathered around the base of a tree. He watched in amazement when rats the size of large dogs appeared and rushed by. It seemed the invasion of the human world had begun. Aware there was nothing he could say to anyone in town they would believe if he phoned to warn them of the imminent faerie threat, he focused on rescuing his daughter and continued to the portal.

On reaching the tail end of the long line of foot soldiers, Deadeye and his comrades flew over their heads. When he reached the front of the column and noticed the cavalry had gone ahead, he led his men above the tree canopy and veered toward Hagstown to intercept them before they reached it.

Sebastian hadn't traveled far when he skidded to a stop on the soft ground, almost toppling face first onto the forest floor when he encountered the faerie foot soldiers.

Faeries and human stared at each other.

The faeries raised crossbows and brandished swords, knives, and spears.

Shaking fearfully, Sebastian slid a jar of salt and iron from his pocket, unscrewed the lid and poured some into a palm.

"What do we do, Sarge?" asked Scratchy Bottom, resisting lowering his crossbow to satisfy an insistent itch.

"It's only one human, we kill it!"

Thorny Briar narrowed his worried eyes at the jar the human held. "What's he got in his hands?"

"Looks like some sort of weapon to me," offered Muddy Molder. "Magical I expect. A devious lot them humans."

"Bottom, kill it!" ordered sergeant Gobshout.

"Oh, why me, Sarge?" moaned Bottom.

"Because I damn well said so."

"It hardly seems fair, Sarge."

"If you wanted fair ya shouldn't have joined the army. Now do as ya told and kill it."

Muttering under his breath, Bottom stepped forward and raised his crossbow.

"And ya better not have one of those magic arrows loaded, Bottom," warned Gobshout.

"No, Sarge." Resting a finger on the trigger, Bottom sighted at his target.

Wondering what they would do and if he should run, Sebastian watched the faeries. When one of them stepped forward and aimed a crossbow at him, he stood his ground. Nothing was going to keep him from rescuing his daughter.

Bottom fired.

Sebastian calmly stepped to the side. The cross bolt whizzed harmlessly past.

"He moved!" exclaimed Bottom, shocked an opponent was allowed to do that.

Gobshout sighed as he turned to his men. "Every soldier in the first five rows, step forward and pepper the human with arrows.

The soldiers moved to the front, spread out, and raised their crossbows.

"The middle five aim at the human," ordered Gobshout. "You five at the end aim to his right in case it dodges that way. The remaining five aim to the left."

"Yes, Sarge!" rippled along the line.

Sebastian gulped at the fifteen arrows aimed at him; far too many to dodge this time. He was about to seek shelter behind the nearest tree when something moving through the forest distracted him. He glimpsed something, swift, tall and pale, speeding closer. It was the ghoul his daughter had told him about.

The Tronk guards tasked with guarding the portal were discussing what Deadeye had told them when the sounds of footsteps thumping on the stone bridge turned them to the source. Amazed at the sight of the charging rat, the ugly hag glaring at them from its back, and other assorted passengers, they wondered if these were the humans they were told to let pass. Undecided whether they should stop them or not, they chose safety over duty and dived aside.

Crowe leaped through the portal and tumbled across the grass when he landed on the other side. Thrown from his back, none of his passengers suffered injuries from their flights or landings.

Panting on the grass, Crowe spasmed with cramp and pain when he changed back to his human form. Glad to be free of the chaffing saddle that had magically disappeared, he gazed around at his companions. Arabella, though looking a little woozy from the effects of passing through the portal, seemed okay. Ellie was back to her tiny self, and Griselda was still ugly. Crowe welcomed the strange normality that now seemed to be part of his life.

"Quick, Crowe," called out Griselda. We need to get the king's head past the briar ring to complete our mission.

Crowe caught the sack she threw to him, ran out of the oak circle, and headed for the tree bridge.

The others dusted themselves down and followed.

"Fire!" Yelled Sergeant Gobshout.

Fingers squeezed triggers. Crossbows twanged. Arrows swarmed through the air like angry bees. Sebastian gulped. Something thudded to the ground in front of him and shoved him out of harm's way so forcefully he slammed into a tree. Dazed by the blow, he collapsed to the ground. Though seven of the fifteen crossbow bolts shot harmlessly into the forest behind Sebastian, the remaining eight came to a halt.

Ghoul looked down at the arrows sticking from his body and then at the faeries responsible for firing them.

"That damn human must lead a charmed life the way it keeps avoiding death," uttered Molder.

"Shall we reload? Sarge?" asked Briar.

Gobshout scrutinized the ghoul yanking the arrows out and dropping them to the ground. They had had no effect whatsoever. "No point. They're useless against the ghoul. We'll have to hack it to pieces with blades."

Bottom nudged Gobshout with his elbow. "I bet it's at times like this that you wish when you told me to return those magic arrows that I disobeyed and hid one in me quiver so I could take it out and look at the pretty patterns now and again?"

With hope on his face, Gobshout turned to Bottom. "Please tell me ya did exactly that."

Bottom shook his head. "I ain't admitting to nothing with those harsh punishments of yours in the offing, Sarge."

"Forget the damn punishments, Bottom. If you did disobey me and have a magic arrow, I'll likely kiss ya."

Bottom screwed his face up. "If that's the case I'm not sure I'd rather have the punishment."

Frustrated, Gobshout twisted Bottom around and pulled the arrows from his quiver. Finding the magic one, he dropped the others, turned Bottom face forward and thrust the shaft into his hand. "Fire it at the ghoul."

"Annoyed by the sergeant's rough treatment and abrupt tone, Bottom muttered under his breath as he loaded the arrow into his crossbow. "Any particular part of the ghoul you want me to aim at?"

"I don't think it matters, just fire the damn thing and make sure you hit it."

Bottom aimed at the ghoul.

Sensing the nearby magic, Ghoul focused worriedly on the silver arrow.

Bottom pulled the trigger.

Concentrating on keeping his balance, Crowe raced across the tree bridge and jumped to the ground. He opened the bloodstained sack, reached in and pulled out the ghastly object by its hair. Like a rugby player scoring the try that would win his team the match, Crowe slammed the head on the ground. Though he wasn't sure what he expected to happen, the unimpressive nothing that did, wasn't it. He righted the head, so it rested on its neck and squashed it into the ground. Still nothing.

"It takes a few moments, Crowe," explained Griselda walking over with the others.

Gathering around him, they stared at the faerie king's head.

Its eyes shot open, as if in shock—a reaction to having your head cut off would definitely produce—and looked at those around it. Resigned to its fate, it opened its mouth and screamed a shrill, piercing cry so loud people in the next county would probably have heard it. A barrier of sound shook leaves from the trees it washed over.

Clasping hands to their ears to block out the sound, the onlookers waited until it had stopped. The king's mouth closed. The head turned gray, shriveled black, and collapsed into a pile of dust.

"That's it. Job done—almost," stated Griselda. "I suggest we head back to the portal, hide behind the oaks, lest we are trampled by the herd of faeries that will shortly be coming our way. When they have all returned to their realm, I'll reseal the barrier."

Ellie fluttered onto a large fallen tree branch. "If you can let the dogs out, Griselda, I'll wait here. They must be wondering what's happening they've been in there so long."

"I'm sure my demon's pampering them; he likes company." Griselda placed her bag by the branch, and as soon as the dogs were out, fastened it back around her waist.

Pleased Ellie was safe, Satan and Lucifer nuzzled and licked her.

"We won't be long," said Griselda to Ellie. "Just keep out of the way when the faeries appear as they'll be in a mighty hurry."

Griselda led Crowe and Arabella back to the portal while Ellie and her dogs fussed over each other.

Aware it was useless trying to avoid the arrow that would follow him until it struck, Ghoul accepted his fate and followed its trajectory ever nearer to its face. Its eyes crossed when it was about to hit between its eyes. Sensing it was about to fulfill its task, the arrow sparkled with magic that would bring about the demise of the ghoul. No one was more surprised than Ghoul when the shaft was cut in two by an arrow. The released magic fizzled out of existence with an unimpressive display of colored sparks. Ghoul blinked when the two halves of the broken arrow struck its face and dropped to the ground.

Bottom sighed. "Unfairness doesn't describe the emotion I'm suffering at the moment."

Gobshout ignored Bottom's whining and concentrated on the group of faeries that swooped down from the sky and placed themselves between his army and their enemy. He focused on the one with a patch over one eye when he stepped forward, his empty bow labeling him as the one responsible for saving the ghoul and upsetting Bottom.

"What's the meaning of this? When I report your traitorous action to Mortgrimmest, he'll have you beheaded."

Smiling, Deadeye rested his hands on the tip of the bow he rested on the ground. "That, sergeant, will be an impossibility as he has suffered that exact same fate."

Though aware no faerie whatever their traitorous disposition would lie about such a serious matter, Gobshout needed confirmation. "The king is dead?"

Deadeye nodded. "He couldn't be deader."

Shocked gasps rippled through the ranks.

"Hemlock is now king," continued Deadeye. "I have already informed the cavalry of this, who should be here shortly, that King Hemlock orders you to cease the attack on the humans and return to the Realm forthwith."

"Forth with what?" asked Bottom.

"It means immediately," explained Thorny Briar.

"If it means we don't have to fight the ghoul I'm up for it. Let's forthwith get ourselves out of here." A hand grabbing his shoulder halted Bottom's eager retreat.

"Stay where you are the lot of ya." Gobshout narrowed his eyes at Deadeye. "The talk of seeking revenge against the humans has been going on for nigh on a hundred years, and ya expect me ta believe it's over, just like that." Gobshout tried to click his fingers for effect but failed miserably. Bottom came to his rescue and clicked his own.

Deadeye shrugged. "Believe me or not, any moment now you'll realize I speak the truth and all of ya will be fleeing back to the realm as fast as ya legs and wings can carry ya."

Gobshout's next words died on his lips when the shrill, piercing cry of the dead king spread through the forest. The invisible sound wave swayed trees, shook boughs and dragged leaves from the ground and carried them in its wake.

Thundering footsteps heralded the arrival of the cavalry rushing back to the portal. They sped by and, as quick as they had arrived, they were gone.

Deadeye smiled at the soldiers when they focused back on him. He raised an arm and pointed back toward the portal. "Run!"

The soldiers turned and ran. Gobshout glared at the one-eyed faerie before joining his fleeing men.

Deadeye glanced at the unconscious human when he crossed to the ghoul. "Go in peace foul ghoul. The time of faeries fighting humans is over. No more will we set foot in the human world."

Staring at the faerie that had spoken, Ghoul shrugged.

"It doesn't understand, Deadeye," stated One Arm the Brave.

To hopefully get his message of peace across, Deadeye held out a hand. Ghoul looked at it for a moment before grasping it. Deadeye shook. Ghoul squeezed and shook vigorously. Fearing his hand was about to be ripped off, Deadeye snatched it from Ghoul's grasp and used his other hand to put the bones back in order.

"Friends?" asked Deadeye, nodding.

This, Ghoul seemed to understand.

"Frriieeenndsssss," replied Ghoul.

"We'd better 'urry back before our heads explode," prompted Twitch, worried about the headache that had begun to make itself known.

The faeries rose into the air and flew away.

Ghoul gave them a wave and turned when the human it had protected, groaned. It walked over, crouched, and stared at him.

Sebastian's eyes blinked open and stared at the blurry form close to his face. When it came into focus, he gasped in shock.

"Frriieeennd," said Ghoul.

Sebastian nodded nervously and unsure if it was a question, replied, "Friend. Definitely a friend."

When the ghoul stood and moved away a few steps, Sebastian climbed to his feet and looked around. Surprised by the faerie army's absence and the lack of their broken, bloodied corpses littering the forest floor, he wondered what had become of them. He turned to the ghoul and waved his arm at where the faeries had been. "What happened to the faeries?"

Ghoul pointed in the direction of the portal. "Gooo hooommme."

"I need to go there too." Sebastian pointed at his chest and then in the direction the army had gone. "I must rescue my daughter."

Ghoul nodded and walked away. Sebastian followed it along the trampled route left by the fleeing army.

Silencing the dogs when the rumble of footsteps reached her, Ellie pulled a leafy weed down to cover them and watched the faerie army rush by. Some flew over the spikey hedge whiles others crossed via the tree bridge.

Hidden amongst the ring of oaks around the portal, Crowe, Griselda, and Arabella watched the faeries atop their rat steeds, the swiftest and thus the first to arrive, disappear through the portal. After a brief spell of inactivity, the panting foot soldiers came next and returned to their realm. Deadeye and his comrades were last to arrive and pass through.

Griselda stepped into the circle. "That seems to be the last of them." She crossed to the gap in the fence. "Crowe, drag the broken fence this side but don't step right through or you'll be back in the Faerie Realm."

Crowe did as he was ordered. He knelt this side of the fence, and when he reached through to grab the fallen fence section, his upper body entered the portal. Glimpsing the tail end of the faerie army moving along the forest track and the one-eyed faerie and his rough looking comrades standing in a group watching him, Crowe nodded at Deadeye as he dragged the fence back into his world. Deadeye returned the nod as he disappeared.

"Now lift one end up," ordered Griselda. Dipping both hands into her bag, they emerged holding a funnel and a large bag of salt.

Never ceasing to be amazed by what she pulled from her bag, Crowe asked, "Is there nothing you don't have in there?"

"Nothing I don't need and everything I want." She looked at Arabella and held out the funnel. "Hold it in the end so I can refill it."

Arabella took the funnel and placed the tip in one of the hollow crossbars. Griselda ripped off the top of the salt bag and tipped the contents into it. When it started pouring from the end of the other crossbar, she stopped and returned the salt and funnel to her bag. The Store Demon made a note of the quantity of salt remaining and placed it on a shelf.

Crowe and Arabella lifted the broken fence section back into place.

"How will you secure it?" Crowe asked.

Griselda rolled her eyes. "Magic of course."

While Arabella and Crowe joined each broken strut to those it had snapped from, Griselda uncorked the bottle of silver, glittery liquid she had pulled from her bag and poured a little on each broken section. As if like magic—which it actually was—they melded together.

"Ya can let go now," said Griselda.

Crowe shook the repaired fence.

Griselda scowled at him. "Ya trying to break it again?"

"Just testing its strength. Good as new, almost."

"Well don't. The last time you mucked about with it, ya broke it." Griselda walked the circumference, sprinkling the liquid over the fence. In her wake, the flaking, rusty metal shrugged away its years of unkemptness to become a shiny silver metallic barrier that looked brand new.

"A few days ago, I would have been shocked by witnessing magic being performed," said Arabella, watching the fence revert to its new state, "but now, after what I've recently experienced, it doesn't seem that strange. Still amazing to witness though."

Crowe understood exactly how Arabella felt. "I'm looking forward to getting back to normality and my writing." It seemed like he had been caught up in this strange adventure for weeks.

"Normality's overrated," muttered Griselda, stowing the bottle back in her bag. "Anyways, we still have Ellie's problem to sort out. The way ya handled yourself in the Realm, though I'm loathed to give ya any praise when you were the cause of it all, ya did good Crowe. We couldn't have done it without ya. The upshot is that we, Ellie and me, would like ya to come back with us to track down this 'ere wizard I believe can cure her."

To put it mildly, Crowe was shocked by the proposal. "Go back!" He looked at the invisible portal. "Into the Faerie Realm?"

"That's the gist of it," confirmed Griselda. "Not straight away as I 'ave preparations to make. Have a think about it while ya rests and writes ya storybook. We'll set off on our second adventure in a few months, with or without ya, but I think we'll stand a better chance of success if you're with us."

Smiling, Arabella nudged Crowe. "Sounds like another fun adventure."

"Fun is the last thing I think it will be. She only wants me to go so I can carry her around."

Griselda tapped Crowe on the shoulder as she walked past. "Think about it is all I ask. Now let's head home, it's been a tiring few days. I want to kick off me boots and put me feet up."

They followed her over the tree bridge.

When they jumped down from the far side, a voice startled them.

357

"Arabella!" called out Sebastian, hurrying over.

Though surprised to see her father in the forest, she was more surprised to see him accompanied by the ghoul, that, on spying the dogs, dived to the ground and let them run over its body as it pretended to try and catch them in its massive hands.

Sebastian hurried over and hugged his daughter. "I'm so glad you are safe, my dear. I had no idea what had become of you or even if you were…"

"It was touch and go for a moment but thanks to my friends, especially Crowe who rescued me from the faerie dungeon, it all turned out good in the end. At times, it was even quite exciting."

"You'll have to tell me all about it. I can't wait to hear about the Faerie Realm." Sebastian then thanked the others for the parts they played in bringing his daughter safely back to him. He approached Griselda. "Griselda Poison, I am so pleased to discover you are not a myth?"

Griselda shrugged. "Maybe not here, but in many places, I do hold mythical status."

"Of that, I have no doubt," replied Sebastian.

With all that had happened lately, Crowe had forgotten about the deadly threat coursing through his bloodstream. There can't be much time remaining. "And she lives up to her name, she poisoned me." He held out a hand to Griselda. "The antidote, please."

"There isn't one," Griselda informed him.

Dread spread across Crowe's face.

"Cease ya fear-filled expression, Crowe. There ain't no antidote 'cause there ain't no poison. I was bluffing so ya did what ya needed to do and correct the wrong ya created."

"You could have just asked."

"If ya remembers, I did just that, and ya was 'aving none of it until ya thought I'd poisoned ya. It was a means to an end, something I'd do again if I thought I could get away with it."

Crowe was at a loss as to how to respond, so he said nothing. With Griselda, that was sometimes the best course of action. Even though they had encountered many life-threatening situations, they had survived. He also had plenty of new and exciting material for his book.

"So, what about this faerie problem?" asked Sebastian. "How can I help?"

"It's done, father," informed Arabella. "The portal is once again sealed, and the faeries say they won't invade our world again, so they are no longer a threat."

"Oh," uttered Sebastian, disappointed. "I was looking forward to meeting a real-life faerie."

"I would have said the very same thing not long ago. But not now," said Crowe. "It's best faeries, and humans remain strangers."

Ellie fluttered from the top of Ghoul's head and hovered in front of Sebastian. "I'm practically a faerie, will I do?" She landed in Sebastian's outstretched hand.

Astonished, Sebastian stared at her tiny form. "My, oh, my. You are amazing."

Ellie smiled. "I know."

"But how? Why..." Sebastian had so many questions he didn't know which one to ask first.

"They'll be plenty of time for chit-chatting later," said Griselda, turning to Ghoul, bush having fun playing in the leaves with Lucifer and Satan who ran over his body as he rolled.

"Ghoul, can you remove the tree fallen across the briar ring?"

The dogs climbed onto Ghoul's shoulders when it rose to its feet and walked over to the trunk. As if it was no more than a twig, it lifted it up and threw it aside. Immediately, the thorny briars crept out to fill the gap. Ghoul dusted off its hands and turned to Griselda.

Griselda smiled up at the lanky ghoul. "Well done, Ghoul. I think that's it for ya now the faeries have been banished back to their realm. You can return back to wherever ya goes when ya not here."

They all noticed the sad expression that appeared on Ghoul's face.

Griselda sighed. "If ya doesn't cease with ya sad eyes and turned down mouth I won't be inviting ya to hang out with me in the depressing bog I call home."

Ghoul's sad expression turned to happiness.

Crowe smiled. "So, the evil witch does have a heart."

Griselda humphed. "It might be black as coal and shriveled like a prune, but it still has a rosy center, but fer how long, who knows. Now let's get out of here."

They set off through the forest.

Sebastian hurried forward to walk beside Griselda. "If you wouldn't mind the company, I would like to visit you," said Sebastian hopefully.

Griselda shrugged. "Your time to waste any way ya choose."

Sebastian beamed.

Arabella walked beside Crowe and slipped an arm through his. "After all that you have been through, and I'm only aware of a small part and hope you'll fill in the rest for me later, what's your plan for the immediate future?"

"A long hot bath, rest for a week at least and then start writing about my adventures in the Faerie Realm." He rolled his shoulders. "I might not be in my rat guise, but I'm still suffering the effects of all the running and fleeing I did while I was back there."

"As you did save me from certain death, the least I can do is give you a massage or two to help ease away your aches and pain."

Crowe grinned. "I'd like that, thank you. I might even make you dinner."

"Then it's a date. I'll come around tomorrow night about seven and this time, I'm hoping things will be a lot more normal than my last visit."

Crowe shrugged. "I can't promise anything, but I'll try."

Satan and Lucifer sat on one of Ghoul's shoulders and Ellie on the other. "Well, Ghoul, we did it. Together we averted an all-out war between faeries and humans."

"Ghoooul haaapppy."

Ellie stroked the side of its face. "I'm glad. Griselda might come across as a crabby old crone, but deep down, she has a good heart. She'll look after you."

Ghoul pointed at Griselda. "Frriieeennd."

Without turning, Griselda smiled. It was nice to have friends again, even if they were a strange bunch. But then, she wouldn't have it any other way.

CHAPTER 38

King Rat

SKIRAX THE WHITE ENTERED the rat dungeon and headed for the guardroom.

When a shadow fell over his plate of mutton stew, the jailor turned to the cause. His cry of surprise at seeing a white rat framed in the doorway, died on his lips when Skirax lashed out a claw, opening three deep gashes across his throat. His face splashed into his stew when he fell forward. Showing no emotion—the faerie jailor had ruled his domain with a cruel temperament, an iron fist, and a sharp stick—Skirax lifted the ring of keys from his belt and left the corpse to rot.

Arriving at the first cell in the long row, Skirax unlocked it. The four rats inside wore puzzled expressions when he opened the cell door.

"Out. You are free," informed Skirax, standing back.

The four rats cautiously moved to the door and peered left and right.

"What about the faeries?" asked Slithe worriedly.

"No need to concern yourselves with them. Their king is dead." Skirax handed Slithe the keys. "Set your comrades free and tell them to gather in the guards' hall where I will speak to them shortly."

Though anxious by what was happening, Slithe took the keys and started unlocking the cells.

Skirax returned to the Jailor's room. His gaze around the small chamber revealed what he was looking for. Though only a few, it was a start. As he gathered up the weapons, he noticed the sharp stick stained with rat blood leaning against the wall. He scowled at the jailor who had wielded it with a vengeance never quashed. Armed with three knives, two swords, and a crossbow bundled under an arm, he snatched up the pointed stick and thrust it into the jailor's back as he passed by to the doorway.

Skirax pushed through the throng of anxious rats who were gathered together and climbed onto a barrel and stood on his hind legs. They had no idea what was happening or what they should do.

"Quit your confused squawking my comrades. I'm here to lead you to a new and better life. No longer will we serve as slaves to the faeries." Keeping a sword for himself, he dropped the other weapons. "Though but a few, we will collect more on our travels until all of us are armed to defend our new-found freedom."

Slithe snatched up the second sword that another rat was about to grab as all the weapons were quickly claimed.

Fearing punishment from their faerie handlers when they returned, a worried mumbling spread through the anxious throng.

"Fear not the wrath of those that seek to control and enslave us, as we will soon be gone from this world. We travel to a new land where the faeries will never find us. However, to achieve this, we need a new leader. Someone strong, cunning, and resourceful." As his gaze swept across the anxious mass of rodents, he spoke out of the corner of his mouth in a fake voice.

"I propose Skirax the White as our leader."

He changed his voice again. "I second that, Skirax for our king."

Like a herd of sheep, the rest fell into agreement.

"Skirax for king."

"Hail the bold and brave Skirax the White."

Skirax raised his paws to silence the crowd and swept the sword over them. "Thank you, comrades. Though this has come as a complete surprise, I accept your proposal if you are all in agreement."

Cheers of acceptance rippled through the pack.

Skirax gave a weak bow. "Then I'll be honored to be your king."

The crowd clapped and hurrahed enthusiastically.

"Hail our new king, Skirax the White," shouted one rat.

"Hail King Skirax," the crowd chorused.

"Long may he reign," called out another.

Bringing them to silence, Skirax voiced his plan. "It is time to leave this foul dungeon and begin our new lives in a greener world filled with tasty scraps to make us all full and fat."

Excited cheers rang out.

"Follow me my loyal subjects, but quietly. We must not alert others to our escape." Skirax leaped from the barrel and headed along a tunnel.

His enthusiastic subjects followed.

Skirax smirked. The Faeries might not be invading the human world, but the rats would be. Excited about the future he had long dreamed of, Skirax led his rat pack through the lower levels of the city. Any concerns his minions had experienced when they were first set free had changed to eager anticipation at the new life of freedom they embarked on.

Entering a space filled with empty wine racks and littered with empty bottles, barrels, and flagons, Skirax headed for the far end of the long room. He halted in front of a stack of barrels, each three yards wide and five long, piled on their sides. All were empty, and some had never been filled, but it wasn't wine Skirax had come here for. His eyes focused on the barrel in the top row in the middle. He spun, almost colliding with Slithe who was being pressed forward by the other rats cramming into the room.

"Back up. Back up!" ordered Skirax.

When they had done so, Skirax pointed at the set of wooden steps on wheels once used to reach the highest parts of the wine racks. "Bring that to me."

Four rats wheeled it over to him and with his instructions positioned it below the barrel he wanted to reach.

Wondering what he was up to, Slithe and the other rats watched they newly elected king ascend the steps and brush the cobwebs from a large barrel.

Recalling the instructions he had read in *Absinia Livingstone's* book, Skirax turned the barrel tap clockwise twice, anti-clockwise once, clockwise half a turn, and pushed it. A click came from the side of the barrel, and the lid opened slightly. Slipping his claws around the edge, he pulled the hinged door open and peered inside at the tunnel that led off from the back of the barrel.

Skirax turned to his puzzled subjects. "We are almost there my comrades. Soon our new lives of freedom and plenty will begin."

Still worried they would be caught by the faeries, punished and locked up again, hushed hurrahs rippled through the pack.

Skirax waved an arm at them. "Follow me."

Slithe was first on the steps. As the others followed him up, Skirax bent his deformed neck and entered the secret tunnel.

Emerging a short distance later into a small cavern, Skirax stretched out his aching back and strode purposefully for the ring of boulders in the center of the cavern. He found it hard to believe he was finally here.

Slithe twitched his whiskers when he saw the stone circle. "Is that a portal?"

"That it is. But not just any portal. It's the lost portal," stated Skirax proudly.

Slithe was impressed. "That's why you spent so long going through the books in the library, you were searching for this?"

Skirax nodded. "It leads to the world of humans in which we will thrive, plunder, and feast like you've never feasted before." He turned to Slithe. "I need a loyal second in command who can be trusted. Is that you, Slithe?"

Slithe jumped at the opportunity. "It is sire."

"Then come. We've spent long enough in this faerie world of pain, misery, and darkness, let's go see if the world of the humans can bring us better fortune." Skirax entered the stone circle, took two steps toward the center, and gradually disappeared.

Those already in the cavern gasped at the strange phenomenon they had just witnessed.

"Calm ya fears my friends. It is a portal to the human world and nothing to be afraid of." Slithe pointed at the stone circle. "All who enter will find a better life ahead. If any of you choose to remain, you know only too well what fate will befall you. The choice is yours. I, for one, know the path I will take." Slithe turned his back on them and entered the portal.

Though nervous about doing so, other rats began their tentative entry into the unknown.

The End

Other Books by Author

A full list of Ben Hammott's books can be found on his author website here:
www.benhammottbooks.com

Hell Ship
The Flying Dutchman

When an ancient document, written by Tom Hardy, the cabin boy aboard the Fortuyn, surfaces, it reveals he was the sole survivor of the stricken Dutch East India vessel and the gruesome events he witnessed that claimed both vessel and crew.

Because the terrible events he witnessed onboard were too fantastical to be believed, Tom kept the truth a secret. However, in an attempt to quell his reoccurring nightmares, he wrote down the events leading to the demise of the crew and the Fortuyn.

It is believed by some that the Fortuyn is the lost ship that haunts the seas and has become known as The Flying Dutchman.

Centuries after Tom's death, and keeping his original title The true catastrophic events of the Fortuyn as witnessed by Tom Hardy, the sole survivor from the aforementioned vessel, the truth can, at last, be revealed.

A ghost ship, also known as a phantom ship, is a vessel with no living crew aboard. These encompass ghostly vessels from folklore and fiction, such as the Flying Dutchman, or a derelict found adrift with its crew missing or dead, like the Mary Celeste.

In maritime folklore, the ghost ship, the Flying Dutchman, has had an impact like no other lost vessel. It has inspired numerous paintings, films, books, opera, etc. The alleged captain, Van der Decken, was on a heading for the East Indies when a ferocious storm overwhelmed them. With sheer determination, he tried to steer his ship through the hostile weather conditions the Cape of Good Hope was famous for but failed miserably even after he vowed to drift until doomsday. Legend declares that since then, ship and crew have been cursed to sail the oceans for eternity.

To this day, hundreds of sailors are credited to having witnessed the Flying Dutchman continuing its never-ending phantom voyage across the oceans.

Tom's account of what happened aboard the Flying Dutchman, however, is considerably more chilling...

Feedback

"The most thrilling, unputdownable book I've read in a long time."

"Crackles with oppressive tension infused with a real sense of dread throughout that had me holding my breath."

"Stunning, scary, and tightly written - a thriller bursting with shivers and edge of your seat horror."

"Brilliant! A thrilling, horrifying, gripping page turner that you want to race through but at the same time don't want to end because you're enjoying it so much."

HORROR ISLAND
Where Nightmares Become Reality

Cocooned in rock, the alien organism was propelled into space when the dying planet exploded.

Dormant for many millennia as it travelled through the cosmos, it headed towards a blue planet.

A fiery spectacle announced its arrival when it entered Earth's atmosphere and crashed to the surface. Trapped on an island it couldn't escape from, it grew, evolved, hunted and spawned.

Time passed. Human's arrived...

More info and concept images at benhammottbooks.com

SOLOMON'S TREASURE 1

BEGINNINGS: A Hunt for Treasure

and

SOLOMON'S TREASURE 2

THE PRIEST'S SECRET

(The Tomb, the Temple, the Treasure Book 1 and 2)

An ancient mystery, a lost treasure and the search for the most sought after relics in all antiquity.

The Tomb, the Temple, the Treasure series, has become an international bestseller.

 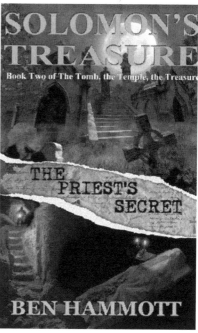

An exciting archaeological thriller spanning more than 2000 years.

More info: www.benhammottbooks.com

ICE RIFT TRIOLOGY
A 3 book action adventure survival horror set in Antarctica.

Something ancient dwells beneath the ice...

Humans have always looked to the stars for signs of
Extraterrestrials.
They have been looking in the wrong place.
They are already here. Entombed in a spaceship beneath
Antarctic ice for thousands of years.
The ice is melting, and they will soon be free.

When a huge rift in the ice is discovered in Antarctica, NASA turns
ones of its satellites upon it and discovers something strange.
Confused by the readings, they call upon a group of scientists
running tests on the ice shelf to investigate. When the scientists
enter the ice rift to check out the anomaly on NASA's satellite scans,
they discover something far more life-threatening than the raging
blizzard trapping them in the rift. They are unarmed and
unprepared for the ensuing threat it poses them and mankind.

More Ice Rift information and location concept images can be found on
the author's website: benhammottbooks.com

Sarcophagus

Their mistake wasn't finding it, it was bringing it back!

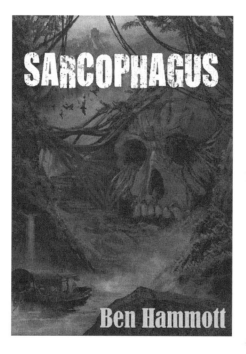

"The Mummy, meets Relic, meets Alien in this scary action driven horror thriller."

Action adventure horror set in the Amazon jungle and London, England.

Concealed in a remote area of the Amazon jungle is something the Mayans thought so dangerous they built a secret prison to entomb it. It remained undiscovered for centuries.

When a maverick archaeologist hears rumors of a mysterious lost city, he heads into the Amazon jungle, determined to find it.

He soon learns that some things are best left unfound.

The dangerous past the Mayans tried so hard to bury, is about to become our terrifying future.

Extended book blurb:

When an archaeologist stumbles across a mysterious Mayan city in a remote part of the Amazon jungle, he informs the British museum funding his expedition of the discovery.

When fellow archaeologist, Greyson Bradshaw, receives news of the discovery, he jumps at the chance to travel to the Amazon jungle to collect artifacts for the forthcoming Mayan exhibition he is arranging.

The two archaeologists explore the city's subterranean levels and enter Xibalba, the Mayan underworld. In a secret chamber, they discover something hidden away for centuries; a sarcophagus.

Realizing its potential as a centerpiece for his exhibition, Greyson transports the sarcophagus and other artifacts back to England.

The past is about to come alive.

(Includes Horror Island sample)

"Hammott is fast becoming the master of monster horror. Read his Ice Rift books and you'll know what I mean. Fantastic escapism."

EL DORADO
Lost City 2 Book series
One of the world's most legendary and elusive
treasures sought after for centuries. . .

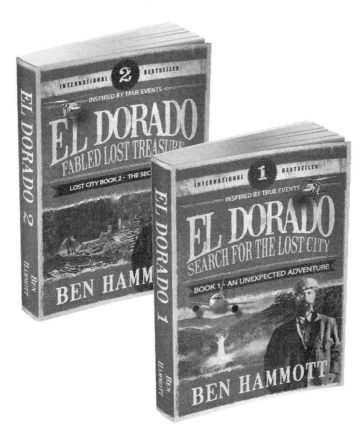

An ancient mystery.
A Lost Treasure.
A Hidden City.
An impossible location.
An unimaginable adventure.

Rumored to be guarded by remote, mist-veiled mountains, the fabulous treasure hoard was hidden from the greedy clutches of Spanish conquistadors somewhere deep inside the unforgiving and mysterious Amazon jungle. As far as anyone knows, it is still there; waiting to be discovered by those brave or foolhardy enough, to try their luck.

Included in Aztec and Mayan legends, Conquistadors had heard rumors of its existence when exploring the New World, but never found it.

During World War 2, Nazi-inspired archaeologists were convinced they had pinpointed its location. They packed a U-Boat with supplies and set a course for the Amazon Jungle. They disappeared!

Many adventurers eager to claim the legendary gold as their own entered one of the most inhospitable places on earth, the Amazon Jungle. Most were never seen again!

And yet the exact location of this fantastic hoard so many have dreamed of finding remains a mystery. Any who may have stumbled upon it never returned to tell the tale.

It was as if someone, or something, was protecting it...

In 1925, Victorian explorer Colonel Percy Fawcett enters the Amazon Jungle to search for a Lost City. Like so many before him, he was never seen or heard from again. Until now!

When a message from the past is discovered washed up on an English beach, it reveals new information about the ill-fated 1925 expedition.

A modern-day expedition sets off to follow in the footsteps of Colonel Fawcett in an attempt to locate the Lost City and its legendary hoard of priceless treasure.

The Lost City Book 1 & 2 will take you inside the Lost City to learn of its many secrets and dangers. A thrilling story of adventure and discovery that weaves together an exciting blend of fact and fiction linked to the legends surrounding the lost Fawcett expedition and the mysterious Amazonian Jungle.

An exciting archaeological mystery thriller with flashbacks to Colonel Fawcett's 1925 Expedition.

Printed in Poland
by Amazon Fulfillment
Poland Sp. z o.o., Wrocław